The choreography was followed precisely. She cried and writhed and fought the bindings; she begged for it to stop; she pleaded. But it continued, past what she thought she could endure, past the pleasure she thought she would gain from it and into something beyond, as had been promised. She rolled and tossed upon the waves of pleasures she had never imagined, she swooned in the troughs and rode the high rolling curls of sensations she had not dreamed. As the tempo increased they approached once again that moment of experiencing each other's breath, that feather of one's essence that no one could alter or destroy. This was it. She was too high, too far, reality was frighteningly small and still receding. She pleaded for it to stop, but it didn't. It was worse, much worse, and for a moment she panicked, almost slid into incoherence before she remembered the safe word. 'Mercy,' she gasped, and waited to be saved. 'Mercy!'

But everything disintegrated in a flare of mandarin red.

Also by David Lindsey:

BODY OF TRUTH
AN ABSENCE OF LIGHT
IN THE LAKE OF THE MOON

Mercy

DAVID LINDSEY

WARNER BOOKS

A *Warner* Book

First published in the United States in 1990 by Doubleday
a Division of Bantam
First published in Great Britain in 1990 by Macdonald & Co
First published in paperback in 1991 by Futura
Reprinted 1991 (five times)
This edition published in 1992 by Warner Books
Reprinted 1992 (twice), 1993, 1994, 1995, 1996

A CIP catalogue record for this book
is available from the British Library.

ISBN 0 7515 0239 1

Printed in England by Clays Ltd, St Ives plc

Warner Books
A Division of
Little, Brown and Company (UK)
Brettenham House
Lancaster Place
London WC2E 7EN

For Joyce
whose 'pacience is a heigh vertu, certeyn.'

Acknowledgments

It is not practical, or even possible, for novelists formally to acknowledge the assistance of others in writing fiction, even though we are constantly thieving the language and behavior and predicaments of our fellow men for our own purposes. As students of human nature, our sources lie as much within ourselves as in the actions of others.

Sometimes, however, we set our stories within a frame of reference that requires a considerable amount of research and which, invariably, entails the help of other people. Inasmuch as I have done that for this novel, I owe a number of persons a debt of gratitude for making themselves available to my incessant queries.

For almost a decade now, Captain Bobby Adams of the Homicide Division of the Houston Police Department has allowed me to pester the men and women in his department who would tolerate pestering. I want to thank him, and them, for their unusual indulgence of me over the course of the years.

For their help in educating me about one of the most extraordinary facets of criminal investigation, I want to thank the following men at the National Center for the Analysis of Violent Crime at the FBI Academy at Quantico, Virginia: Special Agent Alan E. Burgess, Deputy Administrator of NCAVC; Special Agent John E. Douglas, Program Manager of the Profiling and Consultation Program of the Behavioral Science Investigative Support

Unit; and Robert K. Ressler, Supervisory Special Agent of the Behavioral Science Investigative Support Unit. I would also like to thank Special Agent James R. Echols of the FBI field office in Austin, Texas.

For her assistance in helping me understand some of the finer points of forensic evidence, I want to thank Donna Stanley, Serologist in Crime Lab at the Texas Department of Public Safety, Austin, Texas.

I also owe a special word of gratitude to Sergeant Ed Richards, Criminal Personality Profiling, Intelligence Division, Texas Department of Public Safety, Austin. One of the first graduates of the FBI's prestigious NCAVC Fellowship Program, Sergeant Richard's kindness and extraordinary patience with me never flagged over the course of many months. I learned an enormous amount from him, and especially value his friendship.

The danger in beginning an acknowledgement at all is that one inevitably overlooks persons whose names should have appeared. To those I offer my apologies even before I discover the oversight.

While these persons, and many others, assisted me in gathering the facts that provide the underpinnings of this novel, I should emphasize that if there are any misrepresentations of methodologies or procedures or scientific facts, the mistakes are mine alone.

'... such joy thou took'st
With me in secret, that
my womb conceiv'd
A growing burden.'
— John Milton
Paradise Lost, II, 765
Sin to Satan, regarding
their offspring Death.

'But things that fall hopelessly
apart in theory lie close
together without contradiction
in the paradoxical soul
of man ...'

— Carl Gustav Jung
Freud and Psychoanalysis,
CW 4, ¶756

PART
ONE

Prologue

Sandra Moser paused in the broad entryway of her home, a rubber band in her mouth, her arms raised to the back of her head where she was gathering her blond hair in a ponytail. She was wearing a pink bodysuit over white leotards. When she had her hair pulled tight, clasped in one small, pink-nailed hand, she took the rubber band from her mouth and wound it several times around the shank of hair. As she did this, pulling at the loose hair of the ponytail to tighten the band, she listened to the television in the family room across the hallway where her children, Cassie, eight, and Michael, six, were eating hamburgers on TV trays with the family maid.

She had already kissed them goodbye, receiving in-attentive, routine 'byes' from them commensurate with her routine trip to aerobics class. But now she paused again, listening for Cassie's thin, muffled cough. The third grader had received the first of her series of spring allergy shots earlier in the day, and Sandra was hoping they had not waited too long. Cassie was prone to chronic sinus infections when the mold spore count was highest. Tugging at the tight leg of her bodysuit cutting into her groin, she wondered if she should take Cassie's tempera-ture before she left. The kids laughed at something on television, their small voices nearer, louder, than the canned laugh track, and Sandra decided to wait until she returned later in the evening.

Grabbing her monogrammed athletic bag from the closet near the front door, she noticed her husband's umbrella hanging against the closet wall. Andrew refused to take it with him. It just cluttered up the car, he argued, always getting in his way. Besides, he simply never needed it. He parked in a covered garage and walked to his office through the tunnels. She would remind him of the times he had been drenched — it had happened three times in the last three months — but he would shrug off her cautionary examples as 'unusual.' Andrew did not entertain the unusual.

She took the umbrella off the wall and leaned it against the small Chinese table in the entry to remind her to put it in his car when he got home. It was absurd for him not to carry it with him, especially in the spring. Making a mental note to call Gwyn Sheldon about a fund-raising idea for the children's academy — she thought of it because Gwyn's husband had an umbrella with a handle like Andrew's — she hurried out of their two-storied Georgian home nestled in the thick pine woods of Hunters Creek, one of several townships clustered together in west Houston and known as the Memorial Villages. The Villages ranked near the top of the list of the nation's wealthiest suburbs.

A fresh spring rain had moved through the Villages only half an hour earlier, making the woods fragrant and washing the city clean in the dusk. Sandra inhaled deeply of the damp evening smells as she tossed her bag into her dark blue Jeep Wagoneer and climbed behind the steering wheel, flipping on the headlights. It was just now getting dark enough to use them. She started the Jeep, fastened her seat belt, wheeled the Wagoneer around the island of magnolias in front of the house, and drove quickly along the drive bordered by a white fence covered with brambles of pyracantha. When she reached the street, she waited for a car to pass as she checked her watch. It was seven-forty. Her aerobics class began at eight o'clock, and

Andrew was at a weekly business meeting until ten.

Hurrying along the winding street she came to the major north-south artery of Voss and turned left. Within a mile or so she would come to Woodway where she would need to turn left again to go to Sabrina's, an athletic club that catered to the already sleek bodies of the women of the Villages. But Sandra Moser did not turn left at Woodway. Instead she breezed past the intersection and turned left at the next street, San Felipe, and pushed the Wagoneer east through the high-dollar neighborhoods of Briargrove and Post Oak Estates and Tanglewood until she made her first right turn onto the fashionably posh Post Oak Boulevard. Now known as Uptown Houston, the Galleria area was the largest suburban business district in the nation. Its newest pearl was the Pavilion, Saks Fifth Avenue, a multimillion-dollar complex of elegant shops separated from the boulevard by a phalanx of sixty-foot palms that glistened in the light mist that was now moving in on heavy air from the Gulf Coast fifty miles to the southeast.

With the lights of the office towers and high-rise condominiums reflecting back at her from the wet, black boulevard, Sandra Moser whipped the Wagoneer into a median turn lane and quickly cut across traffic to the Doubletree Hotel, a flat-faced structure with an inset glass curtain wall in its center section that fell to two overlapping half-barrel arches that were also made of glass and formed the hotel's porte cochere. She did not stop for the uniformed doorman who stepped to the curb to open her door, but continued past him and drove around to the parking garage gate. She took a ticket from the buzzing dispenser, which opened the gate, and entered the garage, driving up to the third level before finding an available parking space. She snatched her bag out of the Wagoneer, locked it, and walked to the elevator which took her back down to the lobby.

At the registration desk she presented a counterfeit driver's license and told the concierge she wanted to pay in cash. The license was a document that had cost her a

significant amount of money as well as considerable
trouble. Those among them who were married had to
worry about those kinds of things — their wire was
stretched tighter, their balancing act a little more delicate
than the others'. But it had been worth it. It had served
her well for over two years now. She asked for a room
facing the boulevard on the highest floor available. After
signing the registration forms and paying, she declined
the help of a bellboy and walked straight across the cavernous lobby to the elevator, her high-cut bodysuit and
stylish figure turning heads. Sandra Moser was a beautiful woman.

She found her room on the eighth floor not far from
the elevator and slipped the rectangular magnetic card
into the slot above the handle, heard it click, and shoved
it open. She did not turn on the lights, but tossed her bag
and the card on the bed and walked straight to the
curtains and opened them. A little to her left a sweep of
buildings rose up above her, their lights glittering in the
mists like a rainy sky of winking eyes peering at her in
the opened window, their vantage points the envy of
even the most demanding voyeur savant. And across the
shiny boulevard the palm trees of the Pavilion stood
dripping in a surreal desert of green sand.

Sandra Moser walked to the telephone and placed a
call. She spoke only a few words and hung up, then
walked back to the window. Standing in front of it, she
reached up and began taking the rubber band from her
ponytail. But her hands were shaking, the rubber band
was too tight. It snapped, startling her. She raked her
fingers through her hair, tossed the rubber band aside,
and shook out her hair. She took a deep breath. The room
was clean, did not smell of cigarette smoke. It was new
and clean.

From this moment on it would be different from all the
times before. Until now she had been learning. It had
been a long apprenticeship, hampered by her own
anxieties and psychological impediments. She might
never have come to this point at all if she had not had

help, if she had not been coached and coaxed and brought along with patience and understanding. She had reached that stage where she would have to give herself up completely or never know what it might have been like to understand something few people would ever know. It was that simple. It had been explained to her, but she had known anyway, instinctively. The body was the gateway to the mind. She almost had done it before, almost had crossed the threshold, risking her identity until she had grown intoxicated on nothing more than the other's breath, that feather of one's essence that no one could ever alter or destroy.

Her hands were trembling even more now as she pulled off her bodysuit and tossed it out of the way. And then she peeled off the leotards, freeing her body from the tight embracing web, her skin feeling tingly, alive with millions of tiny sensitive fingers. Standing naked in front of the plate-glass window, she let them look at her, let them glitter and wink at her. It was electrifying to have finally made the decision to acquiesce, and for a full week she had been distracted with anticipation. The curtain was about to rise on her repression.

There was a firm knock at the door and she flinched. For a moment she didn't turn around, but remained, nude, facing the night of greedy lights. It really was too late. She picked up the magnetic card from the foot of the bed as she walked by it on her way to the door. For some reason unclear even to her — she had never done it before — she didn't open the door, but knelt and slipped the card into the sliver of light as if she were pushing it out into that promised and anxiously anticipated dimension. Then she backed away slowly, listened to the card slide into the slot and click, listened to the double click of the turning door handle, and watched the sliver of light widen into a harsh brightness burning around the silhouette like a blinding white aura. Then the flood narrowed to darkness again, the light returned to a sliver on the floor, and the figure stood somewhere in the dark passage.

She waited with her back to the room again, facing the window, listening to the sounds of a small leather valise yielding up its contents behind her in the dark room. Almost immediately she caught the thick, musky odor of lipstick and oils, followed by the tinny chinking of buckles, the brittle rustling of new tissue paper, the muffled clacking of ebony wood beads, expelled breath, a waft of Je Reviens. She had planned all this, choreographed these smallest details of sounds and smells in their proper sequence. Not only was she trembling because these things accommodated her imagination, but she was delighted that every detail of her design was being followed. By prearrangement, she controlled the events about to happen and she knew they would continue inexorably, no matter how she pleaded for them to stop. But she could not control her trembling. The rain, it seemed, was coming through the glass.

Like a Noh play it took hours, or seemed to, though it was impossible to know. Time quickly had lost its capacity to be measured. And there was talk, an agitated monologue, a hypertensive soliloquy in which she recognized the familiar disquiet of her own restrained arousal. Even though they had talked it through before, every act and scene, every syllable of dialogue, every postured movement of the hand and tongue and pelvis, there were surprises — of intuition and sensation, the mutual, unspoken decision to sustain the prelude of erotic tension.

Eventually she lay on the bottom sheet of the bed, everything else having been stripped away and thrown into a corner, her arms and legs extended, her wrists already secured. She listened to the gabbling, felt her right ankle being secured. Sometimes she understood, sometimes she didn't, as she struggled against her body's insistence to hyperventilate, though she knew that it was in the act of her surrendering that she controlled the sequence of the play, and achieved a dimension of experience never before realized. As she felt her left ankle being secured, she took long, deep breaths. Trusting was vital.

She remembered: the body was the gateway to the mind. She had never concentrated so hard in her life. When the last buckle was snapped she suddenly felt lighter than air, as if she had been released rather than bound. In that instant she understood that total helplessness, total surrender, was like a black feather, floating, falling into a vast dark emptiness.

The choreography was followed precisely. She cried and writhed and fought the bindings; she begged for it to stop; she pleaded. But it continued, past what she thought she could endure, past the pleasure she thought she would gain from it and into something beyond, as had been promised. She rolled and tossed upon the waves of pleasures she had never imagined, she swooned in the troughs and rode the high rolling curls of sensations she had not dreamed. Sometimes, through it all, to stay in touch with reality she looked to the rain on the window, fixed her eyes on the stippled, fracted, light that formed a complete wall of Brownian motion behind the figure above her. As the tempo increased they approached once again that moment of experiencing each other's breath, that feather of one's essence that no one could alter or destroy. And then she was heaved upon a dark tsunami, a long, swelling high from which she looked down into real fear. This was it. She was too high, too far, reality was frighteningly small and still receding. She pleaded for it to stop, but it didn't. It was worse, much worse, and for a moment she panicked, almost slid into incoherence before she remembered the safe word. 'Mercy,' she gasped, and waited to be saved. 'Mercy!'

But everything disintegrated in a flare of mandarin red.

The first blow broke her jaw.

And she felt herself being bitten and chewed.

She was stupefied. 'Mercy.'

The second blow snapped the cartilage of her nose.

She listened in horror to the gibbering that was faster than comprehension, faster than lips could form words, it seemed, and suddenly she was called by a name she had never heard and was accused of things she had never done.

'Mercy.'

Another blow, and the incredible, dumbfounding sensation of being bitten, the teeth everywhere on her, no place sacred.

She gulped desperately at the blood that poured into her throat from the back of her nose and tried to see through eyes bleary with shock. This was wrong, all wrong. She heard the clicking sound of a buckle and then something slithered under the back of her neck and she felt the naked knees on either side of her chest. The belt was thick, like a high collar, and as it slowly tightened her ears filled with a rushing roar and her heart hammered, rocking her as if it would explode. Then she went deaf and her heart seemed less insistent. She began to drift. She had almost left her body, almost achieved that blessed separation, when she was cruelly brought back through the roar and the hammering and the pain and the unimaginable sorrow of her ordeal.

Then the belt was tightened again.

Time had no meaning apart from her coming and going through these sounds and sensations that filled the verge of consciousness. It all had gone wrong, all of it, this and everything, even the years rolling back over memory. She had granted someone the authority to toy with her life, neither allowing it nor denying it, perversely bringing her back again and again, gabbling faster than comprehension, faster than lips could form words, calling her by a name she had never heard, accusing her of things she had never done.

Only the rain was virtuous, and it was through the rain that she drifted for the last time.

FIRST
DAY

1

Detective Carmen Palma stood in the thin shade of a honey locust on a little shag of lawn near the front steps of the Houston Police Department's administration building. She wore tortoiseshell sunglasses to cut the glare from the hundreds of windshields and thousands of chrome strips on the cars in the parking lots across the street. To her left, within rock-throwing distance of the police station, a backwater loop of Buffalo Bayou wound under the maze of ramps and over-passes of the Gulf Freeway, and the shadow side of the downtown skyscrapers rose against the ten o'clock sun like a massive glass escarpment stretching south beyond the express-ways. Ragged ranks of fat, moisture-laden Gulf clouds drifted to the northwest, but within a few hours they would give way to a hot, ink-blue sky. It was the last week in May, and the temperature had already hit the low nineties seven days out of the last fourteen. An unusually wet and mild winter had given Houston's lush, semi-tropical landscape a head start on summer, and the city looked and felt like a greenhouse with the humidity, like the temperature, settled into the torturous nineties.

She had been in the crime lab in the next building checking the results of an ejector marks comparison test run on a single cartridge found at the scene of a contract killing. She had been hoping they would match the ejector marks on similar cartridges fired from an AMT .45 automatic long slide which she already had tied to another hit. They hadn't.

She was just learning this disappointing news when Birley had called from their office across the drive in the homicide division to say they had to make a scene in west Houston. He was on his way to the motor pool to check out a car and would pick her up in front of the administration building as soon as he could get around there. Palma thanked the firearms examiner, grabbed her Styrofoam cup of coffee, slipped the strap of her purse over her right shoulder, and returned down the stark hallways to the front of the building. Outside, the swampy, tepid air and the gritty traffic pounding by on the nearby expressway turned her stomach against the coffee. She tossed it on the asphalt and carried the empty cup in her left hand, absently punching holes in the rim with her thumbnail as she thought about the circumstances of the second hit and made her way around the corner of the administration building.

At five-ten Carmen Palma was taller than average for a Hispanic woman. High-hipped, and a little more buxom than she wanted to be, she worked out regularly to keep her stomach and hips trim, and, she always hoped, to take a little off her bust. It never happened. Her black hair was kept at shoulder length and blunt-cut, long enough to dress up when she wasn't playing cop yet short enough to be out of her way when she clasped it behind her neck at crime scenes. She never wore lipstick, or much makeup of any kind, a privilege that nature accorded certain types of olive-skinned women whose pigmentation was a lively variety of tint and shade. Her eyebrows were jet and needed no grooming, not even periodic plucking to keep them shaped. She paid cursory attention to liner around her eyes which, as her mother had demonstrated when she was a child by holding a hand-sized chip of wood beside her face in a speckled mirror, were the same color as the sienna heartwood of mesquite.

The morning had started off wrong, even before the bad news from the crime lab, from the moment she had walked into her kitchen half asleep and ripped the previous day's date off the calendar. She had stood there staring at the new number and the note scrawled beneath it, surprised, offended, resentful, angry with herself. Then she had turned away and started making coffee. She made it too strong. She ruined a pair of panty hose while she was dressing upstairs, and then she dropped and lost the tiny back off an earring. Later, in the kitchen again, she sipped the strong coffee and stared out the window to the bricked courtyard and resolved once more to take it in her stride, as she did most things, having learned from her father that a long stride would get you what you wanted more quickly than a short temper. Still, her thoughts kept coming back to it, even crowding in on the negative results of the ejector comparisons which had just destroyed her last hope for making it with a guy who had had such a string of good luck that he could have qualified as an actuarial wonder.

By the time Birley pulled up to the curb, Palma had begun to perspire. After eight years as a detective, four of those in homicide, she had learned her lessons about the practical limits of stylish clothes and police work. In the first place the salary she pulled down wouldn't support the kinds of wardrobes she saw on the leggy career women uptown and, even if it did, the circumstances of the job simply made them impractical. Even the most serviceable and businesslike designer clothes just didn't cut it in the environment where Palma encountered most of her clients.

But it wasn't as if she hadn't tried. During her first year in homicide she had ruined half a dozen of her nicer dresses because she had been determined to dress a little more attractively than was practical, at least occasionally, and had worn them on days when she just 'felt' she wouldn't catch a dirty scene. She had been wrong. The final delusion that this might be possible had passed on a sweltering August afternoon in the far East End when she

and Jack Mane, her partner at the time, had been called
out to investigate the suspicious disappearance of a
neighborhood prostitute. On that afternoon Mane had
decided to be uncharacteristically egalitarian and 'let' her
crawl under the floor of a deteriorating pier and beam house
to confirm their suspicions about the source of a distinctly
putrescent odor. She kissed the price of the dress goodbye
and went in. One lady encountering the bad end of another,
neither of them dressed right for the occasion.

The next day had been her day off and she spent most
of it in a fabric shop. Poring over the pattern catalogs, she
selected a dozen or more classic styles of shirtwaist
dresses and skirts and blouses. Then she turned to the
fabrics. She methodically studied scores of fabrics before
settling on Egyptian cotton as being both utilitarian and
stylishly adaptable. She bought partial bolts in every
conceivable shade and texture, and took it all to a seam-
stress in the barrio where her mother still lived. Now she
had a closetful of dresses that neither sacrificed her
femininity nor caused her too much grief if she ruined
them at a scene.

Birley had the air conditioner cranked up on high as
Palma got in the passenger side and slid her purse off her
shoulder.

'So what did Chuck have to say?' he asked, pulling out
of the drive and heading for the freeway. He had already
shed his suit coat, which was thrown over the back of the
seat, and had loosened his tie.

'It's no good,' she said. 'Apparently it'd been caught
under the rear tire of the guy's car. The asphalt screwed it
up. No match.'

'You've gotta be joking. Nothing?'

Palma shook her head. She liked working with Birley,
though a lot of younger detectives might have chafed at
the older man's professional lassitude.

'What's happened?' Palma asked, closing the over-
loaded ashtray under the dash so the air conditioner
wouldn't whip the ashes. 'I thought Cushing and Leeland
were first out.'

'They are. But they caught something Cush wants us to look at. Said he thought we'd want to see it.'

Palma looked at him. 'That's it?'

Birley grinned. 'It'll be interesting, whatever it is. Cush thinks this is a very nifty thing, getting us out there.'

'Out where?'

'A good address. Just south of the Villages, off Voss.'

Palma took a foil packet from her purse, tore it open and took out a small disposable towelette, and proceeded to wipe the ash-dusted dash. When she had first started riding with Birley he had just quit smoking and hated riding in a car that had been used by a smoker on the previous shift. He would bitch and grumble and empty the ashtrays and wipe the dash with wet paper towels he would bring from the men's room to the garage just in case. For a while he compulsively cleaned every car they rode in. Gradually, after he got his nicotine dependency under control, he stopped the sanitation exercise and eventually even quit worrying about dumping the ashtrays. Palma could let it slide too, everything but the dash.

After she finished, she took a tortoiseshell hair clasp from her purse, pulled back her hair, and clasped it behind her neck.

'Hot?' Birley asked, not waiting for an answer. 'Every year it gets to the blistering point a little bit earlier in the year. I used to think it was my imagination or my age.'

'You don't anymore?' They were passing through the Highway 45 interchange, and she wished she were going straight on to Galveston for the day.

'Not since they discovered this greenhouse effect,' Birley said. 'Fluorocarbons. You know, when Sally's mom died she left us that little cabin up on the Trinity. Last time I was up there the water level had dropped five feet. Big shock. And then I got to thinking about fluorocarbons. I'm convinced my family's a major contributor to this global heat-up. Can you imagine how much hair spray and antiperspirant Sally and those four girls have used during the last twenty-five years?' He laughed.

'Jesus! By the time I retire up there on the lake that cabin's going to overlook nothing but a stinking brown sandbar.'

John Birley was an old dog, not in age but in homicide experience, and he had been Palma's partner for a little over two years. He was fifty-four, just over six feet tall, and beginning to get hefty. He had a pleasant broad face with a small round nose and lifeless brown hair that was thinning but refusing to gray. The lines at the corners of his eyes had already been there for a few years when Palma met him. He had spent much of his career holding down two jobs in order to put his daughters through college, and at times he seemed older than his years. He was seven months shy of a thirty-year retirement.

But the pension hadn't come soon enough. During the last year Birley had burned out. He knew it. Everyone knew it. He had become a detective of the bare minimum. He put in his hours and went home, and his desk cubicle in the homicide division cubbyhole he shared with Palma was decorated with the gaudy, hairy tufts of fly-fishing lures he stuck into the fabric of the walls, his own creations which he studied and revised in his patient search for perfect balance, style, and color. He still did his job, and his work was as thorough as always, but his curiosity was worn out. The veteran detectives recognized Birley's problem and accepted it. He had been a good man for a long time, and no one was going to call his hand because he lost his enthusiasm so close to retirement. It happened.

For her part, Palma was exactly where she had always wanted to be. Her father had been one of the first Hispanic detectives in homicide and would have retired in harness if a traffic accident hadn't claimed him first. Now, at thirty-three she was one of only four female detectives in a division of seventy-five officers, and of the four females she was the only Hispanic. She had had to deal with her share of wiseasses over the years, but luckily John Birley wasn't one of them. He was oblivious to racial prejudices — a rarity in the Southwest — and having grown up as an only boy with four sisters and then gone on to become the father of four daughters, he didn't have a chauvinistic bone in his body. And he harbored no illusions about women, good or bad.

Palma already had worked with Birley long enough to have grown to like and respect him before he started coasting on the job, so she didn't feel any resentment that he wasn't as aggressive as he might have been. As a matter of fact, his gradual disengagement over the past year had unexpectedly worked to her advantage. As Birley's enthusiasm flagged, Palma increasingly took on the responsibility of determining the style of their investigations as Birley tranquilly went along. She had acquired invaluable experience in case management that she might not have gotten if her partner had always insisted on being the 'big boy' of the team, continually asserting his leadership right by virtue of his age, seniority, and sex.

But Birley wasn't always quiet. He had had a lot of experience, and from time to time he had something to say. And when he did, Palma listened. The fact was — and it had taken her a while to realize it — John Birley, while seeming to be not entirely attentive to his business, had managed to carefully guide her development, and as a result he had given her the best training any younger homicide detective could ever have hoped to receive from an older partner. It was in large part thanks to Birley's taking her under his wing that Palma had developed so quickly into one of the division's hottest and most watched detectives with a reputation for grabbing a case and not letting go 'till the devil goes blind,' as Birley liked to say.

Palma had settled back and watched the traffic on the freeway, her thoughts beginning to wander as soon as Birley had started talking. She listened to him with one side of her brain while the other tracked over scenes from her recent past that had been shoving their way to the front of her consciousness all morning. They were the last things she wanted to think about, but she had tried too hard, and now they were the only things she could think about.

By the time they passed Greenway Plaza she was suddenly aware that Birley had stopped talking and was glancing at her out of the corner of his eye. Finally he said, 'Any questions?'

'What?' She looked at him.

'I mean, about what I've been saying. The lake going down, the black bass not biting, the bad problem with mosquitoes up on the Trinity...'

She grinned. 'Okay, sorry.'

'You miffed about the screwed-up shell casing?'

Palma shook her head. The fact was, she was 'miffed' because she was miffed, a response she knew Birley wouldn't think much of as a reasonable explanation. She would have preferred not to talk about it, but Birley was sitting over there waiting for her to get it off her chest.

'Every morning,' she said, looking out across the city, looking at the traffic, flicking something imaginary off her dress, 'I go into the kitchen, go over the calendar, and tear off the previous day's date. Always do that, first thing. And I don't even look at it because I'm gone all day, and at night I don't care. But I do it. And then I make coffee. Anyway, today when I did that I was surprised to see that I'd written — in big green letters: "Divorce final ... six months."' She rolled her eyes. 'For some perverse reason I'd marked it like a damn anniversary. Don't even remember doing it. I can't imagine why...' She fiddled with the clasp in her hair again. 'I went through the entire calendar to see if I'd done any more of that kind of crap.'

Birley turned his head slowly and looked at her as if he were peering over the top of reading glasses.

'I hadn't,' she said.

Birley had been through the whole ordeal with her, the disintegrating marriage, the affair, the lightning divorce. Palma had buried herself with work trying to get away from it, and Birley had watched her, been there when she needed something solid to touch to steady her balance. He hadn't been a father to her, but he had been damn close to it, and she would never forget it.

'Why'd that put you off?' Birley asked, switching lanes without looking back. Palma had already checked her outside mirror. When they traveled in the same car Birley always drove, but Palma always watched the traffic. It was defensive driving by remote control.

'I don't know,' she said. 'That's why I'm "miffed".' Birley was the only person she had ever heard use that word, which reminded her of the 1940s.

Birley laughed. 'Well, hell,' he said, and Palma knew they had reached that point where even his lifetime of experience with ten women wouldn't help him understand.

It was a simple matter: she was furious that she could still be so affected by an unexpected reminder of her ex-husband. Brian DeWitt James III had been — still was — a criminal defense lawyer, which should have told her something about him from the beginning. They had met at a trial where she had testified about a minor aspect of the case he was defending, and Brian had dazzled her and the jury with his quickness, confidence . . . and sincerity. His client, who was as guilty as Judas, was acquitted. Palma, on the other hand, was nailed. He pursued her relentlessly with unabashed adoration. He was gorgeous, with beautiful eyes and teeth, a personal style of dressing and caring for his body that let you know he was squeaky clean without being fussy. He could think on his feet, which made him a superb trial lawyer and a formidable opponent in the other kind of courtship as well. He was quick to flatter, quick to read your thoughts (though not always correctly), quick to defend himself if he believed (as he often did) that he wasn't winning you over, and, unfortunately, he was quick in bed.

The latter attribute didn't even faze her. She couldn't resist him. The relationship had been fast and hot and thrilling, and there had been no time to think it over and no desire to slow things down. But she had to be honest about it, she wasn't thinking anyway. She was *feeling*, and if there had been warning signs she hadn't seen them because her libido had run amok, scattering reason before it. She had married him after four months of heavy breathing.

Any sidewalk philosopher could have told her what would happen next, but Palma didn't even see it coming. It was an old story; she could have read about it in the hundreds of 'relationship' or 'self-help' or 'women's' magazines and books in the pop psychology sections of the bookstores. Women never failed to be caught flat-footed and incredulous about this phenomenon of the Janus-faced new husband. It was like marrying Chang and Chen, the second of the two remaining invisible while you were dating the first, and then mercurially springing to life the morning after your wedding night while the one you had dated proceeded to disappear. The next night you made love to a man you'd never met.

The adoration was gone. Before their marriage Brian had joyfully embarrassed her with flowers (yes, he really had, and yes, she had loved every petal), and gifts (he had impeccable taste, knew what looked good on her, and didn't hesitate to buy it), and surprises (he liked to meet her at the end of her last shift before the weekend with two tickets to Cancún or Acapulco).

But after the wedding, he had undergone a change that had almost given her whiplash. Flowers? Only for funerals, and then *she* had to order them. Gifts? If she wanted something she was perfectly free to buy it. Surprises? His caseload was heavy. It would have to wait, maybe next month (she hadn't seen a beach since).

Before their marriage he spent every moment he could get away from his job with her; after their marriage he suddenly had obligations he seemed never to have had before. He played on the law firm's tennis team which competed every Saturday morning and practiced three afternoons a week. They couldn't have lunches together because he played handball with a group of guys who put him on to clients. It was essential to his career to be attentive to these 'players.' Sundays he was too tired to do anything but lie on the sofa in front of the television set and watch whatever kind of ball game was in season.

He never helped with anything that happened in the kitchen — he only got as far as the dining room in that part of the house. He didn't know how to turn on the washing machine, or even get his dirty clothes from the bedroom to the laundry room. He never went to the cleaners or shopped for so much as a box of cereal — but he knew where the liquor store was and would stop by on his way home. His indifference to such day-to-day practicalities changed only when he was inconvenienced by an interruption in his routine. Then he could be spitefully impatient — with her.

He was still quick in bed, only now he didn't even pretend to postcoital tenderness or even a mild concern for her own satisfactions in such matters. After he had spent himself, he rolled over and passed out like a narcoleptic.

After the first six months she could no longer ignore the fact that this was the way things were going to be. She spent another six months trying to get him to 'communicate' (he didn't believe he wasn't) and another six months paralyzed by the realization that the marriage wasn't going to work. When she caught him in an affair with another lawyer at his firm, a young woman whose ambitions brooked no moral impediments, Palma kicked him out of the house they recently had purchased in West University Place and which Brian had long coveted as an appropriate status symbol. And she made damn sure she got it in the settlement. She wanted it not because of what it meant to her, but because of what it meant to him. It was his idea of the sort of place a man like him ought to live, and it was her idea of getting even to take it away from him. She never regretted it.

She had endured the marriage for eighteen months, had been divorced for six, and was still angry for her astounding lack of good judgment, and — in those moments when she was being brutally honest — not a little embarrassed by having played the part of the stereotypical gullible female.

2

The car leaned into a long climbing curve to the right as Birley left the Southwest Freeway heading north on the West Loop. Palma tried to forget Brian. Actually, it wasn't that easy to do, considering who they were going to see now. Art Cushing was not one of Palma's favorite people.

'Cush didn't say anything except that he wanted us to come out and look at this?' she asked again.

'That's it.'

'You didn't ask what it was?'

'I did, Carmen, but you know Cush. Hell, it was just easier to come out here and look. Big deal. I was getting tired of the office for a change. And besides, the exterminators came through there last night.'

Okay, that made more sense. It probably hadn't taken that much of a call to get Birley out of the office. Still, she didn't like being summoned anywhere by Cushing. In too many ways he was uncomfortably like Brian, though she had to admit Brian was considerably more sophisticated. Cushing looked like a young Italian playboy with a lean, athletic body that of itself consumed about half his salary to feed, to exercise, to tan, to coif, to dress, and to shod. Unfortunately his taste in clothes seemed to have been influenced more by his eight years in the vice squad than by the men's fashion magazines. His wardrobe looked as if it had been confiscated from a Cuban pimp whose cousin fenced Mexican-made knockoffs of Italian ready-to-wear. Cushing's hair was blow-dried, but his manner was oily, and the air of illegitimacy he had picked up from sleazing on the streets had never quite worn off. He was a natural-born scam man.

When Cushing came to homicide, Palma had to deal with his ego within the first three days, which is how long it took this cocky new guy to ask her out for a drink. She accepted, giving him the benefit of the doubt. He took her to an expensive club where they sat at the crowded bar. Two drinks down, Cushing had one hand on her upper thigh and still traveling, as he ran his finest line on her, a stale monologue that would have been transparent even to a convent novitiate. Keeping her eyes on his, she had unobtrusively dropped her free hand down between Cushing's legs and latched on to the tender, knobbed end of his penis as if her hand had been guided by radar. She gripped it in a clinch that launched his eyebrows to his hairline and widened his eyes. Without saying a word or changing her expression, she squeezed him so fiercely she had momentary fears of inflicting permanent damage. But she didn't let go of her eye-watering grip on his glans until he moved his hand from her thigh. Neither of them spoke as they looked at each other, disconnected. Momentarily disarmed and then suddenly furious, and probably in considerable pain, Cushing wheeled around and walked out of the bar, leaving Palma to pay for the drinks and take a cab back to the station to pick up her car.

Cushing never mentioned the incident, never, and neither did she. And he never forgave her. Even now, after three years, Art Cushing could hardly be civil to her. Their mutual antagonism was well known to everyone in the division and was always a good subject for idle gossip, though the speculation about what had happened between them was always more lurid than the facts. No one ever knew the source of their shared animosity. Cushing's machismo would never allow him to relate the story to anyone, under any circumstances, and Palma had long since lost interest in both the incident and Cushing's damaged ego. She thought he at least ought to be grateful to her for that.

'I can't wait to see this,' Palma said.

'Yeah,' Birley grinned and moved into the far right lane for the Westheimer exit half a mile ahead. The traffic grew heavier now and slowed, and to their right the sun was climbing near the meridian, shriveling the Gulf clouds as it rose.

The Hammersmith condominium complex was in a district with the cloying name of Charmwood on the southern bank of Buffalo Bayou and only blocks away from the villages of Bunker Hill, Piney Point, and Hunters Creek. Just off South Voss near Westheimer, the complex was a mingle of small wooded lanes where the buildings were joined together like row houses, different styles and colors butting up against each other in an imperfect harmony, their various rooflines and chimneys bouncing up and down like the individual notes on a musical score. They had been around a while, maybe since the sixties, which in this city of the Modern Way gave them an established air and lent them a kind of comfortable intimacy that in another time and place would have been called a neighborhood.

To the east a little way were the trendy, uptown Post Oak and Galleria shopping districts which were once again exhibiting a grandeur and international popularity that everyone had thought had been irreparably damaged by the oil and real estate disasters of the mid-eighties. But as the new decade came onstage, so did a new city, or at least a city that was beginning to realize the end of its travail was in sight. Houston was making a comeback, and it wasn't apologizing for the lost time. The nouveau riche had evaporated like bayou mist in the harsh sunlight of hard times, leaving the old money behind to take the heat. And they had done it. The hangers-on, who came from nowhere in particular and leeched onto good times wherever they happened to be, were gone. The city had returned to its sanity which, combined with the kind of hard-won experience that comes with the jolting reversal of fortunes, had achieved something approaching wisdom. The worst was over. And if the survivors had anything to do with the future, and they intended to, it would never again be as foolishly sublime, or as gallingly bad, as it had been.

The moment they turned into Olympia Street, Palma saw the police cars and the white crime scene unit at the end of the lane. And she saw, at next glance, the inevitable curious. But they weren't crowding around the police cars or pressing up to the yellow crime scene tape that circumscribed the parameter of violence; they were not aggressive in their inquisitiveness, not pushing to get closer as did their less sophisticated counterparts in whose frayed neighborhoods these sorts of scenes were usually played out. No, these curious were sober and physically remote. Unused to the intrusive sequelae of illegal death, they sensed the inappropriateness of it and wanted nothing to do with it. They hung back, demonstrating their censure by their aloofness. Violent death was a shabby affair. They didn't approve.

When Palma got out of the car, which Birley parked at the curb behind Cushing and Leeland's, the gummy morning heat enveloped her like the tropical, early-day heat of the Yucatán. But instead of the fragrance of bougainvilleas and frangipani, Palma smelled the sweet, weighty breath of honeysuckle and magnolia and jasmine, and heard the spit-spit-spit-spit of a water sprinkler in between the scratchy transmissions of a patrol unit radio.

She was on the sidewalk before Birley, who always took his time, had even gotten out of his seat belt. With her shield hanging from the side pocket of her purse, she hurried past the two young patrolmen manning the yellow-ribboned courtyard and approached the front door, shiny with heavy coats of wine red enamel. Palma noticed that the brass knocker in the center was already dusted with magnetic ferric oxide. The doorknob wouldn't matter. She pushed open the door and was confronted with a heavy wash of cold air. The place was freezing.

Two other patrolmen were standing in the living room talking to Wendell Barry, the storklike coroner's investigator, and Palma spoke to them as she glanced around the light and airy living room with its vaulted ceiling reaching to the second floor. Without hesitating, she passed into a wide corridor and started toward an opened doorway from which she heard the steady, solitary voice of the CSU investigator, Jules LeBrun.

She approached the door, stepped inside the bedroom, and stopped. Art Cushing and his partner Don Leeland, a quiet, thickset man in his late thirties, stood with their backs to her, blocking her view of most of the bed. She could see only the dead woman's feet and her head from the neck up, her eyes open. Both men had their hands in their pockets looking at the woman while LeBrun moved around the bed with an audio-video camera, narrating the setting of the body, pointing the camera at the naked woman on the bed as if she were the catatonic starlet of a porno film. The place was as cold as a meat locker. Palma recognized the faint fragrance of cosmetics that hovers in women's bedrooms.

Almost simultaneously Cushing and Leeland turned around and saw her. Cushing turned back to the bed, but Leeland smiled faintly at her from under his thick, brindled mustache and raised his chin at her. No one spoke or moved for a couple of minutes until LeBrun finished recording his narration and went to another room.

'Hey, Carmen,' Cushing said, turning back to her again, reflexively wiping the corners of his mouth with his thumb and forefinger. He never said hi or hello or whattya say or how's it goin', he said hey. He was wearing a baggy gray suit and black shirt with a dove gray tie. Nodding toward the bed as both men moved apart to make room for her, he said, 'Take a look.'

Palma could feel their eyes on her as she approached, and the instant she glimpsed the body she knew why, even before she had gotten close enough to examine it. She knew because of instinct, that indisputable feminine exertion that tugged at her pelvis and pulled at the sides of her eyes. It took all of her self-control not to react, not to let them know she had seen this before, and that it scared her.

The woman was nude, waxy pale, and only slightly gaseous as she lay in the middle of the bed from which all the covers had been stripped except the bottom sheet. A pillow had been placed under her head, and she had been positioned in a funereal posture, straight out, legs together, her hands placed one on top of the other just below her lolling breasts. Slightly discolored furrows encircled her wrists where ligatures had been, and encircling her neck was a single broader furrow punctuated with small reddish welts where the belt holes had been. Her eyes were open. Her blond hair seemed to have been freshly combed, and her battered and bloated face was freshly made up, the cosmetics expertly applied: eye shadow, eye liner, powder, and glistening lip gloss. Her lower abdomen was only now showing the first faint, blue-green discoloration of internal bacterial decomposition. There were a few bruises, seemingly random, scattered over her body and a widespread stippling of bite marks on her breasts and thighs. Palma knew when they spread her legs they would find others on the insides of her thighs and around her vulva. Both nipples were missing, excised with neat, surgical precision, and the quarter-size wounds had turned black from exposure.

Palma knew what she was looking at, but held her tongue, her thoughts shooting way out on a thin string of probabilities.

'And . . .' Cushing said, stepping back carefully to show her a chair not far from the bed. A woman's clothes were there, fastidiously folded, laid out as if they had been prepared to be packed in a suitcase. Palma looked at Cushing. He was chewing gum, hard, his smoothly shaven jaw muscles rippling in front of his ears. 'It's the same shit, isn't it? What you and Birley came onto a coupla weeks ago.' It was bubble gum; she could smell it on his breath. He was almost smiling, confident, pleased with himself.

Palma turned around, looking for something else. She found the bundle of bedclothes piled next to an opened closet door. She had to give Cushing credit. He must have heard talk around the squad room, and the details stuck with him. They had been out of the ordinary.

'Who is she?' she asked.

'Dorothy Ann Samenov, a sales representative for Computron. Computer software. Offices downtown, Allied Bank Plaza. Thirty-eight years old, according to her driver's license.'

She turned around to face him.

'Patrolman outside the door, VanMeter, found her,' Cushing said, managing to talk and chew his gum at the same time. 'Came here with the victim's friend ... Vickie Kittrie. She works with Samenov. Last Thursday Samenov and Kittrie and others from their office went out for drinks after work. Victim left the bar about 6.30 P.M. That was the last time anyone saw her alive, far as we know. Next morning she didn't show for work. Kittrie called her at home, but there was no answer, and they assumed she was sick. Kittrie called throughout the day, but never got an answer. After work she went by to check. Samenov's car was parked in front out there, just like it is now.'

'Kittrie doesn't live here?'

'Nope. Kittrie knocks on the door,' Cushing continued. 'No answer. She wonders about this, but goes on. Next morning, Saturday, they're suppose to have an exercise class together. When Samenov doesn't show up Kittrie comes by again, still no answer. Car's still out front. She gets worried, calls the police. She tells the patrolman her story, but he doesn't want to enter the place with no evidence of foul play. He asks all the usual questions and suggests maybe that Samenov skipped for a long weekend with somebody. Kittrie admitted Samenov sometimes went out of town for the weekend, but she usually told someone where she was going. Officer suggests Kittrie should try to get in touch with Samenov again on Sunday, and if Samenov does not show up for work on Monday, then call the police again. That's what she did.'

'Have you talked to her?' Palma asked.

'Nope.' Cushing started jangling the change in his pocket. 'What do you think? Same boy, huh?'

'I don't know,' she lied. She knew damn well it was, and it made her queasy. Everything about it signaled brainsick. She turned around. 'John?'

Birley was standing behind them, just inside the door, already looking at the dead woman, nonplussed.

'Hey, Birley,' Cushing said.

Birley moseyed into the room. 'Whatcha got?' he said to Leeland, good-naturedly gripping the top of Leeland's thick shoulder as he went past him, never taking his eyes off the bed. Leeland gave him an amused grin, but didn't say anything.

'Have you guys started in here?' Palma asked.

'Shit! Carmen, it's virgin,' Cushing said, curling his top lip. 'Nobody's been in here but that patrolman, Julie in there, and us. Only thing we've touched is the carpet under our shoes, and not very damn much of that.' Palma was a stickler. Cushing knew exactly what she was thinking: Had they touched anything, opened a drawer, swung a door one way or the other, touched the corpse?

Birley stood beside Palma at the bed, both of them staring at the woman in silence.

'Son of a bitch,' he said. He knew, too.

'Can you believe it?' Palma was fighting a jittery feeling.

'I guess I'd better.' Birley shrugged against the cold.

'What the hell are you two talkin' about?' Cushing tossed his head. 'Is this the same guy's work or what, goddammit?'

'It could be,' Palma said without looking at him.

'Well, very goddamn good,' Cushing snorted. 'Thank you.'

'Some advice, Cush,' Birley said calmly. 'If you don't come up with any more evidence here than we did with the other one, you're going to be in trouble. This guy's going to start doing these as regular as clockwork. He's going to nail you to the wall by your balls.'

'Oh, yeah, ter-rific. You telling me you don't have any leads?'

Cushing's sarcasm made Don Leeland shift his feet. Leeland was Cushing's polar opposite. Of middle height with a physique that would one day be chubby, he had large, sorrowful eyes that, together with his full mustache, reminded Palma of a young walrus. Having a benign demeanor, he kept his head down and did his work, leaving all the razzle-dazzle to his partner. Unlike Cushing, who had developed his knowledge of human nature from working the streets, Leeland was not cynical and combative. He had come to homicide from crime analysis, and his investigative instincts relied more heavily on research and a logical methodology than gut feeling. Together they made a strong team, but Leeland was never comfortable with Cushing's style.

Birley ignored Cushing and moved around to the other side of the bed. 'She's been knocked around a little more. I'm betting this one's got more busted under that makeup than a jaw and a nose.' He nodded. 'And look at the bite marks.'

Palma had already noticed them. She had never been able to acquire an indifference to the sight of teeth marks in a dead woman's flesh. Of the more common types of behavioral evidence in sex crimes, nothing affected her so strongly as these; nothing seemed more primitive or atavistic. Her mind's eye always conjured the image of mating lions, the male mounting the cringing lioness from behind, sinking his bared teeth into the back of her neck as he penetrates her.

She moved closer. 'There're more of them, and they're more vicious. Deeper.'

Birley bent down over the dead woman and sniffed near her face. 'Perfume. The son of a bitch put perfume on her this time.'

Palma nodded.

'She's clean.' Birley was still close to the woman's face. 'I don't see anything that looks like defense wounds.'

Palma looked around the bedroom. 'And he's either meticulous or there wasn't anything to clean up. Maybe she was ...'

'God ... damn ...'

The tone of Birley's voice made Palma swing her head around. Cushing and Leeland moved toward the bed. Birley was only inches away from the dead woman's face now. 'Her eyes aren't open, Carmen.'

Palma looked at the daydreamer's eyes which, now that she studied them, seemed wider than the usual heavy-lidded gaze of the dead. She bent down opposite Birley, caught a waft of the perfume, and saw too much of the tops of the gaping eyeballs. A wash of cold spread over her, colder than the air in the frigid room, as she made out a raw, uneven line running across the upper rear of each eyeball where its sticky tissue joined the socket. The bare, milky orbs were as naked as the woman herself. She had no eyelids.

3

For a moment Palma couldn't swallow. During the past several minutes she had been aware of the lump growing in her throat, at first as some ill-defined sensation that did not require her full attention, then as something she could not ignore or swallow. She knew what it was, but it was no less real for that. She shot a quick look around. It wasn't something she often felt anymore. After the first year or so in homicide she had started checking her emotions at the front door. If she didn't, it simply took too much out of her. But sometimes, with the sexual homicides, she couldn't help it, and a vaguely defined anxiety darkened the veiny back reaches of her mind. It became a burdensome shadow she could not escape, regardless of the mental tricks she played or how fervently she wished to rise above it. And it was happening now, answering to a resonating inner chord. Dread surfaced like something corrosive, and it frightened her. She knew that before she finally beat it down again, it was going to take something out of her; it was going to claim a piece of her.

All of this Palma recognized and understood in an instant. But she was already into it, already committed. It had had something to do with the cold, and with the bite marks. Especially the bite marks.

She bent down, too, and studied the raw lines almost hidden in the mucosa above the woman's eyeballs. This close, she got a strong sense of the perfume, but it was an altered fragrance. Birley had failed to mention the stale smell of death, the first musty odor of the oncoming decay working in the dead woman's bowels.

'Shit, no eyelids?' Cushing dropped his tough-guy act and bent down beside Palma while Leeland, not so curious about the details, craned his neck from the foot of the bed.

'This is precise work,' Palma said. She shifted her attention to the carved breasts only inches away. 'It's hard to tell if it's postmortem ... the way he's cleaned her.' She nudged Cushing aside and, bending close, moved past the wounded breasts to the dead woman's maculated stomach, to the matted caramel wool of her vulva, to the thighs, moving her head from side to side, back and forth, to catch the surface of the body in an angle against the poor lighting. She was trying to find the distinguishing blotches, the scaly, starchy stains of semen. But if she didn't find them, it wouldn't be significant. It didn't always happen; they hadn't found any on Sandra Moser either. However, it would be significant if they could determine if the dead woman had in fact been cleaned.

Birley looked for the same thing around the wounds on the woman's breasts and face. 'He's cleaned her mouth before putting on the lipstick,' he said. 'Maybe this time there'll be something inside.' He checked the sides of her body next to the bed sheet, and then watched Palma's examination. She was thorough.

'I think we're going to find something on the insides of her thighs,' she said, straightening up. 'I believe there's a smear ... going down, just into her left groin.' She straightened up. 'But he's not leaving behind very much.'

'He cut her eyelids last time?' Cushing asked. He was still staring at Samenov's eyes.

'No,' Palma said. 'he didn't, but he cut off one nipple. That was all. But everything else seems the same: the ligature marks, the positioning, the makeup, the removed bedclothes, the victim's folded clothes, the bruises, the bite marks. Only it's more severe this time.'

'The other woman was blond too?' It was the first thing Leeland had said.

Palma nodded and said, 'But there's something else.'

'Yeah, he did something to her.' Birley was still standing beside the bed, his arms folded, thinking. 'He licked her or masturbated on her or something ... else. That's why he's washing them.'

'Fetishist,' Leeland offered soberly. He was writing something on a notepad.

'I could almost buy that if it weren't so damned convenient,' Palma said. 'He's reducing the trace evidence to nil.'

Birley shook his head. 'No, this guy's a mess. He did something to her.' He was still looking at the dead woman. All of them were, standing around the bed looking at her.

'What about the ligatures?' Palma said, noticing again the woman's throat, wrists and ankles. 'There's no evidence of a struggle. A willing victim, maybe. Up to a point.'

'Maybe he's quick,' Cushing said. 'Overpowers them, slaps them down here, and that's it.'

'Still, there should have been more bruises on her, a scratch at least. There's got to be something.' She looked over at a dressing table with bottles of perfume, a jewelry case, nail polish. Then she turned back and looked at the dead woman's swollen face. 'Maybe he knew her,' she said.

'What, you think he knew Moser too?' Birley was shaking his head.

'It would account for the lack of disarray, lack of defense wounds, and the condition of her face,' Palma said.

It was a detective's axiom that when a homicide victim's face had been brutally attacked, the odds were that the killer had known the victim well, perhaps even had been related. It wasn't something anyone pretended to understand, but all too often that was the way it played out.

'I don't know,' Birley said. 'Maybe both women were into this.' He raised his chin at the bed. 'But I doubt if they wanted to be into it this much.'

'He really bit the shit out of her, didn't he?' Cushing said, jangling his change again. 'Jesus, the guy must've really freaked out.'

Palma had noticed that in more than half the bite marks the teeth had actually penetrated the skin, making notched punctures.

'Fine,' she said. 'The bastard made a big mistake. We'll get perfect impressions.' She felt Cushing look at her, and out of the corner of her eye she saw Leeland and Birley exchange looks. She didn't regret the malice in her voice, and she didn't care what they thought. Though she was sure she was missing far more than she was understanding, what she could see of the way this man treated his victims told her more about him than if he had given a lecture on the subject. His intelligence, and his loathing for these women, was evident in every move he had made. For Palma, he was beginning to become something more than just another crazy.

No one spoke for a moment, and then Palma said, 'Where are they?'

'Huh?' Cushing frowned at her.

'The nipples, the eyelids,' she said.

'Hell,' Birley put his hands in the small of his back and bent to one side and then the other to stretch his aching back muscles. 'We didn't find the one he cut off Moser. We won't find these either.'

'He's taking them with him,' she said.

'Probably.'

Suddenly irritated at the cold, she looked at Cushing. 'You know what the temperature is in here?'

'He cranked it down all the way.' Cushing was working his gum between his front teeth, stretching it out with his tongue. 'I checked it. It's almost fifty.'

Birley carefully stepped to the bathroom door, keeping to one side and leaned in, nodding. 'Clean as a whistle.' He paused. 'She's got a bidet in here, for Christ's sake.'

Palma turned and walked out of the bedroom. Cushing followed her. They went a few steps down the hallway to a second bedroom, obviously unused. The closets served as additional storage, the clothes chests were empty, and a second bathroom was furnished with unused soap, unused towels, and an empty medicine cabinet. A guest room without guests. They went back down the hall to the kitchen where Birley and Leeland were looking around. Birley had carefully opened the refrigerator.

'She wasn't a gourmet,' he said. 'Mostly sandwich stuff in here. Some fruit. Diet-drink stuff.'

Leeland was puttering in the trash.

Palma, with Cushing sticking to her side like a pilot fish, walked through the living room and up a staircase to a study that overlooked the living room. There was a large desk, a sofa, a television, and bookshelves. Outside the study was a balcony that looked over one of the complex's central courtyards and offered a clear view of a swimming pool with shimmering blue water. But it had privacy, a trellis of wisteria. As they came back through the study, she noticed that the desk was neat, with one corner stacked with promotional materials from Computron. Though there were few rooms, all of them were spacious and well laid out, making the condo seem comfortably large.

They met back in the living room and milled around for a few moments, everyone pursuing, or pretending to pursue, his own thoughts about what they had just seen. Finally Palma got it out in the open.

'Okay,' she said turning to Cushing and crossing her arms, 'What's the deal? Are you going to give it to us?'

Cushing shook his head, 'No way.' One hand made a preening sweep down his gray tie as he quick-shrugged his shoulders like a self-satisfied street-corner pimp.

Birley and Leeland looked at each other.

'I didn't think so,' Palma said.

'We're going to have to work it together,' Cushing said.

'Together?' Palma smiled. That admission must have

cost him some inner peace despite his confident manner. She studied him for a minute as she tried to guess the reason for his fidelity to this particular case. If the victim had been a sore-ridden addict — even though an obvious serial victim — Cushing magnanimously would have seen the efficacy of turning his case over to Palma and Birley. But in this instance, Palma suspected his motivation to hang on to the case was based on a different set of criteria. 'What do you want out of this, Cush?'

'What the hell's that supposed to mean?' He tried to be indignant, but it wasn't an attitude he carried well. 'This's my job, for Christ's sake.'

'You know we're going to want to keep this out of the media, don't you?'

'The media?' Cushing kept his face straight for a moment, then a slow, skewed grin began to grow, his gum like a plug of pink putty clamped between his bright front teeth. 'You've already been thinking about the media, Carmen?'

Palma looked at him and cursed the bad luck that had made Cushing and Leeland first out that morning. She knew damn well there wasn't anything she could do about it, and Cushing knew it too. The best she could do was to seize the initiative and not let Cushing think he was going to be running the investigation. He had to be impressed with the fact that he was coming into the game late, that the ground rules were already established. To Cushing the guy who killed Moser and Samenov was only the ticket to a potentially flashy case that might — if it got really crazy — be good material for a book or TV movie or a film. To Palma he was something else, something she knew she wanted a hell of a lot more than Cushing wanted to be on the cover of *People* magazine. She wasn't going to let him take it away from her.

'All right,' she said, glancing at Birley, who was standing with an elbow propped on the kitchen bar enjoying their confrontation as if it were a cockfight. 'Since John and I had feared this was a serial killing from the beginning,' she lied, 'we'd better tell you how we've

set up the approach to this whole thing.' She glanced at
Birley again, who was keeping a poker face while
wondering, she knew, if she could pull this off. 'Let's get
Julie in here too.'

Jules LeBrun had finished his solitary video stroll and
narration through the rest of the condo and was already
bringing his equipment back into the living room before
continuing his routine in the bedroom. LeBrun was
young, maybe twenty-six, and took his business very
seriously. Palma had wondered about his name for a long
time; he was clearly Mexican.

She hastily reviewed Sandra Moser's case of the
month before and hit the high spots of their investigation
regarding Moser's background, marital status, their interviews with friends and acquaintances, habits, activities,
everything. And she was honest — she had no choice —
about the dead end they had come to. The leads in
Moser's case had quickly come to nothing. Now,
however, they had a chance to revive the investigation.
Beginning with the scene itself.

'The problem,' she said, looking at LeBrun, 'is that this
guy's work is immaculate. Whatever his reasons —
whether he's a fetishist, or an ex-con who knows what to
clean up and why, or some kind of psycho — he's not
leaving us much to work with. We've got to go to
extraordinary lengths to gather trace evidence and to keep
the scene clean. More than we usually do. There was no
semen at the Moser scene, and only Moser's blood and
very little of it since her wounds were postmortem. No
saliva. Swabs and smears gave us nothing. We did get fair
bite-mark impressions, but we should do better here
because they're more severe.

'Julie, if we catch another one of these we're going to
ask for you personally so you can maintain some kind of
continuity from one crime scene to another, get to know
your man and what he might do, where he might leave
something for us to pick up. Be as creative as possible in
thinking for this guy because he's way ahead of us. Also,
when you take your specimens to the crime lab, make

sure you always give them to Barbara Soronno. She got the material on Moser and we need to keep using her for continuity in the lab work.'

Palma continued in this way for several more minutes, her mind racing to keep ahead of her mouth, hoping she was actually presenting a coherent plan of approach for such an investigation, her eyes occasionally sliding past Cushing to see if he was buying into it.

'That's the general picture,' she said finally. She had rolled the dice, and they were spinning. She waited for them to toss up the right dots. 'What have I missed?' she asked, looking at Birley.

'I think you covered it,' he said. There was a trace of amusement on his broad face.

For a few moments no one spoke, and the only sounds in the room came from Cushing as he nervously jangled the change in his pocket and popped his gum.

'So? Let's get on with it,' Cushing blurted.

A two and a five. She was in.

4

She said to him, 'I slept like a dead woman last night. I didn't dream; I didn't move. Fifteen hours, straight through.'

He said nothing, but turned slightly in his leather armchair and looked at the clock on the bookshelves. She had been lying on his chaise longue for seventeen minutes and these were the first words she had spoken. She lay facing away from him, at an angle, her arms straight to her sides, palms up, fingers relaxed as she looked past her feet, out the glass wall of his office to the woods that sloped down to the bayou, everything suffused in an apple green light filtering through the May leaves.

'I went to a movie and got home around eleven o'clock; I was exhausted. Paul was still out and Emily had already gotten the children into bed. I took a cold shower, and when I got out I dried quickly and lay down on the bed, still damp. The windows were open, and I could smell the woods after last night's rain. I went to sleep.'

He looked at the toes of her stockinged feet, the little tips of slightly darker nylon through which he could see her pedicured nails. Ankles as slim as a gazelle's. The dress was a shirtwaist of silk or rayon, a pastel rose so sheer it required a full slip. Even so, it settled over her body with telling detail.

'It could just as easily have been fifteen seconds as

fifteen hours. I was oblivious.'

She stopped again. After a quiet interval he asked, 'What happened? Why this ... long sleep?'

The question was rote. When they told him they had experienced something for the first time, an emotion or thought or physical sensation, he asked them why they believed it happened. They pondered this question with serious self-indulgence, gratified that someone wanted to know how they felt, that someone cared why they did the things they did, even if he was being paid to do it.

'I haven't slept like that since I was ten.'

Broussard's eyes moved from her rose thighs to her face. She hadn't addressed his question.

'Ten?'

She turned her hands over and placed them palms down, fingers spread slightly, the gesture of a woman suddenly wary, as if the chaise had trembled inexplicably. But she was not frightened; her face betrayed nothing.

'Since you were ten?' he prompted.

Mary Lowe had been coming to Dr. Broussard for a little over two months, five days a week. He hadn't made much progress with her. From the beginning she had been a resistant client, but Dr. Broussard tolerated her recalcitrance, even overlooked the bleak prognosis for success. After all, he was not a strict interpreter of the classic forms of psychoanalysis, and if this woman did not want to cooperate he wasn't going to be rigidly demanding. He already had told both Mary and her husband that the type of therapy she had selected could be time-consuming and protracted. He would let that prove to be so. In the meantime, he was more than content to listen to her recitations which, up to now, had been evasive and vacuous ramblings, a waste of time. But only a waste of time for her. For his own part, he could not have wished for a more pleasurable hour, sitting quietly just out of her peripheral view with the freedom and leisure to let his eyes travel during the course of every sixty-minute session from one end of her long body to the other, imagining the exact texture and tones of the flesh beneath the sheer rose veil.

Dr. Dominick Broussard was forty-eight.

Her hands gradually relaxed, and she turned them over once again, palms up, fingers curled gently without tension.

'When I was nine,' she said, 'I had a doll from Dresden. My father was in the army, and had been stationed there ... or in Germany, anyway, and he brought her back to me. She was porcelain, her face was. I imagine she was expensive, though that didn't occur to me at the time. But thinking back, remembering the delicacy of her features, the detail, the luminous quality of her face, she must have been. She was blond, too, and I thought she was the most beautiful thing in the world. The most beautiful.'

Her tone of voice caused Dr. Broussard to focus his attention on her face. She possessed an exemplary beauty, a firm jawline with high cheekbones and a subtly asymmetric mouth which he found especially appealing because of a small hint of a pucker at the corner of one side. She had a shallow, but distinct, dimple above her upper lip, a fashion model's straight nose, and large gray-blue eyes which she lightly shaded about with a russet shadow that gave them a soulful appearance. Her hair was blond, not the strawy, bleach-punished white of the beauty parlor, but rather the thick, butter-rich blond that occurs only as a genetic gift. Today she wore it pulled back in a loose knot, a style which accented the beguiling qualities of her features.

He found her so wonderfully appealing that he happily would have continued seeing her had she come only to lie on the chaise in silence, staring out at the sun-dappled grounds for an hour before departing in silence. In fact, the idea of that scenario was so appealing to him that he played it out in his imagination: a psychoanalyst has a beautiful client who comes to him three times a week, not to recite her fears and anxieties and to have them analyzed and explicated and demythologized, but to share her silence and secrecy, and through them, perhaps, to share her myths as well. The analysand becomes the analyst, and the analyst, the analysand. The psychoanalyst does not help the woman re-create herself through the emblems of her own words, but rather she re-creates him through the wise compassion of her silence.

But she did speak and, just now, for the first time in over forty hours of consultation, she had introduced the subject of her childhood. Over the years he had heard the childhood stories of many women. There were not many happy ones. After all, they came to him because they had problems, and many of their problems were, tragically, rooted in childhood. Perhaps the most depressing reality he had had to wrestle with in his profession was the banality of his clients' problems. Over the years he had treated hundreds upon hundreds of complaints, the same complaints again and again and again: alcohol and drug abuse; anxiety-based disorders — phobias and obsessive-compulsive neuroses; mood disorders (my God, he could have made a career of depression alone); promiscuity; psychogenic disorders — anorexia, bulimia, ulcers; a plethora of sexual dysfunctions ... But these were not problems, they were only symptoms. Their cause was something else, something more complex than the symptoms, more traumatic. Like a psychic craven, this thing cowered in the deepest fissures of the client's unconscious and sent emissaries — the symptoms — up to the surface of consciousness to harass the bewildered client on his behalf. Like an unsuspecting woman looking into a two-way mirror, the client sees only her own reflection, her own pain, and blames only herself for all that she sees. It was Dr. Broussard's role to break the mirror and to reveal the entity on the other side. It was not a role he always enjoyed, nor was he always successful.

'Actually, I'd gotten the doll when I was five,' she said. 'They'd just divorced.'

Dr. Broussard checked the tiny red light on his tape recorder across the room.

'He drank.' She paused. 'He was a very handsome

alcoholic, and I loved him without reservation. A child can do that, once, anyway. I don't remember anything ... no scenes, no screams, no quarrels. Nothing like that. But she told me about them later, and she showed me scars, which she said he'd made. I don't know if he did.'

'Do you believe she lied to you about it?'

'I don't know,' she said with a trace of impatience. 'I just don't know that he did it. And I never got to see for myself because we ran away. We left him in the middle of the night, in Georgia, in a little town near Savannah. She wouldn't stop until sometime the next morning when we pulled off the highway onto a farm road. She made me stay awake while she went to sleep. When I finally woke her, it was early in the afternoon. We bought some barbecue at a roadside stand and kept driving. We didn't stop until it was night again, and we were somewhere just inside the Mississippi state line.

'And then for a year we lived like Gypsies while mother went through a series of waitressing and clerk jobs, staying for a little while in one place and then another and then moving on, dozens and dozens of cheap apartments, walk-up rooms, "tourist court" motels, different ones all over the South. Mother liked to call it "Dixie." God, I've forgotten how many dirty rooms we stayed in, but I've never forgotten how they smelled. Disinfectant. Uric ammonia in the stale mattresses. The sour odors of other people's sweat and intimacies. At nights she would sob in the dark, and I would hold the Dresden doll, listening to her pitiful whimpering, breathing the smells of those stained mattresses ... I don't know what she was crying about; she was the one who left.'

Broussard looked at Mary Lowe's feet, her right one drawn back, the stocking wrinkling slightly across the top of her ankle. 'You don't seem to have very much sympathy for your mother,' he said, and looked at her face. She had turned her head a little away from him so that he saw her profile from an acute angle, what the artists call a profile perdu, only the outline of her cheek and chin.

'I missed him so much,' she said, ignoring his question. 'Sometimes, in those sweaty beds at nights, the
thought would come into my head that all my internal
organs were slowly detaching themselves from one
another. When I held my breath I thought I could feel it
happening, things pulling away, stretching, little gummy
strings of me getting thinner and thinner, about to snap. I
would grow light-headed, terrified that I would suddenly
blow apart and all the tiny, unrecognizable pieces of me
would zing off in all directions of the universe. They
would never find all of me. There wouldn't be anything of
me left for someone to love.'

She stopped. He could tell from the corner of the one
eye visible to him that she was squinting slightly, remembering.

'I would lie awake in the suffocating darkness of those
nights ... waiting for that idea to come into my head,
dreading it.'

Broussard no longer empathized with these stories. He
had taught himself not to participate, merely to listen. His
understanding of her story was purely intellectual and
associative; he did not actually feel her pain or turn
morose under the burdens of her childish loneliness. He
hadn't always been so detached, but after twice
succumbing to a nervous breakdown himself, he had
learned that to help his clients he had to cauterize his
own natural inclination to take their somber stories to
heart. Like Odysseus, he had to lash himself to the mast
of objectivity to endure the melancholy songs of broken
women, songs that in the past had so easily seduced him.
Still, even now, he often found them bewitching.

Broussard believed that these stories were elaborate
biographies, fabrics of the imagination into the warp and
woof of which were woven fine threads of fantasy and
reality. Every individual fabric had to have a proper
mixture of these fibers to be successful, to give the lives
they represented the stability of the one and the creativity
of the other. But sometimes when the tale is told, when
the fabric was taken from the loom, the storyteller

discovered that she had so skillfully intertwined her strands that she could no longer distinguish between them, and what she was had become indiscernible from what she was not. It was Dr. Broussard's task, an often arduous and tedious one, to help the storyteller unravel the fabric of her imagination.

He was a man of sincere demeanor. He knew that; it was something he cultivated. He owed it to his clients, he thought, to present them with a personality that was receptive to their stories, that did not treat their desperation lightly. Just short of six feet, he cut a handsome figure with a naturally well-developed upper torso which he kept trim with only a modicum of weight management. His complexion was dusky — he didn't have to punish himself in the sun to look healthy — and his hair was thick and wavy, graying at the temples in such a way that he believed it would be difficult to improve upon. He had it clipped slightly, but frequently, so that he never had that awkward appearance of having recently visited the barber. His nails were manicured. His wardrobe was expensive, but not flamboyant, tending toward the rich, sober constancy of European fashion.

'These feelings of panic,' he dutifully persisted. 'How long did they last?' He felt a loose cuticle on his ring finger and unobtrusively took nail clippers out of his pocket and began carefully to nip at the little shred of horny flesh while she continued.

'And you know what I remember?' she asked, again disregarding his query. '"Are You Lonesome Tonight?" Elvis Presley. Jesus. I don't remember if it was on the radio or a record player or what. I was only six or seven. I wouldn't have remembered the song either, except that she never let me forget it. Even after she remarried she would hum that song, or play it on the record player when he wasn't there. I don't know. You would have thought she would have wanted to forget it if it reminded her ... I never hear that song that it doesn't bring back the memory of all those strange, dirty rooms in all those "Dixie" towns. We never stayed in any of them long enough to be anything more than strangers.'

She stopped. Dr. Broussard was quiet, finishing his cuticle, and giving her time. But she was through. He could tell by her mouth, which was her most expressive feature, that she was not going to pursue this any further. He doubted that she realized that she had reached a crucial juncture, or maybe she did and that was why she had stopped. And yet she seemed unmoved. She had spoken as if she had been reading from a book, as if the words had been someone else's.

'What happened to your father?' He unobtrusively folded up the clippers and put them away. The question might have worked, though he had never been able to coax her.

Mary Lowe didn't move or answer. She raised her right hand and looked at her watch. It was small and delicate with an annulus of tiny diamonds around the dial. She wore it with the face on the underside of her wrist.

'It's five o'clock,' she said. She sat up and swung her legs around on the chaise facing him, her knees together, her stockinged feet spread apart to straddle her shoes which were side-by-side on the floor. Raising her arms she tucked at the strands of flax that had strayed loose at the nape of her neck. She bent down to slip on her shoes, and Dr. Broussard watched her breasts fill the top of her scoop-necked dress. She immediately looked up as if sensing what he was doing and met his gaze. He did not try to dissemble, nor did she pretend to be unaware or embarrassed or angered. Instead, she returned to her shoes, letting him look while she finished and maybe, he thought, he hoped, wishing for some sign of complicity, taking a little longer than was necessary.

'We made good progress,' he said as she sat up again. 'It gets easier with time.'

She stood and smoothed her dress across the flat of her stomach. 'Wonderful,' she said without feeling, looking at him as he stood also, putting his notepad facedown on his desk to conceal the fact that it was blank.

She turned away and picked up her purse from the antique Oriental table near the door. Stepping around behind her, he reached for the doorknob to let her out, placing his left hand at the small of her back, flattening it out to touch as much of her as he could.

'See you tomorrow, then,' he said, feeling a stirring of excitement as he cupped his fingers to the curve of her torso. She allowed this, neither stepping forward nor turning slightly to finesse a disengagement. She hesitated a moment. He thought she was going to speak, but then she moved through the door and was gone.

5

The four of them stood in the chill of the bedroom with the naked and funereally posed Dorothy Samenov, who stared up into eternity from startled, lidless eyes, who would go to her grave wide awake, unable to receive that last token gesture that modern men have never exorcised from their archaic past — the closing of their eyes against the awesome unknown. Palma's analytic focus was tested by the pale, lacerated body of this lonely woman upon the cold sheet. As they stood in a circle and talked, Palma was constantly aware of Samenov's waxy, recumbent form in her peripheral vision, as if she were waiting patiently for them to redeem her from humiliation. Her death had cost her more than her life, and the pitifully meek gesture of her politely folded hands seemed to be all that she had been allowed to salvage of her dignity.

Palma had seen enough in her four years in homicide to recognize the distinctions between the particularly intense malevolence of sexual homicides as compared to homicides of other kinds. At first all killings appeared the same insofar as they were expositions of violence. The wounds might vary, but the energy that produced them had a common denominator. Yet the characteristics of sexual homicides quickly distinguished themselves. Though she might forget the details of the hundreds of shootings and stabbings and stranglings she would see during the course of her career, she would never forget the sexual homicides, not even the smallest minutiae. Nor would she forget the eerie intuition she had when she entered the presence of these victims for the first time, as if the mind that produced the horror had lingered behind with the corpse to await its final pleasure: observing the reasonable mind's revulsion at its crime.

The question was one of the division of labors. If the cases were related, and they all believed they were, then Cushing and Leoland were, in a very real sense, behind in their homework. It was decided that the two detectives would stay with Birley, who would take them through the scene and compare its details with those in the case of Sandra Moser two weeks earlier. When it came time for the body to go to the morgue, Cushing and Leeland would follow and attend the autopsy. Birley would continue to go over the scene with LeBrun. Palma, having done most of the interviewing for the first killing, would interview Vickie Kittrie. When Cushing and Leeland got back to the station downtown, they would have to read the report and supplements on the Moser case. After that, the four of them would get together and compare notes.

Leaving them in the bedroom, Palma passed Wendell Barry coming back in, and walked into the living room where the two patrolmen were keeping their distance from the back of the house. She supposed they had done their ogling of the naked woman before she got there and were maintaining this uncharacteristic lack of curiosity for her sake. Sometimes she ran into a peculiar kind of chivalry among the younger men, especially among the patrolmen who didn't often see naked dead women. If the victim was sexually attractive, they were startled to find that death didn't necessarily change anything in that regard, and the inappropriateness of their unexpected arousal could be distinctly disconcerting. Some of them became grave or formal or aloof, or simply stayed out of her way as if they were somehow accomplices with the offender by virtue of their sex and their own poorly controlled chemistry. It took them a while to learn to ignore it, to shut it out, and when they couldn't do that, to joke about it. There were a lot of ways to handle it, but you couldn't afford to take it to heart. Not every time.

'Neither of you are VanMeter?' she asked, approaching them and glancing at their name tags.

'No, ma'am,' one of them said, the stocky one. 'He's outside . . . he's got a red mustache.'

Outside, the late-morning heat was excruciating after the icy condo, and the sweat popped to the surface of Palma's skin as if she had stepped into a sauna. VanMeter was easy to find, standing with his shift sergeant on the thick turf of manicured lawn in the solid shade of a magnolia. A gas lamp burned needlessly in the Texas sun nearby. Neither man was talking, though it was obvious they had been once. As Palma approached she noticed half a dozen cigarette butts against the street curb.

'VanMeter?' she asked, stepping up to the young man and extending her hand. 'Detective Palma.' He was incredibly young, and the blue eyes and fair skin didn't age him any. His handshake was tensely brittle. She shook hands with the sergeant too, and remembered that they had been on a scene together a couple of months earlier. She turned to VanMeter, who was lighting a cigarette.

'You were the officer who found her?'

'Yes, ma'am.'

Palma waited for him to explain.

'Just tell her the way it went down,' the sergeant said to VanMeter. He glanced at Palma, and she realized the kid was fresh out of the academy.

'Basically I just responded to a welfare check,' VanMeter said. His mustache was neatly trimmed, and it suited him. He blew a stream of smoke to the side, away from her, and it hung in the still heat a moment and then vanished. Kittrie had told him her story as Cushing had related it earlier to Palma, and VanMeter had asked Kittrie if she knew of anyone who had a spare key to the condo. Kittrie didn't, but she said Samenov kept a spare set of keys hidden in her car, but the car was locked and

she couldn't get into it to look for them. VanMeter had
then used a door opener from his patrol unit to get into
Samenov's Saab where, after a brief search, he found the
spare key and used it to enter the condo.

'You went in first?' Palma asked.

'Yes, ma'am. I went in and asked her to wait in the
living room while I looked around. I went straight to the
bedroom, I don't know why ... the door was open, and I
found her.' VanMeter's Adam's apple worked uncontrollably, and he swallowed, then took another long drag from
his cigarette.

'Did Kittrie see her?'

'Yeah, well, I must've said something, you know,
surprised to find the dead woman, and she heard me and
came running in. I had taken a couple of steps into the
bedroom, and when I turned around she was standing in
the doorway right behind me.'

'That's when she saw her?'

'Yes, ma'am.'

'Do you remember her reaction?'

He nodded. 'She fainted, dead out. Like she'd been
dropped with a hammer. I had to carry her ... I got her
out of the house. Laid her down right over there in the
shade. A couple who live across the street,' he tossed his
head toward a condo directly across from them, 'must've
been looking out the window. They came right over and
the lady had a damp washrag or something and we got
her to come around. When she got her to her feet they
took her over there.'

'Is that where she is now?'

'Yes, ma'am. I didn't get her name.'

Palma thanked VanMeter, noticing the mist of perspiration that had accumulated on his forehead. She wanted
to reassure him, but she knew better than that. Instead,
she started across the street to the Mediterranean-style
condo with its dun bricks and its front courtyard filled
with frondy sago palms among banks of orangey snapdragons.

When she rang the doorbell the door opened immediately, and a middle-aged man with a head of longish frizzy hair that was thinning toward the front stood looking at her. He was wearing a baggy Hawaiian shirt outside a pair of faded blue jeans. His nose was rather broad, but in a handsome way, and he had extraordinarily long eyelashes.

'I'm Detective Palma.' She held up her shield. 'I understand Vickie Kittrie is here.'

Of course, sure, come on in.' He shook hands with her. 'I'm Nathan Isenberg.' He backed away to let her in. 'She's up here.' He closed the door behind her and preceded her up the steps of the sunken entryway, talking, motioning with his hands. 'Kid's had a hard time. Jesus. Can you imagine?' He stopped, turned to her, and put a concerned hand on Palma's arm. 'Pretty bad over there?' His face twisted in a painted contortion, anticipating her answer.

'Pretty bad,' she said.

'Oh, God!' he hissed, keeping it just between the two of them. 'Poor kid.' He bit his lower lip and shook his head, his wirey hair drifting above him, and then turned and led her on up the steps into a living room separated from the entry by a huge terraced planter of philodendron and monstera. A woman wearing a sarong and the top to a bikini swimsuit had been sitting by Kittrie on the sofa and stood when Palma came in.

The man introduced her as Helena and then introduced Kittrie, who remained seated, red-eyed and clutching a handful of wadded pink tissues. There was an awkward moment, and then the woman, running a pretty hand through her hair, a black bob shot through with gray, asked if she could get anything for Palma, who declined. The man and woman excused themselves, and as they walked out of the living room Palma noticed there was no outline of the bikini bottom under the thin material of the sarong.

Vickie Kittrie was dressed very smartly in a businesswoman's sharkskin blazer of silvery gray rayon and linen and pleated trousers with black heels. A collarless fuchsia blouse of crepe de chine was tucked into the trousers. She was sitting on a sofa behind a coffee table of glazed gold ceramic tiles, kneading the wad of tissues and looking up at Palma with swollen eyes and tear-matted lashes.

'You feel up to talking with me for a few minutes?'

Kittrie nodded readily. 'Of course,' she said, and quickly wiped at her nose.

'I'm sorry about your friend,' Palma said, sitting in a tapestry upholstered chair opposite the coffee table. Kittrie nodded. She had ginger hair with red highlights and a pale Irish complexion. She had cried so much and wiped her face so often with damp tissues that her makeup was disappearing, and a light spattering of freckles was now visible trailing across the top of her nose, disclosing an air of youthfulness that seemed incompatible with the mature clothes she had chosen to wear. She started tugging anxiously at the wad of tissues, her hazel eyes riveted to Palma's. 'Do you have family or friends who can come get you, maybe stay with you?'

'I have friends ... at the office. I've already called them.' Palma was a little surprised at her tone, which had a sharp edge to it.

Ms. Samenov was a friend of yours?'

'Yes.'

'How long have you known her?'

'A long time.' Her voice cracked, but she got control of it. 'Four years, maybe three ... or four. We worked at Computron together.'

'Was she married?'

'Divorced.'

'How long?'

'Uh ... maybe ... I don't know ... five, six years.'

'Does her ex-husband live in the city?'

'Yes.'

'Do you know his name?'

It took her a second. 'Dennis ... Ackley.'

'Did she see him very often?'

She hunched her shoulders. 'It wasn't that kind of a divorce. It wasn't friendly.'

'Do you know where he works, or where he lives?'

'He works ... I think ... at a paint store.'

'Do you know the name?'

She shook her head. 'I only remember her saying that's what he was doing now.'

'Do you happen to know if he was ever in the military?'

Kittrie closed her eyes and shook her head again.

'What about relatives? The coroner's office has to notify someone.'

'There's nobody in the city. I wouldn't bother with Ackley. She's from South Carolina. She was away from home.' Kittrie's eyes were still closed, her hands holding the tissues without fidgeting.

This last remark seemed an odd choice of words in light of the fact that Samenov was obviously in her mid-thirties, had been married a number of years, divorced a number of years, and certainly had lived in Houston long enough for it to be regarded as her home. The phrase would have seemed more appropriate in reference to a college student.

'But ... well ...' Kittrie added, 'I'd like to tell them myself.' She cleared her throat.

'Do you know them?'

'I've met them before. They'd remember me.' Her eyes were still closed.

'I'm sure the coroner's office would appreciate that. You should check with them.' Palma paused, signaling a change of tone in her questioning. 'What about boyfriends? Did she have anyone special?'

'No.' Kittrie opened her eyes. She seemed sure of it.

'Had there been anyone special, in the recent past?'

'No, I don't think so.'

'What kind of men did she date in the last year or so?'

'Oh, I don't know. After a while they all seem the same ... just guys.' Spoken like a woman twice her age. Kittrie couldn't have been more than twenty-three.

'Can you give me the names of some of the men she'd been dating so we can check with them as to when they last saw her?' Palma made it routine.

'I know she dated a guy at Computron, Wayne Canfield. He was in marketing. There was another guy, Gil — I think it was — Reynolds, I met him at her place a few times. I don't remember anything about him.'

She stopped.

'Is that it?' Palma asked.

Kittrie sighed and rolled her eyes to the ceiling. 'Uh, let's see. There was a Dirk she knew from a night class; she took an accounting course at the University of Houston.'

'When was this?'

'Oh, last year, spring semester. For a while she dated a bank vice president ...' she frowned. '... the bank ... I don't know the bank, but I think his last name was Bris ... Bristol. Yeah, Bristol.' She looked at Palma, irritated. 'I don't know. That's all I can remember.'

'She live alone?'

Kittrie nodded, her hands working the wadded tissues once again.

'I understand that on Thursday evening, the last time you saw her, a group of people from your office had stopped off for drinks.'

'Right, at Cristof's. That's near Greenway Plaza. We do that a lot, to wait out the traffic.'

'Who was in the group?'

'The two of us, Marge Simon, Nancy Segal, Linda Mancera.'

'All of you in separate cars?'

'Yes ... no, Marge and Linda were together.'

'How often do you do that? Several times a week?'

'Sure, two or three times a week.'

'At the same place?'

'About half the time at Cristof's. It's on the way home.'

'Do you ever meet men there, or date the men you meet there?'

'Not really.'

'You don't?'

'No.' Kittrie punched a hole in her tissue with a shiny fuchsia fingernail, doubled the tissue, and punched another hole, kneading it roughly.

'Did Dorothy seem concerned about anything that Thursday? Out of sorts? Anything bothering her?'

'Nothing, nothing like that. And I've thought about it, too. Asked myself if I had noticed anything different.' She ducked her head and shook it. 'But this came out of nowhere ... I can't imagine its having anything to to do with her. I mean, that it would be related to anything. I just can't imagine that it would.'

'Was she planning to go home after she left all of you at the club?'

'We all were.'

'She wasn't going to stop off somewhere, the laundry, the grocery? Had she made any offhand references to something like that?'

Kittrie shook her head as she ran a hand through her long ginger hair.

Palma thought of Sandra Moser. The last time she had been seen was by her maid and children as she was leaving home in the evening to go to exercise class. She never arrived. The next time she was seen was when the maid at the Doubletree Hotel on Post Oak went into the room the next morning and found her nude on the bed in the same funereal posture as Samenov.

'You had an exercise class with Ms. Samenov on Saturday morning. Where was this class?'

'The Houston Racquet Club,' Kittrie said, and then pulled some more tissues from the box sitting on the coffee table and dabbed at her nose again.

Sandra Moser had been on her way to Sabrina's, a tony health club off Woodway in the Tanglewood area not far from Moser's home. Whatever else Palma might learn of the man who had killed these two women, it was already apparent that he had rarefied tastes. He was working territory that was squarely in the middle of two suburbs whose demographics placed them among the wealthiest in the nation.

Palma studied Kittrie for a moment. 'Do you have any ideas about this?'

Kittrie's eyes flinched. 'Ideas? Jesus, no,' she said. Her surprise was reflexive, genuine, one of those spontaneous facial reactions that occurred in an unguarded moment and told you more about someone's relationship to a particular person or situation than two weeks of background investigation could reveal. Kittrie ducked her head again, plying the tissues.

Palma decided to go to the heart of the issue. 'What can you tell me about Ms. Samenov's sex life?'

Kittrie jerked her head up and looked at Palma with a mixture of resentment and anxiety. 'Jesus Christ. Do you have to do this?' She started crying again, wiping at her cheeks and eyes which already had been washed of their makeup, revealing them to be paler and smaller and less striking than she would have liked. Her unmade face now seemed at odds with her sophisticated hairstyle and assertive clothes. Her vulnerability was now as visible as her unpowdered freckles.

'The more I know about her, the better chance I have of understanding what happened,' Palma persisted. 'She might have been a random victim; she might not have been. I need to be able to put her private life into perspective.'

'I don't know anything *about* it,' Kittrie blurted. 'I don't know who ... or ... anything. Christ!' She started sobbing uncontrollably and couldn't talk. She buried her face in her hands and her shoulders shuddered rhythmically. Palma didn't believe her. She was too insistent, and her flustered denials seemed out of proportion to the question. She simply could have said she didn't know. But Palma had no doubts about the sincerity of her grief.

There was no reason to try to go any further with her now. Palma looked around for the absent couple, but they were nowhere in sight. Or so she thought, until she glimpsed a wisp of bright crimson in a doorway on the other side of a round Venetian table that sat in the center of the room. She remembered the sarong with its pattern of taupe and gold, and its crimson hem.

6

She left Vickie Kittrie crying on Nathan Isenberg's sofa, wondering if Kittrie's 'friends,' who had not yet arrived, really existed. Helena had come back into the room when she heard Palma closing the interview and walked her to the sunken entrance hall where they visited a minute by the front door. Palma learned that she had seen nothing out of the ordinary, no one coming or going from Dorothy Samenov's home during the past several days. Helena appeared to be in her mid-forties, with dark, kind eyes and the figure of a woman less than half her age. She said she would see that Kittrie got home safely. Palma wondered about these two Good Samaritans and their willingness to help. She had noticed that Helena had worn no wedding ring.

It was almost noon when she walked out into the heat and bright sunlight again and saw the rear of the morgue van going away from her under the overhanging trees at the far end of Olympia. Cushing and Leeland's car was already gone, as well as one of the patrol cars. She crossed the street and nodded at VanMeter and another patrolman still lingering in the shade of the magnolia. They would stay there until it was decided the scene could be left alone. Palma walked into Samenov's condo through the front door, which had been left open. Someone had turned up the thermostat.

She returned to the bedroom where Birley was

standing in Samenov's large clothes closet taking notes.

'How'd it go?' he asked, not looking up from his notepad.

'She was pretty upset. Where's LeBrun? His van's still outside.'

'He's in one of the back bathrooms, getting the sink traps.'

'Was he able to get anything from the bathroom floor?'

'I think so.' He looked at her, his eyes wrinkling with an amused smile. 'That was pretty fancy, what you did earlier.'

'You mean smart aleck,' she said, walking over to him.

'Yeah, that too.'

'Sorry, but I wasn't about to let Cushing take it away from us.'

'Fine with me. You did good. Here,' he said, leaning out of the closet and handing Palma a brown leather address book, the gauzy sleeve of a peach negligee caught on his left shoulder. 'I thought you might like to go through this first thing.'

Which is just exactly what she did. Dennis Ackley's name was there, his address and two telephone numbers. The book obviously was not used for her business accounts because, with the exception of a liquor store, a dry cleaner, a shoe shop, a pharmacy, a hairdresser, and a few other similar, personal-use commercial businesses, all the other names were of individuals. And in most cases only the first names were entered and no addresses were given.

'Kittrie told me about an ex-husband,' Palma said. 'It wasn't a good divorce. He's in here, address and telephone number. I'm going to have a patrol unit go by and see if he's at home.'

'Fine,' Birley said from the closet.

Using the telephone on a bedside table, Palma called the dispatcher and made the request and then dialed the second number under Ackley's name, thinking it might be his business. There was no answer. She dialed the first number, but again no answer. She dialed information, which had no listing for Dennis Ackley and did not show an unlisted number. She put the address book in her purse.

'Kittrie claims she doesn't have the faintest idea of what might have happened here,' Palma said, looking around. She saw smudges of ferric oxide all over the room, like patches of mold that seemed to be everywhere once you began looking for it. LeBrun had already removed the sheet from the bed and sealed it in a paper bag which he had placed near the door along with a number of other paper packets of various sizes, sealed and labeled. 'She really got upset when I asked her if she knew anything about Samenov's "private life."'

Birley looked up from his notebook. 'Oh? She seemed particularly upset about that? You mean her sex life?'

Palma nodded.

'That's interesting,' Birley said, pulling down the corners of his mouth. 'Take a look over there in the bottom drawer of her bureau.'

Palma stepped around the end of the bed, feeling a nagging depression at the sight of the bare mattress and its few sallow stains. No place, no matter how expensive or exclusive, no matter how pure or important its occupants, was free of stains — of one sort or another.

The scattered bottles of cosmetics and perfume on the top of the chest had been disturbed and darkened with more patches of ferric oxide. LeBrun was thorough. She looked in the small top drawer first and saw that LeBrun had taken samples of the lipstick, the eye shadow, everything that might have gone onto Samenov's face. Then she bent down to the bottom drawer and pulled it open. There were some sweaters, cotton ones. She lifted them.

The paraphernalia was diverse, some of it homemade, some of it commercial: soft leather bondage cuffs and keys, panic snaps, a riding crop, nipple clips and clamps, a box of white candles, Tiger Balm, spiky dog-grooming brushes and rakes, a hand dildo and an electric stepped-down low-ampere dildo, enema bag and rubber hose, a straight razor, a variety of weighted nipple rings, K-Y jelly, surgical gloves, a cluttered drawer full of instruments and accessories. She was familiar with all of it from working vice but now, as then, the devices seemed oddly scientific and clinical to her as well as illicit and malign, as if they were the instruments of a death-camp gynecologist.

Kneeling on one knee in front of the drawer, she stared into it. Secrets. Palma would wager that Samenov had never dreamed that strangers — this morning five or six of them at least — would casually go through her hidden cache of erotica. Sudden death, unexpected death, Palma had learned, had a character of its own. It didn't come to every man, only the mysteriously chosen, and it arrived with a large measure of irony. It exposed secrets, *arcanum arcanorum*, as Sister Celeste would have said. In one unexpected instant, sudden death perversely unveiled everything that had been meant to be concealed, hidden things that people jealously guarded with constant vigilance and all the duplicity they could devise. It teaches: you control nothing, not even your own secrets, which at any time can be snatched out of the darkness and thrown into the light like black glitter against the sun.

She thought of Birley behind her, probably with his head bent to his notebook, but with his eyes cut to one side, watching her.

'There was nothing like this with Sandra Moser,' she said needlessly.

'How do we know?'

The question stunned her. Birley had figured it out in an instant. Naturally they had not gone through Moser's home as they were doing Samenov's. She had been killed in a hotel room, and her husband and children were still living in the home. It was true that Andrew Moser hadn't mentioned anything like this in all the lengthy interviews they had had with him, but then he probably wouldn't have. Certainly not if he had been involved himself. And probably not even if he hadn't been involved or even aware, but had discovered something like this while going through his wife's personal belongings after her death. He was pretty much of a straight arrow; he wouldn't have told. He would have carried it around with him as his own personal cross of shame, seeing it, of course, selfishly, as an embarrassing testimony to his own real or imagined sexual inadequacies, proof that she had had to go elsewhere, had had to seek something other than what he could give her. Her secret, and now his secret. Palma understood something of the fragile egos of strong men, that sometimes they had the appearance of stone and the substance of thin glass.

'We need to photograph and dust this stuff,' she said, and then glimpsed the corner of a manila envelope in the bottom of the drawer. She carefully pinched its corner and pulled it out from under the gear, trying to avoid disturbing it. She opened the envelope and dumped an assortment of photographs onto the floor, black and white, and color, some that appeared to be recent, others perhaps several years older and showing evidence of frequent handling. There were seven photographs which she spread out in front of her.

In each of the three black and white eight-by-tens, a woman who appeared to be in her late forties posed nude in a variety of pornographic postures with an anatomically correct male mannequin. The mannequin wore a leather S&M mask and held a straight razor in one of its plaster hands, its partially visible phallus an enormous exaggeration which the woman seemed to accommodate with ostentatious anguish. Each photograph was a positional variation. But Palma was not interested. She had already recognized Samenov's face in the colored pictures.

Samenov was in each of the four colored photographs, which were four-by-sixes and appeared to have been taken with an inexpensive camera. In the first photograph she was tied to a bed with practically every device in her bureau drawer attached to her or inserted in her, her hair pulled up on top of her head and tied to the headboard of the bed, causing her neck to arch in response to the tension as she strained to turn her grimacing face away from the camera. Her body was covered with red blotches from blows or burns or constrictions recently delivered. The other photographs of her were variations of the same pose — in two of them she was tied facedown — the devices variously and ingeniously applied.

But something else arrested Palma's attention. In three of the four colored photographs a second person was partially visible, wearing a black leather hood that masked the face. In the first of these, only the head and part of a shoulder were visible in profile, but so close to the camera that they were slightly blurred and washed out by the flash. In a second picture the same masked head, or one like it, was protruding out from under Samenov's bed, lifting off the floor to look at her, mouth open, tongue extended, eyes rolling white. This time the image was sharp. In the third photograph, the masked head could be seen sticking up from behind the opposite side of the bed, spewing a mouthful of bright red liquid in an arching stream onto Samenov's splayed body.

Was this the reason Vickie Kittrie was so distressed at Palma's questions about Samenov's personal life? Did she know of Samenov's sadomasochism? In light of the pictures and the paraphernalia, it was no longer a mystery as to how Samenov could have been tied up without a struggle.

But what about Sandra Moser? To imagine her in these circumstances was something else again. Palma immediately thought of Moser's two children, a daughter in her third grade, a little boy in the first. She thought of Moser's work in an Episcopalian shelter for the poor and her active membership of the parent groups of her children's private school. She had supported her husband and his career, dutifully entertained his associates at their home when it was expected of her, chaired fund-raisers for the Chartres Academy's music program, and sweated herself into a size eight which she maintained by avoiding most of the things she really wanted to eat. In short, it was doubtful that any woman could more accurately represent the upper-middle-class, all-American woman than Sandra Moser. And she was a sadomasochist? Palma couldn't see it, but she knew a few radical feminists who would argue that Moser's lifestyle, her whole-hearted submission to her husband and his career, certainly qualified her as a masochist at least.

'Damn!' Birley had stepped out of the closet and was looking at the photographs over her shoulder. 'This puts a new face on things.'

After a moment Palma carefully gathered up the photographs and returned them to the envelope, stood, and handed it to him. 'We're going to have to talk to Andrew Moser again. What do you think? You want to bet he hid something like this from us?'

'No, I wouldn't touch it.' Birley shook his head and looked at the envelope.

'But if he was hiding something ...' She stopped, lost in thought, staring at the mattress where Dorothy Samenov had lived her strange pleasures and died her strange death.

Birley nodded. 'Yeah, it would be a break. Something to go on.'

Palma didn't feel exactly right about it, but some part of her was hoping that upon closer examination Sandra Moser would turn out to be as extreme as the Marquis de Sade.

7

So what did it look like?' Frisch asked. He was standing in the doorway of Palma and Birley's office with a sheaf of papers in one hand and a pencil in the other. His shirttail was coming out a little in the back and a frail lock of his thinning sandy hair was sagging over his forehead. He had just come from seeing the captain and had walked back into his office when he saw Palma and Birley come into the squad room. Never taking his eyes off them, he had walked around the plate-glass window behind his desk and out the office door. Ignoring the squad room confusion, he followed them around the noisy, narrow aisle that circled the island of cubicles in the center of the homicide division to their office, one of the many small, windowless compartments which lined the walls like computer-equipped monks' cells in a high-tech monastery.

'It looked like we'd seen it before,' Palma said, sitting down and pushing off her shoes.

'I'll be damned,' Frisch said, and his long face, which always took on the hollow features of a mendicant by the end of the day, registered a respectful surprise. 'I didn't believe him. Cush called in and said he thought he had something like the Moser case you two had caught. Wanted you to come out and look at it.'

'Well, he'd been doing his homework,' Birley said, 'because that's exactly what he had.'

'Where is he?' Frisch looked at his watch.

'Morgue.'

He looked at Palma. 'You got time to tell me about it right now?'

'Sure,' she said, wishing she had stopped by the women's room to wash up.

Frisch stepped outside and grabbed a worn-out typist's chair that was sitting at an empty desk in the squad room and dragged it into the cubicle. He closed the door, put his papers on the side of Birley's desk, slipped the pencil behind his ear, and sat down in the wobbly chair.

As Palma walked him through it, Frisch listened attentively, nodding, interjecting a question occasionally, shaking his head at the description of Samenov's wounds, frowning at the contents of the bureau drawer. But mostly he just looked at her. He had no habits, not gum or cigarettes or coffee or rock candy, and when he listened to you he didn't fiddle with anything, sip anything, or doodle on paper with his pencil. He simply listened, no frills or entertaining nervous tics. He was a good lieutenant. He liked his job and liked his men and had a natural talent for managing detectives. He didn't have any enemies up the ladder or down the ladder and everyone who worked with him felt they could trust both his judgment and his word. He talked straight and didn't play games. You always knew where you stood with him.

When Palma finished, Frisch sat a moment, nodding, looking at her, thinking. 'A married woman and a single woman,' he said. 'Besides the M.O. what are the victim similarities?'

The telephone rang and Palma picked it up. It was one of the patrolmen who had gone to Dennis Ackley's address. Ackley no longer lived there, and the older couple who did said they had bought the place from Ackley nearly six months ago. They didn't know where he was now or how to get in touch with him.

'Geography,' Birley said. 'They lived about a mile or so from each other. Social background. Samenov is a college-educated professional who had to be pulling down some bucks to afford that condo.'

'Age?'

'Moser was thirty-four,' Palma said. 'Samenov's driver's license said thirty-eight. They both were blond.'

'That's good,' Frish said, brightening. 'If they were random targets that could be important. And it's good that they were low-risk victims. Maybe we won't have all this complicated by prostitutes.'

'But that's about all,' Birley said. 'At least as far as we know at this point.'

Birley's telephone rang next. He spoke briefly and hung up. 'That was Leeland. The autopsy's over, and they're on their way in.'

Frisch nodded slowly, thinking. He looked at his watch. 'They can make it in fifteen minutes. When they get here let's meet in my office. We'll just lay everything out and see where we are.' He looked at Palma. 'You've talked it over with them? You're going to work the cases together?'

'Sure,' Palma said. 'We haven't worked out the details, but we've agreed to do it.'

Frisch looked at her. 'This case could attract a lot of heat, a lot of media. Unless we're incredibly lucky it could take a while. Are you and Cushing going to be able to stay away from each other's throats?' It was a blunt question, but Frisch had characteristically gone right to the heart of it. If she couldn't make peace with Cushing, now was the time to get it out in the open.

'I think we've come to some sort of understanding,' Palma said. 'I don't anticipate any problems.' She would have said the same thing about working with the devil. She wanted to be on this case, and she wasn't going to let a question like that bump her off this early in the investigation. If it was necessary, she would deal with Cushing when the time came. Right now he wasn't her big concern.

'Fine,' Frisch said. He got his papers off Birley's desk. 'Buzz me when you're ready.' He pushed the typist's chair out of the office ahead of him and left it in the squad room where he had found it.

Birley looked at Palma. 'Jesus. I'm glad to hear you don't anticipate any trouble.'

'I know,' she said. 'What was I supposed to say?'

'You want some coffee?'

She shook her head. 'I'm going to wash up and get a glass of water.'

In the rest room Palma pulled back her hair with her tortoiseshell clasp, took off her watch, and began washing her hands and arms up to the elbows with soap and cold water. Then she washed her face, rinsing repeatedly, splashing a little of it on the back of her neck until she began to feel her body heat subside and the tension ease in her shoulders. She dried unhurriedly, being careful with the rough brown paper towels from the dispenser. Taking a flacon of perfumed lotion from her purse, she rubbed a small amount over her lips and around her throat. She looked at herself in the mirror above the sink. Slowly she raised a hand and gently touched a middle finger to the carotid artery on one side of her neck. When she found the pulse she lay the thumb of the same hand on the carotid artery of the other side. She stood a moment, feeling the regular, rushing pulse against her fingertips, and then she tried to imagine her freshly washed face without eyelids. It was easy to do. She picked up her purse and returned to the squad room.

By the time she got her glass of water and walked back into the office, Birley was already at the computer typing his portion of the report. Without any further conversation, she sat down at her desk, flipped on her own screen, and set to work.

The meeting in Frisch's office came at the end of the day when blood sugar and energy were ebbing and everyone would rather have been somewhere else. Frisch's office was a large one in a corner of the large squad room. It had two other metal desks besides his own and a number of chairs scattered around. It was often used as a bull-session room, and because of the crowded accommodations in the homicide division the other two desks were variously occupied from time to time by other lieutenants. But when one of them needed it to talk with his men, the others found someplace else to go.

Frisch sat behind his desk and at his back the plate-glass window of the office looked out into the squad room. The four detectives sat in chairs around Frisch, using the corners of the other desks for their files and coffee cups and soft-drink cans. Leeland, who didn't like autopsies but watched every minute that Cushing watched — and Cushing usually watched them from the first incision to the last suture like a bored kid glued to the fifty-fifth rerun of a TV horror movie — nursed a plastic glass of water with a couple of Alka-Seltzer tablets churning the surface. He didn't toss it right down, but sipped it like a martini. Cushing, looking like he wanted a real drink, had the ankle of one leg propped on the knee of the other and was wagging his foot nervously, absent-mindedly, his tie loosened and the collar of his black shirt unbuttoned and open. Birley was eating one of the cafe-teria's old doughnuts on which the glaze had melted to make a soggy surface around the doughnut's tough core. Palma wondered what the long-term effect must have been on his health. He had had one every afternoon about this time, with a bad cup of coffee, for years.

At Frisch's request she opened the meeting by quickly reviewing the Moser case while passing around the photographs from the crime scene. She pointed out the similarities that they had seen that morning with Samenov and noted that as she was going back through the Moser file before the meeting she realized that both women possibly had been killed on the same day of the week, Thursday. Then she reviewed what they knew so far in the Samenov case, her interview with Kittrie, what she and Birley had found in Samenov's condo.

When she finished, Cushing went over the results of Samenov's autopsy.

'The cause of death was ligature strangulation.' Cushing began unbuttoning his shirt sleeves and rolling them up while he read from his notebook propped on his crossed legs. 'Rutledge compared the furrows with the one on Moser and got a perfect match. They weren't all that pronounced, which Rutledge says could indicate the thing was removed as soon as she died. The cartilage in the larynx and trachea was crushed, hell of a lot more than was necessary to kill her.'

Cushing continually shifted in his chair, the snug crotch of his gigolo's pants causing him discomfort. The police department's chairs weren't designed for being cool, and even though he professed disdain for Palma, he couldn't bring himself to openly tug at his crotch for relief as he would have if only men had been present. Palma watched him squirm.

'Temperature in the condo screwed up the time-of-death indicators,' he continued, his words coming out in a singsong fashion from a long sigh. 'And because she was naked, she chilled down even quicker. Rutledge can only call it between three days and a week. But,' Cushing held up an open hand and looked at Frisch, 'we should be able to narrow that down. She'd had a pepperoni and green olive pizza which had just about run its course in her stomach. Don says he remembers a pizza box in the kitchen trash. Maybe we can nail down when it was delivered, or when she picked it up.'

Cushing flipped the pages of his notebook. 'We got swabs and smears on the way to the lab as well as found hair and pubic combings. Rutledge found cotton fibers in her mouth, like from a bath towel, guessing maybe she'd been gagged. We'll need to check these against the towels in her clothes hamper. Her vagina had been roughed up, bruised, but not torn. Rutledge says maybe a dildo. He also said that from the looks of the scar tissue in there she had a history of rough treatment. Same thing in her anus, and weak muscle tissue there, too. He says she'd have to have been into some pretty heavy stuff to get that kind of treatment.'

'Aside from the recent damage, did he have any idea how old these scars were?' Palma asked. 'Years?'

'He didn't say.'

Palma made a note, and Cushing watched her before he continued.

'The wounds,' he paused for emphasis, 'were *ante-mortem*. Nipples and eyelids had been removed with clean cuts, but the eyelid wounds were actually several smooth cuts instead of one single uninterrupted cut like it would have been if you held it up and ran a knife along it. He's guessing scissors. Snip, snip, snip for each eyelid.' Cushing used the forefinger and thumb of his left hand to pretend he was grasping a nipple and stretching it up from a breast while the same fingers of his right hand became scissors. 'Snip. Snip. Once for each nipple.

'Bite marks. Sandra Moser had nine, six on the breasts, three just above her pubic hair. Samenov got *sixteen*, five around the breasts, couple around the navel, three on her right inner thighs, two on the left thigh, and the rest around the pubic area — a couple actually in the hair. These were pretty bad, with suck marks on them. Rutledge said they were also antemortem and were made slowly, not in the heat of struggle as if the teeth had been used as a subduing "tool."'

Cushing closed his notebook and sat back in his chair, trying to tug unobtrusively at his crawling pants legs.

'Aren't the bite marks excessive?' Palma asked, looking at Birley. 'I mean, a lot of them?'

'That's a lot,' Birley acknowledged, swallowing the last wad of doughnut. 'A few times I've seen a hell of a lot more, but not that often. Most of the time, it seems, you know, there're less. I mean, sixteen. The guy was really going after it.'

'What about the severity of them?' Frisch asked. He had been listening with unblinking concentration. 'Did most of them penetrate the skin, or what?'

'Yeah,' Cushing nodded quickly. 'As a matter of fact, they did. About half of them went right through. Once, just inside the parameter of pubic hair at the top, he damn near took a mouthful out of her. Both upper and lower teeth penetrated, and embedded pubic hair into the wound.'

Frisch grimaced.

Leeland sipped his water, which was losing some of its fizz.

'The bites around the navel,' Palma said. 'Did Rutledge remark on those?'

Cushing seemed to be a little irritated that Palma had picked up on that, but he went into it. If he was inclined to hold out on her, he couldn't while Leeland was around. It was the work Cushing did alone that Palma worried about.

'Uh, yeah, as a matter of fact he did,' Cushing said, wrinkling his eyebrows as if just remembering. 'They were placed just right so that they made a complete circle around her navel. Looked like he did it on purpose. You know, put his teeth around it in a certain way. Also, it was the bite wound with the severest sucking evidence. He really went to work on her belly button, like he was trying to suck it out of there.'

'Christ,' Birley said.

Palma imagined that: the man, naked, bent over Samenov's nude outstretched body, sucking on her navel. It must have felt like he was trying to empty her body through her stomach, suck her dry like a spider feeding on a live insect. It was an image she would not forget.

'What about the condition of her face?' Birley asked.

'Right.' Cushing nodded. 'Yeah, she was in bad shape, jaw busted in two places, nose broken, a tooth chipped, a fractured cheekbone, a fractured eye socket.'

'Which one?' Palma asked.

'Uh,' Cushing referred to the report, 'her right one.'

'Could he tell what she'd been hit with? Fists?'

'As a matter of fact, he didn't think so. Maybe something rounded and covered with padding. He didn't see any serious abrasions or evidence of a sharp edge. Something blunt and padded.'

It was clear to all of them that the intensity of the killings, if they continued, was likely to follow an accelerating pattern. It was a grim prospect.

'Samenov's photographs will be ready in the

morning?' Frisch asked.

Birley nodded. 'They'll get them up here tonight, probably.'

'Okay.' Frisch was thinking, looking at Birley. 'Shit,' he said, turning his chair sideways to his desk and throwing a look out into the squad room. He thought about it, ignoring them in his silence, and then said, 'Okay, I'm not going to expand this thing. I'm going to let the four of you go after it. Put all your other cases on the back burner and concentrate on getting a handle as soon as possible. I'll go to the captain when we get through here and tell him what we've got and that I'm going to put the four of you on all the overtime you can handle. That'll piss them off in the chief's office, but if this thing gets away from us, gets out of control, the bad P.R. would be worse for the department than a drain on operating funds.'

He looked at each of them. 'First things first. How do you want to proceed?'

After a brief discussion they agreed to have one of the evening-shift teams follow through with trying to locate Dennis Ackley.

'If they find him,' Palma said, 'I want them to call me. I don't care what time it is. I'd like a little time with him before a lawyer gets in on it.'

Frisch looked at her, and she could see him trying to assess her request. After a moment he nodded without saying anything. She raked her eyes across Cushing, who was trying to decide what she was up to and whether or not he should be there too.

They decided Cushing and Leeland would follow up with Samenov's associates at Computron, including Wayne Canfield, and try to find Gil Reynolds, Dirk somebody, and somebody Bristol, the bank vice president. Palma and Birley would make another call on Vickie Kittrie after she had calmed down and would talk again with Andrew Moser. They would also canvass the neighborhood and check into the question of the time of the pizza delivery, and make a more thorough check of the house.

'One other thing,' Palma said. She was really stepping out in front on this one. Frisch looked at her again. 'I want to get an FBI criminal personality profile on both of these. I've got everything I'll need for Moser — our case report, the photographs, the autopsy protocol and lab reports — and by tomorrow morning I'll have Samenov's photographs. I can pull together a case report. And I'll do the VICAP report for both of them too. If any cases ever justified it, these do.'

Frisch raised his eyebrows in surprised approval. 'Good,' he said. 'This guy sure as hell qualifies for a psychological analysis. Fine, go ahead.' He looked around at each of them. 'I want you to pull out the stops on this one. I'm going to be glued to your supplements, and I want you to feed them to me often. No big lag times. After I brief the captain on this he's going to be on my tail for updates, and I don't want to be empty-handed. What comes down, goes down. So help me out.'

8

Bernadine Mello was forty-two. She was wealthy, living with her fourth husband (who was also wealthy, even before marrying Bernadine), and she was delicious to behold. When she had met with Dr. Broussard for her first interview five and a half years ago, her presenting problem had been 'depression.' It still was.

The chaise longue upon which Bernadine reposed was, professionally speaking, becoming passé. The trend among the more progressive psychoanalysts, especially those who concentrated on short-term therapies, was for the analyst and patient to sit in armchairs across from one another and to interact by means of the analyst confronting the patient face-to-face. It was a more egalitarian approach which Broussard disliked because he preferred the patriarchal advantages of the old Freudian style. And he still favored the chaise — for all their sophistication and addiction to things au courant, his clients were not aware of the academic subtleties that were making the chaise longue obsolete. For his style, for his approach, it was best. Men and women, he thought, had never been more clearly understood than by Sigmund Freud. His tools of psychoanalysis were symbols of their roles — the analyst upright, the woman recumbent — in this posture her mind was most easily penetrated.

The geometric shape which Broussard most often thought of in regard to Bernadine was the oval. Her face

was ovate, with pale gray eyes and a rounded chin that
was the first thing to quiver and show emotion when she
was troubled; her breasts, remarkably elastic for her age,
were as round as the proverbial melons, and when she
lay down they settled to large, wonderfully symmetrical
knolls; her hips were beautiful ellipses which, when she
turned her back to you and bent over with her legs
together, did indeed suggest the perfect heart; her thighs
emerged from her loins like the legs of a Modigliani
woman, though, perhaps, not with as much length as one
would have liked. If an artist were to sketch her naked,
there would not be a straight line within the entire
drawing. She was not a woman of angles, but of cambers.

Of all the women with whom Dr. Broussard had
consulted in the past fifteen years, Bernadine Mello had
to be among the three most vulnerable. She had the
sexual instincts of an Earth Mother, but she had no
children. Her husbands all had been, and were, unfaithful
to her, apparently with little regard to discretion. She
was, in turn, unfaithful to them. But none of her trysts
had ever led to a lasting relationship, and her husbands
— all powerfully driven men who had found her insatiable sexuality an aphrodisiac until marital familiarity
bred, rather than children, boredom — eventually left her.
In fact, Dr. Broussard had been her longest lasting
relationship with a man, and occasionally she made
offhandedly mocking remarks, which were actually in
earnest, to the effect that he wouldn't still be around
either, if it weren't for the monthly payments she made to
him.

She lay on the chaise now in low-cut pink panties and
a thin Bali bra, two straight creases running across her
stomach just above the navel. She was high-hipped. Her
sandy reddish pubic hair darkened the crotch of her nylon
panties, and the aureoles of her breasts were perfectly
centered in each translucent cup of her bra. Her hands,
small with tapering fingers and lacquered nails, were
resting spread out on the flat of her stomach. Her kinky
russet hair was pulled up from the nape of her neck and

rested on the back of the chaise. They had worked up a considerable heat. Dr. Broussard was shirtless. He had pulled on his pants but they were unfastened, and he was bending over, tugging at his sock. His shirt was on a hanger on his closet's opened door, his undershirt was folded neatly on the seat of a chair, his tie folded neatly on the undershirt. He had even put shoehorns in his shoes, which sat side by side underneath the chair that held his undershirt and tie. All of these articles were in the same places every time he had sexual intercourse with Bernadine Mello. Bernadine's clothes, by comparison, were still in a crumpled heap in front of the large plate-glass window that overlooked the sun-dappled lawn that sloped through the trees to the bayou.

'How many times does that make?' Bernadine was looking up at the trees outside, looking at the underside of the illuminated leaves.

'What?' Broussard was straightening the toe seam on a nylon sock before pulling it on.

'How many times does that make for us?' Her voice was a sultry contralto, which he very much enjoyed. She put her red thumbnails under the thin band of her panties and ran them back and forth, flattening out the lace.

He was caught off guard by the question, and before he could respond, she went on.

'Free-association time,' she said, looking at him, her head turned to the side on the chaise. 'One time when I was a child I walked into my aunt and uncle's bedroom in the middle of the afternoon. I was staying with them for the summer. They had two children, two daughters a couple of years younger than me, and sometimes I stayed with them for several weeks during the summers as a companion to the girls, to be an older sister. They liked me. On this afternoon they were taking naps. I was sewing little bonnets for them, little old-fashioned sunbonnets. I'd come across the patterns in a magazine. I'd broken a needle and went to Aunt Ceile's room where I had last seen the sewing basket. I didn't think anyone was in there. I walked in and he was bending over like you are now, exactly like you, no shirt, his pants undone all the way down so that his underwear showed, pulling on his socks. I was startled to see him like that and then I was dumbfounded when he turned his head toward me and it wasn't my uncle. I don't know who he was. Reflexively I looked over to the bed and Aunt Ceile was lying across it on her back, naked, her legs propped up and spread out facing him, and me. Her head was thrown back over the far side of the bed, her breasts pointing upward, and her hands grasping her inner thighs. She didn't see me. The man stopped pulling on his socks, slowly raised one finger and placed it up to his lips, signaling me to be quiet. I backed out of the door and left. That was all there was to it.'

Broussard didn't say anything. He finished pulling on his socks and reached over and got his shoes. He took the shoehorns out of his shoes and put them on.

'I never saw the man again,' she said. 'I don't know why, but I had the impression he was a stockbroker, like my uncle.'

Broussard stood up and slipped on his undershirt, took his shirt off the door and put it on, buttoned it, fastened the cuff links, tucked in the tail, smoothing it over his boxer trunks in his pants, fastened his pants, fastened his belt.

Bernadine watched him. 'I've often thought about that man,' she said, raising her arms and pulling up the hair at the back of her neck, smoothing it. 'I can still see his face perfectly. He smiled a little, almost sheepishly, but frankly. I was twelve.'

Broussard went back to the armchair and sat down without putting on his tie. He didn't believe her. That had never happened. Bernadine could be pitiful sometimes. She was wanting approval of another sort, something more than she was getting through her sexuality, so she was fabricating a story that she hoped he would find pregnant with symbolism. He had never heard this story before. She was so goddamn transparent. Bernadine was so hungry for approval that she would never achieve any significant degree of self-esteem. The only way she knew how to relate to people was by offering herself to be used, and every man she encountered accommodated her. She was beautiful; it was easy to do. Bernadine was going to be pitiful all her life.

He looked at her clothes piled in front of the picture window where he had taken them off her, one piece at a time, and where he had had sex with her, pressing the front of her against the thick glass all the while imagining what it must have looked like from the other side, her heavy breasts, her stomach, her thighs, all the rounded portions of her becoming flat, except for the places where she didn't touch. Woman in intaglio.

'Sometimes when we have sex I imagine myself being twelve,' she said. She cut her eyes at him. 'Just twelve.'

I don't care, he thought, still looking at her clothes. They were silk, very expensive.

She slid one of her feet up alongside the other leg, stopping with her knee in the air, her foot against the inner knee of the other on the leather chaise. With the index fingers of each hand she traced the two creases across her stomach.

'Raymond,' she said, referring to her husband, 'is seeing a woman who has practically no breasts at all.'

Broussard frowned, and took his eyes off the pile of silk. He looked at her. She was already looking at him.

'I hired an investigator,' she explained. 'He's taken pictures of them.' She looked at her own stomach. 'The guy's good. The detective, I mean.'

'Why did you do that?' Broussard was still frowning at her.

'I keep a file. Rather, my lawyer keeps a file. He arranged for the detective. It was his idea. It was okay with me, but it's humiliating going to his office and looking at them.'

'Raymond's going to get the shaft?' Broussard stood and stepped over to a door in his bookcases and opened it. There was a liquor cabinet inside. He took ice from a freezer compartment, put a few cubes in a squatty glass, poured gin over the top of the ice, and came back to his chair and sat down, propping his legs up on a hassock in front of his chair. He didn't bother offering anything to Bernadine, but he knew she was watching him and he knew she wanted him to offer her a drink too, to be nice, and he knew she would be hurt when he didn't. He touched his tongue to the cold gin.

Bernadine swung her legs over the side of the chaise and stood. She ran her red-nailed fingers around the inside of the elastic on the legs of her panties, adjusting them, and then went to the cabinet herself. Her stomach was not flat anymore. He listened to her behind him: the ice into the glass, the chink of the stopper in the lead crystal decanter, the sloshing of liquor. She came back by him and lay on the chaise again in the same position she had been in before she got up. When he looked he recognized the amber scotch. Bernadine was an alcoholic.

'Probably not,' she said. She put the cold glass against the hollow place of her inner thigh near her groin. She held it there a moment before she lifted the drink to her mouth and sipped.

Broussard waited. Probably not. He bet himself Bernadine was getting ready to double her net worth again.

There was a long silence while they sipped their drinks, and he listened to the soft muffled sound of the ice in their glasses.

'Why didn't you offer me a drink?' she asked. She was very still when she asked it, and Broussard could tell she had had to work up the nerve to do it. They had been together so many years that her sessions were now pretty matter-of-fact. He no longer pretended at seduction and she no longer pretended at being coy. He no longer even pretended it was therapy, a travesty that he had stoutly maintained for a few years, referring now and again to their 'therapeutic alliance' or her 'transference resistance' or the necessity of her achieving 'insight into the nature of her unconscious forces.' All of that was gone now, and they had long ago settled into a conjugal familiarity that made her analytic sessions more like a bored married couple's quiet evening at home. She still wanted to be 'nurtured' and continued to cling to the idea that he somehow was going to make her life better. It was something that he, too, had once believed, but Bernadine had been one of his few clients whose personality had continued to baffle, continued to refuse to be broken down and dissected. She was as much a mystery to him now as when she had first walked through his doors. His file on her was enormous, for he had continued to compile notes on her even after they had become lovers. She was that kind of woman: she invited exploration, with a smile, almost as if she dared you to try to figure her out. Sometimes he thought he loved her.

'I really didn't think you should have one,' he said at last.

She fixed her gray eyes on him, looking at him over the rim of her glass from which she had just taken a drink, looking at him as if he had insulted her. Bernadine was easily offended. Batting her eyes, she looked away through the plate-glass wall, through the green haze to the bayou. She let the glass rest on her stomach, directly over her navel.

After a moment she said, 'You don't believe my story about my aunt.'

He didn't say anything. Being a psychoanalyst had spoiled him. He never wanted to talk, and half the time lately he didn't even want to listen. It was amazing how powerful silence was. There were certain kinds of people who simply couldn't tolerate it. They would talk as an antidote, even when they didn't have anything to say.

'You know what?' she said, and a small, ironic smile crossed briefly over her lips. 'It's true. It happened exactly as I told you.' She raised her glass and sipped the scotch. 'It's true, and you didn't know it. And it's significant, and you didn't realize it.'

Broussard was interested now. 'Bernadine, I don't believe you.'

'Dom, what if I stopped seeing you?' she asked.

Now she had his full attention, but he was careful. He

didn't say anything. Nor did she. He waited, sipping his gin. What the hell was she trying to do? Was this a prelude to something? Was she actually going to stop seeing him? Surprised by his own feelings, he was disconcerted to realize that he was actually hurt by her question. Had he grown ... fond of her, this truly disturbed woman whose complexity, whose disarrayed personality was so exceptional that he could count her among the two or three most intriguing cases he had ever had?

'Would you miss me?' she repeated.

'Of course I would,' he heard himself say, and he even heard, to his surprise, an edge of anxiety in his intonation. He was immediately embarrassed by it and was afraid he was going to blush. He frowned at her, tried to put on the face of a scolder in case she should look around.

But she didn't say anything, and she didn't look around. She stared out the window and rolled the bottom of her sweating glass around her navel, forming a wet parameter.

'Haven't we been a lot to each other?' he asked, wanting to hear more of her thoughts, the thinking that lay behind her question. He felt oddly defensive, something he hadn't experienced in a long time. It made him nervous. 'It's not everyone I can relax with like this.'

She looked at him. 'Really?' Her quartz eyes, the very symbol of her personality, indefinable, difficult to be understood, capable of being lost in, fell on him. 'You don't do this with others?'

'No,' he said. 'I don't.' And then he suddenly feared he had said the wrong thing, though he was unsure why it should have been wrong. She studied him, and he had the unusual experience of seeing in her eyes that she was reading the lie. He didn't think he had ever seen that in her before, and he was taken aback. What was happening with her anyway?

'You don't sleep with any of your other clients?'

'Bernadine, no, but you don't have the right to ask me about such things.'

'About what you do with your other clients?'

He nodded.

'Doctor-client confidentiality,' she said.

'Of course.'

'If I didn't see you any more, would someone else take my place ... humping against the glass?' She tilted her head toward the window.

'What kind of a question is that, Bernadine?' It was a vulgar allusion, but Bernadine was earthy, everything about her was elemental. She had the most natural, the most culturally unaffected attitude toward sexuality of any woman — or man — he had ever known.

'It's a question to find out,' she said. She had been watching him, and now she turned her head and drained the rest of the scotch from her glass. She had let her right arm drop to the floor, and set down the glass. She cocked her right leg outward and placed her right hand, cold from the glass, on the indention of her inner thigh where she had held the cold glass before. 'Tell me,' she prodded.

'Bernadine,' he said. 'I don't expect ever to meet anyone like you again.' It was a response which, if it did not directly answer her question, definitely was not a lie. She made him wait a minute or two, her leg cocked to the side, her hand still in place.

'Dom,' she said, 'come here.'

He hesitated, his wrists dangling off the arms of the chair as he studied her leveled gaze. Then he got up and went over to the chaise. She reached out and he knelt beside her and she put her fingers in his hair and pulled him down and kissed him. With her right hand, she guided his head, his face, his lips to the cool spot on the inside of her thigh.

9

Andrew Moser was surprised to hear from her, and he was guarded when she said she wanted to talk to him but wouldn't be specific as to why over the telephone. He didn't want her to come to his home, didn't want to meet her nearby, and didn't want to leave the house until after the children had gone to bed. Since his wife's death, he didn't like to leave the house at nights. They agreed on the 59 Diner on Farnham at Shepherd Drive, just off the Southwest Freeway, at eleven o'clock.

She gathered up the forms she would have to fill out for the FBI and left the office. Even though the Audi had been in the shade of the motor pool parking garage, it was like an oven inside, and she rolled down the windows while she descended the garage ramp and exited out into the compound. She circled the headquarters buildings back to Washington Street and then turned right on Preston, which took her across the northern end of downtown, past the courthouse and the criminal court building and under the West Freeway 59 where Preston Street suddenly became Navigation Boulevard and ran an oblique course into the East End, following the general angle of Buffalo Bayou a few blocks away as it headed toward the Port of Houston Ship Channel.

Palma's mother still lived in the same barrio where Palma had grown up, in a neighborhood where all the streets had Scottish and Irish names and all the residents were Latin. The barrio had been a neighborhood where extended families often encompassed entire blocks of relatives or near relatives, and the grapevine was so rich that rebellious offspring were kept in check by the sheer fact that they couldn't find any privacy to work their mischief. But the barrio had acquired a more sullen air with the changing times, and misfortune of one kind or another had become a way of life for most of the population, rather than an occasional grief for only a few. The drug wars were threatening everything, and the flood of refugees from Central America was introducing an ominous element of uncertainty, as if these thousands of war-weary émigrés were only the first ripples of an impending human flood tide.

But Florencia Palma had raised two daughters and a son in this neighborhood, and she had buried a husband there. That was enough living to have given her title to the place. It was as much hers as the large stucco house that sat square in the middle of two lots that Palma's father, Vicente, had purchased in 1941 from a cousin who was moving his family to California. It was as much hers as the catalpas and oaks and mimosas she had planted, as much as the garden and the lush plantains that cooled the walks in the dead heat of summer. Age, Palma had decided as she watched her mother grow old, carried a great entitlement. If you lived long enough, the things most familiar to you became yours by virtue of the worry you had invested in them. They were yours as surely as memories.

She parked underneath the row of Mexican plums that grew the length of the two lots and shaded the front of the dun-colored house from the afternoon sun. The trees still had a few of their white blossoms scattered among their new green leaves, and they reminded Palma of the numbers of springs she and her brother and sister dutifully had stood beneath the rich flourish of creamy flowers while their mother had taken pictures. How many photographs? How many springs? The children were gone now, Palma's brother to San Antonio, her sister to Victoria, but the trees were still there, and Florencia still took pictures of them every spring. And Carmen still came by to stand obligingly under their white efflorescence to be photographed.

Palma found her mother in the courtyard on the south side of the house, the afternoon sun low enough to cast long, ashy shadows from the massive pecan trees that towered over the opposite side of the house. Smaller than her daughter — Carmen had gotten her height from her father — Florencia was a trim woman with small bones and a face that clearly demonstrated the strain of Tarascan blood in her background, a genetic inheritance that had been dying out for generations and made its last appearance in her handsome sharp features. None of her children carried the distinct characteristics of their mother's Indian heritage. She wore her gray hair long, past her shoulders, and when she was younger she had tended to it with elaborate care, brushing it, braiding it, washing it, grooming it with a diligence that was almost feline. She had done it partly because she was a naturally fastidious woman and partly, perhaps mostly, because Palma's father had a special affection for his wife's thick, dark mane. Now she simply had it pulled back loosely and clasped behind her neck with an ebony wood clasp. It was the only clasp the old woman ever wore now. It had been carved by Palma's father, a little bit at a time in the evenings during the course of one July when Palma was a little girl.

'Look at these,' she said, holding up two clay pots, a hot-pink verbena and a sanchezia, as Palma came through the gate. 'Daughters of daughters of daughters,' she said. 'I planted their great-grandmothers.'

She was standing barefooted on a wet rock walk where she had been watering her flowers, her baggy gardening dress hanging almost to her dusky ankles, her smile as beautiful now as it had been when, as a child, Palma first had become aware that it was something of a gift. Her mother smiled easily, the sort of smile that made

strangers instantly comfortable with her, a disarming
smile that told you she was not a complicated woman, a
misconception you soon would learn to revise. Palma
took a deep breath of the heavy air, the familiar earthy
odors of damp plants and stones. She kissed her mother's
cheek and smelled the faint waft of cheap lilac perfume
the old woman bought in a neighborhood store.

'I got a new letter from Celeste,' her mother said
immediately, setting down the clay pots along the path
and pushing back the wisps of gray hair from her temples
with the backs of her wet hands as she preceded Palma
to a long slatted wood swing that hung from an aging
water oak just off the path near the back patio. Stopping
at the swing, Florencia bent down a little stiffly and took
the hem of her dress and dried her hands. Then she
reached into the torn front pocket of her dress and
produced the letter, its well-worn envelope torn ragged
on one corner, exposing an equally well-worn letter. She
handed it to Palma.

'She's in Huehuetenango now. In the mountains. She
says she has volunteered to go up there, tired of the coast,
tired of the lowlands. She's much happier in the high
country. She says she had to deliver a baby, up — way up
— in the mountains where everything is mist like rain.
This delivery was a very delicate matter because this baby
was turned. A kind of long story.' Palma's mother nodded
at the letter. 'She tells it there, you'll see. Anyway,' a
sparkle of amusement began to pluck at her eyes, 'after a
long and tiresome night the baby is delivered. So. Everything is okay. The child is saved and the mother is saved
— *gracias a Dios*. In celebration, and to honor the good
nun, the parents named the boy . . . Celeste.'

Florencia burst out laughing. '*Un muchacho llamado
Celeste!*' She shook her head, delighted by the whimsical
ways of gratitude, and sat carefully in the tree swing
which Palma held for her. Then, joining her, Palma
dutifully took the letter out of its envelope, unfolded it,
and held it in her lap as if she were reading it while the
swing drifted calmly back and forth, the chain groaning

softly on its leather guides above them.

She came by to see her mother three or four times a week and tried to get over to take her to Sunday mass at least every other Sunday. Even though Palma was the only member of her immediate family still living in Houston, the old woman did not lack for companionship. A large and faithful group of older women, many of them widows, who had raised their families in the neighborhood, looked after one another, old friends that Palma had known all her life and who knew how to get in touch with her if it was necessary. Even so, as her mother's mind began to show the inevitable signs of quirkiness, Palma found herself wanting to keep in closer touch. It was almost as if she could feel that the departure had begun, and as her mother began to slip away from her Palma herself felt the need to move with her, if not to prevent the inevitable then at least to defer it. She knew that this kind of slow separation was part of the human condition, but to acknowledge that didn't make it any less frightening, any less painful.

After Palma had listened to the groaning swing for a minute or two, now and then turning the pages of the letter, which was written on both sides of three sheets, after she somehow had shifted the weight of sadness in her heart so she could carry it and fought back the tears that almost instantaneously sprang to her eyes when she took the letter from her mother, she folded the sheets, slipped them back into the envelope, and handed them back. It was the third time within a week that her mother had shown her this 'new' letter; the third time Palma had 'read' it and listened to the story of the baby boy named Celeste.

'That's a good letter, Mama,' Palma said. 'I know you enjoy getting them.' Florencia smiled and tucked the letter back into her dress pocket and thought a moment.

'I'd like to ask her if she has ever regretted becoming a nun,' she said.

Palma looked at her. The question surprised her.

'I've always been curious,' the old woman mused,

shrugging. 'She was so *beautiful*.'

'You don't think the Sisters of Charity need a pretty nun in Guatemala?' Palma asked, watching her mother.

'She was the prettiest of all your cousins,' her mother said, ignoring Palma's remark. 'She could have been a movie star. A model.'

'You would have preferred that?'

'Oh, no. It's best that she's a nun.' She widened her eyes. 'But I don't understand it.' She waited a moment. 'I'm sure it's hard for the priests, too.'

Palma smiled. Her mother was one of the Almighty's more straightforward creatures. Her faith that God's will would ultimately prevail was firmly grounded in a belief in miracles. It was her conviction that only the miraculous could save man from his considerably flawed nature. Man's only hope was in something greater than himself, something he didn't fully understand, but in which he had an unabashedly explicit faith.

'How do you think Celeste would answer your question, Mama?' Palma asked. A Spanish dove had settled in one of the catalpa trees and had started its languorous, two-noted cooing.

Her mother didn't respond immediately, but stuck out one foot and let her big toe drag back and forth over the stones beneath the swing. Then she looked up toward the dove.

'She would say, I think, that she was sorry that being a Sister of Charity was the only thing she had ever wanted or would ever want.'

'Ah, you're cheating. You're trying to have it both ways,' Palma chided.

'Oh, no. That's an absolutely honest answer,' her mother said earnestly, as if she were defending Celeste's actual words. 'Maybe she feels something is missing, or that something might have been, but doesn't know what it is. But she's curious about it, and sorry she doesn't understand. I'll tell you,' she added, glancing casually toward the catalpa, pretending a casual interest in the dove. 'There isn't a woman alive who doesn't

wonder sooner or later if maybe she didn't take a wrong
turn at some crucial moment in her past. It's in her nature
to wonder about such things. We all do it. Maybe especially pretty little nuns in the jungles of Huehuetenango.'

Palma suddenly had the feeling that they weren't
really talking about Celeste at all. She suspected that her
mother had been thinking about her divorce again. Palma
would never forget the anguished look on the old
woman's face when she had to tell her that her marriage
was over. The expression had had nothing to do with her
mother's own disappointment. Florencia knew her
daughter too well, how long had she waited to marry,
how much it must have hurt her when it came apart. Her
expression had been one of complete, selfless empathy;
her daughter's pain was instantly her own. Palma had
never needed her more than at that moment and the old
woman knew this, even through the thickening fog of her
senility, and she gave her daughter everything she had
from the heart. It had been a crucial time for both of
them, and it had been a lesson for Palma that even this
late in their lives their relationship was still capable of
becoming even richer than it was.

'Anyway,' her mother said, 'how's it going with you?'
Palma came from a family of interrogators. 'I'm doing
fine, Mama.' She urged the swing with her foot against
the stones.

The old woman nodded and let a brown hand go up to
her hair, smoothing it back. 'Good,' she said.

They let the swing run its course from the push of
Palma's foot, the leather groaning on the oak, the little
speckled dove occasionally reminding them of its
presence with a low, moaning whistle from the catalpa.
Palma thought of the woman on the bed, the pale length
of her, the mutilation. What was he doing now, in the
afternoon, waiting out the heat? How did a man who did
things like that wait out the heat? She knew the answer to
that. But she shoved it out of her mind. She didn't want
to think about it now, not here, with her.

Palma asked a few questions about her brother and sister. They communicated mostly through Florencia. It wasn't that they were not close, but they simply were not involved in each other's lives. Palma herself rarely corresponded with them. They visited about Patricio's advancement in the San Antonio police department and about Lina's children, who were now in junior high school. After Palma inquired about her mother's friends and they chatted about the neighborhood, Palma left her standing under the Mexican plums and returned back through the barrio to the expressways.

She drove with her shoes off, one of the air conditioner vents under the dash directed to the floor, her skirt pulled up to mid-thigh. How had it ever happened that women came to believe they were not decently dressed unless they were wearing panty hose? It had been a bleak day for women south of the thirty-fifth parallel. Panty hose were nothing less than instruments of torture in Houston's humid heat, and Palma had mentally threatened to adopt all kinds of alternatives, none of them acceptable, some of them indecent, but all of them considerably cooler. She hiked her skirt a little higher and checked on either side of her for that urban specialist, the freeway voyeur, who rode the city's hot asphalt ribbons in a variety of high-riding trucks, vans, and pickups, keeping a keen eye out for women in lower cars seeking relief from the thermodynamics of panty hose.

She took a deep breath and flipped down the sun visor. The traffic on the Southwest Freeway moved like a sluggish equatorial serpent, worming west under the moist glare of a moribund sun, a copper fire sinking through a hazy atmosphere of ninety-one percent humidity.

Leaving the freeway at the Weslayan exit, she doubled back to the left under the overpass and within a few moments she was entering West University Place, a neighborhood of roughly two square miles that had been an incorporated city since 1925. Immediately west of Rice University, it was a village of older homes on quiet streets crowded with oaks, pecans, magnolias, cottonwoods, redbuds, and an occasional fat palm. The street signs were blue instead of the Greater Houston green, and the streets themselves were patrolled by West University's own police force. Though they accepted gas, electricity, and telephone service from Houston, West University was otherwise fiercely independent, and whereas Houston was distinguished among American cities by having no building code at all, West University was dictatorially vigilant in maintaining its village atmosphere. Fast-food eateries and convenience stores, in fact almost all commercial endeavors, were relegated to the streets that bordered the village, facing the metropolis like jealous sentries holding back the poor taste of commercial progress and town home mentality.

Palma lived in one of the better streets in West University, one of the Yuppie streets where the older homes were being bought up and remodeled or torn down and supplanted by larger 'interpretations' of their styles. She sometimes felt a little out of place here, though she couldn't really put her finger on the why of it. She pulled into the small circle driveway of the two-story brick home, its front door protected from the street by berms of yaupons and scarlet crepe myrtles, its brick drive bordered with flowering clumps of mondo grass. The yard had been made maintenance-free by a solid covering of Asian jasmine and decorative clusters of lantana. She had to admit she liked the way the place looked. Besides grooming himself, it was the one thing Brian had done absolutely correctly.

But she had to admit, too, as she opened the front door, balancing an armful of files as she pulled the key out of the door and closed it with her hip, that the place was too big to live in alone. She laid the files and keys on a hall table and walked into the living room where she lowered the temperature on the air-conditioning thermostat, hesitating a moment, listening for the compressor to click on. She turned on a few lamps, kicked off her shoes again, and picked them up with one hand as she loosened her belt with the other. She walked through the dining room unbuttoning her dress, then back out to the stairway where she started up to her bedroom.

There were times now when coming home to the empty house was the hardest part of the day. She had done it for many years because that was the way she wanted it. Educated and independent, she was very much aware of being a woman of the new age, and even though she dated regularly she relished her independence and had never had a live-in boyfriend. The idea had never appealed to her, for a variety of reasons. And then there was Brian and their marriage and those few good months together before everything turned absolutely wrong. That taste of shared life, of making a forever commitment to someone who loved you enough to make that same promise, of knowing that no matter what else happened in life that other person whom you held so dear would be there to help you endure it or celebrate it, the giddy pleasure of simply being loved by someone who mattered to you more than anything else in the world — all of that had been dangled in front of her just long enough for her to realize it was something she desperately wanted.

And then it was gone. Now there was no hiding from the fact that she missed him — not Brian, but the man he could have been, the man he should have been. It was the most painful experience she had ever been through. Jesus, just to have someone to sleep with, not even the sex, but just someone to bend into when you curled up at night. She really missed that. And somehow she couldn't tolerate the idea of boyfriends. Not now, not yet, not for a long time.

She bathed and washed her hair and put on a thin cotton sundress without underwear. She combed out her hair, but left it wet, and then went downstairs to the kitchen and poured a strong scotch and water before she walked outside to the backyard. It was actually a spacious brick courtyard with islands of yaupons, an abundance of rain lilies in clay pots, surrounded by a tall privacy fence, and totally shaded by a high canopy of oaks that let through dappled sunlight in the middle of the day. It was a refuge, and even when the weather was almost unbearably hot she would sit out here in the late evenings dressed in practically nothing, sipping a cold drink. It almost made the loneliness bearable.

Sitting in a lawn chair, she propped her feet up in another, and hiked her dress above her knees. The drink was tall and had lots of ice in it. She sat a moment, thinking, before she picked up the packet of documents she needed to fill out for VICAP, the FBI's Violent Criminal Apprehension Program, a nationwide computer information center located in Quantico, Virginia, that collected, collated, and analyzed data on specific violent crimes. With a little luck, the data she fed VICAP regarding the Moser and Samenov killings might trigger a computer 'hit' of similar kinds of homicides occurring somewhere else in the nation. If so, she and the detective covering those cases could exchange information and possibly cut short the career of a serial killer. It was a remote possibility, but one she couldn't very well afford to ignore.

Starting at the front of the blue printed crime analysis report form, she read from the first page, not bothering to respond to any of the nearly two hundred items of requested information. Most of the data were case specific, and she would have to refer back to the case report before she could complete it. But she wasn't at it long. When she came to 'Section VII: Condition of the Victim When Found,' she stopped. These were images that were not likely to be far from Palma's consciousness for a long time to come. In fact, she could hardly keep them suppressed.

Suddenly she had no stomach for dispassion or objectivity. It seemed almost a crime itself to grasp these familiar reins of self-control, to use them as an excuse to avoid an emotional investment. She didn't even know why disassociation was a virtue in cases such as these; she didn't believe it was. Not this time, at least, not when she was still numbed by the pale, naked image of a man hunched over Dorothy Samenov's stomach, his face and teeth buried in her naval, not when she could almost feel the lips around her own navel and could see the gnarled ripple of the man's curved spine as he curled in a fetal crouch, knees against her hips, suckling at her stomach with poisoned ardor.

It was too dark to read by the time Palma shook herself loose from such thoughts. She had forgotten her drink, and when she reached for it the tall, sweaty glass was standing in a puddle of its own condensation, the ice having long ago melted, leaving behind an unappealing, warm, off-color liquid. She heard the tremulous purl of a screech owl somewhere in the dense trees of the neighborhood and swatted a mosquito on the side of her knee. She needed to eat something. In a few hours she would have to talk to Andrew Moser.

10

When Palma got to the diner ten minutes early, Moser was already sitting in a booth next to the front windows overlooking the front parking lot. As she walked inside the diner she was relieved for Moser's sake to see that the place was sparsely populated. It was too late for the dinner crowds that characteristically came to this reincarnation of a fifties diner, and it was still too early for the equally faithful late-nighters. Moser was nursing a chunky cup of coffee, looking slightly apprehensive.

He stood as Palma approached his booth. He was a tall, thin man, always neatly dressed, but not a clotheshorse, tending toward Houston's tropical version of the Eastern postcollegiate simplicity. He had a long face and the kind of physiognomy that retained its youthfulness beyond its allotted time and which his wife, had she lived, eventually would have found difficult to compete with.

'Have you got something new?' he asked quickly. The waitress was just on her way over with the coffeepot and an extra cup.

'We don't think so,' Palma said, putting her purse down beside her and crossing her legs under the table. She paused while the waitress poured her coffee and Moser looked at her with puzzled anguish. He was still taking his wife's death very hard, and it didn't help that the circumstances were as strange to him as if she had been swallowed by a python in their church choir.

'You don't "think" so?' he said, leaning toward her as the waitress left. 'What's that mean?' He was agitated, impatient.

'Something has come up in another case and we're wondering if it's related in some way to the circumstances in your wife's death.'

'Like what? What "circumstances"?'

'Let me ask you this,' she said. 'When you were going through your wife's things, did you come across anything that you hadn't known about? Something that she possibly had kept secret from you, that might have seemed totally out of character for her?'

Andrew Moser was not naive. One of the peculiar things about being a homicide detective was that your encounters with the survivors of a homicide victim often took on an intimacy normally reserved for one's doctor, clergyman, or spouse. This was even more likely if the victim was a member of the white middle class, which was rarely touched by such things, and if the murder had sexual overtones, as did Sandra Moser's. The ordeal was so far removed from the normal experience of such persons that the shock of it rendered them emotionally vulnerable for a long time afterward. The homicide detective becomes the 'expert' to whom they can turn for help, from whom they hoped to hear answers to questions they had never dreamed they would have to ask.

Andrew Moser had already had to confront the numbing fact that his wife had probably gone voluntarily to the hotel in which she was found dead. This kind of discovery was not the sort of thing many people ever had to face, and it was not the sort of thing many people would be able to face without extreme emotional strain. Moser had run the gamut of emotions during the last two weeks, and Palma had been with him during much of that time. Even now, he still looked haggard. His wife's mother, a widow, had come from out of state to stay with the children while Moser tried to pick up the pieces and carry on with his life. But the unknown circumstances of his wife's death, the realization that in all likelihood she had had some kind of other life behind his back, were taking their toll on the man.

Still leaning forward, Moser stared at Palma with his expression of impatience frozen on his features, his eyes opened inquiringly, his head cocked slightly to one side. In the ensuing silence between them, while the cook far off in the kitchen began singing a vibrato rendering of Joe Cocker's 'You Are So Beautiful,' while the voices of a man and woman a few booths away rose slightly in argument and then subsided, while the waitresses across the room gathered near the glass-fronted pie cabinets and rested their tired hips against the Formica counter, Andrew Moser's face slowly changed from defiance to defeat as tears welled in his eyes and all the innocence of what he once had thought his life to be passed away from his memory in the dark shadow of disillusion.

'Jesus.' His voice cracked, and his mouth drew tight, betraying the strain he felt as he struggled for self-control. 'Jesus' he repeated, and it was almost a sob, but he caught it, and sat against the back of the booth and quickly looked away as his eyes suddenly spilled over. He wiped them quickly with his fingers and stared stupidly at the glittering lights of the traffic that passed by on either side of the diner.

'I'm not going to have anything left,' he said. 'Nothing. I don't even know who the hell she was anymore.'

Palma ached for him. The man had been dying by degrees, one or two a day for nearly three weeks, drying up inside so that every moist piece of his fiber was growing brittle and crumbling, changing him forever. Cruelly, Palma kept her silence. He had to talk to her, and he had to hurt before he would talk.

He was breathing heavily, almost wheezing, and then he cleared his throat. But he kept his eyes toward the window.

'In any other context they would have been common items,' he said. 'But when I found them together ... in a black lacquer box, for Christ's sake, I knew. A string of large pearls. Small ... clips, rubber-coated. An electric massager ... with an attachment. I don't know ... do I have to go through all of it?'

'No,' Palma said. 'No, it's not necessary. What did you do with them?'

'I threw them away. The box ... all of it.' His head was still turned away. He couldn't look at her. His Adam's apple was working to keep back the sobs building in his chest.

Damn, sometimes what she had to do seemed really just too cruel. 'Can you tell me,' she said, trying to sound controlled, but not dispassionate, 'did you have the impression that these things were ... did any of them seem to be intended for sadomasochism?' She couldn't imagine how that might have sounded to him, and she didn't want to think about it too much.

He didn't react with any particular emotion. Maybe the well was dry; he had already taken a lot out of it. He shook his head wearily and continued to shake it seemingly unaware that he was doing it.

'No, not really,' he said. 'I didn't have that feeling. Just the feeling that ... you know, that ...' His voice thickened. 'Why didn't I know? Why ... would she keep it ...? We weren't prudish about sex. It was good. I mean, I don't think I ever ... denied her anything in that way. Jesus! I've been over it and over it. I can honestly say ... as far as I know ... that it was very good.' He finally turned to Palma. 'I mean, as sincerely as I can evaluate it, it was good for *her*. She never, ever, indicated the slightest ... discontent about it. And I was attentive. I mean, I was aware of the indictment, you know about men's selfishness in that, and I tried to be sensitive about that. I didn't have my head in the sand about those sorts of things. I ... honest to God ... I thought everything was ... very good in that area.'

He stopped and took some paper napkins from the dispenser on the table and rubbed his eyes. He said 'Jesus' again and took a drink of coffee.

'You told us before that you haven't any idea who she might have been seeing. Has that changed now?'

'Hell, no,' he said without anger. 'If I was in the dark about this ... then I'm really at a loss on who she might have been seeing. If you'd found me dead in that hotel room you could have found people willing to speculate. Little flirtations people might have seen at the office or something. I mean, you could have made a case that I might have been seeing someone. But with Sandra, no. And as I say this I realize how it must sound, that it can't carry much weight in light of what I didn't know about her. But I can't think of a single possibility there. I just can't. I've never seen her come on to anybody. It just wasn't her way.'

This of course had been corroborated by countless interviews with her friends, women she had worked with in her charity activities, women who had been in her exercise classes, in the parents' organization at her children's school. Everyone had the same assessment, with one caveat. No one was really close to her, no one really knew her 'that' well. She was a good, responsible mother and wife, fulfilled all her social duties, but had no 'best' friend.

'Have you ever heard of a woman named Dorothy Samenov?'

Moser shook his head, wiping his eyes again.

'How about Vickie Kittrie?'

'No.'

'Was there anything else, however small, you might have come across in her things? Addresses jotted down somewhere that you didn't recognize, telephone numbers that weren't familiar?'

'We've already done this,' he reminded her.

'I know, but sometimes things come to you.'

Palma studied him while he looked at his coffee cup. He looked gaunt. Was he still holding something back? How labyrinthine was this thing? He took a drink of coffee.

'Going through her things,' he said, shaking his head

again. 'I did that when my father died. I went through his things because my mother couldn't do it. It was rough. But this ... At first I just couldn't do it. If you hadn't said it was important I still probably wouldn't have gone through her stuff. The box, I didn't find the box until the last. Actually it was an accident. She'd hidden it at the back of her closet, inside an air-conditioning duct. She hadn't put the vent grill back right.'

Thinking back, he said, 'But then, once I'd found that I couldn't stop. I went through everything again and again. I didn't know what the hell I was looking for, but I was obsessed with finding something else. I even went over the seams of her dresses thinking she might have hidden things in there. I went through every page of her books looking for notes, messages. I took the caps off her cosmetics, her perfume bottles, her eyebrow pencil, nothing was too insignificant. I even ... I even took apart all the tampons I could find. I thought, you know, that she would have thought I would never look in a place like that. And I was terrified the whole time that I would find something. It was like getting it into my head that someone had let loose a poisonous snake in the house. I was afraid to look for it, and afraid not to.'

The waitress dutifully made her rounds, poured fresh coffee for them, and Moser added cream and sugar again, thinking of something else the whole time. Palma didn't know what to ask him next. They had been over everything already and she had even gone back to see him on a couple of fishing expeditions, but the case had been at a dead end right from the beginning. If Moser was right — and telling the truth — the toys in his wife's little black box hadn't had anything to do with sadomasochism. She was just a little more sexually exuberant than he had thought.

Neither of them spoke for a moment and then Moser said, 'It was crazy, but I did it. I don't know if it made me feel better or worse. You know, something like this, it ... it's completely disorienting. At first you're so stunned by the death, and then that it's murder — not a car wreck, an aneurism, or cancer — but murder, then you learn that it's *this* kind of thing. You lose your wife, the one you had, and then you lose the one you thought you had. You end up with a head full of doubts, not even able to hang on to the memories because you're not sure they were valid. What about all those things you said and did together over the years? Which parts of your life with her were truthful, which were the lies?' He stopped, resorted to his coffee again, taking a disinterested sip to wet his throat, which had been tightening. 'I'm not dealing with this very well at all. I know that.'

'No one deals with this very well,' Palma said. 'Not at first, anyway.'

'I'm talking about the whole thing.' The cook started up with Joe Cocker again, and Moser listened for a moment. 'I only returned to work yesterday. I had to take some time off, and they were good about it. And then when I returned everyone bent over backward. But I knew everyone was wondering about it: What the hell was she doing in a hotel? All of them sorry for me, sorry that it had happened, but: What the hell was she doing in a hotel? And Sandra's mother. The woman's dying inside. We don't even talk about it. I can't; she can't. We talk about everything in the world; we talk too much, but not about Sandra. Not about the goddamn hotel.'

He stopped suddenly as if he'd caught himself getting out of line. He looked disgusted with himself, turned away from her and then looked back. 'You said something about another woman.'

Palma nodded. 'That's right. Another victim, there are some similarities of circumstance.'

'She was in a hotel room?'

'No, not that, but other things.'

'What things?'

'I can't really get into that with you,' she said, starting the routine, but then something stopped her. She wondered if she weren't being too cautious. They needed a break, and if she confided in Moser even a little it might scratch the surface of something. 'I'll give you some of it, but you've got to keep it to yourself.'

Moser nodded curtly and frowned at her, impatient for her to get on with it.

'She was four years older than Sandra, a divorcee. She was found at her home, on a bed like Sandra, same marks on her wrists and ankles, same battering, all of that, except this was more severe. She lived alone, worked for a computer firm, and . . .'

'What firm?'

'Computron.'

'Jesus, I know people at Computron. A lot of people. We're one of their largest software clients. What was her name?'

'Dorothy Samenov. I asked you about her earlier.'

'Moser said the name to himself several times. 'Christ! Sammy? She spells it Samme, it's a nickname, but she pronounces it Sammy. Dorothy Samenov. Yeah, I *do* know her. She calls on our division at Sonametrics. I sign off on all our purchases from Computron for our division, and I've seen these yellow-flag notes: 'Thanks . . Samme!' Stuff like that. First time I saw it I didn't know what, you know, it was: Samme, that didn't make any sense to me. I asked about it and the woman who handles the account laughed and told me. And then I met her. That was maybe three years ago. I don't see her much, but I know her. Goddamn.'

'You see her?'

'Not really, but I know who she is. I don't deal directly with the sales people, but I see her at the parties. You know, company parties, Christmas, the annual picnic, holidays.'

'Did Sandra know her?'

'No . . . I mean, I can't imagine she would. Although I guess she might have met her at one of the parties, a Christmas party one time, or one of the company picnics.'

'You don't know, though?'

'I have no idea. But I guess she could've. That's pretty strange, isn't it?'

Damn right, Palma thought. 'I guess it's not all that

unusual,' she said. 'What was she like?'

'Very outgoing, almost aggressive in a way, but very friendly. You don't really get to know anyone at those parties.'

'Did she come alone?'

'I don't know.'

'Do you remember if she associated with anyone in particular?'

'No.'

'I mentioned another woman, too, Vickie Kittrie. She works at Computron with Samenov.'

'Something happened to her, too?'

'No. She found Samenov; they were good friends.'

Moser looked at her. 'No, not at all. I don't know that name.'

'Were there any other circumstances where you and Sandra might have come into contact with Computron employees?'

'No,' he answered without hesitating. 'Just those times. That was it. Maybe two times a year.'

Palma thought a moment. 'Do you think they could have run into each other somewhere else?'

'Where?' Moser's face registered some kind of connection, as if he were reading some significance into this. Palma wondered whether to take it seriously. The significance he saw might exist only in his imagination, like seeing ghosts, or searching the hems of dresses for poisonous snakes. 'What if they did?' he said suddenly.

'I don't know.' She really didn't. But she knew in her own mind that she was going to assume that they had, and then she was going to try to prove it.

'Look,' she said. 'Work on this, give it some thought, but don't talk to anyone about it, okay? It's very important that you don't tell anyone about any of this. If something else comes to you, be sure and give me a call.'

'Sure,' he said, nodding. He was still thinking about his wife and Samenov. He was going to give it a lot of thought. 'I'll call you.'

She picked up her purse and started to open it.

'No, I'll get it,' he said. 'I'm going to sit here a little while.'

'Thanks,' she said. It sounded inane. 'If we come up with anything at all, I'll get in touch with you.'

Moser nodded, and Palma slid out of the booth. She walked away from him, leaving him pondering new possibilities, and went out the front door into the muggy midnight. As she walked to her car through the rippling shadows of the small parking lot she thought about Brian and the attorney with the long chestnut hair she had found him with. She remembered how it had been right after that, how it still was sometimes, wondering over and over about the details, how they had moved and touched, and if he had done the same things with that woman that he had done with her.

SECOND
DAY

11

By six o'clock she was pulling up in the parking lot of Meaux's Grille just off Bissonnet near Rice University. Open around the clock, Meaux's always had a scattering of students and businessmen and was owned and run by a small, henna-haired French woman in her fifties named Lauré. Lauré manned the cash register and looked after her clientele with hawk-eyed efficiency, while the kitchen was run by her husband, a Polish ex-merchant marine named Gustaw. On the morning shift they had two Guatemalan waitresses, sisters — one shy and one flirty — and a Chinese dishwasher and assistant cook called Ling. Gustaw and the Chinese (who, Lauré said, knew more dirty jokes than the whores of Marseilles) laughed and talked incessantly and turned out more good food in less time than any other two cooks in Houston. Inexplicably, they communicated only in Spanish so that the two Guatemalan girls, blushing or laughing lubriciously as suited their personalities, were the only ones who understood what was happening in the kitchen.

Palma parked under the catalpa tree in the parking lot and bought a newspaper from one of the wire cages outside. She went in, took a booth by a window that looked out onto Bissonnet, and ordered breakfast from

Alma, the shy sister. The place was still quiet, with only a
coatless businessman on one of the stools at the counter.
Palma turned first to the section of short articles covering
the police news. After the initial mention of Samenov's
death on Tuesday morning, there had been nothing else
about it, which was unusual. The press, like the police,
tended to pay a little more attention when the victim's
address was in the high-dollar real estate. Mayhem in the
middle class was cause for alarm, perhaps a sign that the
felonious minorities and poor white trash were pushing
their social disorder out of bounds. Still, it was good that
no reporter had yet made the connection, but she couldn't
expect that kind of luck to last very long.

When her food came, Palma folded the paper a quarter
of its size and kept reading while she ate. By the time she
finished, the traffic was beginning to pick up both in the
diner and outside. Leaving a good tip for Alma, Palma
paid Lauré at the cash register, and stepped outside in the
cool morning. She loved this time of day. It was as cool as
it was going to be until the same time the next day. At
this time of morning it was possible to be optimistic.

She was already sitting at her computer terminal when
the seven o'clock shift began arriving. She had been up
until two o'clock filling out what she could of the VICAP
crime analysis report forms for both the Moser and
Samenov cases and now was almost through with
Samenov's narrative summary. Although photographic
services were true to their word and had two sets of
Samenov's crime scene photographs on her desk when
she got there early that morning, the material Palma
would be submitting to the FBI was less than ideal by its
standards. She would not yet have a victimology or
autopsy protocol for Samenov, nor would she have the
crime lab's results on the pubic hair, swabs, and smears.
However, since she did have everything for Moser's case,
and since the police report would make it clear that the
crime scene behavior was obviously similar to that in the
case of Sandra Moser, she felt justified in requesting a
'rough draft' profile in light of the fact that they might

have a possible repeat killer with distinctive ritual behavior.

Palma was beginning her third cup of coffee, her desk was covered with forms and photocopies and photographs and computer printouts of the crime report, and she was folding her leg up under her in her chair when she heard Cushing say, 'You really think this's going to get you anywhere?'

He was standing in the doorway holding a black coffee mug he had ordered from *Penthouse* with a wraparound Asian nude painted on it in pink flesh tones and in such a posture that the mug's handle became a partially penetrated phallus. She had seen the mug before, but only as a pornographic curiosity sitting on the filing cabinet in Cushing's office. He had never actually used it for coffee until this morning. His silk shirt was a little blousy in the arms, and his full, pleated trousers a little narrow at the ankles. The thick scent of too much Aramis followed him into the room.

'What do you think I think, Art?' Palma said, dropping her pencil and turning to him. 'Why am I doing this?'

'No, really, Carmen. I've seen some real screwups in those profiles. Missed 'em by a mile. Not even close. They could get you thinking all wrong about how you should go after this guy. I wouldn't put too much faith in them.'

He casually set the coffee mug on the edge of her desk, pretending he had to tuck his shirttail in a little tighter.

'They've messed you up before?' she asked, looking at Cushing, who was holding back a grin.

'Not me personally, but I've known other guys, yeah.' He picked up the mug again and sucked loudly from it, his lips covering a strategically painted pink breast. 'Selwin, ask Weedy Selwin. He's had dealings with them before. One time they told him his guy ought to be a Swedish bachelor in his forties with a persecution complex and a hairlip, or something like that. Turned out to be a Mexican national who looked like Al Pacino and had four kids.'

'Maybe I should tell Frisch you've decided we ought to

just forget the FBI and get Weedy in on this?'

Cushing shrugged. 'Hey,' he said.

'Right.' Palma nodded and looked at him. The technique was variously praised or maligned, depending upon a detective's experience with it or depending on what he had heard. It wasn't widely used because the kinds of cases in which it was employed were a relatively small percentage of all homicide cases investigated, and even the agent-analysts stressed that the method was never meant to be a substitute for good, solid investigative procedures. It should be used only as an additional tool to supplement everything else available to the investigator. However, the cases in which it was employed were by nature sensational so that the technique had gained a larger-than-life reputation that was easily disparaged by skeptics.

Cushing sucked more coffee from his mug, this time playing with the sound a little bit. They looked at each other a moment and then Cushing, one hand in his pocket, turned unhurriedly and meandered out into the squad room. She watched him go and saw him join two other detectives who had been watching Cushing's conversation with her through the window. All of them were laughing and Cushing was talking, gesturing with his coffee mug.

Then Birley walked into the office.

'Sorry I'm late,' he said, pulling off his jacket and hanging it behind the door. 'Long story ... about a dog and a root canal and Sally and a Peeping Tom garbageman.' He flopped down in his chair, sighed enormously, and looked at a blue Tupperware bowl sitting on his desk that he had brought in with him. He looked at Palma and tapped the plastic. 'Lasagna. Very good last night. Sally swears it'll warm up just fine in the cafeteria's microwave.' He pulled down the sides of his mouth and slowly shook his head. 'It won't.' He looked at Palma's desk. 'The FBI stuff?'

She nodded. 'I'm almost through with it. I've already called Garrett over at the FBI offices and told him I would drop the stuff by there later this morning.'

'This'll be fun,' Birley said. He smiled at her. 'You want this guy's ass, don't you?'

'I do,' she said. 'I really do.'

'You going to get carried away with it?'

'I'm already carried away with it.'

'Work out some little personal vendettas, maybe?'

'I can't think of a better way to do it.'

Birley snorted and shook his head. 'Hell, me either.'

'I talked to Moser last night.'

Birley held up his hand. 'Wait. Let me get some coffee.' He grabbed his mug off his desk and lumbered out to the squad room, around the island of cubicles to the sink and coffeepot just outside Frisch's office. Palma watched him wave at Frisch and a couple of secretaries in Frisch's office, strike up a conversation with several detectives hanging around the coffeepot — he nudged Wyden (probably kidding him about his picture in the paper at a recent homicide scene), grabbed the spare tire at Marley's waistline (probably kidding him about the obvious) — all the time talking, bullshitting, and whipping up his coffee concoction (he used everything).

When he got back to the office he said, 'Okay, let's hear it,' as he came in the door.

Palma told him.

'Poor bastard,' Birley said when she had finished. He drank his coffee and thought a moment. 'This's one bad dream he's not ever going to wake up from.' He looked at Palma. 'Did you believe him when he said he didn't think the stuff was used for S&M?'

Palma smiled to herself. Birley was good. 'Yeah, I'm bothered by some things that I can't quite pin down. Despite what he says, I wonder just how sensitive he really was to his wife's sexual needs. I would almost bet money that the paraphernalia he found was not limited to autoerotic use, but Moser's absolutely incapable of entertaining the idea of her infidelity. Under the circumstances most men's imagination would run wild with something like this. Whatever she was into, it was so foreign to his concept of what she was all about that he has no idea what to do with the evidence to the contrary. There's no doubt that the man's a complete wreck over this, but a lot of stuff doesn't add up. I mean, he didn't find his wife's cache of toys until after we had urged him to go through her things and cautioned him to be meticulous in doing so. We pointed out the importance of finding anything out of the ordinary. Then he threw the stuff away. I don't know.'

'Sure.'

She looked at him. 'What, he was ashamed of it?'

'I imagine.'

'That's what I thought, too. But then why did he finally come across with the information? We'd never have known the difference.'

Birley gave her one of his slow looks, and then turned his eyes to his desk, picked up a pencil, and played with the green feathers of a fishing lure stuck into the fabric covering the cubicle wall. 'Well, you know, there's a difference. On the one hand a guy admits the stuff was there, that it actually existed. He did the stand-up thing. On the other hand he gives the stuff to a bunch of detectives, a bunch of guys who'll paw through it, handle it, look it over, joke about it, the actual stuff his wife had been . . . using.' Without looking at her, Birley jerked his head in a shrug. 'Damn, I don't blame him.'

Palma remembered Moser's reluctance to enumerate the items he had found in the black box, and she felt a pang of discomfort at not having been sensitive to the difference Birley had pointed out. She was so used to the veterans acting as though they didn't have any emotions at all that sometimes they caught her off guard with their unexpected sensitivity, and in doing so made her realize just how frighteningly successful she had been in shutting out her own feelings.

'A guy like that,' Birley added. 'There're things he'll probably never tell us that would be useful to the investigation. But you have to let some things go.'

'Like if he really knew if she might have been having an affair?'

'Maybe. You don't believe he was telling the truth about that either?'

'I don't know,' she said, exasperated. 'I want to blame him for not being observant, for not being sensitive to . . . something.'

'There may be some of that,' Birley conceded. 'But I can tell you when it comes to deceit, neither sex of this species has got a corner on the market. If you want to deceive somebody bad enough you can do it. And for a long time, too. There must have been a lot about her he didn't know, and maybe his ignorance wasn't a result of his being a klutz. I'm guessing that Sandra Moser, in addition to being all the good things her friends claimed, was also a real piece of work.'

'And what do you make of the fact that Andrew Moser knew Dorothy Samenov. At least had met her.'

Birley shook his head. 'Now that's the one that interests me. It's just the kind of thing that could be a fluke, something that seems so obviously a "link" that it throws off the whole perspective of the investigation. Or it could be the real thing. Damn, what a coincidence. You'd almost have to believe it meant something.'

'I need to talk to Cush and Leeland before they go over to Computron. They ought to know about this.'

'Yeah, you should,' Birley said, looking at his watch. 'And I need to get my tail over to Olympia, chat up the neighbors, go through the place, and talk to the pizza folks. It's gonna be a great morning.'

12

It was almost eleven o'clock by the time Palma talked to Cushing and Leeland, took the VICAP forms and profile materials by the FBI offices, and drove out Westheimer to the street where Vickie Kittrie had listed her address. The apartment complex which occupied an entire cul-de-sac was a Mediterranean affair, two stories of white stuccoed arches and terra-cotta tile roofs, fronted by a crescent of tall palms interspersed with crepe myrtle and protected from the high crime rate by a high-tech wrought-iron fence that required security cards to open. Behind the crescent of palms she could see the obligatory swimming pool through a gap in the holly hedge growing against the wrought iron, and behind the pool the complex office.

After showing her badge and assuring the manager that Kittrie was in no way crossways with the 'law,' she received a map of the complex with a penciled *x* marking Kittrie's apartment. She followed the woman's directions through a series of courtyards with elevated redwood walkways, on either side of which palmettos and banana plants glistened in the almost visible humidity. She passed one of several hot tubs indicated on the map and finally entered a courtyard dominated by rose bushes blooming in every shade of pink and red. A pathway of herringbone-patterned bricks crossed the redwood board-

walk. To her right was the wrought-iron fence braided
with roses, and the cul-de-sac; to her left was Vickie
Kittrie's front door. She had not called to see if Kittrie was
there, but she had checked in at Kittrie's office and
learned she had not shown up for work.

Kittrie answered the door after only three rings, which
surprised Palma, who had expected to have trouble
getting Kittrie to talk to her. The girl stood in the doorway
in a crisp, white percale summer robe, squinting into the
bright noon light. Her curly ginger hair was casually
bunched up on her head in no particular style and held in
place with pins. She wore no makeup, nothing to disguise
the fair skin and spatter of freckles across her nose. No
one would ever have doubted she was Irish.

'Hi,' she said. She stood, half behind the door, leaning
on the edge of it. She didn't seem to have a feeling one
way or the other about seeing Palma standing there.

'Do you have a little while to talk to me?' Palma asked.
She studied Kittrie's face. 'I'll try not to take any longer
than necessary.'

'It's sooner or later, isn't it,' Kittrie said. It wasn't a
question.

'I'm afraid so.'

'Come on in.' She stepped back and Palma walked into
the front room of the apartment. It was immediately clear
that all the amenities of the apartment complex were in
the landscaping. The inside of the apartment could have
been interchangeable with any of the millions of cookie-
cutter complexes scattered throughout the city. The front
room was small. It had a fake fireplace and a moderate-
size window that looked out into the courtyard. A bar
separated the living room from the kitchen, and a hallway
led back to the bedroom. Kittrie had done her best to
decorate this Spanish-Mediterranean-style apartment
with an art deco flair, but it was apparent she didn't have
the same size budget to work with that Samenov had
enjoyed. But Palma remembered the dress Kittrie had
worn the previous day. Like many working girls her age,
almost everything she made went into her clothes.

Looking good was right up there near the top on her list of priorities.

Palma sat in an armchair next to the inexpensive, bookless shelves facing the television. To her left was the window looking out to the courtyard and under it a sofa where Kittrie sat down, tucking one of her legs under her and ignoring a man's sport coat of beige raw silk thrown over the pillows at the opposite end. To Palma's right a breakfast bar looked into the kitchen — a Houston Astros baseball cap lay upside down next to a toaster — and in front of her was a glass coffee table scattered with magazines, a bottle of fuchsia nail polish, a pack of Virginia Slims, and an ashtray.

'You've got a nice place here,' Palma said. 'Do you live alone?'

Kittrie nodded and reached for the ashtray and cigarettes.

Something in Kittrie's manner made Palma decide not to treat the girl as a 'sister.' This one wasn't going to let you be friends with her; it didn't seem like the right approach. She got right to the business.

'Yesterday when you were telling me about having stopped off for drinks at Cristof's, you said that besides you and Samenov there were three other women: Marge Simon, Nancy Segal, and Linda Mancera. Did all of them work with Dorothy?'

Kittrie shook her head and exhaled her first breath of smoke. She was holding the ashtray in her lap, and a long pale leg was exposed to mid-thigh by the parting percale robe.

'No. Actually, only Nancy works at Computron, in the Tenneco Building. Marge and Linda work across the street in the Allied Bank Plaza — at Siskel and Weeks. It's an ad agency. Sometimes we all meet at the same deli in the tunnels for lunch, and that's how we got to know each other. We all get off work at the same time. Nancy's the only one, and she doesn't even work in the same department as Dorothy.'

'Do you?'

'I do, yeah.'

'Do you ever see any of these other women at any time other than at lunch or for a drink after work?'

'Not really.'

'What does that mean?'

Kittrie frowned defensively. 'What?'

'What does "not really" mean? You don't see them or you do?'

'Well, sure, some, but I mean not all the time.'

'In what context do you see them?' Palma couldn't tell if Kittrie was dense or giving her a hard time.

'Sometimes we date ... I mean, you know, with guys, to a club or something, or for dinner. Sometimes we might just go to a movie together. It's not all that often.'

'But you did see Samenov more often?'

'Well, yeah. I work in the same office with her, we had exercise classes together, we don't live that far apart. There were times ...' Kittrie had to take a drag on her cigarette, but it had nothing to do with smoking. She was checking her emotions. Palma was a little surprised at this. Kittrie's emotions were closer to the surface than Palma had thought. '... she'd come by and we'd ride to work together. I'm on her way.' She nodded and tried to keep her mouth from puckering. The cigarette was hoisted in the air, her elbow tucked into her side.

'You told me yesterday Dorothy's divorce was not a friendly one. What do you know about that?'

'Not a lot. Dorothy would talk about it sometimes, and I've met the guy.' She dragged on the cigarette again. 'I don't know how Dorothy could have married him in the first place. The guy's a bastard. He used to knock her around. He couldn't hold a job. For a while he was a chemicals-supply sales rep. You know, janitorial supplies to hotels and restaurants. For a while he was part owner of a tire company. He thought that was cool, the best job he'd ever had.' She hit on the cigarette again. '"Where the rubber meets the road." That's what he'd say when he wanted to have sex. He thought that was smart as hell, like it was a unique expression. Dorothy used to imitate

him. She was merciless. The guy was a prick. He wasn't
even good-looking. I mean, I know that's subjective, but
you poll a bunch of women, and he's not going to come
out too good. I didn't like him. Dorothy said she married
him right out of college, graduate school. He was very
macho. That's why she did it.'

'She liked macho men?'

'At that time she did. But not after having lived with
the prick for six years.'

Kittrie mashed out her cigarette in the ashtray, picked
up the pack beside her on the sofa, and lighted another.
She took her time, but her face showed that she was
trying to collect her thoughts on this one. Palma's eyes
scanned the coffee table: a *TV Guide*, *Cosmopolitan*, *People*,
and peeking through two magazines turned on their
backs, a pink-nippled, oversize breast and a cloying
toothpaste smile, and above them the black banner title of
a men's nudie magazine.

Somewhere in the back of the apartment a water pipe
began to hiss softly as someone turned on a bathroom
faucet. A quick twitch skittered across Kittrie's ginger
eyebrows, but she kept her eyes glued on Palma, refusing
to acknowledge what they both had heard.

'Do you remember when you first reported your
concern for Dorothy last Saturday, you talked to a
patrolman who came by but he was reluctant to check
into the house?'

Kittrie nodded, interested.

'He put you off and suggested maybe Dorothy had
gone on a spur-of-the-moment weekend with someone
without telling anyone. You said maybe so. Were you
aware she had done that before?'

'Yeah, she had.'

'Who with?'

'I don't know. Just sometimes I would miss her, like at
exercise class on Saturday, and when I would ask her
about it at work on Monday she'd say she'd gotten an
invitation for a weekend trip and she'd taken it. It was no
big deal.' She angrily ground out her cigarette in the

ashtray. It wasn't even half smoked.

Great, this really wasn't headed anywhere, and Palma had the growing impression that Kittrie was holding out. At the same time she seemed genuinely disturbed by Samenov's death, her nerves just barely under control.

'We found some photographs among Dorothy's things,' Palma said. Kittrie's eyes fixed on her, and she didn't move a muscle. 'They were pornographic, and Dorothy was involved in them. She was tied to a bed in a sadomasochist scenario. There was a guy in a leather hood, a mask. Were you aware of these?'

Kittrie stiffened and shook her head quickly, too quickly.

'Did you know of Dorothy's interest in sadomasochism?'

Kittrie shook her head again.

This time Kittrie's expression had something else in it. She was no longer defiant or evasive or maddeningly uninformative because she had reached the point where her facial movements were operating on their own and she could no more have disguised the fear that showed there than she could have levitated off the sofa. Palma took advantage of it.

'We found some other things too, and there were photographs of other people. I think you understand what I'm talking about. It's not really to anyone's advantage for you to withhold anything on this. This is a homicide investigation, Vickie, and you're liable under the law if you know something that would be helpful to the investigation and you withhold it. We can keep secrets. We do it all the time. What you tell us will be confidential, it's part of the process. You don't have to worry about any of it getting out.'

Kittrie's eyes had grown wider and a little wilder as Palma talked, and she had dropped her hands to her sides on the sofa as if to steady herself.

'What the hell are you talking ... What are you trying to do ...?' she blurted. She slapped her clenched fists down on either side of her on the sofa and shook her

head, her voice rising through clenched teeth. 'What ...
what ... what ...'

'Vickie!' The man's voice, quick and firm, caught them
both by surprise. They turned toward the hallway near
the kitchen and saw Nathan Isenberg standing there. He
was barefoot, wearing white pants and a Jamaican pink
shirt with stripes, the tail out, the long sleeves unbuttoned at the wrist. Helena was a step behind him.

Suddenly Kittrie broke into tears, crying uncontrollably, not hiding her face, just sobbing with her eyes
squeezed tightly shut, tears already streaming down her
pale cheeks past her twisted mouth.

'Let me get her into the bedroom,' Isenberg said to
Palma. It was half question, half statement. With a great
deal of patience and tenderness, he helped the sobbing
girl off the sofa. Supporting her by embracing her with
his left arm, he began crooning soothingly, his voice
taking on the same intonations of an old woman coddling
her spoiled little house poodle.

Standing, Palma watched them leave the room and
then looked at Helena, who hadn't moved a step. She was
trim and tan in a peach cotton tank top tucked into a pair
of tailored khaki shorts. Her girlish figure and bobbed
hair shot through with gray created a striking image.

Before Palma could make sense of what she had just
seen, Helena said, 'Look, I'm sorry to butt in like that, but
... well ... could we just step outside?'

They did, and the midday heat was coming up off the
herringbone bricks with a vengeance. 'Over here, maybe,'
Helena said, stepping up onto the redwood walkway and
going a little way into one of the courtyards near a trellis
of roses. It was out of the sun, but into a pocket of
humidity held close by the surrounding palmettos and
banana trees.

'I'm sorry,' she repeated. 'I guess none of this is my
business, or maybe it is. Anyway, I heard all of that in
there,' she said matter-of-factly. 'I really couldn't help it.
Vickie didn't call any friends yesterday, she lied about
that. I've lived across the street from Dorothy for a couple

of years now. I didn't know her really well, just enough to wave and speak. We saw each other at the pool a lot, but we didn't socialize. She had her own friends, and so did I. I kind of knew Vickie because she was over at Dorothy's a lot and sometimes was out at the pool with her. That's why I came over yesterday when I saw the police. She wouldn't stay at my place, so I came home with her last night and slept in her other bedroom. She didn't have a good night.'

'She didn't have other friends?'

Helena shrugged. 'I just know she wouldn't call anyone. I asked her if she was going to be alone and she said yeah but she didn't care. I tried to get her to stay at my place, but she didn't want to be across the street from Dorothy's.'

She crossed her arms and shifted her weight to her left leg. 'I don't know anything personal about their relationship, okay, but it seems to me that Dorothy was kind of like an older sister to her. Vickie wasn't being very helpful to you in there — this is my impression — and I just thought maybe she didn't want to hear some of the stuff she was hearing. Couldn't deal with it.'

'What do you mean?'

'Maybe she didn't want to hear those things about Dorothy. Look, I'm just giving you my impression. Staying here last night, it seemed to me this girl is not all that independent. I think maybe Dorothy kind of looked after her a little . . .'

Palma studied her, deliberately not saying anything, just looking at her. She was very well made and had a natural way of wearing a minimum of clothes. The low-cut arms on the tank top would have kept a man busy assessing her dimensions, but she wore it like an athlete. Her sure manner reminded Palma of the girls on her swim team in college, comfortable with their bodies, easy in their nakedness.

'Do you work?' Palma asked.

Helena seemed surprised by the question, but not necessarily bothered.

'No.'

'You're home most of the time?'

'Yeah.' Her face portraying a sudden realization. 'Nathan's not my husband,' she explained. 'My last name's Saulnier. I'm sorry, we didn't make that very clear. I'm divorced.' She gave a small, hard smile. 'I got half of everything. The way I see it, I made my payments into the mutual fund. I worked for the man on my feet and on my back for twenty-six years, a lot longer than I wanted to be on either one. The divorce was my retirement party, the settlement was my pension. Now I don't work anymore.' She kind of tossed it off, but Palma could tell it was something that cut to the grain.

'And Mr. Isenberg?'

'Not my live-in,' she smirked. 'Not permanently.'

'There's a sport jacket in there on the sofa,' Palma said. 'Was that Mr. Isenberg's?'

'No.'

'Do you know whose it was?'

'No. Vickie doesn't have anyone special as far as I can tell. But ... she always has someone. The jacket was there when we got there, but the guy's never shown up.'

'Can you remember if you were home last Thursday night?'

Saulnier thought back. 'Thursday night, Thursday ... I was. Yes, I was home. I had rented a couple of movies.'

'We think that's when Dorothy was killed. Maybe around ten o'clock. Did you happen to notice anyone coming or going over there at any time on Thursday?'

Saulnier thought a moment, her eyes staying on Palma, a little dew of perspiration beginning to show on her chest just below the shallow dent in her throat. 'No, I didn't see anything. At least nothing comes to mind.' She frowned. 'Jesus, it was last Thursday? She'd been in there that long? That's horrible.' She paused. 'Did Vickie see her ... like that?'

'Like what?'

'After she was dead ... a while?'

'I think so.'

'How did it happen?'

'She was strangled.'

Saulnier wiped the thin fingers of one hand delicately over her top lip, which was also perspiring now. A cicada's drone swelled and died out in a nearby mimosa. Palma felt a trickle forming between her breasts.

'What happens now?' Saulnier asked.

'We don't have much to go on.'

'I see.' Saulnier was looking toward the pathway around the corner.

Palma reached into her purse and took out a card. She wrote her home telephone number on the back and handed it to Saulnier. 'If anything comes up, day or night, anytime, I'd like to hear from you.'

Saulnier took the card and smiled. It was kind of an odd thing to do.

'I really want to get into this one,' Palma said. 'If you could help I'd appreciate it.'

They walked back toward Kittrie's apartment, and Palma let herself out the wrought-iron gate.

'Listen,' Saulnier said, talking through the bars. 'Don't think too harshly of her. After a time, when she's calmed down some, maybe she'll come up with something.'

Walking back to the car Palma could feel the moisture all over her body as the air she created moved around her. Standing still, she hadn't really noticed. She unlocked the car and left the door open for a moment while she took off her purse and laid it on the front seat.

Before she got in she glanced back across the cul-de-sac. Saulnier was still standing at the gate, watching her. Palma pretended she didn't see her, though she didn't know why.

13

Palma backtracked a few blocks on Westheimer and pulled into a Landry's restaurant. From the telephone booth outside she called Birley at Samenov's condo.

'I did the pizza thing first,' he said. 'Leeland's pizza hunch was good. She ordered a pepperoni and green olive from Ricco's Pizzeria around the corner here. They had a FasFax copy of the order coming in at seven twenty-eight. I called Rutledge, and he said that something like that would pass through her stomach in about one and a half to two hours. According to the autopsy the "tail" of Samenov's pizza was just about to enter her intestines. So it's likely she died somewhere around ten o'clock on the same night she was last seen by Kittrie.'

'What size was the pizza?'

'Right. Small.'

'Doesn't sound like she was expecting company . . . for dinner, anyway.'

'Nope. How was Vickie?'

Palma went over it with him briefly.

'Damn, sounds like Dorothy had some goofy neighbors. We ought to check 'em out.'

'Yeah, I plan to do that. Meanwhile I'm on my way downtown to talk to Linda Mancera at Siskel and Weeks Advertising. Have fun in the neighborhood.'

She quickly ate a shrimp salad with iced tea and then

headed back out Westheimer to the West Loop where she
picked up the Southwest Freeway again. By now the
streets were blistering and the sun splintered a million
different ways off buildings and cars, off chrome and
glass and polished steel. Palma put on her sunglasses and
muscled into the traffic.

She couldn't get Helena Saulnier and Nathan Isenberg
off her mind. She had to admit she had been relieved
when they so suddenly appeared in the hallway and took
charge of the unstable Kittrie. Palma had been in no mood
to play nursemaid to the girl's easily provoked hysterics.
And Saulnier had been helpful, too, in putting Kittrie's
relationship with Samenov into perspective. Helpful, yes,
but in the end it was Saulnier's perspective that Palma
had finally gotten, not her own, and she couldn't shake
the feeling that Saulnier had a vested interest in just
exactly how Palma understood the situation.

The Allied Bank Plaza was a blue glass monolith of too
many stories on the western side of downtown. A
stylized trapezoid with rounded ends, its western face
overlooked the green sward of Sam Houston Park and the
overpass scaffoldings of the Gulf Freeway under which
the Buffalo Bayou made a muddy meander eastward on
its way to the Port of Houston Ship Channel on the
fringes of the city. West, too, was a limitless stretch of
green treetops from which the clusters of skyscrapers at
Greenway Plaza and the uptown Post Oak district rose up
like cities unto themselves. On the eastern face the view
grew hazy toward the fifty vermicular miles of ship
channel encrusted with shipping terminals, petroleum
refineries, chemical plants, and steelworks, all industries
capable of churning out enough effluvia to shroud the
sunrise, which they often did.

Siskel and Weeks was on the sixty-seventh floor. It
was a ritzy place with glass-brick walls and Plexiglas
desks and plastic translucent room dividers in primary
colors and secretaries in forties hairstyles and sparkling
lipstick. All the men wore tailor-made braces on their
pleated suit pants and cut their hair short like the male

models in *Gentlemen's Quarterly*. Everyone was young and clean and busy.

Palma's wrinkled cotton shirtwaist and well-worn shoulder bag did not command immediate attention from the fresh-faced men and women who breezed through the reception area, and the receptionist herself had a serious problem with myopia, which told Palma that she had been sized up as a minority job applicant. She could wait, which she did. She gave the receptionist the benefit of the doubt and three more minutes before she placed her shield two inches in front of the girl's red-framed glasses and stopped a telephone conversation that didn't seem all that important to the firm's fiscal well-being.

The girl's mouth stopped in mid-yap and she rolled her eyes up to Palma, who was looking down on her.

'If you would put that person on hold and buzz Linda Mancera that she is wanted out front, I would appreciate it.'

'May I tell her . . .'

'Carmen Palma.'

Though flustered, the receptionist did a beautiful job, and Palma thanked her and walked over to a leather sofa where she picked up a magazine from a palette-shaped lavender Lucite coffee table.

Linda Mancera came down a long hallway of glass bricks that changed in shade from submarine blue to fluorescent white as it neared the reception area and made her look as if she were emerging from the inside curl of a long surfing wave. Before she got close, Palma could tell she was in her late twenties, built like the women on the cover of *Cosmopolitan*, and dressed like the women in *Vogue*. Frowning and preoccupied, her long, black hair temporarily pulled around over one shoulder, she walked briskly into the reception area and then stopped, brought herself back to the present, glanced around and caught Palma's eye.

'Carmen Palma?'

'Detective Palma,' she said, showing her shield.

'Oh, my God,' Mancera said, raising one red-nailed

hand but stopping short of her mouth. 'Dorothy.'

'Have you got a few minutes? I won't keep you long.'

'I just *heard*, just this minute,' Mancera said, wrinkling her eyebrows. 'A friend called ... she worked with Dorothy, just across the street. Nancy Segal ... she said she'd just talked to the police ... a man.'

Good boy, Palma thought. If Cushing's girl had looked anything like this one, Palma could be sure he had questioned her at length.

'Could we go somewhere with a little privacy?'

'Oh, I'm sorry, of course,' Mancera reflexively reached out, a gesture of apology. 'Let's go to my office,' she said, and Palma followed her into the long watery light, her heels clicking on the dove gray marble.

Mancera's workplace was at the far end of the glass corridor, one of the desirable 'outside' offices that had a ceiling-to-floor view of the southwestern United States. She had a thick plate-glass desk with glass bricks to hold it up and behind her was a wide credenza of similar design with built-in files and drawers. The credenza and part of Mancera's desk were covered with artists' sketches and layouts of ad campaigns, and Mancera shoved them aside as she sat down, her eyes on Palma.

'So what happened?' she asked without ceremony, planting her forearms on the glass and leaning across.

Palma gave her a quick outline of events, enough to satisfy her immediate curiosity, and Mancera listened with an expressive face, reacting to the turn of events with genuine emotion, obviously finding the whole story incredible.

'Jesus H. Christ,' Mancera said when Palma finished. 'This is too much!'

'If she was a random victim there's not a lot we can do from the approach of questioning her friends,' Palma said. 'But if she wasn't, if she knew her assailant, we're hoping her friends will be able to help us identify possible suspects.'

'What? You mean, who do I think could have done this? My God, I can't even believe I know someone this has happened to, much less know who might have *done* it.' Mancera was wearing a linen work smock over a silk blouse and viscose suit skirt. She kept pushing back the baggy arms of the smock. 'Look, if you've been talking to Dorothy's friends you've probably already gotten a good idea of how unpredictable she was. She was one sharp gal, quick, intelligent, but she could be wacky. I mean, she was a free spirit, it opened her up for a lot of ... adventures. I loved her to death ...' Mancera caught the unfortunate reference and looked embarrassed. 'Jesus ... anyway, but she was unpredictable. She easily could have picked up someone on the spur of the moment.'

'Did you, any of you, often do that at Cristof's?'

'Actually, no. Times are changing, you know. We tend not to go around hitting on guys at bars. I mean, *we* don't; people still do, I guess.' She looked at Palma's hands. 'You're not married?'

'Divorced.'

'So what do *you* do?'

Palma ignored the unexpected question, though it seemed to have been asked more out of genuine curiosity than flippancy.

'Did you know Dorothy's ex-husband?'

Mancera nodded, a subtle look of distaste changing the pleasant shape of her mouth. 'I met him once. The guy's an absolute waste. None of us could really feature them together. Totally out of Dorothy's league. Dorothy was ... classy. Very sharp. Guys like that didn't even get close to her. But I understand he went way back, before Dorothy learned a few things.'

'How did they get along?'

'They didn't.'

'How did you happen to meet him?'

Mancera rolled her eyes, remembering. 'It was a strange incident.' She kind of laughed and frowned at the same time. 'Some of us were over at Dorothy's one night, this was over a year ago, and he simply showed up at her door. It was clear she was stunned to see him — later she said she hadn't seen him in almost a year. He just pushed his way in. Nothing she could do about it. I didn't know who he was so I didn't know what the hell was going down. It scared me. He stormed right into the living room and Dorothy jumped up and kind of ushered him back out into the entry. We could hear them arguing. The strange thing was the way Dorothy was acting. She was always so strong, you know. Among us she was kind of the pacesetter. The New Woman. But we could hear them, and she was wheedling, trying to soothe him, calm him. They got quiet — I don't know, this sounds sleazy now, but we were all sitting there petrified, listening to this — they got quiet and we heard this, these, *intimate* sounds. They were kissing, making out. It was crazy. Then suddenly whap! He hit her. It sounded like an open-hand slap. A couple of us jumped to our feet, but *nobody* left the room. The door slammed, and he was gone. Dorothy ran down the hall to the bathroom before anyone could get to her.'

Mancera pushed aside some papers on her desk and found a pack of cigarettes. She lighted one, turned around to the credenza and found a heavy crystal ashtray, and put it in front of her.

'It was crazy,' she said.

'That was it?'

'Well, you know, we tried to get things back to normal, went into the kitchen, made drinks, lighted cigarettes, started trying to clear our heads after that downer. When Dorothy finally came back into the room she apologized. Some of the girls wanted to talk about it, but Dorothy cut them off. It ruined the evening.' She pushed at the smock sleeves. 'All I could think of was those sounds in the entryway. Those were *not* the sort of sounds that should have gone with that little scenario. You hear something incongruent like that, it sticks in your mind.'

Mancera was clearly still bothered by the events of that evening. She didn't know what to do with her eyes so she turned and looked out the glass wall. The hand holding the cigarette was resting on the plate-glass desk, the wrist cocked back, the cigarette trembling.

'Do you know any of the men Dorothy dated?'

Mancera shook her head without even giving it any thought and turned back to Palma.

'I don't know how it is with you and your friends, but with Dorothy and us, the little bunch of us that often go to Cristof's together after work, men just aren't part of the agenda. As participants, anyway. We might talk about them, share war stories, but we aren't interested in being with them in that context. It's just girl talk. You know, kick back and relax, say what you want to, forget the minuet of the sexes.'

She put out her cigarette, only half smoked.

'So to answer your question: no. Aside from that one shabby little episode at her place that night, I know nothing about her men and their relationships. I hope it was better for her with the others.'

Palma liked Mancera. She didn't seem to have anything to hide, didn't appear to be walking on eggshells like Saulnier and Kittrie. But then, she wasn't as close to Samenov. Aside from that, Linda Mancera seemed a more straightforward personality and was simply more confident as a woman.

'Can you characterize the way Dorothy talked about men when you were together?' Palma asked. 'You said you shared "war stories." What were hers like?'

'Oh, I don't know,' Mancera frowned. 'Nothing really sticks in my mind about it except that maybe she seemed a little more independent than the rest of us.' She shrugged and smiled ironically. 'You see, that's the problem. I do think of her as the symbol of the woman of the new age: independent, a successful businesswoman who hasn't fallen into the old clichéd power traps like a lot of women. Too often I've seen women who've achieved a degree of success in 'the men's world' stop being women and simply start acting like men in dresses, miming the old male models, being just as hard-ass, being one of the boys. But not Dorothy. She was true to herself, to being a decent human being. But then there was that episode at her house when she seemed like the sweet, suffering, battered wife. God. I guess I hadn't admitted even to myself how much that had affected me. Listen to me. I can't stop talking about it.'

She stopped and looked at Palma. 'Sorry, I didn't really answer your question, did I? How did she talk about men? I honestly don't remember any particular attitude in a sexual context. I guess she had pretty much the same views as the rest of us. You know, I guess we're all generally less tolerant than maybe we used to be. We don't take the bullshit from them that we used to, demand more, not as willing to compromise.'

'Do you know if she dated a lot?'

'I always had the impression she got around quite a bit.'

Palma watched Mancera closely and asked, 'Were you aware of her interest in rough sex?'

There was a blank expression followed by slowly raised eyebrows. 'Rough sex?'

'We found photographs among her personal things, and some sexual paraphernalia. She was in some of the photographs.'

Mancera swallowed. 'Jeez-us. I never heard anything about that from her.'

'Aside from her ex-husband, do you know any other men in her life?'

Mancera shook her head.

'Have you ever heard of Wayne Canfield or Gil Reynolds?'

'No, sorry.' Mancera paused and looked at Palma, finally realizing what all the questions were adding up to. 'You don't have any leads on this? You're still trying to come up with something?'

'We haven't had a lot of luck so far.'

Mancera hesitated for a second, but went ahead. 'What . . . exactly, were the circumstances?'

'She was strangled.'

'In her home?'

'Yes.'

'They broke in?'

'It doesn't appear so. She might have known the person.'

'Jesus. Oh, I can see ...' She looked at Palma, nodding. 'I'm sorry. I really wish I could be more helpful. Poor Dorothy. You just don't ever imagine these things, not in a million years.'

'Well, I appreciate your taking the time.' Palma stood and laid one of her cards on the plate-glass desk. 'My home number is on the back of the card. If you should think of anything you believe might be helpful to us, please call me. Anytime. I don't care if it's three in the morning.'

Linda Mancera walked Palma back through the aqua corridor to the reception area, saying that she would do anything she could to help, that she wanted to be available if there was any way Palma thought she could use her. She seemed genuinely affected by Dorothy Samenov's death and sincere in her desire to be of service. She was the first glimmer of something positive that Palma had encountered.

14

Mary Lowe was ten minutes late, but she made no reference to it as she came into his office. She was Broussard's last appointment in the afternoon. They exchanged a few brief pleasantries as Dr. Broussard pulled his armchair over nearer the chaise than he normally kept it, and Mary sat on the edge of the chaise and unbuckled her sandals. Today her hair was down, and she wore a polished-cotton chintz sundress with a full skirt and bare shoulders that once again gave him a view of the tops of her breasts. He watched them as she swung her feet onto the chaise and lay back.

'What would you like to talk about?' he asked, crossing his legs and settling into his armchair.

'My father.'

Broussard was surprised. After so many weeks of inanities Mary seemed to be finally wanting to get to the crux of her own psychological story. Perhaps the last session had indeed been a turning point. It had been a long time coming.

The idea that Mary should undergo psychotherapy had not been hers, but her husband's, and Broussard had seen from the beginning that she was going to require a rather complicated therapy. Paul and Mary Lowe had been happily married for four years. They had two children, a boy, three, and a girl, one and a half. Paul was an executive in a successful computer-manufacturing firm with a salary that put them in the higher income brackets. Mary had help with the children and the house; she didn't have to worry about balancing a tight budget. She was attractive, well dressed, well educated, and active in one or two civic organizations with the proper social standing. Her life, by all appearances, was very good indeed.

This was common with his clients. On the surface of things, none of them appeared to belong there.

Then, nearly a year earlier, Mary began making excuses in order to avoid sexual intercourse with her husband. The frequency of their intercourse decreased. At first her husband believed they had let their lives become too crowded with obligations; they needed to set aside more time to nurture their relationship. He told Dr. Broussard he had read about this sort of thing in magazines. They simply weren't spending enough 'quality time' together. Paul Lowe was a good husband. He began to be more attentive to her; he arranged for occasional long weekends during which the two of them would take short trips alone. He did everything that the experts in the magazines said a man should do to revive a flagging marriage.

But nothing changed. Mary persisted in making excuses, avoiding intercourse whenever she possibly could. When her husband confronted her with her obvious disinterest, even aversion, she reluctantly relented to his overtures and tried to discount his concern. But she was still unresponsive and tense. He had sexual intercourse with her — alone — a bizarre feeling that he could not long tolerate. Eventually it became clear to him that she actually was repulsed by intercourse, though she had no objections to lying in bed and holding him, or to being held by him. She seemed to find this comforting, seemed even to desire it, but sexual interaction beyond this simple demonstration of affection caused her immediate anxiety.

Even with all this, Paul could not believe the sexual part of their marriage had come to an end. From time to time he would try to initiate intercourse, believing if he

were gentle enough, delicate enough, understanding
enough, loving enough, then she once again would
become comfortable in their intimacy. The result was that
Mary developed functional dyspareunia, and finally
vaginismus. She developed a vaginal rash she could not
relieve. She told her husband that her gynecologist was
puzzled by her disorders and was trying a variety of
medicines to cure them. But there was no change.

Finally, their damaged relationship and Mary's condition became so unbearable that Paul called her doctor
himself, only to learn that the gynecologist had been
telling Mary for months that in all likelihood her disorder
had psychological and emotional origins, and he had
encouraged her to consult a psychiatrist. He had given
her several names and recommendations, but she had not
acted on his advice. This discovery led to Paul Lowe's
ultimatum that either she sought professional therapy or
he could no longer live with her. Because she truly loved
her husband, Mary was horrified at his threat. But she
refused to see any of the doctors her gynecologist recommended. Instead, a friend gave her the name of Dr.
Dominick Broussard. It was not the best of circumstances
under which to begin a relationship with a psychiatrist,
but it had to do.

He began with a goal-limited therapy to relieve her
anxieties, which were the source of her physical symptoms. But even this took longer than he expected, and
while he was enjoying being with her because of her
remarkable beauty, he was also extremely impatient with
the psychodynamics of her disorders. There was little she
could say or demonstrate that he had not heard or seen in
some other fashion in the context of some other woman's
miseries.

'My stepfather, actually,' she said. Her sundress had a
fabric cord belt and she held the two loose ends of the
cord in her hands, toying with them. The small pucker at
the corner of her mouth tightened ever so slightly. 'He
was an executive with Exxon. When we finally stopped
running, we ended up here in Houston. I remember a

period of time in boardinghouses still, while she was trying to find a job, and then finally she did. My mother is a very beautiful woman, even now. She's only fifty-four. She has a contradictory personality. Though she's very efficient, very orderly, she has blind spots ... about people. She seems very compliant, not pushy, but it's largely a deceptive front. When you stand back and look at what actually happens to her, you see that she always comes out on top of things. She's a very skillful manipulator. She looks out for herself.

'Anyway, she got a job with Exxon, a secretarial job, I think. She met my stepfather there. After a while, a year maybe, they were married. Our lives changed overnight — dramatically. We moved from a boardinghouse in Brookhaven to an enormous ivy-covered home in Sherwood off Memorial Drive. Mother quit working. I was enrolled in a private school. We bought clothes, so many clothes. Douglas, his name was Douglas Koen, didn't deny us anything. He was a kind man, and he must have gotten a great deal of pleasure out of giving us a new life. He spoiled us and we loved it, and we loved him for doing it.

'That first year in our new home was like a dream. It seemed too good to be true, and sometimes I lay in my clean bed at nights and remembered the two years of dirty rooms, and I never ever wanted to live like that again. And I remembered my father too, and wished that somehow he could have been a part of our happiness also. I felt guilty about the fact that he was fading further and further into the back of my mind, that he had become secondary to my own happiness and comfort.'

Broussard looked at Lowe's legs. The hem of her sundress was riding just under her knees, and even though she was not wearing stockings her legs were as smooth and tan as a mannequin's. But her feet betrayed her flesh and blood, especially her blood, for several long blue veins ran along the underside of her ankle and down the top of her foot toward her toes. These were not the swollen veins of older women, but the smooth veins of health, strengthened by several hours of tennis daily. And her skin was fair enough that he knew, too, that if he could see her nude he would see similar veins, though paler, more subtle, in one or two places around her breasts.

'Mother had discovered all the wealth of the Borgias in one prematurely balding executive eight years older than herself,' Mary continued. 'And she was not about to let it slip away. Keeping Douglas happy became her one aim in life, and she made sure that I realized the importance in this too. At her constant urging, I thanked him so many times that first year that it must have been sadly comical. And I was thankful, of course, but Mother had me fawning on him to the point of embarrassment.

'One day when I got out of school he was there waiting for me. He had gotten away from the office early and had called Mother and told her he would pick me up at school. I suspected later that he had planned it so he could talk to me away from her. In the course of our conversation during the drive home, he tactfully let me know that it wasn't actually necessary for me to be so constantly grateful. He said that there was an art to accepting someone's kindness and that there were many ways to express gratitude without having to say thank you all the time. He said he knew I was appreciative and that that was reward enough for him. He said other understanding things too, kind things, as if he knew just how I felt and wanted to put me at ease. He spoke to me as though I were a whole person, worthy of his full attention. I had never been talked to that way before.

'That was a magical afternoon for me, because after that I began to be drawn into a feeling of security that I had never known in my life. He won me over, heart and soul, during that brief drive home from school, and it was never to be the same again. I grew to love the man dearly. I was ten.'

Broussard tensed. Premonition had been an unexpected consequence, an ensuant gift, of his years of practicing psychoanalysis. It was not something he had anticipated or tried to develop, but it came to him as a natural result of his refinement by continual practice of his own innermost abilities. It was not a gift he had come to regard with unmixed feelings. Though it had proved to be an enabling talent that had allowed him to better enlighten his clients, it had also had the effect of oppressing him. He was like a man who had been given a magic sack filled with a hundred pounds of gold coins. No matter how many he spent the sack was always full, but in order to have access to the coins he must carry it on his back. If he ever took it off, the gold and all the good it could do in the world would cease to exist. The blessing, and his ability to use it, was also an inescapable burden.

The prescience was not a clearly defined knowledge, so that when it occurred he was racked with anxiety until he could decipher it, unriddle it, and employ the new understanding to help his client. So it was with a growing sense of dread that he listened to Mary Lowe's story, knowing, surely, that today or the next, or the next, her story would turn dark, very dark indeed.

'Those dreams I dreaded, of disintegrating? They began to go away,' she said. 'Everything was fine for a year.' She didn't go on.

Broussard waited. He looked at his clock. She was capable of extraordinary silences. But not this time.

'You have something to drink here, don't you?' She turned her head toward him.

'Yes.' But he didn't move.

'May I have a little bit of vodka?'

'Stoli?'

'Fine.'

He got up from his armchair and went to the cabinet where he poured a glass for both of them. When he turned around she had gotten up from the chaise and was standing at the window, looking outside. She had gathered her skirt in her hands and was holding it up above her knees as if she were going wading. He walked up behind her.

'Stoli,' he said.

She dropped the left side of her skirt and held her hand up over her shoulder without turning around. He handed it to her, and she sipped without hesitation, still holding half her skirt in her right hand. He was close enough to smell her. She casually moved along the glass wall to the foot of the chaise.

'How long have you had this office?' she asked.

'About eight years.'

'Oh?'

He waited.

'You've heard a lot of stories here, then, spent a lot of afternoons looking down to the bayou.'

'Quite a few,' he said.

'Do you like hearing them?'

'It's not a matter of liking them,' he said. 'I try to use them to help people.'

'You must hear a lot of the same stories,' she said into the plate glass. 'At least, similar ones.'

He knew better than to answer that one. Everyone wanted to believe his story was unique. He was thinking of this, looking at her hair falling across her bare shoulders, when he realized that she had continued to gather the right side of her skirt in her hand until almost her entire right thigh was showing. It was an extraordinary sight.

'What kind of a story do you like?' she asked.

There was a moment, and then he managed to say, 'I don't have any preferences.'

'Everyone has preferences,' she said.

He said nothing, his eyes transfixed on her long, tan thigh. Then her wrist flicked and the hem dropped a little, then a twitch, and it fell a little farther. Her fingers held the rest of it. Then, slowly, she began to gather it again, and the tan thigh emerged from the folds of the sundress with the same erotic impact of total nudity. He didn't know why he looked up just then, but he did, and was startled to see her looking at him from her reflection in the glass. She did not smile or have the vixen-eyed gaze of calculated seduction, but she was watching him. He had no idea what to make of her expression, but it seemed to him — and he was almost sure of it — that she was absorbed in a well-practiced fantasy which had become, through many hours of indulgence, an absolute reality for her. Whatever it was, she was living it as surely as Broussard himself was living this very moment.

15

When Palma got back to her office she found a message to call Clay Garrett. Taking twice the time he should have, Garrett told her he had faxed her request up to Quantico. He said he had already talked to them about the case and that she would be hearing from an agent named Sander Grant. The VICAP forms would be processed overnight, and she should be hearing from one of their analysts within the next couple of days as to any possible matches in the violent crime databank.

Palma thanked him, hung up the receiver, and flipped on her computer. Helena Saulnier was first. A driver's license check: nothing. Person inquiry: nothing, neither of her names showed up as an ID name or an alias. National Criminal Information Center: she was not wanted on any criminal charges. Texas Criminal Information Center: she was not wanted for questioning in any crimes. Pawns: she hadn't pawned anything within the past six months or sold anything to a pawnshop within the last week. Location check: no record of the police ever having been called to her residence on Olympia for so much as a Peeping Tom check. Well, it was a long shot.

She did the same for Nathan Isenberg, Wayne Canfield, and Gil Reynolds. Again, nothing, except that Reynolds had accumulated too many speeding tickets within a ten-month period in 1986. His driving license had been in jeopardy, but then his violations suddenly stopped and he had managed to redeem himself with his insurance agency over the next several years.

Dennis Ackley was a different story. Almost every screen she called up had something to say about Dorothy Samenov's ex-husband. From 1967 to the present he had fourteen moving violations, including three DWIs. He had done time in Huntsville for the last one. He was known under four different aliases and had been arrested seven times, including three times for aggravated assault against his wife, Dorothy Ann Samenov Ackley. All three times she had refused to press charges, though on the last occasion she requested a restraining order against him. He was paroled on the DWI sentence in August 1988 and in February 1989 a warrant was issued for his arrest on the basis of parole violations. He was also wanted by the Dallas Police Department for questioning in an aggravated assault of a woman in Highland Park four months earlier. A month before that incident he had pawned a pair of Zeiss binoculars along with a 9-mm Smith & Wesson Model 459 automatic pistol.

Palma picked up a pencil and made one additional note. When she had begun her investigation of the Sandra Moser case she had checked with Houston's central crime analysis division to see if any other homicides in the city had an M.O. pattern resembling what she had seen with Moser. The search had been negative. Now, considering the fact that Ackley was wanted in Dallas for questioning in an assault on a female, she decided to check with their crime analysis unit as well. Additionally, she wanted to check with the crime analysis office of the Department of Public Safety in Austin, which collected statewide information.

The telephone rang and Palma picked it up. It was Birley, still at Samenov's.

'I'm about to shut down here,' he said, sounding tired, 'but I've made some progress. I found Samenov's financial papers, bank statements, income tax returns, personal correspondence, and a photograph of Dennis Ackley. He looks like a real sleazoid. The gal had strange taste.

Anyway, I went through the bank statements and the checks first, and I think there's something a little screwy here.'

Palma could hear him flipping the pages in his notebook, which she knew he was looking at through his cheap plastic half-lens reading glasses that he had bought off a rack at Walgreen's.

'Beginning in January of last year, she began making periodic withdrawals from one of her two accounts at the Bank of the Southwest. There were eight of these withdrawals last year, and already this year there've been two, one in January, one in March.' He read off the dates and Palma jotted them down. 'I called the bank to see if there had been any since the last bank statement went out and found out there was a three-thousand-dollar withdrawal a week ago yesterday, three days before she was killed. Those earlier withdrawals ranged from five hundred to three thousand a pop. There didn't seem to be any pattern to the time or the amount of the withdrawals.'

'She would get cash?'

'Yep. I wonder if she was feeding them to Ackley?'

'I wouldn't be surprised,' Palma said, and she told him about her conversation with Mancera and of her discovery of Ackley's criminal record.

'Jesus, that figures,' Birley said. 'Anybody who'd let her husband hammer on her that much and not press charges against the bastard is just goofy enough to turn around and give him money too. Women like that, shit.' Birley had a thing about battered women. He didn't understand them, not even a little.

They talked a few more minutes, and Birley said he would bundle up the stuff he had gotten together and take it home with him, see what else he could come up with overnight. He said he would go home from Samenov's and see her at the office in the morning.

Palma sat back in her chair and looked at the notes scattered over her desk. She had checked on Cushing and Leeland, who were still at Computron and were staying until the place closed down at five o'clock. It was well after four o'clock now and the homicide division's evening shift had already come on. There was a new lieutenant, a squad room full of new detectives, and a whole new set of problems.

Suddenly she was exhausted; the sleep she had missed the night before was beginning to take its toll. But she still had to type in her supplements. She called up the appropriate screens and set to work.

It was after five o'clock and she had developed a dull headache by the time she had printed out two copies of her supplement, filed one in the case file, and walked across the squad room and put the other into Frisch's box. Just as she was making the last turn into the aisle that led to her office, she heard her telephone ringing. She ran through the door and picked it up in mid-ring.

'Hey, thought you'd gone home,' Cushing said. 'Have any luck today?'

She told him how their day had gone, beginning with her visit the night before with Andrew Moser. She told him Leeland's hunch about the pizza delivery had been right, and then filled him in on her visit to Kittrie, on her interview with Mancera, and on Ackley's prison and arrest record.

'I like the way this Ackley looks,' Cushing said. 'You checked him out with Dallas yet?'

'Haven't had time. Did you get anything?'

'Samenov's boss said everything good about her,' Cushing said. She could hear him eating something. 'She was conscientious, ambitious, reliable, productive, da-dah, da-dah, da-dah ... He didn't know anything about her private life except that she was divorced. We talked to Canfield.' Cushing kept having to stop to swallow. He was probably eating peanuts. He didn't say where he was calling from, but she would bet it was a bar. 'Also divorced, but he hadn't dated her in over a year. He said she was good-looking, well built, a good sense of humor, and a sharp lady, but she didn't want to get sexually involved. Said he didn't go out with her but two or three times.'

Palma massaged the back of her neck with her free hand. Canfield had said Samenov was attractive, her figure was physically appealing, her personality was enjoyable, and she was intelligent. But she didn't want to get sexually involved. After a few dates he moved on. Christ, he really knew what to value in a woman. He must have been a quality guy.

'We talked to Segal,' Cushing continued. 'She just substantiated what the others had said, nothing really new. But she did say that probably Samenov's best friend, the one who knew most about her, was Vickie Kittrie. And she said that Ackley gave Samenov some flak now and then, that Samenov would sometimes say she wished to hell he would move out of the city. She knew that Samenov had given him money on a number of occasions. Nobody else at Computron gave us anything substantial.'

'That's it?'

'Almost. We got an interesting fluke here. Donny gets smart and pokes around in the records of Samenov's clients. These records are very complete, including frequency of the rep's on-site calls. Over the last year Samenov called on one client a hell of a lot more than any of the others. Maritime Guaranty, Inc., a multinational insurance corporation that underwrites anything that touches water. Their offices are a couple of blocks away. Records showed that Samenov had been there on the Thursday she was last seen. It turned out the contact, guy named Gowen, was not the person she regularly went there to see. She checked in with Gowen, all right, but then she went back into accounting and visited with a woman named Louise Ackley.'

'His wife?' Palma was surprised.

'She's not married. We think maybe a sister,' Cushing said. 'We checked at Maritime but she wasn't there. She'd called in sick on both Monday and today. Her personnel file says she's from Charleston, South Carolina.'

'Ackley's hometown.'

'Right. You wanna talk to her?'

'You haven't?'

'Nope. We located Walker Bristol, though. He's still a VP at a bank downtown. We called him, and he's agreed to meet us at this little place in half an hour.'

This little place. Cushing's euphemism for a bar.

'So you want Sis, then?' Cushing asked. 'She's out in Bellaire.'

'Sure.' She jotted down Louise Ackley's address.

'Also we found Gil Reynolds. He's some kind of executive with a business called Radcom. Radio communications. It's off Post Oak Lane. Since it's out toward Samenov's, you want to talk to him too?'

'Sure,' Palma said again, and wrote down the address. It looked like Cushing was going to stick to Ackley. He knew a good horse when he saw one. 'Those dates when Samenov called on Ackley at Maritime Guaranty, do you have them?'

'Damn right. We photocopied the schedule. Just a sec.' Palma heard him lay down the telephone; the music was distant but it was standard-issue bump-and-grind. Palma hoped Cushing had enough sense not to meet Bristol at *this* little place.

Then Cushing was back on the telephone reading off the dates. Palma took them down, and they hung up. She quickly scrambled through the notes on her desk and found the dates Birley had given her when Samenov had withdrawn money. It took her only a moment to see that Samenov's cash withdrawals corresponded with the dates she had also called on Maritime Guaranty — which was right across the street from the Bank of the Southwest.

She looked at her watch. It was too late to get Reynolds's office. She would call him in the morning before she went out.

16

Louise Ackley lived in Bellaire in a middle-class house in a middle-class neighborhood with scaly-barked cottonwoods in the front yard. A cracked sidewalk led up to a cement front porch with iron railings around it and a lumpy loquat crowding up next to it. A hummingbird feeder hung from one of the branches of the loquat and a dusty, lynx-eared cat lay under a metal lawn chair sitting in a corner of the porch. He watched with lazy-eyed indifference as Palma got out of her car and came up the sidewalk toward him. By the time she stepped up on the porch the cat had decided to ignore her altogether and rolled over on its back and started pawing distractedly at a tag of cloth that dangled from a cushion on the seat of the lawn chair.

The front door of the house was open, as were all the windows that Palma could see from the porch. Through the screen door she could see into the dim living room, though it was difficult to distinguish anything inside. The whirring of an oscillating fan came from somewhere near the middle of the room. She knocked on the wood frame of the door, loudly, because she didn't want to have to do it again. As she waited, she heard no one moving about in the house. A strong odor of stale cigarette smoke wafted through the screen. She knocked again, and heard it echo through the rooms. Still no one answered. She hooked a finger under the screen handle and pulled; it was not locked. She opened it a little more and stuck her head inside.

'Ms. Ackley?' she called.

'I ought to blow your goddamned head off,' a woman's tight, strained voice said without menace, almost casually.

Palma flinched and looked toward the voice, her eyes adjusting to the shadowy room just enough to see the silhouette of a figure on the sofa.

'You're way out of line,' the woman said. There was something thick about her voice that told Palma she was drinking. Palma saw her move her hand up to her mouth and smoke rolled away from the silhouette. 'What the hell you going to do, rob me? I don't think you've got the right equipment to be a rapist.'

Palma already had her shield in her hand and held it up. 'I'm Detective Carmen Palma,' she said. 'Houston police. Are you Louise Ackley?' Palma saw that the woman was sitting at one end of the sofa near an end table. A bottle of beer was profiled against the open windows behind the sofa. The woman reached for the beer and turned the bottle up, taking a long drink. When she sat the bottle down it rocked a little, and she had to steady it.

'Are you Louise Ackley?' Palma repeated.

'Yes, of course,' Ackley said wearily. 'Come on in. You want a Corona? I'm drinking Mexican beer; you'll like that.'

'No, thanks,' Palma said.

'Okay. Sit down, then. Let's get on with this.'

Palma sat in an armchair to the left of the door, across from Ackley. The oscillating fan was on the floor between them, humming back and forth, sucking all the air toward Ackley, blowing her smoke out the windows behind the sofa. Palma could now see that she was wearing only a white T-shirt and was sitting with one leg tucked up under her, the other foot flat on the sofa, the hand holding the cigarette resting on her elevated knee. She wasn't wearing panties, and she did not try to hide what was visible between her splayed legs. From the looks of her tousled black hair and the condition of the T-shirt, Palma guessed that Louise Ackley had been like this for several days.

'What're you here for?' Ackley asked.

'I'd like to ask you some questions about Dorothy Samenov.'

A brief silence.

'That'd be the 'late' Dorothy Samenov?' Ackley's voice was distinctive, slightly hoarse, though not rough or gravelly.

'Yes. How did you know she was dead?'

'I believe I saw it in a little narrow article about four and a half lines long in the cop section of the newspaper. There wasn't very much about it at all. Hardly anything at all. Practically not there.'

'You knew her?'

'I did.'

'What was your relationship with her?'

'Now there's a word for you — "relationship,"' Ackley said, going for her bottle of beer again. She drained the last of the beer and reached over behind the sofa and laid the empty bottle down in the opened windowsill. Palma heard it chink against others already there. '"Relationship" must be a tired word. People have just about used it to death.' She ground out her cigarette in a deep ashtray on the end table. 'Dorothy and I were friends.'

'Did you see her very often?'

'Actually, I hadn't seen her in almost a year. We *used* to be friends.'

'Robert Gowen, your boss at Maritime Guaranty, said that Dorothy Samenov spent nearly half an hour with you at your office last Thursday, the day she was last seen alive, and that she came to see you there regularly.'

'Did that silly man say that? Actually, I'm fond of Robert, and he's a good boss, so I shouldn't contradict him.' Ackley wasn't in the least concerned about being caught in the lie. 'It seems like I remember that he's right — I did talk to her last Thursday. And I did see her regularly, come to think of it.'

Palma could see now that Ackley had a fine narrow nose and high cheekbones, and a seductive mouth that she had a pleasant way of holding slightly open while her tongue lightly touched her upper front teeth.

'Why did she come to your office so often?'

'She liked to talk to me.' Ackley had intended for this to have been as flippant as her other responses, but her voice cracked making the last few words almost a whisper. She squeezed her lips together and turned her head aside with an expression resigned to sorrow. With an elbow on her knee, she ran her fingers into the front of her hair and rested her forehead on the palm of her hand. 'And she liked the way I ... the way I looked,' she said, almost inaudibly.

Close by in the next room to Palma's right, there was a sudden whump! and a bottle — a beer bottle, Palma's senses told her — fell to the wooden floor followed by a rain of coins bouncing and wheeling in all directions and a blurted 'Chingale!' as a man swore in Spanish. Palma flushed with adrenaline. 'This fawkin' ... chit, man ...' Mexican. Palma's heart hammered, but she kept her right hand on the SIG in her purse.

'Oh, shut up, Lalo,' Louise Ackley mumbled wearily, almost to herself. She didn't even look up, her forehead still resting on her palm. She was not acting like a black-mailer, and the tears that suddenly glistened on her face in the oblique light coming from the opened windows were not the tears of an extortionist.

'He's pathetic,' Ackley said. Someone fell heavily onto a bed, the springs squeaking, then silence and a bovine groan of satisfaction. 'Pathetic.'

'Why was she bringing you the money?' Palma asked. She relaxed a little, figuring it was lights out for Lalo. Her tone with Ackley was more curious now than accusatory. 'We thought it was blackmail.'

Ackley nodded, keeping her forehead on her palm. 'It was.' She lifted the tail of her stained T-shirt and wiped her nose, revealing her naked torso and a glimpse of the bottoms of her breasts. 'Blackmail, pure and simple.'

'You were blackmailing her?'

'No, God no, it wasn't *me*,' she said, lifting her head and looking at Palma. Again she raised her shirt and wiped at her nose, then jerked it down in frustration and leaned over and pulled a wad of tissues from a box almost out of reach on the sofa. 'Shit,' she said, wiping the tears off her face. 'I didn't know I had any more left.'

Palma didn't know if Ackley was referring to her tears or to the tissues. 'Who was blackmailing her?'

'Oh, Dennis,' she said, exasperated. 'He was blackmailing both of us.'

'Both of you? Your own brother was blackmailing you?'

Ackley jerked herself up straight, mimicking Palma's surprise, and smiled sourly. 'My "own brother." Yeah. Well, blood is thicker than water, but it's not thicker than sorry, and Dennis is one sorry son of a bitch.' She looked at Palma. 'You find that hard to believe, that he was blackmailing me?'

'Yes.'

'Well, you just learned something, didn't you?'

'I guess I did.'

'Dorothy brought the money to me because Dennis didn't want to see her. I added mine to it and took it to him.'

'Why didn't he want to see her?'

'You know, I'm not sure I can answer that.'

'You mean you don't know?'

'That's right.'

'How long had he been blackmailing you?'

'Let's see, how to answer that ... about eighteen months.'

'You seemed to qualify that before you answered.'

'Eighteen months for money. Before that there was emotional intimidation, all kinds of shit to take from him. He was a bully. It just shows you how really stupid he was that it took him all these years to think of blackmailing us for money.'

'This had been going on for a while, then?'

'Years.'

'How many?'

'Too many.'

Palma was frustrated. How much of this could she believe? Interviewing a drunk was like trying to pick up a drop of mercury.

'How much did the two of you pay out to him?'

'Twenty-eight thousand six hundred,' she said without hesitating. 'Half of that from each of us. But I wasn't doing as well as Dorothy, so she ... paid part of mine. He promised he'd stop at thirty thousand. We were almost there.'

'What was he blackmailing you for?'

Louise Ackley snorted. 'Good try, honey.' She folded her other leg down and sat with them both tucked up under her, yoga-style.

'Are you going to continue paying him?'

Ackley didn't answer.

'You don't have to do that, you know. You've got plenty of documentation to press charges.'

Ackley only looked at Palma with an expression of weary intolerance. She had already been through all the possibilities. If her brother were arrested, everything he was keeping quiet about would come out. It was more important to her to prevent that than to be rid of her tormentor.

'You know where he lives?'

'No.'

'But you said ...'

'Oh, I would just meet him with the cash somewhere. He didn't want Dorothy even to do that.'

'When did you last see him?'

'March twenty-second, last time we gave him some money. He said he was going to Mexico. Good-damned-riddance. I hope he got the worms down there and died. If I don't see him again till the end of time it'll be too soon.'

'He's a suspect in Dorothy's killing,' Palma said.

'I'm sure he is,' Ackley wheezed. 'You seem to be reasonably well informed, so I suppose you believe you have good reasons to suspect him.'

'We know he was arrested three times for aggravated assault and that Dorothy was the victim each time.'

Ackley nodded, sliding her eyes to one side.

'What was their problem?' Palma asked.

'It was a sorry affair, that's all. It was sick.'

'What do you mean?'

'Just that. Wouldn't you call it sick to live with a guy year after year who regularly beat the shit out of you? I mean, he did it all the time. She just called the cops three times. And you *know* he was sick. The whole thing ...' She stopped and shook her head.

'Do you think he did it?'

Ackley began shaking her head, slowly, wearily. 'It was the first thing I thought of when I heard about it,' she said. 'But, really, I just don't know what to think. The silly bastard *could*'ve done it, but ... I just can't believe that he really did.'

'"Heard" about it?'

'Huh?'

'You just said you'd "heard" about Dorothy's death. Earlier you'd said you'd read about it in the paper.'

Ackley was unconcerned. 'Figure of speech, whatever.'

'You don't have any idea where we might find him?'

'No, hell no. He told me Mexico. But I didn't believe him. That'd put him too far away from his sugar titties.'

'You think he's still in Houston?'

Ackley shrugged. She didn't seem to care one way or the other.

'How close were you to Dorothy Samenov?'

Ackley let her eyes settle on Palma and she grew somber, her thoughts far away from either of them. The oscillating fan periodically lifted little wisps of her dyed, black hair on either side of her face as it passed back and forth in front of her.

'Close,' she said. 'I've known Dorothy since before she and Dennis started dating in college. I knew her first.'

Unexpectedly, she smiled.

'Then maybe you know some of the men she's dated in the last year or so.'

'Not hardly.'

'Why do you say that?'

'I wasn't interested.'

'How long had she been into S&M?'

Ackley sat perfectly still. 'I didn't know she was.' She didn't seem surprised, and she didn't seem curious.

'Was your brother involved in S&M also?'

Ackley shook her head and looked at Palma as if she couldn't believe she had asked her such a question. 'Well, now, I just really couldn't tell you about that. S&M and his Social Security number are two things he just *refused* to discuss with me.'

'If your brother didn't kill Dorothy, who do you think might have?'

'Jesus Christ!' Ackley arched her neck and scowled. 'What the hell kind of a question is that? You think I keep company with a whole lot of people who are killers? Something like that? What the hell kind of a question is that? You wanna go arrest ol' Lalo in there? Shit, he's all passed out, go cuff him. He's good-looking, too, make a good killer ... in the papers. He might have done it, fact, he probably did. Yeah ...'

Ackley reached over and grabbed her cigarettes, but the package was empty and she wadded it up and threw it backhanded away from her.

'It was a particularly brutal murder.' Palma persisted. She wanted to touch what she sensed were the tender ends of Louise Ackley's nerves. 'She was strangled and mutilated ... in a certain way. We're having a difficult time getting any leads. Any help, anything at all, that you could do for us would be appreciated.'

Ackley looked at Palma, her head bobbling a little like the unsteady head of an old woman.

'In what particular way?'

'I can't discuss that with you.'

'Why? What if I recognize something about it?'

'What might you recognize about it?'

'I don't *know*. How do I know.' Her voice was wheezy. She started crying. 'Jesus, dear Jesus. Dorothy.' She put her face in her hands, and her shoulders shook as she cried.

Palma thought of Vickie Kittrie, how hard she had cried and how much Samenov's death seemed to have affected her.

'I'm going to leave you a card,' she said, putting her card on a corner table near her chair. 'I've put my home telephone number on the back. I would appreciate your help. If your brother gets in touch with you again, please let me know.'

Palma got up and went to the door and stepped outside.

'Wait,' Ackley said from her sofa, and Palma heard her getting up. She appeared on the other side of the screen, her hair disheveled, her eyes puffy. 'What about ... her ... the funeral? What's being done ...?'

'I believe some of her family are coming to get her from South Carolina.'

'Oh. Really? That's good,' Ackley said, going from surprised to satisfied. She put her hand on the screen between them. 'I don't know, really, which is the best way,' she confided. 'If I knew the details I might think about them, dream about them, or have them pop into my mind when I didn't want them to. But if I don't know the details maybe it'll make me crazy wondering about it. You know, *what* did she go through? What the hell was it? I suppose it's a toss-up. I don't know how you deal with it, but for me it's been bloody hell. I don't know how to leave it alone. They never should happen, things like this ... should never, never happen.'

17

Broussard looked at himself in the mirror of his umber-marbled bathroom just off his consulting room. A hairbrush in each hand, he lightly stroked his graying temples and then leaned close to the mirror and studied the flesh around his eyes. Did he see something subtle there, an as yet indiscernible thickening of the subcutaneous tissue, the precursor of sagging musculature? No, he thought not. Not yet. He surveyed his face above the white collar of his shirt. He had his Lebanese mother to thank for his swarthy complexion. It was bloody well all he could be grateful to her for. She had been a fractious, scowling woman of stern demeanor who had driven his physician father to other women, not as a mere womanizer, but in search of solace, of that elusive peace that lay within the embrace of the vertical smile. And then he drank. And then he killed himself.

He heard the consulting room door open. Bernadine never knocked. He ran cold water and washed his hands and dried them. He turned out the light and opened the door.

She was smiling at him, sitting on the edge of the chaise in a Monet-patterned floral silk jacquard with pleated bodice. If he didn't think of the webby confusions of her depressing psychology, but thought of her instead as something to be consumed like a cool and colorful summer fruit, then he would say that the word 'succulent' suited her completely.

'So handsome,' she said, her contralto languid and seductive. 'How do you see yourself, Dom? When you look in that mirror?'

'What do you mean?' He feigned indifference, but he was curious that she seemed so pleased with herself.

'Do you see the young man you were,' she asked, kicking off her shoes, 'or the old man you're going to be?'

Broussard was deciding not to put on his sport coat which was hanging inside the closet. He would remain in his shirt sleeves. She was the last of the day. He looked at her. Yes, 'succulent,' that was the best word.

'Have you already tuned me out?' She was still smiling. 'I haven't even been laid yet.'

'No, I haven't tuned you out.' Her pale gray eyes were picking up a blue light from the dress. He could almost see through them into her head. And they were always open. She never closed them; even when they made love, she regarded their intercourse with the calm frankness of a mother watching her nursing child. Indeed, with Bernadine he sometimes felt like a child, and he even believed she could sense that and it pleased her, though the idea had never been voiced between them. And if she had ever asked him if it were so, he would have denied it.

'I see myself as I am,' he said, to show her that he had heard every word she had spoken. He walked over to his leather armchair and sat down, 'And sometimes I see myself as I will be. I don't believe I have ever seen myself as I was. I never look back in the mirror.'

'Ohhh. How well balanced of you.'

'It doesn't do any good,' he added, looking at her shins. 'There's no salvation in the past.'

'Salvation?'

'There's no profit in it, I mean.'

'When I look in the mirror,' she said, 'I see something different every time. I'm not sure I've ever seen exactly what I am.'

Yes, he thought, he could well believe that. Her mind was so fractured, so shattered and scattered, she might never see herself — ever. Those pale, limitless eyes would likely never behold the true terrain of their source.

'You don't think an old dog can learn new tricks, do you, Dom?' She was still smiling, as if she knew something amusing about him and was teasing him with it. 'You believe that we are at an impasse here, you and I. Psychotherapy can be a lengthy enterprise, I know. You told me. It takes time, sometimes a lot of time, to gain "insight," you said.'

'That's right,' he said, feeling as if he were speaking to a child. 'And you've got to want to do it. You've got to commit yourself, be dedicated to it.'

He heard echoes in his words of a sincerity long ago abandoned, and it caught him by surprise. Bernadine was the first client he had ever despaired of. It wasn't that he had benefited all the others. Of course not; there had been many over the years he knew he couldn't help. But Bernadine had been the first he had wanted to help so desperately that he had risked his own emotional equilibrium to do so. It had been a fool's endeavor, and that was why she meant so much to him.

'So how do you think I've done?'

'Since when?'

'Overall.'

'You've made good progress,' he lied. As if inadvertently — was it? — her forearms, which rested on her upper thighs as she fiddled with a hair clip, had worked up the hem of her dress, and the little faces of her knees stared back at him like twin creatures guarding the approach to Helen's Well.

'You think so?' she asked, and he thought he detected a mocking tone.

He looked up at her face, and she was still smiling. This was something new for Bernadine, this self-satisfied manner, as if she had eaten the fruit of the tree of the knowledge of good and evil.

'If I had a scotch,' she said, 'I could tell you a story.'

'I think you must've had one before you came here,' he said, observing her.

'Dom-my,' she chided, as if he were a child.

'Jesus.' He hoisted himself out of the deep armchair and went to the liquor cabinet. Why did he let her make him feel this way? His back was to her as he made the drinks — he made one for himself as well and, perversely, he made them both vodka — and he could feel her looking at him. He even thought he could feel a small breath of her on the back of his neck, and any moment he expected to feel the wet flesh of her tongue sliding into his ear. But it didn't. He turned around and carried the drinks over to her. 'Here,' he said.

She took the cold glass, saw that it was vodka, and looked at him standing in front of her. Her smile had faded somewhat, and then faded altogether as he put his right hand on the inside of her left knee and moved it up her thigh under the soft jacquard, along her thickening inner leg until he was almost there. She put a hand on his forearm, her small tapering fingers gripping him, stopping him. She maneuvered away from him and straightened her dress, but left the hem just above the knee. She nodded toward his leather armchair.

'Let's pretend,' she said, 'that I've come here for psychotherapy.'

It was a cutting remark and he felt his face flush, but he knew she didn't mean anything by it. At least, nothing he should be hurt by. But he was, a little. He sipped the Stoli, cold and biting. Unlike Bernadine, it was his first for the day. He returned to his armchair and propped his feet on the hassock.

She sipped her drink, looking at him over the top of her glass the way she liked to do. It was a seductive act, though he knew she didn't intend it to be. But it was. The pale gray stones of her eyes peering at him over the veil of ice and glass and clear vodka couldn't have been interpreted any other way. Bernadine was seductive the way a fox was crafty. She didn't have to be conscious of it; it was her nature. And because of it — again like the fox — she was always in the narrow borderlands of some undefined danger.

'Why have you never married?' she asked.

Broussard felt a flash of anger which he quickly checked; he knew his face hadn't betrayed him. She had done this before, a number of times. Perhaps no other woman had tried more often to dig into his past, and he detested it. At times Bernadine had almost gone too far in this direction, and it was precisely this subject that had almost destroyed their relationship a couple of years earlier.

'Why, Dom, have you never married?'

'Why have you never *stopped* marrying, Bernadine?'

'Oh, no. We talk about that all the time. We've talked about that for five and a half years.' She lowered her glass to her lap where she held it in both hands. 'I want to know about you. I mean, if I'm supposed to listen to you regarding these things, shouldn't you have some credentials, something to establish your authority? Priests, for instance. You know, the stupidity of having celibate men giving sexual and marriage advice. God knows you're more qualified than a priest in matters sexual, but what about in matters marital?'

She kind of laughed at the way she put that, liking it. Broussard looked at her and wondered why she was doing this. Maybe she needed to. It was clear from what she had said about her husband on her last visit that she was on the brink of another divorce. If he had been good for nothing else, he had helped her through two of those — the first had occurred before Broussard had met her. Whatever the reason for her recent capricious mood, he knew that the emotional trials of another divorce would soon take precedence over everything else. She would begin wanting to see him more frequently — Bernadine's divorces were a financial windfall for him, as well as for her — and she would become sexually voracious. This sexual aspect of her divorces had shocked him the first time he realized the relationship. Yes, it had shocked him, but it hadn't prevented him from self-indulgence. The second time he helped her through a divorce he had acted shamefully, like a satyr, and when it was all over he had

had to face the fact that he had peeled back yet another layer of his shadow, and it had nothing to do with creativity. Bernadine had shown him more about himself than he had learned in his own ten-year encounter with psychoanalysis.

'Dom . . .'

'I think,' he blurted, showing more impatience than he had wanted to show, 'that the institution hasn't got much to recommend it.'

'Marriage?'

'Yes. Yes, Bernadine. Marriage. Weren't we talking about marriage?'

'Oh. So you haven't married because you see people like me all the time, so many bad marriages.'

'It gives me pause for thought.'

'But what about most people?'

'What about them?' He had checked his temper, his sudden frustration.

'People who come here . . . we're not like most people.'

'Who the hell do you think "most people" are?' His tone was morose; he couldn't help it.

Bernadine fell silent. She nursed the Stoli, keeping the clear ice cubes back with her lips as she drew the clear liquor from the clear glass, looking at him.

'You *never* married?' she said finally.

'Never.'

Again she fell silent. She swung her legs momentarily, like a child, then drew one of them up on the chaise and he caught a flash of her powder blue panties. Powder blue. She drained her glass with this one leg poised between where it had been and where it was going and she laid the empty glass on a small table on the other side of the chaise. She lay down.

'Would you answer me something, honestly, about yourself?'

'All right,' he lied.

'Have you ever had a homosexual experience?'

'No.'

'Ever wanted to?'

'No.'

'You know that story I told you about my aunt?'

'Yes.'

'That wasn't exactly true, what I said.'

Broussard waited. Bernadine was an arcanum for whom there were no initiates. She knew it, and it horrified her, and made her desperate. 'But you told me it was true,' he said.

'It was, but not exactly.'

'Fine.'

'The truth is that when I walked into the room everything was as I said, but I didn't find a strange man there. It was a woman.'

Broussard swallowed the Stoli in his mouth.

'She was in the chair, but she was completely naked, bending to put on her stockings. She smiled, as I said, and she put her finger to her lips for me to be quiet. But she did it casually, softly, without alarm, as if she had just gotten a baby to sleep in its crib. Nothing in her gestures or her face indicated the least inhibition. It was all perfectly natural.'

'Why did you tell me it was a man?'

'At the last minute I couldn't do it.'

'What?'

'It was all part of a plan, a scenario. The story was only an introduction.'

'An introduction?'

'To ... my own ... story.'

Broussard stiffened.

'Well,' she said. She was staring straight out to the sweep of green grass that sloped gently toward the bayou which, in contrast to the manicured and domesticated lawn, lingered along the margins of the property in a shapeless pool like something feral and vaguely dangerous, overgrown with cattails, and sharp brambles and gnarls of untamed vines, its black mud a womb for brackish water. 'She's younger than me ... I had no idea what I was getting into, what ... beauty I had been missing.'

Her voice had changed and the full-throated huskiness of emotion disgusted Broussard, who scarcely could believe his ears.

'I had never known, never suspected, you see, that I could feel such things, tinglings and quiverings, cool and warm waves washing over me as real as water, electrifying me ... Things I had never, ever, felt with a man. And the peace, a complete absence of anxiety. I hadn't imagined touching another woman like that ... but ... when it came to it I was completely at ease. It is so ... right ... I ... you could never understand how it is. I don't believe it's possible for you to understand. I hardly believe it myself.'

Broussard was speechless.

Bernadine Mello smiled once again, but it was not at Dr. Broussard. She smiled at the incomprehensible good fortune that had come to her at this middle age of forty-two, just as her life once more was about to be uprooted by divorce, and the failure of her fourth marriage loomed before her as confirmation yet again of her unloveliness and of the smallness of her worth. She smiled at the memory of only that morning and of the recent weeks when she had made a discovery as earth-moving and inspirational as anything she had ever experienced in adolescence. Everything she had searched for and longed for in her relationships with men, but which had proved to be so heartbreakingly elusive, she had found in another being whose mind and body were a mirror image of her own.

18

It was half past seven in the evening when Palma turned into the small Weslayan Plaza shopping center near her home and went into Richard's Liquors and Fine Wines and bought two large bottles of white Folonari Soave. She went next door to Randall's and got a couple of chicken breasts, a jar of olives, and a crock of brown mustard. She stood in line oblivious to everyone else around her and thought about Louise Ackley sitting in her dim, smoke-saturated living room drinking beer and grieving over what she had lost and what she had left. They must have seemed like equally empty considerations. Louise Ackley had a great deal to adjust to, and it didn't look as if she had made a very promising start.

Outside, Palma carried her sack of groceries across the parking lot in the copper glow of the streetlamps that had just come on and were creating a metallic haze in the dusk. She put the wine and groceries in the car and pulled out on Bissonnet, drove through the intersection and turned into a Stop 'N Go convenience store to get gas from one of the pumps out front. While she held the nozzle in the tank, she continued to think about Louise Ackley. She had been a surprise all the way around. Obviously, she had been hit hard by Samenov's death, and it seemed to Palma that she had been closer to her former sister-in-law and friend than she had been to her brother. Of course, considering what Palma had learned

so far about Dennis Ackley, that was completely under-
standable. The kind of man who would readily blackmail
his sister and his former wife was not exactly a man of
great heart. Palma also wondered what it was that Ackley
had on the two women that they would continue to fork
over a significant amount of their income to keep it quiet.

The automatic cutoff snapped in the gas pump handle,
startling her and splashing her with gasoline. She swore,
wiped her hands on a pink paper towel she got from a
dispenser beside the pump, and walked inside the store to
pay.

It was only a few minutes to her house, and a blue
evening light was settling in and darkening the trees that
lined the street. She parked in the curved drive at the
front door, got out, unlocked the door of the house, and
shoved it open. Then she returned to the car and wrestled
the grocery sacks into her arms and closed the car door
with her hip. She went inside the house, closed the house
door with her hip also, then walked into the living room,
where she turned down the air-conditioning thermostat,
and then continued through the dining room and into the
kitchen.

Within half an hour she had taken a cold shower and
changed into a cotton sundress without underwear and
was in the kitchen pouring a glass of Folonari, her damp
hair cool as it feathered over the tops of her shoulders.
She had intended to grill the chicken breasts, but now she
thought it was too late and she was too tired to bother.
Standing barefoot at the cabinet, she mixed a green salad
with lettuce, yellow and red bell peppers, cucumbers,
rings of red onions, and olives. She wondered if Louise
Ackley had lied to her about the blackmail. Maybe,
despite, her vituperation against her brother, she and
Dorothy Samenov were actually supporting him, helping
him remain a fugitive. It didn't seem to make sense, but
then Palma had learned a long time ago that 'sense' was a
relative term. It didn't look the same to everyone, and
even the most twisted mind, the mind guilty of the most
unbelievable horrors — she thought of Samenov's lidless

stare — did things because they made 'sense' within the context of its reasoning.

When Palma stopped and looked down at what she was doing, a pile of sliced olives, enough for four salads, was heaped in the bed of lettuce in her plate. Wearily, she picked out the surplus and put it in a small glass bowl in the refrigerator. Cutting a thick slice of bakery bread, she buttered it, put it on her plate with the salad, and took it all into the living room and set it down on the floor in front of the television. She didn't want to think about anything to do with Samenov or Moser while she ate. She grabbed the remote control and flipped it on. Though she refused to watch sitcoms, she would always watch movies, practically any movie, and be satisfied for at least the length of time it would take her to finish the salad.

She found an old Truffaut film and picked up her glass of wine and took a sip. She put her plate in her lap and leaned back against the front of the sofa, her legs straight out and crossed at the ankle as she listened to the French and read the poorly contrasting captions at the bottom of the screen.

The telephone rang seven minutes later. She automatically punched up the time on the television, punched off the sound, and leaned across and dragged the telephone off the coffee table.

'Hello.'

'This is Sander Grant, FBI, in Quantico. Is this Detective Carmen Palma?'

'Yes, it is.' She swallowed the bite of salad and tried to get out from under the plate and away from the glass without dumping everything on the floor.

'I apologize for calling you at home,' Grant said. 'But you said in your application that this would be all right.'

'Sure, it's fine. I appreciate your doing it.'

'Listen,' Grant's voice was mellow and casually precise, like a news commentator or public speaker in private conversation. 'You've got a couple of interesting cases here. Anything new from the labs during the day?'

'Not really, but our primary suspect ...'

'Hold on. Excuse me,' Grant interrupted her. 'But I don't want to know anything about your suspects. It could prejudice me as to what I see in the crime scene. It's best if I read it "blind." All I want to know is what he did, but I want to know as much as I can about that. Nothing new forensically, then?'

'No. There hasn't been time.'

'Okay, fine. I want you to keep me posted, too, regarding victimology. I got a good picture of both victims from your report, but it would help to know anything new immediately.' She heard him shuffling papers. 'Concentrate on her circle of friends — and any men who are known to several of her friends.' He paused, apparently making notes. 'Okay, if anything else comes up, anything you can add to it, call me and fax it up here. I've called only to tell you that I'm sending you some material about the profiling process. Articles, papers. I've Federal Expressed them so you should have them in the morning before ten o'clock. If you read them it'll help us communicate.

'I'm going to concentrate on this tonight and tomorrow, and then sometime tomorrow I'll call you with a preliminary reading. This will only be preliminary. I want to stress that. I'll make a more complete report later, but I think this is something that will need immediate attention.'

Palma couldn't argue with that.

'You think this guy's on a biweekly schedule?'

'Well, I just guessed ... both killings occurred on Thursdays, two weeks apart. I'm going to be a little nervous on the eighth.'

'I'm not so sure you'll have to wait that long. Listen, why don't you ...'

'Wait a minute,' Palma interrupted him. 'Why do you say that?'

'I think it would be best if you read the material I'm sending you first. I'll call you back tomorrow ... tomorrow night, probably, and we'll talk about it.'

'I appreciate it,' Palma said, a little ticked off at the aborted reference.

'No problem. Get a good night's sleep.'

He was off the phone, and Palma was left looking at a silent television screen. A man and a woman were walking away from the camera down the middle of a wet cobblestone street strewn with damp autumn leaves.

THIRD
DAY

19

Palma snapped off the alarm clock radio and threw back the covers. She already had hit the snooze button three times and it was now six-fifty. She sat up in bed and knew even before looking in the mirror that her eyes were puffy. She pulled the chemise over her head, tangling her black hair, and slung it off her arm. After fighting the urge to fall back on the pillows she turned and looked at herself in the mirror over her dresser to the left of the bed. Grim. It was going to take something heroic to make her look decent this morning. She crawled out of bed and walked straight to the shower.

While she bathed she tried to get her bearings. Christ. It hadn't even been forty-eight hours since they had found Dorothy Samenov's body, and she felt as if she had been at it a week. That was the pace and nature of any case that set them to work against the clock. Time smeared, the body clock went haywire, chronology lost its logic of sequence. She thought about Grant's call. The man had been brusque, but not ungracious, and in retrospect it had been thoughtful of him to call since he really didn't have anything to tell her that couldn't have waited. The only thing he did tell her — that he expected the killer would not wait two weeks before his next hit — he would not explain and had left her feeling more uneasy than before he called.

She turned off the water, opened the shower door, and reached for a towel for her hair, wrapping it in a loose knot on top of her head before she got another towel to dry off. She walked into the bedroom, where she had already plugged in the curlers, and finished drying, then dropped the towel and started rolling her hair. While she was doing this she automatically took stock of her body, turning sideways to look at the profile of her breasts — something she didn't mind doing while she was rolling her hair and her raised arms gave them a more attractive lift. She looked at her stomach, holding it in as she turned the other way, and checked her high-hipped waist, tightened buttocks. Not too bad, but she worked like hell for it. Then the images of Sandra Moser and Dorothy Samenov flashed into her mind. She thought of the bite marks, of the frenzy that had caused them, and she turned away from the mirror and dressed.

Before she left the house she called Birley, quickly ran over her interview with Louise Ackley, told him she was going to try to see Reynolds after breakfast, and would come in to the office after that to work up her supplements. Then she tried the Radcom offices. Reynolds wasn't in, but when Palma told his secretary who she was, the woman quickly checked Reynolds's calendar and set up an appointment for ten o'clock.

When she got to Meaux's Grille she was two and a half hours later than she normally arrived, and Lauré's eyes widened as she came in the door.

'Ah, what are the police doing here this late?' she asked, laying down her new copy of *Elle* and smiling, displaying the gold that framed her upper canine and a lower incisor. Lauré, of stumpy stature and the face and hair of a silent-movie heroine, faithfully read the latest French and American fashion magazines. Uninvited, she followed Palma to a table that Falvia had just finished cleaning near the front windows, and the two of them sat opposite each other. Falvia and Alma were busily clearing the dirty tables. The morning had been a busy one.

'They came early this morning,' Lauré said, tossing her head at the dirty tables. 'Like wasps. The girls, poor little bitches, were going mad.' She grinned. 'It was wonderful.'

They visited over coffee as Palma ordered and then ate her breakfast. Lauré kept up with the police section of the newspaper, and always wanted to hear what Palma thought about this or that crime. She worried about the cases printed up in the 'Crime Stoppers' columns, and sometimes would ask Palma weeks after a crime was featured if the 'damned thing' had ever been resolved.

'You have a good job,' she once told Palma. 'Any time you deal with the basic human cravings, it's a good job. People need to eat, they need to make love, they need to pray, and all too often they think they need to kill each other. If you can't own a clean little café, or be a prostitute or a priest, then a homicide police is the best thing.'

She had laughed at this, but Palma felt sure that Lauré believed there was more than a small measure of truth in it.

Palma finished her breakfast, had one more cup of coffee at Lauré's insistence, and then walked outside to her car, where the morning air was already growing heavy with the coming heat.

She made her way to the West Loop Freeway and headed north, the skylines of all three of Houston's 'urban centers' visible through her windshield, rising out of the lush canopies of the city's trees. Downtown was the largest, distant and hazy to her far right and gradually falling behind her; Greenway Plaza on the Southwest Freeway to her near right; and the newer environs of the haute monde, the Post Oak district dominated by the Transco Tower straight ahead. The traffic on the freeways flowed to and from and branched off in the general direction of all three of these centers like concrete causeways connecting island cities in a vast lake of green water.

Palma exited on San Felipe and drove a few blocks, past Post Oak, and then right on Post Oak Lane. Gil

Reynolds's Radcom offices were in a smoke-gray glass building nestled in an inlet cut out of the dense loblolly pines. There was a large artificial pond in front of the building and a fountain in the center of it spewing a single jet of water high into the air so that it feathered out and fell in drifting sheets across the glassy surface of the pond. Radcom occupied the entire top floor of an eight-story building, and as the company's CEO, Gil Reynolds's office was not difficult to find off the main reception area. His secretary politely led Palma into his office, which was large and modern and overlooked a green belt of emerald lawn on the verge of the pine woods.

Reynolds stood as Palma entered and came around his desk to shake her hand, offering her one of the two plush leather chairs in front of his desk. He took the other. A large athletic man in a dark suit, Reynolds was hawk-nosed and handsome with rather longish dun-colored hair. He must have been in his middle forties. His manner was gracious, but straightforward. After the preliminaries he asked, 'How did you happen to come across my name in connection with Dorothy?' He was curious, not defensive.

'It came up during our interviews,' Palma said. 'It's routine to check all the names we get that way.'

'Vickie Kittrie?'

'All the interviews are confidential.'

Reynolds smiled kindly. 'I understand,' he said. 'But I do know Vickie. Can you tell me how she's handling this?'

'Not very well, it seems.'

'No, she wouldn't have. Excuse me,' he said. 'Would you care for some coffee, or a soft drink?'

'No, thank you.'

'I have to have some coffee,' he said, standing and reaching over his desk for a cup and saucer already there. He poured the coffee from an aluminum carafe on a tray and added cream from the same tray, stirred it and sat down again. 'I'm addicted to the stuff,' he said. 'I like it strong, and I drink too much of it.' As he lifted the cup to his lips Palma noticed he was wearing a wedding ring. Holding the saucer and cup of coffee, he crossed his legs. 'Okay,' he said. 'I have my pacifier. Shoot.'

'We understand you had dated Dorothy Samenov for a while.' It wasn't a question. It didn't need to be; Reynolds would know what to do with it.

'It's been about ten months since I've seen Dorothy,' he said, pausing. He gave the impression he was bracing himself to go through with something he had already made up his mind to do. 'I had an affair with her which lasted almost a year. It ruined my marriage.' He looked embarrassed at what he had just said, and winced apologetically. 'Rather, *I* ruined it, because of the affair. I'd been married to a wonderful woman for sixteen years; I have two children just now entering their teens. It's taking me a while to own up to the responsibility of having thrown all that away.'

'You're still wearing your wedding ring.'

He glanced at it. 'Yeah.' He didn't explain.

'Would you tell me what you were doing the night Dorothy was killed?'

'Sure,' he said. 'I've already checked my calendar. I worked here until six o'clock. I didn't want to eat at the condo — I live in St. James condominiums now, can't really bring myself to call them home — so I drove to Chase's over by the Pavilion. I finished there around eight o'clock. Still didn't want to go back to the condo, so I walked across to Loews. I wanted to see *Summer*, but the next feature didn't start for half an hour. I walked around the Pavilion until time, bought a ticket and saw the film. Got out a little after ten-thirty and drove straight back to the condo. Got there about ten-forty or so and was there for the rest of the evening. And have only myself for an alibi.'

Palma didn't say anything to his last remark, but continued routinely. The sooner she got through the list of questions the better.

'Can you tell me what you know about Dennis Ackley?'

Reynolds sipped his coffee before he spoke. 'I met him twice, but practically all of what I know about him — and it's only superficial — I learned from talking with Dorothy. They divorced in 1982. He's a con man, a wife beater, a liar, a thief, a drunkard ... I could go on. He's one of those men who've done just about everything there is to do on the negative side of the ledger. A total loss.'

'How did you happen to meet him?'

'During the months of our affair, I spent a lot of time over at Dorothy's condo. I met him there both times.' He grinned a little, remembering. 'Once he took a swing at me.'

'What?'

'I stayed out of the way, out of sight, really, when he came. He'd come a couple of times before. Four times in all, I guess, over the ten months I was seeing her. He was wanting money. She'd give him some; it was never enough. The second time I met him was the last time he'd come by. He was drunk and slapped her. I was in the next room and came barreling out of there when I heard that. He was surprised, swung at me, and I swung at him, knocked him down. I'd never hit anyone in my life. Broke my little finger,' he held up his right hand. 'Just as he was getting up Dorothy shoved a wad of bills into his hand and shuffled him out the door.'

'You haven't seen or heard of him since then?'

'No. And that last time was several months before Dorothy and I stopped ... seeing each other.'

Palma found Reynold's frankness about his affair, and what it had cost him, a refreshing change of pace from the denials she usually encountered. It was almost as if he had come through a tragic experience of failed integrity with more integrity than he had possessed going in. He seemed determined to confront his failings head-on and not to make excuses for his foolishness. For this reason, Palma felt slightly apologetic about the next question which was, however, unavoidable and which she asked with an uninhibited matter-of-factness.

'Was sadomasochism routine between you and Dorothy, or an occasional thing?'

'Well,' he said, looking at her wryly, 'that was to the point.' He paused. 'Neither.'

'But you knew about her preference for it.'

'Only near the end.'

'How did you find out?'

'She told me.'

'Why?'

Reynolds took another sip of his coffee and then set the cup and saucer on his desk. He wiped his right hand over the lower half of his face, hesitating around his chin, which he rubbed lightly with his forefinger. He did all of this without hurrying, using the time to think.

'Basically,' he said, 'because she had more sense, and a greater understanding of honesty than I did.' He paused again and looked down to his desk, where he put his hand on a bronze lozenge-shaped paperweight and shoved it a couple of inches, then took his hand away and laced the fingers of both hands together in his lap. 'I met Dorothy at a business lunch one day. There were five or six of us. She was a very handsome woman, intelligent, articulate, attractive in a number of ways. We exchanged business cards, and I called her a few days later and asked her to lunch. It was that simple. I found her enormously attractive. I'd never cheated on my wife before, but I began then. Essentially, I began leading a double life. I neglected my business, and my family, and spent as much time as I could with Dorothy. It was easy, as I said, because of her condo on Olympia.' He looked at Palma. 'Cheating is easy. Living with what it makes of you is the hard part.

'I believe Dorothy cared for me — I know she did — but there was always a corner of her that she never wholly gave up to me. There was something she held back. I threw myself into the affair heedlessly. I think I really did go kind of crazy over her. I was ten years older than she was, but she was the one who kept us from getting out of control. I'd lost all sense of perspective.

'Anyway, one day she decided to end it. She told me we had to stop. She didn't have to give me any reasons. I'd been over them a million times in my own mind. There was every reason in the world to stop it and not a single reason to go on, except for my own self-indulgence. But I didn't want to end it. That's when she told me I didn't really understand her, that her life was more complicated than I knew, and she couldn't let it go on the way it was going. I kept arguing with her, and finally she told me about the sadomasochism and Vickie Kittrie.'

Caught by surprise, Palma must have given him a blank look before she could cover it.

'You didn't know that Dorothy and Vickie were lovers?'

'No,' she said, shaking her head and hoping she didn't look as stupid as she felt. Suddenly the whole character of the investigation had changed, and Palma wasn't sure if this new configuration was a big break or a setback.

'I think I was an anomaly in Dorothy's recent history. She'd given up on men years ago.' Reynolds thought a moment. 'To tell you the truth, I'm not surprised Vickie didn't let you in on their relationship. It was a fiercely guarded secret. Dorothy was convinced that her career would be ruined if it was generally known that she was bisexual. And she wanted to protect Vickie in that regard as well. Dorothy was a competitive businesswoman, and she knew what it was like to have to fight sexism. But she thought the fact that she was bisexual was something she wouldn't be able to overcome. She didn't think she'd have a prayer of advancement in the corporate world as a lesbian.' Reynolds nodded. 'She was probably right.'

'Did you ever hear her speak of Dennis Ackley's sister?'

'No.'

'Did you know that Ackley was blackmailing Dorothy?'

It was Reynolds's turn to be surprised. 'Why? You mean using her bisexuality?'

'I don't know. I'm guessing now that's a good possibility. Did you ever hear Dorothy or Kittrie speak of Marge Simon?'

'No.'

'How about Nancy Segal? Linda Mancera? Helena Saulnier?'

Reynolds only shook his head.

'Do you know if Vickie or Dorothy frequented any gay bars, clubs, or organizations?'

'They didn't. It was out of the question. They were completely removed from that scene.' He looked away from her, out to the pine trees, and Palma noticed he had a striking profile. He was a handsome man. Then he turned back to her.

'I'll tell you something,' he said. 'After this happened, after I got over the considerable shock of it and was able to adjust my perspectives about who Dorothy Samenov was, we continued seeing each other for some time, a month or two. In retrospect she must have been trying to let me down easy and to salvage our friendship. We really did enjoy each other. Even without the sex. It was during this period that I met Vickie. Their relationship, in front of me at least, was as steady and conservative as an old married couple's. I would spend evenings with them from time to time, just the three of us sitting around at Dorothy's place talking. We covered everything in the world, but one of the things that happened during those evenings was that I got an education about what it was like to be "different" in this society. I listened to them for hours, and realized that I'd been walking around most of my life with my eyes shut. My life has been, is, the epitome of the status quo, and I hadn't the slightest idea, or concern, of what it was like not to be a part of that system. Not until I fell in love with someone who didn't fit in.'

Up until this point Reynolds had spoken about his relationship with Samenov only as an 'affair,' and Palma had found it a telling inadvertence when he had used the word 'love.' Gil Reynolds had been deeply disturbed by his encounter with Dorothy Samenov, and his stoic determination to make amends with his own conscience didn't negate the fact that what he had felt for a woman who was not his wife was something he would call 'love' only as an unconscious slip of the tongue.

Once again Palma felt a twinge of uneasiness at having to bring up something in that relationship that might cause Reynolds real pain.

'Just another couple of questions,' she said. 'What did Dorothy tell you about the sadomasochism?'

Reynolds nodded, opened his mouth to speak, stopped, then said, 'I guess I've already blown it for Vickie. It was something they didn't want to reveal, the lesbian relationship, I mean.'

'It doesn't matter,' Palma said. 'If it hadn't come from you it would have, and will, come from someone else. It's almost impossible to keep something like that quiet when it's an integral part of a homicide investigation. Things come out.'

Reynolds nodded again, but it was clear he really didn't buy Palma's glib effort at easing his conscience. But he went on, 'The sadomasochism ... it was between them, Dorothy and Vickie. They tried to explain it all to me but ... it was so foreign ... well, I think I pretended to understand it, tried not to be judgmental about it. They said it was something they both understood. That they weren't involved in the shame and humiliation part of it, just pain-pleasure things ...' He stopped, not knowing where to take it from there. He shrugged. 'I don't know. I didn't want to know too much about it.'

'As far as you know,' Palma said, 'were the two of them involved only with each other in this? There was no one else?'

He nodded. 'That's what they said.' He looked at his hands.

'Do you believe them?' she asked.

'Does it make any difference?'

'I'd like to know your feelings about it.'

He didn't answer immediately, his eyes moving restlessly over the top of his desk as if he might find the right words there among the workaday clutter.

'I think,' he said finally, 'There may have been men involved.'

'What makes you say that?'

'You asked for my "feelings."' He looked at her with an expression that told her that was as far as he wanted to go with it. 'I can't give you anything stronger than that.'

20

All the way downtown on Memorial Drive, Palma thought about the way Gil Reynolds expressed himself, how there was almost a feeling of wistfulness about him that seemed edged with the hard acceptance of the realities of his situation. She tried to imagine how much of a shock it must have been to him when he learned that Dorothy Samenov was bisexual, or how much honesty it had taken to admit that there were not only women in Samenov's life, but other men as well. All in all, it appeared that Gil Reynolds had gotten far more than he had bargained for when he decided to place himself in the hands, and between the thighs, of Dorothy Samenov.

It was noon by the time Palma walked into the homicide squad room, maneuvered around the little knots of detectives and civilians and got back to her cubicle. She found them all there. Birley, looking a little tousled, was standing at his desk putting labeled packages of Samenov's personal papers into a ragged cardboard box, his shirttail worked out and sagging over the back of his pants. He was talking to Cushing. Leeland, leaning on the door frame, spoke to her and smiled from under his mustache while Cushing, lounging in her chair, ignored her arrival except to grudgingly move his legs a little so she could get to her desk. None of them looked as if they had had enough sleep.

'Hi, kid,' Birley said, interrupting his dialogue with Cushing as she tossed her purse next to her computer and put down the Pepsi she had gotten from the vending machine outside. With exaggerated weariness, Cushing lifted himself out of her chair and gave it a surly shove toward her with his foot.

She saw the manila package from Quantico on her desk. 'Anybody have any luck here?' she asked, ignoring Cushing's insolence as he moved around and propped an arm on top of the filing cabinet.

'Some,' Birley said, stopping what he was doing and turning to her. Palma sat in her chair, kicked off her shoes, and popped the top on the Pepsi, tossing the tab into the trash can. 'I went through the rest of her financial stuff, which didn't provide any useful information except for the payments to Louise Ackley. Her letters — there weren't many — were all from her folks back in South Carolina. I couldn't see anything there to help us. There were no letters from "significant others" like I was hoping. It was pretty much of a dry run.

'But the address book is interesting,' he added, going back into the cardboard box. 'Aside from the businesses we'd noted earlier, there are a few men's names and numbers. I called them this morning.' He found the book and flipped through it. 'There's a hairdresser, a masseur, an electrical repairman, a guy who raises Dalmatians, a used-car dealer, a plumber, a TV repairman, a clerk at a video store, and a clerk at a bookstore. And then there're several dozen women's names, but only their first names, and the telephone numbers are apparently in code because none of them are working numbers. Some of them aren't even metro exchanges. We need to get this to somebody who can find a pattern here. I can't get to first base with it.'

'Care if I try?' Leeland asked.

Birley tossed him the book. 'I don't know. I think the names are coded too. Except there *is* a Marge in there, and a Nancy and a Linda.' He shrugged.

'Was there a Sandra?' Palma asked.

'I don't remember one. You mean Moser?'

'Yeah.'

'Did you come up with a connection?'

Palma sipped the Pepsi, which was cold and sharp. 'No, just hoping.' She looked at Leeland. 'What did you get?'

Leeland had cut himself shaving around his mustache that morning and had sustained a considerable wound just under his left nostril, which he had managed to coax into a powerful scab. He monitored it occasionally, lightly touching it with the back of his right index finger.

'I talked to the Board of Pardons and Parole in Austin and they're sending Ackley's prison records.' Leeland closed Samenov's address book and looked at her with his large, doleful eyes. 'They're looking for him because he just dropped out of sight, quit checking in with his parole officer. Then, of course, this other stuff came up in Dallas. He tended to hang around with some pretty unsavory characters in the Ramsey unit at Huntsville, all of them still in the pen except one. Guy named Dwayne Seely, also in for aggravated assault, got out within a month of Ackley and also came to Houston. He and Ackley have continued to buddy around together. There's a warrant out for him now on a parole violation. Nobody's heard from him in a couple of months.' Leeland touched the side of his nose. 'And I've put Ackley on the computer and coming out in the next bulletin. That's it.'

Palma looked at Cushing.

'Okay.' Cushing took the paper clip he had been chewing on out of his mouth and turned around to face her. 'I talked to the officer in Dallas who's looking for Ackley. Ackley was seen with an ex-con named Clyde Barbish on the day of the night that Clyde decided to commit mayhem and molestation on Debbie Snider, a student at SMU. Debbie was attacked and raped by two men, but could only make one of them from the files. The second man was always behind her, she said, and when he came around front to do her, he covered her face with her dress. Ackley was in the file along with Barbish, but she didn't make him.'

'The Dallas police think Barbish and Ackley are together?'

'That's what they're guessing. I also had a long conversation with a good man in their central crime analysis,' Cushing continued. 'Guy'd been there forever, one of those photographic memory types. I went over the whole thing, and we talked about a dozen or more cases. None of them really seemed to mesh, but a few were interesting. One of them, a woman with a single nipple removed, the right one, not the left one like Moser's, was also a blonde, but her body was not made up, and she was posed in a sexually suggestive position, not laid out like Moser and Samenov. She was also found in an abandoned house in a sleazy part of town. Not our man's kind of terrain.'

'It's interesting, though,' Leeland put in, 'that SMU's in the swankiest part of Dallas.'

'Snider's rape occurred on the eighth, Birley said. 'And Moser was killed on the thirteenth. That's just five days between.'

'It only takes a few hours to make the drive,' Palma said. 'What about Walker Bristol?'

'Oh, yeah,' Cushing said, sliding his eyes at Leeland. 'Donny talked to him mostly.'

Leeland's calm eyes lingered a second on Cushing, then he picked it up. 'Bristol's a VP at Security National. Fortyish. Married, no children. Claims he dated Samenov two years ago before he married. He's only seen her casually since then. Didn't have any idea about her S&M business, didn't know anything about her during these last three years. Didn't know Dennis Ackley.'

Shifting his feet, Leeland once again touched his finger to the side of his nose. 'I think he's lying. The man was really careful about what he said, tied into a knot about it, but trying to come across cool. We ought to do some background and make another run at him. As for Dirk somebody, there's a woman in the registrar's office at the University of Houston trying to track it down for us.'

'So what about you?' Birley said. 'Did you get to see your people?'

'Yeah, I did,' Palma said, pulling a tissue out of the box on her desk and wiping up the wet spot from the Pepsi. 'There are some surprises.'

She went straight through each of the interviews, Kittrie again at her place with Isenberg and Saulnier, Linda Mancera, Louise Ackley, and finally Gil Reynolds with his astonishing revelation.

'Dykes!' Cushing feigned an exaggerated incredulity. 'These babes are *dykes*? Hey. I don't know about Mancera,' he laughed, his eyes widened at Palma as he shook his head, 'but this Marge Simon is a real baby doll. What a waste!' He cackled again, and looked at Leeland. 'I love it.'

'We don't know about Simon and Mancera,' Palma corrected him. 'The information goes only for Samenov and Kittrie.'

'Shit,' Cushing said, still grinning. 'I don't have to be hit over the head with it. I'll bet they're all cream puffs.'

'Well, that explains why Samenov used first names only for the women in the address book,' Birley said.

'Seems kind of an elaborate system.' Leeland looked at Palma. 'Did Reynolds really think they were *that* secretive about it?'

'He seemed to.' Palma drank the last of her Pepsi. She didn't know why it offended her that Cushing, still shaking his head and grinning, was enjoying the lesbian angle so much. 'I don't think we can assume that Marge Simon, Nancy Segal, and Linda Mancera are lesbians, but even if they are, I don't know where that gets us. We don't have any connection between them and Dennis Ackley. So far they've spoken of him as if he were contaminated. Unless they can be considered potential targets.'

'So what are we supposed to think about Sandra Moser then?' Birley said. 'That the little lady was a closet bisexual?'

'I think we have to,' Palma said. 'Considering the group's composition.'

'There's her S&M stuff,' Cushing said.

'There's not a Sandra in the book.' Leeland was already flipping through the pages again.

'How did Ackley meet her?' Birley asked.

'It's this way,' Cushing speculated, his legs straight out, hips leaned back against the filing cabinet. 'Samenov was lying to Reynolds about her ex being a bastard. Ackley and Samenov are together on this S&M deal. There's the photographs of Samenov — who took the photographs? She procures these women, lesbians, for their trios. They were doing Moser together and she dies, maybe accidentally. They make it look like a psycho job just to screw up the investigation. Later Ackley does Samenov because she's the only witness. Ackley's been around. He knows to clean up after these things. And he stages it to look like the first one.'

'If Samenov was lying to Reynolds about Ackley being a bastard,' Palma countered, 'then Louise Ackley is lying about it too, and so are Linda Mancera and Vickie Kittrie. I think Ackley's criminal record backs them up.'

'Okay, fine. So the guy was a certified bastard, all the more reason why he and his ex-wife were turning S&M tricks together,' Cushing persisted.

'You're missing the point, Cush,' Palma snapped. 'It's not likely any of them would have *wanted* to work with him.'

'Bullshit,' Cushing came back at her. 'You don't know that. People will do anything . . .'

'I think we'd better decipher that damn address book,' Birley broke in. 'And talk to every person listed in there.'

'I'm betting the women's names won't get us that much,' Palma said. 'The main value of that address book is that it *does* list the names of more men. Admittedly the odds are on Ackley, but what if it's not Ackley? There are eight or ten men's names in there who ought to be checked out. Did they have a connection to Sandra Moser? Did the TV repairman repair her TV too? Did she regularly buy video movies from the same store as Samenov? Did she use the same plumber?'

'She's right,' Birley said. 'We need to go through the service records for each one of those names. And we'd better keep our eyes open for *any* woman's name that might come up in the records or client lists of any of these men.'

Palma's telephone rang and she answered it. It was for Cushing, who took it, said yeah and great, and hung up.

'Soronno's got some lab results for us,' he said, going for the door. 'Be right back.'

While Cushing was gone, Birley opened another Tupperware lunch packed by Sally. He ate it without much pleasure, offering some brownies to Leeland, who said he had already eaten. Palma's stomach was rumbling, but she pushed her hunger to the back of her mind as she looked through her notes from the Reynolds interview.

It did not take Cushing long to get back, carrying the report and a fresh Coke. Cushing had a thing about Cokes, and the thing was that he poured a little bit out of each can and spiked it with rum. He thought no one knew it, but Palma and Birley had been keeping tabs on him for a long time, and Palma was sure it was no secret to Leeland.

'Okay,' he said, rolling the typing chair from the squad room ahead of him. 'We've got some things here that tie in.'

He swiveled the typing chair around and straddled it and leaned forward with the back of it against his chest, his legs splayed out toward Palma. The ultimate macho posture, lots of sex appeal. Palma thought it was pitiful that Cushing always had to be on for her, always had to swagger and strut. Having his penis pinched must have done something to his psyche. Maybe Cushing really did have his brains between his legs.

'Fingerprints: they didn't find *any* other than Samenov's in the bathroom and bedroom, though they got some unknowns from other parts of the house, mostly from the kitchen and study. Same with palm prints.

'Footprints: we got some, but they're a woman's, on

either side of the bidet.

'Nothing on the clothes folded in the chair.

'Samenov's blood group: ABO — O; PGM — 2; EAP — BA; Hp — 1. Common as dirt. Even more common than Moser's. All the blood found on the sheet taken from the bed and all the traces found on bath towels matched these descriptors.

'Head hair, unknown: bed sheet submitted to the lab yielded five strands of long blond hair. Four of these hairs matched Samenov's head hair; one definitely did not. Three head hairs were found in the carpet on the right side of the bed, next to the closet, all matched Samenov's. Two head hairs found at foot of bed: one Samenov's, one not. Two head hairs found on left side of bed, next to bath, neither matched Samenov's. Of the four unknown head hairs three match, one is dissimilar.

'Fingernail scrapings yielded only traces of hand soap matching the hand soap in Samenov's bathroom.

'Mouth swab: cotton fibers matching the towels in Samenov's bathroom, not from any of the other bathrooms where the towels were a different color.

'Swabs and smears for mouth, vagina, and anus: no seminal acid phosphatase. Same as with Moser.

'Loose pubic hair: the combings yielded nine pubic hairs of which five did *not* match Samenov's. All the unknown hairs were telogen hairs, third-growth state, dormant, so there weren't any sheath cells that could be blood-grouped. Also, of the five unknown hairs three came from one source and appeared to have been vaginal hair; the other two appeared to have come from another source and seemed to have been from higher up on the pubic bone.

'Since the only unidentified hair collected from Moser's scene was two eyebrow hairs, they couldn't make any match.

'Bite marks: good impressions from Samenov, but because the Moser bite marks were superficial and poorly defined, they're not sure they can make a match. And because Samenov had been washed, like Moser, there was no saliva on the swabs.

'Cosmetics: the makeup on Samenov's face did not match the same source as the makeup in Samenov's room, but it *did* match the same source as the makeup on Sandra Moser's face. It looks like the asshole's bringing along his own stuff.

'That's it,' he said, tossing the report onto Birley's desk and taking a swig of Coke.

'Samenov had had sexual relations with *two* people, then,' Birley said, picking up the paper. 'At some time after her last bath. There could be an eight- or ten-hour differential on that possible time span, depending on whether she usually bathed before going to bed at night or whether she usually bathed after getting up in the morning.'

'And the encounters within that time frame could have been at widely spaced intervals,' Leeland said, 'or at the same time — a ménage à trois.'

'All of the hairs blond?' Birley asked, flipping through the pages.

'All of them. Well, to be accurate, blondish. They're different shades.'

'Like the Moser eyebrow hairs.'

'I guess they couldn't tell what brand of cosmetics any of it was,' Palma said.

'I asked. No way.'

'Damn. Slim pickins,' Birley said. 'But, the guy brings his own ligatures, his own makeup, cleans up after himself like a practical nurse.'

'The thing is,' Leeland said, 'he does a good job with the makeup. He seems to take pains with it. Could be a morgue worker ... beautician ... transvestite ...'

'Theatrics,' Palma offered. 'An actor, a makeup artist.'

'The guy could just be good at it,' Cushing countered. 'Likes to do it. Doesn't have to mean his profession's connected with it.'

'That's true,' Birley put in, tossing his empty Styrofoam cup into the trash. 'Hell, he could also train fleas and sleep with squirrels. It doesn't have to have anything to do with his profession at all. Guys like this ... who the hell knows what makes this boy tick?'

'And Dennis Ackley,' Leeland said. 'Do we know, or have reason to believe, that he'd be particularly inclined to know anything about makeup?'

'Hell, no.' Cushing snorted. 'Guy's a common turd.'

'Okay, then, what *do* we know about him?' Palma was getting impatient. 'He's blond.'

'Don't jump the gun,' Birley interrupted. 'We don't know the guy had anything sexual to do with her. I mean as far as getting his pubic hairs mixed in with hers. There's no evidence of penile penetration — anywhere.'

'He didn't have to penetrate her, John,' Palma said.

'Okay, fine,' Birley held up a hand. 'But don't forget she's bisexual. Plenty of rubbing going on there, I'd imagine. Those hairs could have been a woman's.'

'Sex-type it,' Palma countered.

'Can't,' Cushing checked her. 'Remember, they're telogen, third-stage. No sheath cells. Besides, even if there were sheath cells it would have to be a DNA test and that'd take weeks. And it ain't cheap.'

Palma looked at Birley, and the frustration must have shown on her face.

'We don't know shit about him,' Birley said almost apologetically. 'For sure, anyway.'

'Okay, fine,' Palma said. 'But let's move on something. Don,' Palma addressed Leeland, not wanting to give Cushing the satisfaction, 'do you and Cush want to start checking out the men listed in Samenov's address book, trying to tie them in to Moser?' Leeland nodded. Palma didn't even look at Cushing. 'John,' she turned to Birley, 'what about this? We're checking on these service men. Why don't we go back and get the names of people at the other end of the scale too — doctors, dentists, ophthalmologists, whatever — that Moser and Samenov might have shared?'

Birley nodded. 'Good. I'll do it.'

'I'll go back to Kittrie and get samples of comparison hair since we've got to have exemplars for the unknown hairs found in Samenov's combings. If those hairs are Kittrie's, it's likely she had sex with Samenov after the "happy hour," much closer to the time Samenov was killed. She could very well know something she's not telling.'

The telephone rang again, and this time it was for Leeland. He stepped over and took it at Birley's desk while the rest of them went on discussing their assignments. After a moment Leeland interrupted them to ask for the case file, took it from Birley and turned around, laid it on the desk and started flipping through it as he cradled the receiver between his neck and chin. He named several dates, listened, named a couple more, listened, and started taking notes furiously. 'I'll be damned,' he said, listening and writing rapidly. He said, 'Are you sure?' Listened. 'I'll be damned,' he repeated, and underlined something. Then jotted a few more notes. 'No, we're much obliged. Yeah, well, if you could send us some kind of confirmation on that for our file we'd appreciate it. You bet. Yeah, if you get up this way I'll buy you a chicken-fried steak. Okay, 'bye.'

Leeland turned around, shaking his head and looking at his notes. He stuck his pencil behind his ear and wiped at his mustache.

'That was Texas Ranger John Deaton calling from McAllen down in the Valley. He said he'd been out of touch for several days, working a double murder near Los Ebanos on the border, but had come in last night. This morning he was in the office checking the new TCIC listings that had come on line while he was gone. He caught Dallas's flag on Ackley, and then Dallas put him on to us. He said that a week ago last Tuesday,' Leeland turned and looked at the calendar on the desk, 'that'd be on the twenty-third, nine days ago, three days after Snider's rape up in Dallas, Dennis Ackley and Clyde Barbish held up a liquor store in Mercedes, about twelve miles from the nearest border station. The deal went bad, there was a shoot-out, Barbish was hit but fled the scene and hasn't been heard from since. Ackley killed one of the two liquor store clerks, and almost simultaneously the second clerk blew Ackley's face off with a shotgun. That was two days before Dorothy Samenov was strangled.'

21

'If my father had told me to drink poison, I would have done it,' she said. 'He meant that much to me. I would have done it in a minute.'

Mary Lowe had been talking about her stepfather, how much he had come to mean to her and her mother after having rescued them from their nomadic wanderings through the Southern states, through 'Dixie,' where her mother moved from job to job and Mary had tried to adapt to an endless series of makeshift homes in cheap boarding-houses and third-rate apartments. Broussard noted the slip of the tongue as she substituted 'father' for 'stepfather.' For some reason this made him uneasy, and the foreboding he had experienced during her last session returned.

'We became very close. I was in the third grade. I had missed a year while Mother and I were moving around, so at ten I was a year older than all the others.'

As lean and elegant as a Paris model, Mary was fond of fashionable clothes. Her streamlined body turned everything she put on into haute couture, creating a sleek elegance that caused head-turning responses whenever she entered a room. She was indeed exceptional, and Broussard could easily believe that what she possessed beneath her clothes was equally inspiring. He had spent a lot of time imagining the precise nature of that inspiration. The precise nature of it. But aside from this illicit, if imagined, appraisal of her anatomy, there was his more straightforward appreciation of her fashion sense. He simply liked what she wore, and he had never seen her wear even the smallest accessory that did not seem appropriate.

This afternoon her thick buttery hair was pulled back and tied in the back with a white lace scarf. She wore a surplice wrap dress of rayon challis in a black and white stippling pattern of misty delicacy with a white, lace-trimmed collar that dipped into her bustline. Her stockings were the sheerest white, her shoes, lying at the foot of the chaise, were bone. She lay with one arm at her side and the other draped across her thin waist.

'He became my best friend,' she continued; her right hand touched the skirt of her dress. 'We swam together in our pool, played games; you know, who could swim the farthest underwater, who could pick up the most pennies from the deep end of the pool before having to come up, who could turn the most somersaults underwater. Mother would read by the pool or doze in the cabana. He and I watched a lot of television together, eating popcorn or pizza while we sprawled on the floor or lounged on the sofa. He would get me to snuggle up next to him or lie down with my head in his lap. Lots of times I would go to sleep there. Mother would sit in her own big chair and paint her nails or read magazines, or sometimes she just wasn't there at all. And we cooked together, too. He liked to cook, and he taught me how to help him in the kitchen. I learned everything I know about cooking from him, not from Mother. I don't particularly remember her in the kitchen at all. It didn't interest her.'

The hand that was draped over Mary's waist flattened out and Broussard saw her pressing slightly on her upper abdomen as if she had experienced a slight pain or was trying to ease a tightness. He looked at her face, at the soulful russet shadowing around her eyes, at the subtly asymmetrical mouth with its hint of a pucker at one side. But there was a slight tension between her eyebrows, the faint beginnings of a frown.

'He was my father,' she said. Again Broussard made a note though in this instance it was unclear how she had used the word. She could have meant: 'He was my "father",' or she could have meant: 'He was like a father to me' or 'He became my father.'

'He loved me,' she said. 'He told me so and that made me feel wonderful. I really wanted to be loved and to have that love demonstrated to me. He did everything with me, and we developed a very special emotional bond. It happened very quickly for me because I had this void there, and he stepped right in and filled it. I became his "special girl." At the same time, now that my "emotional needs" were taken care of, Mother seemed to relinquish entirely any attachment to me at all. But she didn't seem to be particularly interested in him, either. My symbiotic relationship with my father seemed to free her to ... simply pay more attention to herself, to indulge her narcissism. She grew increasingly distant, more wrapped up in herself, preening like a solitary white bird. She was very beautiful. And she was also uncommonly self-centered.'

Mary paused and her hand at her side began picking at her dress. It wasn't doing anything, not smoothing the dress or rearranging the way it lay, just plucking at it between her thumb and forefinger. The fingers on her stomach moved slightly, but restlessly.

'I wanted my father to know that I loved him, too. I didn't want him ever to leave me or to drift away from me as my mother had done. I remember being very, very worried that he would do that.

'One afternoon I went shopping with a friend from school and her mother. I bought my first two-piece swimsuit. It was aquamarine, and when I bought it in the store I remember imagining how wonderful it would look in the blue water of our pool. I couldn't wait to get in the pool to see if I would match the water. I imagined that I would be very beautiful swimming in the pool as if I were actually one with the color of the water. I loved the colors, just the pleasure of the colors.

'In the summer we would swim at night, and I especially liked that because the lights under the water seemed very exotic to me. I wore my new swimsuit that night to play water basketball with my father. We were horsing around, and I remember I finally got my hands on the ball and was getting away from him. He chased me, laughing, and grabbed me from behind ... and he held me ... somehow differently. I don't really remember how I sensed it at first. I'd never felt it before, never even given it a thought, but I knew instantly what it was and that it had gotten hard, and he was holding it against the back of my suit bottom, sort of cupping me in his lap. Then he started grinding against me, holding me so tight I couldn't get away. I felt him working that long bulge between my buttocks, and suddenly his hands slipped under the top of my swimsuit, and he began fondling my nipples, massaging them, squeezing them between his fingers.'

Mary stopped and swallowed, her eyes fixed on a distant memory. 'I was so startled ... I didn't really do anything. I just thought, What's this? What's he doing? and then suddenly he kind of shivered and held me tight for another couple of seconds. My mind was a mess of confusion. This was totally alien to me; I didn't understand it at all and I didn't like it. I think I started trying to get away, and then he kind of laughed again and shoved me away, pretending to be playing again, and swam toward the side of the pool.'

Mary's nervous fingers betrayed her agitation and caused Broussard to look at her face. The little pucker between her eyebrows had become a stern frown, but it was more the frown of one straining to hear some faint sound rather than that of a person emotionally upset. Broussard watched her. He had heard a good number of these stories over the years, and wondered how she had handled it as a child, and how she would interpret it as a woman. He said nothing, but he was irritated at the recognition of his own arousal. But he tried not to be self-condemning. After all, it was a biologically normal reaction. The fact that she was speaking as a child didn't bother him, or perhaps it did, and that was the source of his own discomfort.

But there was more at play here than a violation of cultural conventions. The same inexplicable attraction he had felt for Bernadine five years earlier was echoed in the resonance of the emotions that stirred in him at hearing Mary Lowe's story. Not only did he recognize these familiar stirrings, but he discerned, too, an intrusive anxiety. The same feelings of being on the foggy margins of a moral frontier that had emerged as he interviewed Bernadine in those early months after they first met were surfacing once again as he listened to the tortured memories of Mary's childhood, those early memories the Norwegian painter Edvard Munch had characterized as 'the troubled colors of bygone days . . .'

Mary did not continue immediately. In fact, she did not speak again for seventeen minutes, according to Broussard's mantel clock. As always, he remained silent, watching, noticing that Mary's legs moved a little also, almost as nervously as her fingers, but ever so slightly, like someone who had lain in one position too long. But as he watched, she gained control of herself. By a remarkable force of will she calmed every part of her twitching body, settling herself, gaining control so that she could go on.

'As soon as I broke away,' she said, 'I turned and looked at Mother, who was sitting at the other end of the pool with her legs in the water reading a magazine. She hadn't seen anything. I looked at my father, and he sort of frowned and shook his head for me not to say anything. I guess he could tell what I had in mind. It was disorienting — what he'd done. And now this, his not wanting me to say anything about it. It was — disorienting.' Mary couldn't seem to find another word to better describe her feelings. 'He wanted to keep it from her, what he'd done. Even in my child's mind I saw the enormity of what he was suggesting, that it was a kind of point of no return. If I went along with him on this, that put me in the position of a co-conspirator with him. If I agreed, we shared a secret.

'I was still in the water, looking at Mother, her legs moving slowly back and forth in the blue water, her head down looking at the magazine. Behind me I heard my father start calling my name, kind of laughing, Maybe a little nervously. Right there in that moment between them I tried to figure it out for myself. Why did I feel so strange about what he'd done? What *had* he done? I don't know. What's so different about my chest that he shouldn't touch me there, or about his thing that he shouldn't do what he did? What had he done? He kissed me on the lips and patted me on the bottom. What made this so different? I mean, how do fathers act? He *had* been so wonderful to me. I knew he would never harm me. I knew he loved me. And I also knew if I said anything about it, it would be awkward for all of us. It would ruin things.'

In just a few short moments Mary Lowe had worked herself into another state of agitation, but now she couldn't remain lying down. She sat up abruptly and hung her legs over the side of the chaise. She wiped at her face.

'Could I please have a cold washcloth?' she asked.

'I'm sorry,' he said. 'Of course.' He laid down his notebook and went into his bath and ran a washcloth under the cold water, wrung it out, and brought it back to her. Her face was red, and she seemed as if she had been breathing heavily. She took the washcloth and thanked him and put it on her face, unheeding of her makeup. She held it there a moment, hiding her face, and then she lifted it. He stood in front of her watching her, realizing that her agitation excited him. She ignored his closeness and wiped the cloth down into the front of her dress, across her breasts, in between them. Broussard regarded her with an undisguised admiration.

Suddenly she stopped and looked up at him. She glanced down to his crotch, but his sport coat was covering the bulge. It didn't matter. She knew. They both understood.

She thrust the cloth out to him without thanking him. He smiled at her and took it back to the bathroom and left it draped over the sink and returned.

Mary Lowe had gotten her purse and sat it on her lap while she freshened her makeup. Broussard returned to his armchair and watched her. After a moment he said, 'Do you believe that episode just happened out of the blue?' he asked.

'What do you mean?' She was looking at herself in her compact.

'Have you ever wondered if you may have, in some way, provoked this kind of action by your stepfather?'

Her eyes shot up from her hand-held mirror, her expression defiant. He felt as if she had slapped him.

'Sometimes children, little girls, can be provocative without even realizing it,' Broussard persisted. 'Maybe you wanted this episode to happen. Why do you think you bought the two-piece suit? Certainly you'll have to admit this kind of suit is much more revealing, much more . . .'

Lowe lowered her mirror, snapped it shut, and put it into her purse. She looked at him. 'I was a *child*,' she said.

Broussard smiled. 'Of course you were, but do you believe children are completely innocent . . . of such things? Sometimes even as adults we don't know why we do some of the things we do. We're compelled by some unconscious impulse, perhaps never really understanding what we've done until it's over, and we can look back and see that there was more to it than met the eye. Have you never wondered if, perhaps unconsciously, you wanted this isolated incident to happen?'

Mary Lowe stood up from the chaise and looked at Broussard, her pale feet visible in his peripheral vision as they peeped out from under the hem of her dress like two shy creatures whose slight visibility only hinted at the hidden charm that remained concealed higher up under the longer folds of the skirt.

'It was not,' she said, 'an isolated incident.'

22

Vickie Kittrie had not returned to work by Wednesday morning, and her boss at Computron said that she had requested a week's sick leave. Nor was she at home. Palma found her on Olympia, staying with Helena Saulnier.

The three of them sat in Saulnier's living room again, the late morning light throwing a long brassy streak across the dark terracotta tile of the living room that opened out onto a patio crowded with palms and plantains. Whether by chance or by an unconscious need to follow precedents, Palma and Kittrie sat in the same places they had occupied three days earlier, facing each other across the glazed gold tiles of the coffee table while Saulnier, not excusing herself this time, sat in a second tapestry armchair between them. Both women were dressed casually, Kittrie in white tailored shorts and a white safari shirt, and Saulnier in a sarong, as before, and the top of a black bikini. And both women seemed particularly concerned with Palma's third visit in as many days. Kittrie was her usual apprehensive self, but this time Saulnier, too, portrayed genuine concern. Palma thought it was a good opportunity to get straight to the point with them. She had been too cautious too long.

'I'm going to level with you,' Palma said, looking at both of them but settling her eyes on Kittrie. 'I know that you and Dorothy Samenov were lovers.' She pressed on despite Kittrie's round-eyed surprise and the bright pink flush that spread over her freckles. 'I know how Dorothy felt about keeping her bisexuality secret, and I know that her ex-husband had been blackmailing her to keep it quiet. He's dead, incidentally.' Kittrie's mouth dropped open. 'He was robbing a liquor store and was shot. I'll have to admit that he was our main — and only — suspect. Now we're no closer to resolving this thing than we were when we walked into Dorothy's bedroom two days ago.

'Additionally, I need to tell you that a month before Dorothy was killed another woman was murdered in almost the exact manner.' This time both Saulnier and Kittrie reacted with alarm. 'I asked you about her the first time we talked,' Palma said to Kittrie. 'Her name was Sandra Moser.'

'I remember,' Kittrie nodded. 'But I've never heard of her.'

'She was found in the Doubletree Hotel on Post Oak. It was in the papers.'

'Yeah, I remember that,' Saulnier said. 'I just didn't put the names together.' Her expression was sober. 'She was killed ... the same way?'

Palma nodded and opened the manila folder she had brought with her. She pulled out the picture of Moser, and the uncropped copies of the three black and white pictures of the unidentified woman with the mannequin.

'Do you know either of these women?'

Vickie was not as bright as she might have been, and when she got a good look at the pictures she snapped her eyes at Saulnier, who pretended not to notice. Saulnier looked at Palma and shook her head and gave a small shrug. Vickie's face was as blank as an imbecile's.

Palma was furious, but covered it. It struck her as absurd that the three of them were sitting there playing charades.

'I'll give you my opinion,' she said, 'and it's the assumption on which we're conducting this investigation. There are a group of you,' she included Saulnier with her eyes, 'who want to keep your bisexuality, or even your strictly lesbian, preferences secret, for professional or other reasons. You socialize among yourselves in private, but maintain a considerable restrained distance professionally. Maybe you even compartmentalize your lives, some of you knowing the same women without realizing it. In any event, some of you also know, without realizing it, the man who has killed Dorothy and Sandra Moser. He's going to kill others. That's a guarantee, because none of you are cooperating with us and we don't have *any* leads. So he's out there, a husband, a bum, a lover, a friend, a hairdresser, a plumber, an executive ... whatever he is, and he's going to do it again. As long as you maintain this stupid conspiratorial silence, you're sentencing another woman to death.'

Palma stopped and looked at them. Kittrie fidgeted in her cute, cuffed shorts like a reprimanded schoolgirl, her youthful breasts requiring no help to create a seductive cleavage, her permed ginger hair full and bouncy around her face which, even when expressing confused fright as it was now, was a seductive attraction to either sex. Saulnier understood.

'Was the other woman bisexual?' she asked.

'We don't know.' Palma was tired of the game. She nodded at the pictures. 'She's the blonde. We were hoping you could help us find out.'

'I don't know her,' Saulnier said. Then she leaned forward and put a finger on one of the pictures of the unidentified woman with the mannequin. 'But I know her.' She looked at Palma steadily. 'You're sure about this, about the bisexual aspect?'

'I'm not sure about anything,' Palma said. 'That's what we think we've got.'

Saulnier nodded and leaned back in her chair, thinking. The sarong had fallen open, exposing her long tanned inner thigh. She didn't bother to fix the sarong. Her olive face was framed by her straight bangs and the vertical sides of her dark, gray-streaked bob. Only her eyes and something about her mouth hinted at the years she had over Kittrie and even over Palma herself. She was clearly feeling the import of Palma's words, and she was weighing them in the balance against something else at which Palma could only guess.

'It's not exactly a "society,"' she said finally, looking at Palma, 'but it's damned close to it.'

Vickie Kittrie reached for her Virginia Slims on the coffee table. Saulnier pulled herself up in the tapestry armchair and let the sarong fall away from her leg completely now, exposing it nearly to the hip. The very edge of the dark triangle between her legs was visible above the sloping curve of her naked thigh. The gesture seemed to be a declaration of admission. Palma had caught her out, she no longer had a reason for deception. Palma wondered what could be going through her mind. Was she really so comfortable with her nakedness that she did not care that Palma was almost close enough to touch her? Or was the intent of this display to draw Palma into a new eroticism? Or was her intent more selfish; did the titillation flow in the other direction so that Saulnier herself was experiencing a very particular gratification from watching Palma's reaction as she found herself in the uncomfortable position of alternately averting her eyes from Saulnier's exhibitionism, and unavoidably taking in the full, naked length of her handsome body?

'Dorothy actually started this ... group herself, five or six years ago,' Saulnier began, glancing briefly at Vickie before continuing. 'She had been a sexually abused child who had run away from home when she was fifteen to get away from it. She lived in a hospice while she finished high school. She was smart, had spunk, and got a scholarship to go to college. That's where she met Louise Ackley and discovered her sexual affinity for other women.'

Saulnier paused as if she wanted to explain something, then decided against it and went on. Palma thought about the drunken man she had heard swearing in Ackley's bedroom.

'Dorothy recognized early on that this was one aspect of her life she was going to have to hide. That was when she started the prototype of the network. While she was in graduate school she met Louise's brother and, for some inexplicable reason, married him. You know how that turned out. But Dorothy and Louise continued their relationship.'

She paused again, and the tapered fingers of one hand pulled abstractly at one side of her bob. Saulnier's fingernails were perfectly manicured though kept rather short with softly narrowed ends. Palma had never seen them with nail polish.

'Naturally I lied about how well I knew her,' Saulnier said. 'We were extremely close, across the street from each other like this. We were lovers for a while, too, but we were too much alike. Anyway, Louise had been her lover for years, behind Dennis's back. He was such a prick, so wrapped up in himself, he didn't even realize what was going on. And then one day he found them together. He used it against them from then on.

'Except where Dennis was concerned, Dorothy was independent and shrewd. She was professionally successful despite Dennis's hanging around her neck like an albatross, which he continued to do even after the divorce. So she started this networking system to enable other bisexuals and lesbians to associate with each other while maintaining a straight life, if that was what they wanted. Many are professionals whose careers would suffer if their sexual orientation were known. Others are married — happily married, if that's not a contradiction in terms. They don't want to give up their families, but they still long for the kind of affection they can only get from loving another woman. A lot of society women.' She nodded. 'And you were right, the secret to the networking system is its compartmentalism. We don't use our real names when meeting someone for the first time, and some of us may never use our real names. If we keep names and numbers, both are coded. Each woman is responsible for her own coding system.'

'Do you know Dorothy's?'

'No, that's the point,' Saulnier said dryly. 'We never go to lesbian hangouts, and overt role-playing — being butch — is out. There's a fairly wide span of ages, a few are grandmothers, though very well-preserved grandmothers. These women are in income brackets that enable them to take care of themselves. And most of us are feminine.' She allowed herself a wry smile. 'Within our particular network, at least, a woman who wants a woman wants a woman.'

Saulnier stopped and shrugged as if to suggest that was it.

'How large is the group?'

'I don't really know. I guess I could name several dozen off the top of my head, and I'm sure there are a number I don't know anything about.'

'How does the network operate?'

Saulnier nodded as if she knew that would be the next question, but her face was set.

'You realize the problem here,' she said. 'Some of these women are ... prominent, or their husbands are prominent. And their husbands have no idea that something like this exists or that their wives have such needs.' She moved a small, tapered middle finger over a dark arched eyebrow and looked away, thinking, chewing on the inside of her jaw. 'This is volatile. I honestly don't know what to do.'

'You need to consider the possibility that someone's learned of your network,' Palma said. 'And doesn't like what they've found. Maybe a husband or son or friend or lover of one of these women. It's something you've got to consider. *Some*one is on to it.'

Saulnier straightened her back and brushed a small hand over her naked rib cage. She darted her eyes at Kittrie again. The girl had folded her arms and was biting a thumbnail, staring at Saulnier as she smoked.

Palma looked at Kittrie. 'Vickie, you told me that you'd met Gil Reynolds several times at Dorothy's. I know he'd had an affair with her that lasted almost a year. What did you think of him?'

'He was okay,' she said. 'A nice guy.'

'How did he deal with learning that Dorothy was bisexual?'

'He kind of overreacted,' she said. Palma imagined that was a considerable understatement.

'In what way?'

'Well, I just know what Dorothy said, and she said he ran his hand through the wall in her bedroom, the Sheetrock, you know. And he broke up some of her things.'

'What things?'

'All her perfume and cosmetics. Just the stuff in her bedroom. I think they were in there when she told him.'

'Was he easily angered?'

'I don't think so.'

'Did Dorothy ever tell you about the time he knocked out Dennis Ackley?'

Vickie nodded.

'What happened?'

'Oh, I think Dennis slapped Dorothy when Gil was there, and Gil jumped all over him.'

'Hit him once and knocked him out?'

Vickie shrugged, 'Well, that's not exactly what Dorothy said. She said there was a real brawl, and she had to pull Gil off Dennis, that Gil almost ripped Dennis's ear off, and he had to have surgery on it. She said Gil almost killed him.'

'I was led to believe that Reynolds was something of a gentleman,' Palma said. 'Is that how you viewed him?'

'Well, yeah, he was, but he kind of had this other side of him, too. The guy scared me a little, but I don't really know why. It could've just been me.'

Palma could believe that.

'What makes you think Dorothy and the other woman knew their killer?' Saulnier asked, looking back at Palma. 'Maybe they were random victims. You're not even sure the other woman's bisexual.'

'You're right,' Palma said. 'We're not sure. But Sandra Moser willingly went to her hotel, checked in under a

false name, and met someone she *knew*. There's every
indication that Dorothy knew her killer too. She willingly
let him into the house. There was no illegal entry. There
was no struggle, no sign of resistance.'

'But you told me the last time we talked that she was
strangled,' Saulnier said. 'Surely there was some kind of
struggle.'

Palma shook her head. 'That brings us to the next
thing we need to discuss. Both Moser and Dorothy were
strangled ... with a belt, probably the same belt. Their
wrists and ankles had been tied, but apparently there was
no struggle in either case. They had allowed themselves
to be tied. Both were sexually mutilated in the same way.
Sadomasochist paraphernalia was found hidden at both
residences. Do many of the women in this group go in for
that?'

Saulnier shook her head firmly. 'I suspect that what
you found was used for autoerotic purposes.'

Palma was prepared for that. She picked up the manila
envelope again and took out the four-color photographs
of Samenov tied to the bed, her leather-hooded tormentor
aping for the camera. Palma spread the pictures out on
the table and looked at the two women. Saulnier was
dumbfounded; Kittrie blanched, then dropped her eyes
and quickly puffed on her cigarette.

'Vickie, I understand you know something about this,'
Palma said.

Saulnier was quick to check her expression of shock at
this second revelation, but her eyes betrayed a restrained
disbelief as she casually turned to Kittrie, who was
keeping her head ducked as she shook it, denying the
accusation. When Saulnier saw the girl was hiding something — Kittrie was embarrassingly transparent — she
quickly moved to shield her.

'Look,' Saulnier suddenly said to Palma. 'What is it
you want?'

'I want to know who the men were who were involved
with Dorothy in this kind of rough sex.' Palma addressed
her remarks to Kittrie, ignoring Saulnier's protective

intervention. 'I want to know who's wearing the leather hood.'

'No!' Kittrie yelled, her childish face as flinty as she could make it. 'No. Men? No!'

'I was told men *were* involved, Vickie.' Palma raised her voice, stretching the truth, wanting to stretch it more, but checking herself before she overplayed.

Kittrie did not start crying. The extra day had steadied her nerves, and perhaps her resolve. 'I don't care what you were told,' she raised her voice also. 'It was just ... the two of us ... something ... something she asked me to do. I went along.'

'What do you mean? Did you take the pictures?'

'No, but I mean that kind of thing. Dorothy was into that.'

'I can see that.' Palma didn't bother to keep the exasperation out of her voice. 'I want to know who the men were.'

'And I'm telling you there weren't any men.'

'Then who the hell is *this?*' Palma stabbed a finger at the hooded figure.

'I do-not-know.' Kittrie darted her eyes at the still off-balance Saulnier.

Palma stared at Kittrie. Dammit, she believed her. The girl's confusion, her own exasperation, was translating to Palma as a feeling of futility in the face of impossible demands. Palma believed her, but something told her she was approaching quicksand. No one spoke, and Helena Saulnier, stunned, curled up on her tapestry armchair and wrapped her sarong around both legs, sobered, with something to think about that she hadn't had to think about before. Reluctantly she took her eyes off Vickie Kittrie and turned to Palma.

'Look,' she said. 'This scares the hell out of me, but I can't bring myself to give you names. Let me talk to a few of these women ... I'll be honest with you. I don't think any of them are going to talk, to risk it. But let me do what I can.' She looked at the two photographs on the table. Let me talk to her,' indicating the unidentified woman posing with the mannequin.

'Take Sandra Moser's picture, too,' Palma said. 'We've got to know more about who she was seeing. You could be of great help to us.'

There was another silence. After the scene they just went through, Palma was dreading what she had to do next.

'There's one other thing,' she said. 'The crime lab has identified two other persons' hair in Dorothy's room and on her body.' Both women frowned at her, incredulous. Kittrie suddenly looked as if she was going to cry. 'Some of that hair may have come from the killer. There may be other hairs that turn up elsewhere in her bedroom as we continue to investigate,' Palma said, not hitting directly on the mark of truth. She looked at Kittrie. 'Since you were Dorothy's lover and had been in that room many times, we need to know which of those hairs might be yours. We need hair samples from you for comparison.'

'Jesus,' Saulnier said. She seemed on the point of protesting, and Palma was afraid she was going to object on Kittrie's behalf when the girl spoke up.

'That's fine,' she said. 'What do I do?'

Saulnier shook her head as if she couldn't believe Kittrie's foolishness.

'I have to have five head hairs from five different parts of your head,' Palma said. 'The front, the back, both sides, and the top. I have to have ten from the top area of your pubic hair, and ten from the hair around your vagina. The hair has to be plucked, not cut, and I have to witness that they came from you. I've got a package of small self-sealing plastic bags here, and I'll ID the source on each bag. We can go into the bathroom if you want.'

'I don't care,' Kittrie said. 'We'll do it here.'

While Saulnier helped Kittrie, and Palma witnessed the process and marked and sealed the plastic bags, Kittrie proceeded to pluck a total of twenty-five long ginger hairs from the various locations on her head. When she had finished that she stood, unbuttoned her shorts and stepped out of them, peeled off her pink panties, and sat back on the sofa. Bending her head she carefully plucked ten wiry hairs from high on her pubic bone, and then, more slowly, more carefully, she did the same from around her vagina. Palma held the small plastic bags for her as Kittrie dropped in the hairs one by one, and then Palma sealed the bags and marked them.

While Kittrie dressed, Palma finished marking the bags, wrapped them in a bundle with a rubber band, and put them in her purse. Then she picked up the photographs still lying on the gold tiles of the coffee table and returned them to the manila folder, leaving the picture of Sandra Moser. Picking up her purse and the envelope, she stood and looked at Kittrie, who was tucking her shirttail into her shorts.

'I appreciate your doing this,' Palma said. 'It'll help us a great deal.'

'I didn't mind.' Kittrie seemed no longer angry, but subdued. Palma wanted to say something else, but she wasn't quite sure what. The girl was such a strange mixture of innocence and deception that it was difficult to know exactly how to handle her.

Palma turned to Saulnier. 'Do you still have my card and home telephone number?' she asked.

Saulnier nodded, and Palma turned and started toward the entryway. Saulnier followed her around the large potted ficus where the entryway stepped down to the front door. Opening the door herself, she stepped outside, not looking at Saulnier. 'Don't wait too long to use it,' she said without looking back, and walked out of the courtyard past the frondy sago palms and the bright banks of snapdragons.

23

She sat in the swing with her mother and listened to the old woman catalog the recent horrors of the neighborhood, Cynthia Ortiz's middle boy had been arrested for the rape of a girl in Mayfair and they say he was crazy on cocaine, the Linares' youngest daughter is getting married and they say she is three months pregnant, Doris de Ajofín had left her husband and they say her boyfriend is a man of the *coca* trade in Cali, Rodrigo Ruiz has been arrested for the third time for fondling a little girl in Eastwood Park and they say this time he will go to the pen for it, Mariana Flandrau's hysterectomy was botched by her doctors and they say she is suing them for two million dollars, Juana de Cos's baby daughter, Lupita, has died and lies in the Capilla de Tristeza and they say if you bend a little over the casket you can still see the needle tracks on her arms. They say Lupita's boyfriend has tried to kill himself.

They say a lot of things in the barrio, and while Palma listened to the stories of lives surprised by misfortune and redirected by the vagaries of fate, she thought of Helena Saulnier and Vickie Kittrie, whose own lives turned in a world of coded names and double identities and sexual exotica as old as human nature. She thought of Saulnier's long, naked thighs, the dusky smoothness of them, and of how she knew that they were tender where they curved inward toward the dark triangle revealed by the gaping sarong, of how she was curious about Saulnier's motives but unoffended by the brazen sexual content of her actions. Palma herself had virtually no understanding of this kind of woman. When she had worked vice she had learned more than she had wanted to know about the other side of the gay women's world, the leather bars and dyke shops, a crude world of posturing harshness that seemed bitter and desperate and alien.

But Helena Saulnier represented something altogether different. It was not a surprise to Palma that a woman who wanted a woman wanted a woman. She knew that the sterotypical hard-driving dyke and the feminine women who loved them lived on the thin, brittle borders of the mainstream and were only a part of the total picture of female homosexuality, but the picture Saulnier presented of a more prevalent bisexual and lesbian presence in the lives of upper- and middle-class women was one to which Palma had never given much thought. And it irritated her that she had never even considered this hidden world. The bisexual husband and father who lived a double life — sometimes successfully, most of the time disastrously — had long ago emerged as a staple genus in the typology of modern social science. It was indicative, she thought, that even in this recognition of the facts of human sexuality — whether or not they were widely acceptable by popular mores — women had not yet come into their own. So long denied recognition and legitimacy in the more common roles of society, woman's place had not even been conceivable in those areas of the sexually recherché where, with ironic predictability, effeminate men had come into their own before women.

The afternoon heat was settling, and in the shady courtyard where the paths were bordered with lilac liriope and the fragrance of the Mexican broom's yellow blossoms sweetened the still, moist air, Palma listened to her mother gossip of the horrors of the barrio and thought of Vickie Kittrie, a capricious mix of innocence and guile who, in her own peculiar way, seemed to hide more potential perfidy than a woman twice her age. She thought of Vickie Kittrie unselfconsciously stepping out of her pink panties, the milky flesh of her inheritance so readily displayed, bending past her generous breasts, nipples as rose as her panties, to pluck the hairs from her strawberry crotch with locker room familiarity and the aplomb of a woman whose youth and genetics had given her a body that provided no cause for modesty.

And the women. Several dozen, and several dozen more. Women whose bliss was the smell and taste and touch of other women, who admired in another woman even the smallest details of their own form, desired them, and took them with as much passion and abandon — perhaps more, they might say — as they had spent in breeding sons and daughters. Hidden lives, double lives, all the more intriguing because they were not women of the verge, but women of the mainstream, and Palma had a hunch that if she were to walk into a room with these women she would feel as much at home as if she had known them, public and private, all her life.

With the sixth sense that adult children of the loquacious elderly quickly develop in self-defense of their own sanity, Palma's wandering mind quickly snapped back to the present moment. Her mother had stopped talking. She had taken a small white handkerchief from the baggy pocket of her gardening dress and was patting it over her forehead and neck.

'The real summer is here,' her mother said. 'No going back now. No more little cool days.' She waved the handkerchief around her face to stir the air.

Palma looked at the older woman's profile, and her mind overlaid the face she had remembered as a child. Her mother had not changed all that much, or maybe Palma simply wanted to believe she hadn't. It was a curious thing to see a parent aging. Her father had died too young for her to really see it happen to him, but to watch her mother enter old age, step by step, hour by hour, was a humbling thing. Life gradually was taking away what it had gradually given. It was the nature of things, but few people understood their tentative ownership of their gifts until they saw them being taken away from someone they loved. If you were lucky life allowed you that, a preview of the way it was going to be.

'Mama,' Palma said, still looking at her mother. 'Have you ever known any homosexual women?'

Her mother continued to flap her handkerchief with a delicate action of her wrist, showing no sign that she might regard the question as unusual or embarrassing or improper.

'Homosexual?' the old woman said, tilting her head back slightly and staring up into the mottled shade of the water oaks and pecans and catalpas. Palma knew she would take the question and the subject with equanimity. Her mother had never been a prude or pretended that life was anything other than what sensible people knew it to be.

'I've got this case,' Palma said, and instantly thought of her father. That was the way he always began his discussions with her mother. He had talked about the cases that troubled him more than any detective she had ever known. For him, Florencia was his lifeline to sanity. Palma remembered coming into the living room or onto the screened porch late at night and finding them talking, her mother combing her hair or sipping ice water and lime, her father with his shoes off, his shirttail out and his feet propped on a hassock or another chair talking to her, his voice coming solemnly, softly, from deep within his barrel chest. 'I've got this case,' he would begin the conversations, and Florencia would grow still and quiet as though she did not want to distract him, everything she was doing, or might have intended to do, was pushed into oblivion, wiped away, as she gave her total attention to his story.

'Two women were killed recently, and it happens that both of them were bisexual,' Palma said. 'One of the victims was married and had a family, two children. During the investigation I've come across a group of women like the victims, a kind of secret organization whose members lead double lives. Many, maybe most, are married, have families. Most of them are middle- to upper-class . . .'

Palma stopped. She didn't know what it was she expected her mother to tell her, and she didn't know where to take it from there. She couldn't outline the case. There was no point in it really. In fact, now she felt a little foolish for even broaching the subject, so far removed was it from her mother's life.

'There were, in 1968,' her mother said, 'several women living in two houses close together in the area — I forget the street — of Magnolia Park. They were there for some years, and then they left.'

'I mean,' Palma said, 'married women.'

Her mother stopped waving the handkerchief and wiped carefully under her eyes, pulling the skin back toward the temples as she must have been taught to do so long ago that she had forgotten it was something learned. She let her eyes fall from pondering the canopy of shadows to three Spanish doves milling around a shallow fountain near a bank of trumpet vines studded with reddish-orange blossoms.

'Two,' she said, dropping the handkerchief to her lap and giving the swing a little push with her bare feet against the stones. 'One is dead, and the other is too old to gossip about.'

'Here in the neighborhood?' Palma was surprised.

'Yes,' she nodded.

'Did you know them well?'

'Yes, very.' She watched the speckled doves with complete serenity. Her thoughts, Palma could tell, were traveling back in time, gathering memories before them like dark clouds before the wind, gathering strength for stories and rain.

'Lara Prieto and Christine Wolfe,' her mother said flatly.

Palma was shocked. Mrs. Prieto had been the wife of the neighborhood grocer, a woman of quiet, swarthy beauty who kept to herself and, outside of the store, had little to do with others in the community. Christine Wolfe was the barrio's guardian angel. The wife of a well-to-do businessman, she was a great organizer of church bazaars, charity benefits, and seasonal carnivals. She was the closest thing to a socialite the barrio could boast and though she had always lived there — as long as Palma could remember — and lived there still, she had too much money to be accepted on an equal footing with the rest of the women in the community. She was genuinely kind, and they were genuinely polite, but the money was an unbreachable barrier to genuine acceptance. There were many things that wealth could do and a few things it could not do.

'They were lovers?' Palma was incredulous. She could not imagine the two women as she remembered them in these strange new roles.

Palma's mother nodded slowly, thoughtfully. 'They were.'

'How did you know this?'

For a brief instant a flicker of discomfort passed across her mother's face.

'How? I saw them together.'

Palma was surprised by a melancholy note in her voice.

'You *saw* them?'

Her mother nodded. 'At the church of St. Anthony, in the vestry, during the saint's feast day. Years ago. You must have been eight or nine, I guess. Yes, at least. It was that long ago. You remember Lydia Saldano? I had promised her I would put new candles in the altar holders for her. She had called me the night before; her brother was dying in Victoria. It was in the afternoon.' Her mother paused and shook her head slowly, remembering.

'I left the festival grounds and walked across the lawn and through the trees to the church. I came in through a back door to the rooms behind the altar. It was empty, of course, and all the stained-glass windows were pushed open, and I could hear the sounds of the festival across the lawn. As I crossed toward the other side of the church I heard a sound, something scraped or dragged against the floor, and then I thought there were soft voices. It came from the vestry. I wasn't even thinking, my mind was on something else, I don't know what. I turned and went that way. When I came around the corner of the passageway — the vestry is out of the way, at the end of a passage by itself, you know — the door was open. I saw them suddenly. They never even heard my footsteps.'

She paused. She was watching the doves, the three of them pecking at invisible nothings around the damp margins of the fountain.

'I was astonished. You can imagine. They were completely naked, their dresses and underthings scattered on the floor. I was amazed to see this, frozen to the spot. I watched them,' her mother said matter-of-factly. 'Lara. Quiet, meek Lara, was very much in control of their lovemaking, and Christine ... well, she was the *niña*, I suppose. It was as if they had exchanged personalities. I could see it immediately and for some reason, I don't know why, that was as shocking to me as what they were doing. They were very passionate, very sensual and imaginative in the way they touched each other. I had never seen anything like it before.' She stopped, her eyes only incidentally on the speckled doves. 'I could hear them breathing, whispering and hissing in their passion. I could see the perspiration on their skin in the afternoon light that came through the high windows of the vestry.

'I will admit,' she said with a droll smile, her eyes still on the doves, 'I watched as long as I dared, until they had exhausted themselves. For me, this was truly a revelation. Not the kind, I am sure, that God would have chosen to occur in His church, but a revelation all the same.'

Palma was stunned. Her mother seemed to be remembering the event with such detail that Palma could not help but wonder how often she had thought of it in the ensuing years. And why.

'For weeks and weeks I could not get that encounter out of my mind,' her mother said. 'I would find myself thinking about it at all hours of the day and night. I never told anyone about seeing these women, not even your father. In some kind of odd way, by this accident of my arrival and my decision to watch, in secret, the great sadness of their passion, I felt that I had shared this with them and owed them the loyalty of my silence. These two women, I have thought about them over the years as I watched them continuing to live their lives, presenting their masks to the community, to their husbands, to their families. They must have suffered greatly, having to hide so much of themselves from the rest of the world. I know they continued their relationship until Lara died. One would not have noticed. But I knew because I watched them. Little things, you know, became significant. They were such different personalities that when they happened to be at the same place at the same time no one took any notice. But I did. I saw their eyes meet, a brush of their hands in passing. Several times over the years I actually saw them passing notes.'

Something stirred the dark plantains near the fountain and the doves flushed in a whir of whistling, beating wings. But they didn't go far, only to the higher reaches of the catalpas.

'How did you feel about that?' Palma asked, recovering from the surprise of hearing such a story from her mother.

'What, their lovemaking?'

'Yes, the homosexuality.'

The old woman shrugged. 'They call them "gay," I know. What irony.' She paused. 'What was I supposed to feel? Pity? Maybe, but not really, no more than I would feel for the star-crossed lovers of different sexes. Condemnation? The church says it is abominable, but I am sorry, what I saw was not abominable, even though I know that there is more to it than what I saw and so, perhaps, there is an abomination in something else.' She took her handkerchief again and wiped around her hairline. 'But I have to admit to a little prejudice, I guess, because the idea of two women making love has never offended me like the idea of two men. And when I actually saw it, I still was not offended. I don't know why that is. Maybe because I am a woman and can imagine a little more the complicated things that women feel, the small winding ways of their hearts. Over the years, I have given them a lot of thought, Lara and Christine. I do not condemn them. I gave up my license to do that along with my youthful wisdom. I don't even understand it. How can I condemn it?' She shook her head.

Palma looked at her mother. This was one story she could not possibly have anticipated. It never would have occurred to her that her mother had ever given a moment's thought to female homosexuality. She would have liked to have been in her mother's mind at this very moment. Palma could have asked her what she was thinking, but no one, not even a woman as candid as her mother, ever answered such a question with absolute honesty. After a few moments one of the doves returned to the fountain, followed shortly by a second.

Her mother turned to her. 'I will tell you something, Carmen, something it has taken me a long while to understand. A woman is human first ... and a woman second. This fact, I promise you, should not be forgotten.'

24

It was just past eight o'clock when she finished the articles that had arrived in the manila envelope from Sander Grant. She had been sitting at the dining room table with a pencil and pad, underlining passages and making notes as she sipped a glass of Soave. She had eaten a variety of cold salads she had picked up at Butera's deli on Montrose on the way home, and the paper cartons, plastic fork, and napkins she had used were still scattered around the table. And the telephone was there beside her, too, its cord pulled around the corner from the kitchen.

She stretched her shoulders, rounding them forward, twisting them to the left and then the right, and rolled her head from side to side. She wanted a cup of coffee, but she didn't want to go to the trouble of getting up and making it. She looked at the articles scattered in front of her, now heavily underlined and crowded with marginal notations. They were photocopies from a wide range of prestigious professional journals, *American Journal of Psychiatry, Journal of Interpersonal Violence, Medical Science and the Law, Journal of Clinical Psychology, New England Journal of Medicine, Journal of Forensic Sciences, Bulletin of the American Academy of Psychiatry and the Law,* and others. Sander Grant had written many of them and had co-authored most of the others. They were incredible documents, providing stunning insights into the psychology and behavior of sexual killers. Sander Grant, she decided, must have had his share of nightmares. She had just about decided he was going to wait and call her at the office in the morning when the telephone rang. She shoved aside the articles, picked up the receiver, shoved the dirty napkins even farther from her, and turned over a clean sheet on her notepad.

'Hello.'

'This is Sander Grant.'

'I'd almost given you up.'

'Sorry,' he said, sounding a little tired. 'We've been covered up with stuff. So how's it going down there? Have you gotten anything new that'll help us out?'

'Maybe. We learned today that Dorothy Samenov was bisexual, but predominately lesbian. She was very secretive about it. Vickie Kittrie, the girl who found her, was her lover. Samenov had been married, but divorced for about six years. But she still dated a number of men until about a year ago when she went strictly lesbian.'

'What about Moser?'

'Not as far as we can determine at this point, but we're still looking into it. The only thing that connects them so far is the S&M paraphernalia and the fact that Moser's husband was employed at a company that bought computer programs from Samenov.'

'Okay,' Grant said. 'Let me tell you what I see here, and then we'll come back and pick up on this. You read the articles?'

'Yes.'

'Okay. I want to emphasize that for right now I'm going to be talking in generalities, but maybe there'll be something here you can build on, give you some direction.' Without waiting for a comment, he went right into his assessment.

'At first glance, both victims in these two cases seem to be in the low-risk category: Moser, an upper-middle-class housewife and mother, active in community services and attentive to her familial responsibilities; and Samenov, an upper-middle-class professional woman who doesn't hit the singles bars and dates with moderate frequency. Both lived in low-crime areas; both were killed in low-crime areas. Now, the bisexual angle seems to throw a kink in our effort to classify them as low-risk victims, but I'm not sure it does. Statistically, bisexual women are a low-risk group — certainly in comparison to their male counterparts — and especially if they don't frequent the lesbian bar scenes. Okay, that's at first glance. However, when we add to this assessment the presence of sadomasochist paraphernalia found in the residences of both victims, the picture changes. Their possession of that paraphernalia automatically puts them into a higher-risk bracket. This is necessary even though we don't understand how this paraphernalia might have been used, that is, autoerotically, or for the purpose of enhancing innocuous fantasies during sexual play with a partner, or for actual pain-inflicting activities. If either woman used them for the former two reasons, then we can probably put her back in the low-risk category. But if the latter is the case, she's higher risk because to some degree she's leading a double life and her "other" life moves in a high-risk environment.'

There was a slight pause, and Palma thought she heard Grant drink something.

'Normally,' he continued, 'we identify a serial murderer as someone who's involved in three or more separate homicides with a cooling-off period in between. The cooling-off period can be days, weeks, or months. Even though you have only two homicides here, I think we can justifiably anticipate a serial killer because of the distinct behavior. It's highly unlikely that these cases would be unrelated. And they demonstrate the kinds of behavior that we've come to understand are the characteristics of a sexual serial killer. This man doesn't kill because he's involved in a criminal enterprise; he doesn't kill for selfish or cause-specific reasons such as a family dispute, or self-defense, to steal drugs or whatever. He kills for sexual reasons, reasons that have meaning only for him.

'The offender risk in both these cases was moderate to low. Moser, in a private hotel room with no danger of interruption for hours; Samenov, in a private home with no other family members and no immediate danger of interruption.

'Both victims were killed approximately between eight o'clock and ten o'clock in the evening. The murderer had plenty of time to act out whatever fantasy he found necessary for satisfaction, and yet he was not at the scene long enough to run any great risk of discovery — under the circumstances.'

Grant paused for another drink. 'This's hot tea,' he suddenly explained, 'not scotch. Maybe I'll do scotch later,' he kind of laughed. 'Are you with me? I'm barreling right on through it, so pull me up if you want.'

'No, everything's fine. I'm taking notes.' Grant's unexpected aside about the tea and scotch, and his solicitous question about rushing her, took her by surprise. His demeanor up until then had been polite but businesslike, which had already influenced her mental image of him. Now that image softened. It was good to hear that tone of concern in a male voice again; it had been a while. She wanted to reciprocate the kindness, but she was too slow, too long out of the habit, and he was filling the silence before she could speak.

'Okay. Now, as for crime scene scenarios I'm largely baffled,' Grant continued. 'And the major sticking point is not knowing whether Moser was also a closet bisexual. All we *know* so far is that she was heterosexual. If we knew for sure, either way, we could begin building on that as a reflection of something about the killer's personality. But as it stands, we don't know whether it was a fluke — from the offender's point of view — that Samenov happened to be bisexual, or whether this offender is specifically targeting bisexual women. It would make a tremendous difference in constructing his personality if we knew. So, rather than offer you something misleading on this score, I'm going to bypass reconstructing the crime scene scenario. I just don't believe I know enough to do it.

'However, I do see enough here to know you're dealing with an "organized" murderer rather than a "disorganized" murderer, though you have to keep in mind that even though our profiling techniques have identified and categorized sexual killers into these two general classes, in reality the crime scenes are often a mixture of the two characteristics. Still, these killings demonstrate a predominantly "organized" murderer at work.

'Let's go down the checklist of the crime scenes of organized murderers.'

Palma scrambled through her articles to find the section on the distinguishing characteristics of organized and disorganized murderers. There were behavioral characteristics and crime scene characteristics, and she wanted to have them for reference while Grant was reviewing them.

'The killings are planned.' Grant began ticking them off. 'Moser acted according to a prearrangement, checking into the hotel under an assumed name. In both cases the offender brought his own ligatures, and his own cutting instrument, and his own makeup. He knew what he was going to be doing and what he'd need to do it.

'There was no weapon or any physical evidence left by the killer at the crime scenes. Nothing overlooked in haste, none of the ligatures or cutting instruments inadvertently mislaid.

'The killer personalized his victims: both women were near the same age and blond. Both were made up in a specific way. Have you compared the photographs of the two women?'

'Yes, I did,' Palma said.

'What'd you see?'

'The same shade of eye makeup on each, the same hairstyle. The rouge was the same.'

'Exactly the same,' Grant said. 'The *way* he used the makeup was exactly the same. Same style arch to the eyebrows, the same dip to the center of the upper lip when he used the lipstick ... he even did that on

Samenov, though her lips didn't actually follow that configuration. It was almost as if he had painted a face on her. It seems that these women in their natural state — before he touches them — have to conform to a particular "type." But beyond that, after he has completely overpowered them, he "perfects" a preconceived mental image of what he wants them to look like by using makeup.

'The killer controls the situation. Both women *allowed* themselves to be tied by their wrists and ankles. They were beaten after being immobilized, not before. The crime scene reflects overall control by the killer, including the use of ligatures. The folded clothes, the meticulous cleanup. Incidentally, often when a detective sees this sort of "maintenance" at a crime they think ... ex-con. He's cleaning up after himself, covering his tracks. But in sexual homicides you have to consider that much of this may be something compulsive in his behavior that has nothing at all to do with being street smart. He may be doing it to satisfy an *inner* need.

'The killer initiates aggressive acts while the victim is still alive. In these two cases the facial beatings, the vaginal bruising and abrasions, the bite marks, all inflicted while the victim was alive. But in each of your cases there's one exception. The autopsy shows that Moser's nipple was cut off postmortem, probably because this was his first killing and he hadn't perfected his procedure. Also — you don't have the photographs in front of you now, do you?'

'No.'

'Well, I'm looking at my copies and you can see hesitancy cuts, almost scratches, around the nipple — an indication that he was new at it. Sometimes, even with a guy like this, the first time you cut up a human body is a little unnerving. But with these guys, it's usually only the first few moments, from them on they take to it like a duck to water. In fact, this guy conforms to the true character traits of organized killers when he gets to Samenov. He mutilates her *before* she is dead, having to gag her to muffle her screams. Except for the eyelids. Those were removed after death only because he couldn't keep her head still enough to do it before she was dead, and it was important to him *not* to do a messy job of it.'

Grant paused, but it was only for emphasis. Palma quickly adjusted the telephone she was holding between the side of her chin and her raised shoulder. She was frowning. '... he couldn't keep her head still enough to do it before she was dead ... important to him not to do a messy job of it ...' How the hell could Grant make these kinds of statements?

'Fantasy and ritual are paramount for the organized offender,' Grant went on. 'This is very important to remember because it's a window into the guy's mind. There's evidence of it everywhere, both victims are blond, the use of certain kinds of ligatures which he must provide himself, the use of a particular kind of makeup which he must provide himself, and the specific manner of application, the specific funereal positioning of the body, and the removal of the eyelids, which is a far more significant amputation than the removal of the nipples. This guy has a specific fantasy. And watch carefully on the next one: you're likely to see something new with the next victim, something additional as he tries to "perfect" his fantasy.

'Now we come to a couple of anomalies. First: usually an organized murderer will hide the body. He does *not* want it to be discovered, as the disorganized murderer often does. To do this it's usually necessary to transport the body, and of course it wasn't done in either of these cases. Second: often organized killers don't know their victims even though they may have watched or stalked them for hours, or even days, prior to killing them. Their victims are targeted strangers. But in these cases there's every indication that this killer knew both women. Moser checked into a hotel to be with him. Samenov apparently let him into her house. They were *not* strangers to him.'

Grant paused for another sip of tea, for which Palma was grateful. She had been jotting notes as furiously as possible and her finger was aching after having filled several pages in her notepad with wild, hasty hand-writing and a puzzle of arrows, boxes, underlined phrases, exclamation marks, and circled words. Grant was spilling a wealth of information.

'So who are you looking for?' Grant was off again. He was relentless. 'In general, experience tells us that sexual homicides are the exclusive domain of males. There have never been any female sexual killers. All other kinds, yes, but no *sexually motivated* female killers. So we eliminate half the population right away. Crimes of this nature are overwhelmingly intraracial. Not always, but mostly. So, until we know more, we can consider that we're dealing with a white male.

'He's a man of above-average intelligence, socially and sexually competent. He'll be employed in a skilled profession, not a laborer. He'll have a high birth order, the first or second child in a family. He will have used alcohol during the crimes and will have suffered some precipitating situational stress: a divorce, job loss, some emotional trauma that pushed him too far. More than likely he'll be living with a partner and will have good mobility, a car of his own. He will follow his crimes in the news media and may even try to interject himself into the investigation by being a helpful witness, a volunteer of some insignificant information. Also, if you find this guy's home you may find newspaper clippings of the crimes. You may also discover that he's taken a personal souvenir from the victims or their homes — some piece of jewelry or clothing, or even pieces of their bodies.'

Grant heaved a big sigh, and Palma heard the chink of the teacup.

'Questions,' he said.

Jesus, she thought. 'No, everything's perfectly clear.'

There was a pause for a couple of beats and then Grant laughed, an easy laugh that had no urgency about it. 'Okay,' he said. 'I guess I could ease off a little.'

'There's a lot to absorb,' Palma said. 'Two questions. First. What piece of information would help you more than anything else at this point?'

'To know if Sandra Moser was bisexual,' Grant answered. 'That would tell us worlds about the offender. It's such a key attribute. Oddly, in profiling sexual homicides, the more bizarre behavior exhibited at the scene, or in the circumstances surrounding it, the easier it makes our job. Anomalies are always more informative to us than conformities because they're revealing. They're personality markers just as phenotypes are blood markers. And remember, always: behavior reflects personality. What he does is how he thinks.'

'What's the best advice you can give me at this point?' Palma asked, rubbing her eyes.

'Try to crawl inside the guy's mind,' Grant said without hesitation. 'Everything you do, every piece of information you seek or get, every person you interview, every question you ask, should be done for this one purpose. When you're able to start thinking like he thinks, when you can anticipate him, then you've got him, and solved a part of your problem.'

'What? "Part" of my problem?'

'Oh, inside joke,' he said, sounding as if he was going to explain a slip of the tongue. 'If you don't start thinking like him, you've got a problem. If you do start thinking like him, you've still got a problem, only it's a problem of a different sort.'

That was it. Palma didn't say anything. It wasn't much of a joke, and then she realized that was the point of it.

Grant picked up the slack. 'It's not a nice thing, trying to worm your way inside these minds. It's no good. And ... I don't know ... maybe for you, being a woman, it'll be even more painful because of the victims. Or it could be a great advantage. I guess a lot depends on your own personality.'

Her personality? She heard the teacup again, and then Grant said, 'The Bureau doesn't have any women analysts in this unit, although there are a couple who've been through our Fellowship program. The thing is, sexual homicide is a distinctly male activity, and with the exception of homosexual killings, the victims are always women or children. Men against women, men against children, men against everyone, even each other.' He seemed to have grown thoughtful. 'You try to figure that out, and it drives you crazy.'

'How long have you been doing this?' she asked.

'Years,' he said vaguely, though Palma didn't get the impression he was trying to be obscure. The word seemed, rather, to have other connotations for him. 'Look,' he said, smoothly changing the direction of the conversation, 'I'm going to give you my home telephone number. You have my others?'

'Yes.'

'Okay. I'd like you to use this only when there's another killing, but I want you definitely to use it then, immediately. I'm going to want to know if there are any significant changes in patterns in the next one.'

To Palma he sounded as if he had no doubts that there would be others. He gave her the number and she wrote it down, circling it several times. He went on to say something about several days in the following week when he was scheduled to be out of the office, and as Palma listened to him she wondered what he looked like, guessing from his voice that he could be in his middle forties. She wanted to ask him personal questions: Was he married, did he have a family, did he like his job, where had he grown up, how long had he been with the FBI? But she imagined the very hint of such conversation would mean the end of the telephone call, and she didn't want him to get off the line.

'You mentioned the anomalies,' she said quickly. 'He doesn't hide the body; he doesn't transport the body; his victims seem to be people he knows and who know him. How am I suppose to interpret these? How am I supposed to use them?'

'Good question,' Grant's voice was flat. 'Those are serious points, especially the latter one. For a sexual serial killer to know his victims is really quite extraordinary, and therefore it may be the key to this whole thing. I think you've already done the right thing by checking out the men's names in Samenov's address book. It's a good way to start.'

'But ...' Palma anticipated him.

'But I don't think you'll find him among the "general" service employments,' Grant said. 'That is, TV repairmen, plumbers, electrical repairmen. I mean, how logical is it to assume that any group of people — in this case a loosely organized group of bisexual women, if that becomes a valid category for consideration — would use the same TV repairman or plumber? I don't use the same plumber as the other guys in my office. We live in different neighborhoods, for one thing. And if we did recommend plumbers to each other, we'd most likely recommend the same plumbing *company* rather than any one particular employee within that company. I'm thinking that in order for this approach to be valuable to you, you have to look at men whose employment or relative position to the victims has something to do with their bisexuality. The hairdresser, maybe. Do any of the other women own Dalmatians? Does the masseur have a bisexual clientele? You see, the connection must be specifically bisexual — or strictly lesbian — not generic.'

'And if the bisexual angle isn't valid?' Palma asked.

'If it's a fluke,' Grant said, 'then you've got a long investigation on your hands. And the next best chance at getting a breakthrough will be the kind that comes at a high price.'

'Another body.'

'That's it. We need to see the guy do it again.'

25

Palma put the telephone receiver on its cradle and looked at the scribble-filled pages of her notepad scattered around her on the table along with the wadded napkins and empty take-out cartons from Butera's and the underlined articles Grant had sent her. There was a little Soave in her glass and she picked it up and sat back in her chair. Her shoulders had tightened again while she had been taking notes and talking to Grant, and she recognized the beginnings of a first-rate tension headache if she didn't get her muscles to relax. She could take one of the muscle relaxants her doctor had prescribed, but she liked to think she could control these things herself. Or she could begin her own remedy, a warm shower with the water massager pounding on her neck and shoulders followed by stretching exercises on the carpet of the living room floor. But right now she didn't want to take the time that that required. She opted for a third 'cure': the wine. If she drank enough, it would knock her out like Dramamine.

She got up from the dining room table, went into the kitchen, took the green bottle from the refrigerator, and poured another full glass of the white wine. She put the bottle back, closed the door, and sipped it steadily, standing in the middle of the kitchen with the flat of her hand on the back of her hip. She thought about Sander Grant. Actually, she first thought about the articles he had written, and then she thought about the way his voice had sounded over the telephone. It had been unhurried and chesty, for some reason suggesting to her a large man, unflappable, and comfortable in his knowledge of his subject. He had chosen a grisly career for himself, and she wondered how he managed to live with it.

His particular expertise set him apart from the average homicide detective. Palma didn't know how many of the murderers she had dealt with were 'sane' men, but it was the vast majority. Only a few could be considered 'insane' by the Texas Penal Code's definition: men, who at the time of the conduct charged, as a result of mental disease or defect, either did not know that their conduct was wrong or were incapable of conforming their conduct to the requirements of the law. But she guessed that Grant's investigations involved offenders of an inverse ratio in these categories. Sexual murderers, especially those guilty of serial crimes, were often defended with the insanity plea. It was almost as if society found it inconceivable that men of sound mind could commit such atrocities. And indeed, all the true crazies she had seen over the years had been sexual killers or mass murderers. To investigate only these kinds of crimes, to spend your days and nights trying to 'crawl inside the minds' of these men, had to be extraordinarily stressful.

She looked at her watch. It was nine-twenty. She drank some more wine and walked into the dining room and started clearing off the table. She took the telephone back into the kitchen and then returned to the dining room and started gathering up the empty paper containers from the deli. After she had wiped off the table and loaded the dishwasher, she gathered up the journal articles along with the scribbled pages she had ripped out of her notebook. Cradling these under one arm, she went back into the kitchen where she refilled her wineglass. As she left she turned off the light, did the same in the other downstairs rooms, checked the lock on the front door, and went upstairs to her bedroom.

Setting the wineglass on a bedside table, she tossed

the articles and pages on the bed and took off her dress. Opening the closet door, she caught her naked reflection in the full-length mirror on the inside of the door. After her telephone conversation with Grant, she had no inclination to dwell on her figure. Too many other images intruded, and it was too easy to exchange her own face for Samenov's. It was already weird, but it could get out of hand if she dwelt on it; she had to force her mind elsewhere.

She slipped on a white silk pajama top and got into bed, propped both pillows behind her, got a pencil from the bedside table, and started recopying her notes, occasionally sipping the wine and turning to references in the articles scattered around her on the sheets.

At ten-fifteen she went back downstairs for a third glass of wine. Climbing back up in the dark with the oblique light from her bedroom backlighting the balusters, she was aware that she was taking the stairs more slowly, beginning to feel the effects of the Soave. She was glad, but she wasn't sleepy. The grim nature of the articles, and her conversation with Grant had given her too much to think about.

She rounded the top of the stairs and went back to bed, again putting the wineglass on the bedside table. She fluffed the pillows again and lay back on them, shoving the papers and articles aside. Then she realized she was hot. The wine did that to her sometimes. She unbuttoned her pajama top and slipped it off, reached for the wine and took a mouthful and swallowed it, took another mouthful, and set down the glass.

The killings were planned.

Absence of a weapon at the crime scene.

The victim is known to the killer.

He personalizes his victim.

He controls the situation.

Mutilates while victim is still alive.

Her head was lifting now, floating. The pillows cradled her aching neck and enhanced the sensation of weightlessness.

Fantasy and ritual are paramount to the killer.
He is of above-average intelligence.
He will have suffered some kind of precipitating stress.
He will most likely be living with a partner.
May try to interject himself into the investigation.
He is likely to have taken a souvenir . . . a body part.
What he does is how he thinks.
Behavior reflects personality.
Crawl inside his mind.

Her mother was sitting in the swing alone, looking straight ahead and talking. The swing was making regular mechanical sweeps without any effort on her mother's part, almost as if it was one of those wind-up cradle swings for infants. Her mother looked small, even child-like herself in the large swing, the hem of her shabby little gardening dress wafting back and forth in the breeze. The thing was, her mother was saying — though no one was around to listen to her — that in Huehuetenango someone was killing all the nuns. Celeste was having to clean up all the bodies, take their temperature. You didn't know they were dead until the red mercury in the thermometer — which had to go in their vaginas — turned blue. They say it happened very suddenly. It was red and then suddenly it was blue and they were dead. Just like that. Celeste dressed each of the dead nuns in a crisp, yellow habit with yellow wimples and then she took them to the top of a mountain to a tiny meadow surrounded by harsh crags and laid them beside the other dead nuns. There were four now. Celeste sang over them as they lay on stone biers, mist curling up over the crags, Celeste's voice echoing over the jungle valleys. Then her mother said she knew who the man was who was killing the nuns. She said she knew because she had crawled inside his mind and rode in there with him to the killings. And then Palma was standing in the doorway of a tiny nun's cell made of damp stones and she was watching the man kill the nun. He was nude, crouching over the sister who was nude also, except for her wimple. Her eyes were open and she was staring placidly up to the dark ceiling

while the man, his spine curved so that Palma could see
the ripples of his vertebrae, made snuffling noises in her
stomach. Palma wanted to see what he was doing, but his
pale back and buttocks blocked her view. Then Palma
noticed the little body of her mother facing away from her
in the back of the man's head. The man's snuffling grew
louder and Palma could see the nun's naked legs moving,
waggling from his efforts. Then the nun turned and
looked at Palma with a faint sweet smile and the little
figure of her mother in the man's head turned too. She
told Palma that the man would be through shortly and
did Palma notice the man's hips. Palma looked at them
again and they were a woman's hips, but a man's back
and shoulders. The thing was, her mother said, that
women were human first and women second, and men
were human first, too. Then blood started splattering on
the wall behind the nun, splattering from whatever it was
the man was doing, and the nun turned her face back to
the ceiling to wait until he was through. The little figure
of Palma's mother produced a thermometer from her
gardening dress and held it high as if offering it to Palma
and it was so small Palma could barely make it out. Then
her mother started screaming. Her mouth was a tiny
black hole and she was screaming ... screaming ...
screaming ...

When Palma realized it was the telephone, she flailed
at the sound of it and knocked over the wineglass. It was
empty; she didn't remember drinking the rest of it. Her
alarm clock said one-forty. She was sweating, and she felt
slightly nauseous as she grappled with the receiver.

'Hello.' She had rolled over on the papers, her breasts
wrinkling the pages against the sheets. Had she said
hello? She repeated it. 'Hello.'

'Is this Detective Palma?' It was a woman's voice.

'Yes, this is Palma.' What a goddamned dream. Son of
a bitch. She wanted to be sick.

'My name is Claire. I'm the woman in the pictures you
found in Dorothy's condo.' There was a pause as if the
woman expected a reaction. Before Palma could put

anything together, the woman added, 'I'd like to talk to you.'

'Yes,' Palma said. Her mouth wasn't working very well. 'When?'

'Now's the best time.'

'Right now?' Jesus, she thought, of course. 'Fine. Where?'

'At the medical center. Do you know the Baylor College of Medicine?'

'Yes.'

'And the DeBakey Center?'

'Yes.'

'There are trees along Bertner Street there and bus-stop kiosks . . . no, wait. Do you know where the mall is behind the University of Texas Medical School?'

'Yes.'

'I'll be on one of the benches there. We'll find each other.'

'You'll have to give me twenty minutes.'

'That'll be fine.'

The line went dead.

Palma put down the telephone and steadied herself. She crawled over the papers to the edge of the bed and sat with her feet on the floor. Jesus Christ. The goddamned dream. What had brought that on? She hated having that kind of dream, that kind of sick lunacy. She didn't like knowing something like that could come out of her head. She stood unsteadily and lurched to the bathroom. Running cold water, she splashed her face, grabbed a towel, and hurried back into the bedroom, dropped the damp towel on the floor in front of the closet, and grabbed a beige and white striped chambray shirtdress off its hanger. Throwing the dress on the bed, she took panties and a bra out of her dresser and slipped into them, then pulled on the dress. She didn't give a thought to panty hose as she stepped into a pair of woven Mexican sandals and buckled a beige belt around her waist. She ran a brush through her hair, grabbed her purse from the chair by the door, and turned and opened the drawer to the bedside table. She took out her SIG-Sauer, checked the clip, and put it into her purse.

Leaving the light on in her bedroom, she hurried down the stairs, fishing for her keys in the bottom of her purse. By the time she got to the front door she had found them, left the light on at the bottom of the stairs, and stepped out into the damp early-morning darkness. A light fog had moved in during the last several hours.

She switched on the Audi's headlights and pushed the car through the tree-lined neighborhood streets to University Boulevard and turned left. Within moments she was passing the stadium on the western edge of the Rice University campus, and then the Cameron baseball field and the track stadium. At Main the university campus ended and the 525-acre campus of the Texas Medical Center began, its hospital complexes, research laboratories, and medical schools forming its own city of a quarter of a million inhabitants, its lights spreading out in high banks to the left and right, shimmering and disappearing into the fog. Crossing Main, Palma doubled back on Fannin a few blocks and turned right into Ross Sterling Avenue, which became a passageway through the University of Texas Medical School, and then came into the open again adjacent to the mall.

Palma scanned the sprawling compound lighted here and there with the smoky glow of mercury vapor lamps and scattered with the serrated shadows of heavy trees. It was two o'clock by the dial on her dash, and Palma didn't want to take the time to drive over to the nearest of the center's parking lots. She began hunting for a service drive or a staff lot, found one near the Jones Library on the other side of the mall, and turned in.

She walked around the library to the mall and paused on its south end, looking toward the rear door of the medical school. The granite pavers were glistening with the damp and Palma wished she had brought a raincoat. No one was sitting on the benches that were easily visible, and the fog was restricting her depth of vision into the shadows. All she could do was walk across the

mall and hope the woman would see her. The rear door of
the school opened and a solitary, white-coated figure
emerged from the lighted foyer and started across the far
end of the mall with a backpack slung over one shoulder.
It was a girl; a student. Time was all the same to them,
only sometimes you needed lights to see and sometimes
you didn't.

Palma was moving toward the center of the mall,
listening to the precise fall of her own footsteps, when
someone spoke from a cluster of live oaks in a cloverleaf
of sidewalks.

'Detective Palma.'

She stopped and looked toward the trees, making out a
wood-framed kiosk with Plexiglas walls, and then a single
figure on the bench inside. She turned and made her way
to the slight rise of landscaping and approached the
kiosk.

'It's dry in here, at least,' the woman said. 'I'm Claire,'
the woman said, extending her hand from where she was
sitting.

Palma shook it, straining to see the woman's face as
the woman leaned back against the corner of the kiosk at
one end of the laminated wood bench. Palma respected
the subtle message and sat at the opposite end of the
bench.

'I'm sorry you had to come out at this hour,' Claire
said. 'And the fog. But I'm afraid it's the only time I could
do this.'

'It's fine,' Palma said. 'I'm glad you called.' She ran a
hand through her hair and felt the dampness. The spillover from the mercury vapor lamp seventy-five yards
away filtered through the trees and the scarred Plexiglas,
creating a feeble light mottled with thin shadows that fell
across the woman's face like a veil. But Palma's eyes
adjusted, and she recognized her from the photographs.
She must have been in her late forties, with black hair
and a sharp nose that gave a girlish effect to her features
that should have long since faded. She was dressed in
business clothes, complete with makeup and small

jewelry, which made Palma guess that she was on night duty somewhere in the medical complex and had not dressed just for this meeting. Palma also noticed she was wearing a wedding ring.

'Helena called me' Claire said. She crossed her legs at the knee and turned on the bench to face Palma. 'I understand there were pictures of me.'

'Yes.'

'I didn't know they were still around.' The remark was meant to be careless, but there was an underlying note of tension.

'Did Helena Saulnier tell you about our conversations?'

'Yes. I don't know, I guess she told me everything.'

Palma nodded. Claire — Palma did not believe it was her real name — reached into her purse and took out a pack of cigarettes. She took one without offering any to Palma, lighted it with a small lighter that provided too little flame to illuminate her face, and blew a plume of smoke out to mingle with the mist. Though one leg was crossed over the other, she did not swing it nervously as most women would do in such a situation. She seemed very much in control of herself, and in no hurry to get on with the interview.

'Why did you call me?' Palma finally asked.

The woman continued to look at her for a moment, and Palma suddenly thought that perhaps she wasn't so confident after all.

'I thought I might be able to help you,' the woman said.

'In what way?'

'I knew Sandra Moser. I think ... perhaps I was the last one of ... our group ... to be with her before she died.'

26

Claire didn't go on. She pulled on the cigarette, a highly polished fingernail catching a sharp glint of light.

'Then she was a lesbian?'

'Bisexual.' Claire corrected her. 'Most of us are bisexual.'

'When did you see her last?'

Claire again hesitated, her eyes on Palma from the lacy shadows, her knee supporting the hand with the cigarette, a powder blue ribbon of smoke rising from its embered tip.

Palma looked at her and realized what was happening.

'I can't give you the pictures,' she said. 'They're evidence in a homicide. It's out of the question.'

Claire turned her head away and looked through the Plexiglas at the wet paving stones of the courtyard. She seemed to be collecting her composure. She pulled on the cigarette again. 'Those were a lark,' she said. 'I knew it was a mistake at the time. It's my own fault. I should never have let her talk me into it.'

'Dorothy?'

'Vickie, dammit.'

'Kittrie?'

Claire nodded; the bitterness showed in the tense way she held herself and in the tone with which she had spoken Vickie's name.

'Why did she want you to do it?'

Claire didn't answer immediately, seeming to consider how she should frame her response. 'Dorothy always had a special affection for me. A few years ago we'd been lovers, but Dorothy wanted it to be permanent. She knew I couldn't — wouldn't — do that. I had my family, my career. It even went against the philosophy of what this group is all about. It wasn't meant to break up families and wreck lives. But she wouldn't give it up, became possessive. I finally had to break it off completely. And she adjusted to that; she understood. But she never really let go. She would ask the others how I was doing, was I happy, who was I seeing. Things like that.' She shrugged.

'Then, after Dorothy and Vickie's relationship developed, I felt like there was no danger of Dorothy's becoming preoccupied with me again. I stopped avoiding them. I got to know Vickie. She was okay, but I thought she was a little strange, which proved to be true. One night I showed up at a party at a woman's home in Tanglewood. Vickie was there, but Dorothy was out of town. After too many drinks and most of the people had left, Vickie cornered me, started telling me how Dorothy still wanted me, how she talked about me. She talked me into posing for the pictures with the mannequin, something to spice up their lovemaking, she said. I was just drunk enough ... maybe even just a little turned on to Vickie, to do it. The sado theme was her idea, of course.'

'When were the pictures taken?'

'About six, no, seven months ago, just when Vickie started getting Dorothy into this sadomasochist stuff.'

'Vickie? I thought Dorothy was the one who started that.'

Claire smirked. 'Vickie told you that, huh?'

Palma nodded.

'Let me tell you something,' Claire said, tossing her cigarette out into the mist and exhaling smoke toward the open front of the kiosk. 'That little girl is trouble. Her sexual instincts are as warped as any I've ever seen. I don't know what they do to them in those East Texas piney woods, but that girl is spooky.'

'What do you mean?'

'She had very particular tastes.' Clare said. 'Like most of us she liked men also, but she only wanted to do S&M with them. But she always topped with men, and bottomed with women.' She looked at Palma. 'You know about S&M?'

Palma knew enough to know she never knew enough. While she was working in vice she thought she had learned just about everything there was to know about sexual deviancy. And then she went to homicide. A murderer's passions were often closely linked to their sexuality, and sometimes they weren't even conscious of this until they killed. Somehow, in the deepest fissures of the psyche, it was all tied together by dark flowing estuaries, but no one really understood it. The fact that there was an indisputable relationship seemed an awesome enough discovery.

'I know the top is the aggressor and the bottom is the victim,' Palma said. She would leave it at that. Every time she heard someone "explain" these things, she learned everyone understood a different truth.

'In the "play,"' Claire said. 'Right. That's the scenario. But in reality, the bottom calls the shots, the whole scene is for them, for their gratification. The terminology,' she added parenthetically, 'lacks grace, but most of this language comes from a butchy crowd — grace isn't their strong suit. Anyway, the top has simply agreed to play a role and do the bottom's bidding. If you do it right, all of this is agreed on beforehand. The bottom tells the top what she wants done to her — whether it's whipping, cutting, hot wax, choking, the fist, water, whatever — and she outlines the progression of events leading up to the finale. And she establishes a safe word. Essentially the whole drama is orchestrated for her satisfaction. But at the same time, the top derives pleasure from giving the bottom what she wants. Ideally, the pleasure makes a full circle. Though there are some women who will only top, and some who will only bottom, most will easily switch roles in order to accommodate a partner.

'The crucial point of all this, however, is trusting your top. If you don't trust the woman's judgment, then you're crazy to let her tie you up and crawl on top of you with a razor. The top has got to be in control of her own emotions during all this. The risk is that the "punishment" can go too far. So they establish a "safe word" so the top can tell where the bottom's fantasy stops and reality begins once they start role-playing. The top starts the punishment and after a while the bottom is beginning *not* to be treated, the way she really *wants* to be treated, pretending that it's all "against her will" while all the time she's loving it. No matter how much the bottom begs for it to stop, the top is supposed to go right on with it until the bottom either achieves the level of pleasure that she's looking for, or she uses the safe word to signal that it's getting out of hand, going too far for her.'

Palma watched her as Claire leaned forward to dig in her purse for another cigarette and then sat back in the shadow of the corner again. Her movements were graceful, thoroughly feminine, and Palma remembered Helena Saulnier's remark that a woman who wanted a woman wanted a woman.

'Vickie was okay with women,' Claire continued. 'Because she was always the bottom. But when she was with men she couldn't be trusted.'

'Meaning?'

'Meaning that she could be lethal.'

'Do you know any of the men she topped with?'

'You've already talked to one of them, Gil Reynolds.' Palma felt her face flush. The bastard. He had rolled over like a spaniel to get her sympathy and then told her he thought men might have been involved with Kittrie and Samenov. Did he really believe she wouldn't catch him out? Or was he that contemptuous of her? 'Another one was Walker Bristol. Vickie almost killed him, the poor devil. He told me after she'd almost let him bleed to death that she was topping on anger, that she just went berserk with him. Walker has a tendency toward histrionics. He said she had a worm eating away inside her, and it made her mean as hell. I thought that was an ironically Freudian reference. Walker really hated her after that.'

'If Kittrie only tops with men, then Reynolds must have been on the receiving end also.'

'Yeah, well, psychosexually, Gil is a cretin,' Claire said. 'Did you know he was a sniper in Vietnam? He told Vickie once ... he told her that he had orgasms when he saw the heads explode through his scope. That tells you about Reynolds. I think the reason Vickie never went too far with him like she did with Bristol was because she was afraid if Reynolds ever got loose he'd kill her. They have an *un*healthy mutual respect for each other. Sometimes ... sometimes I think they're more alike than any two people I've ever known in this crazy world.'

'In what way?'

Claire inhaled deeply of her cigarette and held it. She looked at Palma. 'They're amoral,' she said slowly, and the two words oozed out of her mouth on a long snake of smoke.

If she had meant the response to be an eerie one, she succeeded. Palma now saw Reynolds's spurious humility as poisonously cynical; in retrospect it seemed especially depraved.

'Do you know if Bristol or Reynolds ever switched the roles so that they were the punishers?'

'Yeah. Reynolds. That's his natural bent. I think he only let Kittrie whip him so he could get her naked. She wouldn't touch him otherwise.'

'Do you know any of the women he punished?'

Claire waited a moment before responding, and for an instant Palma thought she might refuse to answer. Then she said, 'I don't know. You'll have to get that from someone else. Even my rumors are third-rate on that question.' But this time Palma didn't believe her. Even in the marbled shadows of the kiosk Palma could sense the change in Claire's demeanor. The question had more substance than the woman wanted to take responsibility for.

'You can see where this is going,' Palma said. 'I've got to know more about him. If you could just give me a name, someone who'd know, someone who could lead me to someone else.'

In the shadow Claire flicked the ash off her cigarette and for a moment the tip was a single bright eye that suddenly glared at Palma, then clouded over again, and waited.

'You talked to Linda Mancera.' It wasn't a question.

'Yes.'

'Talk to her again.'

Somebody coughed deeply across the courtyard, and they both turned to see another white-coated student in jeans and jogging shoes heading towards the lighted back door where the girl had come out earlier. He cleared his phlegmy throat and spat to the side of the doorway before yanking open the glass panel and disappearing inside.

'What do you know about Helena Saulnier?' Palma changed directions.

'Helena's very straightforward, not too complicated psychologically. She's a manhater. A week after the last of her two children moved away from home for college, Helena walked out on her astonished husband after twenty-six years of marriage. She's got a powerful dislike for anything with a penis.'

'Then how does she tolerate Nathan Isenberg?'

Claire stopped in the middle of pulling on her cigarette and snapped her head around at Palma. She looked at her with round eyes for a moment and then burst out laughing, her voice carrying in the damp air, a muted echo ricocheting off the sheer walls of the surrounding buildings. 'Jesus H. Christ! What a world we live in!' She dropped her cigarette on the cement floor of the kiosk and ground it out with the pointed toe of her shoe. 'I'm sorry,' she said, still laughing. She looked at Palma. 'Nathan hasn't *got* a penis. Nathan is actually *Natalie* Isenberg.'

Palma watched Claire laugh again, Claire who wasn't Claire, laughing about Nathan who was Natalie. Weird lost its meaning with people like this.

'So what about Sandra Moser?' Palma asked. She had almost forgotten.

Claire, who had leaned forward out of the shadows to laugh, leaned back again into the corner. This time her leg did start swinging, and she folded her arms under her breasts.

'I read the papers,' she said. 'It must've been grim.' She paused, not for Palma to affirm her assumption, but to collect her thoughts. 'I've been with her a number of times. She was very sweet, a beautiful body, really wonderful body. She liked to use her mouth a lot; she was very good with it.' Her tone was almost reminiscent. 'But Vickie discovered her ... and liked her. Dorothy wasn't too possessive with Vickie. Really, after a while I think she just tolerated whatever it was Vickie was into. Men, women, S&M. Whatever. She knew she couldn't control her, couldn't demand any kind of reasonable fidelity of her.

'When Vickie came to Houston and found her way into the group, her freewheeling sexuality created something of a sensation. I mean, we were a relatively sedate bunch. Predominantly feminine, predominantly bisexual, avoided the role-playing scenes at the clubs, nobody really kinky among us. Up to then our affairs were deliciously illicit, which was excitement enough for most of us. Nobody was looking for danger, as far as I knew. But Vickie changed all that. She brought a style to the group that many of us hadn't seen before. Suddenly there were secrets everywhere, and a feeling of something perverse and malign crept into some of the relationships.

'Sandra was always a little frisky, and Kittrie recognized her willingness to take a dare. She got her into S&M. Vickie trained her to top, and Sandra liked it. Then Vickie mixed her up with guys like Reynolds and Bristol, and I hear some pretty hair-raising things went on. Sandra's death just seems to me to be an extension of all that. I don't know the details, naturally, but it sounds to me like somebody lost control.'

'Twice?'

Claire shrugged. 'I don't know; that's out of my league.'
She was quiet a moment and Palma could hear the wet
night dripping off the side of the kiosk.

'Who do you think was capable of doing that?' Palma
ventured.

Claire stared out to the darkness across the mall,
beyond the pale gloam of the mercury vapor lamps. She
shook her head, her eyes not focusing on anything in
particular.

'Who could have killed the two of them? I don't know.
I don't know anyone who could have killed them in the
way I imagine they must've died. But none of us know
people like that, do we? We only know people to the
extent they want us to know them.' She shrugged. 'They
interview the neighbors. "He was the nicest guy. Quiet,
kept to himself. Never caused any trouble. I can't believe
this is the same man." Well, hell. It *isn't* the same man
they know.'

She was right, of course. And it was precisely that sort
of invisibility that made a man who did the sort of things
that were done to Dorothy Samenov so mythologically
horrifying.

'Look,' Claire said, her eyes coming back to Palma. 'I
have two boys in high school. My husband is an
ophthalmologist with a private practice. I ... I'm a
gynecologist ... for Christ's sake. Can't you see what
those photographs would do to my career, not to mention
my family?' Her voice had a slight quaver. 'Look.' She
leaned forward, her hands open, palms up, resting on her
knees, side by side. 'I know what you said ... not being
able to do anything about them. But I've cooperated here
... even when you gave me no incentive regarding the
pictures. If ... If there's *any*thing you can do about them,
will you help me out? I'm not going to make excuses for
them ... I know how stupid it was ... I made a mistake.
But ... they were meant to be private. It wasn't like ... I
don't want my life to go down the drain because of those
four photographs.'

Roughly half her face was palely lighted through the net of stringy shadows; the other half was lost in a vague dusk. But Palma could see enough to discern the anxiety that she had managed to hide up to now. She sympathized with Claire. It surprised her, but she did.

'I'll do what I can,' Palma said. 'I can't promise you other detectives won't see them, but I can make sure they don't get out of the division. When this is all over ... I'll get them back to you.'

Claire eased her head back into the denser shadows and was very still, saying nothing. Then, 'If I can help you ... any more ...' she said. 'I know how this must look, my seeming to be more concerned about those pictures than for Sandra and Dorothy.' Her voice was strained. 'But ... they're gone, aren't they? And I'm not. My husband isn't. My family isn't.'

Palma nodded and stood. 'You know how to get in touch with me,' she said. 'If there's anything else, if you just want to talk ... I live alone.'

Claire nodded, but she didn't get up, didn't let Palma see her face again. Palma stepped out into the mist, which was heavy now, wetting her face as she walked briskly across the courtyard. She looked back once, after she'd gotten into the shadow of the library and before she started around the corner to the car. She saw a waft of smoke lift out of the kiosk and drift up through the dancing mist.

FOURTH
DAY

27

Palma called Linda Mancera at her home number early Thursday morning before Mancera went to work. When Palma told her it was important that she see her immediately, Mancera readily assented. But, like Andrew Moser, this time she did not want Palma to come to her office. Instead she asked Palma to come to her home in the north Tanglewood section of west Houston, not far off Woodway.

Mancera's home was a modern two-story condo, one of two buildings inside a spacious walled compound with wrought-iron gates, security card access, and the pretentious name of Cour Jardin. Palma rolled down the car window and picked up a telephone inside a clear plastic cabinet beside the car slot. But the gate was already opening, so she returned the telephone to its cradle and drove between the parting wings of the gateway.

The compound was small, but the grounds were professionally maintained. Already this morning the brick drive had been washed down and the beds of liriope and cape plumbago and sprengeri fern that grew around the courtyard were still wet from a predawn watering of the sprinkler system. The two condos sat at oblique angles to each other facing the drive, and Palma parked in front of the one on the left as she had been instructed. She got out of the car and immediately smelled the heavy odor of woods and damp humus, and followed the crescent-shaped sidewalk bordered by waist-high edges to the front door. Above her, the glass walls of the second floor sloped forward slightly under a deep eave, its view overlooking the courtyard and wooded drive beyond the gates.

Palma had to ring the doorbell twice before it was answered by a stunning black woman a little taller than Palma, her hair pulled back smoothly from her face and hanging in a single long braid over the front of one of her bare shoulders. She wore a long-sleeved ivory cotton-knit blouse and matching skirt that hung almost to her sandaled feet. Her lips were painted a glistening scarlet, and ivory loops with gold bands dangled from each ear.

'Hello, I'm Bessa,' she said with a faint smile. 'Please come in. Linda is making coffee and had her hands in water.' She had an accent, perhaps Jamaican, and had pronounced her name Bay-sa.

They walked through a white living room with white furnishings to a dining room that looked out onto yet another courtyard and adjoined the kitchen where Linda Mancera was coming around the counter drying her hands on a towel.

'Good morning,' she said. 'We'll have coffee in just a minute. Can I get you some orange juice or something in the meantime?'

Palma thanked her, but declined. Mancera was dressed more casually than Bessa in a fitted pearl silk robe. She wore no make-up, and her hair was combed, but not fixed for work. She was completely at ease, as she had been in her office, but was obviously curious as to why Palma had needed to see her so urgently.

They visited a moment, standing around the kitchen while Mancera cut a grapefruit and made toast for Bessa, who had disappeared and returned with a purse and a soft leather briefcase.

'Bessa works for another advertising agency,' Mancera said, smiling. 'Between us we're authorities on the pro-

fessional gossip in this business.' She put the grapefruit
and toast on the table while Bessa stood at the sink and
took a handful of vitamins with a glass of water and then
sat down and started eating while Mancera poured coffee
for herself and Palma. They visited a few minutes more
until Bessa had hurriedly eaten her grapefruit and one of
the two pieces of toast. Then she grabbed her purse, told
Palma goodbye, kissed Mancera, and left through a side
courtyard to the garage.

They settled in the living room, and Palma gave
Mancera a quick overview of where the investigation had
taken her. Mancera's equanimity was slightly shaken, and
she nodded as Palma told her that she had learned of the
lesbian connection. She seemed to have already guessed
that. But as Palma continued, and began talking about the
S&M aspects of the women's relationships, Mancera grew
uncomfortable, several times shifting her long legs, finally
folding them both beside her in the huge, low-backed
armchair she had chosen, her back to a palmetto-filled
courtyard.

'Last night,' Palma said, 'I learned of Gil Reynold's
association with Kittrie, and that he also had had sadistic
relationships with women as well. You told me last time
you'd never heard of Gil Reynolds, but in light of everything I've learned since then, I have to believe you lied to
me. About that for sure, and maybe about other things as
well. But I understand that,' Palma added. 'Right now I'm
only interested in what you do, in fact, know about
Reynolds.'

Mancera took her time. She sat her coffee cup on an
Oriental table beside her chair, leaned her left forearm on
the arm of the chair, and with her other hand massaged
her foot covered by the silk robe.

'I seriously doubt if you understand,' she said finally.
'But, anyway, you've gotten into it, haven't you?' She
shook her head. 'This group of women ... is not easy to
understand. If Reynolds hadn't told you, I wonder if any
of us would have ever given in.' She looked at Palma. 'I'm
glad it wasn't one of us.'

She picked up her cup and sipped the coffee. 'Whoever you talked to last night must've given you a good picture of Reynolds,' she said. 'It was wrong of me not to have come right out with his name from the beginning. But I knew he would lead you into the group.'

Suddenly Palma's frustration spilled over. 'Goddammit. I find that an incredible attitude,' she blurted. 'When I talked to you the first time, you knew — even if I didn't — that both victims were bisexual and that that possibly had something to do with their being victims in the first place. Didn't it scare any of you? I don't understand what the hell you thought you were going to accomplish by keeping your mouths shut. This guy's going to keep coming. It should have scared the hell out of you.'

'It did.' Mancera said evenly. 'But we're *used* to being frightened. Not like that, no, but afraid. If you really think about it ... sometimes there's not a great deal of difference between losing your life and having it ruined. Those of us in the group live every day in fear of the latter possibility. We're not too eager to jump up and throw off the covers and expose ourselves to the outside just to see who's threatening us from the inside. Up to a point, we're willing to take our chances.'

'Up to a point? Really?' Palma said. 'What point would that *be*, if homicide isn't it?'

Mancera looked at Palma, her eyes narrowing, wanting to be understood. 'Can you imagine walking around with a psychological hump on your back the size of another person? That's what it's like, you know, being bisexual or lesbian. You're not really allowed to be an honest person, not if you want a shot at the mainstream way of life. You have to hide half of what you're all about if you want your talents and abilities to be taken at face value. Otherwise, you have to carry that hump around on your back and you soon realize that, for all practical purposes, the hump is all that people see.'

Mancera's anger was quiet but intense. With the wisdom of a survivor, she had learned to control it, to disguise it like she had disguised her sexuality. She smiled softly, icily, and placed a long-fingered hand on her graceful throat.

'What society doesn't realize is that we're in the mainstream anyway. We've learned the value of invisibility. We're doctors and lawyers and teachers and executives and real estate agents ... and detectives. But we're carrying a psychological hump on our shoulders, and the only time we can get rid of it is when we're together. That's what this group was all about. It was the only place we could relax because we were all alike. And the only reason the group was successful was because we were secret; we were protected.'

Mancera picked up her coffee cup, but the coffee was cold and she set it down again. She looked at Palma. 'How could we keep quiet? There was a chance you'd catch the killer, there was no chance society was going to restore our status once we'd lost our anonymity.'

'Unfortunately,' Palma said, 'there's no chance we'll catch the killer either, if you don't cooperate with us.'

Mancera got up from her chair. 'I need some fresh coffee. How about you?'

Palma wanted to slam her back down in her chair, but checked her temper and followed Mancera into the kitchen.

Mancera walked around the corner of the bar and poured her cold coffee down the sink. 'You've got to promise me my background won't be given to the papers if all this comes out. I don't *want* my name in the papers, with or without that kind of appellation.' She picked up the coffeepot and filled Palma's cup, and then her own.

'I can't promise that,' Palma said. 'The case files are open to the homicide division, all the detectives working the case, certain ones in the administration. Right now there are four detectives. But if anyone else gets killed, a lot more people are going to want to dip into it.'

'You think it's Gil Reynolds?'

'I have no idea,' Palma said. 'I mean, all I have on him is a story that he likes to beat up women. Unfortunately, that doesn't make him special.'

Mancera looked out to the palmettos past Palma's shoulder. Palma could see the irises in her eyes shrinking; she could see contact lenses.

Mancera swallowed. 'Denise Reynolds divorced her husband because he was a batterer,' she said. 'She put up with it for years until he did his thing in front of their sons. The boys were in junior high, and one night Reynolds hammered her so badly he put her in the hospital.'

'That would have been in the files,' Palma said. 'It wasn't.'

'She claimed she was mugged, and she stuck with the story. Everyone knew it wasn't true, but she clung to that line like a life raft. But when she got out of the hospital, she divorced him for irreconcilable differences.' Mancera looked at her cup, and rotated it. She appeared to be particularly affected.

'But before Denise divorced him, for maybe a year before, she had belonged to our group. More than a few of us are battered wives.'

Mancera stopped and regarded Palma a moment as if trying to decide how to express herself.

'I assume you're neither bisexual nor lesbian,' Mancera said. 'I don't know how well informed you are, but I can assure you that there's no such thing as "the gay woman" any more than there's "the heterosexual woman." The term encompasses as many moral philosophies and life-styles and political views as does the word "heterosexual." We're not a single-minded entity.'

She hesitated slightly. 'I've known since my first sexual stirrings that I preferred women as sexual partners. I had a normal, happy childhood, no mental or physical abuse. I love both my parents and my siblings, and the love is reciprocated. I'm comfortable with the way I am, despite the fact that professionally I'm forced to live in a world of pretense, appearing to be flattered by the attention I get from the men I work with while being careful not to betray the real pleasure I derive from being around the women.

'But my preference for women as sexual partners is a private thing,' Mancera insisted. 'As all sexual interactions should be. It doesn't dictate my politics or my religion or my morals. It doesn't run my life. It's only a part of it, like my race or my job or my age or my height. Actually, if I weren't compelled to play an absurd game of charades to assure nonprejudicial treatment, the issue of my sexual preference would drop way down on the scale of importance in my life. It shouldn't be a big deal. There are other values of moral concern that are more important.'

Palma did not interrupt the pause created when Mancera stopped to take a sip of coffee. She didn't know where Mancera was going with her explanation, but at least she was talking, and that was often half the battle of a good interview.

'I mentioned abuse a while ago,' Mancera continued, leaning her forearm on the counter next to the coffeepot. 'More than a few women are lesbians because of having been abused as children or wives. A lot of women will vehemently deny that, but their denial has more to do with feminist politics than reality. They don't want to attribute their sexual orientation to a reaction against what men have done to them. That would put men in the driver's seat again: lesbians being what they are *because* of men. They insist that their sexual orientation is a matter of free choice. And they don't like the term "lesbian." They prefer "gay." They feel that "lesbian" carries too many derogatory connotations from old Victorian prejudices.'

She shook her head. 'I've known middle-aged women who had their first lesbian experience after they'd divorced battering husbands and were totally repulsed by anything male. Still others choose a lesbian lifestyle strictly as a political choice, their answer to "patriarchal heterosexism." There's no one reason, no one answer.

'But for Denise Reynolds, turning to women for love was as much a matter of an acquired repulsion for men as anything else. A matter of sanity. She had to find kindness somewhere, genuine love, and she happened to find it with other women. There was no threat there, and there was hope for happiness. Then Gil found out about it and had the boys taken away from her on moral grounds. They're living with relatives now.'

'Where's Denise?'

'She disappeared.'

Palma frowned. 'What do you mean? She just wanted to start a new life?'

'We don't know. At the time, she was living alone, so she'd been gone a week or so before anyone really checked into it.'

'It was reported to the police?'

Mancera nodded. 'Missing persons. But nothing ever turned up. They found a suitcase missing from her place and a lot of her clothes and money. Her car was missing. It just never came to anything. I think the police believe she snapped after the boys were taken away from her. There simply was no evidence of foul play.'

'But you don't believe that.'

Mancera shook her head. 'No. I don't.'

'How did Reynolds get involved with Dorothy Samenov?' Palma asked. Gil Reynolds had been all over the place. The guy was becoming a one-man sideshow.

'That's the strangest part of all this. We all knew Denise by the name of Kaplan. She changed it from Reynolds after the divorce. Shortly after she disappeared Reynolds entered the scene with Dorothy, who was actively bisexual. It wasn't unusual for her to take up with a man. But none of us connected him to Denise. Then shortly after that, Kittrie came into the picture. Dorothy was really taken by her. She was rebounding from an affair with another woman, and Reynolds and Kittrie sort of overlapped their relationships with her.'

Palma found the story amazing. Dorothy Samenov, the pillar of feminist stability, was looking more and more like an emotional derelict, victim of child abuse and husband battering, blackmail, bisexually promiscuous, the unsuspecting prey of a younger woman whose sexual perversions would qualify for her own chapter in Krafft-Ebing, and, finally, murder victim. She had not had a peaceful life. Unfortunately, Palma had seen more than a few Dorothy Samenovs.

'How do Reynolds's sadistic relationships with women fit into this?' Palma asked. Mancera had talked all around it, or maybe all this was prelude.

Mancera nodded, seeming to have decided that she had brought Palma far enough with the preliminaries.

'I used to go with a woman named ... Terry ... She lived with a roommate, nothing sexual, just good friends, close friends. Terry's roommate was a longstanding S&M partner of Reynolds. Some of it involved Kittrie ... and it was bad.'

'Terry heard it from her roommate and told you.'

'That's right. But I'm not going to pass it on. You can talk to the woman yourself. I don't want to have anything to do with it. I don't like it. For the majority of lesbians whose relationships are monogamous and loving, those women are despicable. The worst thing that ever happened to Dorothy Samenov, and the group, was not Gil Reynolds; it was Vickie Kittrie. There wouldn't have been any Gil Reynolds without her. He wouldn't have stayed with Dorothy. She didn't have a mean streak. She may have been a weak and tormented woman, but she wasn't mean. She needed love and constancy, not Vickie Kittrie's schizophrenia.'

'Why do you suppose the woman I talked with last night didn't send me to Terry's roommate in the first place?'

'I don't know. Who was it?'

Palma shook her head. 'Who was the roommate?'

'Louise Ackley.'

'Oh, Christ.'

'I know,' Mancera said, quickly hurrying to mollify Palma, to temper the damage. 'I played dumb when you asked about S&M at the office Tuesday, but you caught me off guard. I had to have time to think.'

'I interviewed Louise after I left there,' Palma said.

'And how did you find her?'

'Drunk. In bad shape.'

Mancera shook her head. 'Look,' she said. 'I owe you, and I want to help out in this terrible mess if I can. I really do. I'm sorry I've given you trouble. Tomorrow night some women are coming over here for drinks. A couple of friends we've known for years in another city are in town and we're just going to have some people over. Why don't you come? These things are very casual and newcomers are commonplace and introduced only by their first names. No one has to know anything else about you. I'll make sure Terry's here and that you have the opportunity to talk to her in private. No one will notice, no one will care. It'll be simple and easy, and it'll give you a chance to meet some of the other women — without the shield — yours or theirs.'

Palma didn't hesitate. 'Fine, I'll take you up on it,' she said. 'But my occupation can't be an "open" secret. I really don't want anyone to know but you and Bessa and Terry.'

'Agreed,' Mancera said, and she smiled a warm, comfortable smile that Palma immediately liked, and then made her slightly uncomfortable.

28

When Palma stopped at a service station on Woodway and called Louise Ackley's home in Bellaire, no one answered the phone. Thinking she might have returned to work, though it would have been unusual, it seemed to Palma, to have returned on a Thursday, she called Maritime Guaranty. But Ackley had not shown up.

Palma waited a moment. She had to talk to Ackley. She wanted to know every sexual twist in the Reynolds repertoire, every quirk and warp in his mind, before she talked to him again. If she had to she would hole up with Louise in her grim little house and buy her as many cases of beer as it took to get the information out of her or, if necessary, she would pay for a twenty-four-hour detox, or however the hell long it took, to get the woman to the point that she could speak either loosely or lucidly about Reynold's sadistic games. After what she had learned from Claire, and now from Mancera, Palma was sure that somewhere in those sick diversions she was going to find traces, like behavioral fingerprints, of the deaths of Sandra Moser and Dorothy Samenov.

She put the quarter back in the slot and called again, but there still was no answer. She wanted to drive to Ackley's at that very moment, but she was already close to overextending herself. Kittrie's hair samples, which were sitting in the car a few feet away, should already be

at the lab. She had the information from Grant's call early
in the night, and then Mancera's interview this morning.
All of it needed to be put into supplements. It would be
stupid to string herself out any further.

Once again Palma drove back downtown on Memorial
Drive, past the joggers sweating in the hazy, late-morning
heat as they pounded, loped, plodded, and fast-walked
along the paths that ran between the winding drive and
the pines of the densely wooded Memorial Park that ran
nearly two miles from the West Loop toward downtown.

She thought of Vickie Kittrie. It had been a distinct
surprise to Palma, as well as to Helena Saulnier, that the
ginger-haired girl who seemed to evoke such protective
instincts in Saulnier, had been — if Claire and Mancera
could be believed — the source of so much menace. What
kind of psychology lay beneath the freckles of that girl
from the small East Texas town, and what had her life
been like that at so young an age she should know so
much about the dark side of eroticism? Palma wondered,
too, if Claire had been totally honest with her. Or perhaps
the more appropriate question would be, which parts of
the things she told Palma were 'adjusted' to lay on one
more misleading flourish to an already baroque investigation? She would not be surprised to learn from someone
else that Claire's 'lark' had actually been in earnest. But
did it matter if the woman had lied to her? It had gotten
her this far, one step deeper into the brackish well of
sadomasochism.

She slowed the Audi as she passed under the Gulf
Freeway downtown, made a quick left on Bagby, another
quick left on Prairie, and then right on Riesner to the
police station. She parked her car on the third floor and
walked over to the crime lab where she filled out the
appropriate form to submit Kittrie's hair samples into the
evidence file of Samenov's case and requested the
comparison tests with the unknown hairs. Then she went
outside and walked down the hot asphalt drive and
around the end of the administration building, the
expressway across the loop of bayou to her left throwing

off heat and noise which she tried to ignore as she thought of the revelations awaiting her in the person of Louise Ackley.

The foyer of the station was crowded with what seemed to be an anachronistic gathering of two tribal families of hippies, their sorely tried women keeping a very loose rein on half a dozen ill-begotten waifs while three of their men with drooping moustaches, bandanna-wrapped heads, and powerful odors argued with several officers about the validity of the inspection stickers on their 'vehicles.'

Birley was not in the office, having already checked in and left her a message that he was going to Andrew Moser's house to talk to Sandra's mother. The children were at school, and Andrew had said that his mother-in-law would know where the names and telephone numbers of Sandra's doctors were. He had asked only that Birley not make the request over the telephone, that he go see the old woman in person.

Leeland was checked out to the University of Houston, and Cushing was running around interviewing hair-dressers.

Palma got another cup of coffee. She had drunk three at Mancera's and she knew she would have to drink them all day long to stay conscious. Her eyes felt grainy, and when she flipped on the CRT she had to squint until she got used to the glare. She dug her notebook out of her purse, turned back through the pages until she got to the point where she had interviewed Kittrie and Saulnier, and started typing.

She typed straight through until she reached the end of her notes with Mancera's conversation, and then immediately printed out her two copies. As she was leaving Frisch's copy in his supplement tray she also checked out, leaving word that she was going back to talk to Louise Ackley.

By two-thirty she had checked a car out of the motor pool and was on the Gulf Freeway again, doubling back through the interchanges to the Southwest Freeway. She exited at Shepherd Drive and had a BLT at the 59 Diner where she had talked to Andrew Moser. Then she was back in the car, back on the freeway and on her way to Bellaire.

It was almost three-thirty in the afternoon when she drove up in front of Louise Ackley's house and looked up the sidewalk to the opened front door. She couldn't see if the cat was in the lawn chair on the concrete stoop. She picked up the hand radio from the front seat as she got out of the car and locked it. She hoped Louise would not be passed out in her bedroom, unable to answer the door, but it wouldn't matter. She had already made up her mind she was going in anyway.

The cat wasn't in the lawn chair, but he had left behind a fresh kill. A half-grown rat that had been killed for the pleasure of it, rather than to eat, was lying on the cloth cushion on the seat of the chair. The rat had a bobbed tail, chewed off close to its rump, but the rest of him was perfectly intact. The only visible signs of violence done to him were rumpled patches of damp hair where the cat had toyed with him. She had seen cats do this, having morbidly wounded and immobilized the rat, they keep it near at hand, seeing its feeble struggles to escape as part of a grim game for their amusement, and they bite and chew the rat as whim and fancy takes them. It could go on for hours, an afternoon, or most of a night, but when the rat dies they lose interest.

She looked at the rat for a moment, started to pick up the cushion, then changed her mind and turned and stepped up to the screen door. After several knocks there was still no answer, and Palma reached for the handle as she had done the first time she was there and half expected to hear Ackley's hoarse admonition. Opening the screen door, she stepped inside. 'Ms. Ackley.' She stood just inside the living room. Nothing had changed. There were three empty beer bottles sitting on the coffee table, the ashtray on the end table at the left of the sofa was still overflowing with butts and ashes, and the inside of the windowsill behind the sofa was still stacked with cords of amber beer bottles. Even the oscillating fan was still sitting in the same spot in the middle of the living room floor, droning back and forth, moving the stale air, occasionally disturbing a dust ball along the edges of the wooden floor.

Then she smelled the feces, and a ripple of fear tripped her heart and set it pounding, and instantly she was short of breath. Her hand went into her purse for the SIG-Sauer and the surging adrenaline sharpened her perceptions. She let her purse slide noiselessly off her shoulder to the floor, as she carefully pulled back the slide on the SIG, easing it softly through the cocking snap. She moved to the wall across from the sofa and to the right of the front door and the chair where she had sat facing Ackley. She was only a foot away from the door frame that led into the bedroom where Ackley's drunken companion had groaned on the squeaking bed springs. The smell of feces was stronger here, and tinged with an unmistakable mustiness. Palma wanted to back out of the house and call for assistance, but she couldn't be sure anything was wrong.

She thought about the street. What cars had been out there? How far down were they? Were they new? Old? No flags went up, but it was no comfort. She could see a few feet away into the kitchen, a dinette against the wall with an open jar of strawberry jam sitting all alone on the bare table. Past that an open door to the left would probably be the bathroom, beyond that at the end of a short hall would be another bedroom. Christ. She took a deep breath and eased her head around the corner to the bedroom and saw the foot of the bed, the covers wadded and limp from the humidity. She heard flies. Next to her face the paint on the door frame was chipped and dirty and tacky to the touch. She waited. The house was absolutely silent, except for the flies. She eased round the corner, through the bedroom doorway, and stopped once more. Then she leaned in.

Louise Ackley was lying on her back on the bed, her filthy T-shirt wrenched up above her naked hips, one leg

cocked, her arms flung out to either side. Half her face
was gone, blown up against the bloody wall behind the
bed, and her one remaining eye, pooched out of its socket
a little, seemed to be on its own, trying to look in Palma's
direction through a welter of flies. Ackley's midsection
and pelvis were arched over a pillow under the small of
her back, and the blood that had gushed from her in the
moments after the gunshot had been trapped on the
opposite side of the pillow so that her head and shoulders
lay in a darkening pudding, abuzz with a swarm of flies.
The wall was spattered nearly to the ceiling. More flies,
working Ackley's inner thighs below the dark patch of
pubic hair, had found the feces.

Palma stared, her lips open, teeth clenched, breathing
through her teeth, not wanting to close her mouth or she
would taste the odor. Suicide? She didn't see the weapon.
To her right the closet door was open. She checked it and
eased around the foot of the bed, looking on the floor for
the weapon. It wasn't there. She glanced at the second
bedroom door that opened into the hallway and looked
through the opposite doorway into the kitchen, this time
toward the cabinets and the sinks. There were some
unwashed pots on the countertops, and an opened can of
chilli. She moved to the side of the bed and looked for the
weapon in the grume and twisted covers. She didn't see
it. Jesus Christ. No suicide weapon? Jesus Christ. And
Her heart hammered even harder, and she felt as vulnerable as if she knowingly had walked naked into the room
with the killer. Then reflexively her mind registered on
the darkening blood. The hit was not recent, not within
the last several hours. It was a rational judgement she
couldn't bring herself to trust.

Still breathing through her teeth, she skirted the foot
of the bed again and stepped into the hallway. She made
her way through the hot, stinking air trapped in the inner
hallway, and checked the bathroom. Ackley kept house
like a bag lady, but the place wasn't ransacked. A hall
closet was open and empty. She turned inside the second
bedroom and suddenly recoiled, falling back and catching

herself against the door frame, bringing down the SIG
and leveling it at the man on the floor. He was face down,
naked, one arm tucked under his body, the other flung
out to his side and clutching a pair of stained jockey
shorts. She saw the relatively small entrance wound in
the thick black hair of the back of his head and knew that
his face, resting just over the edge of a filthy area rug that
had soaked up most of his blood like a paper towel,
would look something like Louise Ackley's. Abruptly she
came to her senses and jerked the SIG around and locked
her eyes on the last closet in the house. It was shut, not
ajar even a little. She swallowed without closing her lips,
which were dry now, and started to step across the dead
man, but stopped. Jesus. She knew better than that. She
backed out of the room, keeping her eyes on the bedroom
door, backed down to the hall to the living room, her legs
tingling, wanting to buckle as she fumbled for her hand
radio tangled in the strap of her purse. Moving to one
side of the living room where she could keep her eyes on
the bedroom door at the end of the hallway, she radioed
for assistance.

29

'**Y**ou're actually a little pissed about this, aren't you?'
'Don't be stupid, Bernadine.'

'You are. You're ... restrained.'

'I'm always restrained. It's second nature to me, part of my training.' He loathed the fact that she was amused with him.

'Yes, but you've never "seemed" restrained. Now you do. This whole thing is upsetting to you.'

'Bernadine, do you think I've never before encountered lesbian relationships?' It was true that he had lesbian clients, but then he had not been having an affair with them for the last five years. It made a difference, by God. Dispassionate objectivity was for analysis. Bernadine was a lover, for God's sake.

'Not like this,' she laughed.

They were drinking, as always with Bernadine — this time she had her beloved scotch — and she had chosen to sit in the other armchair opposite him rather than taking her place on the chaise. She had never done this before. She had always liked the chaise for much the same reasons that he had liked it, because it introduced an aura of seductiveness. The posture was suggestive, and Bernadine knew how to make the most of a provocative attitude.

'We've discussed your lovers at other times,' he said.

'Not my lesbian lovers,' she persisted.

She was absolutely right, but he couldn't possibly let her know that it would make any difference to him, even though he was reeling.

'Surely you understand after all these years, Bernadine, that it doesn't matter. If it's significant to you, if it's important, I'll help you explore it, try to help you understand yourself in light of what it means to you.' It almost gagged him to talk like that, especially with Bernadine. They had long ago gotten past this kind of thing, and now she was wanting him to act like a psychiatrist again. After all those years of intimacy, it was too much like roleplaying. He detested the idea of it. But it was typical of Bernadine not to see the difficulty of what she was proposing. She was wanting to turn back the clock, to start from the beginning because she thought she had discovered some earthshaking truth by making love with another woman. She thought it was the answer. Bernadine had always tried to find the answer to her problems in the person of someone else. She never really understood, or accepted, the idea that she had to look inward.

She looked at him over the rim of her glass, as was her habit, and he could see that she was smiling.

'You know, this has been going on for a while,' she said, smirking. 'And you didn't sense it. On several occasions I even came here within an hour of having been with her, and I had both of you within an hour.'

Broussard couldn't believe she'd said it, and in an instant their past several encounters flashed through his mind as he tried to remember which times it might have been, when he might have sensed something different about her. He sipped his Stoli to cover up the fact that he was going to have to swallow. She shouldn't have told him this. Didn't she see it was humiliating? She had used another woman as a love philter before coming to him, as if she had needed something to prime her for him. It was degrading. He looked at her smile and wondered if he was going to be able to go through with this. She was wanting to talk about it, and he was feeling a tightening claustrophobia. It saddened him that she could be so blindly insensitive; he wished that she were otherwise, that she was more aware of the spiritual issue that had grown between them and had made him a part of her as surely as if they had been one flesh.

'Look,' she said, lowering her glass. 'If you don't want to talk about this . . .'

'Bernadine, please,' he managed to keep his even-keeled, patriarchal tone. 'You know, I believe you're rationalizing, imagining that I am discomforted by this subject and using that as an excuse not to discuss it while all the time it's your own reluctance that you're refusing to recognize.' By sheer force of will he had managed to turn it around.

'No! What do you mean?' Bernadine sat forward in her chair. She started to say something else, but stopped herself. She was frowning, her eyes nailing him, and then the smirk gradually returned to her face and she slowly relaxed and sank back into her armchair. Her mellow contralto laugh moved languidly in her throat.

'Okay,' she said, and she touched her tongue into the scotch, never taking her eyes off him. 'Actually, this has not been my first sexual encounter with another woman.' She shook her head slowly. 'Here's another story. When I was in college — I went to an all-women's university — I had a roommate that I got along with really well. We were together just one semester in my junior year, and then she left to go to another school.

'The last night of that semester a bunch of us went into town and did a lot of drinking, a lot of smoking, and reminiscing about the last few months, that sort of thing. Paula, that was her name, was a little subdued because it was going to be her last time with us. All the rest of us were coming back the next semester. We got back late, drunk and tired, and fell into bed.

'I went to sleep immediately so I don't know how much time had passed before I woke up and realized Paula was in bed with me. She was completely naked and was caressing my breasts. I slept only in panties and she started taking them off. I let her. We lay together for the longest time simply holding each other. I was completely passive at first, letting her caress me, fondle my breasts, massage between my legs. Then after a while I began touching her too, very gently, every small movement an incredible tactile experience, an exploration that I found astonishingly pleasurable. I remember thinking how bizarre it felt to be touching another woman in this way. It was like touching myself, except my body had gone numb while my hands retained their feeling. I was used to a woman's body from the inside, not the outside. I remember two special things: the weight of her breasts ... the very subtle change in texture that became the nipple, and the little hollow place inside her thing, near her vulva. I knew how being touched there affected me, and so I knew what I was doing to her and how she must be feeling. So outrageous a thing to be doing, and yet the most natural thing in the world.'

She looked down at her glass and poked at her ice a moment, shoving it around in a swirl.

'I was already sexually active with men,' she continued. 'That started kind of early, as you know, so I was aware of the different ways I reacted to certain kinds of sexual stimulation. That is, I thought I was aware. Paula was a revelation. It was an extraordinary night, and I didn't sleep a wink. After several hours Paula did go to sleep, with me holding her, but I couldn't. I simply lay there and looked at the two of us. That in itself was exciting. I was already used to seeing my body next to one of another kind, one of different structure and texture and feel. But seeing us, two of the same, thigh to thigh, stomach to stomach, breast to breast, I couldn't get over the unusualness of it. I liked seeing her female shape next to mine. It seemed ... more appropriate.'

Broussard listened with a docile expression, managing to nod every once in a while, though he couldn't have explained why if he had been given all the time in the world. Inside, however, he was being torn apart. It was as if every sexual encounter he had had with Bernadine in the past five years — and they had not been few — had been a deliberate mockery. He was tormented by the idea that during those encounters Bernadine had compared their lovemaking to that which she had experienced with Paula, and had found it lacking. He imagined Bernadine, nipple to nipple, navel to navel, vulva to vulva, with this girl, her lambent, bottomless eyes looking at Paula with the same candid curiosity and untethered pleasure with which she had looked at him — them — time after time after time. He could think of no movement, no caress or gesture, that he would have wanted less to share with another lover than that of Bernadine's clear-eyed and undissembling observance of their lovemaking. To him, it always had been as primitively erotic as her nakedness, the one thing that had made her irresistible to him for more than five years.

A clacking of ice in an empty glass brought him back to the present. Bernadine had drained the last of her scotch.

'But that was it,' she said. 'The next morning I took Paula to the commuter train and stood on the platform and waved her goodbye. I never saw her again.' She thought a minute. 'I don't know why that was an isolated experience ... until recently, I mean. It was the best sex I'd ever had, by far. And yet I never thought of it in terms of anyone else. It was just for us, Paula and me. For years it's been my main sexual fantasy, or I should say my main sexual remembrance, while I masturbate.' She looked at him. 'I think the fact that I've never had another lesbian experience until now is something I'd like to explore.'

Broussard had to scramble to think of something, his mind whirling with his own mental image of the two naked women.

'Did you, at any time during this episode, remember the day you surprised your aunt and her lover?' The question had come to him almost as a reflex and saved him from exposing his disorientation.

Bernadine sat her empty glass on the floor, slipped off her shoes as she got up from the armchair, and walked over and lay down on the chaise. Broussard couldn't have been more surprised if she had flung herself through the plate-glass window. What was this?

'You know, I didn't,' she said, surprised at the idea, raising her hips and smoothing her dress under her, getting comfortable. 'But afterward I did. I mean it was even after I'd taken Paula to the train, and I was driving back to the campus when I first thought of it. I was stunned. Completely. I clearly remember how it affected me. And you know what I became obsessed with? I suddenly wanted, more than anything else, to know who that woman was with my aunt. I even thought about going to see my aunt and telling her everything, asking the woman's name and trying to find her. It was a romantic fantasy for a number of years.'

Bernadine smiled. 'Jesus, I wish I'd done that. It's just occurred to me ... if I had done that, and if I could have found her, she'd more than likely have been younger than I am now. And at that time I was nineteen. We could have had such an affair.' Her smile faded wistfully. 'It would have been entirely possible. It could have happened. That's kind of sad.'

When Bernadine paused, Broussard said nothing. He felt no compulsion to fill the silence this time. His eyes were going over his client as if they had been the curious, probing paws of a baboon. He even felt blue-snouted and cruel. It was as if he had a new client, as if he didn't know her at all and had to start from the beginning. An entire component of her personality had been misrepresented to him and this was not, after all, the woman with whom he had consulted — and bedded — for the past five years. What the hell kind of a deal was this? Was he now going to have to deal with her bisexual identity? Her coming out? With her encounters with homophobia? Her Persephone complex? Lesbian etiology? Lesbian sexual dysfunctions? Lesbian socialization? Lesbian feminist praxis? The lesbian orgasm? The politics of lesbian sexuality? Lesbian power?

'Anyway,' she said, abruptly, interrupting Broussard's grim preoccupation, 'I've spent almost the rest of my life in unsatisfactory heterosexual relationships, always trying to fulfill someone else's desires, trying to be something other than what I was for someone other than myself.'

She turned and looked at Broussard. 'I'm good, sexually I mean, aren't I?' She waited for him to respond, which he did, with a chagrined nod. 'I know I am,' she said, turning her gaze back to the plate-glass window. 'But do you know something? I've never honestly understood what it was men really wanted from sex.'

'What do you mean, Bernadine?' He was sleepwalking through the interview now, barely capable of sustaining continuity.

'I mean, it was never quite the same thing I wanted,' she tried to explain. 'I've always been left with a feeling of: Well, not quite this time. But I never understood quite *what*. What was it that we were supposed to be achieving? Men seem satisfied with what they are going after once they've got it. But somehow, for me, an orgasm has never been quite enough, never quite the end of it. I always feel that somehow we didn't quite achieve what we *could* have achieved.'

Broussard listened to this with absolute dejection. By placing herself once again in the posture of the analysand rather than the lover, but becoming the analysand-lover, she was unwittingly flaying him. If she had actually castrated him, she couldn't have emasculated him with greater skill.

'I met this woman about a month ago,' Bernadine began. 'It was not a chance encounter, although at the time it happened I thought it was. I was on my way here, in fact, and I stopped off at a service station on Woodway to get gas. While the man was servicing my car I went inside to get a package of gum. It was only afterward, when I thought back over it, that I realized that she had followed me in there. I remember her pulling up on the other side of my car at the gasoline pumps just after I did; I remembered her following me into the station and into the aisle where I was looking for gum. I didn't find the kind of gum I wanted right off, and she came up beside me, pretending to look for something also. I remembered that later, too, but at the time it didn't actually catch my attention. Just as I reached for the gum, she did too, and her hand fell on top of mine and stayed there. It didn't move. I looked at her, and she was already looking at me, her eyes holding me steadily, her hand moving slightly on mine, like an embrace. I instantly thought of Paula — for the first time in a long while. She smiled. And I did, too.'

Bernadine's soothing contralto had grown husky as she related this, and by the time she had stopped it was thick with emotion. Broussard listened to it change with growing anxiety. He found it somehow unseemly, while at the same time it stirred something within him.

Bernadine cleared her throat and went on. 'We exchanged a few words. She was obviously much younger than me, by ten years I found out later. She was dressed in a white tennis outfit that did very well by her figure. I was flustered a little, but she was very controlled, as if this open flirtation was very natural to her. Of course it *was* very natural to anyone observing us, two women visiting. There was nothing untoward about it at all; no one even noticed us. But I had felt the electricity between us and was flustered. Very calmly she suggested to me that I tear a deposit slip out of my checkbook so that she could have my address and telephone number. It was the easiest way, she said. She'd obviously done it before. I didn't ask for hers, and she didn't give it to me. After I had done this she smiled again and thanked me. As she brushed past me to leave, she very openly placed her hand on my crotch as she went by.

'I was too weak-kneed to follow her out. I simply stood in the aisle with my back to everyone — there were several other people besides us in the station — waiting to pay at the cash register. The woman left, and I had no idea who she was, or if I really would ever see her again.'

Broussard watched her begin her well-practiced routine. Bernadine Mello liked to remove her clothes as much as any woman he had ever seen, and she did it with style. Even the most experienced stripper had no advantage over Bernadine when it came to technique. The thing that made it so special was that it was clear that she did it as much for her own pleasure as for his, with a subtlety a stripper seldom conveyed.

She didn't say anything else, but now and then her contralto purred — when her bare skin first touched the leather of the chaise, when she flung her dress, when she could look down between her legs and see her own reflection in the plate glass, washed in the green sunlight of late afternoon.

There was not a lot he could do about it. He wouldn't be able to walk away from this no matter how repulsed he had been by her story. He would have to put it out of his mind. Bernadine was quickly wiping out every thought that might have distracted him. It was in her nature, and he let her do it.

He watched her as he slowly, mechanically, began undressing, removing his shoes first and putting the shoehorns inside them, removing his jacket and hanging it on a hanger, then his shirt and trousers, carefully folding them and placing them in the chair, doing everything by feel and habit, unhurriedly tending to the creases as he kept his eyes riveted on her. He knew that she knew what he was doing, that she had time to do what she wanted to do. He watched her hands moving over her own body as if he were guiding them with his mind, as if they were, in fact, his hands. He watched her watch herself in the green reflection of the glass with that peculiar, candid, and dreamy curiosity of the flesh that never failed her. When he was completely undressed, he moved around to the end of the chaise and crouched down with his back to the plate-glass window and looked up at her lengthways from between her legs, replacing her reflection. His eyes absorbed her every detail, slowly, slowly as they had done so many times before, each of them moving exactly as they knew they must, together turning the intricate keys of their own ritual, second nature to them in the foggy confusion of their excitement.

Then at the last moment, at the precise point at which he suddenly would put his face to hers, iris to iris, so that in the culmination of their passion he could fall into her empty, achromatic world, he was stunned to see that she had closed her eyes.

30

Everyone was still there at seven-forty as a humid summer dusk settled over the city, and the street lamps quivered to life and the crickets picked up a steady rhythm in the damp grass and drainage ditches of this less than prosperous section of south Bellaire. Only Louise Ackley and the once handsome Lalo Montalvo had gone, in the back of the morgue van, their stinking bodies zipped up tight in plastic bags that the coroner would have to open so that he could do with them what only a few people in the world could be persuaded to do on a daily basis.

Louise Ackley, as it turned out, had been a saver of letters. This surprised Palma, and depressed her, for the letters Louise had saved had been records of tragedy, and Palma wondered how bleak her life must have been if she had wanted such things for memories. There were stacks of boxes packed with letters, carefully filed in chronological order, some still in tattered and yellowed envelopes, most simply refolded to fit their space, some in pencil or ballpoint pen, some typed. Almost every one of them was from Louise's worthless brother, or from Dorothy Samenov. The letters were a legacy of infamy dating back to adolescence, and covering a dozen states, chronicles of children cheated out of childhood, of incest in which Louise had suffered as much at the hands of her father and brother as if she had been a victim of a pogrom. Their father finally had died in a state mental hospital; their mother, for whom Louise nursed a poisonous and distilled hatred for colluding in Louise's early incest victimization, had disappeared. But the brother and sister clung together both literally and figuratively, sometimes driven apart by their individual passions and sometimes brought together by the same. It was, at best, a relationship of dire needs in which survival, often at a very dear price, always had managed to strike a stalling bargain with despair.

Into this tortured dyad Dorothy Samenov had come as naturally as if she had been a sibling. Helena Saulnier had either lied to Palma or had been lied to by Dorothy, because the letters revealed that Dennis Ackley had never been in ignorance of his wife's affair with his sister. In fact, it had been a ménage à trois from the beginning, and the couplings among the three of them were as indiscriminate as if they had been ferrets. But the absence of boundaries, the denial of limits, had created in each a powerful and complex psychology, and they were destined for the rest of their lives never to be able to sort out their feelings or reconcile their conflicting passions for one another.

It was odd, too, that they had been such letter writers. But there they were, boxes and boxes of letters in which they agonized over their lives over space and time, openly discussing things in their letters that other people only referred to — if at all — in whispered allusions, or buried in the backs of their minds, hoping never to have them resurrected.

Unfortunately, all the pages of correspondence that Louise Ackley had saved were to and from persons who were now dead, and none of it shed even the least bit of light on any of their deaths. Not only that, but there was no evidence, beyond the letters, of Louise Ackley's bisexuality or her penchant for sexual masochism. It was an absence that aroused suspicion.

'I've never seen one of these people that didn't keep *something* around,' Birley said. 'Pictures, paraphernalia, magazines, underground literature. Stuff!'

They were standing in Louise Ackley's disordered
living room, the five of them, Birley, Palma, Cushing,
Leeland, and Frisch. Every light was on in the dingy little
house, and its small rooms were filled with milling
detectives and police officers, including the evening-shift
lieutenant, Arvey Corbeil, and his two detectives, Gordy
Haws and Lew Marley, who were first out that night. By
agreement, they would be picking up the Ackley-
Montalvo case from Palma. Technically it had been
discovered on their shift, and the immediate judgement
was that since it was not strictly one of the female
bisexual killings Frisch would let it pass because he
wanted Palma to concentrate on the serials. And the lab
technicians were still there, two of them, and several
patrolmen who were in charge of keeping the house
secure.

'You think the hitter's job was to get rid of something,
too?' Frisch asked. He looked worn out, his thinning hair
was plastered to his pale skull by the night's humidity.
The spring had been crazy for homicides — the Jamaican
and Colombian coke rings were blowing each other to
pieces with Uzis and Mack 10s and vicious abandon. This
wasn't the only case that was giving Frisch worries. But
right now, it did seem to be the only case on the verge of
getting out of hand.

'Something, yeah, something.' Birley said, sighing and
hitching up his pants. It was hot in the house. There was
no air conditioning, and even though the little oscillating
fan was still doing its job, the muggy, stagnant air it
dragged in from outside warmed quickly under the
incandescent lights and turned stale when it mixed with
the fetid air that seeped from the two blood-soaked
rooms

'Two immediate possibilities,' Palma said. 'Claire: she
could have had something more to fear than just those
pictures, or maybe she feared there would be more like
them. She could have hired it done. Reynolds: pictures
involving him, or his fear that Ackley would disclose

something about their relationship. He could have hired it done.'

'Claire knows Ackley?' Leeland asked. He was standing with his hands in his pockets looking at the stacked boxes of letters they had been going through.

'I don't know.'

'Well, hell.' Cushing had taken out a handkerchief and was wiping his glistening face. 'If the babes in this group are as ritzy as they say, high society an' all, we got a whole club of suspects. The story of this little group gets in the papers a lot of ladies are going to be scrambling to cover their privates.'

'The question is, what has this got to do with the bisexual killings?' Frisch said. 'It could be incidental, coincidental, integral . . .' He looked around at them.

'You think a guy who does what he's been doing to those women would do this, too?' Leeland asked, tilting his head toward the bedrooms.

'Shit, this is something totally unrelated,' Cushing said. When he finished with his handkerchief he put it away and then reflexively wiped his face again in the bend of his arm as if he had been wearing a sweat suit instead of a silk shirt. 'This was to shut somebody up. Maybe it didn't have anything to do with the bisexual killings, but it had something to do with the fact that the bisexual killings were being looked into, and somebody was afraid that something else would be discovered in the process. Probably something to do with somebody's sex kinks. Our goofball just happened to stir up somebody else's water.'

Palma hated to admit it, but she thought Cushing was right on target. Lalo and Louise were a sideshow, or a whole other story. They didn't have anything to do with the deaths of Moser and Samenov.

'I can go along with that,' Palma said. 'With an adjust-ment. Linda Mancera seemed to think Gil Reynold's sadomasochist relationship with Louise Ackley was a pretty rough one. I mean, excessive in relative terms to what they were involved in. I think there was something in the *way* Reynolds came on to Ackley that might have been too revealing. Lalo just happened to pick the wrong night to get drunk with her, but Louise . . .' Palma ran her hand through her hair. She wanted a bath in the worst way, and she wanted her nostrils cleaned of the stale air of the nasty little house. 'I remember Louise asking me in what particular way Dorothy had been killed. I told her I couldn't go into that with her, and she said, well, what if she happened to recognize something about it? I asked, like what? and she said she didn't know, and then she started crying again.'

'Jesus,' Locland said.

'I could've had it right there.' Palma felt sick about it, but she was a realist, and she knew that hindsight was a cheap source for self-reproach. A waste of time. Still, it stung.

'You think this was Reynolds?' Frisch asked.

'You're damned right I do,' Palma said. 'Not the hitter,' she clarified. 'But he hired it. When we get to him, he'll have the time slot for this job solidly alibied.'

'He killed Moser and Samenov, and was afraid Louise would have recognized something about the techniques?' Birley asked.

Palma nodded. 'I think that's exactly what's happened.'

No one said anything for a moment and the low voices in other rooms of the house carried through to them over a faint background of scratchy, halting radio transmission from a handset in the kitchen.

'Look,' Frisch said finally. He had been rubbing his eyes and when he took his hands down from his face the rims of his eyes were red and slightly swollen. 'Corbeil's got this tied down here. We can't do anything tonight. Help me get these boxes into the back of my car, and we'll go home, hash it over again in the morning. Shit, you're all tired. I'm tired. Let's call it quits for tonight.'

'This is Corbeil,' he said. 'Arvey . . .' She was staring at the fluorescent blue digital numbers on her alarm clock, and she had no recollection of picking up the telephone. 'You awake, Palma?'

'Yeah.' Stupidly, she tried to sound alert. 'Yeah, sure. Arvey.' The digital numbers said it was two thirty-seven.

'I think we just got one of your psycho jobs, Palma,' Corbeil said. 'And it's in the Villages, Hunters Creek.'

'How do you know?' Her voice broke like an adolescent's.

'How do I know? The Hunters Creek cop who went to the house recognized the M.O. the second he saw it. Guy'd been reading our metro memos for a change. He called his chief and the chief called me. Said come on in. Hell, they don't want any part of it.'

'Jesus Christ.' Palma's head swam, and she lay back on the pillow.

'Here's the address,' Corbeil said, and he read it out twice, and Palma looked up at her black ceiling and listened to it. 'You get that?'

'I've got it.' Hunters Creek. Her body felt like it was made of lead. She didn't think she could hold on to the phone.

'I'm calling Karl now,' Corbeil said. 'I'll see you there.'

'Ar ... Arvey,' she stammered, her mind suddenly jerking into play. 'You have a crime scene unit on the way out there?'

'Sure.'

'Who is it?'

'Who is it? Uh, Jay ... Knapp.'

'Arvey, call him, call Knapp and tell him not to touch anything. Not to do *anything*. I'm calling LeBrun. He's on these ... we want him to do all of them. Okay?'

'Yeah, I got it. I'll get on the radio.'

She sat up in bed, peeled off her pyjama top, and called Birley and Julie LeBrun.

In less than fifteen minutes from the time she answered Corbeil's call, she was on the Southwest Freeway, her hair, washed before she had gone to bed but not rolled, blowing around her face in a black storm as she let the wind whip through the windows to help her

wake up. The damp night would put ripples in her hair
that wouldn't come out until she washed it again. The
department car was nearing ninety as she braked and
sailed into the turn that took her onto the West Loop.
Christ, she hadn't even asked the woman's name. She
didn't know why she thought of that now, or why it
suddenly bothered her. It was as if she had let the woman
down, breached the unspoken covenant that she was
beginning to feel for these women, as if they were a lost
sisterhood for whom she had assumed the responsibility
of redeeming from a special kind of anathema.

Hunter Wood Drive was in the southeast corner of
Hunters Creek, just off Memorial Drive and a stone's
throw from Buffalo Bayou and the golfing links of the
Houston Country Club. It was also less than a mile from
Andrew Moser's home. The homes here were large and
expensive; set back from the street in the bosky privacy of
pines and oaks that disappeared up into the dark morning
sky. The address was not hard to find, its entrance
through a pair of limestone pillars topped with dimly
lighted lanterns was manned by a Hunters Creek police
car, and through the hedges and woodsy undergrowth
she could see splinters of a police car's cherry and
sapphire flashers.

She showed her ID to the village officer and drove
along the short drive to the front of the house. There were
already five or six cars, including the crime scene unit
van. She had to nose her car into the underbrush to get it
off the drive a little, and then she cut the motor and got
out without locking it. Holding her shield aloft to the
clutch of city and village patrolmen hanging around the
entrance, she walked into the house through the front
door that was standing open.

Corbeil was standing in the entryway talking to two of
his detectives and turned around when he heard her steps
on the slate floor.

'Jesus Christ, Palma,' he frowned. 'You take a chopper
over here?' He nodded toward a living room through
double doors where she could see a mammoth fireplace,

sofas, and armchairs. The Hunters Creek police chief was sitting and talking to a white-maned man in a dark business suit who was also sitting, leaning forward with his forearms on his knees, one hand holding a drinking glass, the other running repeatedly through his thick hair.

'Her husband,' Corbeil said. 'He came home from a trip. San Francisco.' He started walking, and Palma followed him. 'Drove in from Intercontinental, got here a little after one.' They started up a curved staircase with a heavy wrought-iron railing ascending up over the entrance hall. Palma took her tortoiseshell clasp from her shoulder purse and began pulling back her frizzy hair. 'Said they sleep in separate bedrooms; said they always have done since they've been married, which is only a couple of years.' They reached the top of the landing, passed a huge floral arrangement on a French Empire table on the balcony, and turned into a wide corridor. 'Bedrooms are at opposite ends of the hallway. His is here ...' They passed a heavy wooden door opened up to another sitting room. Palma saw a slightly cluttered desk, obviously used for work, not just for interior decorating, which was very much in evidence everywhere in the house. '... and she's down there,' Corbeil wheezed. 'Said he always checks on her no matter how late it is when he comes in from an out-of-town trip.'

They reached the far end of the corridor and walked into a sitting room where Jay Knapp was talking with another homicide detective and Dee Quinn, a medical examiner's investigator. Corbeil extended his arm toward the opened bedroom door on the other side of the sitting room with a be-my-guest gesture, and Palma crossed the room and walked in.

The bedroom was red — the carpet, much of the upholstery on the furniture, and one of the walls, which was covered with an elaborately detailed Indian tree-of-life fabric from floor to ceiling. An ornate gilt French Empire mirror dominated the wall over the dressing table, which was crowded with as many pictures in gold, black, and red lacquer frames as cosmetics. The bed was an

Empire four-poster with a bone silk drapery pulled back and tied at the head of the bed to expose the three open sides.

As before, the bed had been stripped of everything except the single red satin sheet on which the woman lay in the familiar funereal posture. From a few steps away her face was identical to Moser's and Samenov's, almost as if it had been painted with a template. But as Palma got closer, she saw how much of a mask the makeup truly was. The woman's face had sustained so severe a beating that her features were distorted to the point of extreme deformity. In addition, this appearance was made all the more ghastly by the staring, lidless eyes which were the only cleanly defined items in a disfigured field made eerily grotesque by the pasty effects of the heavily applied cosmetics.

The woman's hair was not a true blond, tending more toward russet, with her pubic hair being several shades darker than that. In body shape, she was not as athletically lean as Moser and Samenov, having a kind of pampered attractiveness, high-hipped, full-breasted, and a pale, luminous complexion against which the wounds that had resulted from the removal of her nipples seemed an even meaner violation. They would have been pink ones, rather than dark, Palma imagined. Because the death was recent, and the room temperature was mild, the wounds themselves were still raw and moist.

Palma moved around the bed slowly, inspecting the woman from several angles. She noted that the toenails were painted. She bent down and smelled them. The polish was fresh; the killer had probably done it himself after he laid her out. She walked around to the right side of the bed and bent down again to smell the woman's fingernails. Also fresh. And there was something else. She smelled the hands again, then moved lower and smelled her waist. Bath oil. She moved around the body smelling different areas, all of which gave off the fragrance of bath oil. But it was obvious that the killer had not bathed her after she died. Had she bathed just prior to his

encounter, or had the killer given her a 'dry bath,' wiping
her down with bath oil afterward? Palma made a mental
note to check the washcloths in the bathroom and to see
if the victim had this particular fragrance of bath oil
among her toilet articles.

The ligature marks around her neck and wrists and
ankles were the same as the others. And the bite marks.
But this time the biting had been savage. The killer's teeth
had ripped and torn the flesh, and chunks were bitten out
in three places: the left breast, the inner left thigh, and the
right vulva, where more than an inch of the labia majora
had been bitten away with its hair. Palma was able to
make note of this last bite without touching the body only
because of a slight change in pattern in this victim's
positioning: her legs had not been closed together tightly.
Palma studied this minor variation for a long time, her
concern with the state of the body having grown to such
an extent as to be obsessive. She had begun to believe
that nothing in these homicides, no matter how minute,
was incidental. Could it be that the importance the killer
placed on a particular detail had an inverse relationship to
its size so that the smaller the point of attention, the
greater its significance? But this subtle separation of the
legs truly did seem incidental, except that it attracted
notice to the bite taken from the labia majora.

And then there was the strange treatment of the navel.
Palma bent closer to the woman's stomach and examined
the wound. Again the upper and lower teeth had been
placed precisely around the navel in two different positions to form a complete closed circle. Within that circle
the tissue was turning black from the blood that had been
sucked to the surface of the skin with such force that the
killer had almost extracted blood through the epidermis
itself. What was the fascination this man had for his
victim's navels? Not only did he consistently abuse them,
but he did so with a precision that indicated a ritual
significance. Although the other bites seemed almost
random — aside from the fact that they were primarily
detected at parts of the body that had sexual connotations

— the preoccupation with a precise kind of abuse of the navel was quickly becoming a point of focus for Palma, as it was for the killer.

Straightening up, she moved back from the bed and walked around it, from one side to the other several times, being careful to stay far enough back so that she would not mash into the carpet any hairs that might have fallen during the killer's ministrations. The red satin sheet provided an unusual foil for the victim's positioning and allowed Palma to see something she had not noticed with the other two victims. She made another mental note to check the crime scene photographs of Moser and Samenov. She returned to the left side of the bed, gathering her skirt close around her, holding it in her lap as she bent down once again. The sheet was not completely smooth around all sides of the body, but was puckered along the length of the woman's left side, with a significant bunching of the satin adjacent to her hips. Palma studied the angle of the furrows. Jesus.

He had lain down with her.

And what had he done?

He had tied her up and tortured her; he had mutilated and tormented her while she was still alive; he had strangled her to death; and then he had cleaned her up and carefully, taking great pains, meticulously had applied makeup in a specific manner. What in the hell had he done then? They would find no semen. They would find no discharge other than vaginal fluids she might have smeared on the sheets during their sexual foreplay before the killer had gotten down to business. So what in God's name had he done at this point? Why did he lie down with her?

Palma swallowed. What was it that Claire had said? Even at the time Palma had thought the remark provoked an eerie imagery. Psychosexually, she had said from the shadows, Gil Reynolds was a cretin.

She heard voices coming down the wide corridor outside and recognized Birley and Frisch. They stopped speaking when they entered the sitting room and both were quiet when they walked through the bedroom door. They both looked at Palma, but neither spoke as their eyes settled on the woman on the bed. Frisch stopped a few feet away from the bed, but Birley continued up to the edge, where he stood silently, his experienced eyes ticking off the similarities of the wounds. He shook his head. Palma looked at Frisch, whose long face wore the drawn expression of a lieutenant who knew he was waist-deep in trouble.

'I want to get Sander Grant down here,' Palma said. 'No one here has ever seen anything like this. This is dark water, Karl.'

Frisch, moving stiffly, approached the bed. 'Goddammit,' he said.

'She's right,' Birley said. He grimaced. 'Shit, just look at this.'

'Goddammit,' Frisch's thin shoulders sat at an odd angle, one hand holding a handset emitting short bursts of static.

'I'm going to call him,' Palma said, and walked out into the sitting room where a telephone rested on a gilt-trimmed French secretary. Corbeil was standing in the doorway of the bedroom and a few more people were inching through the hall door into the sitting room. LeBrun still hadn't arrived.

Palma dialed Grant's number, which she had memorized. She looked at Corbeil and then at the cluster of people. 'I'm going to have to have some privacy,' she said. Corbeil started getting them out and shouted out to someone to get everybody the hell downstairs and put crime scene ribbon at the bottom of the stairs with a couple of officers.

Palma heard the phone ringing at the other end and then, remembering, she turned to Corbeil.

'What's her name?'

'Her name? Oh, Mello . . . Bernadine.'

'Hello,' Grant said.

PART
TWO

FIFTH
DAY

31

'Oh, let's see,' Clay Garrett mused, squinting a little at the rain pelting through the low beam of his head lights as he turned off the Sam Houston Parkway onto John F. Kennedy Boulevard that approached the Houston Intercontinental Airport from its south side. Oncoming cars on the other side of the esplanade threw splashes of light over his hook-nosed profile, mottled with shadows from the raindrops on the windshield. 'Sander's kind of a serious sort of fella. I used to work in the same field office with him a *long* time ago, before he was in this BSU business. Like most of us, he doesn't seem to have changed any, just gets deeper and deeper into how he is.' Garrett smiled at that.

Palma waited, looking through the windshield at the rain drifting across the broad, lighted corridor that had been cut through dense pines. They began to pass under the green signs suspended high over the boulevard that told you what airlines were in what terminals. To their left, across the esplanade and the oncoming traffic were the air cargo terminals: Aramco, Conoco, Tenneco, Shell, Exxon . . .

'He's . . . polite. A gentleman, sort of, but not all that easy to get to know.'

The Intercontinental Airport was on the north side of

the city, half an hour's drive out in good traffic. They were almost there and Palma had just now gotten around to asking the question after a lull in conversation. She had been awake only half an hour when Garrett picked her up at her home in University Place. The day had been long and hectic, and she felt the mild disorientation she always experienced when she went to sleep late in the afternoon and woke just as it was getting dark. After staying at the scene of Bernadine Mello's death until Julie LeBrun had finished and taken his findings to the crime lab, and the body had gone to the morgue, Palma had spent the rest of the morning going through Mello's personal effects with Birley.

This latest death had changed the face of the investigation, as everyone knew it would when it finally happened. The media were all over the story within hours, and no matter how tight a homicide division runs its shop, the big picture cannot be kept under wraps indefinitely. Bernadine Mello's death took the covers off. The media didn't know much, but they soon connected the deaths of the three West Houston women who had died in the last few weeks. The headline articles in the late-morning editions of the papers and the lead story on the noon radio and television news didn't hesitate to use the terms 'psychopath' and 'serial killer.' The stories were short, but the reporters smelled fresh meat, and they were swarming.

Karl Frisch was quick to set operational parameters and establish a system of procedures for a task force. Don Leeland's past experience in crime analysis landed him the desk job of case review coordinator. Assisted by another detective, he would function as the central clearing point for all the new information that would come in about the four cases (Ackley and Montoya were considered as a single case) from the task force's investigative teams. He would review and analyze their reports and supplements regarding suspects, victims, witnesses, and physical evidence, looking for new relationships between leads, create files on each witness and suspect (including photographs), create charts and diagrams of the progress of each case, monitoring changes in suspect status, and coordinating follow-up interviews to prevent duplicate contacts or omissions.

Jules LeBrun was put in charge of evidence control and storage and would act as liaison with Barbara Soronno in the crime lab. If there were any screwups regarding evidence, the buck stopped with LeBrun.

Cushing got a new partner and was to continue concentrating on the list of men found in Dorothy Samenov's address book and pursuing any leads that came from those interviews. Palma and Birley's assignments took them in opposite directions. Birley now had to check out Bernadine Mello's physicians as he had done with Moser and Samenov, as well as having the immediate task of familiarizing Manny Childs and Joe Garro with the earlier cases so they could pick up Bernadine Mello.

Frisch himself would be responsible for communicating with the media, working with Leeland to determine what nonsensitive material could be released in careful information bites to satisfy the journalists. The captain would take the heat from the politicos and the police administration. Nobody was looking forward to it.

Palma had to go back to Saulnier to try to get as many names of women in the society as Saulnier could be persuaded to cough up, including Claire's, and she had to try to establish whether Bernadine Mello was also a member of the group. But by the time all that was hashed out it was one o'clock in the afternoon and she was headed home for a few hours' sleep. It seemed she had hardly gotten her clothes off before Garrett was calling to tell her he was on his way, and by four o'clock they were on the darkening, rainy streets headed to the airport to pick up Grant and Robert Hauser, the other agent coming with him.

'But Sander's had a run of hard luck.' Garrett bent forward to read a sign passing overhead. 'He's got twin daughters. Few years ago . . . uh, it's been three, I guess, a little over, his wife died of cancer. It was one of those things where she went in for a checkup and they discovered it and in ninety days she was gone. It was about four months before the girls were to go off to college. They decided they'd sit it out a year, a semester at least, but Sander made them go on. He knew it'd be easier on them to get into something new, not mope around the place with him. They went on. But it was hell on Sander. Had a house full of women, then six months later nobody but him.'

They drove under a runway just as a lumbering airliner was passing across, its engines screaming with a loud, sucking whine, and then Garrett steered the car into the coils of ramps that brought them to the parking garage outside Terminal B. He took a ticket at a gate, and then parked directly across from the terminal doors. He cut off the motor, but didn't move to get out of the car.

'He got depressed,' Garrett continued, pulling the key out of the ignition and draping his wrists over the steering wheel. 'Twins were in school up in New York — Columbia — so they couldn't come home that much. Sander got to where he couldn't stand the house. They lived somewhere around Fredericksburg, big old home, because it was close to Quantico. Twins grew up there mostly. But he couldn't take it. Sold the place, pulled up all his roots, and moved into Washington. That's a pretty good commute down Interstate 95 to Quantico every day.'

Garrett thought a moment, started tapping the key on the steering column, thinking. 'I don't know what happened, exactly, but there was something about him getting involved with a Chinese woman ... some kind of diplomat's wife. He married her. I think she was ... totally out of character for Grant. She was a real knockout, and he just went nuts over her. And then it all blew to hell.'

Garrett shook his head. 'I don't know. Rumors. Hell, Sander never confided in people, that's his problem. That's what Marne was, his confidante. When she died ... screwed up his psychological equilibrium. Guy like that, what he does for a living. It's like being a patho-

logist; dead people from breakfast to supper. Except with
Sander and his boys it's the psychological stuff too, not
just the bodies. With a pathologist he can just walk away
from it, leave it at the morgue. These guys with Sander,
they carry it around in their heads.'

Garrett looked at Palma. 'But I understand he got
through it all right. Chinese lady an' all.'

'How long has that been?' Palma asked.

Garrett shook his head. 'I don't know, exactly,' he said,
reaching for the door handle.

They made their way along the crowded concourse,
past the security checks that took them into the gates.

'There's Hauser,' Garrett said, looking at his watch.
'They're early.'

They approached a good-looking young man with
thick, closely barbered blond hair who was standing by a
small pile of luggage at the edge of the gate's waiting
area, eating a Butterfinger. He recognized Garrett across
the flow of pedestrian traffic in the concourse, took the
last bite of the candy bar, and wadded up the wrapper,
tossing it into the trash. By the time they got to him he
was swallowing and grinning, putting out his hand.

Garrett made the introduction and apologized for
being late.

'Naw, we're fifteen minutes early,' Hauser said. 'Tail
winds.' He pointed his chin at the bank of telephones
across the concourse.

'Sander's over there,' he said, and he and Garrett
quickly fell into a conversation while Palma turned
toward the telephones. There were eight telephones in a
row facing the concourse, and another eight on the other
side, out of sight. All the ones on the near side were busy:
two women, six men. Palma tried to pick him out, but
none of them seemed right to her. She looked at the legs
under the bank of telephones on the other side. Four
men, one in jeans, one in khakis, two in suits. She was
looking at the two pairs of suit trousers when she realized
that the last man on the right was looking at her from
between the telephone boxes. He was talking, but

watching her, and when their eyes met he was not the
one to break eye contact. She pretended she hadn't seen
him looking at her, let her eyes go down the length of the
crowded concourse, and then turned to Hauser and
Garrett, catching Hauser cutting his eyes at her while
Garrett was ending a story that Hauser could have
comprehended quite easily at three times the speed.

'Here he comes,' Hauser said, and both Garrett and
Palma turned to see a man cutting through the concourse
traffic wearing a double-breasted suit. She had never seen
a special agent wear a double-breasted suit. The suit coat
was unbuttoned and Grant was putting a breast pocket
wallet into his coat as he stalled once or twice in the cross
traffic. Palma guessed him at six-two or three, maybe one
hundred seventy pounds. He had dark hair going gray,
and which he wore a little fuller than she would have
expected, combing it back at the temples so that the gray
streaked and was visible from a distance. He wore a
clipped mustache that was slightly darker than his hair.
His nose was not broad, but straight and handsome, or
rather it had been straight. A significant crook in the
bridge signaled its having been broken, perhaps more
than once. His eyes were slightly hooded with the beginnings of crow's-feet at the corners. He walked with his
shoulders back, not with a military bearing but with a
rather loose-gaited, comfortable stride. As he approached,
he smiled and put his hand out to Palma first.

'Detective Palma,' he said. 'It's good to see you,
finally.' He turned to Garrett. 'Clay, I appreciate your
coming out to get us.' They shook hands and then Grant
reached down and picked up his small, soft leather valise
and hanging suit bag, as did Hauser, and the four of them
started walking.

'Sorry about the short notice,' Palma said. 'But I was
afraid this was going to get out of hand before any of us
could get a grip on it.'

'It's okay. We do a lot of short-notice work,' Grant
said. 'Anything since this morning?' They had stepped
out in front of Garrett and Hauser, and Palma was having

to take long steps to keep up with Grant. While they walked down the long concourse she told him about forming the task force and how it was set up.

'That's good,' he said. 'It'll be easier that way. I've got some stuff for you from one of the VICAP analysts. It's not much. They didn't have any strong hits, but there're some things you need to check out. Something in New Orleans, something in Nashville, and a long shot out in Los Angeles.'

They emerged into the main concourse and started across the cavernous terminal lobby, getting separated by the crowds, coming back together, finding Garrett and Hauser ahead of them.

'How're you holding up?' Grant asked, dodging a pair of airline stewardesses quick-walking across in front of them with their luggage on small wheeled cars.

'I don't even know,' she said.

Grant looked around at her and smiled. 'Well, maybe it won't last too long.'

'It's already done that,' Palma said. 'This is my first one of these. I don't like the way it makes me feel. And I'm not talking about the loss of sleep.'

This time Grant didn't say anything. Palma wanted to look at him, but they were already going through the electric doors, out into the drive across from the garages.

On the way into the city Palma turned and leaned her back against the door and reviewed Bernadine Mello's background.

'She was forty-two; her husband, Raymond Mello, is sixty. Mello's a structural engineer. Made a personal fortune on a patented method for testing the tensile strength in construction steel, and still travels a lot doing this. They'd been married just a little over two years. She'd been divorced three times before she married Mello, and he'd been married once before. According to him, this marriage was going under too. Mello's pretty candid and readily admits the marriage hadn't worked out like he'd hoped. He said both of them had had other lovers, in fact her lawyer had hired a private detective to substantiate his affair. He suspected she was about to sue him for divorce. He wasn't sure of the men she'd been sexually involved with, except one, her psychiatrist. When we asked him if he had any reason to believe that his wife might be bisexual, he seemed flabbergasted by the idea. And we didn't find anything in her house that would have suggested it, either.'

'How was he reacting to her death?'

'Genuinely shocked, I think.'

'How long had his wife been seeing the psychiatrist?' Grant asked. The rain on the side windows of the car cast gray spatters over the front of his white shirt as they sped along Interstate 45, heading south into the city.

'Five years.'

'And did the affair predate the marriage to Mello also?'

'He said he thought so.'

'Then the psychiatrist should be able to enlighten you on the bisexual question,' Grant said. 'For our purposes, he'll be more valuable to us than the woman herself. How old is he?'

'I don't know.'

'He hasn't been interviewed yet?'

'No.'

'There shouldn't be any client-doctor privileges now that she's dead. He could be a gold mine in leads, especially if there *is* a connection with her and the other women and their organization.'

Grant had been sitting forward a little as Palma talked. Outside, the stormy late afternoon was as dark as dusk from the lowering clouds, and Grant's face was largely obscured except when it was being illuminated in brief washes of pale light as they passed the freeway lights at regular intervals. Only the left side of his face was periodically visible to her. As she listened to him talk and watched his eyes in the passing washes of mottled light that came through the rainy window, she felt them looking at her with a calm regard that seemed to operate from a different level of consciousness than his words. They did not seem to her to convey an inner world consistent with his personality.

If Sander Grant seemed easily congenial at first meeting, she was sure that she could not trust that assessment. As Garrett pushed the Bureau car through the complex interchanges of expressways that brought them into the city, Palma began to have the feeling that Grant's eyes were what the man was all about, and the amiable personality that greeted her at the airport was only a practiced facade that he presented as a matter of professional necessity. She wondered how long he employed the mask or if, in fact, he ever took it off at all. She hoped he did and that he would do it quickly and get it over with. She didn't look forward to working with a man who held her at arm's length with a bogus cordiality. Nor did she relish waiting for the inevitable moment when, because of tension or competitiveness or unsuppressable egoism, he would yank off the mask of amicability and confront her with whatever it was his eyes were really hiding.

Suddenly, whether justified or not, the prospect of working with Sander Grant took on a slight edge of apprehension that was quite separate and apart from the context of the grisly murders he had come to help her investigate.

32

Holding a black umbrella over his head, Dr. Dominick Broussard stood on the back terrace of his three-story home and looked past a margin of pines at the afternoon mist hovering in the honey locusts and redbuds scattered across the sloping lawn to the bayou below. Accompanied by a big, tawny Labrador that he ignored, he stepped off the terrace and progressed along a stone path that wandered through his property toward a smaller building that architecturally echoed the larger house and which served as his office. This building, which he pretentiously referred to as his studio, was situated nearer the bayou than the main house, and was nestled in a dense wood that extended beyond it some distance before reaching the end of the doctor's property. Woods provided the same seclusion on the opposite side of the large house as well. He had privacy, he liked to remind himself, a great deal of privacy.

For the last half hour Dr. Broussard had been in an emotional free fall, a long descent through his own empty grief precipitated by Bernadine Mello's death — the Asian anchorwoman on the noon news program had said 'murder.' He was staggered, but had had the presence of mind to quickly make three telephone calls canceling his afternoon appointments. He had caught two of his clients, but Evelyn Towne had already left her home to have a late lunch with a friend before his appointment.

She couldn't be reached.

Walking away from the sandwich his maid had prepared for him in the gray light of the sun-room, he had taken his umbrella and in a preoccupied daze had stepped outside. He had intended to go to his studio, but instead was now walking directionless across the lawn until he came to one of the paths that laced his wooded property. He took the first one and followed it. Now, under the canopy of trees, he folded up his umbrella, took off his jacket and draped it over his left arm, and loosened his tie in deference to the heat and humidity. All about him the rain tapped on the huge leaves of the catalpas; it drummed and roared so that he could not hear his own footsteps crunching on the cinder.

The Labrador followed him, blinking in the steady rain, the two of them circling aimlessly along the bayou paths until the dog's hair was matted and Broussard's own thick wavy hair was kinking, his hand-tailored shirt plastered against his thick barrel chest, where the hair showed through the material made translucent by the rain. Finally he stopped. He looked down the path in front of him, at the leaves glistening and shimmering in the rain. Without taking his eyes off them, he reached out to the trunk of a water oak for support. Slowly he leaned against it, letting it take all his weight, and then he began to cry, a dry, awkward sound at first because he was unused to it. The Labrador sat unquestioningly on the wet path, and with a dense curiosity and a slack tongue calmly regarded the pattern of the rain as it stippled the surface of the brown bayou water in overlapping mandalas. Broussard, overcome by the dizzying effervescence of images bubbling up from his memory, overcome by an unexpected fear of loneliness, a queer selfishness that made him anguish more bitterly for himself than for Bernadine, wept like a child.

He slumped against the water oak, submerged in his own self-concern until he was entirely soaked, until his clothes were heavy and clinging, until, even in the stifling heat, he felt a chill grow against his spine and settle in across the back of his shoulders. Pushing himself away from the tree, he wiped his hair out of his eyes and continued on the path toward his studio. With the Labrador lumbering along behind him in the mist, he arrived at the office's back door and paused in an alcove to step out of his soaking shoes. Having left the studio unlocked at noon, he pushed open the rear door which allowed him to come and go to his office without being seen by his clients, who parked in a cinder drive at the front of the building and entered the office from a more formal entrance.

The equanimous Labrador lay down in the alcove with an overweight sigh as Broussard entered the darkened hallway and turned into his office. The glass wall that looked down to the bayou presented a pointillistic scene of hanging mist, as if Georges Seurat had managed to create a picture that possessed an imperceptible motion, one that could not be seen to move, but that could be seen to have moved. The mist — almost a fog — was thick, then sheer, appearing first before, then behind the trees, allowing the bayou now to emerge and now to disappear into its ghostly drifting.

Broussard went into his bathroom, shed his rain-soaked clothes, and took a warm shower. He tried to maintain a blank mind as he washed his hair. He did not want to think about Bernadine either in life or in death. He did not want to remember anything about Bernadine. When he got out, he dried himself and dressed in some of the clothes he kept in the studio closet, a fresh pair of gray trousers, a freshly starched pale blue shirt and dark navy tie. He didn't bother with a jacket. He walked on to the liquor cabinet and poured a Dewars and water and was already standing in front of the plate-glass windows when he remembered he was drinking Bernadine's drink, her beloved scotch. It was nectar to her. She was nectar to him. Jesus. How odd, how surreal, he had felt when he heard, and saw, Bernadine's name on the bright red lips of the newscaster.

No suspects.

He had nearly finished his drink when he heard the front door opening and suddenly realized that he hadn't turned on lights anywhere in the office.

'Dominick. Are you here?' Evelyn.

'Yes, back here,' he called and started turning on his desk lamps, and then the several others in the large office. He had no ceiling light, preferring the more oblique lighting afforded by lamps. He quickly finished his drink as he heard her footsteps in the short hallway, and then she was in the doorway just as he was closing the liquor cabinet.

She looked at him quizzically. 'No lights?'

'I've just come back from lunch at the house,' he said. 'I was just turning them on.' There was a split second when he wanted to blurt out the news of Bernadine's death. But it was only a moment, and when he didn't do it, he knew he never would.

Evelyn looked at him and moved across the room to the windows where Broussard himself had just been standing. She looked out to the rainy landscape for a long time, long enough for her silence to attract his attention and long enough for them to become aware of the small sounds that fill silences: the ticking of the mantel clock on the bookshelves, rain dripping from the eaves onto the glass wall, the sound of their own breathing, the inner turmoil of their own thoughts.

Evelyn Towne was the only one of Broussard's clients whom he totally respected. It was his opinion that she should not be a client at all, and he had told her so. But she had only laughed and disregarded the remark. Despite the fact that Evelyn (she pronounced it with a long initial E) was a woman of pleasing personality and even temperament, Broussard considered her, as she considered herself, a serious person. A woman of extraordinary intelligence and perception, she was not amused by the solitary sound of her own voice. Propriety was important to her, yet it was not her way to be arch or aloof. Social standing meant nothing to her, but correct behavior did, and she respected it wherever she found it, whether in the demeanor of the Mexican *vaqueros* who worked her husband's ranches along the border, or in the attitudes of the powerful men she met circulating among Houston's social elite.

At forty-eight she was tall and erect, with handsome chestnut hair threaded with gray and which she kept in a longer style than most women her age. She took care of herself and still wore the same size dress she wore when she was twenty-five. He had never seen her without earrings, and they were always pearls. During the three years he had been consulting with her, he had seen her wear a wonderful variety of them in every color, shape, size, and arrangement. Today they were irregular drops, rather small, and smoky gray.

Moving with a grace of motion that was bred into her as surely as her eccentric personality, Evelyn turned away from the windows and sat in one of the two leather armchairs. She was one of his few clients who refused to submit to the chaise longue. Broussard sat in his own armchair, crossed his legs, and looked at her. She wore a navy silk jersey dress unbuttoned at her neck just enough to make out the beginnings of a generous décolletage. She wore no necklace. She never did. Her nails were freshly polished, the same shade of red as her lipstick, and when she raised a hand and pushed back a lock of chestnut hair, an antique gold bracelet with bead and reel carvings dangled on her wrist.

'I've had another poem published,' she said, arranging the hem of her dress. 'In *Daedalus*.'

'Congratulations,' he said, trying to sound congenial and undisturbed. 'A long one?'

'Why do you ask that?'

'Curiosity.'

'But *why* do you ask?' Evelyn didn't like him to be imprecise.

'The last poem you published was a long one. Seventy-six lines, I think.' She would admire the fact that he had remembered. 'Much longer than most of your others. I only wondered if you'd continued to do that, or if that last one had been an anomaly.'

She smiled. 'This one was fourteen.'

'A sonnet, then.'

Again she smiled. 'You're on your toes,' she said.

'Shakespearean or Petrarchan?'

'Petrarchan. Do you really know the difference?'

'Only that Shakespearean ones end in couplets,' he confessed.

She laughed outright, a good, full laugh that he always enjoyed because it was the only thing about her that wasn't complicated.

'Jesus, Dominick. I thought for a moment you actually knew something.' She sobered slowly as she cast an eye over his desk and its crowded collection of small figurines, statuettes, and icons of women from history and myth and religion. Today there was something slightly remote about her, something telegraphed in the brevity of the laugh cut off a millisecond too soon, something in the way her eyes did not altogether relax when she looked at him. Evelyn was not a woman to be understood, only studied. Without seeming to, without exhibiting a transparent reticence, she had held more in reserve from him than any client he ever had. She was still largely an enigma, and even after three years he could not say with any certainty why she had come to him in the first place.

'What was it about?' he asked. Evelyn had leveled her eyes at him, waiting for the question.

'Sex and death.'

Two things. Evelyn was incapable of kitsch, and she wasn't smiling any more. Broussard didn't know how to arrange his face. She rescued him.

'Sex, because it's been on my mind a lot lately,' she explained. It was the kind of response that was typical of her: straight to the point, but so provocative that it immediately elicited another question. 'And death, because I want to be rid of it. I want it to leave me alone until it has business directly with me.'

'Evelyn's husband, Gerald, who was twelve years older than she, had been dying of cancer for nearly two years. Broussard knew that she had spent much of her time nursing him, and that rather than having to put him in a hospital she had turned their River Oaks home into a veritable clinic so that he could die at home. Only he wouldn't die. It had been a sad ordeal that dragged on grotesquely. Then, finally, two months earlier, it ended.

'Of course, I wrote the poem before he died,' she said. 'You know it takes forever for these things to be accepted and published, and by some quirk I wasn't notified that they'd taken it. Then, yesterday, the magazine arrived. I sat down in a chair in the entrance hall and read the poem on the spot. Oddly, reading it like that, flat out with no emotional preparation, it seemed to finalize Gerald's death more than his actual dying. Maybe because his death took so long, and the poem,' she averted her eyes again with a preoccupied interest in something unseen, '... only fourteen lines.' Then she looked back to him. 'I want to talk about it.'

'The poem?'

'About what the poem is about.'

Broussard waited as Evelyn crossed her legs at the ankles and again adjusted the hem of her navy jersey. It pleased him to remember what was beneath the jersey, though he did not dwell on it with a recall of titillating sexual images as he often did with other women. It hadn't been that kind of thing with Evelyn.

'Do you want to hear something absolutely primitive?' she said, smiling oddly, almost affectionately. 'Gerald's "cancer" was syphilis.' She paused and gave a rueful shrug. 'Oh, I'd never been in any danger,' she added quickly. And then, 'It was called "latent syphilis" and he had had it for years before it was discovered. By then it was in its third and terminal stage.' The fingers of her left hand idly burnished the antique gold bracelet on the opposite wrist. 'There was a time when he was importing a lot of cattle for the ranches. He thinks, maybe ... on one of his buying trips to Argentina ... in Guatreché, perhaps, or Villa Regina ...'

Broussard was astonished, but not by the revelation of

Gerald's syphilis. He knew that latent syphilis demonstrated no signs or symptoms until its final stage, and
often it went on for decades before it manifested any
physical evidence to its doomed host. Normally it would
not be difficult to transmit the disease to another person.
Normally. But Evelyn had said she had never been in any
danger. So what had been the nature of her sexual
relationship with her husband all these years? How could
he, Broussard, have talked with her regularly for three
years and never have gotten a hint of something so out of
the ordinary? He was appalled. He suddenly thought of
Bernadine's revelation. Jesus Christ. Did he know nothing
about women? But, of course, he did. Still, there were the
few, the rare ones, whose intellects or personalities he
found to be truly riveting, and who lived their lives on
more dimensions than he could identify. These he
studied, these he was drawn to, and even loved, because
their inner lives approached the magnitude of the archetypical.

   'I can imagine what you must be thinking,' she said.

   Broussard almost believed she could. Whereas Bernadine's great attraction for him had been her intuitive and
culturally unencumbered appreciation of human sexuality, Evelyn presented him with an equally fascinating
personality, but from a position at the other end of the
spectrum.

   When he first had begun consulting with Evelyn, he
knew immediately that she was an extraordinary woman.
She was a regularly published poet, born to wealth and
married to wealth, striking in appearance, gracious (if
somewhat proper), uninterested in small talk, childless,
indifferent to playing any role in that uppermost rank of
society where her wealth would have made her an in-
fluential player, at times a little distant, a woman of
privacy who had sought him out and requested only that
she be allowed an altered form of analysis. She wanted no
stated objective or therapeutic technique. It was a request
that required a loose interpretation of 'analysis.'

   Quickly enthralled by her, he had known better than to

try to seduce her. Instead he employed his most calculating subtleties to convey that his feelings toward her could be much more serious than what he was presenting. But he persisted in keeping his distance, never making an overt commitment in even the slightest way. Then one morning nearly eight months after they had their first consultation, she came into his office and proposed an affair. A limited one. She would allow him six 'occasions,' and he could choose the timing — up to three months. Broussard was dumbfounded. It was the most original proposal he had ever received. But it proved to be only the beginning of his surprises. If Bernadine Mello's sexual energy was the most unencumbered, the most natural, he had ever experienced, Evelyn's was surely the most exotic. To his utter astonishment, this proper and mannered woman had proceeded to introduce him to rarefied pleasures, and not only was she electrifyingly creative, but it was soon clear to him that she was practiced at it.

It happened during three weeks in August. Broussard's understanding of her had been profoundly altered, their relationship transformed. It was not only that she had given herself to him in such a singular manner and with such unexpected and undissembling passion that he was overwhelmed and made ashamed of his own cynical design, but that at her own wise choosing what she had given had been all the more dear to him because its duration was predetermined. It had a beginning and an end that were known beforehand, a promise that what they had shared on those sultry August afternoons never would be less than their finest moments. It was a gift, really, of immortality. What they had had together would never age like youth, never fail or fade, never disappoint by becoming something less than what it once had been, as old affairs were wont to do. Evelyn had understood too well the fate that time assigned to all such liaisons, and rather than let it have its way in diminishing theirs, she had cheated it. It had been a sage decision.

All of this he remembered in a matter of seconds, in

the time it took her to pause, and then continue.

'I don't know why, really, I decided to tell you this,' she said. 'Or why I decided to bring it up in such a silly, circumlocutious manner.'

'You're being disingenuous,' he said.

Letting her eyes go to the images on his desk again, she raised her left arm and rested it on the edge of the desk while her hand arched to touch the buttocks of one of the taller statues, the darkened, greenish-stained bronze of the goddess Laksmi, whose hips were cocked in the typical pose of Hindu statuary. Laksmi's tightened buttocks were as round as her naked breasts, and Evelyn's fingers moved over them, circling them tightly.

'You don't know much about women, Dominick,' she said. They had had this discussion before, of course, a number of times. Most often these introductory words were delivered in a tone of good-natured baiting, at times with irony, once with a startling bitterness. But always they were a prelude to a revelation.

'I like to think I have a certain insight,' he said.

Absently, she watched her own fingers on the smooth mounds of the goddess's buttocks.

'A certain insight,' she conceded with a single nod. She let her middle finger go under Laksmi's buttocks and then stop between her thighs. Her eyes slid to Broussard and caught him looking at what she was doing.

'How,' she asked, 'do you think I reacted to the news that Gerald was dying of syphilis, rather than cancer?'

Broussard looked at her. 'You didn't know?'

She shook her head, kept her finger between Laksmi's thighs.

'How did you find out?'

'He told me — after we brought him home from the hospital. The doctors had conspired with him up to that point, up until they knew it was imminently terminal. Gerald then told them he wanted to tell me himself, after he was set up at home.' She pulled her finger away from the statue and rubbed it lightly against her thumb as if drying moisture. Her eyes had lost their focus on him as she remembered.

'We had nurses to stay with him,' she said. 'One afternoon — it was three o'clock in the afternoon, an odd time to do that sort of thing, it seemed to me later — he asked his nurse to leave and asked me to come to his room. I've told you about Gerald. He was a kind man. A gentleman and a gentle man. He treated everyone with the same evenhanded respect, no exceptions. He was a kind of philosopher in that, if you think about it. It was spring, and he was in a room surrounded with windows, as airy as a solarium, and outside every window pink azaleas were creating a gaudy flare of color.' She paused. 'When I see that shade of pink now, I think of syphilis.' She paused again. 'Strange, isn't it, how that sort of thing works . . . the mind.'

She put her hands together in her lap.

'He told me as kindly as he knew how. Told me how long he probably had had it, how he probably had contracted it. He told me how grieved he was that I was going to have to go through this with him. He talked about his life, our life. It was a very gentle kind of soliloquy . . . for it was that. I never uttered a word.

'When he was through I walked over to him, a world of pink azaleas only a foot or two away from us, an embarrassment of beauty under the circumstances. I walked over to him and kissed him. I kissed him on the lips. I forced my tongue into his mouth and gave him the most erotic, most sensuous kiss I had ever given him. And then I turned and walked out of the room. I went straight upstairs and packed a suitcase and drove off within an hour without telling him or anyone else where I was going.'

She was breathing shallowly, oblivious of Broussard.

'I was gone for nine days. I never called him or checked on him or told him where I was. After I came back — I just showed up one day — I dedicated myself to him, nursing him, taking care of him; I cleaned him, bathed him, groomed him, read to him, sat with him when nothing else would do. I was with him every minute of the rest of his life and at the moment of his death five months later.' She stopped, and her eyes went back to Broussard. 'He never asked where I'd gone, or what I did, or why.'

In the silence that followed, Broussard watched the poet's hands crook back gently at the wrists as if to prepare to gesture and in his mind's eye he saw the solarium and the hazy glow of pink azaleas.

'I ... have no earthly idea why I kissed him that way,' she said, and Broussard could see in her face that the memory of that moment was tormenting her. He had never seen her this shaken, and he knew that it was costing her more than it would most people for him to see her this way. 'God knows,' she said, 'I've regretted it.'

Broussard looked at her. 'Neither of you ever mentioned it, I suppose.'

'Of course not ... I think he believed he understood why I did it.'

'And that's what bothers you.'

'Damn right it does,' she snapped. '*I* don't understand it, how could he?'

'You're talking about a dead man, Evelyn.'

'What's that supposed to mean?'

'It's over. He's gone. You'll never know what he thought about it.'

'For Christ's sake, Dominick,' Evelyn said, gaping at him, leaning forward over her crossed legs, a single smoky gray pearl drop glinting at him through a thin web of silver-laced chestnut hair. 'I know all the logic of it. It's the other stuff I'm having trouble with.'

There was a true urgency in Evelyn's voice, but her face showed anger. She was clearly frustrated that the kiss had had more to do with her unconscious than she wanted to admit. It was an interesting thing in a woman that she was so insistent upon everything having a rational basis. But she was not all that terribly logical, and certainly not as disciplined as she would like to believe. There was too much of the poet in her, and from what he

knew of her sexuality, she was fully capable of aban-
doning herself to fey winds.

'What other stuff?' he asked.

She sank back in the armchair and looked away, then
back at him, and then to the collection of statuettes on his
desk.

'I don't know,' she said.

It was an evasive response. He let her simmer. His
heart was not in it. He looked at the pearls through the
wires of gray and chestnut. Evelyn was a complex beauty.
She would never have an indifferent lover. She would
never allow it, dedicated as she was to intensity.

'Why hadn't you ever been in danger of Gerald's
syphilis?' he asked abruptly.

Her eyes moved away from the figurines on his desk
and settled on him like dead weights.

'My God,' she said. Her voice was flat, offended.

'Is that subject inviolate?' he asked. Suddenly he was
angry. What kind of spurious indignation was she
pretending? 'You let slip,' he reminded her. 'You said you
were never in danger of contracting it.'

She shook her head. 'I didn't say that.'

Broussard looked at her. In that one moment of denial
she had diminished herself. The proud demeanor that had
distinguished her, the haughty self-assurance that had
influenced everything about her, including her posture
and the way she spoke and laughed and even made love,
had shattered in one crisp moment like fine crystal.
Broussard had not expected this capitulation to denial. So,
like everyone, Evelyn felt no shame, and it was an
emotion so potent in her as to make her put at risk her
entire persona rather than reveal the source of it.

And then Broussard surprised himself. He backed off.
He hadn't the stomach for it. Whatever he believed about
the unconscious and its demons, whatever revelations
needed to be uncovered to give her an opportunity for
peace through confrontation, he didn't care. He hadn't
the stomach to walk her through the fires of purification.
He wanted no part of her liberation because it would take

its toll on him too, as well as her, and he suddenly had had his fill of the harrowing spirit. This was one journey through hell he would not take; he would be no Virgil to Evelyn Towne. Hers would be a long quest, he could sense it — hadn't she taken this much time just to reach the point of departure, so fearful had she been? He wouldn't do it. He would rather give her up to her own anxieties, and if the truth were known, he would rather condemn her than risk his own sanity. That was what it came down to in the end, wasn't it? Was he really obligated to risk his own sanity to help these women regain hope? Who should be lost, who saved? He had been at it a long while, and now it was the time of sifting. Evelyn Towne would be a casualty of history. In another time, at another place, she would have made it. Another hour this way or that, and he would have taken the plunge with her. But the moment was now, and now he was unwilling. There would be no grand confrontation with Evelyn Towne's unconscious, no journey into the self with a wise companion. He was going to let her go to save himself, an act of spiritual triage.

'It doesn't matter,' he said, shaking his head. 'I was tired; I could easily have misunderstood.'

And Evelyn Towne looked at him with an expression of confused desperation. She knew, he thought, horrified. She knew that he had cut her loose.

33

They parked at the curb under the covered entrance of the Hyatt Regency, and Palma and Garrett waited in the sunken, thirty-story lobby while Grant and Hauser checked into their rooms. Grant had wanted to make the most of his time and asked to go to Palma's office immediately to see the crime scene photographs they had gotten on Bernadine Mello to see how they 'felt' in relation to others. He also wanted to see the crime scene photographs on the Ackley-Montalvo killings as well. Even though they were not the same type murders, Grant was eager to see them in the event they proved to have a spin-off relationship with the killings of the three women. It was a ten-block drive to the police station and a quick walk in the rain across the motor pool compound to the headquarters building.

The homicide division was approaching its evening shift with only one team out at a cantina shooting on Navigation Boulevard near the ship channel. Don Leeland had set up his operation in an office that had been used as a storage room for old equipment since the department's remodelling several years earlier. Space had always been at a premium in the homicide division and now the dusty old desks, outdated computer terminals, and worn-out metal filing cabinets cluttered the already narrow corridor that went around the island of cubicles in the center of the squad room, choking down the walking space to a

single-file passage and making the far side of the squad
room look like a fire sale.

Leeland had gone home to catch a few hours' sleep,
and Nancy Castle, a detective Leeland had pulled from
crime analysis, was sitting at one of the computer terminals plugging in the names that Childs and Garro had
produced in the Mello case, as well as those that were
coming in on the tip sheets. One of the few up sides to
having a high-profile case come out in the open was that
once the police presented the carefully selected facts of
the cases to the public, they usually generated a flood of
tips. It took only one good one to break a case wide open.
In his usual methodical fashion Leeland had set up a
process in which all tips were processed through one
specific person on each shift, and had modeled the tip
sheet itself after the one used by the Green River serial
killings task force in King County, Washington, which
included a cross-indexing system and a method for prior-
itizing suspects and information. The tips operation was
growing by the hour, with the information being fed into
the computer as soon as it came in. Even now a
uniformed officer was at a small corner desk interviewing
a telephone caller in a low monotone and filling in the
sheet.

From the moment they entered the squad room Palma
sensed a shift in Grant's easygoing demeanor. He gave a
quick look around as they threaded their way back to
Leeland's task force office and smiled briefly at Nancy
Castle when he was introduced, but did not speak. His
only interest was getting to Mello's file. Castle got it out
of the locked filing cabinets for them and Palma, Grant,
and Hauser took them into Palma's empty office while
Garret went for coffee.

Grant took off his coat and hung it over the back of
Palma's chair and gave the pictures to Hauser as he sat
down and began at page one of the case report. Hauser
turned square to Birley's desk and started with the first
pictures, which had been organized and numbered in the
chronological order of the investigation from crime scene

to autopsy. Both men turned their backs to Palma, obviously wanting to be left alone. But Palma didn't leave; there would be questions. She sat down in a chair beside the filing cabinets and waited. After a while Garrett returned with four coffees, but Grant and Hauser didn't even look up, eventually reaching for their Styrofoam cups without taking their eyes off their work. In a short while they exchanged files for photographs and continued.

Palma waited. Garrett wandered the squad room, striking up conversations with detectives who didn't know him well enough to avoid him or didn't mind his plodding speech. Grant took a long time with the photographs, studying the same body wounds in photographs that represented them from different perspectives and in different lighting conditions. He took a pencil from Palma's desk and made a few notes, and then turned in his chair to face her, crossing one leg over the knee of the other.

'What do you see different here?' he asked, then sipped from his coffee, which must have been cold at this point. His eyes, she now saw, were an unremarkable brown with hesitant splashes of light green.

'The navel bite marks,' Palma said, 'are not new — we saw them first on Samenov — but it appears he spent more time with them here. The sucking is more severe. He concentrated on the navel more this time. The facial beating is worse. Again, not new, but it got my attention.'

Grant nodded, and Palma thought she detected a slight smile around his eyes.

'The wrinkles in the sheet,' she continued. 'It looks to me like he lay down beside her, probably the last thing he did. I noticed them for the first time with Bernadine — the red silk sheet — but I went back and checked the photographs for Moser and Samenov, and they're there, too. I just hadn't noticed them. I guess the larger picture was dominating my attention. I should have noticed.'

Grant shrugged, as if it was an oversight anyone could have made.

'But I think the fact that he lies down beside them is significant,' she added.

Grant looked at her, and Palma felt as if he was actually reading her thoughts. It was the same way she felt when she knew she was being watched by a man whose sole concern with her was sexual, to undress her, to get next to her breasts and stomach and inner thighs with his mind. Most of the time this sort of thing didn't bother her, but once in a while there would be a man whose eyes and expression almost made her believe that in fact he could see beneath her clothes and, by sheer power of his imagination, place himself next to the tenderest parts of her anatomy. This was the feeling she got from Grant's soft smile, except that Grant's eyes never left her eyes. It wasn't her breasts with which he was being intimate.

He said, 'Why do you suppose he did that?'

She looked at him and hesitated. Out of the corner of her eye, she could see that Hauser was also looking at Grant, and she realized that he was not Grant's equal in this work. He was too young; Grant was his mentor.

'I suppose ... he was working himself up ... maybe masturbating — though there weren't any traces of seminal fluid.'

'But why his way? Why does he put makeup on her, fix her hair — this time he even used hair spray —' he said, looking down at the report. 'Paint her nails ... all that?'

'She's got to look a certain way,' Palma replied, remembering their telephone conversation of two nights before. 'She's got to fit into his fantasy ...'

'The "fantasy,"' Grant said, stabbing the air once with an index finger. 'Come here.' He rolled himself forward with his feet, taking the pictures from Hauser and holding them so both Hauser and Palma could see. He selected one of Mello taken from the foot of the bed so that she lay in the photograph slightly foreshortened like Holbein's pale, dead Christ, her nippleless breasts as voluptuous in wounded death as they had been in life, and the darker wool of her vulva seeming almost a wound itself in

contrast to her blond hair which complemented the
smooth, opalescent surfaces of her skin.

'Most of the time a crime scene like this is a disturb-
ance of a routine,' Grant said, his voice mellowing pen-
sively as if he were allowing her to hear him think. 'Even
when it seems to be a murder committed in extraordinary
circumstances, say, during kinky sex. It's only extraordinary to outsiders, not to the participants. They're
doing something that satisfies them, something they've
done again and again to achieve repeated gratification.
It's a routine.'

Grant used his index finger again and held it up in
front of the photograph as though it were a needle
measuring a response, letting it swing back and forth over
the picture as though it were gauging his words.

'In sexual homicides where there is, at first, a willing
partner — often a prostitute — we actually have the
possibility of two routines,' he explained. 'One is a
scenario designed to achieve their mutual satisfaction. A
scenario the killer has engaged in maybe hundreds of
times before, in reality *and* in his mind, without a fatal
conclusion. And then there's another scenario that inter-
rupts the first and is played out for the satisfaction of only
the murderer. We have to try to distinguish between the
two, and pinpoint the place at which they diverge.'
Grant's finger stopped, tilted to the left. 'Where did
Bernadine Mello's pleasures end,' his finger swung over
to the other side, 'and where did the murderer's begin?'
His finger went down and tapped the photograph. 'And
then we have to establish a chronology of the murderer's
scenario, because it's with this chronology — what he did
and the sequence in which he did it — that we begin to
reconstruct his personality.'

Grant fell silent, holding the photograph, looking at it.
Palma was close to him, close enough to catch a vague,
intimate sense of him: his bulk, his neck and shoulders
thick with the weight of his maturity rather than the hard
muscle of a younger man, his hands large enough to
cover one of hers completely if he had reached out and

placed it there. This close she couldn't look at his face, but she had watched him as he had pored over the photographs. He had a thick beard that was beginning to show through the morning's shave with feathers of stubble growing at the edges of his mustache near the corner of his mouth. The mustache itself was cleanly shaped, as if it had been sculpted, above a thin, rather stern lower lip. He had a strong jaw which, along with the broken ridge of his nose, reminded Palma of the movie version of a rigorous British military officer.

'The hotel room's already back in use, isn't it?' Grant asked, still looking at Mello's body. For a moment Palma didn't catch his meaning.

'Oh. Yes, the Doubletree. Yes, it is.'

'Samenov's condo?'

'Still sealed.'

'Then can we go see it?'

'Yes.'

He turned to her. 'Can Bob get the files on Moser and Samenov? He came along on this deal at the last minute, and he hasn't seen them.'

'Yeah, I'll get them.'

Grant stopped her. 'Can we see Samenov's tonight? And Mello's?'

'Sure. Raymond Mello's moved out for a while.'

The files were brought into Palma's office, and Robert Hauser settled in with a fresh cup of strong coffee from the evening shift's pot. Grant visited a while with Arvey Corbeil in the lieutenant's office, playing the game, touching base with the man in charge. In the morning he would have to step in and see the captain. Palma noticed that Grant was good at this. He didn't come on as Special Agent Grant, and best of all he didn't try to be one of the boys, pretending a breezy camaraderie he hadn't earned and which inevitably rang false with the naturally suspicious homicide detectives. He was not the sort of man to posture, and his unpretentious manner was immediately recognized for what it was.

By seven-fifteen Palma and Grant were once again

maneuvering their way around the mud puddles in the motor pool compound as they crossed in a light rain and went into the garage to check out a car. Grant waited while she signed out and got the keys, and then they took the steamy elevator up to the second level. As they walked through the garage, Grant took off his dripping raincoat and shook it out as they cut across the aisles toward the car, the smell of oil-stained cement and the sluggish bayou waters hanging in the dead air.

'Jesus,' he said. 'Doesn't it cool off at nights down here?'

'Not much,' Palma said, locating the right license plate and going around to the driver's side of the car.

'But shouldn't this rain cool things off?' he asked.

She jammed her key into the keyhole and looked at him over the roof of the car. 'You've never been to Houston?'

'A long time ago, in the sixties. It was December.'

She nodded. 'Well, June is the third-rainiest month of the year down here,' she said, turning the key and popping the latch without taking her eyes off him. 'And it's the third-hottest month of the year, too. The travel books call Houston's climate "humid subtropical." The coast from here to Mobile, Alabama, has the highest effective summer temperatures in the United States.' She grinned at him. 'You're going to love it.'

34

The car windows fogged with the humidity until the air conditioner cooled it down enough to clear them by the time they passed through the Cleveland Park section of Memorial Drive. Downtown hovered behind them, shimmering in the rain, looking massive and otherworldly.

For a while Grant didn't say anything, and Palma assumed it was going to be a silent drive to Dorothy Samenov's, that he was preoccupied with what he had seen in Bernadine Mello's photographs. She didn't feel uncomfortable with that, felt no pull to host a conversation. She wasn't affected by his silence one way or the other, and rather liked him sitting there, keeping to his own thoughts as they swished along the curving drive, rain glittering through the beams of her headlights like shattered glass falling out of the black sky.

'How do you feel about all this?' he asked suddenly.

Their raincoats were thrown over the seat between them, and she felt a wet sleeve against the back of her naked arm. She was surprised by the question, not that she didn't know how to answer it, but that he would ask. There were two cars not far ahead of them as they entered the edge of Memorial Park, and she followed the four ruby taillights into a thickening fog that swallowed the corridor of tall pines almost as quickly as her headlights picked them up.

'No need in trying to pretend a "professional" attitude about it,' she said, slowing a little, keeping her distance from the taillights ahead. 'I'm having a hard time maintaining my objectivity ... Actually, I've lost it completely. This guy is all I can think about. It's been, what, four and a half days since we found Dorothy Samenov, and I suddenly realized what we were dealing with. It seems like a month. Then yesterday afternoon I found Ackley and Montalvo, and early this morning they came up with Bernadine Mello.'

She lifted her foot off the accelerator as they plowed into the white center of the fog and for a moment they were hurtling through a pale dimensionless world in silence and then suddenly the four taillights appeared again five or six car lengths ahead of them.

'I used to be in sex crimes,' she continued, putting her foot on the accelerator again and picking up speed. 'I've seen the work of some pretty sleazy libidos. And since I've been in homicide I've seen a few women hacked up. I've seen worse gore, but I've never seen anything creepier than this guy.' She shook her head. 'I don't know ... I've tried to think him through. I took notes about what you said in our telephone conversation the other night, but Christ.'

It was a moment before Grant asked, 'What bothers you the most about what he's doing?'

'You mean what bothers me the most as a homicide detective or as a woman?'

'As a woman.'

She really hadn't expected him to say that.

'The bite marks. The thing he's doing with their navels. The bite, the actual bite of flesh and hair, he took out of Mello's vulva.'

'Biting is pretty common in these types of killings,' Grant said, looking straight out the windshield.

'I know,' she said.

They were approaching the West Loop, and Palma got into the left lane, which split off to become Woodway, passing under the expressway. She swung onto the access road going south and stayed there, the headlights of the sparse traffic up on the expressway to their left breezing past them in the rain.

She said, 'The guy's going to start eating pieces of them, isn't he?'

'I'd be willing to bet he's already done that.'

'You mean the nipples? The eyelids?'

'I've never seen the eyelid business,' he said, not answering the question. 'That's one of the most interesting things about these cases.'

'In what way?'

'It's just that I've never known eyelids to be considered objects of sexual attraction. Although I've seen just about everything else become an obsession. Anything they do to the sexual organs, externally or internally, doesn't surprise me. I've seen them take away the uterus as expertly as if they'd been surgeons. Same thing with the ovaries. Sometimes these guys' clinical knowledge will astound you. But it's because they're curious, mostly. A lot of them never had satisfactory relationships with women. They were either rejected or felt like they were rejected by their female peers. Their knowledge about women is woefully lacking, really subnormal. They don't really know much about them as human beings, so women become objects of curiosity for them. They literally want to take them apart and see what they're all about. Only their curiosity is limited to the sexual organs and breasts. They want to touch them and feel them and taste them. Inside and out.'

Grant stopped, and she saw him glance at her.

'Go ahead,' she said.

'Well, the point is,' he continued, 'the eyelid thing is different. I think it's another anomaly, which means it's an important indicator for us. It isn't immediately recognizable as a sexual mutilation, but it's obviously symbolic. If it *isn't* a sexual symbol ... well, it would mean we're dealing with an anomaly within anomalies, a new psychology, a wholly different kind of animal.' He paused a moment before he added, 'And I don't mind telling you, I'm skeptical about that. I think what we've got here is a killer with a special kind of wrinkle, not a special kind of killer.'

Palma exited at Post Oak, crossed San Felipe, and entered the straight, glittering heart of the posh district. The new Saks Pavilion with its towering palms dominated their immediate right and beyond that, toward the end of the boulevard, the monolithic Transco Tower rose up into the rainy darkness.

Palma checked her rearview mirror, slowed, and pointed to her left, to the sheer face of the Doubletree Hotel bisected with the recessed glass curtain and the overlapping glass-barreled vaults of the porte cochere.

'That's where they found Sandra Moser. Eighth floor, right side, in one of the rooms facing us. The curtains were still open. If you had been in one of the offices facing the street in Two Post Oak Central,' she said, nodding at an office building with silver-ribboned windows to their right, 'you could have watched the whole thing go down.'

Grant was quiet for a moment, bent forward, looking at the building through the rain. Palma had almost stopped the car. He looked to their right, into the Pavilion.

'Could you pull in here?'

She turned into the parking area in front of the Pavilion and pulled the car up to the landscaping that bordered the drive, the front of the car looking onto the boulevard and the hotel across the way. Grant stared at the hotel through the clean patches made on the windshield by the passing wipers.

'Can you tell me which window?'

She could. She had sat in this parking lot before, staring at the exact window.

'Eighth row up, counting from one floor above the lobby level. Eight windows over from the glass curtain. A nice coincidence.'

Grant nodded, but didn't say anything as he counted eight up and eight over and stared at the window that was identical to the two hundred and fifty-nine others facing them ... identical except for what had happened behind its glass almost at this exact hour twenty-three nights earlier.

Grant was leaning forward, his neck close to the dash, his face upturned and close enough to the windshield for his breath to make a little wavering patch on the glass.

'I wonder,' he said, 'when you first walked into the room that morning and found her, did you have any inkling that this one was going to be different, that it might be extraordinary?'

Because he was leaning forward she had disappeared from his peripheral vision, and had taken advantage of the opportunity to study his profile. She could see the gray streaks in the hair swept back at his temples and the slight ripple in the bridge of his nose.

'I knew it was going to give us trouble, because of her positioning,' Palma said to his profile. 'But I had no idea it would be something like this, a serial killing.'

Grant nodded and leaned back, keeping his eyes on the hotel. 'Okay,' he said.

Dorothy Samenov's condo was warm and a little stuffy. The police had adjusted the thermostat just enough to keep the edge off the heat during the day. Samenov's sister and her husband were scheduled to be back in Houston in the next week to put the condo on the market. The place was exactly as the police had left it, even with the smudges of magnetic ferric oxide.

Grant held his raincoat over his head for the short walk to the front door, and as soon as they were inside he threw the wet coat over a chair in the living room and walked straight to the bedroom as if he had been there before. He stopped just inside the doorway and looked around, then walked into the bathroom. He looked inside the shower, looked on the floor around the bidet where LeBrun had found the footprints. He turned and opened the medicine cabinet and proceeded to examine each item on each glass shelf, turning the bottles around so he could read the labels even on bottles that were easily identifiable, leaving all the labels facing out.

He put his hands in his pockets and stood there, looking at the contents of the cabinet.

'This is a good place to learn about people,' he said. He reached in and took out a flat, clear plastic container and held it up. 'Eez-Thru floss threaders. We had a child rape-murder a few years ago. Prime suspects were twin brothers who were in their early twenties and lived together. We didn't know if one of them did it or both of them, and if it was only one of them we didn't know if the other one knew about it. The psychology between these guys was strange. They were brilliant, but there were little differences in personality. Just about the time we had one of them figured out, the other one would pick up his characteristics and they'd switch. I didn't know what the hell was doing on. We didn't have *anything* on these guys. We were sure it was one of them, but because of their crazy relationship I couldn't settle on a strategy for any kind of proactive intervention.'

He took a hand out of his pocket and reached up and took a wheel of oral contraceptives. He looked to see how many she had taken, and rotated the wheel between his thumb and middle finger, then put it back on one of the glass shelves.

'At the crime scene we'd found a little piece of plastic monofilament, about three quarters of an inch. Nobody knew what the hell it was. Couldn't figure it out, didn't know if it was significant. It sort of slipped to the back of everyone's mind, that little monofilament all by itself in the bottom of the evidence file. One day another agent and myself went to talk to the brothers. While we were there I said I had to go to the bathroom. Sure, go ahead, they said. They had separate but identical bathrooms. I just wandered into one of them, didn't even know which brother it belonged to. I turned on the faucet so they couldn't hear me open the medicine cabinet door, and started going through the things on the shelves. I came across one of these containers, looked inside ... that was it. I knew what we had in the evidence bag. One of the brothers had a partial bridge. That's what these things are used for, to thread dental floss behind bridgework. As soon as we knew that, we went to work on them as if we knew which brother had done the killing. The guy confessed within thirty-six hours.'

He reached into the cabinet again and touched a couple of tubes and a jar, took the jar and put it on the same shelf as the tubes.

'Three different kinds of topical antiseptic,' he said, looking at them, pausing. 'Turned out he was compulsive about keeping his bridgework clean and carried one of these things with him all the time. We didn't know why we never found the looped end of it. But that little piece of monofilament was all the leverage we needed — one sure thing in a puzzle of possibilities. You just never know.'

Grant gently closed the medicine cabinet door and stepped out of the bathroom, turning off the light as he came out. He walked around the end of the bare bed, paused to look at the stains on the mattress, and then went to the dresser.

'Where were Samenov's folded clothes?'

'On the chair beside the bed.'

'That's interesting,' Grant said. 'I wonder why he didn't just hang them up. Closet's right here. I remember from the photographs he took some pains with them, the lapels just right, the pocket on the blouse just right above the fold. Very precise. Military, you'd think, but it wasn't. They don't do it that way in the military. Same as with Mello's clothes. Not military, but very careful.'

With his hands still in his pockets, Grant looked over the cosmetics on the dresser, which were disarranged from LeBrun's finger-printing. He did the same thing with the bottles of perfume and fingernail polish that he had done with the container in the medicine cabinet, turning the labels out.

While he was doing this Palma looked at the bed and remembered Dorothy Samenov. The heavy air in the bedroom contrasted in her memory with the morguelike cold in which she'd been found, and Palma thought how much kinder it had been for Dorothy that the low temperature had been advantageous for the killer. To have lain nearly four days in Houston's heat without the benefit of air conditioning would have done freakish things to Samenov's anatomy. At least she was saved that indignity. The chill had been an inadvertent kindness.

Grant had moved away from the dresser to the closet and was going through Samenov's dresses. He began at the left side of the closet and moved to the right, dress by dress, several times stopping to pull one out and hold it up as if he were shopping. Then he squatted down and went through her shoes on the floor of the closet, even opening each of the shoe boxes stacked at the back. Dorothy had a lot of clothes. It took him a while. When he was through he stood, backed out of the closet, and looked around the room. He looked at the dresser again and then went back to it, took the tops off several of her bottles of perfume and smelled them, replacing them as he finished with each.

He turned to the bed and sat down on it, looking at the opened closet. Almost unconsciously, as if his thoughts were elsewhere as he did it, he reached out with his right hand and pressed on the mattress, testing its firmness.

Then he stood, stepped to the dresser, and pulled open the top drawer and started going through her clothes. As with the dresses in the closet, he did this with considerable scrutiny, as if he were a buyer having to evaluate the quality of the lot, now and then holding up an item to examine it closer. When he came to her lingerie, he didn't pass over it more quickly out of a sense of decorum, but examined it as closely as he had everything else, occasionally holding up a pantie or camisole or bra, sometimes rubbing the material in his fingers. Once he even placed a pair of panties against his face, just briefly, then returned it to the drawer. The gesture startled Palma, and she looked away quickly, and then immediately she was as flustered by her reaction as she had been by what he had done.

'The S&M stuff was in the bottom drawer?' he asked without turning to her.

'Yes, and the photographs.'

Grant nodded, thinking, looking down into the drawer of lingerie. 'You know, you go along for years carrying a lot of baggage — assumptions — about men and women. You can become very comfortable with those assumptions because you don't see anything to make you doubt them. And then one day it hits you straight in the face ... wham! A myth exploded.' He closed the drawer, and turned around and looked at her. 'I think it's a very dangerous thing to be comfortable.' He smiled crookedly, perhaps at himself. 'Let's go to Mello's.'

35

As Palma pulled away from the curb in front of Samenov's and turned into Amberly Court, she looked back across the street to Helena Saulnier's. It was five past eight and the lights were out. There was no doubt in her mind that Helena had watched Dorothy's windows the whole time they had been there.

It was almost two miles through the rainy pine-bordered streets to Bernadine Mello's home. They had to cross Buffalo Bayou and then double back to Hunterwood, which took them almost to the banks of the bayou again before they saw the stone pillars at the entrance of Mello's drive. A Hunters Creek patrol unit was blocking the entrance, and Palma had to show her shield and Grant's ID before the two coffee-drinking officers would move their unit to let them in.

The cinder drive crunched under the tires as they approached the dark house, which was almost hidden from the street by shrubbery, undergrowth, and pines. Only the portico light was burning, leaving the windows on the house as slatey dark and depressing as the damp night.

Inside Palma turned on the entrance hall lights, and as he had done before, Grant started up the stairs without comment as if he already knew where the bedroom was located. Intrigued by his homing instinct, Palma simply followed him, watching him appraise the house as he

moved up the curve of the stairs, easily finding the light
switches on the wall as he came to the juncture of the
mezzanine and the hallway that led to Mello's suite. He
passed the darkened doorway of Raymond Mello's sitting
room and continued to the next one farther down. He
reached inside and flipped on the switch with his right
hand.

'Plenty of room,' he said offhandedly. He looked
around the sitting room a moment before going to the
bedroom, again reaching inside with his left hand to flip
on the light. Having already seen the crime-scene photographs, he did not remark on the red fabric walls, or the
dominant tree-of-life weaving. His eyes were seeing other
things.

As he had done at Samenov's, he proceeded to the
bathroom, a luxurious affair of marble and glass and a
patterned tile shower so large and ornate that it seemed
to have been lifted whole from the baths of Herculaneum.
Grant noted this, but hardly hesitated, making his way to
a long marble table built into the wall and over which
were open glass shelves. Here, Bernadine Mello kept a
plethora of medicines and beauty supplies, a daunting
task for Grant's curiosity. He plunged right into it.

Palma watched him from across the room. His inventory was thorough, and he randomly — as far as she
could tell — opened an occasional bottle and smelled it or
dipped a finger in to rub the cream or liquid between his
thumb and forefinger. He still seemed like a big man to
Palma, and fully clothed amid the mirrors and marble and
fragrances of a woman's dressing room he was out of
place, as if he were the last person in the world who
might understand the woman who had lived in these
surroundings.

'Sometimes,' he said, not pausing in his preoccupation
with Mello's collection, 'I go to a large pharmacy and
simply wander through their aisles. You learn a lot about
the human body that way, as well as the mind. The things
people do to themselves, maybe because they have to, or
maybe because they're hypochondriacs. Or maybe they're

simply obsessed with the way they appear or feel or smell. Americans spend a hell of a lot of money on their bodies. I don't know,' he said, taking the lid off a tiny amethyst flask and smelling its contents, 'they say by 2010 the median age in the United States will be thirty-nine.

She followed Grant into the fiery bedroom and listened to him offer comments from time to time as he methodically worked his way through Mello's closets and chests as he had Samenov's. It took longer here because there was more of it, but Grant never flagged, never grew impatient or hurried past anything. It was as if he had all the time in the world to do this. Palma watched his every move. She noticed what he noticed, saw what made him pause and give a little extra attention, what he seemed to find of no, or little, importance. She noticed what clothes he took time with, what items of Mello's lingerie he rubbed between his fingers, what panties he held up, what chemise he brushed against his face. He was very quickly becoming as interesting to her as the killer he was trying to conjure into life.

'There were no sadomasochistic paraphernalia here, was there?' he asked, closing the last drawer and turning to her.

'None,' Palma said.

'If she proves to be part of Samenov's clique, she'll be a little different in that respect, won't she?'

Palma nodded.

Grant put his hands in his pocket and strolled thoughtfully across to a window that Palma knew overlooked a garden-courtyard. He moved the curtain aside with one hand, looked a moment, then turned into the room, putting his hand back into his pocket. He walked across to her.

'The thing about the psychologist,' he said, 'is that here's a guy — if he's not the killer — who can give us insight not only into Mello, but into all the women — if Mello is one of the clique. He'll know if Mello had sado-masochistic tendencies. Maybe he'll know about her lovemaking with other women, maybe even other men. We can squeeze him for everything he ever told her because the man's gotten himself in a hell of a lot of trouble by having sex with her all these years. He's probably doing the same with other women as well. It could ruin him. You ought to dangle that in front of him in exchange for his spilling his guts about her. Believe me,' Grant said soberly, 'the man knows enough about her to put her mind on a plate for us. And that's exactly what you ought to ask for. We want her complete file, every name she ever mentioned, how she liked her sex — lights on, lights off, on top of spikes with black balloons tied to her toes and needles through her nipples — whatever. Get the lurid details.'

Grant's face hardened as he said this, the preoccupied air with which he had searched the room had dissipated, and something sterner had taken its place. He looked at her, then turned and walked to the bathroom and carefully turned off the light. When he came out again, he folded his arms and ducked his head, thinking, and stopped in the middle of the room.

'You haven't talked about suspects,' he said.

'You said you didn't want to hear about them.'

'That's right,' he almost smiled, his head still down. 'In light of those general guidelines I gave you over the telephone, have you got any possibilities?'

'One.'

He looked up, immediately interested, then nodded. 'Does he fit the descriptors we talked about?'

'About half of them, as far as I can tell. We don't know that much about him yet.'

Grant lifted his chin in a half nod.

'Well, you can add something else to your inventory about the guy,' he said. He looked over to the bed as if Mello were still there. 'I thought at first that he had beaten their faces so severely because he knew each of them intimately ... the old homicide rule of thumb. I actually thought you would find that he might have been the relative of one of them, and a secret lover of the other.' He shook his head. 'But I was all wrong there. You haven't turned up anything like that, and you're not likely to. He may know these women he's killing, but that won't have anything to do with why he's hammering their faces. It's got to do with his fantasy — he's intimate with the woman they *become*. He's destroying *her* over and over. It has nothing to do with who they really are.'

He shrugged. 'In retrospect that may appear to be obvious, but for some reason I didn't think that was a valid reading at first. Maybe I was trying too hard, mixing the behavioral patterns of sexually and nonsexually motivated murders.'

He wiped a hand over his face and touched either side of his mustache at the corners of his mouth with a thumb and forefinger. 'There's just something a little off about these. I can't quite nail it. But it doesn't lend itself to fancy footwork just yet.' He shook his head. 'This guy's killing somebody he loves, and he's seeing her face in the face he's painting on his victims.'

'Someone he loves?' Palma frowned. 'Not someone he resents, someone he's accumulated grudges against, has nurtured a hatred for?'

'Love, hate, desire, repulsion. It's all the same to some of these guys,' Grant said. 'Their emotions are short-circuited. They're not always sure what's driving them. That's why they often leave conflicting messages at the crime scenes. Their emotions are so whacked-out they don't know what they're doing.'

'What about the rest of it? The bath oil, the perfume.'

'I wouldn't be surprised if he's not using the exact cosmetics, same brand and shade of lipstick she uses, same fragrance, same bath oil, rouge, all of it. Jesus. He might even be using *her* cosmetics.'

'What?'

'His mother, if he's unmarried and still living with his parents. His wife. A lover. She's gone, he takes cosmetics, and does his work. Maybe she has a job, has to work on Thursday nights. Let's upscale that a little bit; maybe she belongs to a Junior League-type organization that meets on Thursday nights. A Jazzercise class. Something that gets her out of the home on Thursday nights.'

'She'd have to be gone three or four hours,' Palma said.

'I don't see a problem with that. I could think of half a dozen activities that would keep her out that long.'

Palma thought of Reynolds. He said he lived alone. She simply had taken his word for that, but a girlfriend was easy enough. Walker Bristol was married, and from what little they knew about him he had enough kinks to qualify for a Roman circus, and maybe a brainful of resentments. Who knows what Cushing would find in the list of names from Samenov's address book? And what about Claire's husband? Palma knew she was gone at nights.

Suddenly an idea hit her like a fist in her forehead. Christ! How could she have overlooked it so long? What had she been thinking about? She made a mental note to check it out. She was kicking herself for being so obtuse when she heard Grant's voice.

'Hey.' He was looking at her, eyebrows raised. 'You have an idea or something?'

Palma shook her head. She wasn't sure she liked the tone of his voice. 'Just trying to put things together,' she said. She didn't care if she sounded evasive. She wasn't going to bubble over every time an idea came into her head. On the other hand, what was her problem? He had been pleasant, not overbearing, not even condescending. Why was she reluctant to simply tell him what she was thinking?

Grant studied her and nodded. 'Fine,' he said. 'Come on, let's go.'

They retraced their steps along the broad hallway, then down the sweep of stairs, Grant turning off the lights behind them so that darkness trailed after them at a distance like a wary black dog, and the huge home gradually went dark until there was nothing left but the lighted portico as they drove over the crunching cinders and out into the street.

Again they were on Memorial Drive, the rain slackening to a drifting mist. The digital clock on the dash-
board said 9:50, as Grant loosened his tie and sat back in
his seat in silence once more. She wondered what he was
thinking, but she was no more inclined to ask him than
she guessed he would be inclined to tell her. She accelerated and pushed the car beyond the speed limit, past the
wooded estates of the Duchesne Academy on the left and
then St. Mary's Seminary on their right, heading toward
the West Loop.

Grant looked out the window, and Palma nursed her
own thoughts, beginning to wonder what in the hell she
was thinking, being so arch with him. If she thought she
was being smart, she was making a big mistake. Even if
she felt she was justified on a personal level, it sure as
hell wasn't justified from a professional perspective. She
was defeating every purpose for which she had wanted
him to come down in the first place, and for which she
needed him. And she knew men. If she didn't pick his
brain herself, if she couldn't make him feel comfortable
sharing his insights with her, then it would be very easy
for her to find herself cut out of the information loop
altogether on this thing. It would be only natural for him
to share most of the substance of his observations with
Frisch, falling back on the bureaucratic safety net of
'procedure.' She had seen it happen before. And she
couldn't blame anyone but herself if she let this slip out of
her hands. Christ.

'It's almost ten o'clock,' she said. 'You want to get
something to eat? I guess you haven't had anything since
lunch.' She tried to keep her voice as neutral as possible,
no lingering inflections of impatience or feminine wile.

'Sure, something to eat would be good,' he said.

'There's a pretty good diner on the way downtown.
The food's good and the coffee's guaranteed.'

He looked at her. 'Guaranteed to what?'

Did she detect an edge of sarcasm? Did she give a shit?
She tried to put a little breeze in her voice without
choking on it.

'Guaranteed to keep you awake long enough to eat a piece of Mom's American apple pie, if you don't mind Mom being a bachelor and the American being Polish.'

Grant smiled. 'Sure. Let's see what you call Houston coffee.'

Meaux's Grille had settled into the nighthawk time of late night, coming up on the hours when a different kind of people moved quietly into the almost empty diners and truck stops and grills that never closed. These were coffee-and-cigarette people, the kind who seemed to carry old regrets in the pouches under their eyes like unforgivable sins, whose unblinking, early-morning stares were testimonies to their fear of sleep and its companion ghosts. These were private people, the strange few for whom loneliness was a desirable thing, the better portion of lives of uncertain value.

They took a booth by one of the front windows that looked out to the glistening street and the huge catalpa tree with broad, dripping leaves where Palma had parked the car. The night shift at Meaux's was Salvadoran: a cook who cooked like the inevitable twisted heavy in all the Mexican movies she had seen in the barrio as a girl, a busboy who was beautiful enough actually to have been a movie star, and a waitress named Lupe who had extraordinary, straight white teeth and who had tearfully confided to Palma late one night when the place was empty, except for them, that of all the people in her guerrilla unit that had roamed the mountains around Chalatenango, she had been the best, the absolute best, with the piano wire.

They each ate a blue plate special with a minimum of conversation, and then Lupe brought them fresh coffee and a generous wedge of apple pie for Grant, who ate almost half of it before he sat back against his seat and took a deep breath and a sip of coffee.

'Jesus, that hits the spot,' he said, wiping his mustache with his napkin. 'Very good.' He looked around the grill, watched Lupe a moment as she worked behind the counter, and then he quickly took in the few scattered

solitaires and a couple of Rice coeds conferring conspira-
torily in their booth, their legs folded underneath them as
they leaned toward each other on their elbows. His eyes
came back to Palma. 'Your hangout?'

'Pretty much,' she smiled. 'I don't live too far from
here. It's a good place for breakfast, and for late at night
when there's not enough companionship at home and too
much anywhere else.'

'You're not married?'

'Divorced. Six months ago.'

'Still a tender subject?'

'Not really,' she lied. 'It was over before it was over. I
knew it had to be done long before I did it.'

Grant nodded. He ate another bite of pie and looked
out the window while he chewed it. Then he sipped the
coffee again and looked at her.

'I was married twenty-three years,' he said. 'She died a
couple of years ago after a brief illness. Maybe you were
lucky, didn't have that much of an investment in it. All
those years, then nothing.'

Palma was startled to hear such a statement. It
certainly wasn't what she had expected.

'You call two daughters "nothing"?'

Grant's eyes went flat, and he looked at her with a
dispassionate, level gaze. 'You've done a little research?'

'That's not research. That's just keeping your ears
open.'

He regarded her with an expression that looked very
much like disappointment. 'I guess that's right,' he said.

Palma felt the sting of regret for having a quick tongue.
She had already broken her resolution to back off.

'Look,' she said. 'That was out of line. I . . . it just came
out . . . wrong.'

Grant twisted his head a little in a forget-it kind of
shrug. 'I set myself up for it,' he said. 'I knew better.' He
took another sip of coffee. 'As a matter of fact,' he said,
tilting his head toward the college girls in the booth on
the other side of the room, 'they reminded me of my
daughters when we came in.' He smiled. 'They're in

Columbia. School of Journalism. Setting the world on fire.'

Palma was chagrined, didn't know what to say.

'As for you — four years in homicide. How do you like it?'

'Now that's research,' she said.

'Right. The big FBI vetting,' he said. 'I called a friend of mine, said I was going to be working with this Palma person, what did he hear about her?' This time only his eyes smiled. Now he was the one trying to defuse the tension.

'I like it,' she nodded. 'My father was a detective in this division. I'd always hoped we might be able to be here at the same time, but it didn't work out.'

'Well, you've got a good rep,' he said.

Jesus. He was bending over backward. Rep was a potent thing in this business. If you were lucky enough to have a good one, it went a long way. It opened doors, made things happen. If this was flattery, it had more class than comments about her beautiful eyes.

In the kitchen, Chepe turned up his Japanese portable and the tinny, jerky strains of *conjunto* music strayed into the room. The pretty busboy did some suave, subtle turns and tucked a hand into Lupe's buttocks as he passed her on his way to the kitchen. Lupe didn't even acknowledge the crude gesture; her expression never changed, she never stopped working. The kid was lucky he was on the night shift. That was the sort of thing Lauré wouldn't have missed. She would have fired him for it — after a tongue-lashing.

'It took me a while to get to homicide,' she said. 'Two years in uniform, two in vice, two in sex crimes. But this is where it feels right.'

'Your dad know what you wanted to do?'

'Oh, sure. It was his "fault," according to my mother. I loved his war stories, when he'd tell me how he figured something out, how he "hunched onto" the idea that this was so or that was true, and then how he set about to get it straight. "A good detective sometimes comes in at the back door. You gotta figure out what *didn't* happen." He taught me about liars: "A good liar will make you ignore the evidence." He taught me about eyewitnesses. They were "one of the major flaws in the justice system," he said.' She laughed. 'He said a lot of things.'

'I take it your husband wasn't a cop.'

She didn't know how he managed to 'take' that. 'No, he wasn't,' she said. 'But that's not what ended it. It was more fundamental than that.'

Grant nodded, looking at her, but his mind was somewhere else. She had noticed that it was easy for him to do that, to shuttle his thoughts off in another direction if the topic at hand didn't fully occupy him. Certainly she knew her former marriage wasn't the most riveting subject. Still, after having been so attentive it was a little like a splash of cold water to see him turn you off right in the middle of your response to a question he had asked himself. Working with Grant wasn't going to be all that smooth. Not at all.

36

It was almost eleven-ten when Palma dropped Grant off at the Hyatt Regency and then stopped at a pay telephone only a few blocks away. She dialed the Harris County medical examiner's office and listened to the telephone ring four times before someone answered it. She asked for Dee Quinn.

'Dee? Uh, I think she's out ... what?' The man turned away from the mouthpiece and talked to someone, then back to Palma. 'Just a second, stand by.'

Quinn was on the line immediately. 'Dee, this is Carmen Palma.'

'Yeah, Carmen, you just caught me. We got a cutting.'

'Just give me a minute,' Palma said.

'Shoot.'

'I've got two people, husband and wife, both physicians. They have different specialties, I don't know either of their names, or even if the woman goes by her married name or her maiden name professionally. Is there some kind of physician directory I can go through and look for repeated street addresses or something?'

'That'd be quite a task,' Dee said. She was a tall, lanky woman in her mid-twenties with an unflappable nature and a dogged curiosity about her work. Palma had never seen her without her bright red hair pulled back in a ponytail. 'There's several thousand doctors, and I guess a pretty fair number of them are husband and wife.'

'But is there some kind of directory?'

'There's the Harris County Medical Society Directory,' Quinn said. 'But not all the physicians in Harris County belong to the society.'

'What's in the directory?'

'Doctor's name, address, telephone number, spouse's name — just spouse's first name. But you don't even know their names?'

'No. I only know he's an opthalmologist, and she's a gynecologist. She let it slip out while I was talking to her.'

'On the telephone?'

'What?'

'Do you know what she looks like?'

'Yes, I've met her.'

'You're in luck, then. Their pictures are in the directory.'

'Fantastic. Do you have a copy down there?'

'Sure.'

'Can I come out there and look through it?'

'Sure, but I won't be here. I'll leave it with Dolores.'

'Dee, thanks. I appreciate it.'

Within three minutes Palma was back in her car, ascending the ramps onto the Gulf Freeway and heading south. To her left the entire inner city seemed to rotate in the rain as she passed around it, like a colossal faceted world whirling through a moist space. Then it drifted away from her as she turned sharply southward, heading into smaller worlds, the Texas Medical Center gliding past on her right, its buildings fading in and out of the mist and an encroaching fog as she exited off the freeway and down onto Old Spanish Trail.

The back door of the ME's office was kept locked at nights, and when Palma knocked, Dolores's porcine face peered out of the small window and then smiled in recognition before the latch clacked open, and Palma stepped into the fluorescent-bright back offices of the morgue. The place was empty except for Dolores, who gave Palma the directory and asked her if she wanted coffee, which Palma declined.

Dolores returned to one of several copies of *People* magazine she had on her desk while Palma opened the first page of the directory. There were hundreds of photographs, but of course proportionally fewer women than men. Still, it wasn't until she had paged her way through more than half the book that she suddenly stopped. Claire's face stared back at her from a small, square black and white photograph. She was Dr. Alison Shore, professor of gynecological sciences, Baylor College of Medicine. Palma remembered that she had asked that they meet at the mall outside the University of Texas Medical School, a minor geographical diversion of a hundred yards of lawn and trees. Another diversion was Dr. Shore's hair. It was not dark, but light, either a light taffy or blond. It was difficult to tell in the duo-toned photograph. To Palma she seemed more strikingly attractive as a blonde, even younger. She was, indeed, a handsome woman.

On the page opposite her was Dr. Morgan Shore.

Ophthalmologist.

The dash clock on Palma's car said eleven-fifty when she pulled into the courtyard at Linda Mancera's. She had called from the morgue to apologize for missing Mancera's gathering, only to have Mancera insist she come on. They had gotten a late start anyway, she said, and the party wouldn't be breaking up until well after two.

The circular courtyard in front of Mancera's condo was full of cars, and Palma had to park outside the gates with several other cars along the margins of the wooded drive. She took a moment to freshen her hands and face with a towelette from a foil packet, to brush out her hair, and to rub in a perfumed lotion. It was the best she could do. It had been a lousy day.

She took an umbrella and opened it as she got out of the car. Though the rain had stopped, she could feel a dense fog moving in, hear it dripping off the thick vegetation along the street, and see it beginning to drift between

her and the lights on the condos. She walked through the
drive gates, which were open, and made her way through
the cars to the winding sidewalk. Both floors of Mancera's
home were lighted, and by the time Palma got halfway up
the shrub-bordered sidewalk she could hear women's
laughter. Surprising herself, she acknowledged a slight
shudder of butterflies in her stomach as she approached
the door and rang the bell. She listened, but the level of
conversation she could hear coming from the other side of
the door didn't change at the sound of the doorbell, and
then immediately the door swung open and Linda
Mancera was there in an airy sundress of tropical flowers
in blues and greens and a smile that made Palma forget
the butterflies.

'Great, glad you could make it,' Mancera said, stepping
back and tilting her head for Palma to come in. 'I was
afraid something would come up at the last minute.'

She took Palma's unfolded umbrella and put it in a
corner with others and walked her into the living room
where twenty-five to thirty women were scattered around
in groups or couples, drinking and eating hors d'oeuvres.
There was music, but it was soft — Antonio Carlos Jobim,
she thought — in deference to the main purpose of the
evening, which was conversation. It was a major departure from the usual cocktail party, where you stood
close so you could yell across your drink, not because you
wanted to be close. Here, however, standing close had
another purpose.

A quick scan of the room revealed that the ages ranged
from women in their early twenties to those in their
fifties. Their dress was equally as various, from black
evening wear to poolside casual with a good sprinkling of
Junior League summer cottons and career woman brand
names. Scattered throughout the room, Palma saw
several women with their arms laced through a
companion's or simply holding hands or with an affectionate arm around a waist, none of which even would
have attracted attention at a heterosexual party. But here,
where there were only women, the collective, if minimal,

displays of affection had an altogether different feel about them. On the other hand, there was none of the coarse groping or gratuitous deep kissing that she often had seen at male homosexual gatherings. If Palma had been expecting to arrive at a party for a women's garden club, she wouldn't have seen anything here that would have made her think she was at the wrong address.

'Our den of iniquity,' Mancera said softly, as they started walking through the living room. 'Some of these women have stopped by here — briefly — after an evening out with their husbands or families, others have come just for this, others are on their way somewhere else. Some came as couples ... their night out.'

These women were all on the upper end of the male's ten scale, a fact that struck Palma as remarkable and something that told her as much about the crowd as the price tags on the cars she had seen out in the courtyard. Were there no economically underprivileged or physically plain women in Mancera's circle of friends? By the time they had slowly made their way through a sea of fragrances and fragments of conversations about movies and restaurants and children and bosses and husbands and other women, past a fortune in jewelry and an equal fortune in health-club figures and tennis-court tans, and gotten through the dining room to the kitchen, where Bessa was standing behind the tile bar mixing drinks, Palma had begun to feel distinctly dowdy.

Bessa asked Palma what she would like to drink and then got busy making it. Like Mancera, she was in a tropical sundress, but for her the overlarge flowers were rendered in fiery reds and oranges that set off her cocoa skin in a manner that could only be called erotic. She flashed her smile as she mixed Palma's drink and talked to another woman who was helping her. When she handed the drink over the tile counter, she feathered her dusky fingers over Palma's, a lingering caress that didn't linger at all, perhaps, except in Palma's mind because no one seemed to notice. She felt her heart race and turned away without looking again at the dark Jamaican.

'As you can see,' Mancera said as they moved away to themselves, 'this is a rather innocuous group of women. They're solidly women of the mainstream, and they want to keep it like that. Maybe even a little stuffy because of it. It's the sort of thing, really, that Helena Saulnier would find intolerable. More than half of these women here are living with husbands or boyfriends. This is not their whole life, but it's an important part of it.'

'And their male partners know nothing of this?'

Mancera shook her head. 'Well, let me take that back. You see the woman over there, the one with the red belt talking to the brunette? Her boyfriend knows she has women lovers. She insisted he know when they started living together. If he couldn't handle that, she wanted to know up front. I've never known another woman to do that, but he seems to be handling it. Personally, I can't see how it can last. That seems to be asking a lot of him. But she's definitely a minority of one — and he knows nothing about *this* group.'

She carefully surveyed the room, her eyes darting, sliding, gliding as she sipped her drink and talked. Turning her back to the larger part of the room, she looked at Palma.

'Do you see the two couples over here behind me, talking by the front windows?' Palma nodded. 'The pair with their backs to us have been turned down by their fifth adoption agency. They've been together eight years and they can't convince anyone that it's a permanent relationship or that they can provide a psychologically balanced home for the baby without a man present to serve as a male role model. You can imagine the arguments on both sides. They run the gamut. Well, the woman on your right has recently received her first implant — artificial insemination. The donor is the other woman's brother. They were turned down by three physicians before they found one who would inseminate her. Again, the same arguments surfaced, apprehension that the children raised by lesbian couples may develop negative attitudes towards men, that without the male-female dyad as exemplars they'll grow up with a lack of self-esteem.' She shook her head. 'I don't know. I've read studies. Both sides of the arguments will cover you up with statistics.'

'What about the women here who have families?' Palma asked. 'What do they say about it?'

Mancera smiled and shook her head. 'They come down on both sides. Same observations and arguments you'd get from a group of heterosexuals in a room like this. But then, you've got to keep in mind who these women are. You get a dinner party together with Saulnier's friends, and your discussion on this topic is going to sound a heck of a lot different.'

'Which one of these women is Terry?' Palma asked.

Mancera looked embarrassed. 'She's not here. She was here,' she added quickly, 'but she had to go.' She held up an open hand. 'She is willing to talk to you, though. Here, tomorrow. She wants to meet here for a couple of reasons. She's living with a man now, thinking of getting married, and she's scared to death of Gil Reynolds. She doesn't want to attract attention to her home, afraid that Reynolds is watching her and, at the very least, will talk to the man she's living with.'

Palma looked at Mancera, trying to read whether Terry had really been here or whether this had been only a ploy to get Palma to come by.

'You know about Louise, I assume,' Palma said. 'And Bernadine Mello.'

Mancera nodded. 'We've already been through this. Earlier this evening those deaths were the only topic of conversation for over an hour. We hashed it out. Everyone got involved, everyone had their say.'

'Their say?'

'Look, we're all scared by this,' Mancera said. They had stopped by a ficus tree near one of the courtyard windows. She paused to gather her thoughts before going on. 'I think — and I know this is going to sound callous to you — but I think it's everyone's general feeling that this is not something that concerns us.'

'What?'

'The victims, we think, are all going to be part of Vickie's "crowd." This is an S&M situation. Though everyone thinks this is horrible, a sad thing, no one, none of us here, anyway, feel threatened. The victims may be bisexual, but more importantly they're the pain crowd. You think the key to this thing is bisexuality. It isn't. It's about pain and people who don't want their sex without it.'

'Those are the people you think are going to be the victims?' Palma asked.

'Yes, we do.' Mancera nodded. 'They've always been victims. Do you know about Kittrie's background?'

Palma shook her head.

'It's sordid. She grew up in the deep backwoods bayou country of East Texas. She had a poisoned birth and a poisoned childhood. Her father was her brother. Her mother's husband, the father of Vickie's brother-father, sexually abused Vickie from the time she was three. Her mother colluded in this. When she was eleven her brother, who was her father, began having intercourse with her and then she was shared by these two men until she was fifteen, when she was gang-raped by some assortment of relatives — I've heard uncles, cousins, whoever — in a two-day ordeal that would make you stop believing in God if I told you about it. It made Vickie stop believing in God. She ran away from home, if that's what you call a place like that, and came to Houston. You can imagine, with her beauty and background, what kind of a life she found for herself here. Dorothy came across her in one of the gay bars when Vickie was nineteen.'

Mancera sighed. 'She took care of her as best she could, but I think Dorothy's own life was too damaged for her to have provided anything like a protective wing. Vickie's a woman out of bounds by anyone's definition. Her life has never gone well, and I don't see how it ever will.'

'What about Helena Saulnier? She seems to have appointed herself Vickie's protector as well.'

'I feel sorry for Helena,' Mancera conceded. 'She's in love with Vickie, but she's refusing to admit it to herself. You're right, she sees herself as Vickie's protector, and she has infinite patience with her, much more than Dorothy had. Helena's lesbianism is much more politicized and militant than Vickie's, which gives her a kind of moral fierceness, a sense of purpose that's entirely lacking in Vickie's kind of sick hedonism. Helena wants to be Vickie's advocate, someone to speak for her when she can't speak for herself, to tell her that regardless of what she's been through that she cares for her and that no amount of sin can change that. With a kind of outdated nobility, Helena wants to fill the void that occupies the center of Vickie's heart. It's a magnificent example of tilting at windmills.'

'What about Bernadine Mello?'

'We don't know her. Everyone saw her picture in the papers, and no one we know recognized her. But then we don't know all the women Vickie's involved with, or even the men she's involved with, for that matter. And then there're the code names. If she's new in the group, she's most likely still using one.'

'What if she has nothing to do with Vickie?'

Mancera's face seemed to drain of any expression. 'Are you telling me she doesn't?'

'I'm telling you we think she doesn't,' Palma said, not altogether honestly.

Mancera studied Palma's face, her eyes looking into Palma's as if she were trying to read tea leaves or divine the future in the lines of her face.

'I don't know,' Mancera said. 'I really don't.'

Suddenly but smoothly, she smiled and slipped her arm through Palma's. 'We're getting some sidelong glances,' she said. 'You've been here too long without being introduced to a few people at least. We've huddled to ourselves for too long.' And she deftly turned Palma toward the living room and casually eased into the crowd.

In this way, pulled close to Linda Mancera's side and feeling the cushion of her breasts through the fine

material of her tropical dress, Palma met the elite of
Dorothy Samenov's 'group.' They could have been any
women anywhere and, in fact, they were. Palma was
genuinely interested in meeting them and, even though
she was given first names only, she was able to gather
from overheard conversations to know that being bisexual
for these women had in no way precluded their concerns
in the larger world. Their concerns were the concerns of
women everywhere in their economic class, for it seemed
to Palma that social, rather than sexual, distinctions held
more importance for many of them. They were the true
bourgeoise, in almost every respect. Palma remembered
what Mancera had said about her sexual preference for
women. It did not define her, she had said. It was only a
part of her, like her race or her religion or her occupation.

And yet as Linda Mancera led her around the room of
women, introducing her, allowing her to meet and see for
herself what manner of women they were, she could not
help but feel as though their glances were more than
woman's curiosity about another woman. Women, she
knew, were harsh judges of another woman's appearance, appraising their peers from a distance, looking them
over from head to toe, measuring them with the delicate
calipers of taste of their own manufacture. Women, she
was aware, were masters of the artful seduction just as
surely as she was aware of Mancera's breasts against her
arm and the way Mancera occasionally arched her back to
press them hard against Palma, unobserved by anyone
but themselves, as surely as she was aware of Mancera's
slightly massaging grip of their interlaced fingers, as
surely as she was aware of the now-and-then manner in
which Mancera brought the back of Palma's hand in
touch with Mancera's inner thigh as she bent to speak to
someone sitting or turned in the crowd to look for
someone else. They might be the bourgeoisie, these
women lovers of women, but even the bourgeoisie had
passions that could drive them out of their comfortable
self-satisfaction; even the bourgeoisie could sometimes lose

control of those passions; and even the bourgeoisie —
perhaps especially the bourgeoisie — could have secrets
they would rather die than reveal.

Palma walked down the curving sidewalk from
Mancera's front door oblivious of the wet privet hedge
that was brushing against her dress, soaking her hem and
peppering her stockinged legs. She didn't even think to
put up her umbrella against the heavy fog that was
moving like a warm, moist breath across the city, beading
in her hair and casting halos around the streetlamps. Her
heart was hammering, banging away against her chest.
The room full of women followed her out into the mist,
milled about her as she crossed the courtyard, spoke
softly and touched softly as she unlocked the car and
quickly got inside and slammed the door. She started the
car and turned the air conditioner on high and stuck her
face in front of one of the vents. She unbuttoned the top
four buttons of her dress, pulled it open, and directed
another vent to her chest. Jesus God, she thought.

As the air began to cool the perspiration, she tried to
put the memory of the feel of Linda Mancera's inner thigh
into perspective. Something happened; she had to admit
that, for Christ's sake. She had been caught off guard by
it, allowing herself to be caught up in Mancera's charade
even though, had she been given any warning, she would
have maneuvered to avoid it. But Mancera had simply
grabbed her and they were off, working the room,
smiling, meeting, pretending ... pretending ... It would
not have happened, she thought, if Mancera had simply
taken her hand and continued to hold it, walking from
group to group. But she hadn't done that. Instead, she
would release Palma's hand and touch her back during
one introduction, put her arm around her for another,
take her hand again for yet another, each time bringing
Palma in touch with another portion of her anatomy, the
soft give of her breast here, the strong inner muscle of her
thigh there, and each time the renewed contact with her
warmed flesh vividly re-created a sense of what Mancera
must be like. Or more accurately, it created a heightened

curiosity, a desire to know ... or maybe ... simply ... a desire.

She had understood from the very first moment what Mancera was doing. It certainly wasn't the first time a woman had played her, however subtly, and Palma had developed an acute distrust — even aversion — to the crane dance of modern sexual encounters. Partly it was a result of her longstanding experience with the unabashed insincerity of the singles scene, partly it was the makeup of her personality, and partly, she hated to admit, it was her age. The smooth-tongued magic that might have charmed her as a girl of twenty-two, often had the appearance of cheap tricks to the woman of thirty-three. Whatever the reasons, Palma had a low tolerance level for the presexual rituals of many modern urbans for whom sexual intercourse had become an entertainment as lightly taken and meaningless as going to a movie or ball game. This acquired wariness had not protected her, however, from being seduced by Brian, or from being surprised by her own emotions, as with Mancera only a few moments earlier. Wary though she might be, she was still a creature of her own chemistry, and as she had seen, her chemistry could not be trusted always to comply with her will. She was more than a little rattled at finding herself responding to Linda Mancera's sophisticated sexuality.

Palma took another towelette package from her purse, opened it, and wiped her sweating forehead and across the tops of her breasts. The cold air from the dash made the fresh moisture feel like ice. She put the used towelette in the trash and, leaving her dress unbuttoned, put the car in gear, made a U-turn, and drove away from the women of Cour Jardin.

SIXTH
DAY

37

Palma was awakened at 7:30 on Saturday morning by a telephone call from Frisch's office. There would be a task-force meeting at 9 o'clock. She got out of bed and went straight to the shower without looking at herself in the mirror. She turned on the water, adjusted the temperature to slightly cool, and lay down full-length on the low tile bench built against the back wall. The bench had been Brian's idea when they remodeled the house, and she loved it. It sure as hell beat sitting on the shower floor, which is what she used to do when she would come in at odd hours of the early morning too exhausted to stand on her feet.

Now she lay on the cool tiles, smoothed back her hair away from her face, and let the spray of water pelt her, trickle down her sides and between her outstretched legs. She felt worn out, despite the fact that she had had almost five hours' sleep. Or rather, she had had five hours in bed. Sleep hadn't much to do with it, because there hadn't been much of it. She had tossed and thought of Grant and whether or not they were going to be able to work together; she had tossed and thought of Linda Mancera and what she had done and how Palma had felt about it; she had tossed and thought of Vickie Kittrie's very long, short life, and of how that life had affected the

women around her. She had thought of Helena Saulnier
and her eyes-open compassion, the sort of kindness that
was ennobling to those who could handle it. To love the
unlovely required a brave and honest heart, something
increasingly rare in the world, like visions of saints and
laughing angels. Sometimes all of these people were
mixed together or in varying combinations in a vague,
dream-thought state of semi-consciousness, and then
sometimes she simply woke up and lay there thinking
about one or all of them, or of herself.

Finally, remembering the time, Palma dragged herself
up off the tile bench and started washing her hair. She
finished bathing with cold water, hoping her eyes
wouldn't be as swollen as she knew they would be, and
were, when she finally got out of the shower and looked
at her dripping reflection in the mirror. Jesus. She looked
ten years older. At least ten years. Well, fine. There
wasn't anything she could do about it. To hell with it.

She quickly dried her hair, no time for a hundred
strokes or any of that, and then she slipped into one of
her better-looking Egyptian cotton shirtwaists, grabbed
the Medical Society directory, and ran out of the house.

She had breakfast at Meaux's as she again read over
the information about Dr. Alison Shore. A distinguished
academic career had gained her her position at Baylor,
and since she had been there she had won a number of
national academic honors and awards, as well as being
appointed the chair of one of the university's faculty
committees for curriculum planning. Dr. Shore was no
lightweight, and Palma marveled that with all this and
two teenage sons, she found the time for the kind of
diversions she apparently enjoyed in Samenov's circle.

The other Dr. Shore was as much an overachiever as
his wife, also serving on numerous boards of national
medical organizations, traveling with some regularity to
international medical congresses to give papers on his
special interests in ophthalmic surgery or to study new
methodologies being pioneered in other countries. His
academic past was equally distinguished. It would be

difficult to imagine a couple more professionally engaged and, in the modern sense of the term, fulfilling themselves.

The homicide division showed none of the signs of the lagging pace that usually characterized the weekend shifts. The nine detectives now composing the task force were working around the clock and taking only enough time off to catch a few hours' sleep occasionally and to grab a bite to eat. Frisch had had a late Friday afternoon meeting with the captain, the division commander and the assistant chief in charge of major investigations, which resulted in his being officially assigned the responsibility for task-force operations and relieved of other casework duties until the killings were resolved. The task force was opened up full-throttle, and by this time the new detective teams that had come on in the previous two days had done their homework on each of the cases and were striking out in all directions, wherever their leads took them. The information was coming in fast, and it was increasingly important to keep in touch with developments through Don Leeland's case review coordination.

The meeting in Frisch's office was the first time the entire task force had met together. Cushing and his new partner Richard Boucher; Birley and Palma; Leeland and Nancy Castle; Gordy Haws and Lew Marley, who had taken over the Louise Ackley and Lalo Montalvo killings; Manny Childs and Joe Garro, who were taking on the Mello case. Frisch wanted each team to recap its recent developments, to go over which leads had played out and which were still developing or unresolved, what suspects were sufficiently alibied, and what possibilities remained.

They began with the oldest leads.

Cushing and Richard Boucher had worked their way through about half the list of men's names found in Samenov's address book.

'The hairdresser, masseur, electrician, Dalmatian breeder, used-car dealer. All alibied,' Cushing said. 'All checked out. Car dealer was the only one who'd met any

of the other victims besides Samenov. He'd sold a car to
Dennis Ackley and had met Louise on several occasions
when he'd gone over to Ackley's house to pick up a
payment and one time to pick up a set of keys. One night
he had a few drinks with the two Ackleys and several
other men and women who were over at Dennis's house.
He didn't remember any of the names.'

Cushing slouched in a chair and gave his information
in a sour monotone. Palma guessed that he was more
than a little disgruntled because Leeland had landed in
the catbird seat. Anything that came in went through
Leeland's pudgy fingers, which meant that probably no
one knew more details about the overall course of the
investigation than Leeland and Nancy Castle. Both of
them were tight-lipped by nature, not the sort of people
Cushing could bullshit over a scotch and soda and expect
to get a little gossip. Probably neither of them could be
persuaded to have a scotch and soda with Cushing in the
first place.

'Well, I've got something nice,' Birley said in response
to Frisch's nod. He was wiping his hands on a paper
towel, one bite of a jelly doughnut left on a napkin on the
edge of the desk across from Frisch. His Styrofoam coffee
cup was anchoring the edge of the napkin.

'For a period of five months in 1985, Dr. Dominick
Broussard, Bernadine Mello's trusted psychiatrist and
longtime lover, was also the consulting psychiatrist of
Sandra Moser. According to her husband, Sandra was
referred to Broussard by a friend — Moser didn't
remember who, wasn't sure he ever knew. Apparently
Sandra went to see Broussard regarding a series of
"anxiety-based disorders." Andrew claims he can't be
more specific than that; he just doesn't remember the
details. As far as he knows, Sandra never saw him again
after her five-month series of consultations.'

'As far as he knows,' Palma said.

'What about Samenov?' Frisch asked.

'I've been all through her records. I don't find any
mention of Broussard.'

'But you haven't talked to Broussard yet?'

'Nope.'

Frisch made a note. 'Okay, Gordy, what have you and Lew got on Louise Ackley and Montalvo?'

'Maybe something interesting,' Haws said. Haws and Marley had been together a long time, twelve-year veterans in homicide. They worked like the left hand and the right hand, each knowing what the other was thinking and how the other was thinking, the sort of guys who would get the job done if you left them alone and didn't ask too many questions about whether or not they followed the rule book. Both men were in their late forties. Haws, tallish and swaybacked, consumed two packets of Chiclets chewing gum every day, occasionally changing the color of the packets and the flavor of the tiny, hard-coated gum squares. Several years earlier he had decided not to worry about the middle-aged spread that was gradually changing his appearance and causing him to wear his belt well under a parturient waist and causing his suit pants to hang on his hips and sag in the seat.

Marley would never have to worry about a spreading stomach. Always lean, he was steadily balding, his hair deserting him in a clean line around the crown of his head so that he had come to resemble a carefully tonsured monk. He favored seersucker suits and sport coats, and perhaps to compensate for his loss of hair, wore side-burns that were at least a couple of decades out of style. Together, they were the scourge of fashion and bad guys alike.

'Canvassing the neighborhood, we came across this old geezer, a paraplegic named Jerry Sayles who lives three houses down and across the street from Ackley.' Haws paused and popped two fresh white squares of Chiclets into his mouth. 'Claims he saw an "odd guy" park his car almost across the street from him the afternoon Louise and Lalo got it. Said he was watching Geraldo Rivera on TV in his bedroom — something about a woman who had conceived a baby down around her appendix somewhere — and heard this guy's car and looked out because he didn't recognize the sound of it. Jerry knows the sound of all the neighborhood vehicles,' Haws grinned.

'Anyway, Jerry saw this guy slam the door of his car, a junker '74 Buick. Guy starts walking away from his car, not into the house where he parked. Jerry watches him walk on down the street, wonders what the hell, and then sees him turn onto Louise's sidewalk. Shrugs it off because he said "that woman" had all kinds of visitors. So he goes on and watches Geraldo's freak show. Just as the last commercial is coming on before the end of the show — Jerry knows how many commercials there are for Geraldo — he glances out and sees this character fast-walking back to his car. Jerry says nobody fast-walks in the neighborhood except the old elbow-swinging exercise women in the early mornings. Says the guy gets in the car, cranks her up, and drives off, the old Buick smoking up the street.'

Haws stopped and Marley picked up the story as if they had rehearsed it.

'We got a description,' Marley said, wiping his hand over his shiny pate. Palma noticed the hat Marley had begun wearing was doing its job, giving him a white dome and a two-toned forehead. 'We came back and went over the names that have come up in all these interviews. Got pictures from the files and went back last night. Sayles picks out Clyde Barbish, Dennis Ackley's old buddy that the Dallas police want for raping that girl up in Dallas. Sayles didn't even hesitate on the guy. He's got no doubts. We asked him if he'd ever seen any of the other men there. Finger taps Gil Reynolds.'

'When was the last time he saw Reynolds there?' Palma interrupted.

'He said it'd been weeks, maybe,' Marley said. 'But he said he'd seen him there maybe half a dozen times.'

'Since when?' Palma was impatient with Marley's imprecision. 'In the last year, two years? Six times in the last month?'

Marley looked at her. 'We asked him that, Carmen,' he said evenly, his tone indicating maybe she ought to ease off a little. 'He said maybe five or six months. Said he didn't know for sure. Said he didn't keep a time sheet on everybody that came and went down there. Said it was none of his damn business.' Marley smiled.

'Dammit,' Frisch grimaced. 'Okay, let's put out a general broadcast on Barbish, Lew. Request the maximum time and have them check with me before they take it off.' He thought a moment. 'And start rousting his old buddies. I doubt if the son of a bitch was dumb enough to stay in town, but we'd better run the traps anyway.' He looked at Haws. 'What'd firearms say?'

'Guy used a real hog,' Haws nodded. 'Colt Combat Commander .45 auto pistol with Sierra Power Jacket hollow-point ammo. Probably used a silencer. These babies did *some* kind of damage. The guy didn't just stumble onto this stuff. He knew what he was getting. He was dead loaded.'

Frisch nodded, his nod turning into an exasperated shake. 'Manny, Joe. What've you got on Mello?'

Manny Childs and Joe Garro were both relatively new in Houston homicide, two years each, but both of them had come from homicide divisions in agencies at different ends of the country, Childs from Buffalo and Garro from Los Angeles.

'We've interviewed two of Mrs. Mello's three former husbands,' Garro said. 'The two living in Houston. One guy, her first husband, lives in Hawaii. Second husband, last name Waring, hadn't seen her in five years. He was really rocked back about the homicide, but after talking a while he said he couldn't say it was all that bizarre a thing to have happened to her. He said she was a pretty crazy lady.'

Garro lighted a cigarette while he scanned his notes and picked up a cup of coffee, which he sipped while two streams of smoke curled out of his nostrils. Garro smoked like it was the 1940s, and no one had ever heard of lung cancer.

'He didn't know anything about any bisexual relationships she might have had, but he said he knew she was "addicted" to straight sex. He said she was always randy, and it got her into a lot of trouble because she was just a cat about it, always on the make, always twitching her tail at somebody. He said he cheated on her while they were married, but not until he learned that she'd been stepping out on him. Even so, he said, she was worth it, up to a point. After a while, he decided it wasn't any way to live, so he divorced her. Apparently she took him to the cleaners in the settlement.'

Garro tapped his cigarette with his index finger and popped an ash into the black plastic ashtray he had brought with him into Frisch's office. He put the cigarette back into his mouth and rolled it around on his lips with his tongue while he turned through some pages he had stapled together. Then he took it in his fingers again and continued.

'Husband number three, Ted Lesko. Mello married him eighteen months after divorcing number two. Oh, yeah, Waring owned a bunch of fast-food franchises. Well off. Lesko is in real estate out by NASA. Developed a bunch of that stuff out there years ago. Big money. They were married two and a half years. This Lesko was really upset about her death. He'd read it in the paper. He said he still loved her, no bones about it, just like that. "I still love her." The divorce was Bernadine's idea, and he gave her a generous settlement, too. But he said she didn't ask for it. He insisted.

'I can't imagine this guy beating the shit out of her,' Garro added, looking at Palma, then Frisch. 'I mean the guy fought tears the whole time we talked to him, didn't he, Manny. The guy loved her, even though he sat right there and told us how she prowled around on him. He said she couldn't help it. That was the way she was. Said he lavished everything on her, but none of it was enough. Stuff didn't even mean that much to her. The woman was never satisfied by any one thing or any one man. He said it was sad.'

'Then their divorce was friendly?' Palma asked. 'Did he ever see her?'

'Actually,' Childs nodded, 'the guy'd been seeing her behind Mello's back. He didn't think much of Mello, said he was a pervert. Me an' Joe perked up to that, but all he meant was that the guy screwed around almost as much as Bernadine. Kind of a sick pair, from the way he told it. They just never had any rules from the beginning. He said Bernadine was unhappy from the start. Mello kind of flaunted his affairs, didn't even try to be discreet. But then the bottom line was Lesko claimed he hadn't seen Bernadine for several months.

'Waring's alibi checks out, and so does Mello's. Lesko says he was out working on his boat in its slip at the Houston Yacht Club, but we haven't been out there to confirm it. That's about where we quit to get some sleep.'

Frisch made a few notes, and while he was still writing he said, 'Carmen, what about you?'

Palma looked at Birley. 'You went through Samenov's personal papers. Who was her gynecologist?'

Birley looked at his notebook. 'Dr. Alison Shore.'

'Did Shore show up as anyone else's doctor?'

Birley nodded, looking at her, knowing she was leading to something. 'Moser's.'

Palma explained to them how she had discovered Claire's identity, and gave them some background she had gotten out of the Medical Society's directory.

'This explains why she was so cautious about her identity,' Palma said. 'She's got a lot to lose. But there's another reason. Her husband is Dr. Morgan Shore, an ophthalmic surgeon.'

There was a two-beat pause before someone said, 'Shit,' and then everyone had something to say or grunt or swear, and Palma heard Richard Boucher say, 'Eye surgeon ... he operates on eyes,' explaining ophthalmic to Cushing, who was pulling his neck back and frowning.

'I don't know anything about him,' Palma said to Frisch, anticipating his questions. 'I assume from what his wife says he doesn't know about her bisexual relationships. He's a medical heavyweight, like his wife. Very prominent. I just came across this early this morning and haven't had time to check out alibis on any of the dates.'

'At least that's a little easier to do with a doctor,' Leeland said. 'They're so tightly scheduled that either their secretary or the medical exchange will know where they were almost hour by hour.'

'Or where they're supposed to be,' Birley said.

'We'll need to be careful,' Frisch said. 'Handle this delicately, Carmen. If it gets away from us that we're trying to "nail" a prominent physician as a sex killer, we'd better have something more substantial to go on than that he operates on eyes. By the way, we're not releasing to the press the business about Samenov's and Mello's eyelids. The media's already having a feeding frenzy on this, and the division guys are getting nervous stomachs.' His eyes held on Palma until she nodded.

'One more thing,' Palma said, and she told them of her visit to Mancera's party — with some editing. It was interesting to watch these men's faces when she told about the women at Mancera's gathering. Like Palma and most police officers, their experience with female homosexuals had brought them in contact with a considerably different kind of woman than Palma was describing at Mancera's. They were used to the dyke and baby-doll tandems who hung around Montrose, women who had committed themselves to the 'freak' counterculture. But the idea that there was an 'invisible' community of lesbians and bisexual women, and that female homosexuality might be more common than rare among Yuppie suburban wives and highly paid women professionals, was a concept they were not going to buy very easily.

'You sure these babes weren't indulging in a little wishful thinking?' Cushing grinned, rearing back in his chair. 'I mean, you had a roomful of them there at Mancera's and maybe they got a little carried away with the sisterhood an' all that. "Yes, dammit, there's thousands of us in every neighborhood".'

'I don't know,' Palma said. 'What makes you ask?'

'Well, I've just never heard of something like this
before.'

'*You've* never heard of something like this? You think
you'd be one of the first to know?' Palma felt her temper
rise at Cushing's typical center-of-the-universe self-
regard. 'I don't understand how you arrive at that kind of
deduction, Cush. This has to do with women, not men. In
fact, it has to do with women who don't want to *have*
anything to do with men. What makes you think you'd
have heard of these women? That's pretty smug, even for
you.'

'If it was all that widespread, we'd of known about it by
now.' Cushing dropped his grin.

Palma looked at him, nodding. 'Maybe you do know
what you're talking about. Weren't you among the first to
bring to light the nationwide prevalence of bisexual men
with families leading double lives?' She narrowed her
eyes at him. 'How do you happen to know so much about
the homosexual community, Cush?'

'Getting to the point ...' Frisch quickly broke in as
Gordy Haws snorted and Cushing's face flushed scarlet.
He and Palma glared at each other, and everyone,
including Palma, thought he was going to boil over.

'Getting to the point, Carmen ...' Frisch repeated.

'The point is,' Palma went on, pulling her eyes off
Cushing, 'we have a significantly large group of "invisible" bisexual women, and within this group is a
subgroup that has a penchant for S&M. Mancera seems to
believe that this subgroup is our victim pool.'

'That make sense to you?' Birley asked.

She shook her head. 'I'm not convinced they're the
only targets.'

'Because of Mello?' Garro said.

'Right.'

'You don't think we're going to find that she's
connected to them at all?'

'No, I don't. And as far as I'm concerned that exception makes me doubt the whole theory. Also, Mancera's
theory has the feel about it of whistling in the dark. These

women don't want to admit they can be victims. They can live with this a lot easier if they can convince themselves it has nothing to do with them.'

'Hey, it'd make it a lot easier for us, too,' Garro said, mashing out a cigarette. 'Okay,' he said, taking out his lighter and idly flipping the lid, snap ... snap ... snap. 'Maybe all the victims aren't into rough trade, but three out of four is a pretty good record. I'd still be inclined to look into that angle pretty good.'

'Sure, I think so, too,' Palma said. 'I'll be talking with Mancera's friend tomorrow morning. Apparently she was close enough to Louise Ackley that she knew what went on between her and Reynolds. If she can give us details about Reynold's techniques, we might get a break.'

'You really ought to look at Reynold's military record, too,' Birley said to her. 'That sniper business might have involved some interesting psychological record-keeping.'

Palma made a note. Birley was a smart bloodhound.

With that the major points had been covered and everyone waited for Frisch to proceed. For a few moments no one said anything. There was a cough, some shuffling of feet, and movement of coffee cups. Frisch sat behind his desk, looking at the dirty desk blotter in front of him. One hand was resting on his blue ceramic coffee cup as if he was about to pick it up, the other was simply lying on the blotter. Frisch was the only man Palma knew who didn't feel it necessary to posture. He seemed to have the philosophy that if a body limb didn't have any need to function at any particular moment, then it could just rest in place.

Palma looked at the detectives around the room, all of them used to Frisch's moments of taciturn immobility. All of them waiting, looking at their papers, or pretending to, drinking their coffee or making notes in their notebooks, quietly filling the down time, letting Frisch work it through.

'Okay,' he said finally. 'We have several possibilities. We've got to start narrowing it down, concentrate on some of these guys because we're too spread out. He scooted up in his chair. 'To help us do that we've got a couple of agents down here from Quantico. They're crime analysts from the behavioral science unit. I think you already know what they do, so we're going to get them in here to tell us what they see in this guy's work. They haven't been in here during all this because until they present their initial analysis they like to gather all their information directly from the crime scene and police reports. After they give us their perspective on what's going here, we'll get involved in a lot more give-and-take with them.'

Frisch stood up and grabbed a pile of stapled pages that had been sitting on the corner of the desk.

'Here's Sander Grant's preliminary analysis,' he said, handing out the pages to each detective. 'I'm going to give you some time to read through it, and then we'll get them in here. Whatever you want to ask, ask it.'

38

Grant sat on the edge of the desk with his arms folded, one leg hanging over the side of the desk, the other foot planted firmly on the floor. He was at the opposite end of the room from Frisch and the detectives, all of whom were turned in his direction. Freshly shaved, the graying hair at his temples brushed back, his mustache cleanly clipped, a fresh double-breasted suit, the coat unbuttoned and hanging open for comfort, he didn't seem to be any worse for wear after having been up most of the night.

After Frisch introduced him, Grant gave what Palma assumed was his standard speech about the usefulness of crime scene analysis and behavioral psychology to produce probable profile characteristics of violent offenders, stressing that this technique was not expected to take the place of sound, methodical police work, but was intended to be a supplementary tool in the overall investigative process. He acknowledged that this technique was as much an art form as a science, and then added that as far as he was concerned, if he ever came across a man who could assist him in apprehending murderers by drawing pictures of butterflies, he would use him without blinking an eye, as long as the man's results proved reliable. He didn't care if the method was scientific, artistic, or spiritual, as long as it worked.

'I've worked with a lot of law-enforcement agencies,

and I'm well aware that this technique is not universally admired,' he said. He looked around the room at each detective. 'I know there are skeptics. That's fine. I'm not claiming we've got the answers to all your investigative problems. Like DNA "fingerprinting," this technique is only an additional tool for you to use, and it's only as good as the investigators who back it up. And the technique's not infallible. I'm human, and the killer's human, and that's already twice as much humanity as is needed to screw up a sure thing. So you can either accept it or reject it as you see fit, but you better be damn sure it doesn't have anything to offer you before you turn your back on it.'

He wiped his hand over his mustache and mouth. 'The point is,' he said, pausing, looking at them, 'we're trying to find a man who's killed three women.' Pause. 'Odds are, even with our using every resource available to us, he's going to kill another one or two before we catch him. We have an obligation to bring to bear every investigative technique available to us. If you decide to turn your back on this one, you'd better be damn sure you can live with yourself if it turns out you were wrong.'

Grant picked up the Styrofoam cup sitting on the desk beside him and sipped the coffee, looking around at the detectives, his eyes gliding right past Palma's without hesitation. She was surprised at what he said, and at his tone of voice. This didn't sound like a bureaucrat to her, and she guessed his remarks had struck the others the same way. But for the most part Grant was talking to old hands, and no one was going to be made uneasy by this kind of talk. Comfortably self-possessed and in no hurry to break the silence, Grant took another sip of coffee and continued looking around the room of detectives. It was an interesting moment, with the machismo so thick you could smell it as the detectives refused to show any sign of acknowledging they had been lectured, and Grant refusing to be put on the spot as the unwelcome smart-ass from Quantico. Finally he put down his cup.

'Okay, you've got my criminal profile and crime

assessment there,' he said, nodding at the stapled pages everyone was holding. 'Let's get to the questions.'

Palma had read the pages quickly, much of it being what she and Grant had discussed over the telephone during the past several days and last night. Grant must have written most of the profile and assessment on the plane coming down, working in last-minute observations based on what he saw confirmed or contradicted by the Mello case. The paper was lengthy, fifteen pages.

'A general question.' Gordy Haws was reared back in his chair, his stomach protruding. 'Les and I have the Ackley-Montalvo hits. Since these aren't addressed here in your assessment, I was wondering how you see them in relation to the three women.'

Grant was nodding before Haws finished his question. 'First of all, it's obvious that Ackley and Montalvo weren't killed for the same reasons that the women were killed,' he said. 'But we can't ignore the probability of a relationship because of who Louise Ackley was and the timing of her death. But I'd lay bets it wasn't done by the same man. I'm not saying the deaths aren't related, just that the same man didn't commit all five killings. The Ackley-Montalvo hits seem to me to have all the earmarks of a business transaction. They were a housekeeping matter. No emotion involved. The guy behind the gun wasn't thinking with his dick. He walked in, popped them, and walked out. He was doing business.'

He shifted his position on the desk. 'Now whether that business had anything to do with Moser, Samenov, and Mello is something this investigative technique isn't going to tell us. On the other hand what you find out investigating those deaths could very well play back to us. We've been told Louise Ackley bottomed for Gil Reynolds ... you can read the possibilities there. But that could have been false information. It could have been half false. Or, her death could have been a chance element, another story altogether, one of those loose ends that are inevitable in every case.'

Palma noted Grant's crude reference. It was almost as

if he had read Haws's own personality and knew that he would have used the phrase himself. It was a reference Gordy Haws would recognize and understand immediately. He also would have understood the term 'psychosexually motivated aggression,' but he wouldn't have thought much of Grant for having used it. By acquiring Haws's own manner of expression — but not mimicking him — Grant picked up points, became a nonthreatening cooperative, a fellow hunter, instead of a big boy from Quantico.

Manny Childs waggled his pages, frowning at the floor. 'Uh, I can see where you get some of your conclusions,' he was nodding. 'But you're gonna have to explain why you think the guy's a married man with children.'

Again Grant was nodding before the question was complete.

'Okay. After working through hundreds and hundreds of these kinds of cases we've learned that most organized murderers — and we think this guy falls in that category — live with a partner and are sexually competent,' Grant said.

Still sitting on the edge of the desk, he raised one fist.

'Let's hold on to those two probabilities for a second, keep them over here.' Then he raised the other fist. 'Now over here we have the time elements involved in all three murders. All three deaths occurred on Thursday evenings. The forensic data indicate that in each case the time of death was "probably" around ten o'clock at night. If I remember correctly, Moser was last seen at seven-forty, Samenov at six-twenty, and Mello at six-thirty. In each case the victim was last seen within two or three hours prior to their deaths. This is a very precise — and very consistent — time frame, both as regards the day of the week and the hours.

'If you accept the statistical probability that the man lives with a partner,' he said, holding out the first fist, 'then you have to ask yourself whether these precise time frames would more likely accommodate the living situations of a married man with children, or a man living with a girlfriend or another male . . . not a homosexual.'

He held out the second fist. 'A man without a family could probably be absent at those hours any number of nights a week; life's a little looser for him. You'd have a hard time convincing me that those are the only hours he'd have available each week. A man with a family, on the other hand, has obligations that an unmarried man without children couldn't even imagine: dinner at a certain hour to accommodate the rhythm of the family's routine, household chores that inevitably crop up and can't wait until the weekend, helping the kids with lessons, all those things that have to be done with and for the kids before bedtime — around ten o'clock.

'But — one night a week he has an excuse to be gone: racquetball at the club, bowling with the guys, poker with the boys, Rotary Club meetings, whatever. He has to do it on that one night, and he can't be out too late. He's not out drinking with the guys; he's a respectable family man. He's got to be home at a respectable hour. Odds are a single man has other opportunities, is more flexible, and that flexibility alone would almost certainly mean that out of three murders one would have deviated from the pattern. Otherwise we'd have to believe that this is all a coincidence and the odds, once again, are stacked against that conclusion. And at this point in the investigation, gentlemen, we're playing the odds.' And he brought his fists together and interlocked his fingers in a tight grip.

'But what about a guy with a night job?' Childs followed up. 'Doesn't have to be at work until eleven, twelve.'

'And why on Thursday nights?' Grant anticipated.

Childs looked at Grant and then shrugged.

'That's the way I was thinking, too,' Grant admitted. 'But the whole scenario has to work, not just part of it. I couldn't come up with a good reason why he would do it on that *one* specific night. That night is a bottleneck, we're going to have to go through it, make it a logical part of whatever scenario we create. No way around it.'

Grant stood up from the edge of the desk and crossed

his arms, the crooked finger of one hand stroking his mustache.

'Now it may turn out that you'll be proved right on this because there's something here we can't foresee right now. But using what we do know, my scenario simply plays out better at this point. And there's another element. Our experience tells us organized offenders often have good or above-average intelligence and prefer skilled employment. Disorganized offenders are of average or below-average intelligence and tend to have poor work histories. In general — with the exception of police work —' Grant grinned. 'Night work is often the domain of the unskilled labor force. Therefore, if we accept the judgment that we're dealing with an organized murderer, we're going to have to provide him with a reason — other than employment — for being out of the house every Thursday night. Or, at least, on these Thursday nights.'

Grant stopped and stared at the floor, thinking. 'One other thing,' he said, looking up at them from under his eyebrows. 'Look at the charts I've included with the report about the profile characteristics of the organized and disorganized murderers. Organized offenders are usually socially competent — Ted Bundys, smoothies, non-threatening types. Remember, these victims — all upper-middle-class from the "social" section of the city — all apparently *agreed* to meet this man. They feel comfortable with him.' His voice softened, imitating a reasonableness of attitude. 'He's their kind of people. Hell, they let him tie them up! This is not likely to have happened with a socially immature person who'd probably come across to these women like a misfit, someone who doesn't travel in their circles.'

Grant paused. 'Our man is not going to be a loser, a member of the subculture. He's going to be so "normal" that I guarantee you you'll never look at your next-door neighbor the same again.'

'Sexually competent?' Joe Garro asked.

'Right,' Grant snapped, pausing to turn to the desk,

pick up his cup, and swallow a mouthful of coffee. 'Sexual *in*competence is most often associated with the kind of frustrations we see in spontaneous sexual homicide. A disorganized killer, a disorganized crime scene. But our man has taken control to the extreme. Everything about the crime scenes exhibits control. His motivations for the killings are most likely sexual, that's true, but they're deep-seated drives, not the sorts of things that can be satisfied by merely abducting a woman, killing her, and having sexual intercourse with her body. That's a pretty primitive impulse. This man's more complicated than that. What he does to her, he does *before* she's dead. The sadism is important to him ... he wants her to feel the pain, and he wants her to know that he knows she feels it and that it pleases him.'

Nobody said anything for a moment, and Grant went for his coffee again. He was looking around, wanting more questions. Obviously he enjoyed explaining his reasoning, peeling back the layers of the subject he so far only had imagined, but whom he knew well enough to know how the layers were constructed.

'Yeah, I've got a question.' It was Cushing. Palma had wondered how long he could hold out before trying his hand against Grant.

'Under "Postoffense Behavior,"' he said, frowning at Grant's report in his lap. You say that it's likely that the murderer returned to some or all of these crime scenes and probably kept "souvenirs." I just don't see this. I mean, the guy's so careful, so methodical. It doesn't seem logical to me that a guy who cleans up the crime scene the way this guy does would do something like that. You know, jeopardize his distance from the case. It'd be damn risky to come back to the scene, or to keep something in your possession associated with the victim.'

Grant took another sip of coffee, not because he wanted it, Palma guessed, but because he wanted another few seconds to study Cushing, who had not disguised the challenging tone in his voice, nor the inflection that indicated he thought he had found a loophole in Grant's analysis.

But Grant knew how to handle him.

'You're right,' Grant said, putting down his coffee and walking over a few steps to address Cushing directly. 'That's a good point. The fact is, it *isn't* logical behavior, which brings us to another important factor that I've also mentioned in the paper. But I want to emphasize it — in fact, I can't emphasize it too much in this particular case. That is, the importance to the murderer of keeping alive the fantasy that gave birth to the crime in the first place. This behavior isn't logical to you and me because we don't think like this guy, but it's logical to him because it serves a purpose.'

Grant paused for emphasis, his eyes canvassing the room of detectives as he hunched his shoulders and punched the air with an index finger.

'And that purpose is to sustain the excitement of the murder itself,' he said, emphasizing each word separately and distinctly. 'This need to sustain the excitement is so strong that it overrides self-protective instincts. This fantasy is all-powerful. Returning to the scene, or keeping souvenirs that he can pull out and smell and fondle and taste, provides stimuli that enable him to relive the act, re-create the excitement of the event itself.'

Grant turned and went back to Cushing, looking at him down the uneven bridge of his broken nose, his lips thinner under his mustache because he was tense, putting considerable energy into what he was saying.

'I've seen these men return to the body sixteen, eighteen, twenty hours later to cut off the breasts and take them away. One guy came back to the body several weeks after the killing to engage the body in every form of necrophilia imaginable. Sometimes the desire to be once again physically involved with the body overrides any element of common sense. They'll go back, sometimes simply to see the police discover the body. By doing this, they feel as if they're still controlling the fantasy. It doesn't stop for them. It's the same reason they keep "souvenirs," panties, bras, jewelry, even pieces of the body — I've seen feet, breasts, intestines in cans, jars of blood. One man kept his victim's feet in his freezer, in high-heeled shoes. In the case of our man, he's probably kept their nipples. He takes them out of their box, or wherever he keeps them, and handles them, puts them to his tongue, something like that. They're the catalysts that keep the fantasy alive, and the fantasy drives him and sustains him. The fantasy is all-powerful.'

Grant ended by standing in front of Cushing again, his hands in his pockets, his thick shoulders slightly slumped. He gave the impression of being physically powerful, but unmindful of it, his intensity concentrated in the flesh around his eyes, which sat, warm and placid, in their sockets.

Suddenly he turned and walked back to the desk where he had left his coffee and picked up the Styrofoam cup with his back to the detectives. He took a drink.

'Let me clarify one point,' he said, turning around. 'What we call the items these murderers keep is actually defined by what the items *mean* to the murderer. Most of the time it's the disorganized murderer, the impulsive killer, who keeps "souvenirs." The organized killer tends to keep "trophies," some things that symbolize a successful accomplishment, proof of his skill. However, in this case, even though we have to consider our man an organized murderer, I think the fantasy is so overpowering that we have to consider his collected items as "souvenirs," something that helps him re-create the murders.'

'Jesus Christ.' Richard Boucher had been motionless. He was the youngest detective in the room and had never investigated a sexual homicide. Grant's recitation was opening up a whole new world to him. It wasn't a world for the queasy.

The questions continued for another hour, most of the detectives taking notes, following up on earlier questions, asking for clarifications, elaborations, speculations. There was a break to allow everyone to go to the bathroom and get a fresh cup of coffee, and then they came back and went over the reconstructions of the killings in chronological order, Leeland providing graphic charts while Grant postulated the killer's movements, pointed out how the severity and frequency of the crimes had accelerated and explained what that was likely to mean in terms of future expectations.

At this point Birley asked his only question of the morning. Palma had noticed that he had taken few notes, but then she knew when Birley was concentrating he didn't do anything but concentrate. Clearly, Grant fascinated him, and on several occasions she caught Birley nodding slightly to himself.

'At the beginning you didn't want to know anything about our suspects,' Birley said. His tie was loosened and the recent loss of sleep was showing on him by scoring the flesh around his eyes with deep, seemingly indelible lines, creases that aged him by years and functioned as symbols of the years deducted from his life because he had served long, cruel hours in the company of death. 'At what point can we discuss them with you? It seems to me that we could benefit from a little feedback from you about these characters. How long you gonna want to keep your distance?'

'A few more hours,' Grant said quickly. 'I want to see the video-tapes of the crime scenes first. That'll give you more time to follow up on some more questions and maybe narrow down the suspect list even a little more. I think this whole thing is going to start moving faster now. There's a certain amount of momentum building.' He looked at Frisch. 'Is that all right with you? Let me look at the tapes first, and then I'll be available to do whatever you want.'

'Fine with me,' Frisch said. 'Okay. Everybody check out through Leeland so we don't pass up any interviews. I know some of these suspects have now overlapped into the purview of several different detectives, so you're going to have to work it out among you as to who picks them up. When that's decided nail it down with Leeland or Castle. And check with them about the tips. They're coming in steadily now; they've got to be followed up.'

39

After the meeting broke up, Palma took her time getting her things together, but Grant was quickly engaged in conversation with Frisch and Captain McComb, who had also sat in on the meeting. She wasn't going to be the last to leave the room, or even among the last, so she tossed her Styrofoam cup in the trash can beside the door on her way out and glanced back once through the plate-glass window as she went out into the squad room. Grant had his head tilted slightly, listening to McComb.

'You off to Shore's?' Birley asked from her blind side.

'Claire,' she said, as they walked toward their office. 'But could you help me with the other one?'

'Check out his alibis?'

'That's right,' she said, stepping in front of him as she rounded the corner to the narrow aisle to their cubicle. 'I don't want her to know we're checking up on him,' she said, walking through the door and tossing her notebook on her desk. 'I called over to the medical school early this morning. She's got a seminar lecture this morning.' She glanced at her watch. 'She's supposed to be in her office for about an hour or so after the seminar, so I'm going out there right now, catch her off balance.'

'Do you want me to take him straight on? I don't know that we really have time to play with it.'

'That's fine with me,' Palma said. 'After I talk to her

this morning it's not going to matter anyway.'

'But you don't want me to blow her little secret, do you?'

'No.'

'Great,' Birley said.

The Baylor College of Medicine was at the end of M.D. Anderson Boulevard, almost in the center of the vast Texas Medical Center. Its main building was shaped roughly like a Roman numeral III, with inner courtyards on either side of the central building. Palma parked in the lot across Moursund from the hospital and crossed in a light mist to the college's south entrance. She located Dr. Shore's name on the directory and proceeded through the long halls to the college's departments of obstetrics and gynecology, where the hallways were busier and the air of youth and of academia mingled and humanized the scientific and minimalist feel of the shiny corridors of the hospital. According to the information Palma had received this morning, Dr. Shore should have been in her office nearly fifteen minutes. Palma made her way past the doorways with the right sequence of numbers, and entered a door in the middle of a corridor echoing with the voices of students and the occasional squeegeelike squeal of rubber-soled shoes.

The secretary's office was orderly but very much a place of business, a stack of three cardboard cartons just being delivered by a man with a two-wheeled dolly who had left them to one side of the secretary's desk. She was on the telephone, a woman in her fifties with half-lensed tortoiseshell reading glasses on the bridge of her nose and a gold chain attached to either arm tangling on either side of her neck. She nodded and smiled at Palma as she talked, signing the invoice for the deliveryman while she assured the person on the telephone that the test scores would be posted outside the lecture hall by Wednesday noon. The deliveryman left and the secretary frowned at the boxes, looked again at Palma, rolled her eyes, and thanked the person for calling and ended her call.

'I'm sorry,' she said, hanging up the telephone and

making a note on a slip of paper. 'Can I help you?'

'Yes, I need to see Dr. Shore, please. My name is Carmen Palma. I don't have an appointment.'

'Does she know what you need to see her about?'

'Yes.'

'Fine. Just a moment.' She regarded the boxes again as she picked up the telephone, hit two numbers and looked at the invoice while she waited for an answer. 'Dr. Shore, Carmen Palma is here to see you.' She hesitated, and looked up at Palma. 'Yes. Carmen Palma,' she said more slowly, raising her eyebrows at Palma as if to confirm her name.

Palma nodded.

The secretary frowned and hung up the telephone. 'I think she'll be right out.'

They both heard a door open down the hallway behind the secretary, and Palma saw Dr. Shore step out into the hallway and walk very deliberately, without hurrying, without seeming nervous, toward her. Just before she got to the secretary, she said, 'Ms. Palma,' and motioned to her. She was out of the secretary's field of vision. She waited for Palma to reach her and then turned and preceded Palma the few feet to her office. Inside she let Palma close the door behind them while she walked around and stood behind the desk, crossing her arms.

'I suppose I should have known this would happen.' Her face was ashen. 'Why didn't you just call me? Why did you come here?' she asked sharply.

Behind her the windows looking out over the buildings of the medical complex let in a muted, gray light. Dr. Shore was decidedly blond, and younger than Palma had guessed in the wet night when they first had talked. The dark wig, too, could have seemed to age her. She was an attractive woman. Palma would never have guessed her to have been old enough to have the kind of professional history that she had, or to be the mother of two teenage sons.

'There've been more killings,' Palma said, watching her.

Shore placed her hands on the back of the high-backed chair behind her desk. 'I know it. I read the papers.'

'Did you know Bernadine Mello?'

Shore shook her head, her light hair pulled back in a chignon, a single gold bead in each ear providing just the right amount of accent to her emerald silk dress. She evoked a sense of cool intelligence and an unmistakable sexuality that must have assured a steady attendance at her lectures. She was also nervous and visibly furious.

'What did you think when you read about Louise Ackley?'

'What did I *think*?' She seemed flabbergasted by the question, which she clearly considered absurd. She shook her head and looked away.

'I found her myself,' Palma said. 'I went to Mancera again, as you suggested. She sent me to Louise, but someone had gotten there ahead of me. She was still in bed. She'd been sitting up, and they blew her brains all over the wall.'

Shore quickly looked back to Palma, her eyes wide, not from shock or surprise, but to keep back the tears, sustaining her anger.

'Why didn't you tell me you were Dorothy Samenov's physician, as well as Sandra Moser's?' Palma asked.

'You didn't ask me,' she said.

'You told me a lot of things I didn't ask you,' Palma countered. 'Remember, you're the one who got in touch with me. But I've discovered you were very selective with your information. That makes me cautious.'

'Of *course* I was selective,' Shore said. 'Christ!' She struck the back of her chair with a fisted right hand. '*What* in the hell do you think you're doing here?' It was too loud. She stopped herself, lowered her voice. 'Goddammit. I could've met you somewhere.'

Palma ignored her temper. Reaching inside her purse, she pulled out the photographs of Samenov with her masked partner, stepped to Shore's desk and handed them to her. They were standing close to each other now, just the width of the desk between them. 'Do you know the man?'

Shore took them, and as soon as she saw what they were she swore under her breath. She quickly looked at each photograph, jerking each from the top of the stack and slapping it underneath, jerking another one off the top and slapping it underneath.

'Am I supposed to recognize someone in that ... thing?'

'Somebody had better start recognizing somebody,' Palma said, now having trouble controlling her own temper. She leveled her eyes at Shore. 'Let's get something straight. I'm not a callous person, but I'm not a fool, either. I won't hesitate a second to expose you and everyone else in this thing if I think it'll keep that man from getting his hands on one more woman. I won't lose a minute's sleep over it. I don't want to have to do that, but you people aren't leaving me any choice. And I have to admit, frankly, that I find it disturbing that you seem to value your career more than you do these women's lives. How the hell can you withhold information in a situation like this?'

The photographs in Shore's hands were trembling wildly, and she was fighting tears of rage and frustration. Her jaws were so rigid it seemed to take an incredible effort for her to moisten her lips with her tongue, which she did slowly, barely controlling the shape of her mouth. She spoke steadily, with the taut, hoarse voice of strained emotion, bracing herself against the leather back of her chair, the pictures gripped in one white fist.

'Jesus Christ.' She flung the pictures onto her desk. 'I do *not* participate in nor do I condone this sort of sexuality. Look, I've already pleaded guilty to stupidity for letting myself be talked into posing for the photographs. I regret it — Vickie Kittrie has put a lot of people in touch with regret — but I'm not going to let you pin that S&M crap on me. I've had *no* part in that kind of malignancy.' She glared at Palma, her mouth quivering, her chest fighting to control her breathing. 'Reynolds. Bristol. Dorothy, Vickie, Sandra. Their kind of destructiveness is appalling in whatever form it surfaces. It's life-negating. I

won't be lumped together with that kind of mentality.'
She paused. 'I am a *doctor*, for Christ's sake.' She paused
again. 'I don't know what you think I can give you.'

Shore shook her head, crossed her arms and moved
away from the back of the chair, walked a step or two to
the window and looked out to the monstrous ashen
clouds hanging low over the city, moving slowly inland
from the coast, dragging bands of rain behind them.

'I want to know the names of the women who allowed
Gil Reynolds to "punish" them,' Palma said to Shore's
back. 'I don't give a damn about the fine distinctions of
your sexuality, whether it stretches from pure to profane.
If you were a nun holding out on me like this, I'd still
threaten you, if I could find the leverage. It hasn't got
anything to do with your proclivities or preferences. It's
got to do with a man who's killing women; it's got to do
with stopping him.'

There was a dead silence between them as Shore continued looking out the window. A wind had gotten up
and was beginning to fling rain against the window, a few
drops at first that trickled almost all the way down the
invisible glass, and then more of them, spattering, making
flicking noises in Shore's face. She turned around.

'The only three I knew about are dead,' she said.

'Moser, Samenov, and Ackley.'

Shore nodded.

'But you didn't know Bernadine Mello?'

'No.'

Palma could feel her gut tightening. This case had
nothing symmetrical about it at all. Nothing ever came
around full turn, no definite pattern was discernible
among the ragged threads that made up the tapestry of
the five deaths.

'You knew about Linda Mancera's friend Terry,' Palma
said. 'You sent me back to Mancera for that reason.'

Shore nodded, stepped to her desk, and opened a cigarette box. She took out a cigarette and lighted it, resting
the elbow of the hand holding the cigarette on her other
arm, which she had laid across her waist.

'Did you know Terry yourself?'

'I met her once.'

Palma leaned over and slowly gathered up the photographs scattered on the desk. Shore moved as if to help her and then stopped; there were only a few photographs. She seemed, perhaps, a little self-conscious about the display of anger that had put them there. Noting this, Palma put the photographs in her purse and then looked Shore in the eye.

'Are you absolutely sure your husband doesn't know of your involvement with women?'

Having already permitted herself to feel anything less than defiance and absolute self-assurance, the direct question caught Shore with her guard down. Her mouth dropped open as if to reply, but nothing came out. She simply stared at Palma, a motionless blond portrait with pale doll's eyes against a backdrop of a darkening slate sky. She stayed that way longer than Palma had ever seen anyone lost for words, and then she dropped her hand and mashed out her cigarette in an oval, cut-crystal ashtray. Her head was bent slightly as she did this, and the part in the center of her hair showed blond to her white scalp.

Looking up, she crossed her arms again, her face devoid of rancor or calculation, absent of any role of physician or professor or dauntless professional.

'At one time, maybe three or four years ago, I thought he suspected something,' she said, her voice empty of tension. 'Perhaps he did. But if he did, he came to a solitary reckoning about it. It's not the sort of thing he would have shared with me, his doubts or his suspicions. It was only something I sensed. I can't, now, even recall what made me believe he surmised something out of the ordinary.'

She moved around to the end of the desk, stood close to it, placing her thighs against it, unfolding her arms and touching the dark mahogany with the tips of her fingers. She was almost in profile to Palma.

'He is a good man,' she said, her mouth almost smiling

but having to stop because of the trembling. 'He's brilliant. He is solid and stable and conscientious. He provides me with security. Insurance policies. Stocks. Bonds. Annuities. He always does the right thing by me and the boys.' She spoke as if she were making a checklist, a woman evaluating the qualities of one of several suitors. 'He is good and moral. I would trust him with my life, his hand on the scalpel, even if he knew about my other relationships.'

Palma was startled by a single enormous tear appearing suddenly on the lashes of Alison Shore's right eye, a single one, tumbling down her cheek like a drop of mercury, making a large dark daub on the breast of her emerald dress.

'But somewhere,' she almost choked, 'in the womb, in the cradle, at the breast ... somewhere he was cheated. He was never taught, or never learned ... that very wisest of things ... to express himself tenderly, to demonstrate his love by touch and breath, even — wildest imagination — even passion. Yet I know he loves me. He's told me, years ago. I see evidence of it ... as I told you, in the way he cares for my economic needs, my physical comforts.'

She cleared her throat, looked toward the window again and then back to her hands, the ends of her middle fingers touching lightly the surface of the wood.

'I am a doctor of obstetrics and gynecology solely because he could not show me he loved me. We met in medical school. He was then just exactly as he is now, only I was younger, not so experienced about what men are really like. I thought his strong remoteness was manly, even romantic. I didn't have the maturity to imagine a lifetime of it, or believe that he would remain the same. I must have assumed the tenderness was there, to be drawn out of him by my own strong emotions. Anyway, we married. I quit medical school when I became pregnant with Mark. Our second son, Daniel, was five when I went back to school. By this time, of course, I knew what I'd gotten myself into.

'I was mad with loneliness and longing and indecision.

I had choices. Divorce. Affairs. Turn myself into a mother who loses her own life in those of her husband and sons. It would have been cruel to leave him. He didn't deserve that kind of rejection ... simply ... for being unable to show affection. So small a thing, really, but it had such enormous consequences.

'I plunged into my own career, became an over-achiever. I neglected nothing, neither husband nor sons nor career. And it worked, for a good number of years. I fooled myself for a decade, even more. No extramarital affairs. No whining self-indulgence. We became a remarkable family, touched by the golden finger of prosperity and professional success. He was brilliant. The boys were healthy and intelligent and good-looking — I think,' she said, lifting her eyes to see their pictures on her desk and permitting herself a wan smile.

'Six years ago — the boys were just in junior high school — I had a nervous breakdown,' she said, her voice going slightly brittle at remembering it. 'For absolutely no "reason" at all. Just one of those things. I received coun-seling — a male psychiatrist, "the best," Morgan said. I cooperated, lied to him, and got the hell out as fast as I could. "Recovered" quickly.'

'Do you mind telling me who your psychiatrist was?' Palma interrupted.

'There's a doctor-client privilege,' Shore reminded her.

'I know that. But it turns out that Bernadine Mello and Sandra Moser had the same psychiatrist.'

Shore swallowed, her eyes immobile. 'Dr. Leo Chesler.'

'No,' Palma said. 'I'm sorry, go ahead.'

Shore swallowed again. 'Well, it was during this time of recuperation I met a nurse here at the college who was marvelously perceptive. She ... changed my life. She's gone now, moved to another city, but she introduced me to some of the women in Dorothy's circle of friends. That was in the time before Vickie Kittrie. None of us knew about the really sad story of Dorothy and the two Ackleys. We were all blissfully innocent of that kind of ... tragedy.'

She turned slightly toward Palma. 'I don't expect you to understand; really, I don't. But I can live this ... divided life with more grace than I can live without affection. It's sad that I can't find that kind of comfort with my husband, but I don't condemn him for being unable to provide it. He doesn't withhold himself out of cruelty, but rather out of some extreme deficit in his personality that neither of us can understand. I came to the conclusion years ago that God didn't make any whole people, only broken or chipped ones, all somehow imperfect. I think to achieve completeness we have to commit ourselves to another imperfect person. Not such a bad plan, really, when you think about it. I do that for Morgan. I do love him, and he knows it. I don't deny him anything, sexual or otherwise. He needs me, and I am happy to give him what I can. But what he can't give me, I have to find somewhere else, as a matter of self preservation. Is it a deception? Yes. Is it worse than breaking up the family, hurting him and the boys, destroying careers and the genuine happiness that we do share in being a family? I can't believe it is. This is the way I've worked it out. You can condemn me for it, but you can't be sure you're justified in doing so.'

Palma looked at her. She had delivered a slow, quiet monologue, an effort, perhaps, to achieve many things — to be understood, not to be thought the insensitive woman that she must have believed she appeared to be. It was an effort of sheer will to communicate with Palma woman to woman. She had made the supreme effort in that regard, by freely revealing her vulnerabilities. If she had not been straightforward from the beginning, it would have been the result of more than one kind of fear.

Palma nodded, and snapped the latch on her purse. 'What about the women who are going to die?'

Shore's face showed disappointment. 'You don't give us much credit, do you?' She wiped a hand with a black pearl ring along one side of her smooth chignon. 'From the first day we learned of Dorothy's death, all of us have been in touch. I don't believe there's a single woman who's not aware of the threat.'

Palma looked at her. 'Bernadine Mello was killed the night before last. You don't know if she was part of the group?'

'You know we're compartmentalized but, of course, everyone's curious who the connections were to those who have died. No one I've talked to knows her. And I think,' she said, looking down at her hands again, 'that if she'd been known to anyone in the group I would have heard. Since all this began, our communications have been constant and thorough.'

Palma nodded again. 'Thank you for the time,' she said and turned to go.

Shore stopped her, touching her arm. 'You asked about Morgan.'

'We're having to look at everyone,' Palma said. 'We're not making any presumptions of innocence.'

Shore's face could not conceal her alarm.

'You may not believe it,' Palma said, 'but we're being discreet. The fact is, the bisexual element in all this is something we very much want to keep quiet. For a number of reasons, it's to our advantage.'

Dr. Alison Shore folded her arms once more, and Palma walked out of her office.

40

Palma stood at the large windows that fronted the main lobby of the Baylor College of Medicine, tying the belt on her raincoat and watching the rain being driven by a strong wind across the car-packed parking lots. She looked at her watch. The meeting with Terry at Linda Mancera's was in half an hour. She would give the weather a few minutes to let up. The gusting spring wind wouldn't last long, though now it came in spasmodic blasts, plunging out of the dark sky, hurling sheets of rain like the temperamental outbursts of a thwarted woman's ineffectual wrath. Palma thought of Alison Shore, wondering what she had done after Palma had walked out of her office, wondering if she had turned again to the windows and the stormy landscape, wondering how many women in this one city, their lives invested with men they couldn't talk to, were doing the same, reviewing their destinies, evaluating their decisions to leave or remain with men they had despaired of understanding.

She could not help but catch flashes of her own marriage as she had listened to Shore talk of how she eventually had reconciled herself with her husband's inexplicable and unbreachable distance. The common stories of alienation she had heard from these women during the past week, and even similar stories from the men, seemed to underscore the mutual incompatibility between the sexes that was so elementary and so obvious as to be hardly worth remarking on. It was a disharmony of spirits and perceived mutual good as old as the species, something that men and women must surely have recognized for millennia, but which they seemed no closer to conciliating now than they had from the misty beginning.

Sexual homicide was surely the nadir of this misalignment of the sexes, the ancient antagonism driven to monstrous depths, to regions of legendary depravity. The archetypical images of the male aggressor and his female victim had also become mythologized, an insidious theme that cut across time and cultures, embedded forever in the minds of men and women from Persephone to Picasso.

Suddenly realizing the rain was slackening, Palma pulled up the collar of her raincoat, pushed open the heavy glass doors, and stepped out into the steamy, gray light of the spring storm.

As Palma slowed the car beside the telephone in the Plexiglas box outside the gates of Mancera's condo, she quickly noticed the cherry red Ferrari parked in front. When the gates opened she rolled into the bricked courtyard and parked beside the sports car. She took her time getting out of the plain, boxy department car, adjusting her raincoat against the mist and looked inside the creamy leather interior of the Ferrari. She noticed the rain beading uniformly on its highly polished surface. Terry's life must have improved dramatically from the days when she roomed with Louise Ackley in the dingy little wood-frame house in Bellaire.

As she walked up the sidewalk she tried to ignore the uneasiness in the pit of her stomach. She had already decided she was going to act as if nothing had happened the night before — not a very original plan, but an intelligent one, she thought. Anyway, a lot was happening, and she really wasn't in any mood for games. It wasn't the time for it, and this particular game was not anything she wanted to pursue in any case.

She rang the doorbell, and after a moment Mancera opened the door. She was dressed in a bone white linen skirt and blouse and was already smiling, but Palma thought it was an almost apologetic smile, as if she had realized the morning after that she had probably over-stepped. As they said good morning to each other her eyes lingered a little on Palma's as if she wanted to see something there, some indication of how Palma was feeling, and then it was over and they were walking into the living room where Bessa was sitting on one of the Haitian cotton sofas, her remarkable long-limbed figure set off in a pale lemon bandeau and shorts set.

In an oversized armchair at a right angle to her, a rather small, startled-looking strawberry blonde in a simple pink cotton chambray sundress looked up at Palma. Almost frail in appearance, she stood when Mancera introduced them and extended a narrow-boned and delicate hand and gave a quick nervous smile, and then sat down again in her armchair and resumed fidgeting with a small pastel blue stone egg that she had picked up from a collection on the coffee table in front of her. Though dressed casually, all three women's clothes bespoke individual incomes several times Palma's.

'I'm assuming Linda's brought you up to date on what's happening,' Palma said, sitting on a small settee opposite Terry while Mancera sat on the larger sofa next to Bessa, resting an olive arm on one of the Jamaican's bare ebony thighs. Terry, whose last name had not been provided, nodded curtly, her eyes avoiding Palma's.

'I'm going to get to the point,' Palma started off, and Terry's small eyes, adroitly made up to affect a largeness they did not possess, looked up and fixed on her. 'It's important that you understand that what we talk about here is confidential. At this point, it could easily be a fatal mistake for someone if you tell anyone what we talk about here.' She had been looking at each of them as she said this, but now she stopped her eyes on Terry. 'Gil Reynolds is a suspect. Not the only suspect; one of them. In each of these killings the victims have been brutalized in a particular fashion. Some of it specifically peculiar.' She paused a moment to give their imaginations time to explore the possibilities.

'I understand Louise Ackley confided in you regarding her "discipline" sessions with Gil Reynolds?' she said to Terry. The girl nodded again. She must have been in her late twenties, Palma thought, about the same age as Vickie Kittrie. 'What I'm interested in, and I need you to be specific, is how Reynolds liked to play out these scenarios. Was there one thing he especially liked to do, some technique or physical act? Was there anything that was particularly important to him? Was there a favorite object involved in these episodes with Louise, a favorite "game"?'

Terry swallowed and nodded that she understood, but didn't speak immediately. She continued to fondle the stone bird egg, her narrow fingers turning it over, stroking its smooth, rounded surface.

'It wasn't always the same,' she said, finally. 'Not like the usual sadomaso routines where an elaborate scenario does the trick for them.' She looked at Palma. 'You've been in Louise's place ... you didn't see any of the "dungeon" crap in there. They weren't into role-playing or paraphernalia, and that distinguished them from what you normally see ... in this.'

She leaned forward and put the blue egg on the coffee table and picked up a beige one with brown speckles. Palma caught Mancera and Bessa exchanging glances.

'They were distinguished, too,' Terry continued, 'by the fact that their encounters were not choreographed. There was not the slightest pretense that Louise's desires were actually the ones that were being catered to. There were no safe words. It was very straightforward, hard stuff. Reynolds liked to hurt; Louise wanted to be hurt. He wasn't doing anything particular or special to accommodate her kinks. He was doing what *he* liked. She was simply letting him have his way. Basically, putting an absolute blind trust in him, that he wouldn't kill her or maim her. It was like putting her head in the mouth of the only lion in the cage that she knew to be totally unpredictable. It was Russian roulette — freewheeling sadomaso with no predictable end, the way they both liked it.'

She made a small circle with her curled forefinger and thumb and slowly pushed the egg into it, through it, watching the process as she did it again, more slowly, a prolonged emergence of the narrow end of the egg into the palm of her hand, the middle finger of the other hand pushing it, following it in. Palma cut her eyes at Mancera, who was watching Terry's small hands manipulate the egg. When Palma looked at Bessa, she met the lithe Jamaican's gaze, her eyes, large and long-lashed, fixed on Palma with an unrelieved seriousness.

'I don't know that he had any overriding fetishes,' Terry said. 'None that Louise told me about, anyway. Most of the time she knew when he was coming over, though she never knew exactly what would happen. He could be physically cruel, and later, after he got to know Dorothy better, he used a lot of what he learned about Louise from Dorothy to be psychologically cruel as well. You know, throwing up the incest business to her, using it to hurt her.'

'I thought Reynolds met Dorothy first,' Palma interrupted.

'No, Gil knew Dennis Ackley and some of his creepy buddies first. I don't know how. But that's how he got to know Louise, through them. Then he met Dorothy through Louise.'

Reynolds had really fed Palma a load of lies. The son of a bitch had been good at it, so good that she had shoved him to the back of her mind as a serious suspect. She remembered her father's maxim: 'A crime cannot always be reconciled with the subject.' That is, never believe that any person 'could not have done that.' 'A good liar,' he said, 'will make you ignore the evidence.' Palma had been thinking like a rookie.

'I used to wonder why Louise told me those stories,' Terry said. 'Sometimes they seemed so painful for her to relate, but she wanted to do it. You know, Louise had the lowest self-image of any human being I've ever known. She was punishing herself. I'm sure that's what her maso-trips were all about, punishment, and then she was simply extending that by relating everything to me. I never got used to them, never understood how she could let him do those things to her.'

She held the egg in the cup of her hand and looked at it. Terry was no good at eye contact. She spent most of her time avoiding looking at Palma directly.

'It seems to me there were several basic recurring elements in her stories,' she continued. 'Episodes that concluded with Louise being tied up by him; others where he ended up cutting her with knives or razor blades or broken glass; others that were essentially scatological.' She glanced at Palma to see if she had used a word Palma didn't know. When Palma nodded, she went on. 'She never knew from time to time what to expect, and sometimes he would mix them together, but always he'd leave her in the middle of it.'

She stopped and looked a little surprised.

'Maybe that was a "signature" thing for him, something he always did, regardless of whatever else they did. He always stranded her, left her humiliated. He'd leave her tied, leave her bleeding, leave her covered in feces. He couldn't seem to get enough of humiliating her and always walked out on her in that condition. I don't remember her mentioning any particular object that he favored or any particular technique or scenario. I just recall that these elements recurred. She did remark that he was entirely unpredictable and quirky.'

'Of all these stories Louise related to you,' Palma said, 'which ones stand out in your mind the most?'

Terry had to think only a moment.

'There was one thing he did on two, maybe three, different occasions,' she said. 'There was a certain spot where he could park on the street outside her house and, if she pulled back the living room curtains in just the right place, it was possible for him to see the head of her bed through one of the living room windows. It was just a narrow little line of sight that would be invisible to the naked eye. But Reynolds had worked all this out. He would get outside the house at night in his car and call

Louise on his mobile telephone. While he looked through the telescope sights of a rifle, he'd have Louise adjust the furniture and curtains to create the line of sight.

'When everything was worked out by making marks on the walls to indicate where the curtains should be pulled back, and by marking the place on the bed where Louise would have to sit for him to see her, he was ready. He'd go back into the house and tape Louise's eyes with clear Scotch Tape, pulling them back, you know ...' Terry reached up and demonstrated on her own eyes with her thin fingers '... to make them appear Oriental. Then he'd go back out to the car and sit out there in the dark and watch her through the telescope of his rifle. She had to perform a seductive striptease in that narrow portion of her bed visible to him. When she was finally naked, she had to do certain things that he had instructed her to do, just sexually explicit acts with various objects, incidental things. The whole thing ended with her suddenly bursting a balloon filled with red dye against her forehead. Reynolds watched it all through the cross hairs of his rifle's telescope. Then he'd drive away without even going back inside the house.'

When she stopped, the room was hushed. Mancera's and Bessa's eyes were riveted on the tiny blonde, mesmerized by her solemn recounting of an unbelievably bizarre relationship. Louise Ackley's cooperation with Reynold's sick requests revealed her to be the more aberrant of the two personalities. Her self-hate must have been extraordinary.

'I used to try to imagine what must have gone through her head during these encounters,' Terry said, as though she had read Palma's mind. 'She usually didn't talk about them until late at night, after she'd been drinking quite a bit. They came out of her only at night, like ghosts. I guess she didn't have as much trouble with them in the daytime.'

Terry seemed to think about Louise a moment, looking at her own hands, then she made a resigned gesture with her mouth and continued.

'There was one other crazy thing he did, maybe the most offbeat thing of all,' Terry said. 'It had to do with Louise's eyes.'

Palma's stomach clinched. 'Eyes?'

'Right,' she nodded. 'Weird. One time he showed up at her house, unannounced, at about eleven o'clock at night. He'd brought a complete kit of theatrical paints, you know, face paints, and he made her sit with her eyes closed while he painted her eyelids. It took him a long time, she said, and he was painstakingly particular about what he was doing. When he was through, he sprayed her eyelids with a nontoxic fixative so the paint wouldn't smear when she opened them.

'After they did their thing, he left immediately. When she finally got into the bathroom to clean up, she looked in the mirror and closed one eye to see what he had painted. He had painted another eye. One on each lid, the white, the iris identical in color to her irises, the pupil, all of it. She said they were uncannily accurate and realistic, and gave the effect of her eyes always being open.'

'Was that the only thing you can remember that involved the eyes?' Palma asked.

Terry nodded. 'As far as I can remember.'

'Think about it.'

Terry looked at Palma, realizing that there was something about eyes that was significant to the investigation. 'That's . . . really all I can remember.'

'Do you remember if Louise said what they actually did on that particular occasion?'

Terry looked at the speckled egg. 'I don't know for sure. I think it was bondage. I think he tied her up and beat on her.' She was uneasy having to say it. She shook her head, thinking of it. 'I think that was it; he just beat her up.'

She didn't seem inclined to go on. Still avoiding Palma's eyes, she returned the speckled bird egg to the coffee table and picked up yet another, a light turquoise one with rusty splotches. It was slightly larger than the others, and she closed her hand around it until only the blunt end of it showed through the same hole made by her curled index finger and thumb. She looked at the glimpse of turquoise crowning in the crook of her small fist.

'She couldn't live with the incest thing, you know,' Terry said, studying the end of the egg. She looked at Palma. 'You know about the incest thing?'

Palma nodded.

Terry let her eyes rest on Palma a moment and then they slid back to the egg in her hands.

'She said there were some days when she was able to blot it out, but never for long. Dennis was always there. He treated her like his mistress. I don't know that she ever refused him. It was incredible. She was just a born victim.'

'No. There are no "born" victims,' Bessa suddenly interrupted. She was scowling, and her Jamaican accent cut off her words precisely as she shook a long hand, her golden palm turned toward Terry.

'Listen, girl, that kind of thinking is what killed her. She was lying to herself. If there's one thing we have all learned about it, it's that the finger of blame has to point in the other direction, by God.'

Bessa impatiently pulled away from Mancera, stood, took a cigarette from the ivory box on the coffee table, and lighted it with the thin gold lighter lying beside the box. She sat back down on the sofa again, crossed her long legs, and glared at Palma. Mancera moved away from her, and she and Terry looked at each other as if they knew what was coming.

Bessa inhaled her cigarette several times without saying anything, and then jerked her lovely oval chin at Palma.

'Listen,' she said. 'All of these women, your victims, all of them are victims of sexual child abuse. Dorothy. Sandra. Louise. And there's Vickie, Mary, Gina, Virginia, Meg. All of those women into S&M were victims of sexual child abuse. *Incest.* That's the real secret about these women. *Incest.*'

Bessa dragged on her cigarette angrily. 'I don't know what this madman knows about that, if he knows anything, but I tell you, it's very strange how that woman — Kittrie — has ferreted them all out.'

She shook her head, her eyes flashing at Mancera.

'This was a big topic of discussion at the party last night, before you got there,' Mancera conceded to Palma. 'Some of us think it's a red thread in these killings, but there are a lot of women who simply don't want the subject brought up at all.'

'Why?'

'Despite all the literature about incest that circulates in the lesbian community,' Mancera said, 'the subject is still as much a taboo for us as it is for the rest of the population. Shame has never been in vogue.'

'In what way do you think it's a red thread?'

'Only that it's a common denominator. That and S&M.'

'Are you saying that you think there's a relationship between the two?'

'No, not really, it's just . . .'

'Yes!' Bessa interrupted, addressing Mancera. 'There *is* a relationship, and nobody wants to talk about it because it's not always flattering to women. Politics!' She turned to Palma. 'The abuse of every sort that we've received from men has been so blatant for so long that we've become smug in our self-righteousness as victims. Especially the more militant women among us, the penis-is-Satan faction of the lesbian community. Damn them. These women have no sense of proportion.'

She addressed Mancera and Terry. 'We don't think like that, so why do we let those women bully us into this silence?' Then back to Palma. 'The truth is lesbian battering is a growing problem in lesbian communities all over the nation. That's right. Women battering women, one woman battering her lover in a lesbian relationship. It happens often enough for it to be a widely recognized problem that is so shameful to us that we have kept silent about it. It sticks in our throats to have to admit that in this way women can be just like men.'

Bessa leaned forward and mashed out her cigarette in an ashtray on the coffee table.

'I'll tell you something,' she said, her voice regaining its impatience. 'In our efforts to win some kind of equality with men we've weighted the scales too heavily. The truth is, we aren't any worse than men, and we aren't any better. Our sense of justice is no keener, our capacity for compassion no greater, our spiritual vision no holier; and we can be just as prejudicial as men, just as pitiless, just as wicked.'

She paused and let her eyes settle on Palma. 'And just as violent.' She held up two long, golden fingers of one hand. 'For two years I worked with the child-welfare services in Washington. I've seen what a hell childhood can be. True, in most cases of sexual child abuse men are the offenders. But that one fact is not the whole truth. I saw mothers, too, treat their children like animals, and I saw them sexually abuse them, torture them, and kill them. More often than I had believed possible. It changed my mind about the "sanctity" of motherhood, of woman's "innate" desire and ability to comfort and nurture.'

Palma wasn't sure where Bessa was taking her argument, but she was speaking deliberately now, almost as if she were instructing, and Palma was feeling the giddiness of the beginnings of a new idea. Her thoughts were flying back and forth from her long telephone conversation with Grant to his briefing that morning, from her conversation with Claire to her recent conversation with her mother, from the contents of the Ackley-Samenov-Ackley letters to Bernadine Mello's death scene, from Grant's remark that it was a very dangerous thing to be comfortable in your ideas to his idea that the killer is killing the woman he creates, not the woman he is killing, to her mother's aphoristic observation on the humanity of woman. The pieces were coming together faster and faster like precedent sparks to an inevitable electrical contact, though she wasn't sure why or to what end.

'Sexual child abuse is a special kind of horror,' Bessa

concluded, her voice slowing, softening, the traces of her
British accent clipping her words. 'Do not overlook the
capacity we *all* possess for cruelty, and do not under-
estimate how severely that cruelty can twist the soul of
a child.'

There was a long moment when Bessa held Palma with
her eyes, and Palma felt as if the Jamaican had, without
knowing it, just released the last spark, and now it was
up to Palma, by her own will and reasoning, to stretch
that electrical pulse across the vast chemical distances to
the formation of an idea.

But she could not immediately do that, and at the same
time she was curiously puzzled by the tension she could
feel from Mancera and Terry, who were at this moment
out of her field of vision, but from whom she could sense
an uneasiness as surely as if they had been touching her.
At a loss as to how to direct her further questioning, but
not wanting to let Bessa's pregnant monologue die
without amplification, Palma reached into her purse and
pulled out the copies of the three colored photographs of
Dorothy Samenov stretched out on the bed with the
lurking, hooded figure aping at the camera. She handed
them to Mancera immediately to her right.

'I'd like you to look at these and tell me if you think
you might know the hooded figure, or if you know where
or when the pictures were taken.' She handed them first
to Mancera.

'Oh, Christ,' Mancera whispered, seeing the first of
them. She shook her head, frowning as she took her time
with each one, looking at them as if she had never seen
anything like it, her face undergoing a series of subtle
changes from a stunned vacancy, to unabashed curiosity,
to a soft, sad compassion for Dorothy's splayed body,
which seemed cadaverishly bloodless in the harsh flash of
the cheap camera. She slowly passed each picture to
Bessa after she had looked at it. Appearing drained and
shaken, she handed over the last one and, like Bessa,
reached to the coffee table for a cigarette. She lighted it
before she responded to Palma's question, and used her

free hand to push her black hair back away from her face.

'I don't,' she said, her voice affected. 'Where did you get those?'

'We found them in a drawer in Dorothy's bedroom.'

'Nothing ... there means anything to me. I ... I'm sorry, really.'

Bessa's reaction was more stoic. She looked at the pictures with a frank and clinical dispassion, shook her head, and passed them on to Terry.

Terry was the surprise. 'Yeah,' she said, after oddly cocking her head to study the third photograph. 'That's Mirel Farr's place. That's her "dungeon." '

Palma gaped at her. 'Mirel Farr?'

'Right. She's a professional dominatrix. Dennis Ackley knew her. She was a sometimes girlfriend of one of Ackley's friends.'

'Who was that?'

Terry leaned her head back and squinted, thinking. 'Uh, Barber ... Barbish. Something Barbish.'

'Clyde,' Palma said.

'Yeah, right. Clyde Barbish.'

'Did Dorothy go to Mirel Farr's very often?' Palma did not allow her excitement to show.

'No.' Terry shook her head and looked at the pictures. 'I didn't know she'd ever been there. Dennis and Barbish and Reynolds went to her, but I hadn't heard about Dorothy. I guess it just never came up.' She stood and handed the pictures over to Palma.

'Did Reynolds know Barbish?' Palma asked.

'Oh, yeah. Reynolds slummed with those two. He's just as sleazy as they are, only he comes from the other side of town.'

Palma couldn't believe her luck. 'Do you know how I can get in touch with her?'

'No,' Terry said. 'But if you've got Louise's address book and things, you'll find her under the code name Alyson.' She spelled it for Palma, who was writing it down. When Palma returned the pictures and her notepad to her purse, she pulled out two of her business cards and laid them on the coffee table.

'If any of you hear that Bernadine Mello was, after all, involved with any of the women in the group,' she said, 'I'd like to know about it.' She looked at Terry. 'Listen, I appreciate your help. I may be getting back in touch with any of you.' She stood. 'Don't hesitate to call me about anything at all — anytime. Leave messages if you have to, on my recorder at home or at the office.'

Only Mancera stood and walked Palma to the door, following her outside to the porch, pulling the door closed behind her.

'Listen,' she said, haltingly. 'Last night, I ... I may have been a little too familiar. I do know better than that. I'm going to lay it off on too much to drink before you got there.'

Palma smiled at her. 'That's fine with me,' she said. 'Let's just leave it at that.'

Mancera lifted an eyebrow and nodded with an appreciative smile. 'I don't want to alienate you,' she said candidly. 'I'd like to be friends, real friends.'

'So would I,' Palma said.

It was a congenial parting, one that relieved Palma of a particular kind of tension that more than a few times had delicately played itself out with men, but which she had never had to negotiate with a woman: the mutual understanding that a relationship was based on friendship rather than sexuality. It was surprising to her how many times she had to deal with that in her life, and how difficult it was to come to such an accord.

But Mancera's gesture of honesty was quickly supplanted in Palma's thinking by the excitement of the chain reaction of ideas that Bessa's words had catalyzed in Palma's thoughts. As she hurried down the sidewalk in a fine, drifting mizzle, she was trying to sort it all out, putting a theory into perspective that, for her, would reconcile the discord of evidence that had begun to make her increasingly uneasy with their investigation.

41

Now that the series of women's deaths had been brought out in the open, reporters from every branch of the media were digging into the women's lives, researching 'investigative' pieces, interviewing witnesses, hounding the victims' families, and generally muddying the waters for the detectives. The newspapers were running full-page articles about the victims with pictures of each and skimpy bios, and a map showing where their bodies had been found.

The number and frequency of the deaths, and the upscale lifestyles of the victims, were attracting so much attention that the tip lines were ringing off the wall. To catch up, Childs and Garro postponed their trip to the Houston Yacht Club to check on Ted Leoko's alibi, and stayed in the office to go through the tip sheets to look for anything that might be immediately attractive, and by the time Palma got back to the office Cushing and Boucher had come in from checking out more of the names in Samenov's address book. Someone had brought in sandwiches, and there was an impromptu meeting in Frisch's office, each detective making do with whatever spot he could find to spread out the contents of his paper sack.

Palma had just finished telling them of her interview with Dr. Alison Shore and Terry and looked around the room at the scattering of detectives. Cushing with his spiked Coke had eaten very little food other than salty chips, while Haws, having consumed half of Cushing's smoked ham and Swiss, was now doing the same with the other half of Marley's roast beef on rye. Garro was eating a BLT, a cigarette tucked between his fingers, while Leeland, surrounded by notebooks and file folders, was finishing a barbecue sandwich wrapped in paper stained with barbecue sauce. Hauser was scraping the bottom of a yogurt cup, while Grant, mostly ignoring his half-eaten tuna salad, had turned around at his desk to listen to something Birley was saying. All of them were going on too little sleep and knowing they would have to do it for some time longer, probably days.

'. . . so Dr. Morgan Shore is sewed up tight,' Birley was saying. 'He was making hospital rounds at the time of both Moser's and Samenov's deaths.'

'Reynolds, on the other hand, says he was at home alone at the time Samenov was killed,' Frisch said. 'What about Moser? Where was he when she was killed?'

'I didn't get into that with him,' Palma said. 'My interview with him was early on. We weren't this far along.'

Frisch looked at Grant, who was sitting in one of the torturously uncomfortable metal typing chairs that seemed ubiquitous in the department. He was in shirt sleeves, his hands jammed into his pants pockets, his legs crossed at the knees and stretched slightly out in front of him, a large manila folder in his lap. His eyes seemed tired to Palma, and his broken nose a little more damaged than before. He had spent the morning going through the crime scene videos and photographs, taking notes, and talking with Hauser. He had listened carefully to Palma's report of what Terry had said about Reynold's treatment of Louise Ackley.

'When you interviewed him,' Grant asked her, 'what was his attitude, his demeanor?'

'Self-assured,' she said. 'Gave the impression of being straightforward, unfailingly honest. He readily admitted that it was his fault that his family had fallen apart — a result of his affair with Dorothy Samenov. No excuses. Said it had taken him a while to accept the responsibility for having thrown it all away. He was even still wearing his wedding ring, as if it were a sentimental gesture, an old habit that evoked fond memories. Christ.'

Grant smiled as if she had described one of his old friends with a rakish reputation. 'You feel a little stupid, getting suckered in by him?'

Palma was surprised at the personal note in the question. 'Well, yeah. As a matter of fact, I do.'

Grant grinned. 'If you ever come across another one of these guys, it'll happen again. That's what's so scary about them. They blend in so perfectly with the rest of us. You can't blame yourself for not seeing what isn't there.' Grant shrugged. 'Then you began hearing contradictory stories about him.'

'Right,' Palma regarded him a little more closely as she spoke. 'From Claire first.'

'Did she mention if Reynolds had talked on more than one occasion about his being a sniper?'

Palma shook her head. 'She didn't say. But she did tell me to talk to Mancera if I wanted to know more about Reynolds's sadistic side. And then Mancera put me on to Terry.'

'That's lucky,' Grant said. He was looking at the manila folder, thinking. 'Reynolds sounds good. Has most of the profile characteristics we're looking for.'

Palma winced. She wished to God she had committed herself earlier. Every time Grant took another step in favor of Reynolds, she knew it was going to make her proposal look that much more out of line.

'But if he's got a solid alibi for even one of these numbers, we're going to have to put him aside no matter how good he looks.' Grant took a hand from his pocket and touched the edge of the folder, straightening it on his lap the way some people idly fold and refold paper napkins, while they talked. 'So far we don't have any physical evidence tying him to even one of these. We already know that he's extraordinarily careful. If he's alerted at this point, whatever physical evidence might exist is going to be destroyed immediately. And, if for some reason he suddenly stopped killing, and that's happened to us before, then we're out of it.'

Grant looked at Frisch. 'I'm thinking we ought to keep him completely in the dark about his being a key suspect. Right now he's pretty satisfied with himself. No one's been back to see him so it's likely he thinks he's not in the forefront of the investigation. Safe. He's feeling very secure, very self-confident. He's savoring the fantasy, playing it out.'

'But,' and Grant raised a cautionary finger, 'his cooling-off periods are getting shorter, which means his fantasy is escalating, intensifying. As he gets increasingly carried away with it, the chances he'll get careless will increase also, especially if he believes he's not under suspicion. If we tip him off, it could be like a slap in the face, bringing him to his senses. At this point his own self-confidence is his worst enemy. If we can learn more about him, maybe we could take advantage of it.'

'So how do you want to approach it from here on?' Frisch asked.

'Put him under constant surveillance. Wire his condo and his car. Get a search warrant and go through his place when he's not there. Your probable cause will be the "trophies," but I'll be surprised if we actually find anything directly connected with the murders.' Grant nodded, anticipating their thoughts. 'Yeah, I know what I said before, but after looking through the crime scene videos I'm beginning to feel we're going to have an exception here. These items will be very special trophies. He'll keep them in a special place, well hidden. If he has women to stay over with him at nights, he's not going to want them to stumble onto this stuff. It's sacrosanct. When it's fantasy time, he'll reverently pull them out of hiding. As for the wire, I'd hope to pick up some communication with Barbish.'

'Then what are you really wanting to get out of the search?' Leeland asked.

Grant nodded again.

'Two things. First, I'd like to get detailed photographs

of every room, every piece of furniture, books, insides of drawers of all kinds, closets, everything you've got time to photograph. Maybe we'll get lucky and find the trophies. Fine. But he's shrewd, and chances are we won't get enough evidence to convict him unless we can work on his mind,make him screw up. Men like this are very controlled, and it won't be easy. Therefore, it's to our advantage to do our homework before we make any kind of move at all to try to influence his actions. He's not operating under any feelings of guilt for what he's doing I doubt if he feels any great stress at all, so it'll be hard to jack him up psychologically until we know more about him.

'Second, I want to get the smell of the guy.'

That was it. Grant didn't elaborate, and no one asked him to.

Leeland followed up.

'Carmen's already checked him through vice and intelligence and all the computers,' he said. 'With no luck. I'll go ahead and pull his military records and see if he had any kind of problem with his superiors related to his Nam sniping.'

'Fine.' Grant picked up a pencil and notepad from a nearby desk, flipped open the pad, and started writing. 'Also, we ought to do some backup investigating on Denise Reynolds Kaplan. Especially the "Kaplan" part of her life. Get the missing persons file on her. Find out if she'd ever been sexually involved with any of the victims. We need a good picture of her to see if she resembles the victims *after* they've been made up by the killer. Try to find out what women from Samenov's group were her lovers, and see if they remember anything she might have said to them about her relationship with Reynolds. Anything that might be revealing about his personality.'

'What about trying to verify his whereabouts on the nights of the killings?' Birley asked.

Grant tilted his head and grimaced, indicating a tough call. 'I'm still afraid of tipping him off.' He looked at Frisch, then back to Palma and Birley. 'Actually, I'd rather hold off on that for right now. Let's wait and see what we come up with.'

'One thing,' Garro said, lighting a new cigarette. 'We know that Moser and Samenov and Louise Ackley had done rough scenes with Reynolds. We don't know about Mello. We don't even know if Mello knew him.'

'Yeah, that's true,' Lew Marley said. He was picking his teeth with the sharpened end of a wooden match. 'And it seems to me that if there are other women in the group who've been with him before, they're the ones most at risk. He's going to go back to them.'

Grant was making another note on his pad.

He said, 'Since all of the women have been in touch with each other about this, don't you suppose Reynolds is going to find it almost impossible to make an arrangement with one of them? I'd imagine they're as suspicious of him as we are. He may find himself frozen out, and this may cause some frustrations I hadn't taken into consideration.'

'I don't know,' Birley spoke up, chewing on a bite of a dill pickle still dangling in his fingers. 'I can't believe this guy doesn't have access to other women. You know he does, bound to. Maybe through Mirel Farr, or hell, just from cruising. And shouldn't we get a picture of Mello to Farr to see if there *is* a tie-in there?'

'Yes, definitely,' Grant was now stroking his mustache with his right hand, his brown eyes staring out through Frisch's picture window into the squad room. 'I wonder,' he said, 'if the fact that these women were all victims of childhood sexual abuse has anything to do with Reynolds's thinking. Could he know that about them? I wonder about Bernadine Mello, since maybe she wasn't one of the group. I'd like to know something about her childhood.'

'Dr. Broussard,' Palma said.

Grant nodded without looking at her. 'Yeah,' he said. 'We've got to talk to him ... this afternoon.'

'I'd like to throw something on the table for consideration,' Palma said.

Grant finished what he was writing and looked up, and out of the corner of her eye she could see Cushing stop his Coke halfway to his mouth. Everyone else looked her way with mild curiosity. She did her damnedest not to seem hesitant. She didn't want any of them to realize how intimidated she felt, even though, after her conversation at Mancera's a few hours earlier, she was convinced she was right. Everything had come together in that one enlightening session.

She looked at Grant. 'On the way to Samenov's last night you said that you believed that we had a killer here with a special kind of wrinkle, not a special kind of killer. I'm thinking we do have a special kind of killer ... at least one that's different from what you're used to seeing in this type of crime.' She paused, though unintentionally. She shouldn't have. She plunged on. 'I think the killer is a woman.'

There were several beats of silence before she heard Cushing hiss a sarcastic, 'Shit,' and Gordy Haws gave a snort. Grant's expression didn't change, and he nodded for her to go ahead. She wished she could have seen Birley's face, or even Leeland's. She hoped she would have seen something there besides scorn or a condescending, poker-faced effort at interpersonal diplomacy.

But Palma was ready.

'First, there's the condition of the body,' she said. 'The use of cosmetics, bath oils, painted finger- and toenails, all of that. It doesn't seem quite so bizarre when you consider these are women's tools. In a way, sort of the "natural" thing to do within the context of her mental condition.

'The victim's folded clothes at the crime scenes. Not military-style you said, but it is certainly consistent with someone who's compulsively neat. Perhaps someone for whom "cleaning up" was second nature. A wife, a mother, someone who'd been taught to develop habitual neatness, an attribute that's been distorted under the circumstances of her abnormal psychology. This holds true regarding the general neatness of the entire crime scene, including the washed body.

'Victims willingly meet the killer. None of the women in Samenov's group, or any woman for that matter, would have hesitated to meet another woman. No coercion necessary. No apparent risk. Not even the possibility of a subliminal threat which might arise as a "sixth sense" in the company of even the nicest man in light of recent events.

'There are the anomalies you pointed out,' she continued, still addressing Grant. 'Behavior that doesn't conform to the usual characteristics of organized killers, but which figure logically when you consider a female offender: victims are *not* targeted strangers. Women are not stalkers. The killer is one of the women in Samenov's "group." She knows all the victims — another reason they willingly go to meet her. Victim's body is *not* hidden. No need to. Killings are not conducted in public areas such as a park, lakeshore, or lonely roadside, where men often abduct and rape women. But a woman, especially a woman operating within the context of this "group," would most likely encounter her victims in a bedroom or hotel room. A place of sufficient privacy. Victim's body is *not* transported. Same reason, no need to. But also, the bodies may not be moved because it's something that would be physically impossible for most women to do. The killer circumvented this obstacle by using her brains rather than her brawn. She arranged the killings to occur at places where it would not be necessary to move the body to avoid detection.

'The old saying that women are too squeamish for this sort of violence, preferring poisonings and hired killers, is given the lie by the fact that we're dealing with a group of women who are hard-core S&M enthusiasts used to tying each other up and being tied up. They're familiar with violence, have gotten used to all forms of it, and are willing, even eager, to participate in it. We even have Dr. Shore's testimony that Vickie Kittrie's S&M was so violent it could be "lethal," that she almost killed Walker Bristol.'

There was a snigger from someone, probably Cushing

or Haws again, the only ones who had the bad manners to express their opinion, that she was embarrassingly off-base, with derision rather than silence. But Palma didn't even hesitate.

'The bite marks. I'll admit they threw me at first, since I'd come to associate them with male aggression in sex crimes. I was preconditioned to think of them from a male perspective because I've been taught — and taught by the best, I ought to say, including John and my own father — by males. But it occurred to me that maybe there are some other ways to look at these bites. Given the circumstances of these killings, and from a woman's perspective, it seems that a woman could easily have made the bites as well as a man. It dawned on me that it fits right in with one of the old clichés about fighting women, violent women — kicking, scratching . . . biting women.

'Absence of sperm in swabs or smears or at crime scene. I'm well aware that it's common for sexual homicide scenes not to evidence semen. But I'm offering an alternative reason as to *why* it's absent.

'Timing. You'd mentioned Thursday nights as possibly being a boys' night out. Same goes for women. Club night. Girls' night out. Aerobics class. Moser even had gone out to meet this person in exercise clothes, supposedly on her way to aerobics class.'

Palma stopped. She had never taken her eyes off Grant.

'None of the physical evidence we've gathered so far precludes a woman killer. In fact, there's been no evidence at *all* that suggests a male killer. We've yet to find a single head hair short enough to be male. So far, aside from pubic hair, all we've found is long blond head hair.'

She stopped, then cringed inwardly, waiting for the awkward silence that would follow as Grant tried to think of how to respond. But Cushing, lying in wait for revenge, stepped right in, licking his lips.

'Well, hell,' he said, lowering his chair, which he had reared back on two legs as he listened to her, grinning. He looked around the room. 'I think she's got something here. But I've got a theory of my own that seems to have more credibility. I think it was an impotent orangutan. No sperm at the crime scene. Zoo's closed on Thursday nights. Those big teeth. He's a special kind of . . .'

'Cushing, shut up, dammit,' Frisch snapped, and cut off Cushing as well as a few snickers that were building. Palma kept her eyes glued on Grant, who had dropped his eyes to the folder in his lap, a gesture of neutrality while the locals worked out their personnel problems. Cushing's sophomoric ridicule didn't bother her, but the way Grant and the others handled her idea was going to be crucial. She was curious as to just how far their male myopia would take their response.

Grant looked up. 'What you've pointed out is true. On the face of it.' A qualifying statement that subtly attempted to put Palma's theory itself on the sophomoric level. Obviously there was more to it than just the face of it. 'Everything you've said seems solid.' Seems . . . 'But as I said earlier, we're playing the odds here. It's a little bit like case law. We look for precedents.' He paused a couple of seconds. 'I've been working in the behavioral science unit at Quantico from the beginning of the program,' Grant said, his lips thin and firm under his mustache, 'and I've never seen a woman commit a violent, sexually motivated homicide.'

'How do you know?' Palma wasn't completely successful at keeping the challenging edge out of her voice.

Grant lifted his eyebrows, in surprise at first, and then as a gesture of how the hell was she going to challenge the evidence. 'I'm telling you we've never seen it,' he said.

'Have you cleared every case you've handled?' she asked rhetorically.

Grant waited for her to make her point.

'Every year, nationwide, we have eighteen thousand to twenty thousand homicides,' she said. 'Every year, approximately a quarter of those cases go uncleared . . . forty-five hundred to five thousand cases. *Every* year. Just in the past decade alone that adds up to nearly fifty thousand uncleared homicides. A good portion of them sexual homicides. I don't know what percentage they represent, but I do know from the Bureau's own statistics sexual homicides are on the rise. Are you going to tell me that you *know* that none of those unsolved sexual homicides are committed by women?'

'No,' Grant came back, 'I'm not. But I'm telling you we've never *seen* a female sexual killer.'

'And that gets me back to my original question: How do you know you haven't?' Palma had their attention now, she could feel it, even though she had never taken her eyes off Grant. She could see Leeland, probably the most naturally analytical of all of them, frozen in his seat. 'I understand that historically all the sexual killers you've worked with have been males. You people are rightly credited with being the first to recognize the serial killer, the "lust" killer, the sexually motivated killer. But do you think you really have the definitive story on this phenomenon?'

Grant waited, his hooded eyes resting on her with the cool dispassion of a veteran. No one moved.

'When we were looking through Dorothy Samenov's condo, you made a remark that stuck with me,' Palma said. 'You were talking about assumptions people make about men and women, that they go along for years without these assumptions being challenged, and then suddenly one day something causes them to see things differently and a myth is exploded. You said that it was a very dangerous thing to be comfortable with our assumptions. Well, try to look at your profiling analysis program from another perspective.'

Palma was talking fast, not wanting to be interrupted, wanting to spit it out before she lost momentum.

'The behavioral psychology framework you set up to analyse sexual homicides is grounded in the data you gleaned from extensive in-depth interviews conducted with thirty sexually motivated killers over a long period of time. And you've continued to add to that data base over the years by interviewing other killers. All male. So the behavioral model used to analyse all sexual homicides is based on male psychology. All of your analysts at Quantico are male. So what happens when your analysts get a case they really can't fit within the framework of the behavioral model you've established?'

Grant's eyes telegraphed incredible concentration. He hadn't even blinked.

'Wouldn't your analyst — wouldn't you yourself — try to explain this behavior as an aberration *within* the framework of the behavioral model you've already established for *male* sexual killers? The "case law" assumption that only males commit sexually motivated homicide is so ingrained in detectives — who are mostly male — that even though you may not understand what you're seeing at a crime scene, you automatically exclude the only other suspect possibility available to you.

'Would it ever occur to you, any of you,' she asked, now looking around the room for the first time at the men staring at her with their mouths practically hanging open, 'that you couldn't explain something you'd seen at one of these uncleared crime scenes because it resulted from *female* behavior rather than male behavior? I doubt it.' She turned back to Grant. 'In fact, you've just proved that: you say you don't have a special kind of killer here, you've just got your standard male sex killer with a "special kind of wrinkle," which you haven't figured out yet. It's never even occurred to you that you don't understand what you're seeing because the killer is thinking, and acting, like a woman, not like a man.'

42

After Evelyn Towne left his office, Broussard had somehow made it through the afternoon and well into the night before he had given in to Librium and a strange, dreamless loss of time, until he had awakened to this morning's gray light and the leisurely sound of rain. He was famished and ate an enormous breakfast, and then immediately fell into a deep depression and stood for an hour in the sun room looking out the windows at the slowly drifting mist thickening toward the bayou until it obscured the thick foliage that hugged its margins. Then he had gotten the call on the number to which only his most favored patients had access. Mary Lowe wanted to see him, her session having been canceled by him the day before. She was controlled, he noticed, but her restraint was taut. It was remarkable enough that she should call him at all, under any circumstances, and that she should do so the very day after a canceled appointment indicated an urgency to which she would never admit. He agreed to see her.

He heard the front door to the studio open. Had it been anyone but Mary, he simply would have refused. Even as it was, he would find it difficult to be attentive. But maybe it wouldn't take more than his silence to satisfy her. That was so often the case, that he was wanted only as a human-size ear, an orifice without soul or opinion or judgment, something into which they could

spill their insecurities, their faults, their gloomy intim-
ations, and sometimes lustful dreams.

He was still looking out the windows when she spoke
behind him.

'Thank you,' she said, 'for allowing me to come.'

He turned around and saw her standing just inside the
doorway to his office, unbuttoning her raincoat.

'That's all right,' he said, and watched her slip off the
raincoat and hang it on a brass hook on the wall behind
the chaise. She was wearing a short-sleeved shirtwaist
dress of blue rayon with tiny petal-like designs in white.
He approved of the single strand of tiny pearls that
draped like beads of white liquid between the small
protrusions of her clavicles.

'I want to talk,' she said unnecessarily. He nodded,
and she walked to the chaise and slipped off her flats,
swung her legs up onto the chaise, and leaned back,
raising her hips slightly to straighten her skirt. Broussard
imagined that this was the ideal woman for whom Freud
had introduced the chaise longue. Mary had seemed to
take to it from the beginning, though at first it hadn't had
any effect on her being cooperative. Nevertheless, she
had never hesitated to lie down, to play the role of analysand in posture, if not in spirit.

Broussard settled himself in his armchair out of her
sight and waited a moment for her breathing to become
regular. He reached over where the switches to the recorders were installed under the lip of the desk and flipped
one on. A small red light glowed from the shelves where
the recorders sat in unobtrusive mahogany boxes
resembling cigar humidors. He took a notepad off his
desk and uncapped his fountain pen, turned to a clean
sheet, and waited for Mary to introduce the topic she felt
so urgently in need of discussing.

'It progressed oddly,' she said after a few minutes of
silence. Obviously she was beginning *in medias res*, and
Broussard cast his mind back to the subject of their last
meeting on the previous Wednesday ... the first time her
father had fondled her sexually ... in the swimming pool

... his orgasmic hunching against her childish buttocks under the water.

'I was distant with him for a while after that,' she said. 'I couldn't help it. Even if he did act as if nothing had happened. I knew something had happened. But he was kind, genuinely kind to me, and I didn't doubt in the least that he really loved me. Whatever had happened in the pool ... well, that was maybe bad manners ... or something. Or maybe it wasn't even that.'

Mary's hands rested at her sides on the blue rayon dress, with only her right hand visible to Broussard. He looked at it. She was a very beautiful woman. An image of Bernadine flashed in his mind, and he almost choked on a sob.

'The next time ... we were watching television. I remember it clearly. Over the years all the ... times run together, but this was the first time he went to my vagina ... so I remember it. It was within a week or so of the pool incident. We were curled up on the sofa together, him and me. We were eating popcorn, and I had on my robe but I was in my panties, you know, ready for bed. The popcorn was salted and buttered; he'd go to a lot of trouble to get it just right. I was leaning next to him, and we were watching "G.E. Theater." It was a commercial break and a woman was standing next to a refrigerator which she was opening to show us. He had just eaten some buttered popcorn and his fingers were still slick because he hadn't wiped them on a napkin yet, and he just reached down and slipped his fingers under the edge of my panties.'

Mary stopped, her narrow tapered fingers moving softly on the rayon as if she were mentally going through a piano exercise, only very subtly.

'I was petrified. And I remember feeling a kind of humming spread all over me, and I felt instantly hot and then cold. I didn't even take my eyes off the lady and the refrigerator, although I was wanting to in the worst way. I didn't move. I was too young to have any pubic hair, so his buttery fingers just went round and round my vagina

without any problem, and I remember thinking I might
faint. He kept it up, getting more and more energetic, and
I could feel his hips grinding again like in the pool. Finally
he just made one quick dip into my vagina with his finger
and lunged his hip against my side and kept it there. I
didn't know ... all the signals. But it was over.'

Mary moved her tongue around in her mouth, trying
to stir it to moisture. It didn't seem to work, but she continued.

'After that he was still a minute. Then he pulled his
hand out of my underwear and got up from the sofa and
went into the bathroom. I didn't take my eyes off the television. I didn't stop eating popcorn. I was ignoring the
whole thing as hard as I could. I thought if I stopped
eating popcorn all these things would have to be
confronted. After a while he came back and sat back
down on the sofa, but I had moved over a little way. He
didn't try to get me to come back over to him, and we just
went on watching television until the program was over
and it was bedtime.'

Broussard had been watching Mary's face, the profile
perdu of all his clients who reclined on the chaise, and
when she paused he glanced at her hand again. She had
gathered a fistful of her skirt, squeezing it, the hem on the
side pulled up to her knee.

'I went to bed and lay awake waiting, but neither of
them even came in to kiss me goodnight. I guess he was
feeling ashamed. When I was sure they were both asleep,
I got out of bed and went into my bathroom and washed
between my legs, scrubbed with a washcloth and soap
until it was raw, and then I dried and put perfume around
there to get rid of the butter smell. Then I went back to
bed and lay there a long time staring into the dark before
I started crying and cried myself to sleep.'

Mary released her grip on her dress, and Broussard's
gaze went back to her profile. A single wet rivulet traced
a slightly darker path down the side of her face and into
the blond hairline at her temples. Broussard thought of
the stories Bernadine had told him, all the different kind

of stories. She was the consummate raconteur, a Scheher-
azade who talked to forestall not her death, but her disso-
lution into the dark winds of insanity. That's what all of
them did, together all of them became a composite Sche-
herazade, talking, talking to save themselves. But he was
no sultan, no executioner turned deliverer who, at the end
of a thousand and one nights, could proclaim them libera-
tors of their sex and set them free. And modern life
allowed for no such romantic endings. Their lives were
not redeemed by their cleverness or even by the compassion elicited by their despair.

'It was a month or two before he started coming to my
bedroom,' she said, having once again wadded her skirt
into another tight fist, advancing the hem of her dress still
farther, above the knee, to the beginning muscles of her
long, straight thigh. 'At first he would come only deep in
the night. I would be sleeping, and then I would feel him
lifting the covers and his naked body sliding in beside me.
He taught me how to masturbate him while he played
with my vagina. He was very gentle with me. He didn't
hurt me. He would talk to me, tell me how much he loved
me and how he believed I loved him too. This was the
way we could show our love for each other, he said. He
said that giving each other pleasure like this was a mutual
sharing and sharing was what love was all about. Of
course, he always assumed I was enjoying it; he never
asked me if I was. And I was afraid to tell him otherwise.
I don't know why I was afraid. He never threatened me.

'His penis,' she said, pausing, preoccupied with the
memory of that strange member, filtered through the
mind of the child she had been. 'I'd never felt anything
quite like it, hadn't even imagined anything like it. The
stupid little shape of it. Sometimes he would come into
my room before it was erect and want me to work it up. It
was such a strange piece of anatomy, stuck on the front of
him there, seeming not really to fit anywhere. I always
thought it seemed so out of place, rather like an after-
thought ... just stuck on there. I mean, it seemed ill-
planned, having a life of its own, changing shape the way

it did. As a child, it struck me that way. So there was some curiosity. But mostly, I was just revolted by the whole thing, by the oily secretions and then the ejaculation itself, viscous and noisome.'

She stopped, her eyes having the unseeing glaze of a hypnotic stare that often accompanied a total immersion in recalling the past.

'I was a *child*.' She frowned in incredulity. 'He had no right to acquaint me, however gently, with those sensations. I hadn't the vaguest understanding of what he was going through, and I grew to hate the signs of it that I soon became familiar with. A child, only a child. I didn't understand, but I came to a sad knowledge of the crude signals of his sexual anguish, the moanings and whimperings as I tugged on his penis. I was only a child, yes, but I had an innate understanding of what pathetic meant, and he became the embodiment of it. Whacking him off in those gray nights, I felt overwhelmed by the repulsion and sadness of it all.'

Mary stopped again. Broussard followed the path of her staring eyes, but they were going nowhere. He believed she was looking at the thick coverage of the treetops, the oaks and tallow trees and catalpas where the mist and light rain were sifting down from the lowering sky. What did she see there? Why did she stop? He waited. Her lips were parted slightly, the hint of a pucker at one corner visible to him at this angle. She was laboring to control her breathing, her gray-blue eyes enlarged slightly as if it were part of her effort to gain control of her breathing.

'I had already learned to remove myself from what was happening by thinking of something else,' she began again. 'It was a childish effort, more like daydreaming. I thought of scenes of movies I'd seen. *The Sound of Music*. I was eleven when it came out. I saw it five times, and I retreated into the innocence of that movie many, many, many nights while I hammered away on him. Julie Andrews was all the sweetness that I imagined it possible for people to be. She was so *good*. And she was

completely untainted by the sort of things that went on in
my life.'

She shook her head. 'One time in high school I had a
kind of nervous breakdown, I guess. Back then, though,
the teachers in the public school systems weren't trained
to recognize the symptoms of what I was going through.
But there was one teacher ... she knew. She tried to get
me to go to a state Public Welfare office. I wasn't alone,
she said. There were other girls ... going through this. I
could talk to them, get counseling. I could share this with
other girls, hear their stories. Jesus.

'Well, for me, it wasn't that way.' Mary's voice was
taking on a hard edge. 'I didn't find it any kind of relief at
all to know that there were other kids like me. I didn't
find this enormous sense of comfort in knowing that
there were other kids as abused and sick as me. I
wouldn't have been comforted in the least to learn that
my best friend was going through the same thing I was
going through and would have understood my confusion
and repulsion and desperate desire to be loved differently
than I was being loved. I didn't want any part of that kind
of "comfort." I wanted to think about beautiful Swiss
highland meadows and the clear, smiling face of Julie
Andrews singing "Edelweiss" under blue skies with white
clouds as clean and soft as dreams. She knew *nothing* of
what my life was like, and that was what I wanted. I was
looking for escape, not for a sisterhood of molested,
lonely little girls who could tell me they understood what
it was like to tug away on their fathers' penises at night
while they desperately turned their minds to something
else — anything else.'

As if another thought had swept past and drawn her
thoughts after it, she stopped, her lips slightly parted as
she momentarily followed some other strain of music,
attended to some other story. Then she proceeded.

'We progressed to fellatio. I didn't know ... what it
inevitably would lead to. I just thought if I went along
with whatever he wanted, then at some point he would
be satisfied and leave me alone. Children don't know

anything about the nature of a sexual drive, certainly not one like this. I couldn't have known ... I just couldn't have ... have ... ha ... haa ...'

To Broussard's surprise Mary began stuttering and then suddenly stopped altogether. She whimpered. That was the best word for it, but it was an eerie mewl and reminded him of the *cri du chat*. Rather, it had sexual overtones and was accompanied by Mary's anxiously kneading her upper thigh with her fist in which she still clutched the hem of her dress, which now had worked itself inappropriately high. This continued for some minutes until she once again gained a degree of control. Then she continued.

'And then that was not enough, either, and after a while he was penetrating me. He painstakingly worked up to it over a long period of time. As I think back, he was really quite clever about it. His preoccupation with his own body was enormous, and he wanted me to find it as fascinating as he did. At the time, of course, I didn't realize it, but looking back it's clear that he was almost preadolescent in his fascination with his own penis. It was pitiful. But at the time ... he was my father, and that fact alone had more influence over my mind than anything else. If he said so ... you know, then even if it made me sick, I went on with it. But I cried a lot. God, how I cried.

'The daydreaming ... it just wasn't enough anymore. Not after the intercourse began. At first I was dumbfounded ... all over again.' She paused.

'You wouldn't think that, would you? I mean, a child who has been performing fellatio with her father ... you wouldn't think she would be "surprised" by sexual intercourse. But I was. I just didn't know that this ... these acts were leading anywhere. I mean the stuff before intercourse ... He puts his penis on your stomach and has you tug away on it and then it squirts all over you, hot and gagging you. Incredible. And then he experiments and puts it all over you, different places. And soon he wants it in your mouth. You think, Okay, this is it, it's what he was wanting all along. This is as bad as it's going to get. You can't believe it. It's the most outrageous thing you can imagine. The outer limit ... But no, there's more. Now he wants it in there, where you go to the bathroom. It staggers you to think of it. It can't be. It's too big. He forces it, and you just think, Oh, God, and you cut yourself loose from your body. Let him do it, whatever the hell it is he wants to do if he will just go ahead and get it over with.

'And then later, when it's all over and time has passed and you know he's going to be coming into your room again, the fears start coming at you. How many more places can he think to put it? How many more things can he dream up for you to do to it? You never stop fearing it will somehow get even worse than it is; he will think of something even more grotesque. A child ... you know ... a child has no idea of the progression of events in this ... the enormity of what he is doing simply grows and grows ... and the fear and humiliation ... and the awful, awful sadness.'

Outside a quick wind rose up from the bayou and the sky darkened as the trees began to shudder and then toss, their upper reaches bending and springing as a heavy rain slammed down through their thick canopies with an ominous roar, as if high above them a ranging, angry wind was passing over the city.

Mary Lowe had stopped talking — one of her unpredictable silences — and was lying motionless on the chaise watching the changing tint of bruised light that suffused the woods in the wake of the brief torrent and whipping winds. The harrowing story of her stepfather's sexual abuse, events that had haunted and distorted her life up to this very moment, had left Broussard completely unaffected. He had listened without empathy, staring at her exposed leg as though it were the physical equivalent of the Sirens' song, a temptation of beauty so irresistible that it had bled him of compassion and simple dignity. Her child's anguish that she had carried with her into adulthood like a night terror elicited no stirrings of tenderness in Broussard's heart, at least none so strong as to override the quite different effect of her long naked thigh.

'There was a significant change in the way we related to each other once he began having intercourse with me,' Mary said. Her eyes were still on the darkened landscape, but they were dreamy rather than comprehending.

'He would come to me earlier in the night. I had gotten so that I closed my bedroom door every night, hoping that somehow that would discourage him. One time I actually locked it, but the next day he picked me up after school himself — I usually walked home with friends. He made such a scene of crying and whining and saying I didn't love him, saying that I wasn't grateful for the new life that he had given us, that he succeeded in planting in my mind the fear that he might abandon us if I wasn't more accommodating. That night I left the door unlocked.'

Mary nodded her head slightly as if confirming a point.

'This was a new wrinkle, a new fear for me for the next few years. That is, if I didn't let him have his way with me then he would abandon us. I didn't want to have that on my conscience. I didn't want to be the reason Mother had to go back to waiting tables and living in cheap apartment houses, crying herself to sleep at nights. I began to see myself as the glue that held the three of us together. My mother's happiness, and the three of us being a "family," became my responsibility. If I wanted things to stay the way they were, then I had to give him what he wanted.

'In a way, really, I became the mother. I was the one who had sexual intercourse with him. I was the one who cooked in the kitchen with him and cleaned up after meals with him. I was the one who received his affection. But at nights I would turn my face to the wall and pray that I wouldn't hear the doorknob turning, wouldn't hear the little "chunk" sound of the latch opening. I went to sleep every night with a knot in my stomach, fearing I would wake up to find him pressing his naked body next to me.'

In her agitation she now had gathered the hem of her skirt in both hands, wadding it, worrying it, apparently unaware that she was revealing so much of her body. She seemed not to regard the material as her skirt at all, but as some sort of security blanket that needed handling. Broussard hoped that she would work it high enough for him to get a glimpse of her panties.

'I began to have nightmares,' she said flatly. 'They were vicious, horrifying episodes full of imagery I didn't understand and didn't want to remember. I thought, in my child's mind, that I was being punished for what he was doing to me. That *I* was being punished. That's how a child thinks, you know: *I* was being punished for what *he* was doing to me. I knew instinctively that what we were doing was sick, and because I felt dirty I automatically accepted the guilt. But there were moments of doubt about that ... my guilt. To absorb that much guilt is a horrible burden, and I had to have some relief from it. So I began to question what was happening, and why. If I was being punished, who was punishing me? God? Was it God? Was he sending these nightmares? A child isn't a fool, you know. I knew I was, or was intended to be, an innocent in the world. And I thought: God would do this to *me*? What about my father? What about his penis, his probing fingers, his tongue, and all that ... semen he spilled on me at nights? And God was punishing *me*? That was when I quit believing in God. I decided that somebody had made a mistake about God.'

She stopped a moment. 'And those night terrors. They got so bad I was staying awake all night to avoid them. I began falling asleep in classes; my grades began to drop. The dreams were almost unbearable for about six months, I guess, and then they began to taper off. The images were so vivid I could have drawn them. Certain creatures recurred so that I immediately knew them when they appeared and knew what role they would play in my torment. I dreaded them as intensely as I dreaded him creeping into my room in the dark. To this day when I have nightmares, they come back. The same ones.'

She grew still. 'An astonishing thing happened years later, about those nightmares. The images, the creatures that came to me in those dreams, were particularly grotesque. They were ... fleshy and viscous interpretations of genitalia, personifications that ... slithered and bored and enfolded and suffocated. Incredibly frightening to me. And, in the morning, in the daylight, I felt all the more stained and corrupt because these creations had come from inside my own head. I was quite sure that no one in the world but me could have imagined anything like them. And then one year, while I was in college, I went to an art exhibit, a variety of works of contemporary artists, a touring exhibit from Britain. There, along one wall ... I remember it was a gray wall against which they had hung the exhibit — were the creatures of my nightmares on the canvases of a woman named Sybylle Ruppert. I was stunned. Right there in the art museum, in front of Ruppert's *The Third Sex*, I fainted.'

Mary had opened her hands, her fingers spread wide as she pressed them and the wadded hem of her skirt against her lower stomach. With her legs fully exposed, Broussard now noticed that her legs were not straight on the chaise, but that she had turned her knees slightly inward, was pressing her thighs together defensively. This was a subtle, unconscious gesture, and enormously telling. Then as he watched her, she slowly began relaxing the tension in her legs until they were straight again, and she continued.

'Anyway, as time passed, I found it more and more difficult to get involved with the girls at school. I don't know, their ... lives seemed so ... unrelated, even trivial. They belonged to all sorts of extracurricular activities that I couldn't participate in because my father wanted me to come straight home after school. He always wanted me at home, so I grew more removed from my friends, more distant, more isolated. You know, I think he didn't want me to have any interests other than him. I mean, I was feeling smothered by him. He was kind ...'

She cut her eyes at Broussard. Luckily, he happened to be looking out the window.

'I've said that a lot, haven't I?'

'What's that?' he asked. Broussard never feared sounding as though he wasn't listening to his clients. It did not make them suspicious that he sometimes sounded distracted. They thought it was something to do with technique. Maybe they thought it was some kind of Socratic approach, some kind of Freudian technique for him to ask questions to which he should have known the answer if he had been listening.

'That he was kind to me.'

'Yes. Three or four times already.'

'Well, he was,' she said, turning her eyes to her busily fidgeting hands. 'It was only that he was preoccupied with me. I mean, I was a little girl. I wanted to be with other little girls. But he was all over me, physically, emotionally, every way.'

She paused.

'I started lying to him. Nothing particularly important, but I just quit telling him the truth. It didn't matter what it was, I just lied whenever I had the opportunity. Maybe he'd ask me something like: "What do you want to watch on television tonight?" and I'd name a program that he knew I didn't like. He'd give me strange looks at first, but I went ahead with it. I watched programs I hated. I'd lie to him about the kinds of clothes I liked when he took me shopping, and he'd end up buying clothes I didn't like. And I'd wear them. I lied to him about food that I liked or didn't like. I lied to him about where I'd laid the scissors or whether I'd closed the yard gate or wanted some more iced tea or whether I was too hot or too cold. I also started lying to my friends at school, even when I had to go out of my way to do it. Of course, I was found out a lot and that started alienating people, too.'

Mary put her right hand flat on her bare thigh, the other hand still holding the hem of her skirt, her wrist crooked daintily as though she were raising it coyly.

'I know why I did that. Lying. I've thought about it. It gave me a sense, a feeling of control over my own life. It was something that occurred only when I wanted it to, or didn't occur if I didn't want it to. It wasn't something I did for anyone else, only for myself. It was a realm in which I wasn't helpless. In fact, I was all-powerful. When I lied I became the master of little destinies. Things happened or didn't happen because I said so, and I could exercise this power in front of everyone, and no one could usurp it. By reacting to my lies, other people did things they wouldn't have done otherwise. It was a way to manipulate them, and I got to the point that I would rather lie than tell the truth. I would go out of my way to do it.

'But I went through a pretty bad period for a while, when I was twelve and thirteen. I grew introverted and isolated, daydreaming all the time. Daydreaming became a major preoccupation — another way, I guess, of exercising some kind of control over my own "world." It was the only thing to do, because the real world itself was getting pretty weird. Screwing your daddy will do that to you, turn your world into a hallucination.'

Broussard looked at her. Mary did not often use crude language. It was a sign of disdain, for herself and for what she had done. She delicately reached a long-nailed finger up under the edge of her raised hemline and scratched lightly along her groin. Broussard was suddenly desperate to see her naked hips.

'One night after I hadn't slept for several nights in a row to avoid the nightmares, I couldn't fight it any longer. I passed out, exhausted. I was too far under to wake up when I needed to go to the bathroom, and I wet the bed. Sometime during the night he came and crawled under the covers with me. He woke me, furious and disgusted, and stormed out of the room. Even half conscious, I realized what a discovery I'd made. The next night I wet the bed immediately, knowing I'd be safe sleeping in urine. It worked every night for almost two weeks. I was so starved for sleep that I got used to the smell and feel of it without any trouble at all. By the end of the first week, though, I'd developed a terrible, burning rash on my hips and thighs. Still, I didn't care. I thought I'd found the solution to all my torment — my own urine.

'And then one night he came to me crying, whimpering, wanting to know how I could do that to him, didn't I love him, didn't I want it to be nice for us? Why did I pee on the sheets? He made me get out of bed, and he gave me a damp washcloth he had brought. He made me wash myself while he watched and scolded me for "acting like an animal." That night he did it to me on the floor, with the side of my head bent up against my toy box. And he was deliberately rough. It was the sort of message I'd become good at reading. The next night he came into a dry bed.'

The asymmetrical pucker at the corner of Mary's mouth disappeared as she set her jaw, her expression as hard as Broussard imagined her heart. His eyes were fixed on the highest point of her naked thigh. He adjusted his position in his leather armchair, aware that his swollen member was an ignoble reaction, wishing that he could have remained objective.

It had been his failing as a psychoanalyst, his inability to stand aloof from the sensuality of the women who came to him. Of course, it was often their intention to seduce him. It was part of the process of transference, a roller-coaster ride in which the analyst was not supposed to let his heart leap into his throat at every breathtaking plunge. After all, he had been there many times before, and he was supposed to have his wits about him. But when it came to this kind of woman, he thought, never taking his eyes off her upper thigh where the sinew ran taut into the groin, he often found that clear thinking was as difficult to sustain as a dream in the sunlight.

43

No one rushed in to fill the silence this time, and the only thing that Palma could hear in her head was the sound of her own voice telling Sander Grant that the behavioral psychology model that the FBI's Behavioral Science Unit was using to analyze violent crimes was badly flawed. It would have been a gutsy and audacious charge under formal circumstances, but delivered as it had been pointedly and in considerable heat, Palma was suddenly afraid that it had had the sound of lunacy. Then this weak-kneed fear rising within her like a contrite and groveling Victorian throwback infuriated her, and she summoned up an inner resolve that sustained her through what otherwise would have been a withering silence, enervating enough to have extracted some kind of garbled, equivocal, follow-up from even the hardest detective. But she remained silent, staring at Grant to whom she had addressed her last words.

She didn't know how long they sat that way — it certainly couldn't have been as long as it felt — with Grant's heavy eyes lying on her like a great weight, a weight sure of its density, unperturbed by futile efforts to lift it off. Oddly, she felt that his broken nose gave his British rectitude a kind of humanity on the one hand, while on the other it reflected an integrity of knowledge that had been earned through experience, that means of learning most respected by the fraternity of her peers.

Even as she stared at him she believed, almost against her will, that by his silence Grant had no intention to humiliate her. He was thinking, and she had learned from walking through the crime scenes with him that he didn't care what kind of impression he was making when he was thinking.

With his eyes still fixed on her, he raised his left arm, jerked it a little to reveal his watch and cut his eyes to the dial, then back to her, lowering his arm.

'I just don't agree with you,' he said matter-of-factly. It was as if they had been the only two people in the room. He had been slouching as best he could in the metal typing chair, legs crossed, hands rammed in his pockets, and now he sat up and swung around to Frisch.

'I want to interview Dr. Broussard myself,' he said. 'If it's all right with you and Detective Palma, I'd like her to go along on that.' He turned and raised his eyebrows at her questioningly.

'Fine with me,' she said. That was smooth, very smooth, but she wasn't going to let him get away with that. 'But wait a minute. I don't want to be co-opted here.' She was zeroed in on Grant. 'I'd like a little more consideration to my proposal than that you just disagree with me.'

'Look,' Grant said, squaring around to her again, his tone very carefully walking the thin wire of condescension. 'If we were talking pure theory here, argument for the sake of argument, I'd say you've got as valid a perspective as the next person. But we're talking facts. Odds. And the facts are the odds are lousy to none that this killer is a woman. I don't know what to tell you. It's just not in the cards.'

'You don't think any of what I said has validity?'

'Of course it does, if you're talking theory, if you're going to ignore the historical facts in these kinds of cases.'

'The *known* historical facts,' Palma insisted.

'Okay, fine. The known facts,' Grant conceded. 'But like I said, when you go beyond the known facts then you're speculating, you're into theory.'

Palma looked at him.

'You're not living up to your opening speech,' she said coolly. She could almost feel Frisch's blood pressure accelerating, and hers, too. She was sticking her neck way out on this one, but her indignation gave her the backbone. She couldn't shake the feeling she was being humored by Grant that he would have given any one of the men a better hearing.

'You told us this morning that this methodology you use is as much art as science. You said you didn't care if the method was scientific or artistic or spiritual as long as it works. Well, I think my perspective is just as valid as "drawing pictures of butterflies." You were making a pitch to us not to reject your methodology out of hand, even laid a guilt trip on us, saying if we rejected this methodology we'd better be damn sure we could live with the consequences. To know if a method is going to work you've got to use it. Give it a shot. Fine. As far as I'm concerned, you need to practice what you preach,' she snapped.

Grant stared at her coolly over the crooked bridge of his nose.

'I'm not directing this investigation,' he said calmly.

That was the ultimate male weapon, the one irrational tool they all fell back on when nothing else was working out: equanimity. It was a gesture of superiority that infuriated her even more.

'I came down here to do what *you* requested me to do,' he said. 'I have an expertise you thought you needed. Are you changing your mind now?'

'Don't twist this around,' Palma was quick to come back. She wasn't going to be the first one to lower the rapier. 'Look, all I'm wanting you to do is to consider female suspects as well as male suspects. We seem to have a case in which the circumstances indicate that that's not an unreasonable request.'

Grant's expression was impenetrable. She didn't know if he was going to explode or burst out laughing. He wasn't the least bit intimidated by her aggressiveness nor

did he appear to be afraid of losing face in the confrontation with her. Normally she could tell when she was
putting a man on the spot, when she had gone so far that
he considered himself at risk of having his ego damaged.
But Grant was untouchable. Nothing she had said
changed his expression or his manner, and she was pretty
sure his remarkable self-possession was not an act. She
was confident she could spot an act. Grant was simply
more sure of himself than she had imagined.

Then he started nodding slowly. 'Okay,' he said.
'You've made a good point. I'd like to talk it out with you.
But until we can figure out how to use what you've come
up with, why don't we go ahead and play out what we've
got?'

He paused for her response. It could have been a
gesture of sarcasm, but Grant didn't play to it. He simply
waited. He seemed even genuinely polite. If it was a ploy,
Palma couldn't figure out to what purpose. He was right.
What did she expect them to do, shut everything down
and reorganize?

'Fine,' she said.

Grant turned to Frisch once again. 'Okay with you?'

Frisch nodded. 'Good.' He looked around the office at
the other detectives, who hadn't made a peep during the
entertainment Palma had provided. 'Anything else?'

With a gesture of finality, Grant ran his fingers along
the closed flap of his envelope.

'Okay,' Frisch said. 'Then let's divvy up the chores.'

As she wadded up the paper from her sandwich and
started stuffing it in her sack, Palma had to struggle to
keep from panting. Frisch's voice was way back in her
head, outlining the assignments. When she glanced again
at Grant he was looking at her, and something moved
around the crow's-feet at the corners of his eyes that
might have grown into a smile if he had let it.

She spent the early afternoon at the computer bringing
her supplements up to date and conferring with Leeland
to see if anything she had turned up in her interviews
might connect with any of the information that had come

in on the tip line. The frustration of having to take time off to do the paperwork was making her irritable, as though the investigation was in limbo until she could get back onto the streets.

But the investigation was far from being at a standstill. Though Childs and Garro had gone home for a few hours' sleep, Cushing and Boucher were already out on the first shift of the Reynolds stakeout. Haws and Marley had gone to Mello's residence to get pictures that Reynolds might have had access to and to take them to the dominatrix Mirel Farr to see if Mello had ever been through there, or if she knew anything about Mello's being involved in rough trade, or if by chance she knew whether or not Reynolds knew her. They would also have questions for her about the whereabouts of Clyde Barbish. Birley had drawn the missing Denise Reynolds Kaplan, going through her missing person file and interviewing women in Samenov's group who knew her.

It was three-twenty in the afternoon, and her stomach was growling when Grant finally appeared at the door of the task force room where Palma had been talking to Leeland. He was by himself, his tie undone, his coat draped over one arm as he rolled down his shirt sleeves.

'You at a stopping point?' he asked. 'I'd like to try to catch Broussard.'

'Sure,' she said. 'Let me get my things.'

Grant followed her to her office, where she took her SIG out of the filing cabinet, put it in her purse, and slung the purse over her shoulder.

'Look,' she said, 'I'm sorry, but I'm going to have to get something to eat. We can make a quick stop at any number of places.'

'No, that sounds good to me,' he said, pulling on his suit coat. He seemed a little sober. 'All I've had since breakfast is too much coffee, an RC, and a package of cheese crackers out of the vending machine in the cafeteria.'

'What about Hauser? Is he going to want something?'

Grant shook his head with a crooked grin. 'Hauser's

on his way back to Quantico. Something came up. This was kind of a freebie for him anyway, to give him a chance to get away from teaching cadets for while. He wasn't too happy about going back this soon.'

'You had any Mexican food since you've been here?'

'Nope.'

'Let's go,' she said.

Café Tropical's pink stucco exterior was washed out to a pastel rose in the gray afternoon mist as Palma and Grant made their way through the lush foliage of the courtyard with its palms and banana trees glistening in the mist. The cooking odors of fried rice and corn tostados met them before they even reached the front door, and by the time they were shown to their table near the windows that looked out into the rainy courtyard, Palma could almost taste the cold beer. She recommended a few dishes on the menu and suggested a couple of bottles of Pacifico, which the waiter brought immediately in two tall amber bottles with canary yellow labels.

'This is a regular spot for you?' Grant asked, swallowing his first mouthful of Pacifico.

'Actually, no.' Palma pulled back her hair, gathering it with both hands behind her head to get it out of her way. 'I tend to eat at places a little more "downstream," as Birley says. I grew up in one of the barrios on the east side. Not a lot of pink stucco and fancy tiled patios down there.' She smiled. 'But it's good to keep the fantasy going for out-of-towners.'

Grant's eyes returned her smile and he nodded, understanding. 'You still have family here?'

'My mother still lives in the barrio. And aunts and uncles and cousins, lots of cousins.'

'That's good,' Grant said.

'What about you?'

Grant shook his head, taking another sip from his Pacifico. 'My folks are dead, and I don't have any brothers or sisters. Marne ... has sisters in California. Two. Mostly, it's just me and the twins. And now, of course, the girls are beginning to have interests that tend

to turn their attention elsewhere. I see it coming —
marrying, moving away — and I know it's the natural
course of things. But I don't like it much.'

This time his smile was not so successful, and he
covered it with a shrug, then looked out the window to
the courtyard, glancing around at the shiny wet banana
trees and the white blossoms of the Mexican orange
flowers that were still blooming along the borders of the
walks.

Palma again wanted to ask him about the Chinese
woman. She looked at him and studied his profile in the
gray spring light, tried to imagine him involved in the
kind of mysterious affair with this exotic woman of whom
Garrett had spoken. Grant didn't seem to her like the
kind of man who would have had that affair. Whatever
had happened, she didn't think it had gone well for him.
He did not have the look of a man at peace with himself,
and Palma guessed that an affair that was as tumultuous
as his was reputed to have been would have left him a
little shaken. Just why he was shaken was the story
Palma wanted to hear.

The waiter brought their orders with two new frosty
bottles of Pacifico. As they began eating, it started raining
again and the courtyard was suddenly obscured in a
heavy downpour, the sound of it drumming loudly on the
broad, sagging banana leaves. Grant watched it a few
minutes while he ate. Suddenly he looked at Palma.

'Listen,' he said. 'Let's talk about your theory.'

Palma looked at him. 'What do you want to know?'
She was surprised he had managed to wait this long
before bringing it up.

'When did this idea first come to you?'

Palma was suddenly skeptical. The question was not
what she had expected; it was elementary at worst,
circumlocutious at best. What was he trying to do, put her
at ease? Was this the investigative equivalent of 'Tell me
about yourself'?

'You were expecting something more piercing?' he
asked. He must have read it all over her face.

'No,' she lied.

Grant studied her for a moment, and she didn't have the presence of mind to get on with the answer. She picked up her bottle of beer and drank the last of it.

'You think I have an "attitude" about women?' he asked.

She put down the beer bottle and shoved it aside so she didn't have to look over it or around it to see him.

'I know I was a little pushy back there,' she said. 'But I honestly feel like you've got blinders on regarding this. I hope it didn't come across as a "woman's issue" argument.' She paused. 'It was — is — an honest disagreement.'

'Fine,' he said. 'I accept that. The only thing is, I don't think you believe that I accept it. My question just now was an honest one as well. I just wanted to know when it was you came up with the idea that the killer could possibly be a woman?'

Touché, she thought. But she wasn't going to give him the satisfaction of seeing her backpedal. Rather than say anything at all, she went right into it.

'I'd like to say it hit me in a flash of inspiration,' she said, peeling a corner of the Pacifico label off the bottle and rolling it into a little pellet, watching her fingers. 'But it didn't. It was simply an accumulation of facts and feelings that didn't seem to add up to anything else.' She looked up. 'To me, anyway.' She tossed the pellet against the saltshaker. 'There was the discovery of child abuse among the women in the S&M group. There were those ... wrenching letters we found in Louise Ackley's house. Genuine chronicles of horror. Mancera's pitiful story about Vickie Kittrie's life. Terry's stories about Louise Ackley's hunger for humiliation at the hands of Gil Reynolds. Bessa's disavowal of violence and manhating, her invective against child abuse, and her "advisement" that women could be just as violent as men.'

She looked out the window and was surprised to see the rain had stopped, and across the street, above the trees of a small park, the clouds were separating. The low afternoon sun was coming through in rays of brilliant orange light as if they had been doused with gasoline and set on fire, igniting the rain on the dripping trees.'

'And to tell you the truth,' she said, turning back to Grant, 'there was something my mother said a few days ago. She told me an extraordinary story about two women I'd known all my life, only I didn't really know them, which shouldn't have been any surprise to me, but it was. Anyway, after we had talked about them and we had been sitting quietly for a few minutes, she made the observation that "women are human first, and women second."'

She looked at Grant, half expecting to see the light of revelation in his eyes, but he simply sat there with the same sober dispassion that she now had come to associate with him, and which she was increasingly convinced had as little to do with the real Sander Grant as the booming voice had to do with the real Wizard of Oz. But the light of revelation did not flicker, and Grant continued to wait.

'How about some coffee?' she said to cover up her disappointment.

The waiter brought their coffee and set it down with a small pitcher of cream and then cleared away their plates. Grant offered the cream to Palma, and when she was through he added some to his own cup. He stirred his coffee casually, looking into his cup, and Palma watched as the side of his face began to burn with a soft gold light that grew brighter and harder until exactly half his face, the median line following the crooked course of his broken nose, was frozen in molten gold like the mask of Agamemnon. Outside the wet tiles of the courtyard were glazed in polished bronze.

'I think it has something to do with revenge,' she said. 'It has to do with an abused child and a lifetime of choking on a passionate, deepening hatred.' She sipped her coffee. When she set down her cup she had to pull back the hair at her temples, running her fingers through the tangles created by the humidity.

'One of the women in Samenov's group?' Grant asked.
'I imagine.'

'You don't have a specific suspect.'

'Well, obviously Kittrie. God knows she has reasons.
Saulnier. But I think Kittrie's "faction" must be full of
women harboring resentments against men.'

'Against men,' he said, pausing. 'Then I suppose you
have an explanation as to why we have women victims?'

She nodded. 'The answer to that, I think, lies in something you said.'

Grant registered a mild surprise. She smiled, but not
too much. 'You said, "The killer is killing the woman he
creates, not the woman he is killing." I think you have the
right idea, but the wrong gender. I'm guessing it has
something to do with the role-playing inherent in the
S&M scenarios. Saulnier has said that a woman who
wants a woman wants a woman. Maybe our killer, a
member of Kittrie's group — all victims of child abuse
and proponents of S&M — has a favorite scenario that
involves a fantasy in which her partner is a "man," the
man who taught her about sex when she was only a child.
This early abuse — her "sex education" which has caused
her lifelong emotional pain — is re-enacted in this S&M
scenario in which the victim plays a man. The abusive
man of the killer's childhood. The scenario is played out,
as you said before, up to the point where it begins to
diverge from the original plan. Then it goes wrong, for
the victim. Afterward, "he" is cleaned up and remade into
a woman. An effort, perhaps, to undo what had gone
wrong.

'What she does,' Palma said, 'is she nourishes her. She
takes care of her. Cleans her, gets rid of any blood.
Washes her with bath oils. Combs her hair, maybe the
way she remembered, the way she liked. She sprays it.
Applies makeup, very carefully, very expertly, not
wanting to get it wrong. She lays her out. At first I
thought it was a funereal posture, but I'm not sure
anymore. I have a feeling it's not that at all. The pillow,
her hair on the pillow. The perfume.' Palma shook her

head. 'And then she lies down beside her. She talks to her, maybe touches her near her wounds, apologizes, explains herself to her. Goes over her grievances, tries to get her to understand why she had to do what she did. She really wants her to understand. She cries. If only she had ... or hadn't ... If only she would ... or wouldn't ...'

Palma stopped, looked at Grant. 'I don't know. Something like that,' she said. 'It seems to me it would go along those lines.'

'But made up to resemble the same woman every time?' Grant asked. 'Why the same woman? That's got to be significant.'

'I'm sure it is,' Palma said. 'But I haven't come up with any answer. Maybe she's the ideal woman. The killer's mother.' She shrugged.

Grant stared slowly shaking his head. 'I don't know. When something comes up that doesn't fall within the loop of our behavior models, we usually don't jump to the conclusion that we've discovered another species. Rather, we tend to think we've been reading something wrong, not looking at it the way we should.'

Palma nodded, but didn't say anything. She sipped her coffee, glanced out to the courtyard. The sky was clearing enough now that the day was lightening even though the sun was low in the sky. The tiles in the courtyard were beginning to steam. Grant had put his finger on the curved handle of his spoon and was rocking it lightly, preoccupied, not looking at her but at the spoon and the tiny messy pattern it was making in a droplet of coffee. By this time she realized that she had grown fond of his eyes, even the beginnings of the crow's-feet at the corners.

'What about Reynolds?' Grant asked, looking up. 'How do you look at him now? Have you changed your mind?'

Palma nodded. 'You know what did it for me? When I first noticed those wrinkles on Bernadine Mello's scarlet silk sheet, I instantly knew they were significant, momentously significant. When I finally got back to the office and had the opportunity to look at the crime scene photographs from the Doubletree Hotel and Samenov's condo, I knew we'd been missing something that was important to the killer. Important because it was such a miniscule detail, but one that the killer remained consistent in observing. Then, as time went by and I began to realize what the wrinkles meant ... that the killer was, by lying down with his victim, engaging in an act that was essentially one of compassion, of nurturing. That was the moment when I began to have my doubts about Reynolds.'

'Why?'

'Because I don't believe the man is capable of compassion, even in a sick and twisted way. He's all hate. I have no doubt that Haws and Marley will eventually connect him to Louise Ackley and Lalo Montalvo's death. But is he killing these women? I don't believe so. There's a subtle complexity here that I don't believe Reynolds is capable of devising.'

'Because he isn't that complex?' Grant asked.

'No, because he isn't that subtle.' Palma stopped, her eyes drifting away from Grant to the courtyard as she thought back. 'This morning, at Mancera's; when Terry was telling me about Reynolds's delight in humiliating Louise Ackley, she made the point that Louise had told her that Reynolds *always* left her "in the middle of it." She said he always left her "stranded," left her tied, covered in blood or feces or whatever it was they were doing. This heightened her humiliation, that he would consider her such a nothing that he could walk away from her like that, naked and bound and stinking.'

The entire courtyard was steaming in the heat of the falling afternoon sun which cast its turning light through the hazy humidity and bathed the low palms and banana trees and white hibiscus in a muted copper light that, for some reason, struck Palma as painfully sad. She looked back at Grant, who had not taken his eyes off her.

'Does that sound like the person who washes his victims?' Palma asked. 'Who combs their hair, perfumes them, washes them in bath oils, and then lies down beside them for what must be a strange scene of quiet whispers between the living and the dead? Reynolds hasn't got the touch of delicacy. He isn't capable of the sensitivity required in those last moments with the body.'

Grant was looking at her, still as a basilisk.

Then he said, 'Christ, you've really put yourself into this, haven't you?'

'Yes,' she said. 'I have.'

For the first time since she had met him, she thought she saw a twitch of hesitation in his expression, but she didn't understand what the hesitation connoted. When he responded, he did so obliquely, but it was clear enough she had gotten through to him.

'But I've got to satisfy myself about Reynolds. We've got to go ahead and get the search warrant.'

'I've already filled out the paperwork,' Palma said. 'Frisch is having it taken to Judge Arens now. We'll have it when we get back.'

He looked at her. 'Good,' he said.

'You didn't call and make an appointment with Broussard, did you?' she asked.

Grant shook his head.

'Good,' she said.

44

A smooth, undulating reef of slate gray clouds hung in the western sky just above the tree line as Palma and Grant followed the traffic outbound on the still wet and steaming pavement of Woodway. The rain was moving west, out of the city, and the falling sun was racing the gloomy weather toward the horizon. By the time the clouds were far enough away to clear the sky, the sun was already dropping into the pines and the long shadows came out to meet them on the glistening street. The rain had cleaned the city, which now appeared more three-dimensional than usual, as though viewed through a stereoscope.

Palma and Grant turned into the cinder drive of Dr. Dominick Broussard's estate and immediately veered to the right on a narrow lane that brought them to the small office bungalow isolated by woods from Broussard's home. The cinder drive made a circle in front of the office, where a small black Mercedes 560SL was parked at the door. Palma pulled up behind the car and cut the engine.

'That's about seventy thou worth of paint and metal,' Grant said. 'Is that his?'

'Not according to the records,' Palma said.

'He sees clients on weekends?'

'Not according to his appointment secretary.'

Grant looked at her. 'I talked to her yesterday,' Palma explained. 'In case I ever needed a psychiatrist. This

woman seems to be something of a girl Friday, takes care
of everything for him. I just chatted with her, got a
general layout of the way Broussard works. She wouldn't
discuss fees with me, though. Said I would have to make
an appointment with the doctor. I said that even though
Dr. Broussard had been recommended to me, I was a little
uncomfortable going into "all of this" with a man. Did
Broussard see many women? She said that actually all but
two of his clients were women.'

Grant nodded, still looking at her.

'How did you know he'd be here rather than at his
home over there?' he asked, taking a pen from his pocket
and jotting down the license number on the Mercedes.

'I didn't. I just wanted to see where he met his clients.'

Grant turned and looked through the car window at
the front of the office again. Like Broussard's home, it
was bricked with a vaguely Georgian architectural style.
Ivy was thick on the walls, and the stone walk that led to
the front door was littered with leaves knocked off the
trees by the two days of rain. Water was dripping here
and there off the eaves of the slate roof. 'Well, let's see if
he's busy.'

They got out of the car and Palma slipped her radio
into her shoulder bag and locked the car. There was no
doorbell beside the brass plaque mounted on the brick
among the ivy and engraved with Broussard's name, so
Grant pressed down the ornate bronze latch on the door
and pushed it open. There were no lights on in the waiting
room except for a black light in a large glass case of
orchids covering most of the far wall, its cold, eerie glow
supplemented by the dying gray light of the afternoon
filtering in through the two large casement windows
overlooking the circle drive. Grant looked into the door
that led to Broussard's secretary's office, which was
arranged more like the office of a concierge than a receptionist. Obviously, Broussard wanted his clients to feel as
if they were coming to see him in a domestic setting,
rather than a clinical one.

Grant looked at Palma, made a shrugging expression

with his face, and stepped into the office doorway while Palma went to the doorway that led out into a corridor. She looked to her right and saw a door slightly ajar and revealing a well-appointed powder room. Then she looked to her left and saw a closed door with a dim light coming from under it, and beyond that a French door looking out to an alcove where a large Labrador was sleeping in the blue light.

Just then the door eased open slowly, and Palma quickly hissed at Grant, knocked loudly on the door frame in the hallway, and stepped back, pulling out her shield.

'Hello, anybody here? Hello.' She glanced again at Grant and stepped back into the doorway and looked to her left again. 'Hello?' She caught the silhouette of a barrel-chested man against the blue light of the French door, a handgun raised shoulder high. She fell back. 'Shit. Police!' she shouted. 'Drop the gun! Police!' She stuck her shield out into the corridor, and Grant was instantly beside her with his gun out, frowning at her, trying to read what was happening.

'Police!' he added his voice, and glanced around at the front door.

'How ... How do I know you're the police?' Broussard's voice was unsure.

'Look at the shield!' Palma shouted, and shook her hand dangling the badge. A corridor light came on. 'Sergeant Carmen Palma, Houston Police Department!'

'Yeah,' Broussard shouted. 'Okay. I see it.'

'Put down the gun,' Palma repeated. 'Make sure the safety's on.'

'Okay, fine,' Broussard said. 'Here, now, it's on the floor.'

Grant stepped out into the corridor, now holding his FBI shield in front of him, followed by Palma. Broussard was standing beside the opened door to his office looking uncomfortable, the handgun on the floor in front of him.

'Jesus Christ,' he said as they approached him in the hall. 'What the hell are you doing?'

'We just came by to talk to you,' Palma said. 'The door was unlocked. This is an office, isn't it?'

'Of course. But hell, people make appointments.'

'You always come at unexpected callers with a gun?' Grant asked.

'I've got a security light in my office,' Broussard blustered. 'Comes on when the front door opens. Nobody was scheduled. When the light came on, and I didn't hear anybody, nobody said anything, I thought I was being burgled. I'm not normally here on Saturdays. I thought maybe I was being robbed.'

'Sorry, thought I was loud enough.' Palma said, not putting too fine a point on it.

Broussard looked at her skeptically and then at Grant.

'I'm Special Agent Sander Grant, FBI,' he said. 'If you've got time, we'd like to talk with you.' He was removing the clip from Broussard's automatic. 'You have a license for this?'

'Of course. Damn. Don't you people believe in calling first?' He was still shaken and was trying to control his temper.

'We've been pretty busy,' Palma said. 'We just didn't get around to it.'

'Jesus,' Broussard said.

Grant handed Broussard his gun, but kept the clip. 'Do you have a client in your office?' he asked.

Broussard's face changed, as if he had just remembered her. He stepped back and pulled the door closed softly. 'As a matter of fact, I do.' He looked at Palma, then back at Grant. 'What do you want to talk to me about?'

'Bernadine Mello,' Grant said.

'Oh, my God. Christ.' Broussard was suddenly disturbed all over again, looking at Palma. 'God. Poor ... Listen.' He turned to Grant. 'Can you give me three or four minutes in here? Can you wait in the front room?'

They turned on the light in the waiting room, and it was seven minutes before they heard the back door open and close and saw a woman bundled in a raincoat walking briskly around the side of the bungalow to the

Mercedes. Palma stepped to the windows but could not get a look at her face in the dying light as she unlocked the car door, slipped inside, and in a moment was pulling away on the cinder drive. At that instant Dr. Dominick Broussard appeared in the doorway.

They sat in his office, which smelled faintly of a woman's perfume, Broussard behind his desk, Grant and Palma in leather armchairs facing him. Broussard, calmer and sobered, acknowledged that he had heard of Bernadine Mello's death on the noon news the day before and had read of it in the morning's paper. He controlled his demeanor and facial expressions, but he couldn't as easily command his voice, which grew thick and unpredictable in spite of his repeated clearing it. He told them that Bernadine had been his client for over five years, that he was consulting with her about chronic depression and a number of other things, including alcohol abuse.

'Do you have a specialty practice?' Palma asked.

'Not really,' Broussard said, clearing his throat once more. 'I mean, I don't accept clients with only certain kinds of dysfunctions, but as things have turned out over the years, I've developed a clientele that consists primarily of women.'

'What is your approach with your clients?' Palma asked. 'Aren't there a number of different types of psychotherapies?'

Broussard thought a moment before responding, which seemed an odd thing to Palma.

'I'm a psychodynamic psychotherapist, really,' he said helpfully, 'rather than an interpersonal therapist or a humanistic therapist or a cognitive therapist or a behavioral therapist or a counselor ... whatever. My therapeutic approach to psychological dysfunction is based on psychoanalytic psychology, not one of the newer ... and more popular kinds of therapies available.' He looked at Palma. 'Do you know anything about psychotherapy?'

'Practically nothing,' she said.

Broussard nodded, studying her. 'My approach attributes neurotic, emotional, and interpersonal dysfunctions to unconscious internal conflicts ... usually created in childhood. Originally, the Freudian psychoanalyst sought to reconstruct his client's personality by eliminating these internal conflicts. This was done by helping the patient to delve into her unconscious to retrieve memories and feelings, and thereby gaining "insight" into her problems.'

Broussard spoke very carefully and deliberately but with no studied thought as to what he was saying. It was clear he had done this 'introduction' to his specialty before, probably to clients or prospective clients.

'The effectiveness of this approach relied a great deal on a phenomenon called "transference." As the patient becomes more comfortable with the analyst over a long period of time, the patient will begin to see the analyst in a certain light, projecting attributes onto the analyst that are actually attributes from a person in the patient's past. These attributes will trigger inappropriate reactions from the patient and by subtle questioning the analyst leads the patient to an emotional re-education in which the patient learns more realistic perceptions and ways of behaving.'

Broussard seemed to decide to cut his spiel short.

'Anyway,' he shrugged, 'it's an arduous process. Very time-consuming ... and expensive. But strict psychoanalysis is no longer the vogue, unfortunately. Few people want to invest that kind of time anymore. Recent trends are toward more short-term psychodynamic therapies focusing on a single problem rather than on an exploration of the overall personality. No probing of the unconscious, no striving for insight. Transference is still important, however, but the analyst is more confrontational. The old way adapted to new times.'

'But don't you still have patients who prefer the longer-term approach?' Palma asked.

Broussard smiled slowly. 'Yes, I do. A number of them. Bernadine Mello was one. And there are others.'

'If you read the articles in the paper about Mrs. Mello's death,' Palma said, 'then you know that the police believe she was killed by a person who has killed several other women as well.'

Broussard's countenance sobered, his already swarthy complexion darkening as the sardonic smile soured to what Palma read as a faint look of distaste, rather than commiseration.

'I'll get to the point,' Palma said. 'We believe you can be helpful to us in gaining some insight ourselves, into the mind of this killer.'

Broussard's expression was instantly brittle in the way a person's face becomes brittle when he is caught off guard and believes he is concealing his surprise by holding his expression constant. Few people can actually accomplish this feat, and despite his extensive experience at interviewing, Broussard was not one of them. Though the change was infinitesimal and would have been diffi cult to describe, it was unmistakable.

Palma reached into her purse and pulled out a small notebook which she flipped open and studied a moment.

'Bernadine Mello has been your client since 1983?' She looked up from her notes.

Broussard nodded, his eyes perhaps a little wider than normal. 'About that,' he managed to say. 'I suppose her records are correct. I'd have to check mine.' He let them know that he had guessed how they had gotten their information.

'And Sandra Moser was your client from May to September in 1985?'

Broussard responded more slowly. 'I'd have to check my notes. And for Samenov too.'

Palma felt her face flush, and her stomach went hollow. Jesus Christ. And Samenov too? She managed not to look at Grant, but she could sense, or did she only imagine she sensed, how his mind had locked onto that stunning bit of information so unexpectedly volunteered.

She looked at her notebook. 'I don't have the dates on her,' she said. 'Would it be difficult for you to get them for me?'

Broussard shook his head and turned his chair to an antique Jacobean table sitting in front of the windows overlooking the sloping lawn that was now disappearing into the early darkness of evening. He flipped on a computer terminal and sat before its amber glow, tapping at the keyboard, waiting, tapping, the screen disappearing, reappearing, more tapping until he sat still a moment, and then said, 'I first consulted with Dorothy Ann Samenov on February 14, 1984, and I last consulted with her on December 12, 1984.' He left the screen on and turned back to them.

Palma studied her notebook for a while, letting Broussard watch her. Then she asked, 'When did you first realize that all three victims had been your clients?'

'This morning.'

'Didn't you recognize Sandra Moser's name in the news when she was killed?'

'Of course I did, but that was just one murder. I thought it was extraordinary that one of my clients had been killed. It's never happened to me before. I've had suicides, but not homicides. So I marveled at it, followed the case, but that was all. It was one of those things that happen to people you know. I never knew about Dorothy Samenov until I saw the article in this morning's paper. All three women's names were mentioned. That's when I knew.'

Palma knew that Grant was aware that Samenov's murder had been kept out of the media except for a small mention in the police blotter one morning.

'I'm sure you've already anticipated me,' Palma said. Broussard started nodding, and she went ahead. 'It would help us to know what you thought about these three women. In your opinion, did they have any propensity that would have made them particularly susceptible to this kind of victimization? Do you see a red thread here?'

Broussard leaned his forearms on his desk and interlocked the fingers of his two hands and studied his thumbnails. His arms rested in a clean space in the center of the desk, an area large enough for a leather desk set, a spiral-bound appointment calendar, a telephone, a lamp, an ornate silver Victorian inkwell and pen tray which held four or five well-used ink pens. But on either side of

Broussard, the desk was cluttered with dozens of variously sized figurines, some seemingly antique artifacts of clay, or bronze, or marble, or pitted iron, some of a variety of stones in deep colors of burgundy or black or cobalt or jade. All the figures were of women.

Broussard looked up, preparing to respond, and saw Palma looking at his collection. He tilted his head.

'Recognize any of them?'

'Saint Catherine,' she said.

'Oh, you were educated in a parochial school as a child?'

'Yes, I was.'

'Yes, well, the good and unfortunate Catherine. All of them women out of the mythos of many cultures and spanning many ages, ancient and modern.'

Broussard looked at Grant and then back at Palma. He reached out and touched the marble figure. 'This is multi-breasted Artemis of Ephesus, Queen of Heaven, the Great Goddess, worshiped by Asia and all the world.' He touched the one Palma had recognized. 'Your stoic Saint Catherine, gazing placidly into eternity through the spokes of a wheel of fiery veined stone.' His finger moved. 'A bronze Leda curling her hips to embrace with her heavy thighs the massive feathered body of the swan-Zeus, conceiving in the shudder of her passion yet another woman whose legendary beauty would launch a thousand ships. Here, a pale marble Psyche embracing bisexual Eros; that black one, thin-waisted and heavy-busted Parvati bride of Shiva, Daughter of Heaven, she of the incomparably graceful hips; and squatting beside her there is a steatite Tlazolteotl, Mother Goddess of the Aztecs, whose grimacing face portrays the pain of child-birth and whose parted knees and gaping vagina reveal the emerging head and arms of an offspring race.'

He stopped, bringing his arm back to rest with the other one on the desk in front of him. The collection was a mélange of color and texture and material and form, female archetypes of the graceful and the vulgar, of the proud and the humble, of the beatific and the Satanic.

'I get positively poetic about them,' he said with a
smirk. 'I've been collecting them since I was in college. A
lifetime of women.

'Two things,' he said abruptly, his dusky forehead
wrinkling as he looked up at her. 'I realize that I'm a
common denominator here, and by virtue of my association with these women I'm in something of a compromised position. I'll check my calendar, but I may not be
able to give you alibis for all the nights ... if any. Also ...
I rather suspect that by now Bernadine's husband must
have made you aware that my relationship with her ...
exceeds that of doctor-client. I know that puts my career
in jeopardy should you wish to pursue it as a breach of
professional ethics.'

Broussard sat back in his chair and looked at each of
them in turn with eyes unafraid of meeting theirs. He
shook his head.

'But it wasn't.' Thinking, he shifted his eyes to the
icons. 'I won't say I loved her. It was too complicated. I
don't know that I could call it that, but it was ...
enduring. Over five years, through three husbands. I
collected a fee, yes. For a time I didn't, a year and a half.
But I continued seeing her three times a week, and she
continued analysis. Then one day she started paying me
again because she said I was earning it, regardless of our
relationship.' He smiled sadly and looked up at Palma.
'And she was right; I was. Anyway, Bernadine had a
cavalier attitude toward both sex and money, which was
well enough, I suppose. She had a huge reserve of both.'

Broussard stopped for their reaction.

'We're interested in the homicides,' Grant said,
implying that right now they weren't concerned with the
fine lines of Broussard's professional ethics. Broussard
slowly nodded, perhaps evaluating Grant's response
insofar as it affected his role and what he might say.

'I can give you some other common denominators
besides myself,' he said. 'But I'd urge you to keep in mind
that while women who seek psychiatric counsel may
present broad symptomatic similarities, their histories can

be dramatically varied. And there's no accounting for the quirks of individuality. One, above all, should be cautious about extrapolating from generalities.'

45

'All three women had an assortment of anxiety-based disorders — panic attacks, phobias, obsessive-compulsive disorders,' Broussard said, jerking his chin a little to make his neck more comfortable in the starched white collar of his shirt. Even on a Saturday consultation he had worn a tie, albeit a casual one of russet linen that caught the same highlights in his linen trousers. 'They suffered from mood disorders — sadness, discouragement, pessimism, hopelessness. They were victims of childhood sexual abuse. They were bisexual.' He paused. 'I, uh, on this latter point . . . didn't know about Bernadine's bisexuality until quite recently. And it was latent. She was seduced on one occasion by a college roommate. According to her, and I have no reason to disbelieve her, it didn't happen again until recently, when she met a woman in a service station. The woman approached her without introducing herself, later contacted her. They met and an affair began. A rather serious affair, I think.'

'How recently?' Palma asked.

'Maybe three or four weeks ago.'

'Can you be more specific?'

'I can go back to my notes if you want.'

'We might have you do that later,' Palma said. 'How about the other two women?'

'Samenov, bisexual since her university years. Moser's first experience was after college, as a young career woman, and continued through sporadic affairs on into her marriage.'

'Was there anything unusual about their sexuality, other than their being bisexual?'

'Bernadine's ... enthusiasm ... was noteworthy. I don't think she was, in the clinical sense, nymphomaniacal, but she was addicted to sex. She thought it was the only way people showed love for each other. Non-erotic love was not a concept she understood.

'Dorothy Samenov was probably the most sexually confused of the three women. She almost had developed a multiple personality. Mature, aggressive, self-directed, and self-disciplined in her public-professional life. In her personal life — her sex life, for this discussion — she was weak, regressive, immature, prone to being manipulated. She was totally inept, could not make a mature decision. In her relationships with other people, she was a professional victim ... of both sexes.'

'What was her reason for consulting you?' Palma asked.

'She was having night terrors, losing a tremendous amount of sleep because of it. Ultimately, it tied in to her repressed anxiety about her childhood sexual abuse, her inability to cope with it. We worked through it. I see a significant amount of that in women her age. Childhood sexual abuse is far more widespread than society wants to admit,' Broussard said, addressing Palma. 'You'd be amazed at the percentage of women who live with it buried so deep in their unconscious that it distorts their lives.'

'And Sandra Moser?'

'Very much the same sort of thing, only she was married, living two lives. The stress got to be too much, manifested itself in anxiety based disorders that were putting stress on her marriage. She came to me.'

Palma made a few notes, though she wasn't likely to forget any of what Broussard was telling her. She would have liked to have been inside Grant's mind. He was sitting with one leg crossed over the other, also taking notes, but Palma guessed the note-taking was more an effort to put himself in the role of a benign partner rather than a silent observer, which might have worked on Broussard's nerves. Evidently, Grant had determined that a nonthreatening introduction was the best course initially.

'Did any of the women ever mention to you that they'd been involved in S&M?'

Broussard's reaction was a frown and a subdued, 'No.'

'Would it surprise you if they had been?'

'If they all were, yes. I don't believe Bernadine would have been. Samenov, not so much a surprise. She could have been masochistic easily enough. Moser — no, I suppose not. I can see that both of them could have gone that way. Remember, I saw them in 1984 and 1985. A lot could have happened to them from then to now. Instability is a great catalyst.'

'You don't feel you helped them that much?' Palma asked. 'You believe they were still unstable?'

Broussard almost smiled, as if he knew that Palma thought she had caught him out, and he was going to enlighten her as to her misunderstanding.

'Instability is a relative term,' he said, tilting his head thoughtfully to one side, then straightening it as he spoke. 'As I mentioned before, not many people are willing today to go to the effort of truly exploring their personalities. This is the generation of the quick fix. Dorothy Samenov wanted to be rid of the demons in her dreams. When the night terrors stopped, she broke off the therapy — "cured." Sandra Moser wanted to be rid of her depression, her arousal disorder, that is, her frigidity with her husband. When these symptoms abated, she terminated her therapy — "cured." Both of them still had tremendous problems to wrestle with, but the particular symptoms that had manifested themselves as a result of those problems disappeared, so they thought their problems had disappeared too. They were just squeezing the balloon.'

'Pardon?'

'You compress a bulge in one place, and it simply pops up somewhere else. Whatever "bulges" — or symptoms — emerged after they stopped seeing me were probably more "normal" symptoms. Excessive alcohol consumption, reliance on antidepressant drugs, overeating, promiscuity, peptic ulcers. These forms of "instability" are so prevalent in our society that we tend to accept them as "normal." No need to try to "cure" these, certainly no need to see a psychiatrist.'

Broussard shrugged and flicked his eyebrows.

'How many clients do you see, Dr. Broussard?' Grant's question was asked in a calm, quiet voice as he looked up from his note-taking.

Broussard regarded him for a moment. 'I'd rather not say, if it's not absolutely necessary.'

'Why is that?'

'I just don't believe it's germaine . . . if I understand the purpose of your question.'

Grant nodded. 'Then can you tell us approximately what percentage of your clients have problems similar to the ones we've been discussing for these three victims?'

'Most of them. About eighty percent, I'd say.'

'Anxiety-based disorders, mood disorders, sexual dysfunctions . . . all that?' Grant asked.

'Yes And alcohol and/or drug abuse of varying degrees.'

Grant nodded again, but this time he kept his eyes on Broussard, not looking down to his notepad.

'Well, can you tell me what percentage are victims of childhood sexual abuse?'

Broussard hesitated, perhaps unsure as to how this might infringe on doctor-client privilege. 'Again, most of them.' He thought a moment. 'Actually, among the women, I can't immediately think of one who hasn't been sexually abused as a child.'

Palma didn't interject, letting Grant finish his line of questioning.

'Do you think most psychiatrists have this high a percentage of clients who have been abused as children?'

'If they're seeing as many women as I am, I think it is probable. As I said, I think the public would be shocked to know just how many female children have been through something like this. The experience has varying degrees of long-term effect, but it is always detrimental. Some women get help, some don't.'

'Do you think this factor — childhood sexual abuse — could be the red thread in all these cases?' Grant asked.

Broussard seemed surprised to be asked the question. Again he thought a moment before answering. 'I suppose it could be. You mean, more important than some of the other common denominators?'

'Yes. The most important.'

Broussard slightly rolled his eyes with a half shrug. 'Why do you ask me?'

'You're a psychiatrist, a student of the human mind, of human nature, I thought you might have some insight into the way this man might be thinking.'

Broussard still seemed puzzled by Grant's approach. 'But I don't know anything about ... the case, the actual killings. Surely you have some behavioral evidence that tells you something.'

'We do, yes,' Grant said.

'Well, then, if I knew some details ... I can't just speculate, pull ideas out of thin air.'

'Sure, I understand,' Grant said, 'but unfortunately we can't reveal any of that information at this point. I was just hoping you might ... play with it a little. How might child abuse, sexual child abuse, play a role in such a situation? I don't know ... might the killer have been a victim of child abuse, and is this some kind of delayed revenge? But if men are the perpetrators in the vast majority of child-abuse cases, why is he killing women? Might he be a child abuser himself? If so, why isn't he killing children? Why adult women?'

'You seem already to be making the assumption that child abuse *is* the red thread in these cases,' Broussard said. He nodded, looking at Grant and then at Palma. 'So. First of all, I couldn't agree with your first assumption,

that the "vast majority" of child abusers are men.' He
shook his head. 'You know, in 1896 Freud first committed
himself to his now famous, or perhaps infamous, "seduction theory." In a paper he wrote in that year, he said that
in analysis he had uncovered many instances of childhood sexual abuse in his female clients and that the "villains" in these "grave" and "loathsome" acts were "above all
nursemaids, governesses, and other servants" as well as
teachers and brothers.' He paused for emphasis. 'Not
father. Not even, mostly, men.

'Later, of course, Freud rejected the seduction theory
as the etiology of *all* neuroses. He continued to insist that
some neuroses still grew out of this very common experience, but curiously, in later discussions the 'father'
became the principal villain in Freud's references. It's not
clear how this transition of perpetrators came about, but
never again after that initial observation by Freud himself
were women generally included among the "villains."'

Broussard smiled. 'That is, until recently. The women's
movement has enabled more people to observe life from
radically different perspectives. Some psychologists,
psychiatrists, social workers, counselors have begun to
look at the real facts in these cases and are beginning to
see beyond the often unconscious male perspective that is
almost automatic among many professionals, even
women.

'Example. A fourteen-year-old girl is seduced by a
man. Child abuse. A fourteen-year-old boy is seduced by
a woman. Lucky boy! He's the envy of everyone. Why,
this is the very symbol of the male rite of passage. It's
been romanticized in novels and the cinema many times
over. Do you see the difference? Can you explain to me
why one is a crime, and the other is a marvelous experience that the boy can take with him into adulthood as a
fond memory? It's the old double standard at work again.
Also, our male-oriented society refuses to believe that
such a woman could have a malicious intent in such a
seduction. Women are nurturers, are they not?' He
smiled. 'Caretakers, not tormentors. If they were to do

something like that, surely it would be in a tender
manner. It would be a gift of her own sexuality that she
had *given* to the boy, not something she had *taken* for her
own selfish pleasure. Do we believe that a man can do the
same? His greedy loins know nothing but lust.'

He looked back and forth between Palma and Grant.

'Do you both see it the same way?' Pause. 'Differently,
perhaps?'

He waited long enough for his point to soak in,
grinning at them as though each of them had been caught
out in just the kind of double standard he was describing.

'Anyway,' he said curtly, and then continued more
thoughtfully, 'there are indications that professionals are
beginning to see through our old prejudices. One recent
major survey of adult men who had been sexually abused
as children revealed that only twenty-five percent had
been abused by men. All of the others had been seduced
by women, seven percent by their natural mothers, fifteen
percent by aunts, fifteen percent by their mothers' friends
and neighbors, and the rest by sisters, stepmothers,
cousins, and teachers. In more than three quarters of
these cases, the women performed oral sex on their
victims. Sixty-two percent of the incidents involved intercourse. Thirty-six percent of the boys were abused by two
women at the same time, and twenty-three percent said
they were physically harmed in ways that ranged from
slapping and spanking to ritualistic or sadistic behavior.
In more than half the cases the abuse lasted for more than
a year.'

Broussard stopped. 'Does this sound any different
from the "horrible" crimes committed against little girls,
except that the sexes are reversed?' He answered his
question by shaking his head. 'The marvelous double
standard, again. Men want specific things of women — to
be a Madonna or to be a mistress. The mother of God, or
a whore. But never, never, do they want both of these
things in *one* woman. They want the mother of their
children to be a saint and their mistresses to be whores.
Men themselves, of course, can be partners to both: good

father with a mistress. No problem there. But it upsets their concept of the universe if their women are both. It seems to go against "nature."'

He shook his head at them as if he were chastising children.

'It's a fantasy, of course, to believe that men and women are different in such things. Indeed, it is a mistake to think they are different at all, except in what and how they are taught to conduct themselves by a particular society within a particular culture. But that is learned behavior. Deep in our guts, men and women are alike. For better and for worse.'

When Broussard stopped talking, he was smiling and looking directly at Grant, who had forgotten to pretend to take notes and was staring at Broussard with fascination. It may have been that Broussard was smiling at Grant's expression.

'A second point,' Broussard continued, seeing Grant's interest. 'Sexual abusers of children are typically "tender" in the manner of their abuse. Their narcissism demands love, and it is love they are trying to elicit. A while ago you asked me if I knew whether any of the three women victims in these cases had ever been inclined toward sadomasochism. By that I infer that these homicides somehow involve this activity. It is not a characteristic of child abusers, so I wouldn't think your killer would be a child abuser himself.'

'But a moment ago,' Palma interrupted, 'you said that ... twenty-three percent of the cases in the survey of boys sexually abused by women involved some form of sadistic behavior.'

This time Broussard's smile was a smirk, and he nodded as if Palma's observation were itself proof of something self-evident.

But before he had time to respond, Grant asked, 'You had another point?'

'Point two,' Broussard said, quickly holding up two fingers. 'Fantasy. Sadomasochists are powerfully moti-vated by fantasies, role-playing. "The play's the thing."

They are stimulated by very specific acts, gestures, attire, words. It's the same with sexual killers. But not so with pedophiles. I don't believe your killer will be a sexual abuser of children.'

'Fine. Let's say we rule that out,' Grant was speaking slowly, watching Broussard with an anticipatory curiosity. 'How do you imagine his personality?'

Broussard seemed irritated by Grant's persistence in general and by this question in particular. 'I should think that by now any observant reader of the newspaper or true-crime magazines could answer that. It's a personality type that has been well documented and has almost become a cliché. Introspective, solitary, studious, obsessional, vain. Rarely demonstrates violence to those who know him. A "perfect" neighbor, nice guy, who in fact harbors deep, hidden aggression. If he is a mental patient or a prisoner, he will be a model inmate, never causing trouble, probably becoming a trusty or earning good-behavior time. Most likely he is impotent, and probably feels sexually inferior to women. He has bizarre interests of which his friends — I should say his "acquaintances," he probably has no real friends — are unaware. He is a habitual masturbator and reader of pornography. He probably experiences periods of anxiety or depression.'

Broussard opened his hands and let them fall on the desk in front of him.

'All right,' Grant said. 'Now what do you, as a psychiatrist, know about him?'

Broussard studied Grant, his eyes crimping slightly, as if he was appraising not only Grant's question but Grant himself, as if he suspected Grant was in some way trying to get him to overextend himself. 'Probably nothing,' he said at last.

'You can't speculate?'

'I could. I can't see any benefit in it.'

'Insight, Dr. Broussard,' Grant said. 'You get it from listening to people talk. I can imagine myself as a sexual killer, and I learn something, about myself and about the man I'm imagining. But I learn even more if a trained psychiatrist with years of clinical experience imagines him.'

'Mostly with women.'

'What?'

'My clinical experience has been mostly with women.'

'All the better.'

Broussard continued looking at Grant, his eyes seeming to calculate the meaning and risk of the challenge, the corners of his mouth drawn down slightly, an outward sign of an inward conflict. He slid his eyes away from Grant and reached over and idly picked up a black statue from among the dozens on his desk and set it in front of him.

The Hindus' Kâli Ma,' he said. The female figure was skeletal and hideous, squatting over her consort Shiva, devouring his entrails, a rosary of skulls swinging from her neck. 'Giver of life and devourer of her children.

'Some men, maybe many men,' Broussard began slowly, 'engage in sadistic sexual fantasies to a slight or great degree. But only a relatively few actually act them out. If I am one of the few, why? What factors cause me to act out what most men only flirt with? It is unlikely that there is any single, universal factor. Perhaps I was sexually assaulted in childhood or adolescence. Perhaps my first orgasm occurred during one of these assaults, stunning me with the realization that I was enjoying a wonderous sensation in the midst of despicable degradation. It would have left an indelible scar on my psyche, and forever would have related one of life's most elemental drives — something that should have been good and nurturing — to something harsh and sadistic. I would always equate the two, cruelty and orgasm, because my unformed personality would mistakenly affirm the relationship. The event would have occurred at a crucial point in my sexual orientation. I would have been ... perversely taught.'

There was only one light on in Broussard's office, a desk lamp with an amber glass shade that sat to his right and cast a candle-coloured glow across the varied heads and forms of his mythical women and kept his own face softly alight in the coming dusk. Palma and Grant, sharing little of the lamp, receded farther into the shadows with the failing light.

'My social-sexual relationships would be disappointing as I entered puberty. Nothing would seem to be "as it should be" in my relationships with the opposite sex. I would feel inadequate from the beginning, and as I grew older I would become increasingly frustrated. Unable to control events in the real world, I would turn to fantasizing a different one, one in which I always would be in control. I would develop a pattern of thinking and imagining, scenarios of sexuality that were warped by my earlier experiences. Only now I am in control. I go over the scenarios again and again and again. This pattern of thinking, the scenario, the fantasy, becomes a habit, and I find that I become sexually aroused by fantasies of controlling and dominating. These fantasies become my sole sexual experiences. I retreat into them. Also, eventually, I become bored by them, and I learn that to sustain my sexual arousal I have to alter the scenarios to make them increasingly vivid and provocative. I discover that variety is, indeed, a spice. I may even find myself beginning to act them out, following women at a distance, watching them as I imagine dominating them, humiliating them.'

Broussard rubbed the burnished Kâli, looking at her, his voice quiet and steady, his monologue coming increasingly easy to him.

'I become bolder. I follow a woman home and break into her house while she is away, staying for hours by myself. Trying on her clothes. Or crawling naked under the covers of her bed where her perfume lingers like musk among the sheets. I may "accidentally" meet her, at a restaurant, at a bar, and talk to her. My intimacy with her personal items, her underclothes which I have worn on my own body, her toiletries which I have applied to my own genitals, makes me bold. I know something she doesn't know. I control our meetings. I'm charming enough, my boldness gives me a kind of easiness of manner. In the game of the sexes I am already ahead because I know so much about her, the kind of soap she uses, the name of her perfume, her brand of sanitary napkins. I go home with her. I am at ease, because I know everything about this house that I am pretending to enter for the first time. I enjoy the joke; it gives me confidence. I have confidence and control all the way through it, all the way to the end . . .'

Broussard stopped suddenly in mid-thought and let his eyes slide back to Grant, who was almost swallowed by the darkening shadows. Outside, a lilac evening had slipped into a warm, purple darkness, and below them the sluggish waters of the bayou turned inky and foul in the falling night.

46

Mirel Farr lived in a neighborhood not far from the Astrodome and that for years had been teetering on the brink of decline. Then a couple of years earlier it finally plunged over the edge, and all the homeowners seemed to have decided within an eighteen-month period to sell out to absentee landlords. Now most of the little houses were rental property, and because the people who lived in them had invested neither money nor memories and were themselves teetering on the brink of one kind of disaster or another, the little houses began to reflect the hopelessness of the lives of their occupants. The lawns were unkempt now, and weedy, and burnt to hard, dun-colored bristles, and the buckled sidewalks went unrepaired. Paint had faded to pastels of their former shades and the composition shingles on the roofs were curled and blistered to crumbles under the vicious Texas sun. And another sure sign of 'things going to hell,' as Gordy Haws observed, was that people had taken to parking in their front yards and putting cars up on blocks in their driveways.

Haws and Lew Marley stopped their dark gray department car under the frondy spread of a fat Mexican blue palm across the street from Mirel Farr's house. They looked at the house a moment, its bare yellow porch light casting a jaundiced glow over the cement stoop and thought about the best way to go about talking to dominatrix Farr. Just as they decided that Haws would go around back and Marley would knock on the front door, a black Lincoln sedan eased down the street and turned into Farr's driveway. Its lights went out and the car remained dark and still for a moment, and then a man got out and walked gingerly across the muddy yard to the front door, with his shoulders hunched around his face as if he was warding off a blowing rain. When he got to the front door he simply opened it and walked in.

'Customer,' Marley said, scratching a long sideburn.

'Why don't I check this guy out?' Haws said, jotting down the license number and picking up the radio. He called in the number, and in a few moments the radio scratched and they learned the man's name and address and driving record, all of which were uninteresting. Just a west Houston businessman slumming over to Mirel's for some kinky entertainment.

'It'll take a while,' Marley said. 'Let's go get a burger.' He put the car in gear and they pulled away from the curb and drove to South Main, where they got hamburgers at the American Boy café run by three Vietnamese brothers who took their cross-cultural menu seriously by offering old standard cuisines of several nationalities, jellyfish and squid in steamed vegetables on a bed of seaweed, chicken-fried steak and biscuits and lots of milk gravy, chicken enchiladas, and barbecued brisket. And always, hamburgers and fries.

Marley and Haws took their hamburgers and fries back to the Mexican blue palm across the street from Farr's and settled in to eat, the car windows rolled down to let in the rain-cooled evening air. Their radio was turned low so it wouldn't carry out into the still night.

They had been there only fifteen minutes when the broad, flat muzzle of a giant mixed-breed dog suddenly appeared in Haws's window. Smelling stoutly of wet hair, it draped its great muddy paws over the windowsill and lusted shamelessly after Haws's hamburger, its overlong tongue lathering its purple lips. Unsuccessful in beating the dog away with the window, Haws finally offered a dollar each to two Mexican boys who were passing by if they would tie one of their belts around the dog's neck and lead the animal away. But as soon as Haws gave the boys the money, they bolted and ran away into the dark, and the dog was back up on the windowsill, drooling down on Haws's armrest. Swearing, Haws emptied all of his and Marley's pepper onto the paper his hamburger had been wrapped in and stuck it out for the dog to whiff, which he did mightily. Then he stopped breathing, rolled his eyes and let out a bawl mixed with a sneeze that splattered slobber all over Haws's grinning face, snapped the dog's head back, and whammed it against the top of the window as he scrambled off the side of the car, raking his claws down the paint and knocking his chin against the windowsill. He shot out into the dark, bellowing and snuffling and tossing his head like a mad dog.

Haws and Marley laughed and finished their hamburgers, and Haws told everything that had happened to Marley, even though Marley had been sitting right beside him through the whole thing. Haws told it a couple of times. Later, the cur returned to sit and watch them from the darkness on the other side of the blue palm, but no matter how Haws tried, he couldn't coax the dog to approach the car again.

That was the entertainment.

Then boredom quickly followed and settled in. They had finished their hamburgers, drunk their Royal Crown colas, and eaten their ice, and the man still hadn't come out of Mirel Farr's neighborhood dungeon.

'Je-sus,' Haws said, looking at his watch for the fourth time. 'It's been almost an hour. He must be gettin' an enema.'

'Shit,' Marley said, and slid down in his seat.

Haws laughed at the unintended pun, but Marley didn't even know he had made one and scooted down even more so he could lay his head against the back of the seat.

'Let's go in,' Haws said.

'And interrupt something like that?' Marley asked.

'Why not?'

'You ever interrupted something like that?'

'Well, no, Lew, I haven't.'

'Well, you don't want to.'

'Hell, you haven't either.'

'Right, but Dick Paredes did. Big mistake. He told me about it.'

'Aw, come on.'

'I'm telling you, you don't know what she's doing to the guy,' Marley said. 'She's got him hooked up someway, maybe something tagged onto his peter, something stuck up his ass, maybe electricity involved. We go blowing in there, scaring them, the guy might jump and rip something off or out or down.'

'Down?'

'I'm just saying it's a risk I don't want to take. He'll be out in a minute,' Marley said authoritatively

There was a moment's silence.

Haws looked at Marley. 'What'd Dick Paredes tell you?'

'Long story,' Marley said, rolling his head against the back of the seat, trying to find a comfortable position.

'We're going somewhere?'

Marley sighed impatiently. 'When he was in vice they raided one of these dungeons and caught a little routine in progress. Guy was buck naked, blindfolded, lying on his back with his legs drawn up and alligator clips clamped all over his ass and his peter. Wires were hooked up to a big old truck battery, you know, twelve volts, and this old gal at the controls was buck naked too, except for a rubber Halloween mask of a pig and a pair of high-topped, laced-up roller skates. Paredes and his bunch went blowing in there and scared them all to shit. The gal's skates shot out from under her and she fell on the neck of an upright beer bottle — this is no lie — and it went right up her ass. She screamed and accidentally snapped on the step-down switch she had hooked up to the battery and poured the full force of the juice of that battery into that guy's ass and his peter.'

Haws roared, but Marley never lifted his head off the seat. 'Bad end to the story, Gordy,' Marley said soberly. 'The gal in the pig mask had to go through a bunch of operations. The neck of the bottle broke off in there, and they never got it all straightened out the way it was before. And the guy on the floor, he lost one nut and got the end of his peter burned off. They had to cut most of the rest of it off.'

Haws guffawed again, but stopped before he would have liked to because of Marley's tone of voice, which was serious. Marley was kind of a moralistic guy anyway when it came to sex, and this was clearly a grave warning to any cop who wanted to raid an S&M dungeon while business was in progress. Haws sat back in his seat and thought about the scene Marley had just described and laughed to himself and now wanted more than ever to go bursting into Mirel Farr's place to see what he could discover. Occasionally he would glance out of the window and see the giant cur watching him from the deep shadows under the blue palm.

After almost another half hour of waiting, they heard the front door of Farr's place open, and the man came out, his shoulders once again hunched up around his ears.

'Gee, he's really disguised, huh, Lew?' Haws observed.

The man quick-walked to his car, unlocked it, got inside, turned on the lights, backed out of the drive, and drove away.

Haws and Marley got out of the car and locked it, and Haws made one last effort to call the cur to him, but the dog quickly drifted farther back into the shadows and growled menacingly from the dark. Chuckling, Haws rounded the front of the car, and the two of them walked across to Farr's house. Marley waited for Haws to work his way around the back before he stepped up on the stoop, opened the screen door, and knocked on the wood door behind it. The yellow light falling on his tall, thin frame made him appear slightly malarial. He had to knock loudly three more times before the door opened, and he held up his shield to a woman in a housecoat who looked to be in her late twenties.

'Ms. Farr?'

'Yeah.' She was frowning fiercely.

'Detective Lew Marley, Houston Police. I'd like to talk to you a minute, please.'

'Me?'

'Well, yes.'

'What about?' She had bleached her hair with about an inch of the auburn roots showing down the middle of her part.

'May I come in, please?'

'You got a warrant?'

'Well, I don't need a warrant, ma'am. I just want to talk to you.'

'I don't want to talk to you,' she said petulantly and started to close the door, but Marley's foot was quickly inside the jamb.

'I can radio for a warrant,' Marley said. 'It'll just take a little longer, and it'll probably piss me off.'

The woman looked at him. Her lifeless hair framed a sad face with flat cheekbones and a rather pallid, splotchy complexion. She had a long, sheepish top lip and an unattractive way of quivering the left side of her face. She pulled an overtired face at Marley's remark and backed away from the door, letting Marley push it open himself. He entered a small living room sparsely furnished with two stained cloth sofas, a couple of Goodwill end tables and lamps, and a television and VCR.

'You alone?' Marley asked, keeping his voice low.

'Yeah.'

'Where's your back door?'

'Out the kitchen,' she said, a little worried.

Marley flicked his head for her to go first, and they walked into the yellow-tiled kitchen and he motioned for her to open the back door while he stood at the living room door and looked down a short hallway toward the back of the house.

'Hi, hon,' Haws said as Farr pulled open the back door.

'Got any cookies?'

'Shit,' the girl groaned.

'Show us around.' Marley was all business.

It didn't take her long. They walked through a dining room into a hallway past a bathroom, a bedroom which looked like a bedroom, to a second bedroom which didn't look like a bedroom. On the far side of the room and projecting out into the middle was a platform about ten inches high and eight feet square. It had been built out of plywood and two-by-fours. Attached to the wall over the platform were iron rings and various sizes of pulleys and clips and hasps. A rough cedar beam projected from the wall out to the end of the platform and was supported by an upright pier anchored to the end of the platform and supported by two joists also affixed to the end of the platform. The beam was also fitted with iron rings and pulleys. There were a few benches on the platform. On one of the walls of the room was an 'armaments rack,' where three or four different kinds of whips hung along with chains and ropes, leather straps, rubber hoses, and clamps of various sizes. There was a closet in one corner of the room full of rubber and leather costumes and a nearby rack where some of this clothing was drying.

There were a couple of chairs in the room, and Marley sat on one near the platform and motioned to Farr to sit down. She sat down in the other, and Haws sat on the edge of the platform, looking around the room as he took out a thin box of Chiclets, shaking several into his hand. Farr took a pack of Salems out of her robe pocket and lighted one, tossing the paper match on the floor. Perhaps it was because she had just been through a somewhat rigorous routine with her incognito client, but she seemed rather drained of energy in addition to being clearly nervous. She did not appear to be a woman overly concerned with healthful habits.

'You know, Mirel,' Marley said, looking her in the face, 'we're not interested in busting you on this.' He shook his head. 'Not in the least. We're gonna walk out of here in a

minute and that'll be it. But we really expect you not to
hold out on us.'

Haws nodded and looked at Mirel's crossed legs where
her thin imitation-silk robe was slipping away from her
knees. Well, she was going to give it a try, he guessed.
Why not? He could see inside the loosely draped top of
her robe. Mirel was not going to win the next Miss Big
Cup contest.

'Right to the point,' Marley said. Mirel was cutting her
eyes at Haws. 'Just to set us straight and save some time,
we want to tell you that there are some things we know
and some things we don't know. We'll tell you what we
know, and then you tell us what we don't know. Okay?'

Mirel Farr flicked the ash from her cigarette in Marley's
direction without being too insulting, and some of it got
on his pants leg.

'Good,' he said. 'We know that Sandra Moser has been
here to work out in your little gym. We know that Vickie
Kittrie has been here too, and Dorothy Samenov. We
know that Gil Reynolds has been here. Sometimes with
them, sometimes without them. We know that you are,
off and on, Clyde Barbish's good friend. We know that
you are aware of the tragedies that have lately befallen
these people.'

Marley looked at Farr with a pleasant expression.
'Okay? Let's start with a simple yes-or-no question.' He
reached into a baggy suit-coat side pocket and pulled out
two different photographs of Bernadine Mello. He handed
them to Farr, who took them with one hand and placed
them on her bared knee, one above the other.

'Do you know her?' Marley asked.

Farr held her cigarette aloft and studied the photographs with a certain myopic distance, tilting her head as
if that was going to make a difference.

'Nope,' she said. 'Never seen her.'

'Positive?' Marley asked.

'Sure am.'

'What if she had dark hair?' Haws interjected. He
jerked a felt-tip pen from his shirt pocket, leaned over to

Farr's leg, and stared coloring in Mello's light hair with
broad swishes of his felt tip, his left hand covering a large
part of her naked thigh to steady the photographs on her
knee. When he was through, it took him a second to
steady the pictures again.

Farr didn't move the whole time he was doing his
graphic adjustment of Mello's hair and inadvertently
massaging the top of her thigh. Her eyes locked on him
with a cold, slow burn, and when he was through they
followed him as he sat back again on the dungeon platform. She never looked at Mello's picture again, never
saw Haws's artwork.

'Don't know her,' Farr said to Marley, but she didn't
pick up the pictures to hand them back.

Marley nodded, accepting her acid testimony. He carefully took the pictures off her knee, taking them by their
corners, scrupulously careful to avoid touching her.

'Now, what else we don't know is: What kind of S&M
scenarios did Gil Reynolds like best? When was the last
time you saw him? When was the last time you saw
Clyde Barbish? How well did Barbish know Reynolds
. . .?' Marley paused. 'Well, let's just start with these.'

'What makes you think I know the goddamn answers?'
Farr asked with a strong west Texas twang.

'I told you,' Marley said. 'We know.'

'Yeah?' Farr nodded skeptically, pulling on her short-
ening Salem and looking like she wanted to cry. She
waited a moment, nervously swinging her crossed leg,
which didn't have a suntan but did have a couple of
uneven bruises just above the knee. Finally she blurted,
'He liked to whip up on women. About five weeks ago.
About three months ago. They knew each other purty
good through Dennis Ackley.'

Marley looked at her blankly.

'Oooh,' Haws said. 'Toughy.'

'That's good,' Marley said with elaborate patience.
'Now let's try for a little more in-depth report.'

'Where you guys parked?' Farr asked suddenly.

'Across the street.'

'Jesus. In a police car?'

'It's unmarked.'

'Oh, right. Big deal.' She looked pained. 'I can't just go telling you all this shit. This gets out ... I mean, you know what these people are like? I been at this seven years now. It's my clientele. They know I've talked to the cops I won't even be able to get niggers in here, much less the white trade.'

'You don't really have any choice here, Mirel,' Marley said, almost in the tone of a big brother breaking kind of hard news to his sister, all the time, of course, sympathizing with her situation.

'Okay,' Mirel said, a tremor breaking her voice. 'Okay.' She jerked her robe tight around her chest. No slack, no free looks. She glared at Haws chomping on his Chiclets, then moped a minute while Haws and Marley waited, before she started talking.

47

'Most of the guys come here are masos. They like to be intimidated and humiliated, got their favorite ways to be punished and mastered,' Mirel began. 'And most of the girls, too. They're bottoms — masos. Same thing. That's what Moser was into and Dorothy and Louise Ackley. Most people. Vickie, she bottoms too, but with Reynolds she tops. A very strange couple. Weird. Reynolds only masos with her, but sados with everybody else. Vickie's the only one of the group, Samenov's bunch, that sometimes goes out slumming to bring back fresh meat. Gets out those colored hankies, whatever color she's coding — different things on different nights — sticks it in her rightside hip pocket to signal she's bottoming, and takes off. She cruises the dens, picks up the girls who're into whatever game she's in the mood for, and brings 'em back here.'

'Why doesn't she take them home?' Marley asked. 'I thought you had a set clientele.'

'Hell, I hire out, whatever.' Mirel looked at him like he didn't know shit. 'Anyway, one thing, I got the 'quipment. Another thing, she doesn't want Dorothy to know she goes to the dens. But mainly it's because she bottoms. I mean, she doesn't always know the girls she's picking up, if she can trust them. So she wants me to keep an eye on their game, keep her from getting killed by one of these bitches. But that's what she likes, the risk in it.

Sometimes she doesn't even bother to lay down the rules or get the safe words straight. She just gets right into it, hell for leather. That's when she really needs me. I know when she calls and wants me to do a peeper that it's going to be a wild show and anything can happen. I watch through the mirror in my bedroom wall,' she said, tossing her head toward a full-length mirror opposite the raised platform.

She lighted another cigarette and got it going with a couple of deep tugs.

'What kind of games?' Marley asked.

'She's into fisting in a big way, and rimming, golden showers, and when she's feeling weird she goes riding the rag, or the shit scene, or heavy whipping. Red hankies, dark blue, yellow, maroon, brown, black. Whatever. I watch 'em all, don't matter to me. I been doing this scene so long I'm as good as a doctor at it. I know when they're going too far. I can see 'em gettin' on the vital signs. Some of these bitches don't know Jack-shit about what they're doing. And some of 'em get carried away and don't care. Sometimes me and ... Barbish — what the hell, I know the guy — watch together and drink a couple of six-packs of beer. It's better'n David Letterman.'

She stopped.

'What about Reynolds? What's he like?'

'Sado. That's his thing. All the way. And I used to have a hard time with that 'cause I wasn't always willing to go the distance with the guy.' She looked at Marley. 'To tell you the truth, I had Clyde back me up on him lots of times. But Reynolds didn't know it. He'd of killed me. Clyde sat right there like I did for Vickie, and watched him. Reynolds is not a stable man.' She shook her head. 'Not a stable man.'

'Did Barbish ever have to stop him?'

'Nope.'

'You said you "used" to have a hard time with him. You don't anymore?'

'Nope, 'cause I quit doing it with him. I don't know. I just had a feelin' I needed to shut it down. Which is too bad. The guy paid way more'n anybody else.'

'How did he react to that?'

'What, to my quitting? Pissed him off bad. We had a fight about it one night, but shit, what could he do? I threatened to call the cops. And I would've, too, but it cooled him down, the bastard.'

'Listen,' Marley said, wiping a hand over his balding pate. 'What we need to know about him is, just exactly what did he like most? Was he fascinated by any particular part of a woman's body? I mean not the usual parts, but off-the-wall parts, you know. I mean it might not be a . . . sex part . . .'

'To tell you the truth . . .' Mirel stopped, and her eyes opened wide. All of them heard it and looked toward the doorway and the sound of the venetian blinds banging against the opening back door.

'Mirel. Hey, Mirel,' a man called, and then they heard steps coming across the linoleum floor.

Farr jumped to her feet. 'Clyde! Cops! Co . . .' Marley hit her with all his might with the back of his fist and sent her tumbling back over her chair, feet going over her head, as he came out of his own chair with his .45 already in his hand, racing Haws for the doorway. He burst past the door frame first, going too fast to turn down the hall, and slammed against the wall, hearing Barbish running across the kitchen floor, Haws making the turn first but going too fast himself to make the turn into the kitchen, when he zipped right past and which was lucky, because Barbish fired one-two-three blasts from his Colt Commander .45, ripping fist-size hunks out of the hallway Sheetrock. Marley, who was on his feet again and running, backpedaled wildly at the sound of the shots, sliding on the wood floor right into the line of fire, yelling, 'Shitshitshitshitshit!' as he tried unsuccessfully to reverse the natural law of momentum in an effort to stay out of the doorway, where he finally slid to a stop on his back, firing into the kitchen at whatever the hell was in there, hoping to forestall return fire until he could get out of the way.

By the time Marley realized Barbish was gone, Haws was already pounding across the living room and bursting out the front door into the muggy night. Forgetting about the muddy yard, he bounded off the stoop with the full intention of hitting the ground running and shooting. Instead, his legs squirted out from under him in different directions and slammed him on his back, knocking the wind out of him so that as he struggled to his knees he had no breath and thought he was going to pass out as he saw Barbish stop at the edge of the street, turn, and fire.

Haws went down just as Marley came onto the stoop and yelled, 'Jesus Christ, Gordy!' and saw Barbish running into the street. Marley fired his Smith & Wesson from the stoop one-two-three-four times, and Barbish finished crossing the street on his stomach, sliding face-down into the opposite curb.

Haws was already trying to sit up when Marley got to him.

'Son of a bitch!' Haws squealed.

'Gordy! Gordy!' Marley sounded like he was going to cry.

'Christ!' Haws yelled. 'My leg ... just my leg! Lew! Don't let the bastard get up ... cuff him! Go cuff him!'

Marley jumped up and slogged across the yard and into the street and over to the curb where Barbish was trying to raise his head and which Marley kicked on the run like Tony Zendejas in a Monday night opener. It sounded like he had kicked a cantaloupe, but Barbish's head did not burst open, only hammered down against the cement curb again, putting him out cold. Driven by adrenaline, Marley frantically ran around looking for Barbish's .45, but couldn't find it, gave it up and came back and cuffed the unconscious Barbish's hands behind his back. He left him in the street and ran back over to Haws, who was moaning and holding his left thigh just above the knee and talking on the radio, which was caked with mud.

'Yeah, yeah. Listen *two* ambulances .. I'm not ridin' in

the same ... Lew. Lew, where'd I hit him?'

'Shit!' Marley said, stood again and clomped back across the yard, into the street, where he put a foot under the bleeding Barbish and heaved him over. Barbish's face was all blood and blood was coming from the ear which had caught Marley's flying kick. But his face was only skinned from the trip across the wet street on his nose, which was bleeding profusely. Only one of Marley's four shots had caught him, square in the back of the knee. The lower leg was doubled around at an angle that it normally wouldn't be able to achieve, which meant that Marley's .45 slug had smashed his knee joint. The other inmates would be calling him Crip for the rest of his life.

Marley started to leave Barbish again, but caught the glint of the barrel of his Colt Commander protruding out from under Barbish's hip. 'Son of a bitch,' he swore. Again he put his foot under Barbish and rolled him up enough so that he could pick up the gun without grabbing the barrel. He put the Colt on safety, looked at Barbish's disjointed lower limb, flipping it around so that the foot pointed in the wrong direction. Then he ran back to Haws.

'Where'd I hit him?' Haws groaned, gripping his leg above the wound and looking like a ghost.

'You didn't fire, Gordy,' Marley said. 'But I blew his knee away.'

Haws looked at Marley in astonishment. 'What! I didn't shoot?' He let go of his leg with his right hand and leaned over and got his gun off the muddy dead grass and stared at it. 'Goddamn!' he yelled. 'Son of a bitch! I didn't even shoot?' He groaned and fell back on the grass, ignoring the tiny voice of the dispatcher yelling over the radio.

By this time neighbors were out into their yards and closing in quickly, as they judged the shooting to be over and saw that there were two bodies they could look at. Sirens seemed to be everywhere in the distance as Marley squatted down beside Haws.

'I'm gonna pass out,' Haws said, his eyes closed. He was bleeding profusely, turning the dun-colored grass

and patches of mud black in the faint light from the
streetlamp.

'No ...' Marley laid his and Barbish's guns on the
grass and gripped Haw's wound with both hands. Haws
screamed and his eyes popped open.

'Stopping the bleeding,' Marley explained frantically.
'Gordy!' he yelled, looking at his partner. 'Raise your arm,
Gordy. Point at the goddamn streetlight,' Marley yelled,
trying to keep his partner out of shock. To his surprise
Haws did it, but his Colt was still in his hand and he was
aiming. 'You talk to the dispatcher?' Marley asked.

'Yeah,' Haws croaked, and his hand started to sink.

'Gordy, you son of a bitch,' Marley yelled again. 'Point
at the streetlight!' Haws's hand and nickel-plated Colt
went back up in the air. And that was where they were
when the swarm of radio units converged on Mirel Farr's
house not far from the Astrodome, and the ambulance
jumped the curb and pulled up beside Haws and Marley
on the dead grass.

Palma and Grant were at the intersection of San Felipe
and Kirby Drive returning from Broussard's when they
heard Haws's frantic call for an ambulance. Palma
whipped the car right onto Kirby and headed south as
fast as she could negotiate the traffic, passing under the
Southwest Freeway and following Kirby all the way into
Westwood Park.

The crowd was several people deep around the
shooting scene and the collection of radio units, which
were parked every which way in the curbs and blocking
the street. An officer shooting always attracted a horde of
radio units, and their cherry and sapphire flashers were
bouncing off the crowd and neighborhood houses, giving
the scene an unintended carnival atmosphere. Palma and
Grant used their badges to push through the crowd and
get past the vigilant uniformed officers. The crime scene
unit hadn't even arrived yet, and Palma was the first
detective on the scene. She spotted Marley hanging
around the back of the ambulance that Haws was going

into. As the doors closed, Marley saw her coming over and went over to meet her.

'How is he?' she asked.

'Lucky,' Marley said, looking drained. 'It was Barbish,' he said, turning to look toward the street where the ambulance personnel were having a harder time with Barbish, trying to get him out of the gutter. Marley patiently told them what had happened, going through it chronologically and in some detail. 'The slug missed the bone, but cut an artery, so he bled like hell. He'll be okay,' Marley said, wiping a hand over his thin hair. 'Jesus,' he said. 'I'm a little shaky.'

Palma and Grant followed him over to the stoop of Farr's house where he sat down. Under the sickly porch light Palma could see his clothes were smeared with mud, his shoes so clogged with it that they looked like brogans. He lifted his chin toward Barbish. 'Asshole's okay, too. I blew his knee off.' He looked at Palma. 'I kinda kicked him in the head.' He glanced at Grant. 'Just between us. I think that's their problem over there. I may've vegetabilized him.'

'Farr didn't give you much help about Reynolds?' Palma asked.

Marley shook his head. 'Just that he's a bad-ass who likes to beat up women. We didn't get much past that before Barbish came in. We need to talk to her, though. I'd bet a paycheck she's been letting him stay here. We ought to use that to get more out of her about Barbish's relationship with Reynolds. The way she was talking, I think they may have more to do with each other than we thought.'

Several more police cars arrived and pushed their way through the crowd to park next to the yellow crime scene ribbons. Frisch, Captain McComb, and two of the detectives assigned to the special squad set up to investigate officer-involved shootings got out of one of the cars and started making their way across the pitted and bogged yard, which got more difficult to negotiate with each passing minute as officers swarmed around the house.

Palma put her hand on Marley's shoulder. 'Hang in there, Lew,' she said, and she and Grant moved away as the officers approached, and Marley got ready to tell his story all over again. He would have to tell it more times than anybody would want to.

'Carmen,' Frisch said, veering away from the group and pulling an envelope out of his pocket. 'Reynolds's search warrant.' He handed it to her. 'I talked to Art fifteen minutes ago, and he said he and Boucher have followed Reynolds all the way out to Galveston. He's having dinner with a woman out there at Le Bateau on the waterfront. They've been drinking, just ordered their meal. As soon as they left the city, we had our people go in and wire the place. Before you go up, check with Leeland about the surveillance van so they'll know what's happening.' He handed her a key. 'The wire people had it made. Turn it in to Leeland when you're finished up there.'

'What about Reynolds's car?'

Frisch shook his head. 'They didn't get to it in time. They'll get something in it tonight. Look, you've got a couple of hours at least, if you go right now. That should give you enough time.' He looked at her, and then at Grant. 'Do it right,' he said, then he turned and walked back toward Marley.

'Let's go,' Grant said. 'There's no such thing as "enough time" when you're doing this.'

Palma backtracked to Bellaire Boulevard and turned toward the West Loop. She picked up the radio and called Leeland and told him to let the electronics surveillance people know that they were on their way. Leeland told her that they should identify themselves as soon as they entered the condo, and then do the same when they were leaving.

They parked among a cluster of other cars under the enormous spread of a live oak fifty yards from the phosphorus glow of a mercury vapor streetlamp in the parking lot of the St. Regis Tower condominiums. Though condominium owners were allowed a designated number of slots in the tower's covered parking garage, weekends always found a spillover of cars in the landscaped parking lot in the front of the building. There were a number of large live oaks in the maze of medians and those parking places that fell within the circumference of their canopies were prized spots because they guaranteed shade the next day when the sun would send the temperature inside an exposed car shooting out the top of a thermometer.

Palma got out with the flash camera she had taken from the photo lab at the department that afternoon, and the two of them walked across the front drive of the fifty-six-story tower and into the marble and glass entrance. They took an elevator to the twenty-seventh floor and Palma let them into Reynolds's place with the key that Frisch had given her.

As soon as they were inside, Palma spoke up and identified their entry, and before her eyes had adjusted to the dark foyer she realized that Grant had already left it. He was no longer with her. She started to ask him where he was, then caught herself, not wanting the guys in the surveillance van somewhere outside to know that she was already out of pocket.

She stood in the dark foyer with the uncanny feeling of being in over her head. At first she heard nothing, saw no light, and had the sudden, irrational feeling that Grant wasn't there, that something had gone wrong, and she was walking into a situation that was completely different from what she had left a few minutes before. She shook off the temptation to let her mind run with that fiction. It was too easy to allow that kind of fantasy to dictate to you, make you do something rash. But now she didn't know what to do. Did she wait for him in the foyer? Did she go look for him? Without turning on the lights? Obviously he wasn't using the lights. Maybe if she let her eyes adjust. A few minutes' wait did help, enough to enable her to negotiate the furniture, but certainly not well enough for her to see anything in detail. Then what the hell was he doing?

She moved to the other side of the foyer and started

through what must have been the living room. She could make out sofas and armchairs, a potted palm silhouetted against the Post Oak district skyline sparkling through floor-to-ceiling windows with their drapes drawn back. There was a grand piano, an item of furniture that immediately struck her as incongruous, a bar with a collection of bottles. When she got to the far side of the room near the windows, she turned and looked back, hoping to see the doors to other rooms. To her right was a dining room, and perhaps the kitchen, and to her left she saw an arched doorway and a faint wash of light falling across the marble floors.

Palma moved across the living room toward the light, made the corner, and saw what was probably a bedroom door closed with a bright seam of light issuing from the bottom. She made her way to it, being careful to keep the camera from knocking over a lamp or vase, sliding her feet slowly across the floor like a woman wading in the surf. When she made the hall, she headed for the seam of light, feeling still that she was about to open the door on something completely outside her experience, about to do something that could not be compared with anything she had ever seen or done before.

Almost compelled to knock first, she resisted the impulse and pressed down the door handle and pushed it open. Sander Grant was on his knees beside a king-size bed. She knew he must have heard the door open, though he didn't turn around or speak or acknowledge it in any way, but continued doing something with his hands on the bed in front of him. Palma approached the bed, and even when she knew she was in his peripheral vision he did not indicate that he saw her or knew she was there.

In front of him on the bed were two boxes of bleached white wood about a foot square and four or five inches high. Both boxes were elaborately carved with Oriental motifs, and as Palma looked closer, she could see that in places the wood was mottled as if stained from frequent handling. Grant had gotten one of the boxes open, and

one of each of its four drawers swung out of a different
side of the box and at a different level, forming a spiral
stair, each tray pivoting on a single pin hinge located in
one of the four corners. There were no handles to the
drawers, no latches, no indication of how the drawers
were to be sprung and opened. It was this intricate, but
clever, locking system that Grant was still trying to
discover on the second box.

Palma knelt down beside him and looked at the
contents of the four opened drawers of the first box. The
bottom of each bleached wooden tray was covered with a
piece of bright yellow silk, and mounted on the silk with
thin wire clips were rifle shells, two columns of five each.
On each shell was engraved a date and a location: Tien
Phuoc, 16 May 1968; Thuan Minh, 4 June 1968; Dak Ket,
15 June 1968; Ta Gam, 17 June 1968; Son Ha, 21 June
1968. She went to the next drawer: Rach Goi, 9 July 1968;
Vi Thanh, 23 July 1968; Rang Rang, 3 August 1968; Don
Sai, 10 August 1968.

Palma heard a click and Grant opened out each tray in
the second box. Four more drawers of yellow silk, ten
shells to the drawer: Chalang Plantation, 12 June 1969;
Chalang Plantation, 13 June 1969; Chalang Plantation, 14
June 1969; Bo Tuc, 20 June 1969; Tong Not, 25 December
1969; Dak Mot Lop, 19 March 1970; Ban Het, 22 March
1970; Ban Phya Ha, 9 May 1970; Polei Lang Lo Kram, 23
June 1970. There were eighty shells in all, each of the
same caliber, but differing in subtlety of metal color and
place and date.

Grant stared at the trays and their contents. He said
nothing, did nothing, and his face gave no indication of
what he might be thinking. Then, very carefully, he
closed each of the eight drawers. He stood, still not
acknowledging Palma's presence, and picked up the first
of the two boxes and carried it across the room where he
set it in the floor of the opened closet, careful to place the
shallow, flat legs of the boxes into the same indentions
they had made in the thick carpet. He did the same with
the second box, then came over to the bed and smoothed

it out, adjusting the hang of the bedspread to make sure the seam was even.

Palma stood out of Grant's way while he made himself familiar with Reynolds's bedroom in much the same way he had done at Mello's and Samenov's. He went through Reynolds's clothing, studied the contents of his bathroom, looked through his chests where he found a drawer full of pornographic magazines and videotapes. Seeming preoccupied, he moved out of the bedroom and into the second one, which was furnished but unused, without even towels or soap in the bathroom. She followed Grant into the living room, where he made his way to the far wall and pulled the drapes closed before he turned on the lights and began wandering through the spacious room, which was furnished with an extensive collection of Oriental furniture and objets d'art. Grant left no jar unexamined, no decorative box unopened. He checked under the upholstered bottoms of the chairs and sofas and unzipped the covered foam cushions and probed the sides. There was a small wall of books, and Grant removed each volume and quickly, but thoroughly, fanned through their pages. He spent some time at the bar, looking at the type of liquor Reynolds kept and the kind he had in reserve.

In one corner of the room there was an alcove with a desk surrounded by shelves. Grant pulled open each drawer on the desk and went through it, then carefully went through the few envelopes and papers stacked to one side. Two items were side by side, and he looked at their positioning a moment before he picked up the calendar and set it in the center of the desk.

'Carmen, how much film did you bring?'

'Four rolls, thirty-six exposures each.'

'Great. Let's see how many pages we need to photograph out of the calendar.'

They went through every page, beginning with the last weekend in December of the previous year. Luckily the calendar showed a week on each double-page spread, and Palma was able to get every week up to the present on one roll. There were no notations beyond the present week. Grant carefully replaced the calendar and pulled the address book over in front of them. It appeared to be dedicated to personal use, not cluttered with the names of business contacts as would be his Rolodex at his office. Most of these names were first names only, some with a last-name initial. The book was about the size of a breast-pocket wallet, and Palma was able to get every double page on the next two rolls of film.

Grant had gone through Reynolds's kitchen and was going through a golf bag in the coat closet in the entryway when Palma checked her watch. They had been in Reynolds's condo an hour and forty minutes. She walked to the telephone and called Leeland. Reynolds had left Galveston and was headed back into the city. They were about three miles from Hobby Airport. Palma told Grant they might have another thirty minutes, and he started making one more trip through the condo, this time acting as if he were going through a museum. He turned on all the lights and simply strolled through each of the rooms, pausing and looking at things that Palma couldn't imagine he needed to see again since he had already examined them in detail. But he touched nothing, and sometimes he would turn a lamp off here and there and look around at the effect of the changed lighting on the room, or it seemed to Palma that that was what he was doing. Gradually he worked his way back to the front foyer. Behind them all the lights were out, the drapes over the large glass window overlooking the Post Oak district were once again open, and the lights of the city glittered across the darkness to the foyer.

Twenty-five minutes after Palma talked to Leeland they stepped out into the hallway, and Grant locked the door behind them.

48

Palma and Grant returned to the police headquarters on Riesner and took the rolls of film to Jake Weller in the photo lab, requesting that he print whatever size photographs it took to read the writing on the calendar and the address book. They asked for two copies of each print, one to go to Leeland in the task force control room and one to go on Palma's desk.

Then they went down to homicide, where the main hall was crowded with reporters from all three media branches, none of whom were being let into the squad room itself and all of whom recognized Palma and tried to get her to stop for a few words. Finally making their way into the squad room, they found another, but smaller, crowd of police officials jammed into Frisch's office and spilling out of the open door. Palma also recognized a couple of city councilmen and the mayor's law-enforcement liaison.

With Grant right behind her, she headed into the narrow corridor that took her to the task force room, where a secretary was working at the computer, Nancy Castle was talking on the telephone, and Leeland was hunched over a pile of papers at a crowded desk. Except for Castle's subdued conversation on the telephone and a clerk's fingers clicking on the computer keyboard, the room was the quietest place on the third floor.

They learned from Leeland that both Haws and

Barbish were now in surgery, Haws at Methodist Hospital where he'd asked to be taken and Barbish at Ben Taub. Haws was going to be fine, but Barbish was in serious condition. In addition to his exploded right knee, he had suffered a life-threatening brain concussion, which he apparently sustained when he fell and hit his head against the curb after Marley shot him. Tough luck. If Barbish died or had brain damage, they might never learn the truth about the hits on Louise Ackley and Lalo Montalvo.

'What about Mirel Farr?' Palma said.

'Well, actually, she's at Ben Taub, too,' Leeland said. 'Getting her jaw wired up. Uh, she broke it somehow during all this. I'm not sure of the details. Lieutenant Corbeil's still over there with a couple of our guys and a team from vice. Farr's records could be a lot of help.' He looked at Grant. 'Anything at Reynolds's?'

'I don't think so, at least nothing immediately conclusive.'

That was news to Palma. On the drive back from the St. Regis, Grant had politely but firmly fended off Palma's questions. She had let it go for the moment, but she wasn't any good at being put off. Grant was going to have to cough it up.

'But Carmen photographed Reynolds's calendar and address book,' Grant said. 'They're in the photo lab now, and they're supposed to bring a copy up to you when the prints are ready. Did you get Reynolds's military record?'

'Right here,' Leeland said, reaching for a manila folder which he yanked from under a stack of others. He opened it in front of him and bit his bushy mustache with his lower teeth. 'Was a marine sniper in Nam from February 1968 to July 1971. Three tours. Requested a fourth, but was turned down and shipped home. Discharged in September 1971. He had . . .' Leeland paused for effect, '. . . ninety-one confirmed kills.'

'And an honorable discharge?' Grant asked.

Leeland nodded.

'Any psychological analysis in his medical section?'

Leeland shook his head.

'The Corps protects its own.'

'Have you heard from Birley?' Palma asked.

'Yeah, as a matter of fact . . .' Leeland leaned over and lifted a page on a notepad, 'He's out in Briar Grove right now talking to a woman who spent a lot of time with Denise Kaplan Reynolds during the year before she disappeared. Here's a picture of Denise,' he said, pulling a snapshot from a folder and handing it to Palma. 'She's blond, but beyond that I can't see that she looks anything like the victims.'

Palma looked at Denise. The photograph was made five months before she disappeared by one of the women she had been seeing in Samenov's group. It was a four-by-six color shot. Denise was standing on an empty beach, the shoreline disappearing behind her into the coastal haze. She must have been tossing food to the seagulls, because two of them hovered low in the sky behind her. She was developing a first-class sunburn, and the brisk Gulf air was making her short brown hair stand up on one side of her head. She was not a particularly attractive woman, but she had a kind face and large eyes that sagged slightly at their outside corners, giving her a vaguely doleful appearance.

Palma handed the photograph to Grant, who held it in both hands and looked at it. She watched the miniscule jerky movements of his eyes as he took in the receding shoreline and the floating birds and the sunburned face of the woman who smiled hesitantly, as if by permission, at the photographer. Palma saw Grant's eyes settle on Denise's face and stay there. He looked at her for a long time.

Grant's own face was indecipherable, an attribute that was beginning to get on Palma's nerves. It was not that the man was stone-faced. His face was not expressionless. The real peculiarity about him was that he never showed her anything that she knew damn well he hadn't thought out beforehand and had decided he wanted her to see. When they had met at the airport he showed a convivial smile, a good-humored, pleasant demeanor. When she had confronted him in Frisch's office that morning, he showed a thoughtful seriousness in keeping with his role. When they had lunch together he knew to loosen up a bit, ease back on the formality in order to soothe her ruffled feathers. And it wasn't that he lacked spontaneity. His manner never seemed forced or bogus. But the irritating thing to Palma was that it was when his mind was turning on its most interesting course that his face became the most enigmatic — the most deceptive. She didn't care about the convivial Grant, or the thoughtfully serious Grant, or the eased-back Grant. She wanted to know the Sander Grant who looked at the photograph of the plain and mysteriously disappeared Denise Kaplan Reynolds and was so moved by what he saw that he believed it was necessary to disguise his feelings.

'Birley's talked to two women, besides the one he's with now, who've had sexual relationships with Kaplan,' Leeland said, interrupting the silence. 'And all of them claimed they didn't know whether Kaplan had ever had affairs with any of the victims. Birley said he thought a couple of them were lying, that they were afraid to talk because of the killings.'

Nancy Castle, who had been making and answering telephone calls while they were standing there, hung up the telephone, looked at her watch, made a quick note, and waved the paper at Leeland.

'That was Garro,' she said. 'He and Childs have taken over from Cushing and Boucher, and they've followed Reynolds and his date back to his condo. Garro and Childs have gone into the surveillance van, and one of the electronics men is putting a bug and a listening device in Reynold's car. They'll sit on him there.'

'Cushing and Boucher are gone home?' Leeland asked.

'Said they'd check in again in six hours.'

'Okay, we've talked with Broussard,' Palma told Leeland, and she went over the highlights of the interview, passing on the facts as they had learned them.

'You mean the guy's had all three victims as clients?'

Leeland's solemn eyes widened.

Palma nodded.

'Damn. So how do you read this guy?'

Palma turned to Grant. She wasn't about to answer that. She wanted to hear what Grant had to say. He looked at her; he knew what she was doing.

'Okay, let's talk about Reynolds's condo first,' Grant said, his eyes pulling away from her and going to Leeland. 'You remember I said photographing his place, looking through it, would tell me something about him? Well, it did, but it wasn't what I'd expected. I've known a few men who were snipers in Nam. All of them were long on native intelligence, and tended to be patient, exacting, obsessive. So I wasn't surprised at the sniper shell souvenirs, except for the number of them. After that girl, Terry, told Carmen of Reynolds's rifle scope fantasy involving Louise Ackley, the souvenirs were almost expected.

'What I didn't expect was that Reynolds would go down a notch on my suspect list.'

Leeland looked at Palma, but she kept her eyes on Grant.

'I've said several times that sexually motivated killers were souvenir keepers,' Grant began explaining, 'but the sniper shells don't count. Not in this particular context, anyway. If we were investigating sniper killings, okay. But they mean nothing in these cases. I don't doubt that Reynolds has problems, but I don't think they're our problems. Not on the serial killings, anyway.'

'Then you didn't find anything?' Leeland couldn't believe it. Lack of sleep had puffed his eyes and emphasized his weighty jowls, giving him the countenance of a mildly surprised walrus.

'That place was empty as far as any reference to these cases is concerned. Nothing. But Reynolds is one cold individual — no picture albums, no mementos or references to his family, no letters to anyone or from anyone ... nothing of any personal nature at all. The place could have been a motel room occupied by someone different every night. I imagine,' he said to Palma, 'the rifle Terry told you about is kept in his office or the trunk of his car.'

'Couldn't he be keeping his souvenirs there too?' Leeland asked.

'I just can't feature it,' Grant said, folding his arms across his chest and standing swaybacked to relieve the tired muscles in his lower back. 'He'd have kept them at home, well hidden maybe, but they'd be in that condo. We were there a little over two hours. I've had a lot of practice looking for those sorts of things. If they'd been there, I think I would have found them.'

'Broussard, on the other hand ...' Palma said, as if cuing him.

Grant nodded. 'Exactly. This guy we've got to look into. Aside from the obvious facts we've already mentioned, there were a couple of things that really impressed me. The facts he gave us about child abuse ... female offenders.' He looked at Palma. 'That must've done your heart good. But the point is,' he addressed Leeland again, 'he wasn't expecting us, and even if he had been I doubt if he could have anticipated our line of questioning. Yet he rattled off those percentages of various abuses as if he'd just looked them up. Two possibilities: either he was mightily impressed by those facts and figures when he read them somewhere and took special note to remember them, or he has a specific interest in that subject and has a ready recall of the statistics. I'm guessing the latter.'

'He did say almost all of his clients were women,' Palma reminded him. 'It seems logical to me that he'd be up on those kinds of studies.'

'Right.' Grant nodded warily as if knowing she was going to say that. 'But the next point isn't so easy to explain. When I kept after him to speculate about what kind of thinking process our murderer might follow, he was reluctant to do it. Didn't want to at all. But when he finally *did*, his observations were expressed in the first person, not the third person. It's true I'd asked him to try to put himself in the killer's place. Still, the choice of pronouns was significant. Additionally, his assessment was perfect, accurate in every aspect. I don't think this can be explained by way of his being a psychologist. Criminal psychology *is* a specialty. Unless a psychoanalyst had a particular interest in criminal psychology, he'd have to do considerable reading before he could rattle off the information Broussard gave us this evening. But he had a ready grasp of it, and of this *precise* criminal typology — the sexual killer.'

Grant said this with unmistakable satisfaction. Obviously, Broussard was tracking true to form.

'The interesting thing,' Grant added, 'is that he gave it all to me. Straight out. He made no effort to blow smoke at me. It was as if he was saying, "Okay, here's my life, here's what it's all about. But even knowing this won't do you any good because I'm still more clever than you by half." He was challenging me. And that's what I was waiting for.'

'Christ, when you think of it, he was extraordinarily cooperative,' Palma said. 'Victimology, volunteering that he was Samenov's doctor.'

'Exactly,' Grant said again. 'We've got a lot of work to do on this guy.' Suddenly he turned back to Leeland. 'Anything new from the lab?'

'Oh, yeah, there is.' Leeland reached around to his desk and shuffled through his files until he found a yellow-tagged report from the crime lab. 'LeBrun brought it over shortly after five o'clock.' He flipped over the cover sheet and read a moment.

The telephones had been ringing steadily, keeping Castle and the clerk busy. When both of them were on the telephones as they were now, Leeland and Palma and Grant had to move a little closer together to cut down on the noise level.

'Okay,' Leeland said. 'Remember we had five unidentified pubic hairs collected off of Dorothy Samenov's bed. Of those five, three came from one source and the other two came from another single source. Well, the three pubic hairs matched Vickie's.'

'I'll be damned,' Palma said. 'But we still have a

chronology problem. A bath or shower most likely would have washed away any hair she picked up from sexual partners. If it was her habit to bathe in the mornings, then the period of time during which she could have had sexual relations would have spanned, say, from six in the morning until the time she was killed at approximately ten o'clock that night.'

'She might have bathed when she came home from work,' Grant said. 'Then she would've picked up those hairs within about three hours' or less, assuming it would have taken her, say, forty-five minutes to drive home from Cristof's and bathe.'

'You might be able to account for her workday hours,' Leeland said. 'She might have been with someone practically every minute of the day, which would confirm she was clean until she drove away from the club.'

'Which would put both sexual encounters within that three-hour period,' Grant said.

'Birley and Leeland speculated from the beginning that she might have had a ménage à trois,' Palma said, looking at Leeland.

'But I didn't have any idea that one of them would be Vickie Kittrie,' Leeland said. 'Damn, we didn't even know we were talking about women.'

'We still don't,' Grant picked up the lab report from Leeland's desk and looked at it. 'We still have two unknown pubic hairs. These women are *bi*sexual.'

Palma was disappointed. if Grant was seeing any validity at all in her theory — and she hoped that his elimination of Reynolds as a major suspect was an indication that he was — then he was not letting go of the traditional male killer theory very easily. But, realistically, she couldn't expect him to.

'And these were all telogen hairs?'

'That's right,' Leeland said. 'No sheath cells, can't be DNA-tested, can't be sex-typed.'

'Still, it's likely that Kittrie had been sexually involved with her within, at least, three hours of her death,' Grant said.

'Unless Samenov hadn't bathed that evening and she had been with Vickie sometime earlier in the day,' Palma interjected. 'Or unless she, for some reason, didn't bathe that morning or even the night before and she was with someone twenty-four hours earlier in a ménage à trois or separately, twenty-four to thirty-six hours apart.'

'Or,' Leeland said, 'unless someone planted the hairs there, either Kittrie's or the others, or both.'

'Reynolds,' Palma said. 'He would've, and could've done that. He's had access to Kittrie's hair.'

But Grant wasn't interested in Reynolds anymore. The evidence might well eliminate him as a suspect later on or, as was likely, implicate him in the Ackley-Montalvo deaths, but as far as Grant was concerned he was out of the picture on the serial killings. It had been a quick reversal, but Grant didn't waste any time on rehashing previous miscalculations. Broussard now commanded his full attention.

'For all we know right now, Broussard could've had access to her hair too,' Grant said. 'I think we're going to find the good doctor's sex life very interesting, and I'm not going to be too quick to exclude any of these women from having a part in it.'

'How realistic is it to believe that Broussard would've thought of something like this?' Leeland asked.

'Hell,' Grant said, 'whoever's killing these women would have had the intelligence, and probably the inclination, to have thought of everything we can think of, and I'm quite sure much more. You bet he could have planted the hair.' He thought a moment, tossed the lab report onto Leeland's desk, and reached out and pulled up a straight-backed metal chair. He propped one foot on a bottom back rung.

'On the other hand,' he said, gripping the back of the chair with both hands, his arms straight out, 'I'm wary of getting too fancy here. It's easy to fool yourself with speculation. I've screwed up more than once doing just this sort of thing. It's too easy to do, especially when you know you've got a formidable adversary. But we've got to keep

it clean.' He looked at Palma with the first genuine grin
she had seen from him. 'We ought to take your dad's
advice, Carmen. We need to decide what *didn't* happen.'

Leeland nodded thoughtfully, his eyes staying on
Grant, who was now loosening his tie as he studied the
flowcharts of events that Leeland and Castle had
diagramed on a chalkboard behind Leeland's desk.

'You're right,' Leeland said. 'But I'll tell you, I've never
seen anything quite like this. The facts accumulate, but
they don't seem to add up to anything.'

'They will,' Grant said. 'They always do. We ought to
do a couple of things, and unfortunately, I guess we'll
have to wait until Monday now, but we need to check
with the American Psychiatric Association and the American Psychoanalytic Association to see if either of them
have ever had any grievances filed against Dominick
Broussard. Also,' he said, 'even though he lives in a ritzy
neighborhood and those areas are usually pretty tight-
lipped when it comes to giving out information about
each other, we ought to have people out there knocking
on doors. See if Broussard has domestic help. These
people ride the same bus lines together, and talk about
their employers is often a major pastime. They're good
sources. We've got to find out more about him.

'I thought it was interesting, too, that he felt compelled
to tell us that he's likely not to have alibis for the nights
in question. Actually, he already knows he doesn't. He
realized that when he read the newspaper account of
Mello's death which summarized all three murders and
gave the dates.

'My back's breaking,' he said, taking his foot off the
chair rung, turning the chair around and sitting in it.
'Christ,' he groaned.

Palma sat down on the edge of Castle's desk beside her
purse, and Leeland sat in his own desk chair.

'And we have to do something with Vickie Kittrie,'
Grant said, crossing his legs a little stiffly

'What we do with her is we make her a suspect,' Palma
said. 'Once more,' her voice was tight with frustration,

'we're working awfully hard to avoid the obvious. We've just been through all kinds of contortions with the chronology of Samenov's last day to try to explain how Kittrie's and someone else's pubic hair got mixed in with Samenov's — except to conclude that she was with Samenov when she died. That's ludicrous. Why the hell don't we *consider* the obvious that Kittrie was with Samenov when Samenov died and that Kittrie might have killed her? It's really wrongheaded to keep avoiding this possibility.'

'But Jesus, Carmen,' Leeland said, 'she gave you her pubic hair without so much as a mild complaint.'

'Oh, come on. What was she going to do, make me get the search warrant? Was that going to look suspicious, or what?'

'She called the police *herself*,' Leeland persisted. 'You said in your own report that she was practically distraught over Samenov's death. She fainted when she saw the body, for Christ's sake.'

Palma looked at Leeland. 'Yeah, I wrote that. And she *was* distraught. And even if she did faint, neither of those occurrences is even half a decent reason to eliminate her as a suspect. I know women who don't need a reason to cry. It's their first response to everything unexpected. Vicki has cried *every* time I've seen her. And do you think that rookie who was with her when she fainted would know a theatrical faint if he saw one? I talked to him too, and he was as shaken at finding the body as Kittrie seemed to be.'

'Look, I don't see any reason to go through this kind of thing,' Grant said to Palma. 'Just go after her. Start with her alibis and keep going. Let's find out if she knows Broussard. How is she to interview?'

'Tough. She runs the gamut from cooperative to hysterical. She can be intractable, but not bitchy, not dykey. She's completely feminine, so her resistance to cooperation comes on like little-girl stubborn.' Palma gave an apologetic twist of her mouth. 'I'll admit, after what I've learned about her in the last couple of days her bimbo act seems to have been pretty calculating. Which convinces me all the more that we'd be making a serious mistake to overlook her simply because she doesn't fit the formula.'

Grant hung his head in thought a moment. 'We need to talk to Mirel Farr as soon as the doctors will let us. She ought to be able to give us considerable insight on Kittrie. I think we can make it clear to her that she's in enough hot water that it would be to her benefit to cooperate with us a lot more than she was willing to cooperate with Marley and Haws.' He looked at Leeland. 'Would you call us as soon as the interview's possible?' Leeland nodded, making a note.

'But most important,' Grant said, 'is that it's essential to get a round-the-clock surveillance on Broussard. What are our chances of getting that? What's the mood of the administration? Are they going to want to put up the money to cover this?'

Leeland grimaced and flicked his head toward Frisch's office across the squad room.

'That's what's going on in there right now,' he said. 'My feeling is they'll go for it. Frisch anticipated we might need several surveillance teams, so he's already pitching for it. You're not thinking we should pull them off Reynolds?'

Grant shook his head. 'No, he's still your best candidate for the Ackley-Montalvo hit, using Barbish. When he finds out tomorrow that Barbish has been picked up, he's likely to do something rash, or if not rash, then he's likely to tip us to something. I'd have your surveillance people get into Reynolds's car trunk tonight, too. Before he hears about Barbish's arrest. What about Barbish's gun?'

'It's the same type weapon used in the hit,' Leeland said. 'But they'll have to wait until in the morning to run the tests.'

Grant nodded, thinking. 'Okay,' he said, standing. 'Can you let us know about the Broussard surveillance?'

Leeland nodded, already making another note.

All three telephones in the task force room rang at the same time and Leeland, Castle, and the clerk-typist answered them simultaneously.

49

Strange bedrooms are intrinsically erotic. I've known that since I was a child, long before I knew the meaning of 'erotic.' I have never been here before, and I have come early so that I can enjoy the subtle but potent pleasure of entering someone else's home alone. I do not turn on the lights. This is an older home, and the woman who lives here has decided to save on her electric bill by turning off her air conditioner and throwing open the windows, taking advantage of the lower night temperatures and the recent cooling rains.

I have quickly walked through it, moving carefully in the blotchy pools of light filtering through the windows in every room, imagining the woman who lives here and the way she moves from room to room as I have just done. At first I deliberately avoided the bedroom itself, teasing myself the way a stripper teases a roomful of men who want to be teased, knowing the way of the game. Not yet. Every room but the bedroom. I passed by, feeling the pull of it, but not going in. Not yet. I glimpsed its opened door from another room and felt the first quiverings between my legs, then moved to yet another room and looked back at it, anticipating the sweet aches that were still to come on the other side of that inviting doorway.

But now I stand here, looking into the bedroom. From the windows on the other side of the room where sheer curtains have been pushed aside and the black silhouettes of palm fronds peep around the edges of the dirty glass, a madder blue light comes into the room and glazes all the hard surfaces as though they were porcelain and penetrates the curtains and the sheets on the unmade bed as though they had been stained in dye.

The closet door is open, and I walk over to it and catch the subtle weight of aged perfumes. It is a particular kind of odor, this fragrance of perfumes on dresses hanging in closets. It is the olfactory equivalent of pastels, the breath of an essence, rather than the essence itself. I step to the closet and run my hand along the blue dresses, the whole length of them in front of the opened door. And then I smell my hand. It is a kind of intercourse that I smell there, her fragrance on my flesh. An intercourse without her knowing, as if I were a deity and could disguise myself as a cloud or a mist of gold and in that form could partake of her sex, wherever I wanted, whenever I wanted. She could not deny me.

I find two empty hangers in the closet and begin removing my clothes. When I am completely naked I hang my clothes on the hangers and place them among her blue dresses. Later, when I take them out to put them on again, they will smell ever so faintly of the pastel fragrances of her dresses.

There is a chest of drawers near the closet, and I go there and open the drawers until I find the lingerie. Piece by piece I take it out and hold it up to the blue light. All of it is blue, lighter and darker shades of blue. Each piece I take between my lips and, rubbing my lips together, feel the smooth fabric gliding against itself, nylon and silk. When I have put every piece between my lips I pull out all the drawers and drape the lingerie over the drawers. I hang the bras horizontally. There are not enough drawers so I hang them from the doornobs, from the pictures and lamps, from the mirror, from the back and seat of a chair, everywhere I can find the space until it is all displayed, all having passed between my lips.

I go to the unmade bed, very much aware of my excitement and what it is doing to my body. The tumbled sheets are cool, the heat of the last body to lie here long dissipated. But not the odors. Naked I crawl into the madder blue sheets and smell the woman who lives here. Once again I am like a deity, a blue immortal entering between the sex of this unknowing woman, the folds of her sheets like the folds, the innermost folds, of her sex. I pull the sheets around me, between my legs, under my arms, around my neck and feet, only my head sticking out of her blue vagina with the dark shadows of the surrounding room like the dark pubes of her vulva. I feel bright in my face and secure in my soul, riding between the legs of this woman, inside her, looking out at the world and imagining what we must look like, big she and little I, as though we were a painting by Frida Kahlo.

The sheets quickly grow warm in the muggy night, then hot. When I am thoroughly drenched in perspiration, I come out of the sheets, slick with sweat I come out of a blue birth. I kick at the covers and fling them off, get them away from me, strip them loose at the foot of the bed, and throw them in a corner. Then I lie back on the bare bottom sheet, the only one left, spread out my arms and legs, and lie in the center of the bed, alone, feeling the engulfing tickling spreading over every tiny millimeter of me as the perspiration evaporates and leaves me cooled. But I still smell the sheets, which I now have made some part of myself as well as of her, by virtue of the moisture of my recent blue birth.

And I wait.

She has a key, too, and I hear it in the lock of the front door. Though she does not live here she has been here before, and I hold my breath and listen to her step onto the wooden floors. The door closes behind her. I have not turned on any lights nor does she, knowing she mustn't change anything. Whatever she finds, she accepts. But her steps are slow as she moves through the barely dark, negotiating shadows and faint patches of pale light. Silence as she crosses a rug, and then her footsteps again on the wooden floor through the rooms to the bedroom doorway, where she stops. The light here is bluer, but more telling. I know she sees me on the bed. I begin to breathe again, my mouth closed, sucking the much-wanted air through my nostrils with whooshing gusts I know she can hear because they fill the room.

I hear a tap as she kicks off one of her heels. A double tap as the other falls. I hear the sound of clothes, the soft thup of buttons yanked through their holes, a zip, a snap, the slump of clothing sliding to the floor and the muted pop of elastic against bare flesh.

When I roll over to face her she is close, within arm's reach, bathed in the madder blue light coming from the window behind my back. She has already begun to work on herself, her legs bowed slightly as though she were playing a cello, her right elbow out away from her body, moving ever so subtly from the action of her hand. Her head is tilted back, her hair hanging long over her shoulder and behind her as her left hand cups the bottom of a lavish breast with an indigo nipple.

When I was a child I used to watch my mother do this, precisely this.

Soon, in the pale light I can see that she is perspiring, that her hand is moving more vigorously, her legs are bowing even more. Hyacinth rivulets are streaming down the sides of her forehead, one, two, down her arched neck, headed toward the indigo nipple of the breast that is rolling free, the one she is not holding. Her legs continue to bow until she is almost on her knees, panting as I had panted after holding my breath, only she is making sounds in her throat as well, hurried, sad sounds that suddenly make me want to cry.

I turn away from her to the madder blue windows and the black palms. I feel them coming, coming, coming from way down inside my heart, crowding up into my chest like a sob, gorging through the narrow channel of my neck, scattering frantically up through the fissures of my face and into my eyes. I lie listening to her, to the quicker, frantic, ululating approach to her climax, and when it happens, when she gasps as though she is being stabbed and stabbed, the tears spring from my eyes in quick

streamlets, limpid, profuse ejaculations that run down my
face and take me back to my childhood, to my mother
slumped against the bed in exhaustion. Then for an
instant, for a clean, fleeting instant, I feel exactly as I did
then, my emotions a moil of fear and desire and disconso-
lation . . . of a longing for something I did not then understand, nor do I understand it even now.

I lie still. Her head is on the bed and a great luxurious
sweep of her hair is touching my naked hip.

I would, and do, go to great lengths to recapture that
brief, precise emotion from my childhood. Great lengths,
and my abiding fear is that someday I will not be able to
reproduce it just exactly as I remember it. Indeed, it is
becoming more difficult to do with passing time, and this
has caused me hours upon hours of anxiety. _Why_ is this
threatening to elude me? What would my life be like
without it? Thinking of it panics me. I have tried to re-
create the emotions of that moment by simply casting my
mind back to those childish years when the emotion itself
was born. A few times I have actually done it. But more
and more it requires a woman, young as my mother had
been young, her breasts as ample as her breasts had been,
her flesh as smooth and taut as hers had been when she
first invited me to share. It has required this. And the
aftermath. It works now only when I know in the lower
substrates of my mind that the aftermath is coming,
though I do not think of it or anticipate it consciously. The
aftermath is my gift to her. Bittersweet. And I think she
would understand it. I know she would. For she is the
one who taught me what I know, and made me what I
am. She was the one who blurred the borders between
love and lust, who stole my childhood, and taught me
while I was still too young to know, the meaning of
betrayal.

The woman has recovered her strength now, and I feel
her moving against the bed, getting up and going to the
bag that I have brought and set down beside the bedroom
door. I hear her open it, her hands moving among the
things that I keep. I know what she is doing and a warm

liquid begins to flow inside me, spreading out through all my limbs until I vibrate. I keep my eyes on the black palms.

When I feel the bed moving I know she is climbing onto the bare sheet, the bed sinking here and there under the weight of her knees, shifting as she positions herself, knees on either side of me. And then I look around. She is a tall girl, long-limbed, high-hipped, and breasty. I love her breasts, which in the madder blue light, I can see are still streaked with perspiration. Her stomach is drawn flat with excitement, and she is smoothing back her hair, which has become wildly tousled. Dangling from her raised arms I can see the ropes she has tied to her wrists, and I know that others are around her ankles as well, though I cannot see them because they are doubled back behind her, alongside my own legs.

She is magnificent, and I can feel the ache beginning within my own groin, the ache that will take us beyond anything she has ever experienced. I rise up and embrace her body, my arms around her buttocks and I pull her vulva to me and feel its wiry lubricity against the depression in my throat, smell the singular fragrance of her sweat. I take my tongue from the top of her pubes, up the center of her stomach to the depression that is her navel. I encircle it with my lips and begin to nurse, feeling her stomach against my face, feeling her fingers thread themselves into my hair.

Of the things I am about to do to her she has no intimation, though she thinks she knows why she is here and what is going to happen. It will be a rare thing. For her, a singular event. For me it will be yet another sequel, the price of reliving that haunting passion from my childhood, the price for keeping it alive though it has caused me more anguish in my life than if I had been possessed by devils.

50

By the time they had made their way through the crowded hallway, down the elevator, and across the lobby and out to the front of the administration building where Palma had double-parked, it was a quarter past ten o'clock. Palma pulled out onto Houston Street and pushed the department car under Memorial Drive and quickly up onto the Gulf Freeway. They were always circling south of downtown and Palma was easing over to the right to pick up the Southwest Freeway before either of them spoke.

'Tired?' Palma asked.

'Yeah, that too,' Grant said, looking out the window toward the twin cluster of skyscrapers that distinguished Greenway Plaza and the Post Oak district of downtown.

'In the mood for any particular kind of food?' Palma asked.

'No, you decide. I'll eat whatever you want.'

'Then I'm going home,' Palma said. 'How do sandwiches strike you?'

'Oh, sure, that'd be perfect.' He was surprised, looking around at her. 'But wouldn't you rather not go to the trouble? A diner's fine with me.'

'If it's all the same to you,' she said, 'I'd really rather go home. At my place, we don't have to keep our shoes on.'

It wasn't until she was unlocking the front door with

Sander Grant standing beside her that Palma had a moment's apprehension. All of Grant's talk about what you could tell about a person from their surroundings, from what they kept on their bookshelves and in their closets, in their refrigerators and in their medicine cabinets. She had the sudden feeling that she was giving everything away, giving Grant the advantage from the moment they walked through the door. The advantage to what? To hell with it, she thought, and pushed the door open.

She invited him to make himself at home, and offered to take his suit coat and hang it up, but Grant just shook his head as he pulled it off and draped it over the back of one of the dining room chairs.

'There's a guest room and bath through there,' Palma said, motioning past the stairs as she laid her purse on the dining room table.

'Yeah, I'd like to wash up,' Grant nodded. 'Thanks.'

Palma just about had everything pulled out of the refrigerator when Grant came back into the kitchen, rolling up his sleeves.

'What can I do?'

'That's okay,' Palma said. 'Just pour yourself whatever you want to drink. There's some wine and beer in the refrigerator, and some iced tea, I think.'

'What about you?' he asked.

'Wine is fine,' she said. 'Glasses are up there.'

Grant got the glasses out of the cabinet and poured one for each of them and set one beside her on the tile counter. Then he leaned against the cabinets and watched her slice the roast beef and smoked ham, and lay out a platter of green onions and olives and cheeses and celery and tomatoes and sliced boiled eggs. Grant started nibbling. Neither of them spoke, which didn't seem odd to her at all, but comfortable. She was in no mood to chat, and if he didn't have anything to say she didn't want to be worn out any more than she already was by trying to exchange niceties. But Grant didn't say anything, just stood there watching her, taking an olive or pickle, drinking and thinking. She would have liked to know what he was thinking, though, without having to bother to pull it out of him.

'After being married,' he said without preamble, 'how do you like living alone?'

Jesus, she thought. She tilted her head and laughed a little. 'I wasn't married that long.'

'Well, you'd gotten used to it, though, hadn't you?'

'Yeah, I had,' she conceded, finishing slicing the bread. 'Here it is. Help yourself.'

They started making their sandwiches.

'I don't have much of a frame of reference,' he said, spreading Dijon mustard on his bread. 'A good number of the men I work with are divorced. Sometimes you hear people talk about their divorces, how tough it was or how they've remained good friends with their ex-wives. It's hard to imagine, to put myself in their place.'

'It's hard to imagine even when it's happened to you,' Palma said, sipping her wine, this time watching him. He made his sandwich with the preoccupied air of a man who had made a lot of them and didn't need to give his full attention to what he was doing. When he finished he took one of the knives and cut the sandwich diagonally.

'You've gotten used to it, though, living alone?'

'You get used to anything,' she said, and the second she said it she knew that Grant hadn't found that to be the case. But he nodded and stepped around her for a bottle of Soave and refilled their glasses. They took their plates and glasses and the bottle into the living room, where they set them on the small table in front of the sofa. Palma kicked off her shoes.

He grinned and sat on the edge of the sofa and untied his shoes too, and slipped them off. Then he pulled out his shirttail and the two of them sat on the floor. Palma leaning back against the front of an armchair and Grant leaning back against the sofa, their legs stretched out in front of them, almost toe-to-toe. Grant sipped his wine and looked at Palma again. Then he smiled.

'I appreciate this,' he said.

They ate for a few minutes in silence and Palma noticed that even though Grant's mind quickly wandered, he truly seemed to be enjoying himself. She was glad she had guessed that he would have wanted to do this sort of thing. She knew he traveled a lot, doing exactly what he was doing here, a job that in itself must be something of a burden, a chain of ghosts. And she knew that motels and hotels, at least the kind you often had to stay in on government budgets, could be excruciatingly depressing. She was glad she had read this much correctly, that he seemed to be at ease. She was glad that he had stood at the cabinet and nibbled off the plate, and that he had pulled out his shirttail. All of those little things she had noted while pretending not to, all of them as welcome and comforting to her as the memory of an Eden that never was. 'Yeees-ter-days, yees-ter-days, day I knew as happy, sweet, sequestered days.' For all her man troubles, Billie Holliday knew what men should have been, even if they never were.

'Maybe men and women handle this sort of thing differently,' he said, and when she looked around he was already looking at her. She didn't catch his meaning, and he saw it in her face.

'About getting used to anything.'

'Oh, listen,' she said. 'That was kind of a flippant remark. Besides, divorce is different . . .'

'Different from what?'

Palma looked at him, caught off guard. 'Well, I . . . thought . . .'

'No, I know what you're talking about,' he said quickly, as if he wished he hadn't questioned her.

Palma looked down at her sandwich, put her plate aside, and picked up her wineglass.

'But, about being alone,' she said, looking at him. 'Women do handle it better.'

'Yeah, that's what I read, too.' Grant put his plate aside also and reached to refill his glass. He offered her some, but she waved him off. He had already polished off three while she was still on her second. Pulling up one leg, he rested his forearm on his knee.

'I'm not that big on machismo,' he said. 'But I used to think I could handle a few things most people couldn't. But those things didn't have anything to do with loneliness. When I confronted that ... well, it cut me down to size. Never experienced anything like it. Never.'

He stopped, gave a little self-conscious laugh, and took a drink. 'Don't worry,' he said. 'I've already worked through "maudlin."'

Palma looked into her wineglass. She was sorry he was suddenly self-conscious, protective of getting into something too personal, something that might bore or offend her. She didn't want him to get away from the thing that had prompted him to talk in the first place, to make shop-talk out of it. More than anything else she wanted him to talk about Marne. It didn't offend her. It wasn't like he was talking about an old girlfriend. This was different. Grant was different, and she wanted to know what he wanted to say. She wanted to know what he would choose to tell her, and what he would choose to keep to himself.

'It's been three years since she died?' Palma asked.

'And three months.'

'You ever think about remarrying?'

'Yeah, that's a funny thing,' he said. 'For a year or so, no. It would have been like adultery, worse. Then at one point ... at one point, it got to where I didn't think of anything else. I thought I *had* to remarry. Thought I'd go nuts if I didn't remarry. Actually, I panicked, a sort of psychological hyperventilation. I sold the place where we'd lived for years, where the girls had grown up, and moved into Washington. Georgetown. It was a joke. After all those years being married, I didn't even know how to go about meeting another woman. The thought of going out to bars or clubs was laughable to me. I couldn't see myself doing it. I was still invited to all the same homes and all the same parties Marne and I used to go to. But of course, I was odd man out. Then they started inviting a single woman, a widow, a divorcée. They had to be one of the two, to be my age. She'd just be there. Hell.' He grinned, remembering. 'It was ridiculous.'

'So you never dated anyone?'

Grant drank his wine. 'No one they intended for me to date. No one they knew.'

'Then you did? Or do?'

'Yes, I did,' he said, sobering.

She waited, but he didn't continue, and he didn't act as if he was going to.

'A bit of a scandal,' she said.

His eyes shot up at her.

'I'll tell you what I know,' she said, realizing it was a bold thing to do, knowing she was risky offending him rather than breaking down more barriers and getting closer. But she remembered that Garrett had said Grant had gotten through it all right. Chinese lady and all. And she wanted him to know she really didn't know anything.

'She was a Chinese diplomat's wife. Beautiful. You fell in love with her, very seriously. You married. It ended suddenly. That's it.'

'Jesus Christ,' Grant said, looking at her. He didn't seem surprised, didn't even seem shocked, or offended. 'The rumor mill. I don't know whether to be amazed by the fact that it got down this far, or by the fact that that was all of the story that survived.' He drank some more wine, almost finished the glass.

She had made up her mind in the split second after she told him what she knew that she wouldn't go a step further with it. If he didn't want to speak another syllable about it, then she would let it go, reluctantly. But she didn't want to crowd him. She still didn't know enough about him to do that, and she was quickly gaining a kind of admiration for his honesty that she hadn't anticipated. She didn't want him to feel anything he didn't want to feel, maybe develop a feeling of obligation to go on with his story, or to quickly change the subject and get him off the hook. Then again, who was she kidding? Did she think that any conversation they might have was going to make Sander Grant talk about anything he didn't want to talk about? He had been in his line of work a lot longer than she had, and reading human nature was the brick and mortar of his profession. If he didn't want to talk about it, he wouldn't, and he wasn't going to feel guilty about it.

'I'm surprised you didn't get a lot more detail,' Grant said. 'There was certainly plenty of it.' He finished off his wine and set the glass down. Stretching his legs out in front of him again, he crossed them at the ankles and interlaced the fingers of his hands.

'I met her at a Bureau function, the sort of Washington social thing I never went to before Marne died,' he said. 'But I'd moved into Georgetown by then, the girls were up in New York, I was sick of television, and I couldn't concentrate enough to read a book. So I went to this thing. Black tie. I hadn't worn one in fifteen years. Went to the tailor, had everything put in shape. If nothing else, I thought I would get in some good people-watching, better than airports.

'The party was in Georgetown, too, so I didn't have far to go. I hadn't been there ten minutes, obligatory drink in hand, other hand in pocket, feeling one hundred and ten percent out of place, when I ran into a guy I used to know before I went to Quantico. He was now in counterintelligence, and I hadn't seen him in years. We talked a long time, and then I guess he thought it was time to circulate so he steered me around and introduced me to a number of people. One of them was a Chinese woman.'

Grant fiddled with his watch, adjusted the leather band, wound it. He reached for his glass and poured it about half full, then held it in his lap without drinking.

'I was caught off guard,' he continued. 'And to be honest, it didn't take much to do that at that time. She was married ... to a diplomatic liaison attached to the Chinese Embassy. Educated in Beijing, then Oxford, she had several degrees and was taking courses at Georgetown University. Her husband wasn't at the party that night, and I hate to think how I must have acted. In appearance she was Marne's polar opposite.'

He looked at his glass, as if his allusion to the physical comparison of the two women had been a painful slip of the tongue.

'I think it's fair to say that if someone had tried to keep us apart I would have risked my career to continue seeing her. But no one did, no one knew what was happening, at least that's what I thought. The affair was nothing less than a shared frenzy to be together. It was something we didn't even have to articulate, and never did.

'It was late winter in Washington, the time of year when the snow seems interminable and you get restless for spring. We met most of the time at my place because I lived alone and no one in the neighborhood knew me that well yet. She was an artist of discretion. We squandered time.'

Grant had to swallow with emotion, but he raised his wineglass to his mouth to have a reason.

'Long afternoons in bed, watching the winter light change in the room, the shadows on the ceiling growing longer as the hours passed. I was ... absolutely ... spell-bound. In that relationship, reality had no place whatsoever. For either of us. When we met alone, whether at my place or a country inn in Virginia for the weekend, even a hotel, we stepped through a doorway to another time, another place.'

Grant cleared his throat. 'I never even asked her how she managed to steal so many hours away from whatever life she had apart from me.

'By spring our affair was a nonsecret. It caused problems, for her, for me. She was already in the throes of a divorce. But we didn't stop. Never in my life had I been so ... reckless. Then one rainy afternoon — it was in the middle of April — her divorce was finalized. We were married within twenty-four hours.'

Grant put the wineglass to his lips once again and drank, holding the Soave in his mouth a moment before swallowing it slowly.

'Everything was wonderful for a while, maybe several

months. She was back in school. But the affair should
have remained an affair. She was brilliant, an intellectual,
really, but the impetuosity that had excited and ... ignited
me during those stolen, sex-driven afternoons turned out
to be something quite different when I saw it up close
twenty-four hours a day. She was so beautiful, and she
was impossible to live with. She was manic. She went to
school all day, studied all night, went to plays, films,
museums. She never slept, never stopped. She was
always cheerful, often euphoric, which was infectious if
you were an acquaintance or friend ... or lover. But when
you got to know her well you realized that there was
something pathological about her incessant zeal, as if she
were hungry to find something, something ill-defined
except that she expected it to be just over the horizon, in
the next lecture, or book. Or affair.

'As to that,' Grant said, pausing, 'I honestly believed
she loved me.' He paused again. 'If she could have
stopped long enough to think about it. But I couldn't
satisfy her, not any more than any one book or play or
friendship could satisfy her. It wasn't long before I knew
she was having affairs. It almost killed me when I realized
what was happening. But the maddening thing was that
by then I was beginning to understand her, and I couldn't
bring myself to condemn her for something I knew she
couldn't help. With something like that ... you just
endure it. It's a one-way hurt. You know it'll never be
anything but pain.'

Grant seemed to be at the end of his story. It was the
sketchiest sort of introduction, but Palma was spellbound,
even shocked, that he had been so brutally honest about
his own feelings, about her unfaithfulness. If Grant had
thought this brief story of his affair would satisfy her, he
was sorely mistaken. All it did was set fire to a thousand
questions. But she asked only one.

'Did you love her?'

He didn't move, and for a moment he didn't reply. His
expression did not seem to convey that he was considering how to answer the question, only that he was

remembering. Finally he said, 'Inordinately.'

He looked at her. 'Five months ago, I guess it's nearly six now, because it was ten days before Christmas, I got home from Quantico around eight o'clock in the evening, a little late. It had been dark several hours. She was gone. She'd left a letter that was meant to explain everything, but of course it was no help. She had plans and dreams, things she wanted to do and other people she wanted to do them with.

'There was an extraordinary thing about her leaving,' Grant said, almost as if he expected Palma to understand it. 'She left nothing behind. There was not any little thing of hers for me to ... have. You would have thought there would have been something, if only left by accident, a comb that might have slipped down behind a sofa cushion, a belt in a closet or drawer, a sock in the clothes hamper ... a nail file.' He shook his head. 'There was nothing. And I looked, too. There were some photographs, snapshots we'd taken of each other. They were gone. I couldn't even find a strand of hair. It was as if she had never existed.'

He shook his head again, remembering. 'The girls had gone home with school friends for the holidays. It was a hell of a Christmas.'

He looked at Palma without any kind of macho act of shrugging it off or self-conscious smile of mild embarrassment at having talked too much about himself and shown his vulnerabilities. He told it straight out of a weary bewilderment, seemingly unafraid to show the kind of blunted emotion that comes in the aftermath of a tragedy when you are worn out with grieving and tired of long suffering and the first glimmerings of objectivity have begun to color memory and experience. He seemed, if nothing else, relieved to have had the opportunity to say the things he said, and Palma suspected that this was as much as he had ever told anyone about it.

'What did your daughters think of the marriage?' she asked.

This time Grant did smile, if only a little sadly.

'They saw it for what it was,' he said. 'They met her several times. It wasn't that they didn't like her, it was just that they knew instinctively that it was going to end in disaster. It was the first Christmas I hadn't spent with the girls since they'd been born. I didn't tell them she had left. As a matter of fact, I didn't tell them for a couple of months. It wasn't until recently that I think I realized why they chose this Christmas to spend away. And I'm pretty sure of this now. She and I had gone up to New York to see them about six weeks before the holidays. I think they sensed that it was unraveling. I think they made themselves scarce, thinking it would be the merciful thing to do, not to be around when everything went to hell for me. They knew me that well. And they were right. You make a fool of yourself on a grand scale, you need a little time to lick your wounds. Talk to yourself, get a grip on the loose ends of your frayed psyche.'

'Is that what you did?'

'That's what I'm doing,' Grant clarified. 'I'm not as resilient as I used to be.' He gave a humorless snort. 'Hell, I was never as resilient as I used to be. The thing is, I was dependent on Marne for twenty-three years, emotionally dependent. I suppose unconsciously I knew that, but I really never admitted it, brought the fact out in the open and looked at it for what it was. I took her for granted in that respect. This work, these people are so goddamned bizarre that you need emotional stability more than anything else in the world. You crave normalcy. You *need* it. Marne was my steady second self. When I immersed myself in this work, when I had crawled around in the brains of grotesque minds so long that my own hands started shaking and I couldn't stop them, I could go home and put them in Marne's and know that I'd be all right. As long as she was there I knew I'd never get so far out that I couldn't get back, that she couldn't bring me back. I never had to worry that she'd lose sight of true north. When she died I had to learn to navigate by the stars. So far I've made a lot of miscalculations ... but I'm getting better at it.'

Grant was looking at her when he stopped, and just for a moment he seemed to look at her, really see her, for the first time. It was as if she could feel his eyes like a blind man's fingers feathering lightly over her features, feeling the planes and slopes, the curves and textures of her face. Then he stopped, and his eyes went back to her eyes.

'One more glass,' he said, leaning forward to the small table and pouring nearly a full glass of the white wine. He held the bottle up and looked at it against the lamp light. 'There's a couple of more glasses in there. How about it?'

She nodded, and against her better judgment extended her glass for Grant to fill.

Leaning back against the sofa, he let a smile slip past his mustache. 'It was good of you to ask the questions,' he said.

51

He began the process as if it were a tantric rite. And in a very real way it was in fact a re-enactment of those exercises before the image of the lingam-yoni in the secret sect of the Vratyas, the sacred harlots. Recognizing woman's superior spiritual energy, men knew that they could achieve realization of the divinity only through sexual and emotional union with the Vratyas. That was very much what it was like, what he was doing. Certainly the lingam-yoni was never more perfectly embodied.

But that was only a fancy fantasy, a pedantic extrapolation of his own feelings. With his training, there was hardly anything he could say or see or do that did not somehow echo a mythological meaning. And certainly this act was a perfect example of the historicity of ideas. Carl Gustav Jung had said of the anima, 'Every mother and every beloved is forced to become the carrier and embodiment of this omnipresent and ageless image, which corresponds to the deepest reality in a man. It belongs to him, this perilous image of Woman; she stands for the loyalty which in the interests of life he must sometimes forgo; she is the much needed compensation for the risks, struggles, sacrifices that all end in disappointment; she is the solace for all the bitterness of life.'

The whole thing was, really, too perfect.

He reached for the squatty little pot of concealer, dipped his finger into the cream, and began rubbing the smooth emollient under the eyes. The eyes were very important, maybe the most important. Of the Great Goddess Shakti, it was said that whole universes appeared and disappeared with the opening and shutting of her eyes; and in Syria the eyes of the Goddess Mari were her means of searching into the innermost reaches of men's souls. The power of the eyes. He worked the cream lightly, gently. The eyes were delicate.

Then the foundation mousse. He had spent a lot of time locating the right kind of foundation, something delicate enough to match the subtle color of the skin and yet dense enough to conceal the contrasting dark lines. They had made improvements in foundations over the years, whether cream or liquid or mousse, but for his purposes the mousse, this particular mousse, was best. It also took time, but not for the same reasons. He had to apply it down the neckline, unable to stop along the chin and underside of the jaw as so many women preferred, because of the darkness. He was careful on the forehead and around the temples, lightly feathering it in around the hairline.

Eye-shadow base, to hold the true color of the shadow.

Loose powder. Translucent. A dusting of it to set the makeup, the mink brush dancing around the eyes, the cheeks, the angles of the nose, the chin, tickling the corners of the mouth. It seemed like such a little thing, but it made a difference.

Powder blush. His favorite moment, returning blood to the new face, making the transformation breathe again, giving life. A delicate step, a real blush was what he wanted, not the harsh, feverish look of a whore. Too many women turned themselves into whores at this point. They think that if a little is good, a lot is better. No, it wanted a light touch.

Eye shadow. The subtleties of hue and tint and shade and tone. Again, what was wanted was pastel, the hazy effect of an old movie, a suggestion of something, not the thing itself. If an observer's attention was attracted to the shadow first, it had been misapplied.

Eyeliner. He had shopped a long time before he found the right one, a tiny soft brush, a roundish thing that could be rotated in the fingers to a fine point. The bristles, so fine and delicate they moved as one, laying down a smooth umber line next to the eyeball.

Mascara. Nothing elaborate here either. Only a shallow, graceful curve to the lashes and one or two strokes with the cylindrical brush.

The woman was almost there; he had almost re-created her, and with every tiny movement came a sense of increasing well-being, a deep peacefulness that he no longer tried to understand. He simply welcomed it, was grateful for it, and accepted it as a peculiar gift of the psyche. It was no longer the curse that it had been for so many years. The emerging woman was some part of himself that lay in the deep regions of his anima. Once he had fought with her chaos. He had struggled and agonized; he had suffered trying to understand. But now the curse had turned.

He took a silver hair pick and touched up the bouffant blond hair, lightened it around the face. It was an especially fine job, he thought. He liked what he saw. He almost smiled at what he saw.

Standing slowly, he looked at the new *point d'esprit* stretch teddy with elaborate lace insets. He had gotten a small cup and his nipples showed through the dusky lace. It had been an experiment, this body-clinging spandex, a successful experiment, he told himself, as he turned sideways and regarded his buttocks, the way his beefy chest actually filled the tiny cups of the bra. He cocked one leg forward, bent the knee with a practiced coyness. Jesus, he was pleased. Watching himself, he bent down to the corner of the bed and picked up the garter belt, a mink-colored affair that he had looked for forever. He spread it open, flattening the lace, and, again watching himself in the mirror, stepped into it with pointed toes, his hair falling across the corner of his face with a springy, sexy bounce. He tossed it back with a flip of his head — a gesture he loved — and then stepped into the garter belt with the other leg. With his thumbs inside the elastic, he pulled the belt up over his stomach and flattened it around his waist.

Sitting in front of the dresser, he faced the mirror and watched himself slip the toe of one raised leg into the gathered stocking. He watched himself pull and smooth the stocking over his foot, over the ankle, tightening it from behind with a caressing gesture of his cupped hand, slowly stretching it up his calf, the dark silk playing out of his hand in a sheer envelope as sweet as liquid, over the knee and up to the dark top of the stocking. Never moving his eyes off the mirror, he used both hands to smooth and tighten the stocking one last time and then stretched down the elastic straps and hooked the stocking, first in front and then, reaching behind his thigh, in back.

The second leg followed quickly; after all, he had had years of experience. He had only taken his time with the first one because it pleased him so much to watch the natural grace of his fluid movements, and because he would never, never tire of the feel of fine silk embracing his straightened leg.

He got up quickly and went over to the side of the bed and took the dress off the padded hanger. For this evening he had chosen a Victor Costa straight skirt of rayon crepe and matching surplice jacket with slightly padded shoulders. It was a leaf print, tropical leaves, white on black with black trim on the surplice and hem of the jacket. He stepped into the skirt and slipped on the jacket, and while he was still fastening the jacket he walked over to the dresser mirror. He had already picked double-twisted strands of black and white pearls as a choker, which he quickly fastened. Tilting his head to one side and then to the other, he screwed on two large pearl earrings bordered with tiny chips of onyx. Finally, he stepped into black Amalfi low-heeled calfskin pumps. He snatched a soft kid purse off the edge of the dresser, struck a last pose for the mirror, and saw a woman who pleased him enormously. Feeling totally at ease, free of anxieties and tensions for the first time that day, Dr. Dominick Broussard allowed himself a smile for the mirror, and then turned and stepped out onto the mezzanine and started downstairs. He would take a drive, have a couple of cocktails in a dimly lit club somewhere, enjoy the incomparable pleasure of simply being himself. Then he would come home and have dinner.

He ate alone, of course, a dinner that Alice always prepared for him on Saturday mornings before she took off at noon for the rest of the weekend. He heated the meal in the microwave — it was always a complete dinner, tonight veal Basquaise with lightly sautéed vegetables — and put it on a table also set by Alice that morning. Tonight he felt very glamorous and opened the terrace doors and ate by candlelight, overlooking the lawn that sloped to the bayou and beyond which the lights of the city rose up on the other side above the black trees. The air was heavy after the rains, but not too hot, just warm enough to enhance the tropical mood of the evening. He put on several albums of Brazilian music, the varied feminine voices and favored rhythms of Alcoine, Gal Costa, Elis Regina.

He had done more drinking than eating, but when he had finally had enough of the veal Basquaise, he took his glass and the bottle of Santa Sofia Valpolicella and drifted out on the terrace, where he placed the wine bottle on a marble-topped iron table and sat beside it in one of the chairs. Crossing his legs at the knee, he pulled the liquid hem of his dress up over his knee, and felt the warm air wash over his thighs, felt it touch his bare flesh between the top of the stocking and the bottom of his panties. He was heady with the wine, thrilled at the thought of himself sitting in the dark, but covered in the luxuriant white tendrils and small fingers of the tropical flora of his dress, the voices of the dusky Brazilian women purling and soaring, floating and sinking and wafting, maybe even reaching to the distant glitter on the far, black margin of the night.

'Dominick!'

His eyes popped open, and at the same time he almost lost consciousness, the effect of the woman's voice calling his name stunning him as effectively as if he had been hit over the head with a mallet.

'Dominick?' It was a hoarse, questioning whisper.

He forced himself to come around. It was real. Jesus. The dress. The glass slipped from his hand and shattered on the terrace floor. He froze. The Brazilian voices had stopped and nothing was audible but his own heart and the sea of crickets that flowed in the bayou. Did she think *he* was Dominick? Or that he was there with Dominick, and Dominick was somewhere on the terrace?

'This is Mary,' she said. She was still out of his sight in the shrubbery next to the terrace. Why didn't she come around? Did she think she was interrupting something? He was stone, not even turning his head her way, only knowing where she was because of her voice. Jesus God. Did he try to get out of this?

Broussard lowered his crossed leg and felt the glass grind under the Amalfi pump. He desperately wished he hadn't drunk so much wine because the way he was he couldn't be sure of any of his movements, if they were too slow, too brittle. He couldn't even be sure if he was doing the right thing, whatever it was he was doing. Did he appear drunk to her from her vantage point in the shrubbery? What *did* he look like? What was she thinking?

'I'm sorry,' she said, 'but I knew Alice was gone ... I saw the lights, and I just came around by the wall, around to here. I thought I might see you from here.'

He simply couldn't move. His thinking on this was ... blank.

'I ... I don't care ... if ... you're dressed up,' she said.

Christ Almighty! What a strange thing to say. He wondered how long she had been there.

'Not in the least,' she said.

And what a strange reaction to what she was seeing. He imagined what she was seeing; he got out of his body and walked down to where she was and looked back at himself, sitting there bolt upright, gripping the arms of the wrought-iron chair, his blond wig, perhaps, phosphorescing in the darkness.

'Is it all right if I come up?' she asked.

Not even Bernadine had seen him 'in dress.' Not after all the years of kinky sex, not even after Bernadine came to him in a man's suit with a dildo tied between her legs. Not even then, and not even after . . .

'I'm coming up,' she said tentatively. He couldn't even get his throat to work to protest. Besides, he didn't know what kind of voice to use. His heart was hammering so hard he thought his ears would explode and shoot out a stream of blood.

Then it was too late, and in the corner of his right eye he saw her move around the end of the steps below him. Ever so slightly, he adjusted his head and turned his eyes to meet hers. She was wearing a calf-length dress, light-colored, probably a summer beige, that buttoned down the front from neck to hem, allowing her to adjust the amount of bust and leg she wanted to show. Right now, with one foot on the bottom step, it seemed to him she was showing quite a bit of both. And then as he looked at her he became slowly aware of a vague air of disorientation about her and, even, he thought, an intimation of something uncanny. Her hair was in slight disarray, a definite feel of wild uncertainty about her.

'I don't care . . . I don't care about the dress,' she said, one lovely pale hand on the limestone banister of the terrace steps as she raised her other leg and mounted the first step. 'I had to talk to you . . . a drastic, a drastic thing, I know. But this afternoon I wasn't through . . . We had to stop . . . the interruption.'

If Broussard lived through all the lives of Tiresias, from sex to sex and back again, he would never forget this moment.

'I went to meet someone tonight,' she said, mounting another step. 'I should have told . . . should have told you . . . more about the little girl, you know, me, and . . . even, now, how it is. I lied, or it was like a lie because it never came out . . . really came out.'

She was up another step now and moving with less hesitation and more quickly. He was still frozen in the chair beside the bottle of Valpolicella. He had yet to make a sound.

'But it's nothing to me,' she said. 'The lie. It's all the same to me, all of it . . . all the same.'

She was only a step from the top, maybe fifteen feet away, close enough for Broussard to see her face clearly and the effort she was making to control it. The dress was most likely a cotton jersey, a beautiful thing, the sort of stylish garment that Mary Lowe possessed by the closets full.

She approached him across the small distance, and he saw her face more clearly in the weak light coming from behind him. She stopped in front of him, her legs slightly parted, and the sound of crickets came up from between them like a birthing of cunning music. Her cheeks quivered as she made an effort to smile, and he tried to read her eyes, to decipher what she must be thinking as she looked at him, and he looked at her through a purple haze of wine and from behind the woman in white leaves.

'There are bound to be mistakes,' she said, for no reason that he could imagine. And for no reason, he nodded.

'How long do you think I should have let him come to my bed at nights?' she asked, and she slowly sank to her knees and walked on them until she touched him. She put a hand on either side of his skirt and began pushing it up. 'All through my twelfth year? Until I was thirteen? Fourteen?' She was working the skirt past the top of the stockings, past the garter belt, above his *fleur-de-lis* panties, and finally, free and around his waist. 'Fifteen?'

Broussard was going wild inside. How many times had he dreamed and yearned for this to happen to him, for these clothes — the satin surfaces of silk and nylon and lace, the tiny ribbing on the panties, the buckles and snaps, the colors of flesh through colors of lingerie — to be taken from him as she was now taking them. He felt the garter belt give way on each leg and he felt her fingers go into the tops of his stockings and peel them off, like a skin, the heavy air of the bayou night refreshing on the lengths of his newly naked legs.

His eyes closed, and his mind's eye followed the removal of his garter belt and panties. He loved the way his face must have looked to her.

'Sixteen? Seventeen?'

And then there was nothing left below his waist but his excitement.

'But there was one more surpise,' she said, and Broussard heard her voice move and he opened his eyes. 'There came the time — and I was twelve, still twelve — of the worst part. The worst part of it all.'

Standing before him, she began unbuttoning the cotton jersey from the top and when she reached the last button her eyes were riveted to him like Bernadine's, the way he liked, wide open to the things that they would do. A small shrug of her white shoulders sent the jersey falling to her feet, and she stood in front of him as he had often imagined her with a body so remarkably perfect that it was a pure thing, as pure as death.

She stepped up to him, placed one hand on each of his shoulders to steady herself, and then raised one naked leg and slipped it through the inside of the arm of the chair and then swiftly raised the other one and placed it through the other arm, straddling him.

'The worst part of it was,' she said, taking him in her hand, slowly settling into him, and leaning down until he felt her heavy breasts against his chest, until he felt her lips feathering his ear, until he felt the warmth of her breath, warmer than the bayou air. 'The worst part of all ... was the night my daddy came to me in my bed ... and I enjoyed it.'

SEVENTH
DAY

52

Saturday night at Ben Taub General Hospital, the city's largest charity hospital, located on the northern border of the Texas Medical Center, is like a war zone — every Saturday night. Janice Hardeman, a surgical nurse in one of the hospital's emergency operating rooms, had been pulling the night shift at the hospital five nights a week for over five years, and during that time she had seen a lot of human damage. But the immediate satisfaction she received from helping trauma patients, stunned and bewildered by finding themselves suddenly in the red midst of a life-threatening tragedy, was more than enough compensation for the spent adrenaline and the constant visions of human slaughter that all too frequently approached the absurd.

By three o'clock this Sunday morning Janice Hardeman had assisted while surgeons removed an icepick embedded in a twenty-two-year-old woman's left breast, its tip passing through her left lung and coming to rest one and a half centimeters from the exterior wall of her heart's right ventricle. She had assisted in an unsuccessful effort to save the life of a woman who had received a single gunshot wound in the stomach, which had exploded her pancreas and celiac artery. She had run down the hospital's long, shiny halls beside a stainless-steel gurney with her right thumb jammed into a man's slashed throat, trying to stanch the hemorrhaging of his right carotid artery; she had delivered by cesarean section a cocaine-addicted baby from its mother, who was dying of crack-induced convulsions; she had assisted in the removal of a four-year-old boy's left arm, which had been crushed in a car wreck; and now she was going home early because her period had started and the cramps that had begun plaguing her during her last four or five periods were making it impossible for her to stay on her feet any longer.

With her shoes squeaking on the polished floors, she left the nurses' lounge thankful that she wasn't the little boy's mother and didn't have to tell him about his arm when he woke up in the morning. And she was worried about her cramps. Her periods always had been easy, even from the very beginning, but lately they had begun to be unusually painful. The cramps only lasted the first eighteen or twenty hours — she had made mental notes about the duration — but they were unusually sharp. Or so it seemed. She really had nothing to compare them with.

Walking out the back door of the hospital, the smell of hot asphalt and oil-stained parking lots replaced the hospital odors of alcohol and disinfectant. There was a faint waft of something rancid coming from the Dumpsters at the far end of the building, and Janice felt a sudden momentary queasiness. She recognized the irony and laughed to herself. Blood and vomit and urine and feces hadn't fazed her for the past six hours, but the smell of rotten fruit was too much.

She hurried across the lot to her car and stood by the door, fishing her keys out of her purse. She usually remembered to have her keys ready when she left the building to avoid this delay in the deserted lot, but tonight she had forgotten, the little boy and the cramps taking their toll on her concentration. The predawn air was cool and Janice was thankful that every day she was able to experience these early-morning hours. You could almost understand the city when you saw it like this. With the millions of tiny glistening lights coming from the looming buildings of the surrounding complex, she saw the city at its best. It wasn't always harsh and hectic and mean and hot. It wasn't always merciless.

Getting inside her new Toyota, Janice locked the doors and then pushed the buttons that rolled each of the windows down a few inches. She pulled out of the hospital parking lot and onto the loop that took her to the Outer Belt, the boulevard that separated the north side of the Texas Medical Center from the south side of Hermann Park and the Houston Zoo just through the trees. She took the Outer Belt to Main Street across from Rice University and turned left and followed along beside the campus until she got to University Boulevard, where she turned right and headed into the empty streets toward the quiet village of West University Place.

She lived alone in the southwest quadrant of the village, just inside its limits. Having recently split up with her boyfriend, she was enjoying her newly recovered privacy, not having to worry about looking out for another person's clothes — either clean or dirty — or another person's books or records or combs or socks or favorite cookies or bicycle or breakfast cereal. Everything was hers again, only hers, and she knew where she put things and why. If she got lonely she would have a friend over, or she would go over to a friend's without having to worry about whether he was going to feel excluded or, if he went along, whether their personalities were going to clash or if he might decide to be boorish because he hadn't wanted to go in the first place, but didn't have the resourcefulness to stay at home alone and entertain himself for a change. In short, she was once again enjoying the pleasures of selfishness.

Just as she turned into her street, she met the paperboy tossing white rolls of newspaper through the morning darkness into dew-dampened yards, and with her windows down she heard the faint whumps as an occasional paper hit a tree or slammed into front porch steps.

She pulled into her driveway, rolled up the windows, and got out and locked the car. Exhausted, she walked across the damp grass, picked up her newspaper, and walked up the sidewalk to the front door of her small wood-frame house. It was painted a light green with forest green trim and forest green canvas awnings. She had mortgaged the house with her own salary, and it was made energy-efficient on a payment plan. She mowed the small lawn herself. She was proud of the place and liked the neighborhood.

Unlocking the front door, she pushed it open, kicked off her white nursing shoes, and tossed the newspaper over onto the sofa across the small living room. She would look at it right there in that spot in a few hours, with a cinnamon roll from the neighborhood bakery and a nice strong cup of coffee. But right now all she wanted was to take a long shower with lots of scented soap to wash off the emergency room odors, and then to crawl between the cool sheets.

Unbuttoning the blouse of her white uniform, she stepped across the small hallway off the living room and turned the corner into her bedroom. The moment before she flipped on the light, she smelled the perfume — not her perfume. That simple fact registered like a cold blade of fear going into the back of her neck at the very same instant that the ceiling light flung up the naked, pasty cadaver of a woman in her bed, her face painted like a great grotesque doll, eyes staring round and bulging, bloody breasts, and a queerly refined and proper posture.

Prim horror.

The telephone rang four or five times before Palma fought her way to the surface of consciousness and groped for the receiver. As she said, 'This is Carmen,' she saw that the digital clock read three fifty-five.

'You're man's done another one,' Lieutenant Corbeil said.

'Jesus Christ.' Her mouth was dry, and Corbeil's words had the effect of the first roiling sensations of nausea.

'What ... what about Reynolds?'

'He didn't move.'

'Palma swallowed. 'He didn't move? He ... what about Broussard?' She was holding her head in her hand. 'Did they get the tail on Broussard?'

'Yeah, but he didn't go anywhere either,' Corbeil said.

Palma was incredulous. 'Are they *sure*? I mean, who was on him?'

'Martin and Hisdale, but I don't think I'd question their ...'

'Goddamn, Arvey, it was just a question.' God, how could it not be either one of them?

'And there's something odd about your victim,' Corbeil said. Palma was irritated that Corbeil kept saying 'your man' and 'your victim.' Why the hell had he started that? 'Victim doesn't live in the house where she was found. Place belongs to a single woman, a nurse who found her when she came in from her shift at Ben Taub about twenty minutes ago.'

'She doesn't know the victim?' Palma asked, sitting up on the edge of the bed, looking at her wrinkled dress, trying to remember.

'Says she doesn't know if she does or not. Couldn't tell with the makeup and all,' Corbeil said. 'Thirty-twenty-six Blane. Practically in your own back yard.'

'Jesus Christ,' Palma said again. 'Okay, I'm on my way as soon as I wash up.'

'Say,' Corbeil said quickly, 'you know where Grant is? I've called his room at the hotel, but he doesn't answer.'

'I don't know,' she said crossly. 'Try it again.' She hung up and ran her fingers through her hair, cursing Corbeil's impertinence. Or she thought it was impertinence. She stood up slowly and went into the bathroom and washed her face with cold water, came out patting her face with a towel, ran a brush through her hair, and started down the stairs, still dabbing her face. She went into the living room and saw their plates still on the coffee table, and then she turned and went across the hall to the guest room. The door was open and she stepped in and saw Grant standing at the bathroom sink in his suit pants but without a shirt, washing his face.

'I listened on the telephone down here,' he said quickly, turning off the water. 'I'll be ready in a few minutes.'

She stared at him. When she didn't leave the doorway, he turned and looked at her.

'You all right?' he asked.

'Yeah,' she said, holding the towel to her mouth. 'I don't remember going up to bed.'

'I carried you up,' he said, trying to act as if it was nothing, quickly turning back to the mirror to comb his hair. 'You kind of conked out.'

'I passed out?'

'I'd say you just went to sleep.'

Palma looked at him a moment. 'I, uh, I don't drink too well,' she said.

'I'm sorry you had to sleep in your dress,' Grant said, striding out of the bathroom and grabbing his shirt from the back of the chair near his bed. Palma noticed his bed had been slept in. She also noticed his build, surprised at the thickness of his chest and shoulders. He slipped on the shirt and hurriedly started buttoning it. 'But I thought . . . you'd rather.'

Palma nodded. 'Right,' she said stupidly. 'It'll take me just a second to throw on some fresh things.' And she turned and hurried out of the room.

Blane Street was not exactly in Palma's back yard, as Corbeil put it, but it was eighteen blocks away, just inside the city limits of West University Place. As with the murder of Bernadine Mello in Hunters Creek, the village police were well aware of the serial killings and contacted Houston homicide immediately. Because of their proximity, Palma and Grant were the first ones there except for several radio units, their doors flung open, radios barking, flashers bouncing off the small neighboring houses in the predawn darkness.

'Stop back here,' Grant said quickly, and Palma slowed and pulled to the curb, cutting her lights and stopping several car lengths back from the house. Grant quickly got out of the car and stalked toward the house, reaching for his shield to hang outside his suit coat pocket. He headed straight for the patrolman stringing plastic ribbon around the entire perimeter of the yard to the front sidewalk.

'Excuse me,' he said, stopping the officer, laying a hand on his shoulder. He introduced himself. 'Anybody inside?'

'One officer, just inside the front door. Officer Saldana over there in the patrol unit with the homeowner was first on the scene.'

Grant nodded. 'Listen, I think it'd be a good idea to put that ribbon all the way across the street to the opposite curb. Maybe two car lengths either side of the property. Move your patrol units outside the ribbon, too. It's likely this guy came and left by car, maybe stopped out here somewhere, maybe raked something out into the street when he got out. Could've dropped something along the curb. We want to keep it restricted, keep people from driving all over it until we've had time to search it properly,' he said. 'Give us plenty of room.'

Immediately other patrol units started arriving and the patrolman and Grant started waving them back away from the front of the house, recruiting another officer to help them enlarge the scene.

Palma walked over to the patrol unit parked behind a car in the driveway. Its doors were open for air, its interior lights making it a lighted bubble in the morning darkness. Palma saw that the officer was a woman and that the woman with her was wearing a nurse's uniform. She approached the car and motioned for the officer to get out. A stout Chicana, Officer Saldana wore a practical ponytail and had an efficient manner.

She told Palma the woman's name was Hardeman, gave her occupation and the circumstances surrounding the discovery of the body. She confirmed the fact that Hardeman didn't know who the victim was, and that the house was locked when she arrived home. She said when

she arrived at the scene and saw what it was, she simply
got Hardeman out to the car and closed up the house. She
didn't even look to see if the victim had a purse so she
could check ID. Palma thanked her as Grant walked up,
and the two of them started up the sidewalk to the open
front door where they spoke to the officer guarding the
door and went in.

Palma quickly looked around Janice Hardeman's living
room and what she could see of the dining room and
kitchen. The windows of the house were thrown open,
causing the temperature to be ambient with the cool early
morning. Because the air was not being filtered, the
humidity enhanced the surrounding odors, and pungent
smell of older furniture and the specific redolence of old
houses that differs with each one as distinctly as fingerprints.

Hardeman was not an exacting housekeeper, certainly
not as organized as the businesslike Dorothy Samenov,
nor was she as conscientious about picking up a blouse or
slip that she shed as soon as she came in the front door as
Bernadine Mello's maids had been about looking after her
casually tossed clothing. The rooms were not sloppy or
ill-kept, only comfortably lived in with an apparent I'll-
get-to-it-later lifestyle.

Palma's stomach was already tightening in anticipation
of what she was going to see as she and Grant crossed
the hall to the bedroom. She smelled the perfume almost
immediately at the bedroom door, and then she saw the
pallid body in the same funeral posture she already had
seen three times before. By now Grant knew the details of
the killer's techniques by heart, and together they entered
the room looking for the familiar telltale mannerisms or
any deviations from them.

The bedroom was not large, and the bathroom was not
contiguous, but was around the corner in the hall. There
was a large closet without doors so that the clothes hung
on the racks open to the bedroom. A long, low clothes
chest was against one wall across from the foot of the
bed, and in the corner between the end of the chest and

the wall was the top sheet and bedspread that had been stripped off the bed. On its far side, the bed was relatively close to a row of windows, and an old wooden armchair sat between the bed and the windows. It appeared to serve as a makeshift table for reading material, since it was stacked with magazines and a couple of books. On top of the books and magazines was a neatly folded set of women's clothes. On the near side of the bed was a bedside stand, a junk store 'antique' with a marble top and a compartment below. The little table held a telephone, alarm clock, and a box of tissues.

They both moved to the bed. Grant stood beside her, hands in his pockets, his own thoughts shrouded in a grim frown. Then he broke the silence.

'Sandra Moser was thirty-four. Dorothy Samenov, thirty-eight; Bernadine Mello, forty-two. I thought we had something going there, each woman getting older. But this one,' he really couldn't tell anything about her face, 'from her general physique it looks like she's twenty-three, twenty-four.'

Palma was beginning to feel strange. The body was vaguely familiar, the build of it, the long legs and even the woman's groin, the color of her pubes . . . the color of her pubes . . . Stunned, Palma jerked her eyes sideways to the woman's hair. She was not a true blond, for her hair had a sandy, reddish cast to it, the color of ginger.

'My God,' she said, and reflexively put a hand out to touch Grant's arm, then quickly withdrew it. 'Jesus.' She studied the woman's dollish face and tried to see beneath the makeup, beyond the distortion caused by the swelling, beyond the distracting gape of the lidless eyes. 'I think this is Vickie Kittrie,' she said.

'You think?' Grant's voice was calm.

'I recognize . . . the hair.' She had almost said 'vulva.' These deaths were spreading their strangeness even into her own life. Could she ever have imagined that she would one day identify another woman by the general nature of her vulva? She remembered — two, three days earlier? Four? — sitting in the tapestried armchair in

Helena Saulnier's house and watching Vickie, willingly naked from the waist down, pluck her own pubic hair, one at a time, from her carefully barbered pubis. She looked at Vickie's groin now and remembered that, remembering noting the overall effect of that scene, the long, milky thighs that Vickie had to spread slightly to get to the hair on the outer lips of her vagina. Had that incident made more of an impression on her than she wanted to admit? Had she been moved unconsciously by what she had seen, while consciously she had not given it a second thought, had even 'forgotten' it? How the hell could she recognize a woman's groin if it had not made an extraordinary impression on her?

'It's Vickie,' she said, and her eyes were already taking in the quarter-size wounds where Vickie's nipples had been and the discolored suck marks that dotted her abdomen and inner thighs like the maculae of typhus, symptoms of a sickness. These were the signs of a singular disease, a fatal virus that never killed its host and never infected its victims. Her eyes quickly had passed over all these wounds and scars, markers of the killer's mind, and had locked onto Vickie's navel and the distinctive bite and suck marks that ringed it — and one additional, and grotesque, feature that she had not immediately recognized in her surprise at identifying Kittrie. The navel itself, the inner coil, the snubbed end of what once had been the umbilical tie between the lives of mother and child and through which they had shared genetics and life, past and present and future, was a moist, extruding wound where the killer had sucked out the cicatrix.

From the corner of her eye she was aware of Grant looking over at her, perhaps alerted by her silence, then following her eyes to Kittrie's stomach. He quickly moved around closer, buttoning his double-breasted coat to keep his tie from getting onto the body when he bent over. He examined the wound where her navel had been, tilting his head this way and that like a curious bird. Palma did not have to examine it so closely; she did not have to see

the minute rippled impressions left by the serrated edges
of his teeth that she knew lay in the subsurface of the
scalded ring of his bite. Those were the fait accompli, and
she had already memorized those. What her mind craved
was the images she could never have, the sight of him
bent over her stomach, the words of their strange foreplay, the sounds of sexual urges gone awry and that had
led to an even stranger death. But what she could not
witness, she could not avoid imagining. Vickie's senses,
the coppery taste of raw fear, the smells of their sweaty
intercourse, sounds of his distorted sexual greed, what
she saw him do to her as she strained in disbelief over the
top of her breasts, what she felt when he placed his
mouth over her navel and bit and sucked with enough
rage to eviscerate her.

Grant straightened up, had a second thought, and bent
down again and felt the sheet along the edges of the body
on both sides.

'It's still soaking,' he said. 'And discolored. He washed
her, used a lot of water. There was probably a lot of blood
this time. Looking at the wounds, the navel, the nipples,
even the eyelids ... I think all of these will prove to be
antemortem. The breasts are like the head, tremendous
vascular density. You cut the head or breasts, and you're
going to shed a lot of blood.' Grant nodded to himself.
'He came into his own with this one. He went all the way.
Full-blown sexual sadism. She felt everything.'

Palma thought his voice was different somehow,
perhaps a little more hushed, more grave.

He stood looking at Vickie, craned his neck forward,
and then bent again and brought his face right down to
her vulva. Then without saying anything straightened up
again, looked around the room. He went to the closet and
got an empty wire coat hanger and returned to the bed,
straightened the hooked end of it with his hands. Again
he bent over the body and with the straightened wire he
very carefully, like a surgeon, reached down between her
crotch, fished a moment in her hair, and pulled up the
end of a thin white string protruding from her vagina. He

laid it on the small pad of hair. 'Menstruating,' he said.

He stood back again and shook his head, his eyes still on the body, his jaw muscles working down towards his mustache.

'This isn't all that much mutilation,' he said. 'I've seen this small amount before ... on single sexual homicides. Usually it's more, a lot more, especially if it's a serial killer. It tends to get worse with every victim, complete evisceration, body parts strewn all over the place.' He shook his head, looking at Kittrie. 'But this small amount of mutilation — eyelids, nipples — in a serial killer is unexpected. Bite marks, suck marks, even this many, okay. The facial beating, okay. But this small amount of mutilation ... and the parts he chose to mutilate ... I don't know. This just isn't tracking in a way you'd expect. It's just not a pattern I've seen before, in its relative moderation, in its selectivity. They usually want to get inside them, take them apart, look at every little thing. This guy, he's not showing the kind of curiosity in the female sexual body parts we usually see.'

Palma looked at Grant. His head was tilted slightly as he looked at Vickie on the bed, the coat hanger dangling from his left hand, his right hand thrust back into his pocket, his double-breasted coat still buttoned. Still, she could see that his shirt was terribly wrinkled as if he had slept in it, and it would be clear to anyone that his suit was working on its second day of wrinkles. His posture reflected his consternation, and the dim light of the bedroom accented the shadow of his beard.

They heard sirens and raised voices outside, car and van doors opening and closing. The window curtains on the other side of the bed were flushing blue and cherry, blue and cherry. In the next few minutes the three of them would lose their privacy.

'When we get through with this,' Grant said, 'I'd like to run something by you. Just the two of us. This isn't looking good at all.'

53

As the predawn sky lightened to gray, then pearl, Janice Hardeman's bedroom became the focal point of intense scrutiny. Until she and Grant had had time to work through the scene again and again, Palma would not allow the body to be moved or anyone to enter the small bedroom except Jules LeBrun, who went through his arcane and solitary chores with the studied precision of a *tai chi chuan* master, pausing occasionally to consult with Palma and Grant as to the particulars of their special requests.

Palma watched the color in the room change, as clean, pale daylight overrode jaundiced incandescent and, with the changing light, Vickie's nude body seemed to evolve from a symbol of mysterious and perverse sexuality to something banal and even tawdry, evoking not excitement, but depression. Palma found herself oddly affected by this transformation, her perceptions unexpectedly recast in much the same way that they are when one sometimes is surprised to hear a perfectly ordinary word in a peculiarly different way, so that it seems altogether new and unfamiliar. The dead woman became *una cosa de muerte* — a thing of death — her father's term, by which he meant that the human element had disappeared. She was something dead, formerly warm-blooded but otherwise unrecognizable, a pale and gaunt, split-finned thing with a doll's head slapped onto its grisly, elongated torso, its lidless eyes staring at all that moved and didn't move with the same mindless detachment.

Palma resisted this mirage of disassociation. Homicide detectives were famous for creating these mirages, a mother becomes a case number, a daughter becomes 'the girl in the landfill,' a sister becomes 'the coat hanger case,' a wife becomes 'the woman in the Dumpster.' But Palma was finding it impossible not to empathize with these victims. For her, the four women were mother, daughter, wife, sister and, try as she might, they could not be depersonalized to the peripheries of her emotions. She was in it up to her heart, and she didn't want it to be any other way. The woman on the bed became *una cosa de muerte* only momentarily before she returned to the reality of what she had been and was still.

Like the dead woman in her bed, Hardeman had to give up hair samples from various parts of her body, one of her towels was taken to match with fibers in Kittrie's mouth, her sheets were taken from the bed, her bedroom floor selectively vacuumed, and the occasional dust balls that she had allowed to drift along the edges of the hard-wood floors and accumulate around the legs of the bed and corners of her closet were gathered for microscopic examination, a ridiculous idea in any other context, but which suddenly had accrued to a major element in a grim methodology because of what had happened on her bed within the last twelve hours.

When the three of them were finished, they left Kittrie to the coroner's investigator and walked out through the living room to the front yard, where the sky had achieved the bird's egg blue of a new morning, and Corbeil and Frisch were waiting for them with other detectives and uniformed officers within the taped-off parameters fronting Hardeman's house. A throng of reporters and cameramen had made camp outside the yellow ribbon and had been joined by a sizable neighborhood crowd, some of them sipping mugs of coffee, a few women in housecoats, and a number of kids who looked as if they were going to be late for their first class, if they made it to school at all. A gathering of grackles had begun to shriek and snap and whistle in a tall and bulky mulberry at the corner of Hardeman's house, and the almost subliminal sound of early traffic on Kirby Drive a couple of blocks away was audible in the background.

Ignoring the shouts from the reporters and turning their backs to the cameras, Palma and Grant held their necessary debriefing with Corbeil, who was now working past the end of his shift, and Frisch, who had been called early to his.

'Vickie Kittrie,' Frisch said, looking over at the house as if he might see her there. He was holding a cup of coffee, too, in an insulated paper cup.

Palma nodded. No one was going to say it, but Palma knew what they were thinking. The main suspect in her fancy female-killer theory was now a victim, which essentially pulled the plug on her credibility. Grant had never been seriously challenged.

'She have any idea why Kittrie was here?' Frisch gestured with his paper cup toward Janice Hardeman, who was still sitting with the policewoman and had been joined by a neighbor.

'We haven't had the chance to interview her.' Palma said.

Corbeil was looking at Grant, probably drawing conclusions about how he had gotten to the crime scene so quickly.

'I got something for you on the two stakeouts,' he said, turning to Palma. 'Reynolds sure enough didn't leave his condo. The electronic surveillance verifies that. Broussard has never come out of his place, so we're assuming he's in there. You two left the station last night about ten-fifteen, and by ten-forty Martin and Hisdale were sitting a few drives away from Broussard's house. At ten-fifty a woman driving a Mercedes registered to Broussard entered his drive. She hasn't come out yet. At eleven-forty another woman driving another Mercedes — this one registerd to a Paul Lowe — entered Broussard's drive, and she hasn't come out yet either.'

'You checked on Lowe?' Palma said.

'Lives on Brookmore. Hunters Creek. No police record, a few speeding tickets. He's thirty-eight and married.'

'Could have been his wife, a sister, sister-in-law, friend,' Palma said.

'But Broussard's not married, is he?' Frisch said.

Palma shook his head. She was preoccupied, not caring too much about what Frisch or Corbeil might conclude about her theories from their questions or by what they had seen or hadn't seen. Like Grant, she thought something was terribly wrong here, and she couldn't keep her mind from going over and over it. Nor could she keep her thoughts off Vickie Kittrie and her extracted navel.

Jeff Chin, the coroner's investigator, stepped through the front door of Hardeman's house and came over to them along the sidewalk. The earphones of a Walkman were hanging around his neck, and he was wearing a mexican *guayabera* outside his jeans and cowboy boots, which were the color of butter.

'I'm going to be a little longer in there,' he said looking around at all of them, but his eyes finally settled on Carmen as he fished on the breast pocket of his *guayabera* for a pack of cigarettes. 'But at this point I'm guessing that she died an hour either side of ten-thirty last night.' He jogged up a cigarette, lipped it out of the pack, and lighted it with a red Bic. 'Rigor mortis is extreme. Under ordinary circumstances — woman dies of natural causes in room temperature conditions — rigor mortis usually reaches its full development anywhere from six to fourteen hours after death. However, those aren't ordinary circumstances in there. She was tied up, bitten, cut, chewed, beaten, adrenaline squirting everywhere. From all that we can assume her antemortem emotional and muscle activity was strenuous and that contributes to a more rigid onset of rigor mortis and would also push the timing closer to six hours than to fourteen.'

He drew on the cigarette and frowned. 'Livor mortis is well developed, which takes about three or four hours. It reaches its maximum degree of development in eight to twelve hours. But I think she's still got a way to go, so I'm going to go with the lower numbers. Her liver was only one degree below normal. The house is open, so the ambient temperature was — what was it last night? — seventy-four, seventy-six, which is okay. So, considering the postmortem temperature plateau of four to five hours, it looks like she could have been dead about six hours, give or take one. Ten-thirty's still a good guess.'

'You feel good about the time, then?' Palma said.

'It's a good *guess*,' Chin said.

'Can you do the autopsy this morning?'

'The sooner the better?'

Palma nodded.

'Will do.' He nodded at them, slipped his headphones on as he turned on the sidewalk, and started back toward the house, adjusting the radio in one of the fat pockets of his *guayabera* and taking a few last drags off the cigarette before he went back inside.

No one spoke for a moment, and then Frisch said, 'Jesus!' and tossed his cold coffee out onto the damp grass.

'He could have been in the trunk,' Corbeil said, talking about Broussard. 'Or just lying down in the seat. Woman drives in past Martin and Hisdale, and he's lying down in the seat.'

'Then there'd be more than one person involved,' Palma said.

'I don't understand how he got her,' Frisch said, turning the subject back to Vickie. 'How could she have been that stupid?'

'She had a bigger problem than fear,' Palma said. 'And she'd been afraid before. I think she rather liked it. When you think about it, it had to be Vickie sooner or later. If we're surprised by anything it should be that it didn't happen to her sooner. I should have seen it coming. I really should have.'

'You?' Frisch looked at her. 'Don't start talking like that. We knew the odds were that he'd get another one,

or two — or more. We can't be responsible for a bunch of
women who don't have enough goddamned sense to ...'
He stopped himself. 'Shit,' he said.

'We ought to see what we can get from Hardeman,'
Palma said. They were wasting time just standing there.
What Frisch was thinking about — how to handle the
press, what and how to tell his superiors what was
happening, how best to use the men he had and how to
get more — was not Palma's concern. Not at this
moment, anyway.

Frisch looked at her and then nodded. 'Yeah, go
ahead.' He caught her eye before she turned away, and
Palma guessed that Corbeil had shared his inaccurate
deductions.

After Palma and Grant introduced themselves to Janice
Hardeman, the patrol officer and neighbor made themselves scarce and Hardeman asked if she could get out of
the car to talk. They stood at the front of the car, and she
folded her arms and leaned her hips against the front
fender. She wore a small utilitarian chrome wristwatch
that Palma had seen on so many nurses that she imagined
they must be as regulation as the uniforms.

'The woman was Vickie Kittrie,' Palma said flatly.

Hardeman's eyes widened and she gasped, thrusting
her head forward.

'Then you did know her?' Palma asked.

Hardeman frowned and swallowed, but she didn't
answer. She straightened her stance against the car,
unfolded her arms, and pushed back her black hair from
her temples. She had a pale, almost luminous complexion
that she apparently had been careful to protect from the
harsh Southwestern sun. It wasn't the sort of nature-girl
look that went best with a swimsuit, but it was flawless
and elegant, and rare. Her lips were the color of washed-
out lipstick, with a slightly redder ring around the edge
where she hadn't chewed it all off yet.

'You've been reading the papers?' Palma persisted.

Hardeman nodded. Her hands were braced against the
fender behind her and she was looking down at the ground.

'Then you've read the names of the victims?'

Hardeman looked up.

'We'll find out anyway, you know. There's nothing to be gained from holding out; it'll only waste time, cause all of us a lot of trouble.' She paused a couple of beats. 'Besides, it's a felony to withhold information in a homicide investigation.'

Hardeman looked suddenly tired. She shifted her white-stockinged legs, bending one knee, putting all her weight on the other leg. Her face bore the hard expression of an overstressed woman who was getting close to pulling the plug on her emotions. There was a limit. She nodded, a gesture of resignation.

'Yes. I knew her.' Hardeman's voice was subdued.

'But you didn't know she was coming here last night?'

'No, of course I didn't. I hadn't seen Vicki in ... maybe two months.' She saw Palma's questioning look. 'She had a key to my place. When we broke up she gave it back, but I guess she could have had a duplicate made.' She ran her fingers through her hair again.

'Why did you stop seeing her?'

'Well, I really hadn't known her that long. Four or five months. I didn't know about her ... proclivities. When she started trying to get me involved, I put her off. But she kept at it, really wouldn't let it alone. She was even getting rough in our own relationship, trying to ease me into it. I just ... couldn't do that. I see too much pain in my work. I don't want it in my sex life, too. I just quit seeing her.'

'Has she ever done anything like this before? Come into your home while you were away? Use your place to meet men, or other women?'

'No. Not that I've known about, anyway.'

'I guess you don't have any idea who might have been here with her.'

'God. I can't even imagine.' She cringed, as if remembering what had happened. 'This is too, just too bizarre.' She glanced over her shoulder at the crowd of neighbors in the early-morning sunlight. 'Look at them. I don't believe this is happening to me.'

'Who did Vickie do most of her S&M with?'

'Oh, hell,' Hardeman said wearily, and Palma saw tears glistening at the corners of her eyes. 'Uh, there were the women in the paper . . . who've been killed. Dorothy, Louise, Sandra. Uh, and there was Mirel Farr.' She shook her head. 'I think those are all the names I remember.

'Did you know all these women?'

Hardeman nodded. 'Only by sight, really. But not because of this. Just as friends of friends. You know, some of the women we knew.'

'What about Bernadine Mello? Did you know her?'

'No, I didn't know her. I saw her name in the paper, but I didn't know her.'

'Do you know anyone who knew her?'

Hardeman shook her head.

'What did you think,' Palma asked, 'when you read about the killings in the paper?'

'What did I think?' Hardeman frowned. 'What do you mean? I was scared, for Christ's sake.'

'Why were you frightened? Did you think you had a reason to be?'

'Well, after Dorothy was killed, yeah. It doesn't take a genius to see a connection there. I mean, two people you know are murdered and the only reason you know them is because of . . . your mutual sexual interests. You don't think we'd be scared, all of us?'

'You think this could have happened to any of you, then?'

'At first I did, sure. But then we've all been talking about it, in groups, among ourselves. We've picked over it, thought it out some more, and came to the conclusion it's confined to the S&M crowd. We were convinced of it.'

Palma looked at her. 'I guess you speculated about who it might be.'

'Sure. Every guy those women messed around with was a candidate, as far as we were concerned.'

'But wasn't a lot of it strictly between women? Lesbian S&M?'

'It was, right.

'But you didn't suspect any of the women?'

Hardeman looked at Palma. 'Well, yeah. There was some talk about that.' She shifted on her feet again and once more glanced around at the crowd. Palma felt sorry for her. She was wiped out. Palma guessed that after working a night shift in a Ben Taub war zone and then coming home and finding a friend butchered in your bed that you would have just about emptied every drop of adrenaline your body was capable of producing. She wasn't going to be able to stay on her feet much longer.

'And who were your candidates among the women?'

'Well, shit,' Hardeman said, nodding toward her house. 'The number one vote-getter is right in there.'

'Any one else?'

'Some mentioned Mirel Farr, but I couldn't go along with that. Mirel's in the business. It's her trade. She does it for money. Whoever does that ... in there, they do it because it's a passion with them, not a business.' She bent her head over and started rubbing the back of her neck. 'That's the way I see it, anyway.'

'You think a woman could have done that sort of thing?' Palma was going to get it straight from the horse's mouth for Grant, who, so far, hadn't made a peep.

Hardeman stopped rubbing her neck and cut her eyes up at Palma with a tired but amused smirk. 'You've got to be kidding.' She slid her eyes to Grant and then back to Palma. 'Jesus!' She shook her head. 'Listen,' she said to Palma, 'you ought to take the boys down to Mirel's. Get them a comfortable chair behind her two-way mirrors and let them watch what goes on there for a week or so. Change their attitudes. Only difference between men and women's S&M — aside from the anatomical differences — is that women never spit between their teeth.' She looked at Grant. 'That's distinctly male behavior.'

'What about the men?' Grant asked. If he was put off by Palma's setup and Hardeman's sarcastic response, he didn't show it in the least. 'Who were they?'

Hardeman said, 'A guy named Clyde, and a businessman

... uh, Reynolds. And Louise Ackley's brother. I remember I found that pretty incredible. Louise's brother, for God's sake. They're the only ones I ever heard her talk about. Like I said, I didn't want to hear about it too much. It was too off the wall.'

The grackles shrieked in the top of the mulberry, where the first rays of the morning sun were turning the blue leaves to green. In a few hours the oppressive heat would be unbearable as the rain-soaked city began steaming under a bright clear sky.

'Do you know if Vickie had ever sought psychiatric help?' Palma asked.

'I don't know. She sure as hell should have, but I can't say that she did. I just don't know.' Two men from the coroner's office unloaded an aluminum gurney from the back of a morgue van and took it up the sidewalk toward the front door. Hardeman's shoulders slumped even more. 'Jesus, I'm not believing this. I'm really not.'

'Have you got someone you can call to stay with today?' Palma asked. 'Our lab technicians are going to need some time in your house.'

Hardeman nodded. 'Sure. But what about clothes? I've got to pack some clothes. Shoes. Things from the bathroom.'

'We'll get Officer Saldana to go with you. I'll talk to her,' Palma said. 'I know this is a bad time to put you through the questions. I'm sorry we had to do it.'

'It's okay,' Hardeman said wearily, shaking her head. 'I'll have to buy a new bed,' she said to Palma, as if Palma was going to help her plan what she should do next. 'No way can I sleep in that bed again.' She shook her head, and again turned her face toward the house. 'I can't do it,' she said, and her voice cracked. She snapped her eyes around at Palma as if to see if Palma caught it, heard the revealing slip of vulnerability. But it was too late. The tremor in her voice had been the sound of the last shred of strength she had left. With an anguished look at Palma, she buried her face in her hands and started crying, her shoulders hunching with the quiet, wrenching effort of it.

Without a word, Grant turned and walked away. Palma didn't even look at him as she stepped over and put her arms around Hardeman and held her, feeling the deep sobs coming up from the pit of her stomach, requiring something from every inch of her body. It was only then, holding her, that Palma realized Hardeman wasn't even wearing shoes.

54

When Broussard opened his eyes to see the oblique angle of the sun seeping through the cracks of the tall shutters in his bedroom, he was gripped with a sudden sense of paralysis, and an obfuscated memory of something tragic. The high, white ceiling of the room floated in a hazy world of mote-filled morning light. He remembered she was beside him before he actually felt her, and then, remembering, he became aware of the weight of her on the mattress, though he was not actually touching her. His right arm lay on top of a single silk sheet, and without looking at her he reached over with his right hand and placed it on Mary's buttock. He could feel that she was naked under the peach silk sheet, and from the shape and angle of her taut hip, he could tell that it was cocked in his direction as she lay facing away from him with one leg pulled up a little, the other extended. He moved his right foot ever so slightly and felt her long leg. Christ Almighty. Through his own perfume he smelled hers, milder, less sweet, almost as if it were the natural fragrance of her body. He could believe that, that cologne spurted through her veins instead of blood, and her flesh wafted an associate perfume as a vessel smells of its contents. After last night, he could believe anything about her.

He could believe that she was dead. He held his breath and watched the folds in the sheet that stretched from her to him across his chest. They moved, lightly, lightly with her breathing.

He could believe she was the embodiment of all the women he had ever tried to redeem, that coming last she was in fact first, the after-image of a prototype, an anomaly so extraordinary that she became a paradigm.

He could believe that she did not lie. And, actually, he believed she didn't. That was the thing about Mary, she no longer knew the difference between reality and her own fantasies. She told the truth that was Mary's truth, the truth in Mary's head.

He could believe that last night had never happened, that he had not seen her do the things she did, but only had wished them fervently, so fervently that he had dreamed them more vividly than dreams.

Slowly he raised his left hand and looked at his painted fingernails. The uneasy sense of dread returned, the pall of a vague remembrance — or was it a premonition — of something tragic.

Broussard tried to put himself into the context of the moment. He lowered his hand and felt his head. The wig was gone. Hesitantly he wiped a finger across his lips, and it came away smudged with crimson. Stirring under the sheet, he felt that he was naked, and then he was aware that his right hand was still resting on Mary's buttock. He left it there and raised his other hand again, held it straight above him. Looking at his fingernails, he let the focus of his eyes slide away to the ill-defined regions of the ceiling again. It was a world of transition, fantasy lay behind them, reality was undesired and yet to come.

He carefully lifted his right hand off her and cautiously turned on his side to face her back. He feathered his left hand over the top of the sheet up to where it formed a cuff across her white shoulders. He pinched the cuff in his fingers and began pulling it down slowly, revealing the buttery whorls of her hair bunched around her neck, the ambit of her shoulder, her profile perdu so often observed on the chaise longue, the long angle of her arm, the first swells of her breasts whose actual beauty even his practiced imagination had failed to envisage, the fall of her ribcage that quickly rose again to her hip, her top leg bent for balance, the bottom one extended, showing him the inside of her thigh where he wanted to put his mouth.

She was extraordinary, more beautiful than any other woman he had ever known.

He placed his mouth at the first subtle rise of vertebrae that showed itself from beneath her hair and kissed it. And then he kissed the next one, moving down her spine and counting them, feeling the roundness of each with his lips, imagining that he and she were floating in the lambent upper reaches of the morning, suspended, unencumbered by weight and gravity, able to touch wherever they wished without contortion, down he traveled until the ripples disappeared between the two dimples above her buttocks, and he felt the beginnings of her dividing flesh.

Still floating, carefully, carefully, he placed his left hand on the flat of her stomach above her pubis and pressed gently to turn her over, his right hand guiding her shoulder. He watched the weight of her large breasts shift upon themselves, her pink, conical nipples riding upon their liquidy surfaces, seeking their centers of gravity as she rolled over onto her back. He kissed her navel, feeling the dusty wool of her vulva against his Adam's apple.

'What are you doing?' she asked.

Broussard flinched. He raised his eyes from her navel, looking up between the slopes of her breasts, and met her stare. He imagined how the overnight smear of his makeup must seem to her. Her expression conveyed nothing in particular, just a calm, steady gaze that reminded him uncomfortably of Bernadine's candid perusals of their intercourse.

'Where's your wig?' she asked.

Her sex had been like that too, straightforward, unabashed, even aggressive. It had been wild and extravagant, and when it was over she had gone to sleep as soundly as if she had been drugged. Now she looked at him with blue-gray eyes that were slightly swollen. He noted again her asymmetrical mouth, and the little pucker at the corner of one side which, when seen straight on, became a more curious detail than he had remembered it in profile. All those hours he had studied her as she lay upon the chaise longue, imagined her undressed, imagined her in ways that he believed only he could imagine her, had not prepared him for the reality. This time his imagination had fallen short.

He lay between her legs, his elbows on the sheet on either side of her hips, her pubis against his chest, and in the gauzy, filtered light of the room he watched her russet-hooded eyes as she studied him. At that moment if all the money he possessed could have bought her thoughts — her authentic thoughts, holographs as it were, from the id, not something refined through her superego — he would have paid it in an instant. There were things inside those eyes he wanted to discover, things he wanted to taste, new savors he was sure he had never known before.

She kept her eyes on him and reached down to his upturned throat and lightly, slowly, raked her fingernails up the length of it to his chin, continuing up his face over smeared lipstick, the morning bristles of his beard no longer hidden by base, over blush and smudged mascara and shadow and liner, her sullen blue-gray eyes watching him, watching her own hands, her own nails. When she reached the top of his head, she moved her hands around in back and haltingly pulled his face back down onto her stomach, pressed his lips into her navel as he felt her lifting her pubis firmly up against his neck.

'Secrets,' she said hoarsely, and then suddenly with one quick thrust of her hips against his throat she hooked her nails under the backs of his jaws and urged him up until he felt his chest against the largeness of her breasts and heard her breathing through her teeth, quick, sucking breaths, as though she were bracing herself against anti-

cipated pain. They clung to each other, and she pulled
him to her tightly, more tightly than he would have
imagined she could, as he buried his face in her neck,
breathing of her blond hair, hair like fragrant spiders'
webs. Resisting a sudden desire to crush her, to snap her
back, he concentrated on letting her take him; he concentrated on the slow drift of their intercourse as they
ascended through the high, hazy light, buoyed on a
rushing sound of whispers.

When he got out of the shower and walked into the
bedroom with his towel around his waist, he discovered
she already had dried her hair and was sitting naked on
the window seat, framed by the shutters thrown back, the
windows pushed open to the late-morning heat building
in the green woods along the bayou below. She was
leaning forward, her arms wrapped around her knees, her
breasts silhouetted in the rhomboid space created by the
angles of her body. Her head was turned away from him
as she looked outside, listening to the mournful burbling
of the tiny Spanish doves who gathered in the cool, dark
canopies of the magnolias and live oaks.

He didn't know how she felt, how it would be for her
now. For him, it was over. The cautious self-conscious-
ness that characterized his daily life had returned, and he
already had withdrawn into the persona of Dr. Broussard
in the name of social expediency. He knew she had heard
him come into the room, but she didn't look around as he
opened his closet, his other closet. He felt that it wasn't
entirely fair to her that he should return completely to his
tightly controlled role without a sense of transition. He
was used to it, years of living a divided life had made him
accustomed to neck-snapping transitions, but at this
moment he felt it was inappropriate. So he compromised.
He left his suits and ties in the closet and took down a
pair of casual silk trousers, dropped his towel and
stepped into them, then followed with a contrasting silk
shirt, which he left unbuttoned.

Barefooted, he walked over to the window seat where

she was sitting, hesitated, then reached for a chair, pulled it over next to her, and sat down. Still she didn't look around. He crossed his legs at the knee and glanced down to the sloping lawn. A sluggish breath of warm air moved through the opened windows and the sharp sunlight made him squint. He heard a sudden swooshing noise and below them the sprinkler system sprang to life, sending a thin mist up into the air above the lawn where it hovered momentarily before falling in a slow, sparkling dance. The system was computerized, and the gardener had forgotten to turn it off. Broussard would have to speak to him. It was stupid to water the lawn after two days of rain.

He looked at her. She hadn't the slightest inhibition about her body. He supposed that her rather bold preference for nakedness now, with him, was a kind of willful liberation from the self-imposed modesty that she insisted on when she was at home with her husband. Her shins and bare knees faced him, and behind her thin ankles he saw the fawn triangle of her vulva. Just then she suddenly turned her head and caught him looking at her.

'Did you know that I'm bisexual?' she asked, pushing back her hair and resting her eyes on him.

'I didn't know that,' he said.

She continued looking at him. 'Are you surprised?'

'No,' he said.

She didn't change expressions for a moment, just let her eyes stay on him, and then she smiled. Broussard was taken completely by surprise. It was the first time ever he had seen her smile, but he was equally surprised by the realization that he never before had noted this omission.

'You guessed?' she asked. 'How'd you guess?'

He shook his head. 'I didn't guess. I almost expected it.'

Her smile quickly faded.

He would tell her straight-out. He always told them straight-out when the subject finally came up, though he never brought it up himself.

'It often happens that women who have been victims of father-daughter incest are bisexual, or even exclusively lesbian,' he said. 'It happens more than you might think.'

Mary squinted at him, resting her chin on her bare knees.

'Is this going to be an obvious psychological calculation?'

'Such as?'

'Defiled by her father as a child, she rejects men in favor of women.'

'No,' Broussard shook his head. 'You missed it. It isn't obvious.'

Mary's eyes shifted to a guarded opacity, which settled over them like the hooded defense of a serpent's eyes. He could almost sense her challenge, the dare to unriddle her.

'The Persephone complex,' he said.

'Persephone.'

Broussard nodded.

'As in Greek mythology.'

He nodded again. 'Goddess of Spring.'

'Yes, I remember.' She rolled her eyes upward. 'Uh, she was carried away to the underworld by . . .'

'Hades.'

'. . . the god of the underworld.'

'Her uncle.'

'Oh, really?' She regarded Broussard. 'Something to do with spring,' she said vaguely.

'Her mother was Demeter, goddess of the earth and fertility. When her daughter was stolen, Demeter was furious and withheld her favors. The earth became barren until Zeus intervened and forced Hades to allow Persephone to return to her mother on earth. But Hades did not give her up permanently. One third of every year she must return to him. When she does, Demeter withholds her favors from men, the earth ceases to be fruitful. All the time she is with Hades, Persephone longs for her mother, and she is destined to relive this longing over and over for all eternity. Before the seduction, mother and daughter had been inseparable. The seduction destroyed that bond forever. In the mythological stories about Persephone and Demeter, sorrow is the central theme.'

Though it was his intention to relate more informally with Mary, Broussard almost mechanically slipped into the language of his professional manner. Like many men, he was an animal of habit — and of inhibitions — and Mary Lowe was the kind of creature from which he unconsciously protected himself. It would have taken a resolute effort for him to have lowered his defenses in her presence without the benefit of his feminine persona.

'Freud,' he continued stiffly, 'though he really didn't understand women very well, at least revealed to us the invaluable discovery that every child's initial erotic attachment is to its mother. For males, this eventually causes a conflict with the father — Oedipus complex. In females, however, this separation from the mother takes a different form. She turns to her father, but this change from mother to father is prolonged and painful. Her pre-Oedipal attachment to her mother is extraordinarily intense, and she does not find the changeover an easy one to make. In fact, it is never adequately resolved. Therefore, women never satisfactorily develop a demanding superego, and this results in a developmental lacuna, a feminine deficiency: a less discriminating ethical construct.'

Broussard paused. Mary was following his cursory explanation with a fixed, passionless stare. It was as if she had turned off all her emotions, though the fact that she was absolutely motionless belied her intense interest. There was something pathetic about the lack of feeling in her face. In the quiet moments he perceived this; he was also aware of the first rich fragrances of the rain-dampened woods borne through the opened windows on the warm late-morning air.

'For a number of years now,' Broussard said, 'most of my clients have been women. A majority of these women have been either lesbian or bisexual. And a majority of *them* have been victims of childhood sexual abuse, mostly incest.'

Mary Lowe very slowly moved her toes and leaned her head forward to rest her chin on the tops of her bare knees. It was her only movement, and it was done in such a way that it reminded Broussard of a cat.

'Incest is a very complicated thing,' he continued cautiously. Mary's eyes did not move. They were light enough to see into, to see through, as if they were openings to another world. 'Whereas a boy's first sexual attraction is to a person of a different sex, a girl's first attraction is to a person of the same sex, and because of this it creates a bond that is much stronger than that which occurs in the male. And since it occurs so early in the girl's life, it forms an unbreakable link that always underlies subsequent sexual attachments to men.'

He paused, surprised by a sense of growing apprehension, though he had no intention of stopping.

'One of the primary tragedies of father-daughter incest is the damage that is done to the mother–daughter bond. When incest is initiated early in a little girl's life, this bond is interrupted much earlier than it would normally occur in the natural course of a girl's emotional development. The relationship with the mother is cut short and forever leaves the daughter with an intense longing for a nurturing relationship with another woman. This early break with the mother is natural for little boys, but not for little girls, whose attachment to their mothers is normally extended for a longer period ... except in cases of incest.

'Like Persephone, abducted by her uncle (the father figure), the little girl incest victim is torn too early from her mother by her father. She is forever marked by the double wounds of paternal betrayal and maternal loss. Like Persephone, the incest victim is doomed to return, through memory, to her father, who is her betrayer, her abuser, her lover — to Hades, a symbolic hell. Memory and guilt will hound her unrelentingly for the rest of her life, unless she learns to resolve the discord of her imagination.'

55

Vickie Kittrie came out of Janice Hardeman's front door headfirst in a thick, black plastic bag, and everyone standing behind the yellow crime scene ribbon finally got to see what they had been waiting for. They saw where her feet punched up the narrow end of the bag, and they saw how the weight of her shifted in the bag as though she were still pliable, which she was, as the morgue attendants bumped the legs of the aluminum gurney against the back of the morgue van, making them fold up as they slid Vickie Kittrie out of sight and closed the doors.

Palma watched the trip from the door of the house to the door of the van and wondered, as she had done more than a few times before, what it must be like to be zipped into such a bag, listening to the barking static of the police radios and surrounded by the muffled crackling of the thick plastic bag as it moved around you. It was the kind of primitive wondering that the living often did about the dead, the sort of thing that had more to do with emotion than reason. Palma knew that, of course, but still she sometimes found herself wondering all the same.

Janice Hardeman left the crime scene with a couple of friends after being allowed to go into her bedroom with Officer Saldana and collect enough clothes for several days. She was told the police would notify her later in the day about when she would be allowed back into her house. Palma thought about that too, about Janice Hardeman selling her bed. Murders, especially murders like these, played havoc with reason. In fact, the act of murder was a symbol for havoc, in the mind of the murderer as well as in the public psyche. Reason had to marshal all its forces to deal with it, and even then it was a close contest.

Nothing was found in the street in front of Hardeman's house that gave them any help, and the crime ribbon was pulled back to encompass only the little plot of yard in front of the house. With the removal of Kittrie's body and the traffic once again moving by on the neighbourhood street, the crowd began to disperse and most of the police cars moved on to their regular beats.

Before Frisch started back downtown he stood in the shade of an old honey locust near the curb and brought Palma and Grant up to date on the other facets of the investigation.

'Gordy's in good shape,' Frisch said, backing well into the shade of the tree. At ten-thirty the sun was already high and white in a cobalt sky, and the humidity was so heavy it appeared like a glaucous vapor in the distance.

'He's going to be gimpy for a good while, but no permanent damage. Good excuse to make him lose a few pounds. Uh, Barbish is fine, too. He's out of danger, and the doctors tell us they expect him to be in good enough condition to be interviewed in another twenty-four hours. It ought to be an interesting conversation, because we've got a lot to tell him.'

'The ballistics information was good?' Palma anticipated him.

Frisch nodded. 'Yeah, the Colt Combat Commander checked out. It was the same weapon that fired the Power Jacket hollow points into Ackley and Montalvo. Barbish is not too smart. Like a lot of other thick-skulled cowboys, he loved his damn weapon too much. He should have gotten rid of it. He's going to have to have a damn good lawyer to keep him from taking the needle in Huntsville. I imagine Gil Reynolds can just about feel the injection

himself. The electronic-surveillance guys picked up
Reynolds's reaction at the breakfast table when he saw
the morning paper about Barbish's being wounded in a
shootout with police. And then when he got to the part
about Mirel Farr he got real quiet, and his overnight girlfriend started asking him what was wrong, what was
wrong. She couldn't figure out what had gotten into him.
She kept pestering him until he yelled at her, and she
started crying and they had a yelling fight. She ran off
into the bedroom, and it's been quiet there ever since. But
so far he's sitting tight.'

'What about John?' Palma asked. 'What have you
heard from him?'

'Birley's not having any luck getting anything new
from Denise Kaplan's lovers,' Frisch said, taking out a
notebook from his coat pocket. 'But the guys we've got
beating the bushes in Broussard's neighborhood finally
came up with the name of his housekeeper and cook. This
was called in just about fifteen minutes ago.' He looked at
his notes. 'Alice Jackson, a fifty-eight-year-old black
woman living not far off Wheeler Avenue near Texas
Southern University. Maples and Lee came on to her
through another domestic a few houses away. This
woman said Jackson had worked for Broussard ten or twelve
years. Said Jackson didn't talk about the man too much
except to say that he was "particular" about his privacy. She
claimed Jackson was as closemouthed as they come.'

Frisch tore the sheet of paper off his notepad and
handed it to Palma.

'What have you heard about Farr?' Grant asked.

'Her doctor said she could be interviewed later this
afternoon,' Frisch said. 'He sedated her pretty good for
the jaw-wiring, and he wanted her to have time to lose
some of the swelling. Maybe around five o'clock. Even
then, he's not going to give you much time with her.'

Grant nodded. 'Okay, then. I guess it's Alice Jackson.'

Grant wiped a hand over his face, and Palma could
hear the scratchy sound of the night's growth of beard
against his hand. Now that they were in full daylight,

Palma could see that Grant's eyes were redder than they should have been, and the crow's-feet at the corners of his eyes looked as if they had been chiseled into his face. She was glad that the wine could have its effects on him as well.

'I'll be frank with you,' he said to Frisch, loosening his tie. 'I'm not sure what the hell's going on here.' He looked at his watch. 'I've been here a little over thirty-six hours. Ackley eliminated himself before I got here, Reynolds and Barbish eliminated themselves only hours ago, and *no* other suspects have come to the forefront besides Dominick Broussard, who fits only a smattering of the characteristics in my profile. And, to tell you the truth, I didn't see anything today in Kittrie's case that would make me change my mind about what I've already concluded. It's going to take some more digging but, honestly, I don't think he's going to give us much time before the next one. This guy's really on a tear, his fantasy's pinging around like a pinball machine and pretty soon he's going to explode. I think he'll screw up, completely lose it. In the end, he's going to get so crazy he'll practically give himself to us. But not before he kills another woman ... or two.'

'Then you don't think it's Broussard,' Frisch said.

Grant shook his head. 'He's the only guy in sight,' he conceded. 'And there are some things I liked about him — we talked about them last night with Leeland. But I've been going over it and over it since then, and I'm going to back down a little.The man just doesn't add up to the profile characteristics we're used to seeing in these kinds of cases. My cop nose tells me that if a guy has intimate knowledge of every one of the victims, then that's more than coincidence, and I put him right up there at the top of the list. But my experience with sexually motivated killers tells me he's not what we're looking for.'

Grant was standing in the edge of the shade so that the rising angle of the sun was catching the back of his left shoulder. Beads of perspiration were popping up all over his forehead, and even though he had unbuttoned his double-breasted suit coat it looked hot. Palma remembered his pulling out his shirttail and leaning back on her sofa with his shoes off.

'On the other hand,' he said, looking at Palma and then back to Frisch, 'countering each of those "hunches" are old maxims that I'm finding hard to ignore. The first maxim: "A chance element will sometimes send you on a wild goose chase." The fact that Broussard knows each of the victims could be nothing more than chance. After all, the man specializes in their particular emotional disabilities. Maybe we're stacking the deck against him because we desperately need a good hand. The second maxim: "There are no absolutes in human behavior." Just because I haven't seen it before, even after thousands of cases, doesn't mean I won't see it now. Anything's possible when you're dealing with the human personality. The variables are incalculable.'

Palma took Grant to the Hyatt Regency, where she waited in the coffee shop while he quickly showered and shaved and put on a clean change of clothes.

While she waited, she went over the scene in Hardeman's bedroom. She stood at the door again and very carefully went over every move they made around the stiffening remains of Vickie Kittrie. She recalled their conversation, Grant's face, her own thoughts. Her own thoughts, imagining once again the man bent over the body, the bare buttocks, the rippled spine, what he did.

Suddenly she stood and walked out of the coffee shop, stopping at the cash register to tell her waitress not to clear her table, that she was only going to make a phone call. She hurried across the lobby to the bank of telephones behind the glass elevators. She took two quarters from her purse. With the first quarter she called Jeff Chin. With the second one she called Barbara Soronno in the crime lab.

They had a late breakfast sitting at a table that looked out onto Louisiana Street and had their first cups of coffee in a long morning that already seemed like it had been a full day.

But Grant was fresher after his shower, and certainly appeared more alert than Palma felt, though after making her telephone calls she had gone by the women's lounge and spent some time trying to make up for what she hadn't done before they left the house that morning in the dark.

'I'd mentioned to you I wanted to run some things by you,' Grant said after several sips of his coffee. Palma noted that he was wearing another double-breasted suit — a summer gray — and a fresh white shirt with a spread collar. Very polished, she thought, and she wondered if he had dressed this way when his first wife was alive, or if this was a result of the Chinese woman whose name Grant had never told her. Either way, he wore these rather proper clothes very well, not the least bit self-conscious of them. She looked at his face, squeaky clean from his fresh shave, his British officer's mustache immaculately trimmed.

'But first I'd like to get your reaction to what you saw this morning.'

'My reaction? To what part of it?' Palma asked.

'Any part of it.'

She hadn't expected the question, and her own questions were largely intended to give her time to think. How much of her 'reaction' did she really want to share with him? Actually, Grant's query was wide open. It could encompass Palma's entire emotional reaction to all these cases, to all that she had seen in the past two weeks, or it could simply be a response to the physical evidence they had seen that morning, whether or not it demonstrated any deviation from what they understood so far about the murderer's habits with the bodies. Palma knew that how she responded would reveal as much about herself as it would about her understanding of the cases, and it made her wonder what was really behind Grant's simple inter-rogatory. She decided to be straightforward about it. She always decided to be straightforward.

'The main element that's affected me from the beginning of these cases,' she said, 'has been the bite marks. I know they're common in sexual homicides, but these aren't common sexual homicides. Not to me, anyway.'

'Not to you?'

'I don't mind admitting to a strong personal reaction to these from the beginning. It's not anything I can focus on, I mean I can't identify any key element that makes them different for me, but something's there. And the bite marks, well, I've seen bite marks before, but these turned my stomach. Then with Bernadine Mello I saw the deliberate centering on the navel, then this morning ... the whole thing ... gone.'

She turned her head, looked out to Louisiana Street, where the cabbies were lined up outside the hotel. Some of them were sitting in their cars with their doors open, out of the sun but not out of the heat, the buses and the traffic throwing up as much as the sun was throwing down, and the asphalt and the cement, already heated to capacity, weren't taking any more and were reflecting it back like heat lamps.

She turned back to Grant.

'You've been in this business a while, seen a lot of things,' she said. 'Maybe you've seen eyelids cut away before. I haven't. Maybe you've seen navels sucked out of people's bellies. I haven't. But for me, the missing eyelids don't hold a candle to that eviscerated navel.' She lowered her voice, unable to keep out the tonal strain of her tightening throat. 'He didn't remove the eyelids with his mouth,' she said with deliberation. 'But that's damn sure the way he took out her navel.'

She saw that Grant's eyes were leveled at her with the same seeing-unseeing gaze that he had when he was looking at the picture of Denise Kaplan, his mind having gone way beyond the immediate focus of their concentration, and his next question sent a hot rush up from her stomach.

'How do you know that?' he asked.

Palma looked at him. Neither of them blinked. Jesus Christ, she thought.

'That's what it's like,' he said. His face was an odd mixture of grim knowing and restrained excitement. 'It doesn't always happen, doesn't always come to you like this, but when it does, there's really nothing like it. When you tap into one of these guys ... there's really nothing like it.'

Palma reached for her glass of water and took a long drink to quench the fire in her stomach. She was stunned. She remembered what Grant had said during their second telephone conversation. He had told her that her objective ought to be to start thinking like the killer. Jokingly, she had replied, 'No problem.' But Grant had not been that amused. It was too late for her *not* to have a problem, he had said. If she didn't start thinking like the murderer, then she had a problem. And if she did start thinking like the murderer, then she still had a problem, only it was a problem of another sort. At the time, she really hadn't known what he was talking about. Now she was afraid she did. What in the hell had she gotten herself into?

'Look,' Grant said, bringing her back. He was talking slowly, as if he were coaching her through it, knowing what she was feeling and wanting to reassure her. 'You've just discovered something about yourself that's extraordinary. It's an unnerving realization for anyone, in whatever field of human endeavor, to come face-to-face with a special ability ... a gift. It sets you apart in secret ways, in ways that you know you can't explain, or even admit to anyone else. And it presents you with a burden, and a choice. Either you pick up the burden and carry it, or you don't. It's a choice you can't afford to make lightly, because it's going to have lifetime consequences. All I'm trying to say is that it's nothing magical or freakish. It's just ... just like having a hunch, only it's more intense than that. You've got to have the guts to give it free rein, to let it get into you and develop. Accept it. If you can do that, if you've got that kind of genius and don't use it ... it would be wrong. You can't afford to be afraid of it.'

Palma fought a sense of suffocation. A warm, feverish glow spread over her, and she was sure she was flushed.

She took another drink of water, and then looked at him.

'You're saying ... that you think he actually did that?' she asked.

'*You* told *me* that's what he did,' Grant said.

Palma nodded. She *had* been convinced, but now she realized it had been an unconscious certitude until Grant had pointed it out to her.

'Yeah, I believe it happened that way,' Grant affirmed. 'Or at least it's so close to the way it happened that we can begin predicating some of our investigative decisions based upon that "theory." That's the way it works. You play it down. You follow your "hunches," and they prove to be remarkably accurate. People will accept that kind of prescience if you call it a "hunch." Cops are proud of their hunches. But you can't say what it *really* feels like, that it's as if you'd been there yourself.'

He took a drink of water himself and then shoved aside his half-eaten breakfast and looked at her as a wry grin eased onto his face.

'The fact is,' he said, 'I had sensed that you were getting more out of this than I was. I'm stumped here, but you seem to be connecting on a different level. I *still* think my profile analysis is correct; I can't see anything I'd change. But I have to face the fact, too, that it isn't meshing with our primary suspect. This whole thing seems to be drifting in the wrong direction for me. I think you can put us back on course.'

Palma was uneasy. Grant was making it sound like she had all the answers, that breaking the case was up to her. 'I'll have to be honest with you,' she said. 'I don't think I understand what's going on here as much as you seem to believe I do. It really is only a hunch. You're making it sound much more ... developed than it is. I mean, I'm sticking with my gut feelings on this ... but if you haven't noticed, I'm still having mixed signals. I said "he" took out Kittrie's navel with "his" mouth. But I'm sticking with the idea of a female killer. It *feels* consistent.'

Grant came back at her quickly, with a steely urgency. 'Intuition, this kind of "insight," is not an exact thing,' he said. 'It has to be ... accommodated. It's a slender vision of another mind, and you have to have the strength and the faith to let it guide you to ideas you've never imagined. That's why it seems amorphous, unclear. You're following, not leading. It requires a rare courage to give yourself to an inner voice.'

Grant was leaning on the table, his eyes leveled at her with a slight, crimped earnestness. His brief exposition had been ardent, a word she normally would not have associated with him. It was disconcerting.

'Let's at lest double-check Broussard against the list of the profile characteristics you gave us,' Palma said, wanting to reduce the wire-tight tension she was beginning to feel in her brain. She wanted something mundane, something routine and structured to concentrate on. 'Good intelligence.'

'Check,' Grant said. He seemed to understand what she was feeling. 'Broussard obviously has that.'

'Socially competent.'

'My gut tells me he's in the cellar on that,' Grant said. 'We don't know that yet, but that's what we're going to find out. Let's say I'm right. That's a negative.'

'Sexually competent.'

'My nose tells me the same thing. Broussard's as screwed up as the women he consults.'

'Inconsistent childhood discipline.'

'That we don't know. Again, my gut tells me it was a mess.'

'Living with a partner.'

'No.'

'Follows crime in the news media.'

'If we can believe him, he says no.'

'Precipitating situational stress.'

'We don't know, but I'd say we'll find something there.'

'The man's married and has children.'

'Not Broussard.'

'Kept souvenirs from the killings.'

'Of course, we don't know. But with Broussard — as

opposed to Reynolds — we'll find some. I'm sure of it.'

'The importance of fantasy.'

'I'm dead-solid on that one. Broussard's a fantasizing fool.'

She stopped. 'That's most of them.'

'By my count,' Grant said, 'Broussard fits four out of ten of the characteristics this killer should have. We never expect to have all of them right, but we hope to have a better ratio than that. And I, personally, usually have a hell of a lot better ratio than that.'

Palma took another sip of water. The thought of the coffee she had badly wanted half an hour earlier nauseated her.

'I think you're being a little hard on yourself,' she said. 'You guessed at many of those characteristics. We simply don't know Broussard that well. I think we ought to have this conversation again after we talk to Alice Jackson. With a little luck, things could look a lot different.

56

Alice Jackson lived less than a dozen blocks from Texas Southern University, which was established by the Texas legislature in 1947 as the Texas State University for Negroes. The legislative move was not, as it might seem, the result of an educationally enlightened state political body, but rather an effort by Jim Crow politicians to stave off ambitious blacks who more and more were beginning to go to court to obtain admission to the state university. As it was, blacks were not admitted to the Texas state university system of schools until 1950, but the efforts to prevent them from doing so established a university that now had an enrollment of more than eight thousand predominantly black students, most of them from the city of Houston.

The neighborhood had fallen on hard times. In fact, no one there could remember anything but hard times, though there were many who now claimed that in addition to hard, things were also getting mean, too damn mean. Just a few blocks to the east of Alice Jackson's street, the Gulf Freeway kept up a constant roar of traffic going to and from the coast, and a few blocks to the west the South and Southwest freeways kept up a constant roar sending traffic south toward Mexico. Alice Jackson never went to either place. She stayed close to home and watched the things that used to be pass away and the things that shouldn't be take their place. Not too far away in Emancipation Park the kids of the ward worked their way to hell at nights, giving each other cocaine and heroin and new diseases and drug-ridden little babies that the welfare system had to clean up and their grandmamas had to raise. Hope was the name of a few of the older girls in the local high schools, but that was all any of the kids knew about the word. And even the grown-ups had let the word slip out of their vocabulary in recent years. There weren't any Hopes below the eighth grade.

Alice Jackson watched this strange, sad pageant of her neighborhood from the front porch of her small brick house that distinguished itself from all the other houses on her street by its neatness. Not only did Alice's tiny front yard have grass on it, but the grass was mowed. The front porch railings were painted. She regularly killed the persistent weeds that sprang up in the cracks of her cement driveway, even though she didn't have a car to park in it. She washed her windows. Three times a week she went to church at the River of Jordan Baptist Church around the corner, and it was only because of this regular and highly emotional exposure to the idea of the possibilities of a better world that Alice Jackson was able to look upon all the decay that went on around her with a kind of philosophical composure. She kept her backbone straight and her heart soft and waited with the rest of the congregation for that day 'farther along when we'll understand why.'

Pink and mauve and lavender petunias were blooming in faded clay pots on the steps of Alice's front porch when Palma and Grant pulled up to the curb in front of her house around twelve-thirty. Palma took in the derelict street and Alice's neat little brick house and began to form judgments about the woman she was about to interview. The petunias had been recently watered and the dark patches on the cement steps were still glistening in the sun as they made their way up to the porch and knocked on the screen door. The cooking smells of a Sunday meal wafted out to them on the warm air.

'Baked ham,' Grant observed in a low voice, and Palma

thought of the different smells she remembered in a different part of the city, smells of the barrio instead of the ward.

Before she had a chance to say anything, the face of Alice Jackson appeared on the other side of the screen door, a dark face with sharp, chiseled features arranged in a questioning expression and the amber palm of a long-fingered hand placed cautiously on the face of the screen.

'Ms. Alice Jackson?' Palma asked.

The woman nodded. 'I am.'

'My name is Carmen Palma and this is Mr. Grant.' Palma pulled her shield out of her purse and held it up for Alice Jackson to see. 'I'm with the Houston Police Department, and Mr. Grant is with the FBI. Would you have a few minutes to talk to us?'

Alice Jackson hesitated. 'Regarding what, ma'am?' She spoke slowly, politely. She wore a dark Swiss-dot dress with a broad white collar. Her hair was long and pulled back in a bun, and at the front of her hairline and to the left side of the off-center part was a broad streak of gray that was combed back toward her bun in a gentle, wiry wave.

'We're part of a team of detectives who are investigating a series of homicides in the city,' Palma said. 'We're questioning people who live or work in Hunters Creek, where some of the victims lived, and we understand you're employed in that area.'

'Yes, I am,' she said. She looked at Grant, regarded him leisurely, and nodded. 'I sure am.' She looked back at Palma. 'I guess you better come on in.' She pushed open the screen and stepped back.

As tall as Palma, Alice Jackson was a thin woman with a slow, proud carriage, and a gentle manner. She offered them seats on a small sofa in a pin-neat living room and offered them something to drink, which they both refused. Sitting forward in an armchair opposite them, she very naturally crossed her low-heeled feet at the ankles and folded her hands in her lap. She did not appear to be uncomfortable having these two white police detectives in her home, despite the fact that she lived in an area where neither the police nor white people were common visitors, and when they were they were universally unwelcome. She cocked her head slightly forward and waited for Palma to explain further.

Palma spent a minute or two asking general questions and making notations in her notebook, giving Alice a chance to watch her and draw some conclusions about her, and in turn getting a feel for how she thought Alice might react to the touchier questions that were soon to follow. Within a few minutes she decided that the circumspect older woman was not only fully capable of coping with the awkwardness of discussing her employer, but also that she had already begun to suspect that Dominick Broussard was in fact the very reason they were there. She was not a woman who needed to be humored or coddled along, either emotionally or intellectually.

'Ms. Jackson,' Palma said finally. 'I think it's probably best if I'm simply straightforward with you.' Alice Jackson gave a half nod. 'I'm going to need to ask you a number of rather personal and confidential questions about Dr. Broussard. But I want you to understand that in the natural course of an investigation like this we ask questions about a lot of people. Naturally, most of the people we make inquiries about are not guilty of homicide, but we have to make the inquiries all the same. It's true that in a criminal trial the person who is charged with the crime is presumed innocent until proven guilty. But it's also true that before the trial there's the investigation, and as a general rule there are always far more people suspected of a crime than are ultimately charged with it.'

'I understand what you're saying, Detective Palma,' Alice said. 'I understand it. Go ahead.'

Palma smiled. 'Okay. How long have you worked for Dr. Broussard?'

'Eight years. Or a little over eight years.'

'And you work five days a week?'

'Five and a half. I come in on Saturday mornings and

stay until noon. Often he sees clients on Saturday morning. I get his Saturday supper for him. A microwave meal. I cook French dishes; he taught me a number of dishes. I fix them for him to heat in the microwave after I'm gone. A complete meal, so all he does is warm them. That's what I do mostly, is cook. There's not much house-keeping, him being a bachelor. Nothing gets messed up much. He's a very neat man.'

'You do that every Saturday?'

She nodded. 'For years. Regular as a new moon.'

'You commute to work? You ride the bus?'

'In, in the morning; out in the evening.'

'What time do you leave at in the evenings?'

'Seven o'clock. I start his suppers for him. That's later than most domestics, but he pays me well for that. And in the summertime there's still plenty of light to enjoy when I get home.'

'What do you know about Dr. Broussard's habits in the evenings? Does he go out regularly?'

'I don't know about that,' she said.

'Have you ever met any of the women he's dated?'

'No, ma'am.'

'Do you know anything about his social life at all?'

'Not hardly.'

Palma didn't know whether Alice meant of course not, it was out of the question, or not very much. It was an interesting response.

'Is Dr. Broussard homosexual?'

Alice Jackson didn't respond immediately, but she didn't seem shocked by the question. She was giving it some thought. She looked toward the screen door, where the bright sunshine of midday threw a burnished path across the linoleum floor from the threshold of the door to her chair, and she seemed to regard it with mild curiosity while her mind was more specifically occupied with Palma's question. Outside, the day was sweltering and the voices of children playing under the row of chinaberry trees across the street wafted in on the hot air. Alice Jackson's hands still rested in her lap, but they did not fidget or betray a sense of uneasiness. Finally she turned back to Palma.

'I don't know how to answer that, really,' she said. 'Keeping house for people, you know, is a funny thing.' She looked at Palma. 'Down here, in the South, people's housekeepers are usually black or Mexican. Any of your people ever housekeepers?'

'No,' Palma said. 'I don't believe so.'

'Well.' Alice's eyes glided in a smooth circle toward Grant and back again to Palma. 'It's an interesting thing. Dr. Brousssard's a psychiatrist, knows a lot about human nature.' She tilted her head at Palma. 'Police, they know a lot about human nature. Dr. Broussard sees a lot of strange human nature, and I guess you do too.' She nodded to herself, thinking.

'Well, domestics — I usually say "housekeeper," employers like to say "domestic" — they know something about human nature too. I don't know what it is, but when people pay someone to take care of their personal things, you know, "personal" things, then it seems to me they kind of have to separate themselves from those people somehow, because it's embarrassing to pay a stranger to do something you would otherwise do for yourself, or someone close to you would do for you, a mama or a wife. So what happens is they pretend, maybe, that you are not a full-fledged person. Pretend you're deaf or blind and don't hear and see things they say and do. You know, you're just the "help."

'The point is,' Alice continued, 'Dr. Broussard is a very kind man, always very good to me. But, sometimes, he thinks I am deaf and blind.' Alice looked at Grant. 'I'm sorry,' she said, 'if this sounds roundabout. It's just that that's a serious question, and I think I have an answer, but I'm not sure what it means. It needs some understanding.' Then back to Palma.

'For eight years I have taken care of Dr. Broussard's house,' she continued. 'I don't believe he has ever married. Lifelong bachelor. I clean his house, but as I said he does not live in it too hard, and so the only things that

regularly need attention are his things. His bedroom. His
sheets. His laundry.' She paused and started to look over
again at the sunny path coming in through the screen and
then decided to look at her hands instead. She raised
them a little and lightly patted her thighs as if she were
resolving to continue. 'He likes women, all right. Sometimes one has been there in the mornings when I get to
the house. Sometimes they are still in bed till late
morning. I have heard them, but I act deaf. I have seen
them, but I act blind.' She smiled a little, as if she had
proved her earlier point.

Then she gathered her brows and frowned. 'But in Dr.
Broussard's upstairs bedroom there are two very large
closets. One of them is full of Dr. Broussard's suits and
pants and shirts, all his clothes. The other one, well, it is
full of women's dresses and a low shelf with wigs. He has
two very large dressers. One of them is filled with his
underclothes and other personal items. The other one is
filled with women's underclothes. He keeps his cologne
on his dresser with a few other things, a set of clothes
brushes, a set of shoe brushes. He's a very dapper man, if
you've noticed. On the ladies' dresser is a full set of
perfumes and cosmetics. A wide variety of them. For a
long time I thought he had a special lady, and that these
women's clothes and cosmetics were hers. But of course, I
learned very soon that wasn't the case at all. He had lots
of women friends, and they were not all of them the same
size or would have used the same makeup. So I was
curious, and I began to notice. The makeup was used
regularly. The dresses were worn frequently. The dresses
were all the same size, rather large. But the labels were
tony, and they were very pretty dresses, very smart.
Dinner dresses, almost all of them. Nothing casual. And
every once in a while a new dress would show up, and an
older, less stylish one would disappear.'

Alice Jackson looked straight at Palma. 'The thing was,
you see, there was times I was washing ladies' underwear
when there wasn't any ladies there, and hadn't been any
ladies there for weeks at a time.'

'How long had you been working for him at this time?'
Palma's heart was pounding. She imagined that Grant's
mind was churning, trying to place this newly discovered
piece into the fragmented psychological mosaic of the
murders.

'You mean when I first noticed all this? Well, from the
very start is when.'

'So you've known all these years that he was cross-
dressing?'

'If that's what it's called, yes.'

'What color are the wigs?' Palma asked. She could
hardly keep her voice in a normal register.

'Blond, mostly. There's a light brown one, I think, but
mostly blond.'

'How many of them are there?'

'Seems like five, maybe.'

'Have you ever seen him cross-dressed?'

Alice looked blank for a moment and then she was clearly
embarrassed, looking to the side, moving in her chair.

'Once,' she said. 'A couple of years ago. It was on a
Thursday evening. I had ridden my bus home, and when I
got off at my street I realized I had left at Dr. Broussard's
a gift that I had bought for my little niece who was
coming over that evening. I just stood right there and
waited for the next bus coming the other way and rode all
the way back into town and went back to the house. I
rang the front doorbell, but he never answered, and I
thought he was at the office, you know, through the
woods there. So I let myself in with my key, went into the
little dayroom where I keep my things, and got the toy.
As I was walking back through the house, I heard music
start up on the terrace. I stepped into the dining room and
looked out. He was out there, all dressed up, drinking
wine and walking back and forth on the terrace in this
flowing evening dress.' She smiled. 'It was very strange
to see him. I couldn't help myself. I stood and watched
for some time, him prancing and gliding around in that
dress, drinking and listening to the music.' She shook her
head, remembering.

'But you know, the strangest thing. Dr. Broussard is not an easygoing man. He is a bit ... aloof. Often he is tense, preoccupied. Kind of surly. But while I stood there watching him, it was very clear to me that he was completely at ease. He was not awkward in that dress. Did just fine in those heels. And he was graceful! Lord, I was just hypnotized by him. He seemed to be comfortable and at ease for the first time since I had been working for him. I believe that man would be better off as a lady. A lot happier.'

She turned to Grant again. 'So you see what I mean? Homosexual? Oh, I don't think so. I'd say his personal life with ladies is pretty healthy. But the man dresses up like a lady. All the time. I don't know the fine details of a homosexual, but I think Dr. Broussard just likes ladies so much he wants to be one.'

'You're very observant,' Grant said. It was the first time he had spoken, and Alice Jackson sat a little straighter. 'I think your information is going to be a lot of help to us. You mentioned Dr. Broussard's office; do you clean that as well as the house?'

'Oh, no. He has a service to do that. He says he can take it off his income taxes.'

'Have you ever met any of his clients?' Grant asked.

'I've seen them. I haven't met them.'

'Have you seen them at his home?'

'Yes.'

'How did you know they were clients?'

'I told you, he acted like I was deaf sometimes. He talked to them like he was talking business, like I imagine a psychiatrist would talk.'

'And then you think he had sexual relations with them?'

'It seemed that was what was going on.'

'Do you have any reason to believe that his sexual relations with the women he brought to the house were in any way unusual?' Palma asked. She wondered how a question like that might strike an older woman who had been unmarried all her life.

'Unusual,' Alice said. 'Now that is a loaded question. It seems to me that the word gets harder and harder to define every year.' She looked at her hands again and shook her head. 'What goes for "unusual" in this neighborhood has changed ... so much. Everywhere, too, it seems to me.' She shook her head. 'I am afraid that more things look "unusual" to me than they might to the next person. But, no. I don't have any reason to believe that anything "unusual" went on with Dr. Broussard's women.' She looked up at Palma. 'But you understand, I really don't know.'

57

'So you know a lot about women, then?' Mary Lowe said. She was still resting her chin on her bare knees, her arms wrapped around her legs.

'I know a good deal about some types of women.'

'Some types.'

Broussard nodded. He was aware of the warm breeze coming in the window. It penetrated the hair on his chest, got next to his skin. He was aware of the wet hissing of the sprinkler system.

'Victims of father-daughter incest,' Mary said.

Broussard nodded.

'About me.'

'To a certain degree.' And then he thought to himself that possibly, of all the women he had ever had as clients, he knew the least and was destined to continue to know the least about Mary Lowe. She was *sui generis*, and this sense that he had of her distinctiveness did not follow from reasoned deductions, or from analysis. Rather it came from his emotional center. It was a gut feeling.

'What do you know about me?' Mary asked.

'In general?'

'No. Me specifically. As a subcategory of the "type" you just mentioned.'

Broussard caught the scent of damp, sun-heated grass, and it seemed to him as erotic as Mary's perfumed flesh. Suddenly he thought of himself standing on the other side of the room looking at himself and Mary Lowe. It was an intriguing picture, and he liked the way they looked. Himself in summer linen. Her, naked. Blond and naked, framed in the tall opened window like a Renaissance woman with a landscape stretching out past her in the early summer heat. If he had seen this picture in a book or magazine without any caption or explanation, he would have enjoyed the opportunity to create a scenario of explication.

'You tend to isolate yourself,' Broussard said, moving his attention from the outward swell of her hip to her eyes. 'I would say you have no close adult women friends. You tend to rebuff the approaches of friendship from the mothers of your children's schoolmates. You are a good mother and wife, and you are extremely conscientious in your responsibilities in these roles, though you are perhaps not as affectionate as you might be. To others, you appear to be the model parent and wife.'

Broussard uncrossed his legs and pulled his chair closer to her. She had moved her face slightly so that her mouth was hidden on the back side of her bent knees and she gazed at him over the tops of them as though she were spying on him. Having pulled his chair as close to her as the window seat would allow, he leaned forward only slightly until his lips touched — just touched – the front of her knees and their eyes were only inches apart. When he spoke, his lips feathered against her flesh.

'You are a daydreamer,' he said huskily. 'You are a compulsive masturbator. You are a chronic liar. You have a long history of self-loathing which you often deal with by projecting hostility. You vacillate between repressing your sexual feelings and indulging them promiscuously. You distrust your own desires and needs, and often tell yourself you are not entitled to the care and respect your husband gives you. You have nightmares, often of a sexual nature, sometimes violent.' He paused. 'I would guess, too, that your sexual experiences with women have often been violent ... and in those instances ... you have preferred a masochistic role.'

She did not respond when he finished, but remained motionless, looking at him across the tops of her knees. He waited. And then, as though it were a slender crimson serpent, a tiny rivulet of blood wriggled slowly down the side of her knee and made a bright scarlet path across her white thigh. It continued its wavering course until it reached the crease created by her upper thigh and groin, where it ran into the groove and then out again, proceeding down the round ambit of her hip to the window seat.

In the inside corner of each of her eyes a single oily tear clung to its source. Broussard stood and walked into the bathroom and returned with a damp washcloth. Mary had turned her head aside, back toward the mist on the lawn, and said nothing while he cleaned the blood off the window seat and then from her hip, pressed the cloth into the crease of her groin, wiped it the long length of her thigh, up to the wound, the ringlet of teeth marks. Mary allowed him to clean her as if she were an animal, a pet that he was grooming, washing. Broussard was a long time at his task. He didn't want a trace of blood to remain. He wiped and wiped, folding the cloth to a clean spot until she was immaculate. He chose not to cover the bite mark with a bandage, but left it visible, like a rosette, a mandala, the yoni symbol, the vertical smile. Mary was oblivious of his ministrations.

When he was through he returned to the bathroom, where he rinsed out the washcloth and draped it over the side of the sink. Then he came back to the bedroom and his chair beside the window seat. Mary had sat back against the deep sill of the window seat, away from the wound on her leg. She was breathing heavily, and Broussard wondered if it was because of the pain of the wound or because of the sexual excitement that she must have derived from it.

'I guess you were right about some of that,' she said self-consciously. She lowered her legs, stretched them out in front of her, and crossed them at her ankles. 'Most of it.' Her breasts were looking at him, both pink aureoles, the buttery triangle of ringlets covering her vulva reached toward her lower stomach from between her legs.

'What do you think about it?' she asked.

'What do *you* think about it?'

Mary was breathing deeply, laboriously, seeming to have difficulty in getting enough air. Broussard could not imagine what must be going through her thoughts.

'I ... think ... I should ... never have discovered ... sex ... that way ... and ... and that ... I ... should never, never have experienced that pleasure ... with him.' She smothered a sob, and her face contorted for only an instant and then she was in control again, her stomach sucked in, her eyes widening to defy the tears.

Broussard regarded her calmly, unaffected by her pain, unmoved by the apparent disorder of her emotions. There was no way this woman could be made unattractive, not in her grief or her shame or, even, in her humiliation.

'You should understand,' he said, his own voice a little hoarse, though he didn't know why, 'that you cannot be expected to be responsible for your biological responses. If someone touches you in a certain way, if someone stimulates you sexually, your body will respond regardless of who is stimulating you. The responsibility for what you were feeling lies with your father, not with you. He betrayed a trust as old as the human family. He is responsible for your response being inappropriate because the source of the stimulus was inappropriate. A child cannot be expected to know what is unfitting ... cannot be expected to understand ...'

Broussard stopped. What could not be expected of a child? He had built a career on telling clients what could not be expected of a child, but, really, he didn't know, did he? That was how he had come to be a psychiatrist, searching for such answers. Eventually he had come to the end of his quest, and they had given him his third academic degree. Yet he was still in ignorance, but too ashamed to admit it. So he began to hide behind the shield of wisdom, and he began explaining things that he himself did not understand. But people believed him,

especially the women who were always so eager to
believe, and he lost respect for them because they were so
easily gulled and because they had the emotional instincts
of lemmings.

A child is even more innocent than adults believe. But
he is more cunning, too. Adults deceive him, but he is not
deceived. What did a child know? More than logic told
him, more than science, more than biology. He remembered this: her large breasts ... large breasts like ... some
of the other women ... like Bernadine's ... like Mary
Lowe's ... his face smothered into them, his nose buried
in her cleavage, the softest thing to touch in the world. He
remembered the smell of them, the feel of them against
the back of his neck as she leaned over him, dressing him
from behind, pulling on the panties, pulling them tight,
the elastic tight around his little legs, the silk and nylon
pressing his little penis against his stomach. She clucked
and cooed over him, the pastel dresses, and starched
pinafores. That was what made her happy, and he would
do whatever made her happy. Whenever his father was
away traveling, whenever they were alone, even for three
or four hours, any chance she got, she took off his clothes
and dressed him in girls' clothes. And as time passed he
changed and the clothes changed, but she never changed,
until he was fifteen. And he liked it, too. He liked the way
the nylon felt, and the silk, because it felt like her nylon,
her silk, which were forbidden to him because they clung
to her so intimately. Even as she held him close, his face
in the crevice of her large and fragrant bosom, they were
forbidden. But he could be near them, and he could
imagine what lay in that dark triangle that he could see
through her sheer panties. She had no inhibitions about
what she herself wore as she dressed him in girls' clothes.
Two girls in their underwear. And when she had dressed
him, then she would embrace him, and while she
embraced him his hands were free to feel her, all of her
private parts, and she let him do it then, but not when he
was not dressed as a girl. She would let him — she must
have encouraged him — to probe her and lick her. But

didn't he want to do it? Wasn't *he* the one who, time after time, became more adventurous, more adventurous until they ... regularly ... went beyond those misty borders of son and mother. But *she* had dressed him. *She* had given him the opportunity. *She* had pulled his face into her breasts and held it there, offering her hardened nipples to his adolescent mouth. *She* had been the one who first had held him in such a way that he could not avoid that dusky space between her legs.

Mary Lowe was staring at him.

He heard the sprinkler system shift, another station kicking into operation on another section of the lawn, somewhere, he guessed, nearer the bayou.

'Clinical evidence suggests,' he said automatically, sounding like a textbook, 'that some women respond to the trauma of incest by rejecting heterosexuality in early adulthood, or even later in life. They become bisexual, or exclusively lesbian.'

Had he already said that? Was he repeating himself?

Mary was staring at him.

'Sometimes when the incest involves ambivalent emotions — when positive feelings of pleasure, of being loved, coexist with the negative ones of offended conscience — the trauma often is greater than when the experience is totally unwanted.' He didn't believe he had said that before. He was spitting out formulas of clinical psychology like an automaton, falling back on rote knowledge to avoid his own emotional turmoil. 'When the emotions are confused, conflicted, the damage is greatest because there is no clear moral demarcation. The child feels personally responsible for committing an act that "seems" wrong to her — even the offending adult telegraphs that something is amiss in what they are doing by his conniving manner — but which she nevertheless enjoys. The child never forgives herself. And when she becomes a woman she never forgives herself, though she may have relegated the experience to her unconscious so that she no longer remembers. She still is haunted by a lingering, ill-defined uneasiness that reminds her ... reminds her of something horrible she has done. At some point ... the experience will surface, usually at a time of stress, and she has to confront the incest.'

Broussard saw with relief that Mary took her eyes off him and began studying the bite mark above her knee. He was aware of perspiration on his top lip, of the gummy moisture that had suddenly dampened the hair under his arm. Had Mary seen something in his manner that made her divert her eyes? What happened? Why had she begun studying her bite mark? Surely ... surely he could not have been so transparent as to ... have overstepped ... He had practiced a lifetime of restraint. He had trained himself.

Without preamble Mary began talking. 'I really don't hold any ... feelings of malice toward my father,' she said. 'People can't live without some kind of love, some kind of affection. If he sought it from a child ... I just find it ... impossible to condemn him.' She flicked her eyes at Broussard and then returned them to her wounded leg. 'I think I told you he was never anything but kind to me. Always he was tender. Even after I was older and we had intercourse, he was kind and tender and loving.'

Broussard watched her. She was lying. Only the last time they had talked she had told him of her father's — was it her father after all, and not her stepfather? — coarse penetration of her. She had said, 'After lying still and panting a little bit, he would get off me, pull up his pants, and walk away without a word and without looking at me, like always.' Like always.

'Maybe it wasn't the kind of love I was supposed to have,' Mary continued, 'but it was all the love I was getting. And I guess it was all the love he was getting, too. I don't believe it's possible for human beings to live without love, and if they don't get it, then they get something else and lie to themselves about it.'

She moved her eyes from the bite mark and let them rest on Broussard. Suddenly he wanted to kiss her eyes. He wanted to put his tongue on them, on the lenses themselves, as he had often wanted to do with Bernadine.

'When I think of this I always remember the little monkey I saw in a film in a psychology class in college,' Mary said. 'For some reason, which I've forgotten, this baby monkey was being raised in isolation. Some kind of experiment. The lab technicians put this crude rubber tube into the cage with the baby monkey and on it they had painted these stupid round circles for eyes, and they tied a rag around the rubber tube to give it some softness. This pitiful little creature fell in love with this hard rubber tube. It became passionately attached to it, holding it, cuddling it, stroking it, grooming it. He convinced himself that the tube loved him, even though the tube, of course, never demonstrated that it loved him in any way at all. It was just there. But he convinced himself that the tube loved him, and he loved the tube. He was terrified of being separated from it, never let go of it. Then one day they separated him from it ... they took it away from him. He was distraught, grief-stricken. He stopped eating. Wouldn't sleep. Eventually, he actually got sick and died.'

Mary looked at him again. 'Some kind of love. If you don't have the genuine thing then you'll create something to take its place. You'll lie to yourself, convince yourself that that thing is not bogus, that it's the genuine article. People have done a lot of grotesque things and called it love, but they've done it because they've had to.'

'What about revenge?' Broussard asked suddenly.

Mary slowly drew her legs up like before, only this time her back was resting against the wall.

'Don't you ever want revenge?' Broussard persisted.

Mary looked at him. 'No,' she said. 'He couldn't help it.'

She was clever. She knew perfectly well what he was getting at. Broussard himself understood revenge. He understood what an adult's selfishness and a failure to nurture could do to a child. Narcissism was a failure to nurture. Even though the child was involved, the seduction was for the narcissist; the child received none of the incestuous parent's affection. It was all inner-directed, and the child was little more than a rubber tube in a monkey's cage. A thing to be used. Broussard remembered his mother's embrace, the soft depths of her breasts, the nylon between them, and her saying to him that he was the prettiest little girl she had ever held and then how he would touch her and she would lay her head back and let him do what he wanted. It all had been for her. And she had never gotten enough. He never had been able to do enough for her, no matter how greedily he satisfied his own priapic curiosity.

58

'I don't know that much about them,' Palma shouted against the traffic as she turned her back to the afternoon sun coming in through the phone booth glass glazed with dirt and oxidized smog. She had stopped at the first pay phone she could find after she and Grant left Alice Jackson's house, which meant they had driven only a few blocks and were still deep in the environs of the Third Ward, working their way back under the expressways toward Montrose. She was talking to Leeland.

'We just know he cross-dresses and wears several different styles of blond wigs. The main thing right now is to find out if the unidentified strands found at Samenov's were wig hairs. I do know that most expensive wigs are made of real human hair. Some of it comes from Indonesia, usually Korea, and some of it comes from Europe. The Korean hair has coarser strands and is less expensive than the European hair, which is a finer texture. Both kinds are often bleached and redyed. But when natural hair color is wanted it has to be European, since Indonesian is only black. Both kinds are used to make blond wigs.'

Palma stopped a moment while a line of trailer trucks pulled around the corner and headed up the ramps to the expressway, their diesel engines laboring and their stacks belching black, oily smoke. When the last one was gone, she continued shouting at Leeland, watching Grant in the car through the dusty glass.

'Since we don't have a sample of Broussard's wigs, all we can really determine at this point is whether the hair is wig hair.'

'But if it's human hair, how do we do that?' Leeland's voice was faint, even though she could tell he was shouting.

'I'm not sure.' Palma wiped her mouth. She was burning up in the booth, even with the door open. 'But I'm going to give you the name of a hairdresser I know who can give you the answer. This is her home phone.' Palma read the number out of her address book. 'Or maybe Barbara Soronno already knows the answer to that. Listen, I'm getting out of this booth. I'll get back with you after a while.'

Palma hung up the telephone, her hands feeling grimy from holding the filthy receiver. She quickly got inside the car, which she had left running with the air conditioner going, and turned the vent into her face.

'They're going to check it out,' she said, getting a disposable towelette from her purse. She tore open the foil packet, wiped her face with the small damp cloth, and then turned the dash vent toward her and put her face in front of it.

'I don't know which is worse,' Grant said, watching her. 'The heat and sweat down here, or the cold and frostbite back home.'

'The cold and frostbite,' Palma said, putting the car in gear and pulling out onto the street.

Grant watched the traffic for a few minutes and then said, 'You know, that was a damned balanced assessment from a woman like that.'

'What do you mean, "a woman like that"?' Palma asked.

'It was pretty amazing, in fact,' Grant said. 'She probably didn't have a college education, even an elementary course in psychology. I would imagine her only exposure to transvestism has been with drugged-out male prostitutes. Not exactly good recommendations for cross-dressing. But she knew, she knew in her gut that Broussard's cross-dressing was a benign disorder. She wasn't indignant; she wasn't horrified. She even seemed to "understand."'

'"Domestics know something about human nature, too,"' Palma said. Having to stop at a traffic light, she looked out her window at a group of grade school boys lounging in the shade of a chinaberry tree at the side of a vacant house. They were lolling around on a tire swing, the empty shell of a barbecue pit, and the detached rear end of a taxicab, passing around a tiny joint, holding their breaths like the big dudes.

She turned to Grant. 'You're awfully damned sure of yourself,' she said.

Grant shook his head. 'It won't hurt to have them check out the hairs,' he said.

'But Broussard's not our man.'

'I'm not saying that.' Grant was tired, his tone a little edgy. 'Cross-dressing may give you the creeps, but it's not something that ought to trigger suspicion in sex crimes.'

'Except for the male prostitutes.'

'Yeah, but true transvestic fetishism, which seems to me to be what she was describing, is a harmless disorder, unless you're married to the guy. It's rare in women, and these guys are almost exclusively heterosexual.'

'And the underlying causes?' Palma didn't know what the hell to think anymore.

Grant shrugged. 'Psychologists think maybe it's a conditioning model problem. Something occurred when he was a small child that, perhaps inadvertently, taught him to associate female dress with acceptance, made him believe that acceptance was contingent on his "becoming" a girl. This misconception — or maybe it was a reality — continued until puberty and became associated with sexual gratification. Stimulus-response. The pattern was set. It's a hell of a rigmarole to have to go through in order to become sexually excited, but there's nothing threatening about it.'

'Then you don't see any possibilities here?' Palma asked. 'I mean, homicide and the psychology behind transvestism, even the possibility that somehow it's gotten garbled in his mind? Maybe he accepts the fact that his sexual life has been made unbearably complicated by this. He blames it on his mother, a sister, an aunt — whoever — something she did, something she didn't do, which he directly relates to his situation.

Grant looked at his watch. 'Look, I didn't eat much of the breakfast, and it's already approaching two o'clock. Could you go for a hamburger?'

'Sure.'

'Meaux's have good hamburgers?'

Palma turned back on Montrose and headed toward Bissonnet.

'The thing about transvestic fetishists,' Grant continued, 'is that, apparently, his only sexual preoccupation is related to female clothing. It isn't dependent on another person's emotional response, therefore the interpersonal element is minimal. You give them a woman's clothes, and they're perfectly happy. They don't have to have the woman. But, equally as often, they function perfectly well heterosexually, only they're wearing women's clothes instead of men's. It's kind of a hard thing for a woman to go along with, but if she can handle it they can be perfectly happy as a couple. Two thirds of these guys are married and have children.'

Grant looked out of the window. 'The point is,' he said, trying to put it to rest, 'this is not the sort of thing that promotes high levels of aggressive anxiety. It would be a low-motive ingredient for aggressive acts against women.'

'Even if it's coming from a guy who's got other problems, a lot of problems, and this is just one of them?'

Grant was silent a moment. 'No. You can't dismiss the guy in a situation like that. Look, I'm only saying that cross-dressing shouldn't draw any more attention to Broussard regarding these murders than acne or buck teeth. It's that harmless. It's that irrelevant. Whatever else

is in the guy's brain is another story. That's what we'd
hoped to learn from Alice Jackson. Maybe some hint of an
interest in sadomasochism, some kind of sexual kink that
involved a specific kind of emotional interaction with
another person. But, damn, cross-dressing . . .'

Grant shook his head, and slipped on a pair of sunglasses. Palma let it go, but something lodged at the back
of her mind like a small grain of sand that wouldn't wash
away in the sure current of Grant's dismissals. She
glanced at Grant as he stared out to the harsh light of the
street from behind his sunglasses. She believed there was
something else that needed explaining regarding Dominick Broussard's cross-dressing. And she had the feeling
that despite Grant's ready explanations, he also was
rethinking the possibilities.

Because they had missed the lunch hour rush, Palma
found a parking place in the shade of the catalpa tree in
front of Meaux's, and they again found a window booth
looking onto Bissonnet. For some reason Lauré was not
there, but Alma, the shy Guatemalan sister, waited on
them, casting prolonged glances of curiosity at Grant
whenever she was far enough away from them to believe
she was unobserved. Palma rarely came here with a man
other than Birley, whom they all knew and whom the
Guatemalan sisters treated with the same affectionate
goodwill they would allow a barnacled uncle. But Grant
was a different thing, and it wasn't just her usual friendli-
ness that caused Falvia, Alma's spicy sister, to make
several passes by Palma's table to speak and flash a
dazzling smile.

Grant was not noticing and gave most of his attention
to Gustaw's hamburger and Polish home fries. Both of
them kept their thoughts to themselves until they were
through eating, and Alma had come by to top up their
coffee cups. Outside the catalpa leaves hung still and limp
in the afternoon heat.

Grant sat back and looked at Palma until she felt it and
looked back at him. He pulled a paper napkin from its
worn black holder next to the window and wiped at the

empty space where Alma had cleared away their plates.
He was thinking.

'Okay,' he said finally. 'How far have you gotten with
it?'

Palma sipped her coffee, looking at him over the top of
her cup. She was going to tell him, by God. She thought
she was right. And if she was, they were both right.

'I think I know why your profile analysis isn't tracking
like you thought it would,' Palma said. Grant nodded for
her to go ahead.

'The killer's a woman,' she said.

Grant looked at her with a blank expression, and then
a slow, crooked smile grew on his face, and he shook his
head. 'For Christ's sake,' he said. He looked at her,
studied her, and as he did she suddenly knew she had it.
He started nodding. 'Go ahead,' he said.

'In one of our very first telephone conversations you
pointed out some basic assumptions we could make about
these killers,' she began. 'The broadest assumption, the
one invariable in crimes of this nature, is the gender of
the killer. He is male. His victims are female. Sometimes
his victims are children, and they can be male or female,
but the killer is *male*. Never otherwise, not in sexual
homicides. Women do not kill for sexual reasons, no
matter how distorted or sick.

'For nearly twenty years the Bureau's been developing
behavioral models of investigation that have been based
on a psychology that is exclusively male. The killers think
the way men think, they behave the way men behave.
Men dominate the crime, the investigation, and the
assessment. You've said yourself that this business is
really about playing the odds. No one's going to argue
with that. But you don't really believe that you win every
time, do you? Your uncleared cases prove you don't.

'How many of those uncleared cases do you suppose
could have been committed by women? How well do you
think a behavioral model based on male psychological
perspectives and interpreted by male investigators is
going to work when applied to a case where the unknown

subject is female? How many of your unsolved cases do
you suppose you might've misread because they were
committed by women and you were looking at the behavioral evidence as if the subjects were male and what you
saw didn't make any sense to you so you never made any
headway? You claim that your one invariable is the fact
that only men commit sexual homicides. How do you
know that? Because you've never proved that a woman
killed for sexual reasons? You've said yourself that when
you're dealing with the human personality the invariables
are incalculable, that presuppositions are dangerous. Yet
you begin every sexual homicide investigation, every one
of them, with an enormous presupposition: that the
unknown subject is male.'

Palma stopped.

Grant regarded her in silence and then asked, 'Which
one of the women in Samenov's group is it?'

'None of them.'

Grant smirked, his lips thin under his mustache, and
waited.

'This morning you told Frisch you really didn't understand what was happening,' Palma reminded him, 'that
your profile didn't jibe with any of the suspects, which by
now have been whittled down to Broussard. But you said
that after examining Vickie Kittrie you really didn't see
any reason to adjust your analysis. Well, you were
expressing your doubts about how you saw the cases
developing long before you talked to Frisch. Yesterday
when we were having that late lunch at the Café Tropical,
you said you were concerned about the "contradictions"
you were seeing between the behavioral evidence and the
suspects.'

Palma took a pen and a notepad out of her purse,
shoved her coffee cup and glass of water aside and wrote
'#1' on the notepad.

'What puzzled you then, what seemed to stick most in
my mind at that time, at least, was what the murderer did
to the victim *after* she was killed. If he conformed to the
usual behavioral characteristics of an organized murderer,

the killing itself would have been sadistic. His perverted sexual motivation would have been satisfied by the sadistic and ritualized act of the murder itself. The disorganized murderer, on the other hand, would have continued "exploring" the body: his first sexual act would have been with the body after death, dismemberment, even a return to the body at a later date, hours, days later, to do more of the same.'

Palma jabbed the '#1' with the tip of her ballpoint. 'You said that you were puzzled because this "organized" murderer had, uncharacteristically, continued to "nourish" the body. He cleans her, grooms her, lies down beside her. You said, "He treats her like a child would treat a doll, dresses and undresses her, pretends that she's real ..." Palma leaned toward Grant. 'Who plays with dolls, Sander?'

Palma caught herself. It was the first time she had ever called him by his first name, ever called him anything at all. She went on. 'Girls play with dolls. Girls. Not boys ... or at least damn few of them. "Nurturing" is typically considered a woman's role, and this killer "nurtures" the body.'

Palma made a '#2' on her notepad. 'Broussard volunteered from the beginning of our interview with him that his clientele was almost exclusively female. He considered himself something of an expert on female psychology. He's immersed in the feminine mind. Remember the clutter of feminine statuary he described to us with such relish? He was able to quickly give us "common denominators" for the victims. He brought up the subject of child abuse himself, and said he couldn't think of one of his women clients who *hadn't* been a victim of child abuse. He gave us a little lecture about Freud's seduction theory, about how at first Freud had attributed childhood sexual abuse to "nursemaids, governesses, and other servants and teachers," traditional women's roles. He went into the whole idea that women, as well as men, sexually abuse children, but that cultural mores refused to accept it. He quoted statistics from a study about the number of women who were sexual abusers of children. He mentioned that a significant percentage of these female abusers indulged in sadistic behavior with their victims. He made the same point that you did that the personality of child molesters does not lend itself to sadism, so it was unlikely that our murderer would be a child molester. But he didn't say anything about the killer possibly being a *victim* of child abuse. He talked about the importance of fantasy in the lives of sexual killers and sadomasochists and then, when you asked him to "imagine" the killer's personality, he protested, but then very easily slipped into that imagined role.

'The point is, you've said that fantasy is the compelling element of these recurring murders, and Broussard is a consummate practitioner of fantasy, as he imagines himself in the minds of his female clients — victims of child abuse — and as a cross-dresser, a woman.'

Palma laid down her pen and crossed her forearms on the table. 'If Broussard is killing these women, he's doing it from within the personality of the woman he becomes. Therefore, his behavior is a hybrid. You're not sorting out this thing because your motivational models are predicated on male psychological behavior. What you've got here is a woman, at least a woman as a man perceives her. He's probably reading most of his "female" behavior incorrectly, but he's got enough of it right to skew your analysis.'

'One more thing,' Palma said. 'Do you remember what he said about "men" and "women"? "It's a fantasy," he said, "to believe that men and women are different."' She nodded. 'You've been right all along. You've just been dealing with a killer with more than one gender.'

When Palma finally stopped, Grant's smirk had disappeared, and he was staring at her with one hand bracing his chin and mouth, his elbow on the table. The forefinger of his hand was stroking his mustache. He was no longer amused; his hooded eyes were deadly serious.

She reached for her coffee. It was almost lukewarm, but it hardly fazed her. She was watching Grant.

'It's a pretty wild scenario,' he said. He took down his

hand, put his fingers on the paper napkin and pushed it around in a drop of water that had fallen off the bottom of the glass. He shook his head. 'I don't know,' he said.

She said, 'It's fancy, isn't it?'

Grant nodded, but he was thinking about it, pursing his lips. 'I'd feel a lot better about it if we could connect him to some form of violence.'

'For the sake of argument,' Palma said, 'let's say it isn't fancy. Let's say it accounts for the behavioral contradictions in the evidence, and we intend to move on it. What kind of proactive measures would you suggest?'

'Okay, fine. I'd guess he's running at full tilt by now. His cooling-down periods are growing shorter and shorter, practically down to nothing now. He's getting careless selecting his victims. If he holds true to pattern, the next one will be a client, a member of Samenov's circle. A blond ... all the stuff we've been through before ...'

'The two women Martin and Hisdale saw drive into Broussard's last night,' Palma said. 'The one driving his car was him.'

'Possibly.'

'The other one was a woman named Lowe.'

'Right.'

'She's still there, as far as we know.'

'Even if he's flipping out, he wouldn't kill her at his place,' Grant said. 'He wouldn't do that. He's pressured, but he's still methodical. He'll make a mistake, but it won't be something like that. It'll be more like an indiscretion. He'll still think of himself as coolly methodical, similar to the way an experienced heavy drinker thinks he's perfectly under control when he's drunk. He'll drive the speed limit; he'll stay on the right side of the street, but he'll forget something simple, elementary, like turning on his headlights.

'But we need to move,' Grant conceded. 'We're not too far away from the Ben Taub Hospital, are we? We need to talk to Mirel Farr. If we get the right answers from her, I think we can do something.'

He didn't tell her what the questions were.

59

Mirel Farr was pissed off. She was sitting up in her hospital bed, which she had cranked up like a chair, and her auburn-rooted bleached hair was spewing stiffly in all directions, looking as if she had not made the slightest attempt to comb it the entire time she had been in the hospital. Her left eye was bruised and the swelling in her flat cheeks, which would usually make someone else look like a chipmunk, only made Mirel look normal. Her collarless hospital gown had a spatter of ocher stains down the front where her ungenerous breasts made little knobbly appearances in the thin material.

Though Mirel's jaws were wired shut, she was not in the least inhibited from talking. Her West Texas twang issued with relative clarity through the network of stainless-steel wires.

'I jus' got through talking to my lawyer,' she said waspishly. She was holding a can of Diet Coke with a ribbed hospital straw sticking out the top. 'We're gonna *sue* the fuckin' Houston Police Department. Sonofabitch cop slugged me. I jus' said, "Clyde? Is that you?"' Her twang imitated a question of whining innocence. 'At's all I said. "Clyde? Is that you?" and the son of a bitch cop slugged me! Mother-fucker!' She demonstrated how Marley had punched her and sloshed some of the Coke on her lap and then quickly pinched the wet spot in her fingers and flapped it. 'Suing for everything. Damages.

Cost plus. Individual liberties. Emotional distress. Over-head. Work loss. I mean!'

'I'm sure your lawyer will take care of it,' Palma said. She and Grant had only introduced themselves before Mirel launched into her legal rights speech.

'I mean!' she snapped, and her dull eyes flashed as best they could. She was pissed.

'All we want to do is ask you some questions about one of your customers,' Palma said. Grant was standing behind her near the door, and Mirel kept glancing at him.

'I don't have to answer any questions about my "clients."'

'Lieutenant Frisch tells me you've already discussed your situation with him. He tells me you've come to an agreement with him and the DA's office about your role in this investigation. He tells me you have agreed to answer questions.'

Mirel narrowed her eyes. 'Well, my lawyer will have some things to say about that.'

'It's my understanding that he's already said some things about that, and he believes you had better co-operate if you want to avoid indictment as an accessory.'

Mirel glowered at her straw. She sucked on it, grabbed a tissue from a square flowered box on the chrome tray swung over her bed and dabbed at her mouth with a wince. 'What client?'

'Dominick Broussard.'

Mirel frowned. 'Shit. I don't know anybody by a name like that.'

'He probably uses a false name. He knew Samenov and Moser and Louise Ackley. And Vickie Kittrie.'

Mirel snapped her head around. 'Vickie?' She looked at Grant over by the door, and then back at Palma. 'Vickie get killed?'

'Late last night. They found her body this morning.'

'God almighty damn,' she said slowly. 'Vickie.' There was awe in her voice. She looked out her dusty window at the wall of another wing of the hospital. She had a good view of the compressors of the air-conditioning

system, and the lime-fouled roosting site of thirty or forty
pigeons who seemed to have taken a great liking to one of
the ugliest spots in the entire 525-acre medical center.
Mirel's expression took on a faraway look of seriousness
that was distinctly different from her former anger.
'That's a lot of 'em. Girls I knew.' She looked back up at
Palma. 'God *damn*. This's weirder'n shit. This guy's Billy
Berserko.' She paused. 'What? You think this Grussard's
doing it?'

'Broussard. He's one suspect,' Palma said. 'There are
others.'

'He's into S&M?'

'We think so. That's what we wanted to hear from
you.'

'Well, can you tell me something about him, for God's
sake? I mean. What's he look like?'

'He's about forty-six, forty-eight. Six feet. Dark
complexion like a Hispanic, though he's clearly not
Hispanic. He's a cross-dresser. He's got black hair but . . .'

'Wears blond wigs, expensive dresses, and does a
damn good job with his makeup.' Mirel smirked. ''At's
Maggie Boll. Margaret. He insists on Margaret, but I call
him Maggie to his back. This joker's the best cross-
dresser I've *ever* seen. I mean. Thing is, he's not really
built for crossing — he's a little thick for it — but the
guy's got such style you can't believe it's a man. Makes
kind of a sultry babe.'

'Why does he come to you?'

'To watch. Likes to see women whip up on each other.
Most crossers like to see men. Well, actually, most cross-
dressers I get are gay. So.' Mirel shrugged. She sipped
from the accordian straw and then blotted the pink tissue
to her swollen mouth. At first Palma found it difficult to
understand her through her clenched teeth, but now she
was getting used to the twang. 'But his deal is women.
Sits behind the two-way mirror, always in the act,
watching. Sometimes I watch him.' She cut her eyes at
Grant. 'I got another peeking place so I can peek on the
peekers. Some of these crossers whack off while they're

watching, but not Maggie. He just sits there, always in the act, watching. Just like it's a movie. I mean he doesn't show any emotion, nothing. Might as well be a documentary about skydiving. He don't show *nothing*.'

'That's it?'

Mirel nodded with exaggeration, her strawy spray of hair wagging stiffly.

'How often does he come in?'

'Every six or eight weeks. Something like that.'

'How long does he stay?'

'Most of an hour.'

'Has he been around more frequently lately?' Grant asked.

Mirel looked at him. 'Not really.'

Grant moved up closer to the bed. 'When he watches the girls, does he do anything in particular? I know you said he just sits there, doesn't do anything, but what exactly does he do? Does he hold his hands in his lap? Does he cross his legs? Chew gum? Rub his arm?'

Mirel Farr regarded Grant with sullen eyes and thought about this. She clicked her fingernails against the aluminium Coke can and thought and thought. It seemed an odd thing for her to apply this much attention to Grant's question. The other responses had been snappy, almost flippant. But now she deliberated with some gravity. Then she began to nod tentatively, then with more conviction.

'Yeah. Come to think of it, I guess he does,' she said. 'What he does is he holds himself. I mean, not his dick, but like a woman holds herself. You know, kind of wraps her arms around herself. He does that, and then he kind of leans forward like he's got the cramps, leans forward just a little.' Mirel leaned forward a little, too.

'That's it?'

'Well, yeah. And it seems to me like maybe he sort of pressses his hand into his stomach the way you do when you've got a stomachache, or a cramp. Menstrual cramps. Maybe Maggie thinks she's having her time.' She tried to grin at the idea, but it was a stiff effort, and she gave it up. 'Not much fun to peek at, though. Some of those other guys, the peepers, damn, you wouldn't believe the kind of kinko shit they go through when they're peepin' but don't know *they're* being peeped.'

'Could you see Broussard's face when he was doing this?' Grant asked.

'Sort of.'

'What was his expression like?'

'Oh, hell, I don't know. I mean, he had makeup on.'

'Who did he watch?' Palma asked. 'Anyone in particular?'

'Yeah. Shit, yeah! Goddamn!' Her eyes widened. 'That was the special thing. Certain women. Yeah, you bet.' She was getting excited. 'He gave me a list. Some of the girls that's been killed. Dorothy was there. Jesus. And Sandy Moser. Vickie. And then he saw Louise Ackley with Dorothy once, and he put her on the list, too.'

'These women knew he was watching them?' Grant asked.

Mirel cocked her head self-consciously. She didn't answer right away and spent some time touching the tiny faded blue flowers on her gown. 'He gave me a pretty good boost to let him do that. Top dollar. They never would've done it if they'd known. When they called to schedule a time, I'd let him know. If he showed up, I got top dollar. He wouldn't always show up.'

'Were there very many women on his list?'

She shook her head. 'At first only Dorothy and Louise. Then he saw them with other women. If he liked them, he'd ask me who they were, and he'd add them to his list too.

'How many?'

'Six, seven.'

'We'll need the names,' Palma said reaching for her notebook in her purse. 'There's Dorothy, Louise Ackley . . .'

'Yeah, and there was Vickie Kittrie and Sandra Moser. Uh, that's four. Nancy Seiver. Cheryl Loch. Mary Lowe.'

Palma's hand jagged like a polygraph needle, but she

kept her head down. Christ! They were catching up with
him, getting closer and closer to the kills.

'I don't know,' Mirel shrugged. 'There wasn't that
many of them. I was probably the only place in town for
this kind of thing, so there wasn't *that* many of them.
This is not exactly a widespread recreational kind of
entertainment. I was lucky to hit onto this group of nuts.
Never seen anything like them. I used to be in LA for a
while, and San Francisco, too. But this little group of gals
here beat 'em all.'

'Mary Lowe,' Palma said. 'What do you know about
her?'

Mirel cocked her head and parted her dry lips from her
clenched teeth. She was uncomfortable and looked like
she wanted to brush her teeth.

'Mary is a class act. Of all these gals, even Dorothy,
Mary's the one with something that makes you wonder
why she's in this league. High society. Almost all of these
women are upper-class, you know. West Side. The
Villages. River Oaks. Junior League. Charity organizers.
Wear whatever color's in for the season. I coulda made a
fortune blackmailing 'em. Mary's built like a model,
maybe her tits are a little big, but *what* tits! Married. Two
kids. Big modern house in Hunters Creek. I went and
looked at the house. I do that sometimes. I like to see how
far down they're coming when they come to my place.'
She paused. 'Mary, she does all the right things at all the
right places. Very savvy gal.'

'Did Broussard ever demonstrate any special interest in
her?'

'No, but she's a turn-on for all the others, I can tell
you. I mean. She'd turn a woman's head as fast as a
man's, has these dykey types drooling. But when she
does her thing she does it with femmes. Never dykes.'

'Did she prefer to control or be controlled?' Palma
asked.

'I seen her do both, but mostly she bottoms. She does
it like it's a modern-dance performance or something. I
mean, she's graceful whatever she does.' Mirel nodded,

almost trying to smile again. 'She's a class act. People wouldn't believe it, you know. Seeing her at my place, doing what she does. I mean. Shit. People wouldn't believe it.'

Everyone was quiet for a moment, and the only sound was that of Mirel Farr's straw vacuuming the last few drops of Diet Coke as she reached the bottom of the can. Palma looked at Grant, who was watching Mirel with that expression in his eyes that told her he wasn't seeing what he was looking at. Then he caught Palma looking at him.

'Do you know,' Grant said to Mirel, 'if Broussard — or Doll — ever saw any of these women aside from these instances?'

'Well, you know, I'm not sure about that,' she said. 'I wondered about that myself. I mean, he asked to see Dorothy the first time, so I guess he knew her from somewhere. Let's see, then he saw Louise with Dorothy, and Vickie with Dorothy. Then he asked to see Sandy Moser, so I guess maybe he knew her somehow, too. Uh, I think he saw Nancy Seiver with Moser, or maybe Kittric, or maybe that was Carol Loch. But I know he asked to see Mary Lowe, because she was a pretty recent addition.'

'Did any of them ever mention him, Dominick Broussard?'

'Nope.'

'Do you know anything else regarding his interest in sadomasochism besides his coming to your place and watching these women?' Grant asked.

'Nope.'

'How did he happen to learn about you?' Palma asked. 'Did he just walk in one day?'

Mirel shook her head again 'Nobody jus' walks into my place,' she said with evident pride, though perhaps not everyone would understand the cause of her smugness. 'It's not like I was in the Yella Pages. References. Somebody's got to put you onto me. And I don't accept *any*body, either. I mean,' she snorted.

'So who recommended him to you?'

Again Mirel squirmed a little with embarrassment,

which she then immediately attempted to cover up with a cocky explanation.

'Look, I've been around the block with people like this,' she said. 'I see 'em walk in the door I know if they're masos or sados or some kind of jerk-off combination. You got to trust your gut with them people 'cause they don't think like the rest of us. They got hang-ups you wouldn't believe. Reason I'm alive right now is 'cause I know my way around these people, can smell a screwball a mile away. Maggie gets in touch with me, I know exactly what I'm into. Just a harmless peeper. Not even all that weird. Offers big bucks to watch a lady he knows. I can tell. No problem here. And there's big bucks. One thing he wanted was that they didn't know he was watching. Fine. I know he's not going to pull anything funny. I mean, I'm watching *him*. My instincts told me all I needed to know. Guy was harmless. Hell, if he knew Dorothy ...' Mirel shrugged as if that was self-explanatory.

Palma looked at her. Listening to Mirel's 'explanation' of how her reference system worked — that is, not at all — made her furious. The woman was despicable. She jabbed her pen and notebook into her purse.

'I'll tell you what,' she snapped. 'I think you'd better have your instincts examined. And you'd better hire yourself another lawyer. I don't think one is going to be enough.'

If Mirel's mouth could have dropped open it would have, but as it was she simply rolled her head and widened her eyes at Palma's back as Palma strode out of the room without looking at Grant.

She waited near the nurses' station halfway down the hall while Grant probably thanked Mirel for her help, going through all the crap that goes along with having to be a public servant. Sometimes Palma found the stupidity of people like Mirel Farr too infuriating to deal with rationally. With every year that passed she was finding it increasingly difficult to convince herself that each person on earth had as much intrinsic worth as the next. She had grown up with that concept persistently impressed upon her by her mother, whose unflagging religious faith had, admittedly, carried her through many thin and arduous times. But there were many days when Palma just didn't swallow the idea. Some lives evidenced no discernible value whatsoever. It would be difficult to ascribe any positive worth at all to Mirel Farr.

Palma's beeper startled her. She checked the number, saw it was Frisch's, and walked up to the nurses' station and asked them to tell the man who would be coming out of Farr's room that she had gone down to use the telephone outside the waiting room.

Frisch sounded tired.

'How's it going?' he asked.

Palma brought him up to date on what they had learned about Broussard from Alice Jackson, and what they had just heard from Mirel Farr.

'I'd be surprised if Grant doesn't have some proactive suggestions after this,' she said. 'He's being very cautious about it, but Broussard's been all over these women for a long time. He's known some of them as long as they've known each other. He knows a hell of a lot about them, and I don't think he'd have any trouble getting next to them, even during all this scare. Besides that, these women aren't the kind who scare too easily anyway.'

She looked out the glass door of the booth and saw Grant waiting, leaning against the wall with his hands in his pockets. He was staring straight ahead, lost in thought, facing away from the waiting room, which looked like a scene from a refugee camp. Because Ben Taub was a charity hospital, certain of its waiting rooms were often crowded with the indigent friends and relatives of the indigent patients. It was no trick to grow depressed simply staring into the passive faces of people who seemed perpetually exhausted.

'Grant's outside now. We haven't had time to go over Farr's interview. Let us hash it out, and we'll get back to you in half an hour, or we'll be back to the station to talk. Anything happening?'

'Nothing,' Frisch sounded irritable. 'Reynolds hasn't budged, and his girlfriend's still with him. Nothing's moved at Broussard's. I hope to hell he isn't laying her out in there.'

'Grant swears it won't happen. Not at his place,' Palma said. 'It'll have to be somewhere else.'

'Shit.' Frisch was impatiently skeptical. It was rare for him either to swear or be rude, or even show that much emotion. She could imagine what the atmosphere was like at the station and was glad she wasn't there.

'Anybody turn up anything canvassing Hardeman's neighbors?' she asked.

'Nothing.' Frisch turned away from the telephone and she heard him tell someone to shut the damn door, and then he was back on. 'Nobody saw anything. This guy's got to be the luckiest bastard going. Vickie's car turned up in the parking lot of the Houston Racquet Club.'

'What about the lab reports on her?' Palma asked. 'Did LeBrun come up with anything? What about the autopsy?'

'Yeah, actually we have gotten something from the lab, just a few minutes ago.' Frisch turned away from the telephone again, and she heard him asking someone for the lab report. She looked outside at Grant. He hadn't moved, literally. He looked like a mannequin. 'Yeah,' Frisch said to somebody, and she could hear him shuffling papers and someone, she thought it was Leeland, talking to him. 'Okay, here it is. On the head hair Le Brun found on Hardeman's bed with Kittrie, we've got a matchup with the unidentified head hair found at Samenov's. LeBrun also picked up pubic hairs on Kittrie that match the two unknown, single-source, pubic hairs found on Samenov. However, they can't tell us whether the unknown head hair and pubic hair found on Samenov and Kittrie came from the same person or whether they're male or female.'

'So the hairs could be from two people or from one person.'

'Right.'

'And they don't know the sex.'

'Right. But we do know — regardless of whether it's one or two people — that he or they were with both Samenov and Kittrie sometime shortly before their deaths.'

'And they don't know if it's wig hair yet?'

'No, but they know that wig hair has been treated with some kind of preservative. They're trying to nail that down now, and then they can test for it. It's going to take a while.'

'What's a while?'

'It depends on what the preservative chemical is.'

'Damn. The pubic hair,' Palma said suddenly. 'Broussard's hair is black. If it's his, it'll have to be bleached or dyed. Have them check it.'

Frisch made a few muffled remarks to someone. 'And one more thing,' he added. 'They found a couple of fibers in Kittrie's dress. They think they're pieces of a fiber mesh, stuff that kinda of looks like horsehair, that some foreign-car manufacturers use to mold their car seats. Mercedes people use it, Volkswagen people use it, or used to. Anyway, they're trying to narrow down the possibilities.'

'Broussard drives a Mercedes.'

'Yeah, we know. We're trying to determine if we can risk sneaking somebody up to the house to snatch some of it. Anyway, listen, get back to me soon.' Frisch had to raise his voice because of the background noise. 'Leeland's being flooded with calls from people turning in their creepy neighbors, and we've got a dozen of our guys trying to follow these up. But aside from that and what you two are coming up with, the investigation's ground to a standstill. The media are all over us, and the politicians, and as of this afternoon some women's organization says we're not pursuing this with enough conviction. And I suppose a charge of ineptitude and mismanagement will be coming soon from the guy who wants to be the next police chief. The people in Hunters Creek have formed some kind of female buddy patrols and the village police are being run ragged checking out peeper calls, false reports of bodies in the bayous, all that sort of thing. We're catching a lot of heat, and we're seeing a lot of brass in the squad room now. Everybody looking in personally, that sort of thing. Everybody wants in on the big one.'

Palma hung up and looked at Grant again. This time he was looking at her, and she opened the door.

'Give me one more minute. They've got some interesting lab results. One more quick call.'

She closed the door again and put in another quarter. This time she dialed the number that rang on Barbara Soronno's desk.

60

Palma didn't say anything right away. She wanted a moment to try to sort out how the information fit in, and now that her hunch had paid off and she had the results she expected to find, she also wanted time to examine her own intuition, to understand what it was that had made her ask Barbara Soronno to conduct such an unusual test in the first place. It was an eerie feeling, especially in light of the fact she didn't know what leap of logic had put her onto the startling discovery.

'What's the matter?' Grant asked.

'Nothing,' she said, stepping out of the booth and coming across to him. 'Just trying to understand the data, where they fit in.' She told him everything that Frisch had said and watched his face as he assimilated the information and factored it into his own peculiar arrangement of what he knew of the four murders. Palma had the feeling that, like her, Grant was not telling everything he was thinking.

A child shrieked in the waiting room, and a shouting match broke out between a furtive Vietnamese clan and a trio of stocky black women whose dusky scowls, flared nostrils, and flashing ruddy tongues made them formidable adversaries for the smaller Asians.

Grant bowed his head in thought and moved slowly around the corner to the long antiseptic hallway where the odors of alcohol and medication replaced the human odors of the overcrowded waiting room.

'Vickie Kittrie and an unknown person had been with Dorothy Samenov before she died,' he mused. 'An unknown person had been with Kittrie before *her* death. The unidentified head hair is blonde — wig or not — and the pubic hair is also blond.'

'Dyed or natural,' Palma said.

Grant nodded without saying anything, his eyes fixed on the far end of the glistening hallway.

He said, 'But no physical evidence from a third person on Vickie's body, or any of the other victims, for that matter.'

This was as far as Palma could let him go without telling him what Barbara Soronno had found. Palma didn't know what Grant was puzzling out, but it had to do with a third person, and Palma had come up with physical evidence of a third person with Vickie Kittrie.

'There was a third person in Vickie's case,' she said outright. Grant stopped. He looked at her. They were halfway down the length of the long hall, midway between another nurses' station and an intersecting hallway. Grant put his hands in his pockets again and leaned against the painted wall. In a room not far away an aspirator was sucking noisily at some kind of human fluid, keeping cadence with a rattily, uneven respiration. Grant waited, regarding her from behind the crooked bridge of his nose with a becalmed concentration, prepared for something revelatory. In the sterile white light of the hospital corridor his hazel eyes complemented the brindled colors of his graying mustache.

'I just learned this a moment ago, when I made the second telephone call,' she said. 'I would have told you about it, but it was such a ... crazy long shot, and I didn't want to appear ... unreasonable.' Grant was as unresponsive as a sphinx. 'This morning, just before we left Janice Hardeman's, I grabbed Jeff Chin and told him to take special care of the tampon in Kittrie's vagina. I told him to mark it for Barbara Soronno's attention. Then I called Barbara and asked her what the chances were of getting a clean type from it. It all depended on how saturated the tampon was. When she got it, Barbara cut into it and took some fibers from the very center of it and typed it. It was clean. It wasn't contaminated.'

Grant's face was already registering surprise. 'It wasn't Vickie's type?

'No,' Palma said. 'It wasn't.'

'Broussard's blood type is on his medical records,' Grant said quickly. 'We can get it.'

'It's not his blood either,' Palma said.

'You know his blood type?'

'No. But after Barbara determined the blood inside the tampon wasn't Kittrie's, I asked her to run an additional test. The blood on the interior of the tampon contained no plasminogen and no fibrin, which means it didn't have the ability to coagulate. It was menstrual blood, but not Vickie's.'

'Je-sus Christ,' Grant said. He looked at her. 'You knew this?'

Palma shook her head. 'No. Of course I didn't. I don't know why I even asked her to run the test. It wasn't even an official assay. Barbara did it on the side, as a favor.'

'Well, what in the hell did you have in mind?' Grant was astounded. He seemed to be as amazed at why she had asked for the test as he was at the test's results.

'I told you.'

'Did you *think* it would be menstrual blood?'

'I just thought ... maybe, I don't know, that we ought to type it.'

'And when it wasn't Vickie's type ...'

'Then I just wondered where in the hell he'd gotten it. And then I wondered if it was his blood. Did he cut himself to get it? I wondered what his reasoning was. If it wasn't his blood, and if it wasn't Kittrie's blood, then was it human? If it was human, was it a man's blood or a woman's blood? I thought about the bites around the navel, about the extracted navel, and it seemed to me that he was trying to tie this in somehow with ... maybe, birth, the umbilical cord, the obsession with the victims' navels.'

Palma paused, not knowing where to go next. 'I don't know. I just thought it ought to be tested.'

'You didn't simply make the assumption that it was Kittrie's?' Grant asked.

'For some reason I never thought that it was.'

'I'll be damned,' Grant looked at her as if she had begun speaking in tongues. 'You're *unbelievable*,' he said. 'What . . .' He seemed to be groping for a way to frame his question, and then he seemed as if he wasn't even sure what the question should be. He shook his head incredulously and looked away toward the nurses' station, the small figures of women in white dresses. He kept his gaze on them for a moment, completely encompassed by his own thoughts, as isolated as if he had been alone at sea.

Palma was uneasy, but she didn't really understand why. In an odd sort of way, she almost felt apologetic for her prescience. And at the same time, she was thrilled at being close to the killer. She thought they had him, though they might not understand exactly how yet. But they were close, she knew they were close. It was a matter of not letting up, of not fumbling the details.

Grant shifted his weight against the wall. 'What in the hell have we got here?' he said, his eyes still on the little white forms of the distant nurses. It was a rhetorical question, and it wasn't addressed to Palma. Then he turned back to her but kept his head down, looking at the toes of his shoes. 'Did your friend Soronno give you any other kind of data about the blood?' He looked up. 'Did it appear to be old? None of the other victims were menstruating, were they? I don't remember seeing it in their autopsy reports.'

'No. Barbara couldn't determine anything about how long the blood had been on the tampon. She said it seemed to be consistent with having been in place when the body was found. And no, none of the other women was menstruating.'

'So he couldn't have gotten it from them and saved it to use in Kittrie. It hadn't been a souvenir,' Grant said. 'So he either got it from a living acquaintance or, perhaps we could surmise that he killed someone else earlier in the evening and took it from her and inserted it in Kittrie. Or, maybe it was Janice Hardeman's. He could have found it in her trash.'

Palma was shaking her head. 'I wouldn't think so. I noticed in her bathroom that she used pads, not tampons.'

'Why would he do that?' Grant's voice was edged with incredulity. 'What kind of fantasy is this guy working ...?' Grant stopped suddenly and looked at Palma. 'Anything strike you odd about Mary Lowe's being at his place all night last night and all day today?'

'Farr said she had a husband and two children.'

Grant nodded. 'So how does she manage this?'

'The same way other people manage adultery,' Palma said. 'Lies. I wouldn't think she's been gone from home longer than they had expected her to be gone, for whatever reason. At least they haven't contacted missing persons. They're on tap to get in touch with homicide the second anything resembling these cases comes through.'

'We've got to get inside that house,' Grant said.

Frisch sat behind his desk with his forearms resting on the arms of his chair, a limp lock of thin, sandy hair sagging over his forehead. His long face looked drawn and monkish in the white fluorescent lighting of his office. To one side Captain McComb and Commander Wayne Loftus of major investigations sat in swivel chairs. McComb's suit was so wrinkled it looked like it was made of crinoline, while Loftus was wearing a knit shirt and a pair of khaki pants and Topsiders, having been called in from home where he had been stealing a few hours' sleep because it had looked like nothing was going to develop over Sunday night. Like McComb, Loftus's career had been built on years of street experience and a judicious sense of what was right for the boys in the division. Assistant Chief Neil McKenna wore a fresh suit and tie, ever sensitive to the media and their potential impact on his own career ladder. Younger than the other two men, McKenna was part of the new breed. Wielding a variety of degrees in law and criminal justice, they spent fewer years on the street and advanced rapidly. McKenna had been in charge of investigative operations for three years.

They had just listened to Palma run down the information she and Grant had garnered thus far from Alice Jackson and Mirel Farr, as well as the most recent data from the crime lab, including Palma's unexpected discovery. Regarding Broussard, all of the information was damaging from the point of view of his professional integrity, but adding up to little more than a sordid story. At most, Dr. Dominick Broussard could be sanctioned by the professional organizations to which he belonged for breaching the trust of his patients and, after the proper panels and hearings, he could be barred from practicing psychotherapy in the state of Texas. He also could be sued by any woman with whom he had had sexual intercourse during the time he was seeing her as a client.

But as regards the investigation of the serial homicides, Broussard was remarkably untainted. As of yet there was absolutely no physical evidence that connected him to any of the crime scenes, and the only evidence that they had any hope of developing against him hung in the balance by a few short hairs.

'But the circumstantial evidence is so heavily weighted against him,' Palma concluded, 'that we don't have any doubt that we'll eventually develop the physical evidence that we need. Unfortunately, it's only been in the last eighteen hours that Broussard has come to our attention as a suspect, and it has only been within the last seven hours that we've come to focus on him as *the* suspect. There just hasn't been enough time to develop very much of a case other than the circumstantial evidence we've just given you.'

'He's with this Lowe woman right now,' McComb said to Loftus. 'Been there all night last night, all day today. She's got a husband and kids, but they haven't reported her missing so we're guessing they think she's out of town, gone to Mama's or something.'

'Damn,' Loftus said, 'you're sure he's not chopping her up in there?'

'Hell, no, we're not sure,' McComb said, showing a little heat. 'That's why we've got to come to some kind of decision here ... how much we're willing to risk legally and politically, and whatever the hell else, to get in there. Maybe we'll barge in and bust up a cozy little weekend of adultery that they'd had to plan for a month to put together, and it'll turn out Broussard's just a horny psychiatrist whose business has got a lot of fringe benefits. *Or* we may find him cutting her up and putting her in the freezer, for Christ's sake.'

'Actually,' Frisch said calmly, 'Grant thinks he won't kill her in his own home.' He looked at Grant for further explanation.

Grant was sitting on the edge of one of the desks, his arms folded. Palma thought he was beginning to look more than a little worn. They all were, some of them wearing out a little faster than the others. Frisch looked like he ought to be on sick leave. Palma herself could feel that the muscles in her shoulders were as tight as they were going to go.

'That's my feeling,' Grant said. 'But I've got a caveat. In any given case the suspect naturally will deviate from the behavioral models we've come to associate with these kinds of sexually motivated murderers. There's no such thing as complete predictability, but there are variance tolerances. Broussard has stretched these tolerances to the limit. Insofar as we've been able to anticipate certain kinds of behavior, there's some degree of predictability. Naturally, the better we know the suspect the better we can anticipate his actions.' He looked around the room at each of them. 'We know practically nothing about Broussard. Additionally, so far his behavior has deviated from this behavior model more than any other suspect I've ever investigated.'

'What's all that mean?' Loftus snapped. He wanted bottom-line deductions.

Grant looked at him evenly. He didn't like being snapped at.

'It means that I don't think Broussard will kill her in

his home, but if it was up to me I wouldn't bet the woman's life on it. I'd get her out of there.'

'Fine,' Loftus said. He had one leg crossed over the other with an Astros baseball cap on his knee, and one hand dropped down picking at a tag of rubber coming off the sole of his aged Topsider. 'I don't know what your experience is with these society shrinks, Grant, but I suspect he could get bent out of shape real bad if you're wrong about him. I don't know. Hell, I know a preacher in Pasadena who for the last three years has been responsible for leading his congregation to provide more than half the full-time support for two orphanages here in the city. He also collects lesbian sex magazines. I don't know what he does with them, but I'm sure he doesn't use them to level up all his wobbly tables. I know an Exxon executive who personally collected over a million bucks in charity money last year and every four years supports a new indigent kid through four years of college. He also wears ladies' panties instead of boxer shorts. What this means to his brain I do not know. But these guys' strange quirks haven't prevented either one of them from being useful citizens. Point is, weird don't count for shit anymore. You can't arrest people for being weird.'

Grant nodded. Palma knew he wasn't going to get into that kind of an argument with a local commander. She also knew Loftus was intelligent enough not to beg the question or miss the point, both of which he seemed to be doing, so she could only believe that this was a serious case of jurisdictional jealousy. Loftus resented having a hot-shot from Quantico coming down to Houston telling him how to run his investigations.

There was a moment's pause before Frisch said, 'I'm going to go with Palma. She's been following this from the beginning, and I trust her judgment. They need physical evidence and, as far as I'm concerned, they've got probable cause. That's our recommendation. That's what we're going to do unless some of you want to over-rule us.'

Palma wanted to jump up and hug him. Frisch never

failed to cut through the bullshit. He didn't want to see a simple decision bog down in a committee decision process.

'Okay,' McKenna said abruptly. He knew exactly which course of action the administration would consider the most politically hazardous. 'I'd rather run the risk of an invasion of privacy lawsuit from a pissed-off psychiatrist than be caught sitting on our asses while the guy kills another woman. Get a search warrant, probable cause being the accumulation of the circumstantial evidence against Broussard and the possible jeopardy to the woman, and go in.'

61

Through the long, rising heat of the afternoon they had talked, about love and the lack of it, about revenge and the lack of it, about incest. And Mary had lied to him, and he had listened to her with as much interest in her lies as he had had in the slim threads of her truths, knowing that she no longer acknowledged the difference anyway and that it was all the same to her in the tangled skein of her mind. What he had suspected before had been confirmed to him today as he had listened to her talk from the window seat, that it probably had been years since she had had any concept at all of the meaning of truth. Long ago, years ago, she had abandoned reality for something less brutal, something more imaginative and compassionate. And until now, she had functioned reasonably well, playing the role of a person playing a role. The acting had been effortless because she had grown accustomed to being something other than herself. But in her unconscious, the lies had been unraveling silently until they had frayed beyond restraint, and the increasingly complex patterns of her imagination had overwhelmed her. Chaos had overcome design.

She had put on her panties and bra, but nothing else, and he had remained in his casual linens, his shirt unbuttoned so that his thick, hirsute chest was exposed to her, a display of bohemianism that he did not easily accommodate. They had gone down to Broussard's kitchen, and

from the richly eclectic stock of his pantry they had gotten
several bottles of Valpolicella, breads and cheeses and
patés and olives and fruits. They had taken it all upstairs
to his bedroom, where they spread a linen cloth over the
deep mahogany window seat that looked out the opened
windows onto the wooded bayou below. They dined al
fresco, leisurely, Broussard slicing the apples and pears
into thin wedges with red and pale green borders, the
aroma of the red wine wafting on the warm air, and, for
Broussard, the exquisite sight of Mary's long limbs, the
rosy daubs of her nipples through the sheer cups of her
overfilled bra, the tuck of her navel above the lace band of
her panties, the red bite, like a vicious birthmark above
her knee.

Behind them, on the other side of the city, the sun
seared a trace of orange fire into the horizon where its
impact spewed a radiant carnelian dust high into the sky,
while in the east a mauve haze rose from behind the
silhouette of the city's skyline, and the heat of the afternoon settled into the darkening margins of the magnolias
and the great, lowering oaks.

As the light failed, Broussard listened to Mary's lies
with the taste of apples and wine on his tongue, and
watched her as she began to blend into the waning
evening like a ghost, her pale figure growing translucent
as if she were an afterimage, visible only if he didn't look
directly at her. So, for him, her voice became Mary in the
twilight, whereas her body had been Mary in the light,
and her lies became the life-sustaining lies of her sex,
tales of survival and cunning, the verbal archetypes of all
her sex, the fables of all the modern Scheherazades.

Broussard waited until Mary in the twilight had
finished another halting and painful recounting of her
awakening sexual appetite as first experienced in intercourse with her father. Her voice had grown strained as
she finished the story, and the two of them sat in silence.

They drank more wine, and for a long time Mary was
quiet, sitting across from him in her bra and panties,
which looked pale blue in the dusk. As heartbreaking as

her story had been, Broussard's mind had often
wandered. He had heard heartrending stories before.
They did not leave him gasping with surprise. Nothing
surprised him anymore. Nothing. And it was during this
time that he began to wonder why Mary had not yet
mentioned his cross-dressing. She had not even alluded
to it. From the first moment when she had found him on
the terrace until now, she had accepted his uncommon
predilection as though it had been the ordinary practice of
every man she new. Certainly it had not perceptibly
affected her sexual interaction with him. She did not seem
to have found sexual intercourse with a man who was
dressed as a woman as something to which she had
needed to adjust. Nor had it appeared to have affected
her ardor.

But this lack of surprise, or even curiosity on her part,
made him uneasy, and at the same time he recognized the
irony of his restiveness. All his life he had wished for a
woman who would accept his cross-dressing with the
complete nonchalance with which Mary had in fact
accepted it, a woman whose erotic reciprocity would
accommodate even his compulsion for the texture and the
sound and the color of women's clothing. No woman, at
least none since his mother, had been able to accept this.
None of them. And even in all the years he had been
intimate with Bernadine, he had never had the courage to
tell her about his fetish until near the very end, until after
she had revealed her recent bisexual encounters. Even
then, he had found her to be far less open-minded about
his sexual heterodoxy than he had been about hers.

And now, this late, he had found Mary and, having
gotten what he always had longed for, he was disappointed to discover that he could not escape a feeling of
something being not quite right. That was the way it had
been with his mother, too. Eventually there had arisen
between them something disquieting, something he had
never fully understood or resolved, that had brought their
symbiotic relationship to an abrupt end. That same sense
of vague uncertainty was what he was now feeling with

Mary Lowe, and he thought it eerie that it had returned at
the precise point at which he had found a woman who
could have meant as much to him in regard to these
things as his mother.

While they talked, dusk slipped into night, and the
Mary who was disappearing in the twilight reappeared in
the dark as the glow of the city lights flared off the black
sky and came in through the tall windows, limning her in
pale blue. The distance between them on the window seat
was small and filled with the smell of wine and apples.

'I really never could bring myself to hate him,' Mary
said. 'I pitied him, felt repulsion and disgust for him, but,'
she shook her head, 'I couldn't hate him. Even though I
was only a child I knew he was pathetic, that he didn't
deserve my hatred. Sometimes, in flashes of intuition, I
sensed the real absurdity of what he was doing to me and
felt as though we both were victims of some huge and
awesome evil. The other face of God maybe, something
that he didn't understand any more than I did.'

Broussard watched her bend forward and pick up one
of the wine bottles, and he heard it burbling into the
shallow glass. Her movements were graceful; it was as
natural to her as the raw sex that she enjoyed, as natural
to her as the sweet scent of her veins, as natural as lying.

'He was the only one who offered me any kind of real
relationship, even if it was a sick one,' she said. 'What
was I supposed to do, reject the only intimacy available to
me, reject the only sign of affection that had ever been
offered, however imperfect? At least there was a sense of
tenderness there, evidence that to *some*one I was something of value.'

Mary looked at him. He could not see the arrangement
of her features, whether she regarded him skeptically or
scornfully or indifferently, but he was sure she didn't give
a damn about his explanations. He sensed it. He had to
remind himself that she had not come to him voluntarily,
as a grieving victim. Rather, she had come as an actress
approaching one more role, denying the real Mary to play
the Mary everyone wanted her to be, knowing that as

long as she was acting, the real life offstage would not catch up with her. There was no time for reality; acting kept her alive. By agreeing to come to Broussard, she had been acquiescing to a condition of her husband's ultimatum. She was not interested in reconstruction. She was not interested in emotional growth. She was not interested in wholeness. She was incorrigible. She was *sui generis*. It seemed to him that Mary had decided to be only a fragment of a woman, to be only some ragged piece of what she could have been, and should have been. Wholeness would have cost her too much. She did not long for it; she only feared it. Mary would never be whole. Her childhood had been torn into too many pieces, and when she had patched the pieces together she had done it imperfectly, as a child would do.

Broussard's psychiatric platitudes and his half-baked explanation of the Persephone complex lost its meaning in the face of what he felt happening to him. If he had ever believed in the reconstruction of Mary's psychological integrity, that belief gradually took a position of secondary importance as he looked at her sitting across from him in the hyacinth blue light of the city night. Though he could not truly distinguish the shade of her eyes, he saw them nonetheless, the never-closing blue-gray specula of her psyche through which he saw another, stranger universe, and through which, he knew, he could be sucked into the vast, haunted spaces of Mary's world.

She was still looking at him, motionless, the fine asymmetry of her mouth communicating its own mute erotica. For all her silence, Mary's body was one of extraordinary expressiveness. As with Bernadine, she understood everything through her sexuality, like the serpent that understands the world through its tongue. Incest had taught her child's mind that relationships were inherently sexual. It was the most tragic lesson she had ever learned.

Broussard had seen this again and again with his clients, and he had never been able to deny himself the opportunity of taking advantage of this misfortune. He knew what was coursing through her unconscious, and he knew he could turn it to his own purposes. And why shouldn't he? After all, they both were children of misfortune. If comfort was what they longed for, why should they deny themselves? Nothing could make up for what they already had lost, and how did it affect Mary anyway, if he understood what was about to happen on a higher plane? For Mary, the momentary escape from the unrelenting burden of her internal loneliness was all that mattered. If that was all he gave her, then fine. It was all she was looking for. If it ended here, then fine. It was as far as she wanted to go.

It had been dark a good while now, and the obscurity that followed close onto dusk had given way to night sight so that even in the vague illumination Broussard could see her, all but her finest features, all but the furrowed brow and the imagined shadings of her flesh that in normal lighting showed through the gauzy nylon.

She watched him without comment as he rose from his chair beside the window seat and began carefully to move the tablecloth away from them. Deftly she reached for the bottle of Valpolicella before he slid the cloth along the mahogany out of reach. She filled her glass, then put it on the windowsill with her right hand and watched him as he came and stood beside her, the linen of his trousers leg touching her long, bare thigh. He took off his shirt and tossed it away into the dark room, and then he unbuttoned his trousers and dropped them, kicking them out of the way. She was eye-level with his waist now, and as he took off his underpants she turned away and drank from her glass, her head tilted back and her long graceful throat making a fine white line in the hyacinth light. When she finally lowered the glass, he saw that she had spilled it. Dark purple lines streaked the sides of her mouth and glistened on the tops of her breasts and stained the front of her bra. She immediately refilled her glass.

He knelt beside her, her face slightly above his as he

gently took her thighs in his hands and turned her around until she faced him. Her legs hung over the edge of the window seat, and she sat facing him, her shoulders squared, the full glass of wine in her right hand balanced on her thigh. He reached behind her and unhooked her bra, slowly pulling it until it fell away from her breasts. He was instantly erect at the touch of the lace in his fingers. He looked at the bra, at its filigreed borders, at the sheer film of its cups, and he turned it around and slipped his arms into the straps, streched the elastic sides and reached around in back and hooked it.

Mary watched him. Her only reaction was to raise her long-stemmed glass and stop it halfway to her mouth, the blue light from the window reflecting on the surface of the dark wine. In her face, turned slightly toward the glit tering city in the cobalt distance, Broussard imagined that he saw the taut-muscled expression of desire. Or was it yearning? Or, even, grief? Then she brought the glass to her mouth, and he thought, desire, and she drank all of the wine in the glass. It took her several swallows, and then she reached out and back a little and dropped the glass out of the window. Broussard heard it fall with a swish into the hedges. It was a crystal wineglass, and he imagined it resting lightly, glinting in the tiny leaves of the boxwood.

Broussard could feel his body humming, tingling as he touched the sides of Mary's hips and felt the place where her panties cut into her skin. Hooking his fingers into the nylon near the back, he began pulling them down, and when he got to the window seat she raised her hips, first on one side and then the other, to allow him to pull them off the rest of the way, peeling them down her thighs, her calves, and off her ankles. Then he stood and took his time unwadding the twisted panties, the feel of them delightful, enormously arousing, until finally he had them straight. Then he stepped into them and felt a magical transformation. This was the way it was meant to be. These were the clothes he was meant to wear. Though they were too small for him, he pulled them up tightly around his waist, the feel of the nylon, the tightness of the elastic around his groin, sending erotic jolts through his veins.

He disappeared into the darkness of the room and returned with a handful of makeup. Mary scooted back on the window seat, and he dumped the makeup between her parted legs. She understood everything, even this. There was no need to explain anything. It was too dark to see in detail, but he could adjust his work to the gloam in the room. Like actors on a stage, their features would be exaggerated, larger than life. This life, anyway.

Without having to be instructed, she leaned forward. His hands were unsteady with excitement as Broussard began painting their faces. There was no particular order of application this time. It was only ritual anyway — and she seemed to understand this, too, the symbolism of it, the rite of it — lipstick on her lips, the same on his, eyeshadow on her lids, the same on his, the fragrance of cosmetics winding him tighter with every inhaled breath. He felt the tender aureoles of her heavy breasts brushing against his forearm as he worked on her face, and their hyacinth world lifted and drifted, freeing him at last, bringing him to the familiarity of moments lived for and longed for, the time when Dr. Broussard no longer existed, and Margaret Boll was born.

Their faces were close enough for Broussard to feel her breath, thick and aromatic with wine. His own breathing was difficult to control and came in unpredictable shudders

'I have rope,' he said, and he felt a fine mist of perspiration forming across his forehead.

Mary looked at him without any change in expression, no indication of how she was reacting.

'Do you want me to tie you?' he whispered.

'I've never done it,' she lied, and Broussard's brain reeled with the memory of Dorothy Samenov standing over Mary with a laver of heated oil, dropping strings of it onto Mary's naked body as she lay bound with saffron scarves; with the memory of Sandra Moser suddenly losing control over Mary's outstretched body and an alarmed Mirel Farr rushing into the room to stop her; with the memory of . . .

'Do you want to tie me . . . first?' he asked.

'I've never done it,' she lied, and Broussard's brain flashed up the memory of Mary straddling Louise Ackley, the most grievous masochist of them all, both of them glistening with sweat from the closeted heat in Farr's shabby little dungeon as Mary skillfully skated a straight razor across Louise's stomach, leaving thin carmine trails straight down into her pubis; the memory of Mary and the lanky, jet-haired Nancy Seiver, whose passion for needles and steel balls Mary had pushed to the outer limits of bizarre.

'I've got scarves,' Broussard coaxed. 'Saffron . . . scarves . . . all of them silk.'

Mary lifted her face and kissed him, lightly, as light as a butterfly kiss, and then more vigorously until he could taste the lipstick on their tongues and breathed the wine of her breath.

'We'll take turns,' she said, lips against his lips.

The feel of her and the feel of her nylon was making him lightheaded.

'Turns . . .' He was almost incapable of speaking. 'Yes, of course,' he said. 'We'll take turns,' and his mind once again played back the sweaty memories of the things he had seen Mary do at Mirel Farr's.

It was unimaginable.

Rather, until now, it had been *only* imaginable. Years of fantasizing were turning into reality and, paradoxically, he felt as if he were dreaming. With their faces painted identically, Mary naked and him wearing the undergarments he had removed from her, he lay in the center of the stripped bed while Mary hovered over him, patiently combing and grooming his favorite wig so that it lay naturally around his face. They had thrown open all the tall windows along the side of the room that overlooked the bayou, and Broussard's perfume hung thick in the heavy air. Through the windows, the dust of city lights lay scattered across the nightscape like a summer frost.

She tied his ankles first, jerking the saffron scarves into tight knots. But they were not uncomfortable. Silk, even constraining silk, was never unpleasant, and the idea of being splayed and bound with silk was a temptation he could not have resisted, even if he had been suspended over an abyss. Straddling his stomach, she leaned over him to tie his wrists, the nipples of her breasts brushing across his face. Like a Venetian courtesan, she had accommodated his every wish, nothing surprised her, nothing caused her to hesitate, nothing was taboo as she lavished her attentions upon him, indulged him as though he were a sultan.

When he was firmly bound and his eyelids were heavy with the narcotic of anticipation, time turned slower and slower until it stopped, and he was aware of silence and stillness. His eyes fluttered, and through the screens of his lashes he saw her straddling him, her arms raised, the fingers like pale combs thrust into the sides of her long golden hair as she pulled it away from her face, looking down at him. She was so beautiful, honey to the eyes, every dimension, every tint and shade of her.

'Margaret,' she said, and she had pulled her hair to one side, the long, thick bulk of it falling over her left shoulder. My God, Broussard thought, she was wonderful. She was preternatural.

'Margaret,' she repeated to him, 'I have a story to tell you. It's not an analysis story ... it's just ... my story.' She twisted her neck in a dipping motion to the side as though she were trying to relieve a stiffness. 'If you don't know my story, you won't understand.'

It was not what he had expected — what had he expected? — but he didn't question it for a second. For him she was magic, and magic had its own peculiar course. He waited.

There was a moment while Mary continued simply to look at him and pull her fingers through her blond hair, her eyes gradually losing him as she remembered, casting back into her story.

'Oh, I must have known it from the beginning,' she said, as if she were answering a question. 'From that first night in the pool when she sat with her legs in the water, smiling at me across the turquoise water, her silly red lips parted from her bright, white teeth.

'I must have known it the night he first put his buttered fingers into me while we watched television. She was there, sitting a little to one side in an armchair. Her hair was fixed, sprayed and coiffed as though she was ready to go out. She was never sloppy. And he did it, and I was petrified. My eyes were glued to the woman advertising refrigerators who was smiling at America like she had smiled at me across the turquoise water, white teeth and red lips. But I didn't look at her, though I wanted to more than anything, to see if she was seeing what he was doing to me. But I didn't.'

Margaret sensed a change of mood, feeling the insides of Mary's thighs against his hips, her buttocks resting just below his navel.

'Because I was afraid.'

Margaret opened his eyes to see her more clearly.

'I was dying, him doing that to me,' Mary continued. 'I was ignoring everything but the woman and the refrigerator on television. I was ignoring the fact that she would have had to be blind, or unconscious, not to have seen what he was doing. I was ignoring the fact that she wasn't doing anything about it — that she was probably even watching him.'

Mary was motionless.

'She didn't come and kiss me goodnight that night. In fact, she never did it again. I noticed that. I noticed that she stopped coming to kiss me goodnight after he put his buttered fingers ...'

She stirred on his stomach, shifted her weight a little and seemed to collect her thoughts, to gather her resolve.

'It wasn't long afterward that he began coming to my bed late at nights to put his hands all over me ... and into me ... and to teach me how to masturbate him. I managed to convince myself that she didn't know about his visits either, because he was coming in so late that he was obviously waiting until she was asleep. I attached my sanity to that little bit of deductive reasoning, told myself he was the only aberration among us, the only betrayer. It sustained me for a while, all too brief a while, as it turned out. Before long he was coming to me earlier in the night, early enough so that I knew she still had to be awake, had to feel him slipping out of bed, if he even bothered to "slip" at all. He came earlier and stayed longer. And she knew. When she went shopping and left us at home on Saturday afternoons, she knew. When the two of us were missing for half an hour or so in the evenings, she never asked where we'd been. She knew.

'As time went on we settled into a routine in which I essentially supplanted her role as wife. She read magazines and watched television and manicured her nails and pampered her hair. She gradually became more alienated from me. She never touched me anymore, never spoke kindly to me, if she even spoke at all. There were times when just the two of us would be in a room together, and she would act as if I wasn't there. I became invisible to her. She didn't even see me.

'And that was when I began the lying I told you about. I lied to her, too. I lied to her most of all.'

Margaret looked at Mary's face. She was staring at him but her eyes did not make contact with his, and her voice had the flat inflection of one hypnotized.

'I never told her how I felt,' Mary said. 'I couldn't. How could I? I no longer knew how to act around her.' She paused. 'I started spying on her,' she said matter-of-factly. 'I don't remember why, or how I got the idea, but it was after I had started lying. One afternoon when she went out to the pool to sunbathe, and I knew she would be gone a while, I went into her bedroom. She always had made it clear to me that her bedroom was out of bounds, so I had rarely been there, and when I went in it was like entering a stranger's room, and immediately I felt the excitement, the giddiness of offending the boundaries of a sanctum, of breaking taboo. The room was lush with the uninspired furnishings of a self-indulgent woman, the fuzzy fripperies of poor taste. But I was a child, and I thought it was a wonderfully beautiful place. I looked through all her clothes drawers and closets, looked through her folded underwear, touched all of it. It was while doing that that I felt a strange intimacy with her that surprised me, something I had never experienced before. It struck me as peculiar in the extreme, even then, as a child, to feel closer to her when I handled her under- wear than I felt when I was physically near her. I remember thinking — and this was childlike, without insight — that maybe I would find something there among all those trifles of her tacky Sybaritism that would explain things to me.'

Mary stopped, emitted a jerky sigh, and once again started rolling her head on her neck, her hair falling around her head in ever looser canary waves until her face was lost in the tangling webs of it. She stopped and sat still, her arms hanging loose at her sides, long, pale fingers touching Margaret's naked hips, her face obscured behind the veil of disordered hair.

'I found an electric dildo.'

Outside the tall windows behind her, nighthawks flitted like black fireworks against a cinder sky.

Then, slowly, she raised her arms and cleared her hair away from her face, and Margaret felt the beginning moisture of perspiration where Mary's crotch rested across his stomach.

'What a thing for a child to find,' she said with bitter hoarseness. 'It was a realistic instrument, not just a plastic tube, but "anatomically correct," of pliable, flesh- colored latex. By this time, I was only too familiar with the real thing, and it took me only a moment to under- stand the grotesque irony in what I had found. The differ- ence between us, between what she was doing and what I was ... doing.'

Margaret was still, his preoccupation with his own erotic stimulation suddenly arrested by the queer timbre of Mary's voice and by his own sobering prescience.

Mary nodded slowly and rose a little on her knees so that Margaret felt air penetrate the moist band across his stomach where she had been sitting. But Mary was unaware of this delicate sensation, and the muscles in her thighs reacted to something unrelated to what was happening between them.

'Then ... it was then that I finally admitted to myself that I hated her,' Mary said. 'And I wanted her to know that I hated her. It was easy enough. At this time my father was wanting to have sex with me at every turn, and I spent a lot of time talking him out of it, pushing him away, making excuses. As time went on his approaches were often totally inappropriate ... even within the context of the unreality that had become our status quo ... when she was in the next room, or when we were out by the pool and he'd follow me into the house on the flimsiest of pretexts. It was just too obvious. How ... how ... what I did was, I just stopped fighting him off every time.'

She had to stop to swallow.

'So one night we'd been watching television. That damned television ... we used it as a narcotic so we wouldn't have to talk to each other. A program was coming on she didn't want to watch, but her favorite show was scheduled right after it. I don't even remember what it was.' She paused. 'That's interesting, my not remembering ... what it was. Anyway, she decided to bathe and come back in half an hour for her show. As soon as she left, he started whimpering and pawing at me. It was just too much; I decided this was the time to do it.

'I fought him off for a long time because I knew if I let him go ahead he'd be through by the time she came back. I held him off and held him off, right there on the sofa in front of the damned television. Finally, he was really grunting for it, and it was about ten minutes before her program started. I let him start undressing me. I even let him take everything off like he always wanted to do at these times, but I'd never let him. I wanted him to commit

himself so far that there couldn't be any misunderstanding about what she found when she walked in.

'I gave up, closed my eyes, and disassociated myself,
just floated off into another world, but I heard her
walking through the kitchen toward the family room, her
shiny gold slippers flapping against the floor — slap-slap-
slap-slap. And then they stopped. At this point he was
really carried away, so crazy he wouldn't have heard a
gunshot in the room and wouldn't have stopped if he
had. I was out of my body, my eyes squeezed tight, aware
only of her footsteps and the sudden silence, imagining
her standing there. I wanted desperately to open my eyes
to see her expression, to know that she was seeing him,
but I was too afraid I'd see myself and him on top of me,
and I dreaded that even more than I wanted to see her
face. So I didn't look. But suddenly I heard those quick
slap-slap-slap-slaps fading into another part of the house,
and just then he finished.

'I remember feeling sick to my stomach, and I honestly
thought I was going to throw up on him. I didn't know
what this would mean, that I'd made her see, and I was
full of dread for days.' She paused. 'I was always full of
dread.'

Margaret moved uneasily on the bare sheet, subtly
testing the saffron knots, his mind's eye widening at the
possibilities that had begun to parade across the screen of
his inner vision like the evolving creature-men in Escher's
Encounter. Reality was proving to be, and not to be, what
it seemed. Responding to his movement, Mary lowered
herself again onto his stomach, her flesh as warm as the
summer night, her weight restricting him.

'How do you think she reacted to what she saw?' Mary
asked, looking at Margaret from her cowl of golden hair.
She smiled at him, a sardonic and self-mocking smile.
'How do you think?' It was a rhetorical question. She
wasn't expecting an answer, and he couldn't bring
himself to speak anyway.

'After lying still and panting a little while, he finally
rolled off me,' she continued. 'He pulled up his pants and

walked away without a word, without looking at me, like always. It was pathetic. Him. Me. Her. All of us. What we were and what we were doing. I went to my own bathroom and cleaned up, and then forced myself to go back to the family room — Jesus, "family room" — just to see how she would handle it. She was already sitting in her usual armchair, watching her television show.' Mary leaned a little forward over Margaret's face. 'Eating ice cream,' she said in a stage whisper, and he felt her wine-heavy breath upon his eyes. She straightened up a little. 'I remember. She had a big dish of it, three different kinds. I was stunned — I mean, three different kinds — that she even would think to do that, to get three different kinds of ice cream, after what she'd seen, was mind-boggling. She didn't speak to me when I came in and sat down. She didn't look at me. I know, because I never took my eyes off her.'

Mary sat back again, and tossed her hair out of her face. 'And my father?' she asked, raising her eyebrows at Margaret as if he had asked the question. 'Yes, he came back into the room, too ... carrying a bowl of ice cream. I don't remember how many kinds. It was just too bizarre. I mean, it was bizarre to me. Why wasn't it bizarre to them? He asked me if I wanted some ice cream too. He said he'd get it for me. I just shook my head. I thought I would die right there, of hurt, or just from the sheer desolation of grief.'

Margaret looked at Mary. His heart hammered so fiercely he thought she would feel it where her inner thighs were spread against his stomach. He was perspiring and, for some reason, he didn't want her to see it. It was running out of the edge of his wig and down the sides of his forehead. He didn't move. He thought if he moved he would snap the fine strand of his life, that single gossamer filament by which he existed.

'I'll never forget that night,' Mary continued. 'Because that was when I realized ... that I'd been bargained off. I was humiliated and frightened. All of a sudden I didn't think there *was* going to be an end to it. I was afraid that it would all lead to something even more unimaginable. How far was it going to go? How far *could* it go? I felt like a fool for taking so long to catch on. I hurt so much. I didn't think I'd live through it.' Mary stopped. 'But I did, of course. After a while you learn that you live through everything. Nothing is too terrible for people to do to you, and if they don't stop your heart, you can endure anything. Your spirit doesn't die, so it can be tortured without end and you just go on and on and on. Nothing is so terrible that it simply stops of itself, because the sheer horror of it has reached the point of the unimaginable. It's not that way at all.' She shook her head. 'And that's the secret of life: that suffering is infinite.'

Margaret looked down the length of his chest at the golden wool of Mary's vulva resting over his navel. He thought of the vagina dentata that had haunted ancient man. What if, in the too brief space of one's dying moment, all the laws of reality disintegrated and one passed through a world where such mythologies actually existed?

'At first ... I was despondent,' Mary's voice again resumed its flat inflection. 'I was sick, stayed home from school a few days — four days. From that day on I lied to her as an established rule. I've never told her the truth about anything significant from that day to this. It seemed reasonable, lie for lie. The first two days I couldn't keep any food on my stomach, couldn't keep anything down. He took off from work and looked after me. Or tried to. I didn't give him much cooperation. She never came into my room. By the second night I was holding down crackers, so the next day he went back to work.

'But, being home alone with her all day, well, I had the opportunity to spy on her in a way that I couldn't do on Saturdays or after school. It was on the third day that I actually watched her use the dildo for the first time. She had a ritual with it that was ... theatrical.' Margaret felt Mary's thighs widen from his sides in an unconscious imitation of what she was seeing in her mind. 'In front of the mirror.'

'On the fourth day, I devised another part of my retaliation. She decided to go shopping and left me at home alone. When I was sure she was gone, I went into her bedroom. Her dresser was covered with perfume bottles, every kind imaginable, lined up like votive fragrances. I had brought a little plastic pitcher with me from the kitchen. I put it in the middle of her bathroom floor, lowered my panties, squatted over it, and urinated until I was empty. Then I spent the next half hour opening every perfume bottle that I could get the top off without its being detected and pouring some of my urine into each bottle. Not enough that she could tell, but enough for me to know that every time she sprayed some of it on her she was spraying herself with my urine, too. On her face and neck, at her hairline, on her arms, behind her knees. She was soaked in my urine every day for months and months. She used a lot of perfume. I was so despicable to her that she wouldn't even look at me, refused to see what she had done. But I was with her anyway, intimately, every day. I was in her pores. She breathed me. I was all over her, in private places and in private ways. And the lies and regrets stacked up between us like a high, thick wall, solid and impenetrable.'

Margaret could feel Mary's thighs trembling against his sides. Her voice had grown hoarse, as if she had screamed all of this from the bottom of her lungs, as if these words of malice had scoured the cords of her throat like a real and brutal acid. The construction of Margaret's thoughts began to discompose, his ideas failing to comprise intelligible relationships. A fatal mistake. The fragments of Mary's disintegrated personality tumbled out of his mind like tiny naked and crippled creatures, distorted and aborted little things that plummeted toward him out of a blood-black void, made for revenge, furious at him for their deformities, the stubs and clefts and malformed orifices of which they thrust at him in lewd predictions of the coming horror of his own last moments.

'It was humiliating, you know, not having your mother

love you.' Mary turned her head and looked out to the large, hollow night. 'I thought there was a reason, that there was something wrong with me that made me unlovable. That was what I honestly believed. Years passed before it occurred to me that maybe it wasn't my fault. Even when I started hating her for withholding her affection — I was so messed up — I thought, Well, it's my fault, but still, unreasonably (I thought) I wanted her to love me in spite of myself, because I was a child. I gave myself some benefit of the doubt, you see; I knew that I couldn't be expected to think and act like an adult, yet at the same time, I held myself to adult responsibilities. But I wanted desperately to be a child, to be carefree, as other children seemed to be. And I wanted her to tell me it was all right to be that way, that I shouldn't worry myself about anything at all, that I should just go out and play. But she never did that. She never told me I didn't have to worry.'

Mary fell silent, her face still turned toward the tall windows, toward the phosphorescing city in the humid belly of the night. Unaware of what she was doing, she had dropped her hands to Margaret's stomach and was twining her fingers in the kinky hair that grew there. In rigid stupefaction, Margaret fixed his unblinking eyes on Mary's profile as if he believed, against all reason, that salvation lay in absolute immobility.

'At the same time ... I felt protective of her,' Mary continued, turning back to Margaret. 'I felt responsible. That's why I went along with his whining demands from the beginning. I couldn't forget the itinerant life we'd led in those shabby rooming houses all across Dixie, those long, hot nights when I listened to her cry herself to sleep and nursed my own fears as best I could by comforting a doll with a porcelain face. So I let him have what he wanted, and we didn't have to go back to that kind of life again. And she knew.'

Mary paused, and her two manicured fists began kneading Margaret's stomach, kneading and twisting, then pinching, pulling at it fiercely until Margaret's eyes burned with tears that ran black with mascara.

Margaret was catatonic. Unable either to blink or swallow, saliva suddenly and inexplicably sprang into the pockets of his jaws in such astonishing volume that his gaping, painted lips instantly overflowed with limpid, viscous ropes of it that draped his powdered neck and festooned the blond tresses of his wig. But he was oblivious of this glandular effusion. He saw and knew only Mary, and her ineffable and lethal beauty.

'She abandoned me,' Mary said hoarsely, spreading her fingers out over his stomach. She emitted a quick, muffled gasp. 'Even in the womb, she abandoned me.'

She bent forward and began stroking Margaret's wig, a gesture so unexpected and tender that it momentarily broke through the numbing paralysis of his hysteria. But he was mute. She lowered her head. He was dumbfounded. He felt the weight of her breasts upon his hips. It was ending. Her mouth began to suck at his sternum. He had wanted to understand the essence of Mary Lowe. He had longed for it, had fervently wished to know it. She began to gnaw at him, to bite him, her teeth gashing fiery gobs of him. Margaret arched his neck and made a sound in his throat through the well of saliva; he rolled his eyes in bewildered horror at such an indescribable sensation as Mary worked her way down his stomach.

62

Everyone agreed that the search warrant should be obtained with the knowledge of as few people as possible. Palma called Birley and asked if he wanted to go along to back up her and Grant, an acknowledgment that Birley had an investment in the case and a gesture of a partner's respect. Art Cushing and Richard Boucher were already there, since they had picked up the stakeout from Maples and Lee at the end of their shift. Leeland, who had had the patience not to chafe at being deskbound during the investigation, asked at the last minute if he could go along with Birley, a request that was readily granted.

It took them nearly an hour to get organized. While they waited for Birley to drive in from his home in Meyerland, Palma had to go through an ordeal to find the proper judge to sign the warrant. She finally located him at Brennan's Restaurant, where he had taken his wife for a birthday dinner. Palma and the judge retreated from the dining room to a wrought-iron table outside in a secluded corner of the walled courtyard, where the humidity and heat worked its will on the judge's shiny forehead and starched white shirt. Palma brought him up to date on the investigation and he, being a careful and politically astute man, had asked a number of questions after making it clear he did not want to be humored with glib responses. Eventually he consented to sign the warrant, using the side of Palma's purse to write on.

Followed by Birley and Leeland in a second car, Palma and Grant once more drove west through the tall pines of Memorial Park, the car's headlights flitting through wispy streaks of night humidity which hung in the air like ribbons of smoke. It had been almost forty-eight hours since she had picked him up at the airport and taken him this route to see the hotel where Sandra Moser had been found, the condominium where Dorothy Samenov had died, and the large red bedroom in Hunters Creek where Bernadine Mello had had her last affair. But Palma's preoccupation with the case had been so intense it had warped her sense of time, and Grant might have been there a week, or even a month.

They had not spoken since they left the police station, and just as they were passing the drive to the Houston Arboretum and approaching the West Loop Expressway, Grant shifted in his seat.

'How do you feel about it?' he asked.

'What part of it?'

'Confronting Broussard, now that we know a little more about him.'

'I'm thinking that if we don't find anything in his place that nails him, it's going to scare the hell out of me.'

Grant didn't respond and it was a moment before Palma asked, 'I didn't say the right thing?'

'You said exactly the right thing. That's what it does, scares the hell out of you.'

'When you don't catch them?'

'That's right. In the dozen or so years I've been doing this, there's been a fair number of cases we've never cleared. In the beginning I consulted on a few that were never resolved, which bothered me, nagged at me, but the first time I was in charge of a case that wasn't cleared it nearly drove me crazy. Damn thing plagued me. Couldn't stop thinking about it. Dreamed about it. Daydreamed about it. It turned me inside out. It was the first real job-related stress that came between me and Marne. That was our first taste of it.'

Grant looked out the window to the darkness, and then back at the headlights through the windshield.

'That first one almost changed the rest of my life, and then somehow I learned to cope with it. Me and Marne.'

Grant stopped talking until they had passed under the West Loop and got onto the tighter, narrower Woodway with the dense woods coming close up to the street.

'And then there was a second one,' he said. 'And eventually others. Now there's a collection of them.' He tapped his head.

'They're lodged in there like tumors turned silent and benign. You know they're there, but you try not to think about them. If you think about them, draw psychic attention to them, they might come to life again ... start killing again.'

'Are you trying to prepare me for something?' Palma asked. She was leaning toward the windshield, trying to find her turnoff.

'I've just been thinking about all those uncleared cases you mentioned earlier today,' Grant said, without answering her question. 'Four, five thousand a year. Some are cleared eventually, but most aren't. It adds up to numbers you don't like to think about.'

'Here we are,' Palma said, and turned right onto a heavily wooded street where the houses were set far back into the dense pine and undergrowth. The only visible signs of habitation were the openings of narrow asphalt drives disappearing into thick vegetation. Occasionally a drive would be bordered with low curb lights casting eerie green splashes as they reflected off the low shrubbery, and occasionally a pale candescent glow would illuminate the magnetic card box of a security gate.

Palma slowed, and turned left into a corridor of thick pines and sapling oaks. She cut to her parking lights and immediately turned right into the drive that led to Broussard's office. Her parking lights picked up Cushing's car sitting in the darkness, and in her rearview mirror she caught the twin beads of Birley's car right behind her.

They stopped perpendicular to Cushing, who had

pointed his car toward the front of Broussard's house so he and Boucher could watch the rest of the drive and the exit gate without having to crane their necks. Palma turned off the ignition, and she and Grant got out of the car. In the still, muggy darkness she could hear the muffled snapping of car door latches as Cushing and Boucher in front of her and Birley and Leeland behind her got out of their cars, and then a quartet of single snaps as the same doors were pushed closed to the first latch. Footsteps crunched over the gravel drive until everyone was standing at the front fender of Palma's car.

'Nothing shakin' in there, far as we can tell.' Typically Cushing was the first to speak, but he kept his voice low and soft. They were standing in a loose circle around her, close enough for her to smell Cushing's cologne. 'Place had been totally dark until about an hour ago when Rich noticed a dim light come on in the upstairs window.'

He turned and they all looked through the trees, where a faint glow identified the upper-floor window. 'We took a little walk through the woods to get the layout of the place. Circle drive in the front comes out here,' he nodded to the entrance they had just come through, 'and a wall goes out from either side of the house with a gate on this near side so you can get to the back. We looked through there, big lawn sloping down to the bayou. Big terrace thing on the back.'

'What about the light upstairs?' Palma asked. 'It looks like it's in a corner room.'

'Yeah,' Cushing nodded. 'Top floor, left corner. Matter of fact, it looks like the room runs along the whole far end of the house 'cause we could see light along there. Looked like the windows were open; they're the tall kind, big ones.'

'What's below the windows?'

'Uh, I think, a hedge close to the house, about fifty or sixty feet of yard, and then the woods, all sloping down to the bayou.' Cushing looked around., 'Hey, what is this, a raid? I thought you was just giving the guy a warrant.'

'We don't expect him to answer the door,' Palma said.

She was hoping no one would actually come right out and ask her if she planned to try very hard to get Broussard's attention. 'Cush, why don't you stay with the cars in case there's an effort to avoid us through the drive here?' The possibility of a car chase would appeal to Cushing and would keep him away from seeing anything she might decide to do that wasn't strictly by the book. 'Don, could you and Rich get outside the windows at the far end of the house? If they're open, there could be an effort through there.' She didn't know Boucher that well and didn't want to trust him with a crucial exit site by himself or, like Cushing, with the opportunity to see her do something outside regs. 'John, can you take the terrace? There are probably French doors back there, maybe a lot of them, something to allow a view to the lawn and bayou. If Broussard's in the dark, he could see you coming up on the terrace.' Suddenly she realized she didn't have to tell him that, but he nodded anyway. She was doing what she was supposed to do.

'Grant and I will go in the front,' she concluded. 'If there's no answer, we'll go ahead and enter and try to get back to the terrace doors and get you inside as soon as we can,' she said to Birley. 'Everybody keep your handsets on.' She looked at Leeland and Birley. 'We'll wait here until you let us know you're in place.'

Neither she nor Grant nor Cushing spoke as they waited for the other two men to get in place. Grant hadn't said anything since they had gotten out of the cars, and she wondered what he was thinking of the way she was handling it. She wondered if he always took the backseat in these situations or if he was doing so in this instance because of her. She decided it was his character. It would have been an insult to him to believe otherwise.

It seemed like a long wait, but it was actually less than ten minutes before, 'Leeland, ready,' came over the radio, followed a minute later by, 'Birley, ready.'

Leaving Cushing with the cars, she and Grant walked up the drive toward the front of the house. As they approached the rear of the two Mercedeses, Grant moved to the edges of the cars and looked inside while Palma walked up to the front door. The doorbell was not lighted, and Palma looked around at Grant, who was now looking in the other side of the cars. She reached in her purse and took out her set of picks, an expensive set that had been her father's and which she had learned how to use while she was still in high school. She already had the picks working up the pins when Grant joined her on the steps, and before he could say anything she felt the rotor moving and the lock clicked open.

'I didn't hear the doorbell,' she explained, adhering to the letter of truth if not the spirit, and the moment she spoke it occurred to her why Grant had stayed behind and shown so much interest in the two parked cars. He had worked with a lot of law-enforcement agencies, both large and small, and with all kinds of officers, straitlaced and devious. He probably had learned a long time ago that sometimes it was best for special agents acting as advisers to local agencies not to know all the details of the way the local officers ran their operations. Unoccupied cars and doorbells that couldn't be heard. There was, after all, a relationship.

Palma was aware of perspiration soaking through her Egyptian cotton by the time she pushed open the door and felt the waft of cold air from Broussard's air-conditioning system. She was reminded of the morning she had walked into Dorothy Samenov's condo and the chill of a lowered thermostat had foreshadowed a deeper, stranger chill of another kind.

If the entry had activated an alarm system, Cushing would intercept the call or the investigating officers. Palma and Grant stood in the foyer, letting their eyes and ears get used to the darkness and the silence in the house. Simultaneously they both readied their handguns, Palma remembering the incident in the hallway of Broussard's office when he had confronted them. She knew they ran that risk here as well, but chose to gamble for the chance of catching him unexpectedly. She saw the entry into the dining room and another room past that with the glow of me city sky seeping in through the dozens of small panes of the French doors that lined the far side of the living room beyond.

She looked at Grant, who nodded at her, and then she started toward the dining room, pausing at a transecting hallway and looking both ways before she continued, skirting the table and dining chairs around to the other side, where she paused before entering the living room. It was a long room, stretching across much of the bottom floor, with its length contiguous with the terrace. Waiting a moment, she scanned the long line of French doors and then saw Birley standing where two door frames came together and provided a thin barrier for him to stand against. She carefully crossed the room and approached the doors, running her hand up the facing until she found a latch, turned it, and opened the door for Birley. She saw the glint of his Colt in the faint light.

Now that the glow from the city sky was at their backs and illuminating the room in front of them, they moved quickly back through the living room and dining room to Grant, who was still waiting in the entry hall. A long stairway went up to the second floor from either side of the entry, and Grant motioned to his left, meaning that was the direction that would take them to the end of the house where the bedroom window was lighted. Palma nodded, and he let her pass him and start up the stairs first. She felt a warm spot growing hotter in the center of her chest as she mounted the stairs carefully but without hesitation.

When she reached the landing, there was no confusion about which way she should go along the mezzanine. To her right the mezzanine continued across the foyer below and toward the stairs on the other side of the entry and to bedroom doors beyond that. To her left, maybe fifteen feet away, a door was open and a lemon light spilled out into the hallway. Palma noted the color of the light and decided it was much too yellow to have been the result of a small-wattage bulb. There was another explanation.

She moved aside to let Grant and Birley gain the

landing also, and then motioned to them that she wou.
go ahead. The three of them approached the openec
doorway and waited, listening, trying to get some audible
bearing. The bedroom door opened in a corner of the
room, and along the wall to Palma's left were the
windows that had been visible to them from the front of
the house. On the other side of the door, on Palma's
right, a short wing wall created a mini-foyer before the
room itself opened up on the same side and ran the depth
of the house.

Palma moved carefully, grateful for the thick, expensive carpet, and actually stepped through the bedroom
doorway into the small foyer behind the wing wall. As
soon as she did so, her heart sank as she smelled the
familiar perfume that had pervaded each of the rooms
where the other victims had been found. But here, mixed
with it, there was another smell too, a faint pungent odor
as if something were scorching. And then she heard
something familiar, the hissing sibilants of whispering.
With adrenaline punching her nerves like a hot prod, she
looked around as Grant and Birley moved in close behind
her. Then with a sharp nod she stepped out from behind
the wing wall and took a firing stance with both hands,
her arms pointed straight out to the bed across the room
as Grant and Birley burst past her and did the same, one
right after the other so that all three of them were
crouched in standing firing positions, looking down the
lengths of their arms and over the tops of their guns at
the macabre sight on the bed twenty feet away.

The room was poorly lighted by a single lamp that sat
on a reading table beside the bed. Several yellow scarves
had been thrown over the lampshade, one draped directly
onto the bulb, which was creating the scorched odor.

Palma could not immediately understand what she
was seeing on the bed, stripped of all its cover except its
top sheet, but what she saw in the next few seconds
confused her and then numbed her so quickly that she
forgot herself, forgot to move, or even to breathe. There
were two naked bodies, both with long blond hair, both

ith faces painted like all the previous victims. The body
.hat lay on its back was thickly set, its eyes wide open
and glassy. Two huge and irregular circular wounds
appeared where the breasts had been and the body had
been so severely bitten that from where Palma stood, the
person appeared to be thickly covered with smallpox
welts. A single stringy, gray entrail extruded from the
navel and lay across the stomach, and the pubic region
had been completely resected so that the gender of the
victim was obscured. Or would have been if Palma had
not had such a grim familiarity with the mutilated human
anatomy. The thick set of the waist and the narrow hips,
the almost right angles of the abdominal muscles and the
dark patterns of body and leg hair told her the mutilated
body was a man, and even as she comprehended this her
eyes were shifting to the second nude figure, a body as
exquisitely lovely as the other was nauseous. The woman
lay on her side beside the corpse, ignoring them, her
attentions fixed hypnotically on the painted, mutilated
man, the foot of her top leg stroking his ankle seductively,
her head resting beside his on her bent arm while the
long, graceful fingers of her free hand traced idly around
the two wounds on either side of the man's chest. Her
own long, buttery hair mixed with the flowing locks of
the man's wig as she arched her neck to keep her lips
next to his ears. Transfixed by the discordant imagery of
what she was seeing, her emotions in disarray, Palma was
startled to feel a sob rising in her chest, and then she was
startled again to feel it stop. In the near silence the three
of them stood in stunned awe listening to Mary Lowe's
whispered gabblings to Dr. Dominick Broussard, apologies and groanings and supplications, reminders of the
way it once had been for them, before their long flight
through the dingy towns of Dixie, before the seductions
and the betrayals, before she had become her father's
whore and her mother's venging angel.

Epilogue

The media storm that followed Mary Lowe's arrest was unprecedented and, within twelve hours, international. The idea of Lady Cop Gets Lady Killer with its facile double entendre and sex-and-death formula made the case immediate headline and lead-story material. The moment Mary Lowe was booked, the security was stepped up at the police department and then at the county jail, where she was taken to the women's ward only half a dozen blocks away on the northern edge of downtown and on the southern bank of Buffalo Bayou. For the first few weeks everyone even remotely connected with the case was hounded by the media, looking for a wedge, however small, by which they hoped to open up the story. As the days passed and the police department released enough information to bleed off the intense pressure created by a breaking story, the supporting cast received less and less attention.

Practiced at dodging the media in sensational cases, Sander Grant had worked round the clock in the seclusion of the homicide division to complete his report and then, within forty-eight hours, was on a plane back to Quantico.

But Carmen Palma was not so fortunate. From the time the murders first came to light she had been identified as the central detective in the investigation, and the fact that she was a woman homicide detective had intrigued the media from the beginning. For weeks after the story broke she was besieged by reporters from newspapers large and small, by writers from magazines on both sides of the Atlantic, by newsmen from the networks and talk-show bookers, by personality agents and movie producers waving contracts and talking stars and package deals, and by aspiring bestselling authors promising percentages and household recognition.

Palma refused them all. The scene she had blundered onto at Broussard's home that hot June night had embedded itself in her mind, and for months afterward it was seldom out of her thoughts. The women, both living and deceased, she had gotten to know during the investigation, the issues she had confronted, the new coils of psychology she had discovered both in the killer and in herself, all had worked together to disturb her peace of mind and prevent her from going back to her life as it was, even without the turmoil produced by the media's insatiable appetite. For a while her days were filled wrapping up loose ends and helping the DA's office prepare its case. And, of course, there were her other cases as well. Her world had not begun and would not end up with the bizarre career of Mary Lowe.

Paul Lowe's money had gotten the best defense team it could buy, and the court was immediately swamped with motions and continuances and every manner of delay imaginable. The legal procession to Mary Lowe's trial promised to be convoluted and protracted.

Through the DA's office, Palma was kept informed of the slowly developing posture that Mary's lawyers were planning to make in her defense. She would readily admit to having an affair with Dr. Dominick Broussard, but in this, they would insist, she was more victim than accomplice. She had put her trust in him, and he had taken advantage of her exploiting the very thing for which she had gone to him in search of remedy. Broussard's records were seized, and it was discovered that with the astonishing poor judgment one sometimes sees in the private affairs of men known publicly to be perspicacious, he had

kept a 'secret' record of all the affairs he had had with h.
patients over the years. There was ample evidence t
support Mary's claims that Broussard had abused his
professional relationship with her.

As to how she had come to be naked in bed with the
dead Broussard, her explanation was straightforward and
simple. At Broussard's request, she had agreed to meet
him at his home, where he proceeded to drug and assault
her. The next thing she knew the police were bursting
through Broussard's bedroom door. When the police
entered Broussard's house that night, they were in effect
'rescuing' Mary from a long, vicious enslavement to the
insidious Dr. Broussard. Regardless of whoever else
Broussard had lured to his bedroom that night, Mary
herself was lucky to have gotten out with her life. Broussard's own housekeeper could testify to the fact that the
doctor regularly enticed women to his home, where he
apparently forced them to participate in his sordid sexual
rituals, just as he had Mary Lowe.

The unidentified pubic hairs and the few strands of
head hair that came from Sandra Moser, Dorothy
Samenov, and Vickie Kittrie matched Mary Lowe's. Her
lawyers nodded. They admitted up front that Mary was
having affairs with women. Once again, her inexplicable
bisexual tendencies were something she was seeking
Broussard's help in 'correcting,' instead his sexual abuse
had only served to exacerbate them. It may have been
unfortunate coincidence that she had had sexual relations
with each of the victims before they were killed — they
were, after all, a rather small and closely knit group — but
certainly it was nothing more than that. Because of the
regular sexual intimacy among them, the evidentiary
strength of finding Mary's hair on the victims was greatly
weakened.

Mirel Farr's testimony regarding Mary's sadomasochist
play at her 'dungeon' would be weakened by Farr's own
tarnished reputation and by the fact that she was testifying for the DA's office, which had offered her a 'deal' in
exchange for not being indicted as an accomplice for

...ding Clyde Barbish in the Louise Ackley and Lalo Montalvo killings. By now, Barbish had recovered enough to understand the full import of what was about to happen to him, and he plea-bargained for a lesser charge in exchange for testifying that Reynolds had hired him to kill Louise Ackley who, having learned one more form of deviant behavior from her brother, was threatening to blackmail him.

It was true that there were those who could testify that Mary often went to Mirel Farr's to participate in sado-masochist scenarios, but these were only prime examples of how thoroughly she had succumbed to Broussard's spell. Didn't he go there to watch her in these acts? There was apparently no limit to the extent to which he was willing to corrupt his clients in order to satisfy his own deviant pleasures.

But the coup de grace to the state's case against Mary Lowe, the defense would argue, was provided by the investigative expertise brought to bear by the state itself. Federal Bureau of Investigation Special Agent Sander Grant, a veteran member of the Behavioral Science Unit of the National Center for the Analysis of Violent Crime, FBI Academy, Quantico, Virginia, would be subpoenaed to testify that in all his years of experience with violent crime, after analyzing thousands of cases of murder, including serial killers, he had never seen a case in which a woman had been the perpetrator of a sexually moti-vated homicide of this kind. Never.

The state, of course, would have their counterargu-ments, their own witnesses and manner of presenting the evidence and arguing the case, but the fact remained that the case against Mary Lowe, 'victim,' was far from being a cinch for successful prosecution. It was unlikely that they could get convictions on the deaths of Moser, Samenov, Mello, and Kittrie. The evidence was pro-minently circumstantial. And even in Broussard's case they would have to conduct a careful and intelligent *voir dire* and then sweat blood to bring it off. And if it appeared to the defense that the jury was actually going

to be convinced by the paltry show of evidence presente
by the state, they simply would switch their defense to
temporary insanity, which, in light of the bizarre setting
in which Mary had been found at Broussard's that night,
certainly would seem to be a credible defense. As
Broussard's victim, Mary simply had been pushed too far,
to the very limit of her sanity, and temporarily had lost
control of her senses and killed him. And who could
blame her? Wasn't this even, in the true sense of the
meaning, self-defense?

The fact was, in not being sure who they were
pursuing, in not having a solid suspect, in being kept off
balance by the contradictory evidence, and by being
caught off guard when the last killing, that of Dr.
Broussard, had presented them with an unavoidable
suspect, the police had not been able to build a solid case
as the investigation progressed. The defense could and
would, challenge them at every turn, point for point,
leaving the jury to decide if this much-abused mother of
two could possibly have commited the heinous sexually
motivated killings of which she had been accused, the
kind of killings that, by the FBI's own historical records of
criminology, had never before been committed by a
woman.

While the two sides laboriously prepared their legal
arsenals for a trial that was still many months away,
Palma kept to her business, locked into a routine of
steady work that she had sought in an effort to keep her
head clear of the craziness. She had had to change her
telephone number twice and had developed a reputation
among the writers and movie people still pursuing her of
being an eccentric (for turning down the publicity and
inevitable fame), of being a fool (for turning down the
money), of being a bitch (for hanging up on them,
ignoring their letters and telegrams, refusing to answer
her door), and of being a class act (for sticking to her
guns). But Palma had no noble feelings for avoiding all
that had been coming her way, whether it might have
proved to be good or bad.

The truth was, after what she had been through, Palma had discovered that she could not shake a feeling of restlessness, maybe even of vague apprehensions. Peace of mind was no longer possible. It could not be conjured up by going over and over the crime scenes or thinking through the interviews for the hundredth time or second-guessing for the hundredth time the way she had handled her investigation. It could not be acquired through long weekends of solitude in which she dwelt upon the surprises she should have anticipated in the case, or in the people she had met, or even in herself. It could not be summoned from the jugs of her Italian table wine or in the last of the fancy green bottles of Tanqueray gin that Brian had left behind. To Palma's increasing consternation, the world had changed. Or she had changed. Nothing was the same, no smell or sight or sound or emotion was as it had been, nothing satisfied. It was true that she had discovered something within her that she had never known was there, and that she was wary of it, perhaps even fearful. But her uneasiness was more than that. Something was missing, and a sense of emptiness pervaded every moment.

Then, near the end of August, when a fierce heat had settled over the bayous and stands of loblolly pines, and a perverse, subtropical doldrum had appeared overnight from the Gulf of Mexico to keep down the coastal breezes that normally could have relieved the blistering city, Palma spent a Sunday afternoon alone at her mother's, who was visiting her other daughter in Victoria. Palma had fled the loneliness of her own house in West University Place and had come home, where even the empty rooms were not empty because of the memories, where everything perceived by her five senses was familiar, and nothing changed. Here everything had been settled. There were no surprises to disturb the past or taint the future.

She had gone to her old bedroom and peeled off her underwear and slipped on a loose-fitting sun dress, left her shoes in the middle of the floor and walked barefooted and idly through the house, looking at each of the empty rooms as if she were visiting an old friend who reminded her that at one time things had indeed been simpler. When she came into the kitchen she took two limes out of the hanging basket where her mother kept them near the windows next to the back door. She got ice from the refrigerator and put it into a glass and squeezed both limes over the ice and added water from the faucet at the sink. Stirring it with her finger, she took the drink out the screen door to the courtyard, where the cicadas droned so fiercely that they completely drowned out the noises of the city. She might have been in the middle of a jungle.

With a water hose she sprayed the stone walks and the plantains and hibiscus that grew along the borders until the courtyard smelled of damp earth. Then she sprayed her feet and legs, and bent down and ran the stream across her face. Without bothering to wipe off the water, she turned off the hydrant and with a dripping face walked back to the swing. She sat in it sideways, stretching out her legs on the slatted seat and leaned back against the arm and the chain. With a slight bow forward she set the swing going, the long chains groaning softly on the leather guides wrapped around the mammoth limb of the water oak. She sipped the cold lime-flavored water and reached back and gathered her long hair and held it in a pile on top of her head.

She lost track of time, which was what she had wanted to do most of all. In the last month it had been a surprisingly difficult thing to achieve. Everything she did, everything she thought, reminded her of some aspect, recent or remote, disquieting or numbing, about Mary Lowe and the women who had died.

She had drunk all the lime water and had started eating the ice when she thought she heard a car stop in front of the house. The garden wall blocked the street except for the deep green canopies of the Mexican plums, but she listened to the car door open and shut. There was a brief silence until the footsteps hit the stones of the front walk, and then she listened to their progress toward the front of the house, then stop before they reached the porch. They paused, and then by some instinct or deduction, they changed direction and took the walk that led around to the garden gate.

Palma waited, eating ice, looking at the wrought-iron gate where the person would appear between the two scarlet bloomed hibiscus that flanked either side of the gate. Sander Grant stepped into the frame of flowers and wrought-iron gate and looked through the bars into the courtyard. He saw her immediately, sitting with her feet propped up in the swing.

'My God,' she said.

'Hello.' He pushed open the gate. He was wearing suit pants and a white shirt without a coat. His tie and collar were loosened and his sleeves were rolled to the elbow. He closed the gate behind him and approached her at the same pace he had walked up the front sidewalk. Speechless, Palma watched him come through the dappled shade and plantains, his broken nose as welcome a sight as she could ever have hoped to see. She had the presence of mind to lower her legs before he was close enough to see her bottom.

He smiled at her as he approached. 'Surprise, huh?'

She steadied herself and swung her feet onto the stones to stand.

'They told me downtown you might be at your mother's if you weren't home,' he said, stopping a few feet from where she stood with the backs of her legs against the front of the swing. The cicadas roared in her ears. 'I hope it's all right,' he said.

'Of course.' She didn't know whether to reach out and shake his hand or embrace him. Grant put his hands in his pockets and smiled again, as if he knew how she felt.

Her eyes couldn't get enough of him. She gestured with her glass. 'What are you doing here?'

'You have any more of whatever that is?' he said, lifting his chin at her glass.

'Oh, God, sure. I'm sorry. Here,' she said. 'Sit down.'

She stepped away from the swing and then thought how she must look. She thought of her bra and pant tossed on the bed in her old room. She laughed self consciously. 'I can't believe you just showed up like this.'

Grant nodded with a shrug and sat down in the swing, looking up at her. Suddenly she felt naked. The sundress had not been designed to be worn without underwear.

'I'll get us another drink,' she said. 'It's only lime and water. It'll take just a second.' And she turned and walked into the house and went straight to her bedroom.

'I've never written such a lengthy and detailed report,' Grant said. 'I worked on it for several weeks, incorporating graphics and photographs, technical reports from the autopsies and crime lab. Everything I could get my hands on has gone into it. It was hell to organize. But it's a landmark case as far as we're concerned.' The two of them were sitting in the swing. He had been doing most of the talking, stopping every once in a while to sip the lime and water and touch the sweaty glass to the side of his face. 'I must've presented the case half a dozen times already, to the other agents in the unit, to the cadets, to the officers in the Fellowship program, to anyone who'd sit still long enough.'

Palma had been listening, turning her head away once in a while to look across the mottled shadows of the courtyard, dropping her eyes to her glass, afraid that she was looking at him too much.

He sipped from his glass again and dabbed at his mustache with the light green paper napkin she had brought out with his glass.

'Rankin, her attorney's, already gotten in touch with you?' Palma asked, moving a bare foot over the stones under the swing.

'Yeah,' Grant nodded. 'Hell of a twist, isn't it? Makes the whole thing even worse.' He wasn't uneasy about looking at her. He had hardly taken his eyes off her.

'It's months before this thing goes to trial,' she said. 'A lot can happen in that time. Maybe it won't come to that.'

Grant snorted and looked away toward the gate where
had come in. She raised her eyes from her glass,
studied his broken nose, his British soldier's profile, the
brindled gray at his temples, the thickness of his chest.

He turned back and caught her looking at him.

'What I'd like,' he said, 'is for you to consider coming
to Quantico for a while. We'll have a new Fellowship
program starting in the fall, actually next month,
September. I've recommended you for one of the positions.'

Palma was surprised. She hadn't seen it coming. He
saw her hesitating.

'The new course begins in about three weeks. You
don't have that much time to think about it.' He looked at
his glass and rattled the ice. 'It's a year-long course.
You'll be there a year.'

'I'm not sure I can do that,' she said.

'I've taken the liberty of checking this out with Captain
McComb,' Grant added cautiously. 'They know how I feel
about your abilities. Only a select few get into the Fellowship program. If you accept, they'll give you the necessary leave of absence, with pay.'

Palma was taken aback. 'I ... I'm surprised,' she said.
'I'm flattered, I guess, that they'd do that.' She paused.
'But that's not what I meant. It's the course. I'm not sure I
can ... handle that. That's primarily what I'd be doing,
isn't it? When I finish the course? I'd be profiling?'

'Right. Violent crime analysis. You'd be obligated to
dedicate at least the next three years to practicing what
the Bureau has trained you to do.'

She looked away again, shaking her head, uncertain.

'Look,' Grant said. 'You owe it to yourself to explore
this. You've ... got unusual abilities. If ... if nothing else,
you've got to learn how to live with them, to understand
them better. They're not going to go away. I know. If you
want to get away from them, you're going to have to get
the hell out of the business. Get completely out of police
work, because now that you've used them they're not
going to leave you alone. It's like an artist recognizing

that he's a gifted colorist. He can't help himself. It's just going to happen. You might as well learn how to control your gift, discipline it.'

Palma held the cold drink in her hands and looked at the brilliant orange and yellow blooms of lantana across the path from her. High in the water oaks and catalpas the cicadas rasped against the dead heat of late summer, the throbbing, metronomic rhythm of their droning reminding Palma, as always, of loneliness. She didn't know what to say or she would have said it. She didn't even understand what she was feeling.

'I'd like you to consider it,' he said again. 'It's a year,' he repeated.

She took her eyes off the lantana and looked at him. 'Is this why you're down here?' she asked. 'To tell me this?'

He gave a short nod. 'I came to talk to you,' he said.

She continued looking at him, and for a moment she thought he wasn't going to say anything else. Then he said, 'Look, I just don't want to seem totally irresponsible, is all. You know what I've gone through this past year, and it seems to me I might have come across to you as pretty frivolous ... or, maybe, I don't know. I just don't want ... you ... to misunderstand me. We'd have a year. You could get to know me in a year.'

Palma looked at him. Yes, she thought, she could get to know him in a year, but she didn't think she could possibly feel any differently about him then than she did at this very moment. With an enormous sense of relief, the first she had felt in over two months, since Grant had returned to Washington, she was thankful that he had been wiser about their silence than she had been. If he hadn't come back, she wasn't sure she would ever have understood what had happened between them.

BODY OF TRUTH

David Lindsey

In a remote country with no rules, people – and
the truth – just disappear.

Lena Muller, daughter of a wealthy Houston businessman,
went missing in Guatemala. Now, six weeks later,
homicide detective Stuart Haydon receives a phone call
from Guatemala City. Lena is alive – and in trouble.

But Guatemala is synonymous with trouble. Thirty years
of guerilla warfare have turned it into a surreal and violent
netherworld where fear rules; where no one can be trusted;
where a small coterie of American expatriates is deeply
involved with the corrupt military and an elusive guerilla
faction, and where everything is tainted by
greed and cynical political motives.

When Haydon arrives he finds himself embroiled in the
menace, the complex mystery and the tension of life in
Guatemala. He also finds that Lena Muller is not the
young woman either he or her parents thought her to be –
and that he is searching for a harsher truth
than he dared imagine . . .

'It is, as a thriller should be, precise and immediate'
Independent

'Entertains, educates and breaks the heart'
Chicago Tribune

FICTION
0 7515 0109 3

IN THE LAKE OF THE MOON

David Lindsey

The first five photographs were perplexing; but the sixth –
the sixth seemed to be the chronicle of a death foretold.

Houston detective Sam Haydon opens the anonymous
envelopes to find two photographs of his late father, and
three photographs of a beautiful woman he doesn't
recognise. All five seem to date from around fifty years ago.

Photo number six is of Haydon himself, taken a few days
earlier, and is marked with a felt-tip pen to show the
trajectory of a bullet into his right eye and the resultant
explosion of blood from the back of his head.

It's not the first time Haydon has had a death threat, but
as it becomes clear that this one could well be his last,
Haydon is flung into a desperate search for the murderous
maniac who's tracking him down – a search that leads to
the sprawling mass of Mexico City and the unknown world
of his father's past.

Gripping, utterly compelling, *In the Lake of the Moon* is a
superbly constructed thriller from the bestselling author of
Mercy and *Body of Truth*.

'Chilling'
New York Times Book Review

'One of the most unusual and fascinating thrillers I
have read'
Hammond Innes

FICTION
0 7515 1428 4

AN ABSENCE OF LIGHT

David Lindsey

Marcus Graver, an officer in the Criminal Intelligence
Division of Houston Police Department, is understandably
concerned and upset when a colleague
commits violent suicide.

But when the inevitable investigation begins to unearth
worrying details about the dead man's apparently
unremarkable life, Graver realises his concern should be
more professional than personal. The evidence points to a
betrayal of terrifying import, forcing Graver to face the
murkier realities of modern information technology, where
everyone's privacy is for sale – at a price.

And as the trail leads him nearer and nearer the dark core
of a vast criminal intelligence network, Graver has no
choice but to acknowledge an uncomfortable truth: that
when men's desires are shaped in an absence
of light, only the corrupt survive . . .

As gripping as the clutch of a drowning man, *An Absence of
Light* is a dazzlingly superior thriller from the acclaimed
author of *Mercy* and *Body of Truth*.

FICTION
0 7515 1279 6

☐ Body of Truth	David Lindsey	£6.99
☐ In the Lake of the Moon	David Lindsey	£5.99
☐ An Absence of Light	David Lindsey	£5.99

Warner Books now offers an exciting range of quality titles by both established and new authors. All of the books in this series are available from:

Little, Brown and Company (UK),
P.O. Box 11,
Falmouth,
Cornwall TR10 9EN.

Alternatively you may fax your order to the above address.
Fax No: 01326 317444
Telephone No: 01326 317200
E-mail: books@barni.avel.co.uk

Payments can be made as follows: cheque, postal order (payable to Little, Brown and Company) or by credit cards, Visa/Access. Do not send cash or currency. UK customers and B.F.P.O. please allow £1.00 for postage and packing for the first book, plus 50p for the second book, plus 30p for each additional book up to a maximum charge of £3.00 (7 books plus).

Overseas customers including Ireland, please allow £2.00 for the first book plus £1.00 for the second book, plus 50p for each additional book.

NAME (Block Letters) ....

....

ADDRESS ....

....

....

☐ I enclose my remittance for ....
☐ I wish to pay by Access/Visa Card

Number ☐☐☐☐☐☐☐☐☐☐☐☐☐☐☐☐

Card Expiry Date ☐☐☐☐